HOUSE
OF
EARTH

Pearl S. Buck

HOUSE
OF
EARTH

The Good Earth

Sons

A House Divided

THE JOHN DAY COMPANY
NEW YORK
AN INTEXT PUBLISHER

THE GOOD EARTH

Copyright © 1931, 1949 by Pearl S. Buck
Copyright renewed 1959 by Pearl S. Buck

SONS

Copyright © 1932 by Pearl S. Buck
Copyright renewed 1960 by Pearl S. Buck

A HOUSE DIVIDED

Copyright © 1935 by Pearl S. Buck
Copyright renewed 1963 by Pearl S. Buck

The John Day Company, 257 Park Avenue South, New York, N.Y. 10010
An Intext Publisher

CONTENTS

THE GOOD EARTH

I

I T was Wang Lung's marriage day. At first, opening his eyes in the blackness of the curtains about his bed, he could not think why the dawn seemed different from any other. The house was still except for the faint, gasping cough of his old father, whose room was opposite to his own across the middle room. Every morning the old man's cough was the first sound to be heard. Wang Lung usually lay listening to it and moved only when he heard it approaching nearer and when he heard the door of his father's room squeak upon its wooden hinges.

But this morning he did not wait. He sprang up and pushed aside the curtains of his bed. It was dark, ruddy dawn, and through a small square hole of a window, where the tattered paper fluttered, a glimpse of bronze sky gleamed. He went to the hole and tore the paper away.

"It is spring and I do not need this," he muttered.

He was ashamed to say aloud that he wished the house to look neat on this day. The hole was barely large enough to admit his hand and he thrust it out to feel of the air. A small soft wind blew gently from the east, a wind mild and murmurous and full of rain. It was a good omen. The fields needed rain for fruition. There would be no rain this day, but within a few days, if this wind continued, there would be water. It was good. Yesterday he had said to his father that if this brazen, glittering sunshine continued, the wheat could not fill in the ear. Now it was as if Heaven had chosen this day to wish him well. Earth would bear fruit.

He hurried out into the middle room, drawing on his blue outer trousers as he went, and knotting about the fullness at his waist his girdle of blue cotton cloth. He left his upper body bare until he had heated water to bathe himself. He went into the shed which was the kitchen, leaning against the house, and out of its dusk an ox twisted its head from behind the corner next the door and lowed at him deeply. The kitchen was made of earthen bricks as the house was, great squares of earth dug from their own fields, and thatched with straw from their own wheat. Out of their own earth had his grandfather in his youth fashioned also the oven, baked and black with many years of meal preparing. On top of this earthen structure stood a deep, round, iron cauldron.

This cauldron he filled partly full of water, dipping it with a half gourd from an earthen jar that stood near, but he dipped cautiously, for water was precious. Then, after a hesitation, he suddenly lifted the jar and emptied all the water into the cauldron. This day he would bathe his whole body. Not since he was a child upon his mother's knee had anyone looked upon his body. Today one would, and he would have it clean.

He went around the oven to the rear, and selecting a handful of the dry grass and stalks standing in the corner of the kitchen, he arranged it delicately in the mouth of the oven, making the most of every leaf. Then from an old flint and iron he caught a flame and thrust it into the straw and there was a blaze.

This was the last morning he would have to light the fire. He had lit it every morning since his mother died six years before. He had lit the fire, boiled water, and poured the water into a bowl and taken it into the room where his father sat upon his bed, coughing and fumbling for his shoes upon the floor. Every morning for these six years the old man had waited for his son to bring in hot water to ease him of his morning coughing. Now father and son could rest. There was a woman coming to the house. Never again would Wang Lung have to rise summer and winter at dawn to light the fire. He could lie in his bed and wait, and he also would have a bowl of water brought to him, and if the earth were fruitful there would be tea leaves in the water. Once in some years it was so.

And if the woman wearied, there would be her children to light the fire, the many children she would bear to Wang Lung. Wang Lung stopped, struck by the thought of children running in and out of their three rooms. Three rooms had always seemed much to them, a house half empty since his mother died. They were always having to resist relatives who were more crowded—his uncle, with his endless brood of children, coaxing,

"Now, how can two lone men need so much room? Cannot father and son sleep together? The warmth of the young one's body will comfort the old one's cough."

But the father always replied, "I am saving my bed for my grandson. He will warm my bones in my age."

Now the grandsons were coming, grandsons upon grandsons! They would have to put beds along the walls and in the middle room. The house would be full of beds. The blaze in the oven died down while Wang Lung thought of all the beds there would be in the half empty house, and the water began to chill in the cauldron. The shadowy figure of the old man appeared in the doorway, holding his unbuttoned garments about him. He was coughing and spitting and he gasped,

"How is it that there is not water yet to heat my lungs?"

Wang Lung stared and recalled himself and was ashamed.

"This fuel is damp," he muttered from behind the stove. "The damp wind—"

The old man continued to cough perseveringly and would not cease until the water boiled. Wang Lung dipped some into a bowl, and then, after a moment, he opened a glazed jar that stood upon a ledge of the stove and took from it a dozen or so of the curled dried leaves and sprinkled them upon the surface of the water. The old man's eyes opened greedily and immediately he began to complain.

"Why are you wasteful? Tea is like eating silver."

"It is the day," replied Wang Lung with a short laugh. "Eat and be comforted."

The old man grasped the bowl in his shriveled, knotty fingers,

[5]

muttering, uttering little grunts. He watched the leaves uncurl and spread upon the surface of the water, unable to bear drinking the precious stuff.

"It will be cold," said Wang Lung.

"True—true—" said the old man in alarm, and he began to take great gulps of the hot tea. He passed into an animal satisfaction, like a child fixed upon its feeding. But he was not too forgetful to see Wang Lung dipping the water recklessly from the cauldron into a deep wooden tub. He lifted his head and stared at his son.

"Now there is water enough to bring a crop to fruit," he said suddenly.

Wang Lung continued to dip the water to the last drop. He did not answer.

"Now then!" cried his father loudly.

"I have not washed my body all at once since the New Year," said Wang Lung in a low voice.

He was ashamed to say to his father that he wished his body to be clean for a woman to see. He hurried out, carrying the tub to his own room. The door was hung loosely upon a warped wooden frame and it did not shut closely, and the old man tottered into the middle room and put his mouth to the opening and bawled,

"It will be ill if we start the woman like this—tea in the morning water and all this washing!"

"It is only one day," shouted Wang Lung. And then he added, "I will throw the water on the earth when I am finished and it is not all waste."

The old man was silent at this, and Wang Lung unfastened his girdle and stepped out of his clothing. In the light that streamed in a square block from the hole he wrung a small towel from the steaming water and he scrubbed his dark slender body vigorously. Warm though he had thought the air, when his flesh was wet he was cold, and he moved quickly, passing the towel in and out of the water until from his whole body there went up a delicate cloud of steam. Then he went to a box that had been his mother's and

[6]

drew from it a fresh suit of blue cotton cloth. He might be a little cold this day without the wadding of the winter garments, but he suddenly could not bear to put them on against his clean flesh. The covering of them was torn and filthy and the wadding stuck out of the holes, grey and sodden. He did not want this woman to see him for the first time with the wadding sticking out of his clothes. Later she would have to wash and mend, but not the first day. He drew over the blue cotton coat and trousers a long robe made of the same material—his one long robe, which he wore on feast days only, ten days or so in the year, all told. Then with swift fingers he unplaited the long braid of hair that hung down his back, and taking a wooden comb from the drawer of the small, unsteady table, he began to comb out his hair.

His father drew near again and put his mouth to the crack of the door.

"Am I to have nothing to eat this day?" he complained. "At my age the bones are water in the morning until food is given them."

"I am coming," said Wang Lung, braiding his hair quickly and smoothly and weaving into the strands a tasseled, black silk cord.

Then after a moment he removed his long gown and wound his braid about his head and went out, carrying the tub of water. He had quite forgotten the breakfast. He would stir a little water into corn meal and give it to his father. For himself he could not eat. He staggered with the tub to the threshold and poured the water upon the earth nearest the door, and as he did so he remembered he had used all the water in the cauldron for his bathing and he would have to start the fire again. A wave of anger passed over him at his father.

"That old head thinks of nothing except his eating and his drinking," he muttered into the mouth of the oven; but aloud he said nothing. It was the last morning he would have to prepare food for the old man. He put a very little water into the cauldron, drawing it in a bucket from the well near the door, and it boiled quickly and he stirred meal together and took it to the old man.

[7]

"We will have rice this night, my father," he said. "Meanwhile, here is corn."

"There is only a little rice left in the basket," said the old man, seating himself at the table in the middle room and stirring with his chopsticks the thick yellow gruel.

"We will eat a little less then at the spring festival," said Wang Lung. But the old man did not hear. He was supping loudly at his bowl.

Wang Lung went into his own room then, and drew about him again the long blue robe and let down the braid of his hair. He passed his hand over his shaven brow and over his cheeks. Perhaps he had better be newly shaven? It was scarcely sunrise yet. He could pass through the Street of the Barbers and be shaved before he went to the house where the woman waited for him. If he had the money he would do it.

He took from his girdle a small greasy pouch of grey cloth and counted the money in it. There were six silver pieces and a double handful of copper coins. He had not yet told his father he had asked friends to sup that night. He had asked his male cousin, the young son of his uncle, and his uncle for his father's sake, and three neighboring farmers who lived in the village with him. He had planned to bring back from the town that morning pork, a small pond fish, and a handful of chestnuts. He might even buy a few of the bamboo sprouts from the south and a little beef to stew with the cabbage he had raised in his own garden. But this only if there were any money left after the bean oil and the soybean sauce had been bought. If he shaved his head he could not, perhaps, buy the beef. Well, he would shave his head, he decided suddenly.

He left the old man without speech and went out into the early morning. In spite of the dark red dawn the sun was mounting the horizon clouds and sparkled upon the dew on the rising wheat and barley. The farmer in Wang Lung was diverted for an instant and he stooped to examine the budding heads. They were empty as yet and waiting for the rain. He smelled the air and looked anxiously

[8]

at the sky. Rain was there, dark in the clouds, heavy upon the wind. He would buy a stick of incense and place it in the little temple to the Earth God. On a day like this he would do it.

He wound his way in among the fields upon the narrow path. In the near distance the grey city wall arose. Within that gate in the wall through which he would pass stood the great house where the woman had been a slave girl since her childhood, the House of Hwang. There were those who said, "It is better to live alone than to marry a woman who has been slave in a great house." But when he had said to his father, "Am I never to have a woman?" his father replied, "With weddings costing as they do in these evil days and every woman wanting gold rings and silk clothes before she will take a man, there remain only slaves to be had for the poor."

His father had stirred himself, then, and gone to the House of Hwang and asked if there were a slave to spare.

"Not a slave too young, and above all, not a pretty one," he had said.

Wang Lung had suffered that she must not be pretty. It would be something to have a pretty wife that other men would congratulate him upon having. His father, seeing his mutinous face, had cried out at him,

"And what will we do with a pretty woman? We must have a woman who will tend the house and bear children as she works in the fields, and will a pretty woman do these things? She will be forever thinking about clothes to go with her face! No, not a pretty woman in our house. We are farmers. Moreover, who has heard of a pretty slave who was virgin in a wealthy house? All the young lords have had their fill of her. It is better to be first with an ugly woman than the hundredth with a beauty. Do you imagine a pretty woman will think your farmer's hands as pleasing as the soft hands of a rich man's son, and your sun-black face as beautiful as the golden skin of the others who have had her for their pleasure?"

Wang Lung knew his father spoke well. Nevertheless, he had to struggle with his flesh before he could answer. And then he said violently,

[9]

"At least, I will not have a woman who is pock-marked, or who has a split upper lip."

"We will have to see what is to be had," his father replied.

Well, the woman was not pock-marked nor had she a split upper lip. This much he knew, but nothing more. He and his father had bought two silver rings, washed with gold, and silver earrings, and these his father had taken to the woman's owner in acknowledgment of betrothal. Beyond this, he knew nothing of the woman who was to be his, except that on this day he could go and get her.

He walked into the cool darkness of the city gate. Water carriers, just outside, their barrows laden with great tubs of water, passed to and fro all day, the water splashing out of the tubs upon the stones. It was always wet and cool in the tunnel of the gate under the thick wall of earth and brick; cool even upon a summer's day, so that the melon vendors spread their fruits upon the stones, melons split open to drink in the moist coolness. There were none yet, for the season was too early, but baskets of small hard green peaches stood along the walls, and the vendors cried out,

"The first peaches of spring—the first peaches! Buy, eat, purge your bowels of the poisons of winter!"

Wang Lung said to himself,

"If she likes them, I will buy her a handful when we return." He could not realize that when he walked back through the gate there would be a woman walking behind him.

He turned to the right within the gate and after a moment was in the Street of Barbers. There were few before him so early, only some farmers who had carried their produce into the town the night before in order that they might sell their vegetables at the dawn markets and return for the day's work in the fields. They had slept shivering and crouching over their baskets, the baskets now empty at their feet. Wang Lung avoided them lest some recognize him, for he wanted none of their joking on this day. All down the street in a long line the barbers stood behind their small stalls, and Wang Lung went to the furthest one and sat down upon the stool and motioned to the barber who stood chattering to his neighbor.

[10]

The barber came at once and began quickly to pour hot water, from a kettle on his pot of charcoal, into his brass basin.

"Shave everything?" he said in a professional tone.

"My head and my face," replied Wang Lung.

"Ears and nostrils cleaned?" asked the barber.

"How much will that cost extra?" asked Wang Lung cautiously.

"Four pence," said the barber, beginning to pass a black cloth in and out of the hot water.

"I will give you two," said Wang Lung.

"Then I will clean one ear and one nostril," rejoined the barber promptly. "On which side of the face do you wish it done?" He grimaced at the next barber as he spoke and the other burst into a guffaw. Wang Lung perceived that he had fallen into the hands of a joker, and feeling inferior in some unaccountable way, as he always did, to these town dwellers, even though they were only barbers and the lowest of persons, he said quickly,

"As you will—as you will—"

Then he submitted himself to the barber's soaping and rubbing and shaving, and being after all a generous fellow enough, the barber gave him without extra charge a series of skilful poundings upon his shoulders and back to loosen his muscles. He commented upon Wang Lung as he shaved his upper forehead,

"This would not be a bad-looking farmer if he would cut off his hair. The new fashion is to take off the braid."

His razor hovered so near the circle of hair upon Wang Lung's crown that Wang Lung cried out,

"I cannot cut it off without asking my father!" And the barber laughed and skirted the round spot of hair.

When it was finished and the money counted into the barber's wrinkled, water-soaked hand, Wang Lung had a moment of horror. So much money! But walking down the street again with the wind fresh upon his shaven skin, he said to himself,

"It is only once."

He went to the market, then, and bought two pounds of pork and watched the butcher as he wrapped it in a dried lotus leaf, and then, hesitating, he bought also six ounces of beef. When all had been bought, even to fresh squares of beancurd, shivering in a jelly upon the leaf, he went to a candlemaker's shop and there he bought a pair of incense sticks. Then he turned his steps with great shyness toward the House of Hwang.

Once at the gate of the house he was seized with terror. How had he come alone? He should have asked his father—his uncle—even his nearest neighbor, Ching—anyone to come with him. He had never been in a great house before. How could he go in with his wedding feast on his arm, and say, "I have come for a woman"?

He stood at the gate for a long time, looking at it. It was closed fast, two great wooden gates, painted black and bound and studded with iron, closed upon each other. Two lions made of stone stood on guard, one at either side. There was no one else. He turned away. It was impossible.

He felt suddenly faint. He would go first and buy a little food. He had eaten nothing—had forgotten food. He went into a small street restaurant, and putting two pence upon the table, he sat down. A dirty waiting boy with a shiny black apron came near and he called out to him, "Two bowls of noodles!" And when they were come, he ate them down greedily, pushing them into his mouth with his bamboo chopsticks, while the boy stood and spun the pennies between his black thumb and forefinger.

"Will you have more?" asked the boy indifferently.

Wang Lung shook his head. He sat up and looked about. There was no one he knew in the small, dark, crowded room full of tables. Only a few men sat eating or drinking tea. It was a place for poor men, and among them he looked neat and clean and almost well-to-do, so that a beggar, passing, whined at him,

"Have a good heart, teacher, and give me a small cash—I starve!"

Wang Lung had never had a beggar ask of him before, nor had any ever called him teacher. He was pleased and he threw into the beggar's bowl two small cash, which are one fifth of a penny, and

[12]

the beggar pulled back with swiftness his black claw of a hand, and grasping the cash, fumbled them within his rags.

Wang Lung sat and the sun climbed upwards. The waiting boy lounged about impatiently. "If you are buying nothing more," he said at last with much impudence, "you will have to pay rent for the stool."

Wang Lung was incensed at such impudence and he would have risen except that when he thought of going into the great House of Hwang and of asking there for a woman, sweat broke out over his whole body as though he were working in a field.

"Bring me tea," he said weakly to the boy. Before he could turn it was there and the small boy demanded sharply,

"Where is the penny?"

And Wang Lung, to his horror, found there was nothing to do but to produce from his girdle yet another penny.

"It is robbery," he muttered, unwilling. Then he saw entering the shop his neighbor whom he had invited to the feast, and he put the penny hastily upon the table and drank the tea at a gulp and went out quickly by the side door and was once more upon the street.

"It is to be done," he said to himself desperately, and slowly he turned his way to the great gates.

This time, since it was after high noon, the gates were ajar and the keeper of the gate idled upon the threshold, picking his teeth with a bamboo sliver after his meal. He was a tall fellow with a large mole upon his left cheek, and from the mole hung three long black hairs which had never been cut. When Wang Lung appeared he shouted roughly, thinking from the basket that he had come to sell something.

"Now then, what?"

With great difficulty Wang Lung replied,

"I am Wang Lung, the farmer."

"Well, and Wang Lung, the farmer, what?" retorted the gate-man, who was polite to none except the rich friends of his master and mistress.

"I am come—I am come—" faltered Wang Lung.

"That I see," said the gateman with elaborate patience, twisting the long hairs of his mole.

"There is a woman," said Wang Lung, his voice sinking helplessly to a whisper. In the sunshine his face was wet.

The gateman gave a great laugh.

"So you are he!" he roared. "I was told to expect a bridegroom today. But I did not recognize you with a basket on your arm."

"It is only a few meats," said Wang Lung apologetically, waiting for the gateman to lead him within. But the gateman did not move. At last Wang Lung said with anxiety,

"Shall I go alone?"

The gateman affected a start of horror. "The Old Lord would kill you!"

Then seeing that Wang Lung was too innocent he said, "A little silver is a good key."

Wang Lung perceived at last that the man wanted money of him.

"I am a poor man," he said pleadingly.

"Let me see what you have in your girdle," said the gateman.

And he grinned when Wang Lung in his simplicity actually put his basket upon the stones and lifting his robe took out the small bag from his girdle and shook into his left hand what money was left after his purchases. There was one silver piece and fourteen copper pence.

"I will take the silver," said the gateman coolly, and before Wang Lung could protest the man had the silver in his sleeve and was striding through the gate, bawling loudly,

"The bridegroom, the bridegroom!"

Wang Lung, in spite of anger at what had just happened and horror at this loud announcing of his coming, could do nothing but follow, and this he did, picking up his basket and looking neither to the right nor left.

Afterwards, although it was the first time he had ever been in a great family's house, he could remember nothing. With his face burning and his head bowed, he walked through court after court, hearing that voice roaring ahead of him, hearing tinkles of laughter on every side. Then suddenly when it seemed to him he had gone through a hundred courts, the gateman fell silent and pushed him into a small waiting room. There he stood alone while the gateman went into some inner place, returning in a moment to say,

"The Old Mistress says you are to appear before her."

Wang Lung started forward, but the gateman stopped him, crying in disgust,

"You cannot appear before a great lady with a basket on your arm—a basket of pork and beancurd! How will you bow?"

"True—true—" said Wang Lung in agitation. But he did not dare to put the basket down because he was afraid something might be stolen from it. It did not occur to him that all the world might not desire such delicacies as two pounds of pork and six ounces of beef and a small pond fish. The gateman saw his fear and cried out in great contempt,

"In a house like this we feed these meats to the dogs!" and seizing the basket he thrust it behind the door and pushed Wang Lung ahead of him.

Down a long narrow veranda they went, the roofs supported by delicate carven posts, and into a hall the like of which Wang Lung had never seen. A score of houses such as his whole house could have been put into it and have disappeared, so wide were the spaces, so high the roofs. Lifting his head in wonder to see the great carven and painted beams above him he stumbled upon the high threshold of the door and would have fallen except that the gateman caught his arm and cried out,

"Now will you be so polite as to fall on your face like this before the Old Mistress?"

And collecting himself in great shame Wang Lung looked ahead of him, and upon a dais in the center of the room he saw a very old lady, her small fine body clothed in lustrous, pearly grey satin, and upon the low bench beside her a pipe of opium stood, burning over its little lamp. She looked at him out of small, sharp, black eyes, as sunken and sharp as a monkey's eyes in her thin and wrinkled face. The skin of her hand that held the pipe's end was stretched over her little bones as smooth and as yellow as the gilt upon an idol. Wang Lung fell to his knees and knocked his head on the tiled floor.

"Raise him," said the old lady gravely to the gateman. "These obeisances are not necessary. Has he come for the woman?"

"Yes, Ancient One," replied the gateman.

"Why does he not speak for himself?" asked the old lady.

"Because he is a fool, Ancient One," said the gateman, twirling the hairs of his mole.

This roused Wang Lung and he looked with indignation at the gateman.

"I am only a coarse person, Great and Ancient Lady," he said. "I do not know what words to use in such a presence."

The old lady looked at him carefully and with perfect gravity and made as though she would have spoken, except that her hand closed upon the pipe which a slave had been tending for her and at once she seemed to forget him. She bent and sucked greedily at the pipe for a moment and the sharpness passed from her eyes and a film of forgetfulness came over them. Wang Lung remained standing before her until in passing her eyes caught his figure.

"What is this man doing here?" she asked with sudden anger. It was as though she had forgotten everything. The gateman's face was immovable. He said nothing.

"I am waiting for the woman, Great Lady," said Wang Lung in much astonishment.

"The woman? What woman? . . ." the old lady began, but the slave girl at her side stooped and whispered and the lady recovered herself. "Ah, yes, I forgot for the moment—a small affair—you have come for the slave called O-lan. I remember we promised her to some farmer in marriage. You are that farmer?"

"I am he," replied Wang Lung.

"Call O-lan quickly," said the old lady to her slave. It was as

[16]

though she was suddenly impatient to be done with all this and to be left alone in the stillness of the great room with her opium pipe.

And in an instant the slave appeared leading by the hand a square, rather tall figure, clothed in clean blue cotton coat and trousers. Wang Lung glanced once and then away, his heart beating. This was his woman.

"Come here, slave," said the old lady carelessly. "This man has come for you."

The woman went before the lady and stood with bowed head and hands clasped.

"Are you ready?" asked the lady.

The woman answered slowly as an echo, "Ready."

Wang Lung, hearing her voice for the first time, looked at her back as she stood before him. It was a good enough voice, not loud, not soft, plain, and not ill-tempered. The woman's hair was neat and smooth and her coat clean. He saw with an instant's disappointment that her feet were not bound. But this he could not dwell upon, for the old lady was saying to the gateman,

"Carry her box out to the gate and let them begone." Then she called Wang Lung and said, "Stand beside her while I speak." And when Wang had come forward she said to him, "This woman came into our house when she was a child of ten and here she has lived until now, when she is twenty years old. I bought her in a year of famine when her parents came south because they had nothing to eat. They were from the north in Shantung and there they returned, and I know nothing further of them. You see she has the strong body and the square cheeks of her kind. She will work well for you in the field and at drawing water and at all else that you wish. She is not beautiful but that you do not need. Only men of leisure have the need for beautiful women to divert them. Neither is she clever. But she does well what she is told to do and she has a good temper. So far as I know she is virgin. She has not beauty enough to tempt my sons and grandsons even if she had not been in the kitchen. If there has been anything it has been only a serving man. But with the innumerable and pretty slaves running freely about the courts, I doubt if there has been anyone. Take her and use her well. She is a good slave, although somewhat slow and stupid, and had I not wished to acquire merit at the temple for my future existence by bringing more life into the world I should have kept her, for she is good enough for the kitchen. But I marry my slaves off if any will have them and the lords do not want them."

And to the woman she said,

"Obey him and bear him sons and yet more sons. Bring the first child to me to see."

"Yes, Ancient Mistress," said the woman submissively.

They stood hesitating, and Wang Lung was greatly embarrassed, not knowing whether he should speak or what.

"Well, go, will you!" said the old lady in irritation, and Wang Lung, bowing hastily, turned and went out, the woman after him, and after her the gateman, carrying on his shoulder the box. This box he dropped down in the room where Wang Lung returned to find his basket and would carry it no further, and indeed he disappeared without another word.

Then Wang Lung turned to the woman and looked at her for the first time. She had a square, honest face, a short, broad nose with large black nostrils, and her mouth was wide as a gash in her face. Her eyes were small and of a dull black in color, and were filled with some sadness that was not clearly expressed. It was a face that seemed habitually silent and unspeaking, as though it could not speak if it would. She bore patiently Wang Lung's look, without embarrassment or response, simply waiting until he had seen her. He saw that it was true there was not beauty of any kind in her face—a brown, common, patient face. But there were no pock-marks on her dark skin, nor was her lip split. In her ears he saw his rings hanging, the gold-washed rings he had bought, and on her hands were the rings he had given her. He turned away with secret exultation. Well, he had his woman!

"Here are this box and this basket," he said gruffly.

Without a word she bent over and picking up one end of the

box she placed it upon her shoulder and, staggering under its weight, tried to rise. He watched her at this and suddenly he said,

"I will take the box. Here is the basket."

And he shifted the box to his own back, regardless of the best robe he wore, and she, still speechless, took the handle of the basket. He thought of the hundred courts he had come through and of his figure, absurd under its burden.

"If there were a side gate—" he muttered, and she nodded after a little thought, as though she did not understand too quickly what he said. Then she led the way through a small unused court that was grown up with weeds, its pool choked, and there under a bent pine tree was an old round gate that she pulled loose from its bar, and they went through and into the street.

Once or twice he looked back at her. She plodded along steadily on her big feet as though she had walked there all her life, her wide face expressionless. In the gate of the wall he stopped uncertainly and fumbled in his girdle with one hand for the pennies he had left, holding the box steady on his shoulder with the other hand. He took out two pence and with these he bought six small green peaches.

"Take these and eat them for yourself," he said gruffly.

She clutched them greedily as a child might and held them in her hand without speech. When next he looked at her as they walked along the margin of the wheat fields she was nibbling one cautiously, but when she saw him looking at her she covered it again with her hand and kept her jaws motionless.

And thus they went until they reached the western field where stood the temple to the earth. This temple was a small structure, not higher in all than a man's shoulder and made of grey bricks and roofed with tile. Wang Lung's grandfather, who had farmed the very fields upon which Wang Lung now spent his life, had built it, hauling the bricks from the town upon his wheelbarrow. The walls were covered with plaster on the outside and a village artist had once been hired in a good year to paint upon the white plaster a scene of hills and bamboo. But the rain of generations had

[19]

poured upon this painting until now there was only a faint feathery shadow of bamboos left, and the hills were almost wholly gone.

Within the temple snugly under the roof sat two small, solemn figures, earthen, for they were formed from the earth of the fields about the temple. These were the god himself and his lady. They wore robes of red and gilt paper, and the god had a scant, drooping mustache of real hair. Each year at the New Year, Wang Lung's father bought sheets of red paper and carefully cut and pasted new robes for the pair. And each year rain and snow beat in and the sun of summer shone in and spoiled their robes.

At this moment, however, the robes were still new, since the year was but well begun, and Wang Lung was proud of their spruce appearance. He took the basket from the woman's arm and carefully he looked about under the pork for the sticks of incense he had bought. He was anxious lest they were broken and thus be an evil omen, but they were whole, and when he had found them he stuck them side by side in the ashes of other sticks of incense that were heaped before the gods, for the whole neighborhood worshipped these two small figures. Then fumbling for his flint and iron he caught, with a dried leaf for tinder, a flame to light the incense.

Together this man and this woman stood before the gods of their fields. The woman watched the ends of the incense redden and turn grey. When the ash grew heavy she leaned over and with her forefinger she pushed the head of ash away. Then as though fearful for what she had done, she looked quickly at Wang Lung, her eyes dumb. But there was something he liked in her movement. It was as though she felt that the incense belonged to them both; it was a moment of marriage. They stood there in complete silence, side by side, while the incense smouldered into ashes; and then because the sun was sinking, Wang Lung shouldered the box and they went home.

At the door of the house the old man stood to catch the last rays of the sun upon him. He made no movement as Wang Lung approached with the woman. It would have been beneath him to notice her. Instead he feigned great interest in the clouds and he cried,

"That cloud which hangs upon the left horn of the new moon speaks of rain. It will come not later than tomorrow night." And then as he saw Wang Lung take the basket from the woman he cried out again, "And have you spent money?"

Wang Lung set the basket on the table. "There will be guests tonight," he said briefly, and he carried the box into the room where he slept and set it down beside the box where his own clothes were. He looked at it strangely. But the old man came to the door and said volubly,

"There is no end to the money spent in this house!"

Secretly he was pleased that his son had invited guests, but he felt it would not do to give out anything but complaints before his new daughter-in-law lest she be set from the first in ways of extravagance. Wang Lung said nothing, but he went out and took the basket into the kitchen and the woman followed him there. He took the food piece by piece from the basket and laid it upon the ledge of the cold stove and he said to her,

"Here is pork and here beef and fish. There are seven to eat. Can you prepare food?"

He did not look at the woman as he spoke. It would not have been seemly. The woman answered in her plain voice,

"I have been kitchen slave since I went into the House of Hwang. There were meats at every meal."

Wang Lung nodded and left her and did not see her again until the guests came crowding in, his uncle jovial and sly and hungry, his uncle's son an impudent lad of fifteen, and the farmers clumsy and grinning with shyness. Two were men from the village with whom Wang Lung exchanged seed and labor at harvest time, and one was his next door neighbor, Ching, a small, quiet man, ever unwilling to speak unless he were compelled to it. After they had been seated about the middle room demurring and with unwillingness to take seats, for politeness, Wang Lung went into the kitchen to bid the woman serve. Then he was pleased when she said to him,

"I will hand you the bowls if you will place them upon the table. I do not like to come out before men."

Wang Lung felt in him a great pride that this woman was his and did not fear to appear before him, but would not before other men. He took the bowls from her hands at the kitchen door and he set them upon the table in the middle room and called loudly,

"Eat, my uncle and my brothers." And when the uncle, who was fond of jokes, said, "Are we not to see the moth-browed bride?" Wang Lung replied firmly, "We are not yet one. It is not meet that other men see her until the marriage is consummated."

And he urged them to eat and they ate heartily of the good fare, heartily and in silence, and this one praised the brown sauce on the fish and that one the well done pork, and Wang Lung said over and over in reply,

"It is poor stuff—it is badly prepared."

But in his heart he was proud of the dishes, for with what meats she had the woman had combined sugar and vinegar and a little wine and soy sauce and she had skilfully brought forth all the force of the meat itself, so that Wang Lung himself had never tasted such dishes upon the tables of his friends.

That night after the guests had tarried long over their tea and had done with their jokes, the woman still lingered behind the stove, and when Wang Lung had seen the last guest away he went in and she cowered there in the straw piles asleep beside the ox. There was straw in her hair when he roused her, and when he called her she put up her arm suddenly in her sleep as though to defend herself from a blow. When she opened her eyes at last, she looked at him with her strange speechless gaze, and he felt as though he faced a child. He took her by the hand and led her into the room where that morning he had bathed himself for her, and he lit a red candle upon the table. In this light he was suddenly shy when he found himself alone with the woman and he was compelled to remind himself,

"There is this woman of mine. The thing is to be done."

And he began to undress himself doggedly. As for the woman, she crept around the corner of the curtain and began without a sound to prepare for the bed. Wang Lung said gruffly,

"When you lie down, put the light out first."

Then he lay down and drew the thick quilt about his shoulders and pretended to sleep. But he was not sleeping. He lay quivering, every nerve of his flesh awake. And when, after a long time, the room went dark, and there was the slow, silent, creeping movement of the woman beside him, an exultation filled him fit to break his body. He gave a hoarse laugh into the darkness and seized her.

II

THERE was this luxury of living. The next morning he lay upon his bed and watched the woman who was now wholly his own. She rose and drew about her her loosened garments and fastened them closely about her throat and waist, fitting them to her body with a slow writhe and twist. Then she put her feet into her cloth shoes and drew them on by the straps hanging at the back. The light from the small hole shone on her in a bar and he saw her face dimly. It looked unchanged. This was an astonishment to Wang Lung. He felt as though the night must have changed him; yet here was this woman rising from his bed as though she had risen from it every day of her life. The old man's cough rose querulously out of the dusky dawn and he said to her,

"Take to my father first a bowl of hot water for his lungs."

She asked, her voice exactly as it had been yesterday when she spoke, "Are there to be tea leaves in it?"

This simple question troubled Wang Lung. He would have liked to say, "Certainly there must be tea leaves. Do you think we are beggars?" He would have liked the woman to think that they made nothing of tea leaves in this house. In the House of Hwang, of course, every bowl of water was green with leaves. Even a slave, there, perhaps, would not drink only water. But he knew his father would be angry if on the first day the woman served tea to him instead of water. Besides, they really were not rich. He replied negligently, therefore,

"Tea? No—no—it makes his cough worse."

And then he lay in his bed warm and satisfied while in the kitchen the woman fed the fire and boiled the water. He would like to have slept, now that he could, but his foolish body, which he had made to arise every morning so early for all these years, would not sleep although it could, and so he lay there, tasting and savoring in his mind and in his flesh his luxury of idleness.

He was still half ashamed to think of this woman of his. Part of the time he thought of his fields and of the grains of the wheat and of what his harvest would be if the rains came and of the white turnip seed he wished to buy from his neighbor Ching if they could agree upon a price. But between all these thoughts which were in his mind every day there ran weaving and interweaving the new thought of what his life now was, and it occurred to him, suddenly, thinking of the night, to wonder if she liked him. This was a new wonder. He had questioned only of whether he would like her and whether or not she would be satisfactory in his bed and in his house. Plain though her face was and rough the skin upon her hands, the flesh of her big body was soft and untouched and he laughed when he thought of it—the short laugh he had thrown out into the darkness the night before. The young lords had not seen, then, beyond that plain face of the kitchen slave. Her body was beautiful, spare and big boned, yet rounded and soft. He desired suddenly that she should like him as her husband and then he was ashamed.

The door opened and in her silent way she came in, bearing in both hands a steaming bowl to him. He sat up in bed and took it. There were tea leaves floating upon the surface of the water. He looked up at her quickly. She was at once afraid and she said,

"I took no tea to the Old One—I did as you said—but to you I . . ."

Wang Lung saw that she was afraid of him and he was pleased and he answered before she finished, "I like it—I like it," and he drew his tea into his mouth with loud sups of pleasure.

In himself there was this new exultation which he was ashamed to make articulate even to his own heart, "This woman of mine likes me well enough!"

It seemed to him that during these next months he did nothing except watch this woman of his. In reality he worked as he always had. He put his hoe upon his shoulder and he walked to his plots of land and he cultivated the rows of grain, and he yoked the ox to the plow and he ploughed the western field for garlic and onions. But the work was luxury, for when the sun struck the zenith he could go to his house and food would be there ready for him to eat, and the dust wiped from the table, and the bowls and the chopsticks placed neatly upon it. Hitherto he had had to prepare the meals when he came in, tired though he was, unless the old man grew hungry out of time and stirred up a little meal or baked a piece of flat, unleavened bread to roll about a stem of garlic.

Now whatever there was, was ready for him, and he could seat himself upon the bench by the table and eat at once. The earthen floor was swept and the fuel pile replenished. The woman, when he had gone in the morning, took the bamboo rake and a length of rope and with these she roamed the countryside, reaping here a bit of grass and there a twig or a handful of leaves, returning at noon with enough to cook the dinner. It pleased the man that they need buy no more fuel.

In the afternoon she took a hoe and a basket and with these upon her shoulder she went to the main road leading into the city where mules and donkeys and horses carried burdens to and fro, and there she picked the droppings from the animals and carried it home and piled the manure in the dooryard for fertilizer for the fields. These things she did without a word and without being commanded to do them. And when the end of the day came she did not rest herself until the ox had been fed in the kitchen and until she had dipped water to hold to its muzzle to let it drink what it would.

And she took their ragged clothes and with thread she herself had spun on a bamboo spindle from a wad of cotton she mended and contrived to cover the rents in their winter clothes. Their bedding she took into the sun on the threshold and she ripped the coverings from the quilts and washed them and hung them upon a bamboo to dry, and the cotton in the quilts that had grown hard and grey from years she picked over, killing the vermin that had flourished in the hidden folds, and sunning it all. Day after day she did one thing after another, until the three rooms seemed clean and almost prosperous. The old man's cough grew better and he sat in the sun by the southern wall of the house, always half-asleep and warm and content.

But she never talked, this woman, except for the brief necessities of life. Wang Lung, watching her move steadily and slowly about the rooms on her big feet, watching secretly the stolid, square face, the unexpressed, half-fearful look of her eyes, made nothing of her. At night he knew the soft firmness of her body. But in the day her clothes, her plain blue cotton coat and trousers, covered all that he knew, and she was like a faithful, speechless serving maid, who is only a serving maid and nothing more. And it was not meet that he should say to her, "Why do you not speak?" It should be enough that she fulfilled her duty.

Sometimes, working over the clods in the fields, he would fall to pondering about her. What had she seen in those hundred courts? What had been her life, that life she never shared with him? He could make nothing of it. And then he was ashamed of his own curiosity and of his interest in her. She was, after all, only a woman.

But there is not that about three rooms and two meals a day to keep busy a woman who has been a slave in a great house and who has worked from dawn until midnight. One day when Wang Lung was hard pressed with the swelling wheat and was cultivating it with his hoe, day after day, until his back throbbed with weariness, her shadow fell across the furrow over which he bent himself, and there she stood, with a hoe across her shoulder.

"There is nothing in the house until nightfall," she said briefly, and without speech she took the furrow to the left of him and fell into steady hoeing.

The sun beat down upon them, for it was early summer, and her face was soon dripping with her sweat. Wang Lung had his coat off and his back bare, but she worked with her thin garment covering her shoulders and it grew wet and clung to her like skin. Moving together in a perfect rhythm, without a word, hour after hour, he fell into a union with her which took the pain from his labor. He had no articulate thought of anything; there was only this perfect sympathy of movement, of turning this earth of theirs over and over to the sun, this earth which formed their home and fed their bodies and made their gods. The earth lay rich and dark, and fell apart lightly under the points of their hoes. Sometimes they turned up a bit of brick, a splinter of wood. It was nothing. Some time, in some age, bodies of men and women had been buried there, houses had stood there, had fallen, and gone back into the earth. So would also their house, some time, return into the earth, their bodies also. Each had his turn at this earth. They worked on, moving together—together—producing the fruit of this earth—speechless in their movement together.

When the sun had set he straightened his back slowly and looked at the woman. Her face was wet and streaked with the earth. She was as brown as the very soil itself. Her wet, dark garments clung to her square body. She smoothed a last furrow slowly. Then in her usual plain way she said, straight out, her voice flat and more than usually plain in the silent evening air,

"I am with child."

Wang Lung stood still. What was there to say to this thing, then! She stooped to pick up a bit of broken brick and threw it out of the furrow. It was as though she had said, "I have brought you tea," or as though she had said, "We can eat." It seemed as ordinary as that to her! But to him—he could not say what it was to him. His heart swelled and stopped as though it met sudden confines. Well, it was their turn at this earth!

He took the hoe suddenly from her hand and he said, his voice thick in his throat, "Let be for now. It is a day's end. We will tell the old man."

They walked home, then, she half a dozen paces behind him as befitted a woman. The old man stood at the door, hungry for his evening's food, which, now that the woman was in the house, he would never prepare for himself. He was impatient and he called out,

"I am too old to wait for my food like this!"

But Wang Lung, passing him into the room, said,

"She is with child already."

He tried to say it easily as one might say, "I have planted the seeds in the western field today," but he could not. Although he spoke in a low voice it was to him as though he had shouted the words out louder than he would.

The old man blinked for a moment and then comprehended, and cackled with laughter.

"Heh-heh-heh—" he called out to his daughter-in-law as she came, "so the harvest is in sight!"

Her face he could not see in the dusk, but she answered evenly,

"I shall prepare food now."

"Yes—yes—food—" said the old man eagerly, following her into the kitchen like a child. Just as the thought of a grandson had made him forget his meal, so now the thought of food freshly before him made him forget the child.

But Wang Lung sat upon a bench by the table in the darkness and put his head upon his folded arms. Out of this body of his, out of his own loins, life!

III

WHEN the hour for birth drew near he said to the woman, "We must have someone to help at the time—some woman."

But she shook her head. She was clearing away the bowls after the evening food. The old man had gone to his bed and the two of them were alone in the night, with only the light that fell upon them from the flickering flame of a small tin lamp filled with bean oil, in which a twist of cotton floated for a wick.

"No woman?" he asked in consternation. He was beginning now to be accustomed to these conversations with her in which her part was little more than a movement of head or hand, or at most an occasional word dropped unwillingly from her wide mouth. He had even come to feel no lack in such conversing. "But it will be odd with only two men in the house!" he continued. "My mother had a woman from the village. I know nothing of these affairs. Is there none in the great house, no old slave with whom you were friends, who could come?"

It was the first time he had mentioned the house from which she came. She turned on him as he had never seen her, her narrow eyes widened, her face stirred with dull anger.

"None in that house!" she cried out at him.

He dropped his pipe which he was filling and stared at her. But her face was suddenly as usual and she was collecting the chopsticks as though she had not spoken.

"Well, here is a thing!" he said in astonishment. But she said nothing. Then he continued in argument, "We two men, we have no ability in childbirth. For my father it is not fitting to enter your room—for myself, I have never even seen a cow give birth. My clumsy hands might mar the child. Someone from the great house, now, where the slaves are always giving birth . . ."

She had placed the chopsticks carefully down in an orderly heap upon the table and she looked at him, and after a moment's looking she said,

"When I return to that house it will be with my son in my arms. I shall have a red coat on him and red-flowered trousers and on his head a hat with a small gilded Buddha sewn on the front and on his feet tiger-faced shoes. And I will wear new shoes and a new coat of black sateen and I will go into the kitchen where I spent my days and I will go into the great hall where the Old One sits with her opium, and I will show myself and my son to all of them."

He had never heard so many words from her before. They came forth steadily and without break, albeit slowly, and he realized that she had planned this whole thing out for herself. When she had been working in the fields beside him she had been planning all this out! How astonishing she was! He would have said that she had scarcely thought of the child, so stilly had she gone about her work, day in and day out. And instead she saw this child, born and fully clothed, and herself as his mother, in a new coat! He was for once without words himself, and he pressed the tobacco diligently into a ball between his thumb and forefinger, and picking up his pipe he fitted the tobacco into the bowl.

"I suppose you will need some money," he said at last with apparent gruffness.

"If you will give me three silver pieces . . ." she said fearfully.

"It is a great deal, but I have counted carefully and I will waste no penny of it. I shall make the cloth dealer give me the last inch to the foot."

Wang Lung fumbled in his girdle. The day before he had sold a load and a half of reeds from the pond in the western field to the town market and he had in his girdle a little more than she wished. He put the three silver pieces upon the table. Then, after a little hesitation, he added a fourth piece which he had long kept by him on the chance of his wanting to gamble a little some morning at the tea house. But he never did more than linger about the tables and look at the dice as they clattered upon the table, fearful lest he lose if he played. He usually ended by spending his spare hours in the town at the story-teller's booth, where one may listen to an old tale and pay no more than a penny into his bowl when it was passed about.

"You had better take the other piece," he said, lighting his pipe between the words, blowing quickly at the paper spill to set it aflame. "You may as well make his coat of a small remnant of silk. After all, he is the first."

She did not at once take the money, but she stood looking at it, her face motionless. Then she said in a half-whisper,

"It is the first time I have silver money in my hand."

Suddenly she took it and clenched it in her hand and hurried into the bedroom.

Wang Lung sat smoking, thinking of the silver as it had lain upon the table. It had come out of the earth, this silver, out of his earth that he ploughed and turned and spent himself upon. He took his life from this earth; drop by drop by his sweat he wrung fruit from it and from the fruit, silver. Each time before this that he had taken the silver out to give to anyone, it had been like taking a piece of his life and giving it to someone carelessly. But now for the first time such giving was not pain. He saw, not the silver in the alien hand of a merchant in the town; he saw the silver transmuted into something worth even more than itself— clothes upon the body of his son. And this strange woman of his, who worked about, saying nothing, seeming to see nothing, she had first seen the child thus clothed!

She would have no one with her when the hour came. It came one night, early, when the sun was scarcely set. She was working beside him in the harvest field. The wheat had borne and been cut and the field flooded and the young rice set, and now the rice bore harvest, and the ears were ripe and full after the summer rains and the warm ripening sun of early autumn. Together they cut the sheaves all day, bending and cutting with short-handled scythes. She had stooped stiffly, because of the burden she bore, and she moved more slowly than he, so that they cut unevenly, his row ahead, and hers behind. She began to cut more and more slowly as noon wore on to afternoon and evening, and he turned to look at her with impatience. She stopped and stood up then, her scythe dropped. On her face was a new sweat, the sweat of a new agony.

"It is come," she said. "I will go into the house. Do not come into the room until I call. Only bring me a newly peeled reed, and slit it, that I may cut the child's life from mine."

She went across the fields toward the house as though there were nothing to come, and after he had watched her he went to the edge of the pond in the outer field and chose a slim green reed and peeled it carefully and slit it on the edge of his scythe. The quick autumn darkness was falling then and he shouldered his scythe and went home.

When he reached the house he found his supper hot on the table and the old man eating. She had stopped in her labor to prepare them food! He said to himself that she was a woman such as is not commonly found. Then he went to the door of their room and he called out,

"Here is the reed!"

He waited, expecting that she would call out to him to bring it in to her. But she did not. She came to the door and through the crack her hand reached out and took the reed. She said no word, but he heard her panting as an animal pants which has run for a long way.

The old man looked up from his bowl to say,

"Eat, or all will be cold." And then he said, "Do not trouble yourself yet—it will be a long time. I remember well when the first was born to me it was dawn before it was over. Ah me, to think that out of all the children I begot and your mother bore, one after the other—a score or so—I forget—only you have lived! You see why a woman must bear and bear." And then he said again, as though he had just thought of it newly, "By this time tomorrow I may be grandfather to a man child!" He began to laugh suddenly and he stopped his eating and sat chuckling for a long time in the dusk of the room.

But Wang Lung stood listening at the door to those heavy animal pants. A smell of hot blood came through the crack, a sickening smell that frightened him. The panting of the woman within became quick and loud, like whispered screams, but she made no sound aloud. When he could bear no more and was about to break into the room, a thin, fierce cry came out and he forgot everything.

"Is it a man?" he cried importunately, forgetting the woman. The thin cry burst out again, wiry, insistent. "Is it a man?" he cried again. "Tell me at least this—is it a man?"

And the voice of the woman answered as faintly as an echo, "A man!"

He went and sat down at the table then. How quick it had all been! The food was long cold and the old man was asleep on his bench, but how quick it had all been! He shook the old man's shoulder.

"It is a man child!" he called triumphantly. "You are grandfather and I am father!"

The old man woke suddenly and began to laugh as he had been laughing when he fell asleep.

"Yes—yes—of course," he cackled, "grandfather—grandfather—" and he rose and went to his bed, still laughing.

Wang Lung took up the bowl of cold rice and began to eat. He was very hungry all at once and he could not get the food into his mouth quickly enough. In the room he could hear the woman dragging herself about and the cry of the child was incessant and piercing.

"I suppose we shall have no more peace in this house now," he said to himself proudly.

When he had eaten all that he wished he went to the door again and she called to him to come in and he went in. The odor of spilt blood still hung hot upon the air, but there was no trace of it except in the wooden tub. But into this she had poured water and had pushed it under the bed so that he could hardly see it. The red candle was lit and she was lying neatly covered upon the bed. Beside her, wrapped in a pair of his old trousers, as the custom was in this part, lay his son.

He went up and for the moment there were no words in his mouth. His heart crowded up into his breast and he leaned over the child to look at it. It had a round wrinkled face that looked very dark and upon its head the hair was long and damp and black. It had ceased crying and lay with its eyes tightly shut.

He looked at his wife and she looked back at him. Her hair was still wet with her agony and her narrow eyes were sunken. Beyond this, she was as she always was. But to him she was touching, lying there. His heart rushed out to these two and he said, not knowing what else there was that could be said,

"Tomorrow I will go into the city and buy a pound of red sugar and stir it into boiling water for you to drink."

And then looking at the child again, this burst forth from him suddenly as though he had just thought of it, "We shall have to buy a good basketful of eggs and dye them all red for the village. Thus will everyone know I have a son!"

IV

THE next day after the child was born the woman rose as usual and prepared food for them but she did not go into the harvest fields with Wang Lung, and so he worked alone until after the noon hour. Then he dressed himself in his blue gown and went into the town. He went to the market and bought fifty eggs, not new laid, but still well enough and costing a penny for one, and he bought red paper to boil in the water with them to make them red. Then with the eggs in his basket he went to the sweet shop, and there he bought a pound and a little more of red sugar and saw it wrapped carefully into its brown paper, and under the straw string which held it the sugar dealer slipped a strip of red paper, smiling as he did so.

"It is for the mother of a new-born child, perhaps?"

"A first-born son," said Wang Lung proudly.

"Ah, good fortune," answered the man carelessly, his eye on a well-dressed customer who had just come in.

This he had said many times to others, even every day to some-one, but to Wang Lung it seemed special and he was pleased with the man's courtesy and he bowed and bowed again as he went from the shop. It seemed to him as he walked into the sharp sun-shine of the dusty street that there was never a man so filled with good fortune as he.

He thought of this at first with joy and then with a pang of fear. It did not do in this life to be too fortunate. The air and the earth were filled with malignant spirits who could not endure the happiness of mortals, especially of such as are poor. He turned abruptly into the candlemaker's shop, who sold incense also, and there he bought four sticks of incense, one for each person in his house, and with these four sticks he went into the small temple of the gods of the earth, and he thrust them into the cold ashes of the incense he had placed there before, he and his wife together. He watched the four sticks well lit and then went homeward, comforted. These two small, protective figures, sitting staidly under their small roof—what a power they had!

And then, almost before one could realize anything, the woman was back in the fields beside him. The harvests were past, and the grain they beat out upon the threshing floor which was also the dooryard to the house. They beat it out with flails, he and the woman together. And when the grain was flailed they winnowed it, casting it up from great flat bamboo baskets into the wind and catching the good grain as it fell, and the chaff blew away in a cloud with the wind. Then there were the fields to plant for winter wheat again, and when he had yoked the ox and ploughed the land the woman followed behind with her hoe and broke the clods in the furrows.

She worked all day now and the child lay on an old torn quilt on the ground, asleep. When it cried the woman stopped and uncovered her bosom to the child's mouth, sitting flat upon the ground, and the sun beat down upon them both, the reluctant sun of late autumn that will not let go the warmth of summer until the cold of the coming winter forces it. The woman and the child were as brown as the soil and they sat there like figures made of earth. There was the dust of the fields upon the woman's hair and upon the child's soft black head.

But out of the woman's great brown breast the milk gushed forth for the child, milk as white as snow, and when the child suckled at one breast it flowed like a fountain from the other, and she let it flow. There was more than enough for the child, greedy though he was, life enough for many children, and she let it flow out carelessly, conscious of her abundance. There was always more and more. Sometimes she lifted her breast and let it flow out upon the ground to save her clothing, and it sank into the earth and made a soft, dark, rich spot in the field. The child was fat and good-natured and ate of the inexhaustible life his mother gave him.

Winter came on and they were prepared against it. There had been such harvests as never were before, and the small, three-roomed house was bursting. From the rafters of the thatched roof hung strings and strings of dried onions and garlic, and about the middle room and in the old man's room and in their own room were mats made of reeds and twisted into the shapes of great jars and these were filled full of wheat and rice. Much of this would be sold, but Wang Lung was frugal and he did not, like many of the villagers, spend his money freely at gambling or on foods too delicate for them, and so, like them, have to sell the grain at harvest when the price was low. Instead he saved it and sold it when the snow came on the ground or at the New Year when people in the towns will pay well for food at any price.

His uncle was always having to sell his grain before it was even well ripened. Sometimes he even sold it standing in the field to save himself the trouble of harvesting and threshing to get a little ready cash. But then his uncle's wife was a foolish woman, fat and lazy, and forever clamoring for sweet food and for this sort of thing and that and for new shoes bought in the town. Wang Lung's woman made all the shoes for himself and for the old man and for her own feet and the child's. He would not know what to make of it if she wished to buy shoes!

There was never anything hanging from the rafters in his uncle's crumbling old house. But in his own there was even a leg of pork which he had bought from his neighbor Ching when he killed his pig that looked as though it were sickening for a disease. The pig had been caught early before it lost flesh and the leg was a large one and O-lan had salted it thoroughly and hung it to dry. There were as well two of their own chickens killed and drawn and dried with the feathers on and stuffed with salt inside.

In the midst of all this plenty they sat in the house, therefore, when the winds of winter came out of the desert to the northeast of them, winds bitter and biting. Soon the child could almost sit alone. They had had a feast of noodles, which mean long life, on his month birthday, when he was a full moon of age, and Wang Lung had invited those who came to his wedding feast and to each he had given a round ten of the red eggs he had boiled and dyed, and to all those who came from the village to congratulate him he gave two eggs. And every one envied him his son, a great, fat, moony-faced child with high cheek bones like his mother. Now as winter came on he sat on the quilt placed on the earthen floor of the house instead of upon the fields, and they opened the door to the south for light, and the sun came in, and the wind on the north beat in vain against the thick earthen wall of the house.

The leaves were soon torn from the date tree on the threshold and from the willow trees and the peach trees near the fields. Only the bamboo leaves clung to the bamboos in the sparse clump to the east of the house, and even though the wind wrenched the stems double, the leaves clung.

With this dry wind the wheat seed that lay in the ground could not sprout and Wang Lung waited anxiously for the rains. And then the rains came suddenly out of a still grey day when the wind fell and the air was quiet and warm, and they all sat in the house filled with well-being, watching the rain fall full and straight and sink into the fields about the dooryard and dip from the thatched ends of the roof above the door. The child was amazed and stretched out his hands to catch the silver lines of the rain as it fell, and he laughed and they laughed with him, and the old man squatted on the floor beside the child and said,

"There is not another child like this in a dozen villages. Those brats of my brother notice nothing before they walk."

And in the fields the wheat seed sprouted and pushed spears of delicate green above the wet brown earth.

At a time like this there was visiting, because each farmer felt that for once heaven was doing the work in the fields and their crops were being watered without their backs being broken for it, carrying buckets to and fro, slung upon a pole across their shoulders; and in the morning they gathered at this house and that, drinking tea here and there, going from house to house barefoot across the narrow path between the fields under great oiled paper umbrellas. The women stayed at home and made shoes and mended clothes, if they were thrifty, and thought of preparations for the feast of the New Year.

But Wang Lung and his wife were not frequent at visiting. There was no house in the village of small scattered houses, of which theirs was one of a half dozen, which was so filled with warmth and plenty as their own, and Wang Lung felt that if he became too intimate with the others there would be borrowing. New Year was coming and who had all the money he wanted for the new clothes and the feasting? He stayed in his house and while the woman mended and sewed he took his rakes of split bamboo and examined them, and where the string was broken he wove in new string made of hemp he grew himself, and where a prong was broken out he drove in cleverly a new bit of bamboo.

And what he did for the farm implements, his wife, O-lan, did for the house implements. If an earthen jar leaked she did not, as other women did, cast it aside and talk of a new one. Instead she mixed earth and clay and welded the crack and heated it slowly and it was as good as new.

They sat in their house, therefore, and they rejoiced in each other's approval, although their speech was never anything more than scattered words such as these:

"Did you save the seed from the large squash for the new planting?" Or, "We will sell the wheat straw and burn the bean stalks in the kitchen." Or perhaps rarely Wang Lung would say, "This is a good dish of noodles," and O-lan would answer in deprecation, "It is good flour we have this year from the fields."

From the produce, Wang Lung in this good year had a handful of silver pieces over and above what they needed and these he was fearful of keeping in his belt or of telling any except the woman what he had. They plotted where to keep the silver and at last the woman cleverely dug a small hole in the inner wall of their room behind the bed and into this Wang Lung thrust the silver and with a clod of earth she covered the hole, and it was as though there was nothing there. But to both Wang and O-lan it gave a sense of secret richness and reserve. Wang Lung was conscious that he had money more than he need spend, and when he walked among his fellows he walked at ease with himself and with all.

V

THE New Year approached and in every house in the village there were preparations. Wang Lung went into the town to the candlemaker's shop and he bought squares of red paper on which were brushed in gilt ink the letter for happiness and some with the letter for riches, and these squares he pasted upon his farm utensils to bring him luck in the new year. Upon his plow and upon the ox's yoke and upon the two buckets in which he carried his fertilizer and his water, upon each of these he pasted a square. And then upon the doors of his house he pasted long strips of red paper brushed with mottoes of good luck, and over his doorway he pasted a fringe of red paper cunningly cut into a flower pattern and very finely cut. And he bought red paper to make new dresses for the gods, and this the old man did cleverly enough for his old shaking hands, and Wang Lung took them and put them upon the two small gods in the temple to the earth and he burned a little incense before them for the sake of the New Year. And for his house he bought also two red candles to burn on the eve of the year upon the table under the picture of a god, which was pasted on the wall of the middle room above where the table stood.

And Wang Lung went again into the town and he bought pork fat and white sugar and the woman rendered the fat smooth and white and she took rice flour, which they had ground from their own rice between their millstones to which they could yoke the ox when they needed to do so, and she took the fat and the sugar and she mixed and kneaded rich New Year's cakes, called moon cakes, such as were eaten in the House of Hwang.

When the cakes were laid out upon the table in strips, ready for heating, Wang Lung felt his heart fit to burst with pride. There was no other woman in the village able to do what his had done, to make cakes such as only the rich ate at the feast. In some of the cakes she had put strips of little red haws and spots of dried green plums, making flowers and patterns.

"It is a pity to eat these," said Wang Lung.

The old man was hovering about the table, pleased as a child might be pleased with the bright colors. He said,

"Call my brother, your uncle, and his children—let them see!"

But prosperity had made Wang Lung cautious. One could not ask hungry people only to see cakes.

"It is ill luck to look at cakes before the New Year," he replied hastily. And the woman, her hands all dusty with the fine rice flour, and sticky with the fat, said,

"Those are not for us to eat, beyond one or two of the plain one for guests to taste. We are not rich enough to eat white sugar and lard. I am preparing them for the Old Mistress at the great house. I shall take the child on the second day of the New Year."

Then the cakes were more important than ever, and Wang Lung was pleased that to the great hall where he had stood with so much timidity and in such poverty his wife should now go as visitor, carrying his son, dressed in red, and cakes made as these were, with the best flour and sugar and lard.

[41]

All else at that New Year sank into insignificance beside this
visit. His new coat of black cotton cloth which O-lan had made,
when he had put it on, only made him say to himself,

"I shall wear it when I take them to the gate of the great
house."

He even bore carelessly the first day of the New Year when his
uncle and his neighbors came crowding into the house to wish his
father and himself well, all boisterous with food and drink. He had
himself seen to it that the colored cakes were put away into the
basket lest he might have to offer them to common men, although
he found it very hard when the plain white ones were praised for
their flavor of fat and sugar not to cry out,

"You should see the colored ones!"

But he did not, for more than anything he wished to enter the
great house with pride.

Then on the second day of the New Year, when it is the day for
women to visit each other, the men having eaten and drunk well
the day before, they rose at dawn and the woman dressed the child
in his red coat and in the tiger-faced shoes she had made, and she
put on his head, freshly shaven by Wang Lung himself on the last
day of the old year, the crownless red hat with the small gilt Buddha sewed on front, and she set him upon the bed. Then Wang
Lung dressed himself quickly while his wife combed out afresh her
long black hair and knotted it with the brass pin washed with silver
which he had bought for her, and she put on her new coat of black
that was made from the same piece as his own new robe, twenty-
four feet of good cloth for the two, and two feet of cloth thrown in
for good measure, as the custom is at cloth shops. Then he
carrying the child and she the cakes in the basket, they set out on
the path across the fields, now barren with winter.

Then Wang Lung had his reward at the great gate of the House
of Hwang, for when the gateman came to the woman's call he
opened his eyes at all he saw and he twirled the three long hairs on
his mole and cried out,

"Ah, Wang the farmer, three this time instead of one!" And then seeing the new clothes they all wore and the child who was a son, he said further, "One has no need to wish you more fortune this year than you have had in the last."

Wang Lung answered negligently as one speaks to a man who is scarcely an equal, "Good harvests—good harvests—" and he stepped with assurance inside the gate.

The gateman was impressed with all he saw and he said to Wang Lung, "Do you sit within my wretched room while I announce your woman and son within."

And Wang Lung stood watching them go across the court, his wife and his son, bearing gifts to the head of a great house. It was all to his honor, and when he could no longer see them when they had dwindled down the long vista of the courts one inside the other, and had turned at last wholly out of sight, he went into the gateman's house and there he accepted as a matter of course from the gateman's pock-marked wife the honorable seat to the left of the table in the middle room, and he accepted with only a slight nod the bowl of tea which she presented to him and he set it before him and did not drink of it, as though it were not good enough in quality of tea leaves for him.

It seemed a long time before the gateman returned, bringing back again the woman and child. Wang Lung looked closely at the woman's face for an instant trying to see if all were well, for he had learned now from that impassive square countenance to detect small changes at first invisible to him. She wore a look of heavy content, however, and at once he became impatient to hear her tell of what had happened in those courts of the ladies into which he could not go, now that he had no business there.

With short bows, therefore, to the gateman and to his pock-marked wife he hurried O-lan away and he took into his own arms the child who was asleep and lying all crumpled in his new coat.

"Well?" he called back to her over his shoulder as she followed him. For once he was impatient with her slowness. She drew a little nearer to him and said in a whisper,

"I believe, if one should ask me, that they are feeling a pinch this year in that house."

She spoke in a shocked tone as one might speak of gods being hungry.

"What do you mean?" said Wang Lung, urging her.

But she would not be hastened. Words were to her things to be caught one by one and released with difficulty.

"The Ancient Mistress wore the same coat this year as last. I have never seen this happen before. And the slaves had no new coats." And then after a pause she said, "I saw not one slave with a new coat like mine." And then after a while she said again, "As for our son, there was not even a child among the concubines of the Old Master himself to compare to him in beauty and in dress."

A slow smile spread over her face and Wang Lung laughed aloud and he held the child tenderly against him. How well he had done—how well he had done! And then as he exulted he was smitten with fear. What foolish thing was he doing, walking like this under an open sky, with a beautiful man child for any evil spirit passing by chance through the air to see! He opened his coat hastily and thrust the child's head into his bosom and he said in a loud voice,

"What a pity our child is a female whom no one could want and covered with smallpox as well! Let us pray it may die."

"Yes—yes—" said his wife as quickly as she could, understanding dimly what a thing they had done.

And being comforted with these precautions they had now taken, Wang Lung once more urged his wife.

"Did you find out why they are poorer?"

"I had but a moment for private talk with the cook under whom I worked before," she replied, "but she said, 'This house cannot stand forever with all the young lords, five of them, spending money like waste water in foreign parts and sending home woman after woman as they weary of them, and the Old Lord living at home adding a concubine or two each year, and the Old Mistress eating enough opium every day to fill two shoes with silver.' "

"Do they indeed!" murmured Wang Lung, spellbound.

"Then the third daughter is to be married in the spring," continued O-lan, "and her dowry is a prince's ransom and enough to buy an official seat in a big city. Her clothes she will have of nothing but the finest satins with special patterns woven in Soochow and Hangchow and she will have a tailor sent from Shanghai with his retinue of under tailors lest she find her clothes less fashionable than those of the women in foreign parts."

"Whom will she marry, then, with all this expense?" said Wang Lung, struck with admiration and horror at such pouring out of wealth.

"She is to marry the second son of a Shanghai magistrate," said the woman, and then after a long pause she added, "They must be getting poorer for the Old Mistress herself told me they wished to sell land—some of the land to the south of the house, just outside the city wall, where they have always planted rice each year because it is good land and easily flooded from the moat around the wall."

"Sell their land!" repeated Wang Lung, convinced. "Then indeed are they growing poor. Land is one's flesh and blood."

He pondered for a while and suddenly a thought came to him and he struck the side of his head with his palm.

"What have I not thought of!" he cried, turning to the woman. "We will buy the land!"

They stared at each other, he in delight, she in stupefaction.

"Buy the land—the land—" she stammered.

"I will buy it!" he cried in a lordly voice. "I will buy it from the great House of Hwang!"

"It is too far away," she said in consternation. "We would have to walk half the morning to reach it."

"I will buy it," he repeated peevishly as he might repeat a demand to his mother who crossed him.

"It is a good thing to buy land," she said pacifically. "It is better certainly than putting money into a mud wall. But why not a piece of your uncle's land? He is clamoring to sell that strip near to the western field we now have."

"That land of my uncle's," said Wang Lung loudly, "I would not have it. He has been dragging a crop out of it in this way and that for twenty years and not a bit has he put back of manure or bean cake. The soil is like lime. No, I will buy Hwang's land."

He said "Hwang's land" as casually as he might have said "Ching's land,"—Ching, who was his farmer neighbor. He would be more than equal to these people in the foolish, great, wasteful house. He would go with the silver in his hand and he would say plainly,

"I have money. What is the price of the earth you wish to sell?" Before the Old Lord he heard himself saying and to the Old Lord's agent, "Count me as anyone else. What is the fair price? I have it in my hand."

And his wife, who had been a slave in the kitchens of that proud family, she would be wife to a man who owned a piece of the land that for generations had made the House of Hwang great. It was as though she felt his thought for she suddenly ceased her resistance and she said,

"Let it be bought. After all, rice land is good, and it is near the moat and we can get water every year. It is sure."

And again the slow smile spread over her face, the smile that never lightened the dullness of her narrow black eyes, and after a long time she said,

"Last year this time I was slave in that house."

And they walked on, silent with the fullness of this thought.

VI

THIS piece of land which Wang Lung now owned was a thing which greatly changed his life. At first, after he had dug the silver from the wall and taken it to the great house, after the honor of speaking as an equal to the Old Lord's equal was past, he was visited with a depression of spirit which was almost regret. When he thought of the hole in the wall now empty that had been filled with silver he need not use, he wished that he had his silver back. After all, this land, it would take hours of labor again, and as O-lan said, it was far away, more than a *li,* which is a third of a mile. And again, the buying of it had not been quite so filled with glory as he had anticipated. He had gone too early to the great house and the Old Lord was still sleeping. True, it was noon, but when he said in a loud voice,

"Tell his Old Honor I have important business—tell him money is concerned!" the gateman had answered positively,

"All the money in the world would not tempt me to wake the old tiger. He sleeps with his new concubine, Peach Blossom, whom he has had but three days. It is not worth my life to waken him." And then he added somewhat maliciously, pulling at the hairs on his mole, "And do not think that silver will waken him— he has had silver under his hand since he was born."

In the end, then, it had had to be managed with the Old Lord's agent, an oily scoundrel whose hands were heavy with the money that stuck to them in passing. So it seemed sometimes to Wang

Lung that after all the silver was more valuable than the land. One could see silver shining.

Well, but the land was his! He set out one grey day in the second month of the new year to look at it. None knew yet that it belonged to him and he walked out to see it alone, a long square of heavy black clay that lay stretched beside the moat encircling the wall of the town. He paced the land off carefully, three hundred paces lengthwise and a hundred and twenty across. Four stones still marked the corners of the boundaries, stones set with the great seal character of the House of Hwang. Well, he would have that changed. He would pull up the stones later and he would put his own name there—not yet, for he was not ready for people to know that he was rich enough to buy land from the great house, but later, when he was more rich, so that it did not matter what he did. And looking at that long square of land he thought to himself,

"To those at the great house it means nothing, this handful of earth, but to me it means how much!"

Then he had a turn of his mind and he was filled with a contempt for himself that a small piece of land should seem so important. Why, when he had poured out his silver proudly before the agent the man had scraped it up carelessly in his hands and said,

"Here is enough for a few days of opium for the old lady, at any rate."

And the wide difference that still lay between him and the great house seemed suddenly impassable as the moat full of water in front of him, and as high as the wall beyond, stretching up straight and hoary before him. He was filled with an angry determination, then, and he said to his heart that he would fill that hole with silver again and again until he had bought from the House of Hwang enough land so that this land would be less than an inch in his sight.

And so this parcel of land became to Wang Lung a sign and a symbol.

Spring came with blustering winds and torn clouds of rain and for Wang Lung the half-idle days of winter were plunged into long days of desperate labor over his land. The old man looked after the child now and the woman worked with the man from dawn until sunset flowed over the fields, and when Wang Lung perceived one day that again she was with child, his first thought was of irritation that during the harvest she would be unable to work. He shouted at her, irritable with fatigue,

"So you have chosen this time to breed again, have you!"

She answered stoutly,

"This time it is nothing. It is only the first that is hard."

Beyond this nothing was said of the second child from the time he noticed its growth swelling her body until the day came in autumn when she laid down her hoe one morning and crept into the house. He did not go back that day even for his noon meal, for the sky was heavy with thunder clouds and his rice lay dead ripe for gathering into sheaves. Later before the sun set she was back beside him, her body flattened, spent, but her face silent and undaunted. His impulse was to say,

"For this day you have had enough. Go and lie upon your bed." But the aching of his own exhausted body made him cruel, and he said to himself that he had suffered as much with his labor that day as she with her childbirth, and so he only asked between the strokes of his scythe,

"Is it male or female?"

She answered calmly,

"It is another male."

They said nothing more to each other, but he was pleased, and the incessant bending and stooping seemed less arduous, and working on until the moon rose above a bank of purple clouds, they finished the field and went home.

After his meal and after he had washed his sunburnt body in cool water and had rinsed his mouth with tea, Wang Lung went in to look at his second son. O-lan had lain herself upon the bed after the cooking of the meal and the child lay beside her—a fat, placid child, well enough, but not so large as the first one. Wang Lung looked at him and then went back to the middle room well content. Another son, and another and another each year—one could not trouble with red eggs every year; it was enough to do it for the first. Sons every year; the house was full of good fortune—this woman brought him nothing but good fortune. He shouted to his father,

"Now, Old One, with another grandson we shall have to put the big one in your bed!"

The old man was delighted. He had for a long time been desiring this child to sleep in his bed and warm his chilly old flesh with the renewal of young bones and blood, but the child would not leave his mother. Now, however, staggering in with feet still unsteady with babyhood, he stared at this new child beside his mother, and seeming to comprehend with his grave eyes that another had his place, he allowed himself without protest to be placed in his grandfather's bed.

And again the harvests were good and Wang Lung gathered silver from the selling of his produce and again he hid it in the wall. But the rice he reaped from the land of the Hwangs brought him twice as much as that from his own rice land. The earth of that piece was wet and rich and the rice grew on it as weeds grow where they are not wanted. And everyone knew now that Wang Lung owned this land and in his village there was talk of making him the head.

VII

WANG LUNG'S uncle began at this time to become the trouble which Wang Lung had known from the beginning that he might be. This uncle was the younger brother of Wang Lung's father, and by all the claims of relationship he might depend upon Wang Lung if he had not enough for himself and his family. So long as Wang Lung and his father were poor and scantily fed the uncle made muster to scratch about on his land and gather enough to feed his seven children and his wife and himself. But once fed none of them worked. The wife would not stir herself to sweep the floor of their hut, nor did the children trouble to wash the food from their faces. It was a disgrace that as the girls grew older and even to marriageable age they still ran about the village street and left uncombed their rough sun-browned hair, and sometimes even talked to men. Wang Lung, meeting his oldest girl cousin thus one day, was so angered for the disgrace done to his family that he dared to go to his uncle's wife and say,

"Now, who will marry a girl like my cousin, whom any man may look on? She has been marriageable these three years and she runs about and today I saw an idle lout on the village street lay his hand on her arm and she answered him only with brazen laughter!"

His uncle's wife had nothing active in her body except her tongue and this she now loosed upon Wang Lung.

"Well, and who will pay for the dowry and for the wedding and for the middleman's fees? It is all very well for those to talk who have more land than they know what to do with and who can yet go and buy more land from the great families with their spare silver, but your uncle is an unfortunate man and he has been so from the first. His destiny is evil and through no fault of his own. Heaven wills it. Where others can produce good grain, for him the seed dies in the ground and nothing but weeds spring up, and this though he break his back!"

She fell into loud, easy tears, and began to work herself up into a fury. She snatched at her knot of hair on the back of her head and tore down the loose hairs about her face and she began to scream freely,

"Ah, it is something you do not know—to have an evil destiny! Where the fields of others bear good rice and wheat, ours bear weeds; where the houses of others stand for a hundred years, the earth itself shakes under ours so that the walls crack; where others bear men, I, although I conceive a son, will yet give birth to a girl —ah, evil destiny!"

She shrieked aloud and the neighbor women rushed out of their houses to see and to hear. Wang Lung stood stoutly, however, and would finish what he came to say.

"Nevertheless," he said, "although it is not for me to presume to advise the brother of my father, I will say this: it is better that a girl be married away while she is yet virgin, and whoever heard of a bitch dog who was allowed on the streets who did not give birth to a litter?"

Having spoken thus plainly, he went away to his own house and left his uncle's wife screaming. He had it in his mind to buy more land this year from the House of Hwang and more land year after year as he was able, and he dreamed of adding a new room to his house and it angered him that as he saw himself and his sons rising into a landed family, this shiftless brood of his cousins should be running loose, bearing the same name as his own.

The next day his uncle came to the field where he was working. O-lan was not there, for ten moons had passed since the second child was born and a third birth was close upon her, and this time

[52]

she was not so well and for a handful of days she had not come to the fields and so Wang Lung worked alone. His uncle came slouching along a furrow, his clothes never properly buttoned about him, but caught together and held insecurely with his girdle, so that it always seemed that if a gust of wind blew at him he might suddenly stand naked. He came to where Wang Lung was and he stood in silence while Wang Lung hoed a narrow line beside the broad beans he was cultivating. At last Wang Lung said maliciously and without looking up,

"I ask your pardon, my uncle, for not stopping in my work. These beans must, if they are to bear, as you know, be cultivated twice and thrice. Yours, doubtless, are finished. I am very slow—a poor farmer—never finishing my work in time to rest."

His uncle understood perfectly Wang Lung's malice, but he answered smoothly,

"I am a man of evil destiny. This year out of twenty seed beans, one came up, and in such a poor growth as that there is no use in putting the hoe down. We shall have to buy beans this year if we eat them," and he sighed heavily.

Wang Lung hardened his heart. He knew that his uncle had come to ask something of him. He put his hoe down into the ground with a long even movement and with great care, breaking up the tiniest clod in the soft earth already well cultivated. The bean plants stood erect in thrifty order, casting as they stood little fringes of clear shadow in the sunshine. At last his uncle began to speak.

"The person in my house has told me," he said, "of your interest in my worthless oldest slave creature. It is wholly true what you say. You are wise for your years. She should be married. She is fifteen years old and for these three or four years could have given birth. I am terrified constantly lest she conceive by some wild dog and bring shame to me and to our name. Think of this happening in our respectable family, to me, the brother of your own father!"

Wang Lung put his hoe down hard into the soil. He would have liked to have spoken plainly. He would have liked to have said,

"Why do you not control her, then? Why do you not keep her decently in the house and make her sweep and clean and cook and make clothes for the family?"

But one cannot say these things to an older generation. He remained silent, therefore, and hoed closely about a small plant and he waited.

"If it had been my good destiny," continued his uncle mournfully, "to have married a wife as your father did, one who could work and at the same time produce sons, as your own does also, instead of a woman like mine, who grows nothing but flesh and gives birth to nothing but females and that one idle son of mine who is less than a male for his idleness, I, too, might have been rich now as you are. Then might I have, willingly would I have, shared my riches with you. Your daughters I would have wed to good men, your son would I have placed in a merchant's shop as apprentice and willingly paid the fee of guaranty—your house would I have delighted to repair, and you I would have fed with the best I had, you and your father and your children, for we are of one blood.'"

Wang Lung answered shortly,

"You know I am not rich. I have the five mouths to feed now and my father is old and does not work and still he eats, and another mouth is being born in my house at this very moment, for aught I know."

"You are rich—you are rich!" his uncle replied shrilly. "You have bought the land from the great house at the gods know what heavy price—is there another in the village who could do this thing?"

At this Wang Lung was goaded to anger. He flung down his hoe and he shouted suddenly, glaring at his uncle,

"If I have a handful of silver it is because I work and my wife works, and we do not, as some do, sit idling over a gambling table or gossiping on doorsteps never swept, letting the fields grow to weeds and our children go half-fed!"

The blood flew into his uncle's yellow face and he rushed at his nephew and slapped him vigorously on both cheeks.

"Now that," he cried, "for speaking so to your father's generation! Have you no religion, no morals, that you are so lacking in filial conduct? Have you not heard it said that in the Sacred Edicts it is commanded that a man is never to correct an elder?"

Wang Lung stood sullen and immovable, conscious of his fault but angry to the bottom of his heart against this man who was his uncle.

"I will tell your words to the whole village!" screamed his uncle in a high cracked voice of fury. "Yesterday you attack my house and call aloud in the streets that my daughter is not a virgin; today you reproach me, who if your father passes on, must be as your own father to you! Now may my daughters all not be virgins, but not from one of them would I hear such talk!" And he repeated over and over, "I will tell it to the village—I will tell it to the village . . ." until at last Wang Lung said unwillingly, "What do you want me to do?"

It touched his pride that this matter might indeed be called out before the village. After all, it was his own flesh and blood.

His uncle changed immediately. Anger melted out of him. He smiled and he put his hand on Wang Lung's arm.

"Ah, I know you—good lad—good lad—" he said softly. "Your old uncle knows you—you are my son. Son, a little silver in this poor old palm—say, ten pieces, or even nine, and I could begin to have arrangements with a matchmaker for that slave of mine. Ah, you are right! It is time—it is time!" He sighed and shook his head and he looked piously to the sky.

Wang Lung picked up his hoe and threw it down again.

"Come to the house," he said shortly. "I do not carry silver on me like a prince," and he strode ahead, bitter beyond speech because some of the good silver with which he had planned to buy

[55]

more land was to go into this palm of his uncle's, from whence it would slip on to the gambling table before night fell.

He strode into the house, brushing out of his way his two small sons who played, naked in the warm sunshine, about the threshold. His uncle, with idle good nature, called to the children and took from some recess in his crumpled clothing a copper coin for each child. He pressed the small fat shining bodies to him, and putting his nose into their soft necks he smelled of the sun-browned flesh with easy affection.

"Ah, you are two little men," he said, clasping one in either arm.

But Wang Lung did not pause. He went into the room where he slept with his wife and the last child. It was very dark, coming in as he did from the outer sunshine, and except for the bar of light from the hole, he could see nothing. But the smell of warm blood which he remembered so well filled his nostrils and he called out sharply,

"What now—has your time come?"

The voice of his wife answered from the bed more feebly than he had ever heard her speak,

"It is over once more. It is only a slave this time—not worth mentioning."

Wang Lung stood still. A sense of evil struck him. A girl! A girl was causing all this trouble in his uncle's house. Now a girl had been born into his house as well.

He went without reply then to the wall and felt for the roughness which was the mark of the hiding place and he removed the clod of earth. Behind it he fumbled among the little heap of silver and he counted out nine pieces.

"Why are you taking the silver out?" said his wife suddenly in the darkness.

"I am compelled to lend it to my uncle," he replied shortly.

His wife answered nothing at first and then she said in her plain, heavy way,

"It is better not to say lend. There is no lending in that house. There is only giving."

"Well I know that," replied Wang Lung with bitterness. "It is cutting my flesh out to give to him and for nothing except that we are of a blood."

Then going out into the threshold he thrust the money at his uncle and he walked quickly back to the field and there he fell to working as though he would tear the earth from its foundations. He thought for the time only of the silver; he saw it poured out carelessly upon a gambling table, saw it swept up by some idle hand—his silver, the silver he had so painfully collected from the fruits of his fields, hoping to turn it back again for more earth for his own.

It was evening before his anger was spent and he straightened himself and remembered his home and his food. And then he thought of that new mouth come that day into his house and it struck him with heaviness that the birth of daughters had begun for him, daughters who do not belong to their parents, but are born and reared for other families. He had not even thought, in his anger at his uncle, to stop and see the face of this small, new creature.

He stood leaning upon his hoe and he was seized with sadness. It would be another harvest before he could buy that land now, a piece adjoining the one he had, and there was this new mouth in the house. Across the pale, pearl-colored sky of twilight a flock of crows flew, sharply black, and whirred over him, cawing loudly. He watched them disappear like a cloud into the trees about his house, and he ran at them, shouting and shaking his hoe. They rose again slowly, circling and re-circling over his head, mocking him with their cries, and they flew at last into the darkening sky.

He groaned aloud. It was an evil omen.

VIII

IT SEEMED as though once the gods turn against a man they will not consider him again. The rains, which should have come in early summer, withheld themselves, and day after day the skies shone with fresh and careless brilliance. The parched and starving earth was nothing to them. From dawn to dawn there was not a cloud, and at night the stars hung out of the sky, golden and cruel in their beauty.

The fields, although Wang Lung cultivated them desperately, dried and cracked, and the young wheat stalks, which had sprung up courageously with the coming of spring and had prepared their heads for the grain, when they found nothing coming from the soil or the sky for them, ceased their growing and stood motionless at first under the sun and at last dwindled and yellowed into a barren harvest. The young rice beds which Wang Lung sowed at first were squares of jade upon the brown earth. He carried water to them day upon day after he had given up the wheat, the heavy wooden buckets slung upon a bamboo pole across his shoulders. But though a furrow grew upon his flesh and a callus formed there as large as a bowl, no rain came.

At last the water in the pond dried into a cake of clay and the water even in the well sank so low that O-lan said to him,

"If the children drink and the old man have his hot water the plants must go dry."

Wang Lung answered with anger that broke into a sob,

"Well, and they must all starve if the plants starve." It was true that all their lives depended upon the earth.

Only the piece of land by the moat bore harvest, and this because at last when summer wore away without rain, Wang Lung abandoned all his other fields and stayed the day out at this one, dipping water from the moat to pour upon the greedy soil. This year for the first time he sold his grain as soon as it was harvested, and when he felt the silver upon his palm he gripped it hard in defiance. He would, he told himself, in spite of gods and drought, do that which he had determined. His body he had broken and his sweat he had spilled for this handful of silver and he would do what he would with it. And he hurried to the House of Hwang and he met the land agent there and he said without ceremony,

"I have that with which to buy the land adjoining mine by the moat."

Now Wang Lung had heard here and there that for the House of Hwang it had been a year verging upon poverty. The old lady had not had her dole of opium to the full for many days and she was like an old tigress in her hunger so that each day she sent for the agent and she cursed him and struck his face with her fan, screaming at him,

"And are there not acres of land left, yet?" until he was beside himself.

He had even given up the moneys which ordinarily he held back from the family transactions for his own use, so beside himself had he been. And as if this were not enough, the Old Lord took yet another concubine, a slave who was the child of a slave who had been his creature in her youth, but who was now wed to a man servant in the house, because the Old Lord's desire for her failed before he took her into his room as concubine. This child of the slave, who was not more than sixteen, he now saw with fresh lust, for as he grew old and infirm and heavy with flesh he seemed to desire more and more women who were slight and young, even to childhood, so that there was no slaking his lust. As the Old Mistress with her opium, so he with his lusts, and there was no making him understand there was not money for jade earrings for his favorites and not silver for their pretty hands. He could not comprehend the words "no money," who all his life had but to reach out his hand and fill it as often as he would.

And seeing their parents thus, the young lords shrugged their shoulders and said there must still be enough for their lifetime. They united in only one thing and this was to berate the agent for his ill management of the estates, so that he who had once been oily and unctuous, a man of plenty and of ease, was now become anxious and harried and his flesh gone so that his skin hung upon him like an old garment.

Neither had Heaven sent rain upon the fields of the House of Hwang, and there, too, were no harvests, and so when Wang Lung came to the agent crying, "I have silver," it was as though one came saying to the hungry, "I have food."

The agent grasped at it, and where before there had been dickering and tea-drinking, now the two men spoke in eager whispers, and more quickly than they could speak whole words, the money passed from one hand to the other and papers were signed and sealed and the land was Wang Lung's.

And once again Wang Lung did not count the passing of silver, which was his flesh and his blood, a hard thing. He bought with it the desire of his heart. He had now a vast field of good land, for the new field was twice as large as the first. But more to him than its dark fertility was the fact that it had belonged once to the family of a prince. And this time he told no one, not even O-lan, what he had done.

Month passed into month and still no rain fell. As autumn approached the clouds gathered unwillingly in the sky, small, light clouds, and in the village street one could see men standing about, idle and anxious, their faces upturned to the sky, judging closely of this cloud and that, discussing together as to whether any held rain in it. But before sufficient cloud could gather for promise, a bitter wind rose out of the northwest, the acrid wind of the distant desert, and blew the clouds from the sky as one gathers dust from a floor with a broom. And the sky was empty and barren, and the stately sun rose each morning and made its march and set solitary each night. And the moon in its time shone like a lesser sun for brightness.

From his fields Wang Lung reaped scanty harvest of hardy beans, and from his corn field, which he had planted in despair when the rice beds had yellowed and died before ever the plants had been set into the watered field, he plucked short stubby ears with the grains scattered here and there. There was not a bean lost in the threshing. He set the two little boys to sifting the dust of the threshing floor between their fingers after he and the woman had flailed the bean vines, and he shelled the corn upon the floor in the middle room, watching sharply every grain that flew wide. When he would have put the cobs away for fuel, his wife spoke out,

"No—do not waste them in burning. I remember when I was a child in Shantung when years like this came, even the cobs we ground and ate. It is better than grass."

When she had spoken they all fell silent, even the children. There was foreboding in these strange brilliant days when the land was failing them. Only the girl child knew no fear. For her there were the mother's two great breasts as yet filled for her needs. But O-lan, giving her suck, muttered,

"Eat, poor fool—eat, while there is yet that which can be eaten."

And then, as though there were not enough evil, O-lan was again with child, and her milk dried up, and the frightened house was filled with the sound of a child continually crying for food.

If one had asked Wang Lung,

"And how are you fed through the autumn?" he would have answered, "I do not know—a little food here and there."

But there was none to ask him that. None asked of any other in the whole countryside, "How are you fed?" None asked anything except of himself, "How shall I be fed this day?" And parents said, "How shall we be fed, we and our children?"

Now Wang Lung's ox he had cared for as long as he could. He had given the beast a bit of straw and a handful of vines as long as these lasted and then he had gone out and torn leaves from the trees for it until winter came and these were gone. Then since there was no land to plough, since seed, if it were planted only dried in the earth, and since they had eaten all their seed, he turned the ox out to hunt for itself, sending the eldest boy to sit upon its back all day and hold the rope passed through its nostrils so that it would not be stolen. But latterly he had not dared even to do this, lest men from the village, even his neighbors, might overcome the lad and seize the ox for food, and kill it. So he kept the ox on the threshold until it grew lean as its skeleton.

But there came a day when there was no rice left and no wheat left and there were only a few beans and a meager store of corn and the ox lowed with its hunger and the old man said,

"We will eat the ox, next."

Then Wang Lung cried out, for it was to him as though one said, "We will eat a man next." The ox was his companion in the fields and he had walked behind and praised it and cursed it as his mood was, and from his youth he had known the beast, when they had bought it a small calf. And he said,

"How can we eat the ox? How shall we plough again?"

But the old man answered, tranquil enough,

"Well, and it is your life or the beast's, and your son's life or the beast's and a man can buy an ox again more easily than his own life."

But Wang Lung would not that day kill it. And the next day passed and the next and the children cried out for food and they would not be comforted and O-lan looked at Wang Lung, beseeching him for the children, and he saw at last that the thing was to be done. So he said roughly,

"Let it be killed then, but I cannot do it."

He went into the room where he slept and he laid himself upon the bed and he wrapped the quilt about his head that he might not hear the beast's bellowing when it died.

Then O-lan crept out and she took a great iron knife she had in the kitchen and she cut a great gash in the beast's neck, and thus she severed its life. And she took a bowl and caught its blood to cook for them to eat in a pudding, and she skinned and hacked to pieces the great carcass, and Wang Lung would not come out until the thing was wholly done and the flesh was cooked and upon the table. But when he tried to eat the flesh of his ox his gorge rose and he could not swallow it and he drank only a little of the soup. And O-lan said to him,

"An ox is but an ox and this one grew old. Eat, for there will be another beast one day and a far better one than this."

Wang Lung was a little comforted then and he ate a morsel and then more, and they all ate. But the ox was eaten at last and the bones cracked for the marrow, and it was all too quickly gone, and there was nothing left of it except the skin, dried and hard and stretched upon the rack of bamboo O-lan had made to hold it spread.

At first there had been hostility in the village against Wang Lung because it was supposed that he had silver which he was hiding and food stored away. His uncle, who was among the first to be hungry, came importuning to his door, and indeed the man and his wife and his seven children had nothing to eat. Wang Lung measured unwillingly into the skirt of his uncle's robe a small heap of beans and a precious handful of corn. Then he said with firmness,

"It is all I can spare and I have first my old father to consider, even if I had no children."

When his uncle came again Wang Lung cried out,

"Even filial piety will not feed my house!" and he sent his uncle empty away.

From that day his uncle turned against him like a dog that has been kicked, and he whispered about the village in this house and in that,

"My nephew there, he has silver and he has food, but he will give none of it to us, not even to me, and to my children, who are his own bones and flesh. We can do nothing but starve."

And as family after family finished its store in the small village and spent its last coin in the scanty markets of the town, and the winds of winter came down from the desert, cold as a knife of steel and dry and barren, the hearts of the villagers grew distraught with their own hunger and with the hunger of their pinched wives and crying children, and when Wang Lung's uncle shivered about the streets like a lean dog and whispered from his famished lips, "There is one who has food—there is one whose children are fat, still," the men took up poles and went one night to the house of Wang Lung and beat upon the door. And when he had opened to the voices of his neighbors, they fell upon him and pushed him out of the doorway and threw out of the house his frightened children, and they fell upon every corner, and they scrabbled every surface with their hands to find where he had hidden his food. Then when they found his wretched store of a few dried beans and a bowlful of dried corn they gave a great howl of disappointment and despair, and they seized his bits of furniture, the table and the benches and the bed where the old man lay, frightened and weeping.

Then O-lan came forward and spoke, and her plain, slow voice rose above the men,

"Not that—not that yet," she called out. "It is not yet time to take our table and the benches and the bed from our house. You have all our food. But out of your own houses you have not sold yet your table and your benches. Leave us ours. We are even. We have not a bean or a grain of corn more than you—no, you have more than we, now, for you have all of ours. Heaven will strike you if you take more. Now, we will go out together and hunt for grass to eat and bark from the trees, you for your children, and we for our three children, and for this fourth who is to be born in such times." She pressed her hand to her belly as she spoke, and the men were ashamed before her and went out one by one, for they were not evil men except when they starved.

One lingered, that one called Ching, a small, silent, yellow man with a face like an ape's in the best of times, and now hollowed and anxious. He would have spoken some good word of shame, for he was an honest man and only his crying child had forced him to evil. But in his bosom was a handful of beans he had snatched when the store was found and he was fearful lest he must return them if he spoke at all, and so he only looked at Wang Lung with haggard, speechless eyes and he went out.

Wang Lung stood there in his dooryard where year after year he had threshed his good harvest, and which had lain now for many months idle and useless. There was nothing left in the house to feed his father and his children—nothing to feed this woman of his who besides the nourishment of her own body had this other one to feed into growth, this other one who would, with the cruelty of new and ardent life, steal from the very flesh and blood of its mother. He had an instant of extreme fear. Then into his blood like soothing wine flowed this comfort. He said in his heart,

"They cannot take the land from me. The labor of my body and the fruit of the fields I have put into that which cannot be taken away. If I had the silver, they would have taken it. If I had bought with the silver to store it, they would have taken it all. I have the land still, and it is mine."

IX

WANG LUNG, sitting at the threshold of his door, said to himself that now surely something must be done. They could not remain here in this empty house and die. In his lean body, about which he daily wrapped more tightly his loose girdle, there was a determination to live. He would not thus, just when he was coming into the fullness of a man's life, suddenly be robbed of it by a stupid fate. There was such anger in him now as he often could not express. At times it seized him like a frenzy so that he rushed out upon his barren threshing floor and shook his arms at the foolish sky that shone above him, eternally blue and clear and cold and cloudless.

"Oh, you are too wicked, you Old Man in Heaven!" he would cry recklessly. And if for an instant he were afraid, he would the next instant cry sullenly, "And what can happen to me worse than that which has happened!"

Once he walked, dragging one foot after another in his famished weakness, to the temple of the earth, and deliberately he spat upon the face of the small, imperturbable god who sat there with his goddess. There were no sticks of incense now before this pair, nor had there been for many moons, and their paper clothes were tattered and showed their clay bodies through the rents. But they sat there unmoved by anything and Wang Lung gnashed his teeth at them and walked back to his house groaning and fell upon his bed.

They scarcely rose at all now, any of them. There was no need, and fitful sleep took the place, for a while, at least, of the food they had not. The cobs of corn they had dried and eaten and they stripped the bark from trees and all over the countryside people were eating what grass they could find upon the wintry hills. There was not an animal anywhere. A man might walk for a handful of days and see not an ox nor an ass nor any kind of beast or fowl.

The children's bellies were swollen out with empty wind, and one never saw in these days a child playing upon the village street. At most the two boys in Wang Lung's house crept to the door and sat in the sun, the cruel sun that never ceased its endless shining. Their once rounded bodies were angular and bony now, sharp small bones like the bones of birds, except for their ponderous bellies. The girl child never even sat alone, although the time was past for this, but lay uncomplaining hour after hour wrapped in an old quilt. At first the angry insistence of her crying had filled the house, but she had come to be quiet, sucking feebly at whatever was put into her mouth and never lifting up her voice. Her little hollowed face peered out at them all, little sunken blue lips like a toothless old woman's lips, and hollow black eyes peering.

This persistence of the small life in some way won her father's affection, although if she had been round and merry as the others had been at her age he would have been careless of her. Sometimes, looking at her he whispered softly,

"Poor fool—poor little fool—" And once when she essayed a weak smile with her toothless gums showing, he broke into tears and took into his lean hard hand her small claw and held the tiny grasp of her fingers over his forefinger. Thereafter he would sometimes lift her, all naked as she lay, and thrust her inside the scant warmth of his coat against his flesh and sit with her so by the threshold of the house, looking out over the dry, flat fields.

As for the old man, he fared better than any, for if there was anything to eat he was given it, even though the children were without. Wang Lung said to himself proudly that none should say in the hour of death he had forgotten his father. Even if his own flesh went to feed him the old man should eat. The old man slept day and night, and ate what was given him and there was still strength in him to creep about the dooryard at noon when the sun was warm. He was more cheerful than any of them and he quavered forth one day in his old voice that was like a little wind trembling among cracked bamboos,

"There have been worse days—there have been worse days. Once I saw men and women eating children."

"There will never be such a thing in my house," said Wang Lung, in extremest horror.

There was a day when his neighbor Ching, worn now to less

than the shadow of a human creature, came to the door of Wang Lung's house and he whispered from his lips that were dried and black as earth,

"In the town the dogs are eaten and everywhere the horses and the fowls of every sort. Here we have eaten the beasts that ploughed our fields and the grass and the bark of trees. What now remains for food?"

Wang Lung shook his head hopelessly. In his bosom lay the slight, skeleton-like body of his girl child, and he looked down into the delicate bony face, and into the sharp, sad eyes that watched him unceasingly from his breast. When he caught those eyes in his glance, invariably there wavered upon the child's face a flickering smile that broke his heart.

Ching thrust his face nearer.

"In the village they are eating human flesh," he whispered. "It is said your uncle and his wife are eating. How else are they living and with strength enough to walk about—they, who, it is known, have never had anything?"

Wang Lung drew back from the deathlike head which Ching had thrust forward as he spoke. With the man's eyes close like this, he was horrible. Wang Lung was suddenly afraid with a fear he did not understand. He rose quickly as though to cast off some entangling danger.

"We will leave this place," he said loudly. "We will go south! There are not everywhere in this great land people who starve. Heaven, however wicked, will not at once wipe out the sons of Han."

His neighbor looked at him patiently. "Ah, you are young," he said sadly. "I am older than you and my wife is old and we have nothing except one daughter. We can die well enough."

"You are more fortunate than I," said Wang Lung. "I have my old father and these three small mouths and another about to be born. We must go lest we forget our nature and eat each other as the wild dogs do."

And then it seemed to him suddenly that what he said was very

[68]

right, and he called aloud to O-lan, who lay upon the bed day after day without speech, now that there was no food for the stove and no fuel for the oven,

"Come, woman, we will go south!"

There was cheer in his voice such as none had heard in many moons, and the children looked up and the old man hobbled out from his room and O-lan rose feebly from her bed and came to the door of their room and clinging to the door frame she said,

"It is a good thing to do. One can at least die walking."

The child in her body hung from her lean loins like a knotty fruit and from her face every particle of flesh was gone, so that the jagged bones stood forth rock-like under her skin. "Only wait until tomorrow," she said. "I shall have given birth by then. I can tell by this thing's movements in me."

"Tomorrow, then," answered Wang Lung, and then he saw his wife's face and he was moved with a pity greater than any he had had for himself. This poor creature was dragging forth yet another!

"How shall you walk, you poor creature!" he muttered, and he said unwillingly to his neighbor Ching, who still leaned against the house by the door, "If you have any food left, for a good heart's sake give me a handful to save the life of the mother of my sons, and I will forget that I saw you in my house as a robber."

Ching looked at him ashamed and he answered humbly,

"I have never thought of you with peace since that hour. It was that dog, your uncle, who enticed me, saying that you had good harvests stored up. Before this cruel heaven I promise you that I have only a little handful of dried red beans buried beneath the stone of my doorway. This I and my wife placed there for our last hour, for our child and ourselves, that we might die with a little food in our stomachs. But some of it I will give to you, and tomorrow go south, if you can. I stay, I and my house. I am older than you and I have no son, and it does not matter whether I live or die."

And he went away and in a little while he came back, bringing tied in a cotton kerchief a double handful of small red beans, mouldy with the soil. The children clambered about at the sight of the food, and even the old man's eyes glistened, but Wang Lung pushed them away for once and he took the food in to his wife as she lay and she ate a little of it, bean by bean, unwilling except that her hour was upon her and she knew that if she had not any food she would die in the clutches of her pain.

Only a few of the beans did Wang Lung hide in his own hand and these he put into his own mouth and he chewed them into a soft pulp and then putting his lips to the lips of his daughter he pushed into her mouth the food, and watching her small lips move, he felt himself fed.

That night he stayed in the middle room. The two boys were in the old man's room and in the third room O-lan gave birth alone. He sat there as he had sat during the birth of his first-born son and listened. She would not even yet have him near her at her hour. She would give birth alone, squatting over the old tub she kept for the purpose, creeping about the room afterwards to remove the traces of what had been, hiding as an animal does the birth stains of its young.

He listened intently for the small sharp cry he knew so well, and he listened with despair. Male or female, it mattered nothing to him now—there was only another mouth coming which must be fed.

"It would be merciful if there were no breath," he muttered, and then he heard the feeble cry—how feeble a cry!—hang for an instant upon the stillness. "But there is no mercy of any kind in these days," he finished bitterly, and he sat listening.

There was no second cry, and over the house the stillness became impenetrable. But for many days there had been stillness everywhere, the stillness of inactivity and of people, each in his own house, waiting to die. This house was filled with such stillness. Suddenly Wang Lung could not bear it. He was afraid. He rose and went to the door of the room where O-lan was and he called into the crack and the sound of his voice heartened him a little.

[70]

"You are safe?" he called to the woman. He listened. Suppose she had died as he sat there! But he could hear a slight rustling. She was moving about and at last she answered, her voice a sigh,

"Come!"

He went in, then, and she lay there upon the bed, her body scarcely raising the cover. She lay alone.

"Where is the child?" he asked.

She made a slight movement of her hand upon the bed and he saw upon the floor the child's body.

"Dead!" he exclaimed.

"Dead," she whispered.

He stooped and examined the handful of its body—a wisp of bone and skin—a girl. He was about to say, "But I heard it crying —alive—" and then he looked at the woman's face. Her eyes were closed and the color of her flesh was the color of ashes and her bones stuck up under the skin—a poor silent face that lay there, having endured to the utmost, and there was nothing he could say. After all, during these months he had had only his own body to drag about. But this woman had endured what agony of starvation with the starved creature gnawing at her from within, desperate for its own life.

He said nothing, but he took the dead child into the other room and laid it upon the earthen floor and searched until he found a bit of broken mat and this he wrapped about it. The round head dropped this way and that and upon the neck he saw two dark, bruised spots, but he finished what he had to do. Then he took the roll of matting, and going as far from the house as he had strength, he laid the burden against the hollowed side of an old grave. This grave stood among many others, worn down and no longer known or cared for, on a hillside just at the border of Wang Lung's western field. He had scarcely put the burden down before a famished, wolfish dog hovered almost at once behind him, so famished that although he took up a small stone and threw it and hit its lean flank with a thud, the animal would not stir away more than a few feet. At last Wang Lung felt his legs sinking beneath him and covering his face with his hands he went away.

"It is better as it is," he muttered to himself, and for the first time was wholly filled with despair.

The next morning when the sun rose unchanging in its sky of varnished blue it seemed to him a dream that he could ever have thought of leaving his house with these helpless children and this weakened woman and this old man. How could they drag their bodies over a hundred miles, even to plenty? And who knew whether or not even in the south there was food? One would say there was no end to this brazen sky. Perhaps they would wear out all their last strength only to find more starving people and these strangers to them as well. Far better to stay where they could die in their beds. He sat desponding on the threshold of the door and gazed bleakly over the dried and hardened fields from which every particle of anything which could be called food or fuel had been plucked.

He had no money. Long ago the last coin was gone. But even money would do little good now, for there was no food to buy. He had heard earlier that there were rich men in the town who were hoarding food for themselves and for sale to the very rich, but even this ceased to anger him. He did not feel this day that he could walk to the town even to be fed without money. He was, indeed, not hungry.

The extreme gnawing in his stomach which he had had at first was now past and he could stir up a little of the earth from a certain spot in one of his fields and give it to the children without desiring any of it for himself. This earth they had been eating in water for some days—goddess of mercy earth, it was called, because it had some slight nourishing quality in it, although in the end it could not sustain life. But made into a gruel it allayed the children's craving for a time and put something into their distended, empty bellies. He steadfastly would not touch the few beans that O-lan still held in her hand, and it comforted him vaguely to hear her crunching them, one at a time, a long time apart.

And then, as he sat there in the doorway, giving up his hope and thinking with a dreamy pleasure of lying upon his bed and sleeping easily into death, someone came across the fields—men walking toward him. He continued to sit as they drew near and he saw that one was his uncle and with him were three men whom he did not know.

"I have not seen you these many days," called his uncle with loud and affected good humor. And as he drew nearer he said in the same loud voice, "And how well you have fared! And your father, my elder brother, he is well?"

Wang Lung looked at his uncle. The man was thin, it is true, but not starved, as he should be. Wang Lung felt in his own shriveled body the last remaining strength of life gathering into a devastating anger against this man, his uncle.

"How you have eaten—how you have eaten!" he muttered thickly. He thought nothing of these strangers or of any courtesy. He saw only his uncle with flesh on his bones, still. His uncle opened wide his eyes and threw up his hands to the sky.

"Eaten!" he cried. "If you could see my house! Not a sparrow even could pick up a crumb there. My wife—do you remember how fat she was? How fair and fat and oily her skin? And now she is like a garment hung on a pole—nothing but the poor bones, rattling together in her skin. And of our children only four are left —the three little ones gone—gone—and as for me, you see me!" He took the edge of his sleeve and wiped the corner of each eye carefully.

"You have eaten," repeated Wang Lung dully.

"I have thought of nothing but of you and of your father, who is my brother," retorted his uncle briskly, "and now I prove it to you. As soon as I could, I borrowed from these good men in the town a little food on the promise that with the strength it gave me I would help them to buy some of the land about our village. And

[73]

then I thought of your good land first of all, you, the son of my brother. They have come to buy your land and to give you money —food—life!" His uncle, having said these words, stepped back and folded his arms with a flourish of his dirty and ragged robes.

Wang Lung did not move. He did not rise nor in any way recognize the men who had come. But he lifted his head to look at them and he saw that they were indeed men from the town, dressed in long robes of soiled silk. Their hands were soft and their nails long. They looked as though they had eaten and blood still ran rapidly in their veins. He suddenly hated them with an immense hatred. Here were these men from the town, having eaten and drunk, standing beside him whose children were starving and eating the very earth of the fields; here they were, come to squeeze his land from him in his extremity. He looked up at them sullenly, his eyes deep and enormous in his bony, skull-like face.

"I will not sell my land," he said.

His uncle stepped forward. At this instant the younger of Wang Lung's two sons came creeping to the doorway upon his hands and knees. Since he had so little strength in these latter days the child at times had gone back to crawling as he used in his babyhood.

"Is that your lad?" cried the uncle, "the little fat lad I gave a copper to in the summer?"

And they all looked at the child and suddenly Wang Lung, who through all this time had not wept at all, began to weep silently, the tears gathering in great knots of pain in his throat and rolling down his cheeks.

"What is your price?" he whispered at last. Well, there were these three children to be fed—the children and the old man. He and his wife could dig themselves graves in the land and lie down in them and sleep. Well, but here were these.

And then one of the men from the city spoke, a man with one eye blind and sunken in his face, and unctuously he said,

"My poor man, we will give you a better price than could be got in these times anywhere for the sake of the boy who is starving.

We will give you . . ." he paused and then he said harshly, "we will give you a string of a hundred pence for an acre!"

Wang Lung laughed bitterly. "Why, that," he cried, "that is taking my land for a gift. Why, I pay twenty times that when I buy land!"

"Ah, but not when you buy it from men who are starving," said the other man from the city. He was a small, slight fellow with a high thin nose, but his voice came out of him unexpectedly large and coarse and hard.

Wang Lung looked at the three of them. They were sure of him, these men! What will not a man give for his starving children and his old father! The weakness of surrender in him melted into an anger such as he had never known in his life before. He sprang up and at the men as a dog springs at an enemy.

"I shall never sell the land!" he shrieked at them. "Bit by bit I will dig up the fields and feed the earth itself to the children and when they die I will bury them in the land, and I and my wife and my old father, even he, we will die on the land that has given us birth!"

He was weeping violently and his anger went out of him as suddenly as a wind and he stood shaking and weeping. The men stood there smiling slightly, his uncle among them, unmoved. This talk was madness and they waited until Wang's anger was spent.

And then suddenly O-lan came to the door and spoke to them, her voice flat and commonplace as though every day such things were.

"The land we will not sell, surely," she said, "else when we return from the south we shall have nothing to feed us. But we will sell the table and the two beds and the bedding and the four benches and even the cauldron from the stove. But the rakes and the hoe and the plow we will not sell, nor the land."

There was some calmness in her voice which carried more strength than all Wang Lung's anger, and Wang Lung's uncle said uncertainly,

[75]

"Will you really go south?"

At last the one-eyed man spoke to the others and they muttered among themselves and the one-eyed man turned and said,

"They are poor things and fit only for fuel. Two silver bits for the lot and take it or leave it."

He turned away with contempt as he spoke, but O-lan answered tranquilly,

"It is less than the cost of one bed, but if you have the silver give it to me quickly and take the things."

The one-eyed man fumbled in his girdle and dropped into her outstretched hand the silver and the three men came into the house and between them they took out the table and the benches and the bed in Wang Lung's room first with its bedding, and they wrenched the cauldron from the earthen oven in which it stood. But when they went into the old man's room Wang Lung's uncle stood outside. He did not wish his older brother to see him, nor did he wish to be there when the old man was laid on the floor and the bed taken from under him. When all was finished and the house was wholly empty except for the two rakes and the two hoes and the plow in one corner of the middle room, O-lan said to her husband,

"Let us go while we have the two bits of silver and before we must sell the rafters of the house and have no hole into which we can crawl when we return."

And Wang Lung answered heavily, "Let us go."

But he looked across the fields at the small figures of the men receding and he muttered over and over, "At least I have the land —I have the land."

X

THERE was nothing to do but to pull the door tight upon its wooden hinges and fasten the iron hasp. All their clothes they had upon them. Into each child's hands O-lan thrust a rice bowl and a pair of chopsticks and the two little boys grasped at them eagerly and held them tight as a promise of food to come. Thus they started across the fields, a dreary small procession moving so slowly that it seemed they would never be to the wall of the town.

The girl Wang Lung carried in his bosom until he saw that the old man would fall and then he gave the child to O-lan and stooping under his father he lifted him on his back and carried him, staggering under the old man's dry, wind-light frame. They went on in complete silence past the little temple with the two small stately gods within, who never noticed anything that passed. Wang Lung was sweating with his weakness in spite of the cold and bitter wind. This wind never ceased to blow on them and against them, so that the two boys cried of its cold. But Wang Lung coaxed them saying,

"You are two big men and you are travellers to the south. There is warmth there and food every day, white rice every day for all of us and you shall eat and you shall eat."

In time they reached the gate of the wall, resting continually every little way, and where Wang Lung had once delighted in its coolness now he clenched his teeth against the gust of wintry wind that swept furiously through its channel, as icy water will rush between cliffs. Beneath their feet the mud was thick and speared through with needles of ice and the little boys could make no headway and O-lan was laden with the girl and desperate under the weight of her own body. Wang Lung staggered through with the old man and set him down and then went back and lifted each child and carried him through, and then when it was over at last his sweat poured out of him like rain, spending all his strength with it, so he had to lean for a long time against the damp wall, his eyes shut and his breath coming and going quickly, and his family stood shivering and waiting about him.

They were close to the gate of the great house now, but it was locked fast, the iron doors reared full to their height and the stone lions grey and windbitten on either side. Upon the doorsteps lay cowering a few dingy shapes of men and women who gazed, famished, upon the closed and barred gate, and when Wang Lung passed with his miserable little procession one cried out in a cracked voice,

"The hearts of these rich are hard like the hearts of the gods. They have still rice to eat and from the rice they do not eat they are still making wine, while we starve."

And another moaned forth,

"Oh, if I had an instant's strength in this hand of mine I would set fire to the gates and to those houses and courts within, even though I burned in the fire. A thousand curses to the parents that bore the children of Hwang!"

But Wang Lung answered nothing to all this and in silence they went on toward the south.

When they had passed through the town and had come out on the southern side, and this they did so slowly that it was evening and near to darkness, they found a multitude of people going toward the south. Wang Lung was beginning to think of what corner of the wall they had better choose for sleeping as well as they could huddled together, when he suddenly found himself and his family caught in a multitude, and he asked of one who pressed against him,

"Where is all this multitude going?"

And the man said,

"We are starving people and we are going to catch the fire-wagon and ride to the south. It leaves from yonder house and there are wagons for such as we for the price of less than a small silver piece."

Firewagons! One had heard of them. Wang Lung in days past in the tea shop had heard men tell of these wagons, chained one to the other and drawn neither by man nor beast, but by a machine breathing forth fire and water like a dragon. He had said to himself many times then that on a holiday he would go and see it, but with one thing and another in the fields there was never time, he being well to the north of the city. Then there was always distrust of that which one did not know and understand. It is not well for a man to know more than is necessary for his daily living.

Now, however, he turned doubtfully to the woman and said,

"Shall we also then go on this firewagon?"

They drew the old man and the children a little away from the passing crowd and looked at each other anxiously and afraid. At the instant's respite the old man sank upon the ground and the little boys lay down in the dust, heedless of the feet trampling everywhere about them. O-lan carried the girl child still, but the child's head hung over her arm with such a look of death on its closed eyes that Wang Lung, forgetting all else, cried out,

"Is the little slave already dead?"

O-lan shook her head.

"Not yet. The breath flutters back and forth in her. But she will die this night and all of us unless—"

And then as if she could say no other word she looked at him, her square face exhausted and gaunt. Wang Lung answered nothing but to himself he thought that another day of walking like this one and they would all be dead by night, and he said with what cheer there was to be found in his voice,

"Up, my sons, and help the grandfather up. We will go on the firewagon and sit while we walk south."

But whether or not they could have moved none knows, had there not come thundering out of the darkness a noise like a dragon's voice and two great eyes puffing fire out, so that everyone screamed and ran. And pressing forward in the confusion they were pushed hither and thither, but always clinging desperately together, until they were pushed somehow in the darkness and in the yelling and crying of many voices into a small open door and into a box-like room, and then with an incessant roaring the thing in which they rode tore forth into the darkness, bearing them in its vitals.

XI

WITH his two pieces of silver Wang Lung paid for a hundred miles of road and the officer who took his silver from him gave him back a handful of copper pence, and with a few of these Wang Lung bought from a vendor, who thrust his tray of wares in at a hole in the wagon as soon as it stopped, four small loaves of bread and a bowl of soft rice for the girl. It was more than they had had to eat at one time for many days, and although they were starved for food, when it was in their mouths desire left them and it was only by coaxing that the boys could be made to swallow. But the old man sucked perserveringly at the bread between his toothless gums.

"One must eat," he cackled forth, very friendly to all who pressed about him as the firewagon rolled and rocked on its way. "I do not care that my foolish belly is grown lazy after all these days of little to do. It must be fed. I will not die because it does not wish to work." And men laughed suddenly at the smiling, wizened little old man, whose sparse white beard was scattered all over his chin.

But not all the copper pence did Wang Lung spend on food. He kept back all he was able to buy mats to build a shed for them when they reached the south. There were men and women in the firewagon who had been south in other years; some who went each year to the rich cities of the south to work and to beg and thus save the price of food. And Wang Lung, when he had grown used to the wonder of where he was and to the astonishment of seeing the land whirl by the holes in the wagon, listened to what these men said. They spoke with the loudness of wisdom where others are ignorant.

"First you must buy six mats," said one, a man with coarse, hanging lips like a camel's mouth. "These are two pence for one mat, if you are wise and do not act like a country bumpkin, in which case you will be charged three pence, which is more than is necessary, as I very well know. I cannot be fooled by the men in the southern cities, even if they are rich." He wagged his head and looked about for admiration. Wang Lung listened anxiously.

"And then?" he urged. He sat squatting upon his haunches on the bottom of the wagon, which was, after all, only an empty room made of wood and with nothing to sit upon, and the wind and the dust flying up through the cracks in the floor.

"Then," said the man more loudly still, raising his voice above the din of the iron wheels beneath them, "then you bind these together into a hut and then you go out to beg, first smearing yourself with mud and filth to make yourselves as piteous as you can."

Now Wang Lung had never in his life begged of any man and he disliked this notion of begging of strange people in the south.

"One must beg?" he repeated.

"Ah, indeed," said the coarse-mouthed man, "but not until you have eaten. These people in the south have so much rice that each morning you may go to a public kitchen and for a penny hold as much as you can in your belly of the white rice gruel. Then you can beg comfortably and buy beancurd and cabbage and garlic."

Wang Lung withdrew a little from the others and turned himself about to the wall and secretly with his hand in his girdle he counted out the pence he had left. There was enough for the six mats and enough each for a penny for rice and beyond that he had three pence left. It came over him with comfort that thus they could begin the new life. But the notion of holding up a bowl and begging of anyone who passed continued to distress him. It was very well for the old man and for the children and even for the woman, but he had his two hands.

"Is there no work for a man's hands?" he asked of the man suddenly, turning about.

"Aye, work!" said the man with contempt, and he spat upon the floor. "You can pull a rich man in a yellow riksha if you like, and sweat your blood out with heat as you run and have your sweat freeze into a coat of ice on you when you stand waiting to be called. Give me begging!" And he cursed a round curse, so that Wang Lung would not ask anything of him further.

But still it was a good thing that he had heard what the man said, for when the firewagon had carried them as far as it would and had turned them out upon the ground, Wang Lung had ready a plan and he set the old man and the children against a long grey wall of a house, which stood there, and he told the woman to watch them, and he went off to buy the mats, asking of this one and that where the market streets lay. At first he could scarcely understand what was said to him, so brittle and sharp was the sound which these southerners made when they spoke, and several times when he asked and they did not understand, they were impatient, and he learned to observe what sort of man he asked of and to choose one with a kindlier face, for these southerners had tempers which were quick and easily ruffled.

But he found the mat shop at last on the edge of the city and he put his pennies down upon the counter as one who knew the price of the goods and he carried away his roll of mats. When he returned to the spot where he had left the others, they stood there waiting, although when he came the boys cried out at him in relief, and he saw that they had been filled with terror in this strange place. Only the old man watched everything with pleasure and astonishment and he murmured at Wang Lung,

"You see how fat they all are, these southerners, and how pale and oily are their skins. They eat pork every day, doubtless."

But none who passed looked at Wang Lung and his family. Men came and went along the cobbled highway to the city, busy and intent and never glancing aside at beggars, and every little while a caravan of donkeys came pattering by, their small feet fitting neatly to the stones, and they were laden with baskets of brick for the building of houses and with great bags of grain crossed upon their swaying backs. At the end of each caravan the driver rode on the hindermost beast, and he carried a great whip, and this whip he cracked with a terrific noise over the backs of the beasts, shouting as he did so. And as he passed Wang Lung each driver gave him a scornful and haughty look, and no prince could have looked more haughty than these drivers in their rough work coats as they passed by the small group of persons, standing wondering at the edge of the roadway. It was the especial pleasure of each driver, seeing how strange Wang Lung and his family were, to crack his whip just as he passed them, and the sharp explosive cut of the air made them leap up, and seeing them leap the drivers guffawed, and Wang Lung was angry when this happened two and three times and he turned away to see where he could put his hut.

There were already other huts clinging to the wall behind them, but what was inside the wall none knew and there was no way of knowing. It stretched out long and grey and very high, and against the base the small mat sheds clung like fleas to a dog's back. Wang Lung observed the huts and he began to shape his own mats this way and that, but they were stiff and clumsy things at best, being made of split reeds, and he despaired, when suddenly O-lan said,

"That I can do. I remember it in my childhood."

And she placed the girl upon the ground and pulled the mats

[83]

thus and thus, and shaped a rounded roof reaching to the ground and high enough for a man to sit under and not strike the top, and upon the edges of the mats that were upon the ground she placed bricks that were lying about and she set the boys to picking up more bricks. When it was finished they went within and with one mat she had contrived not to use they made a floor and sat down and were sheltered.

Sitting thus and looking at each other, it seemed less than possible that the day before they had left their own house and their land and that these were now a hundred miles away. It was a distance vast enough to have taken them weeks of walking and at which they must have died, some of them, before it was done.

Then the feeling of plenty in this rich land, where no one seemed even hungered, filled them and when Wang Lung said, "Let us go and seek the public kitchens," they rose up almost cheerfully and went out once more, and this time the small boys clattered their chopsticks against their bowls as they walked, for there would soon be something to put into them. And they found soon why the huts were built to that long wall, for a short distance beyond the northern end of it was a street and along the street many people walked carrying bowls and buckets and vessels of tin, all empty, and these persons were going to the kitchens for the poor, which were at the end of the street and not far away. And so Wang Lung and his family mingled with these others and with them they came at last to two great buildings made of mats, and everyone crowded into the open end of these buildings.

Now in the rear of each building were earthen stoves, but larger than Wang Lung had ever seen, and on them iron cauldrons as big as small ponds; and when the great wooden lids were pried up, there was the good white rice bubbling and boiling, and clouds of fragrant steam rose up. Now when the people smelled this fragrance of rice it was the sweetest in the world to their nostrils, and they all pressed forward in a great mass and people called out and mothers shouted in anger and fear lest their children be trodden

upon and little babies cried, and the men who opened the cauldrons roared forth,

"Now there is enough for every man and each in his turn!"

But nothing could stop the mass of hungry men and women and
they fought like beasts until all were fed. Wang Lung caught in
their midst could do nothing but cling to his father and his two
sons and when he was swept to the great cauldron he held out his
bowl and when it was filled threw down his pence, and it was all
he could do to stand sturdily and not be swept on before the thing
was done.

Then when they had come to the street again and stood eating
their rice, he ate and was filled and there was a little left in his
bowl and he said,

"I will take this home to eat in the evening."

But a man stood near who was some sort of a guard of the place
for he wore a special garment of blue and red, and he said sharply,

"No, you can take nothing away except what is in your belly."
And Wang Lung marvelled at this and said,

"Well, if I have paid my penny what business is it of yours if I
carry it within or without me?"

The man said then,

"We must have this rule, for there are those whose hearts are so
hard that they will come and buy this rice that is given for the
poor—for a penny will not feed any man like this—and they will
carry the rice home to feed to their pigs for slop. And the rice is
for men and not for pigs."

Wang Lung listened to this in astonishment and he cried,

"Are there men as hard as this!" And then he said, "But why
should any give like this to the poor and who is it that gives?"

The man answered then,

"It is the rich and the gentry of the town who do it, and some
do it for a good deed for the future, that by saving lives they may
get merit in heaven, and some do it for righteousness that men
may speak well of them."

[85]

"Nevertheless it is a good deed for whatever reason," said Wang Lung, "and some must do it out of a good heart." And then seeing that the man did not answer him, he added in his own defense, "At least there are a few of these?"

But the man was weary of speaking with him and he turned his back, and he hummed an idle tune. The children tugged at Wang Lung then, and Wang Lung led them all back to the hut they had made, and there they laid themselves down and they slept until the next morning, for it was the first time since summer they had been filled with food, and sleep overcame them with fullness.

The next morning it was necessary that there be more money for they spent the last copper coin upon the morning's rice. Wang Lung looked at O-lan, doubtful as to what should be done. But it was not with the despair with which he had looked at her over their blank and empty fields. Here with the coming and going of well-fed people upon the streets, with meat and vegetables in the markets, with fish swimming in the tubs in the fish market, surely it was not possible for a man and his children to starve. It was not as it was in their own land, where even silver could not buy food because there was none. And O-lan answered him steadily, as though this were the life she had known always,

"I and the children can beg and the old man also. His grey hairs will move some who will not give to me."

And she called the two boys to her, for, like children, they had forgotten everything except that they had food again and were in a strange place, and they ran to the street and stood staring at all that passed, and she said to them,

"Each of you take your bowls and hold them thus and cry out thus—"

And she took her empty bowl in her hand and held it out and called piteously,

"A heart, good sir—a heart, good lady! Have a kind heart—a good deed for your life in heaven! The small cash—the copper coin you throw away—feed a starving child!"

The little boys stared at her, and Wang Lung also. Where had she learned to cry thus? How much there was of this woman he did not know! She answered his look saying,

"So I called when I was a child and so I was fed. In such a year as this I was sold a slave."

Then the old man, who had been sleeping, awoke, and they gave him a bowl and the four of them went out on the road to beg. The woman began to call out and to shake her bowl at every passerby. She had thrust the girl child into her naked bosom, and the child slept and its head bobbed this way and that as she moved, running hither and thither with her bowl out-stretched before her. She pointed to the child as she begged and she cried loudly,

"Unless you give, good sir, good lady—this child dies—we starve—we starve—" And indeed the child looked dead, its head shaking this way and that, and there were some, a few, who tossed her unwillingly a small cash.

But the boys after a while began to take the begging as play and the elder one was ashamed and grinned sheepishly as he begged, and then their mother perceiving it dragged them into the hut and she slapped them soundly upon their jaws and she scolded them with anger,

"And do you talk of starving and then laugh at the same time! You fools, starve then!" And she slapped them again and again until her own hands were sore and until the tears were running freely down their faces and they were sobbing and she sent them out again saying,

"Now you are fit to beg! That and more if you laugh again!"

As for Wang Lung, he went into the streets and asked hither and thither until he found a place where jinrikshas were for hire and he went in and hired one for the day for the price of half a round of silver to be paid at night and then dragged the thing after him out to the street again.

Pulling this rickety, wooden wagon on its two wheels behind him, it seemed to him that everyone looked at him for a fool. He was as awkward between its shafts as an ox yoked for the first time to the plow, and he could scarcely walk; yet must he run if he were to earn his living, for here and there and everywhere through the streets of this city men ran as they pulled other men in these. He went into a narrow side street where there were no shops but only doors of homes closed and private, and he went up and down for a while pulling to accustom himself, and just as he said to himself in despair that he had better beg, a door opened, and an old man, spectacled and garbed as teacher, stepped forth and hailed him.

Wang Lung at first began to tell him that he was too new at it to run, but the old man was deaf, for he heard nothing of what Wang Lung said, only motioning to him tranquilly to lower the shafts and let him step in, and Wang Lung obeyed, not knowing what else to do, and feeling compelled to it by the deafness of the old man and by his well-dressed and learned looks. Then the old man, sitting erect, said,

"Take me to the Confucian temple," and there he sat, erect and calm, and there was that in his calmness which allowed no question, so that Wang started forward as he saw others do, although he had no faintest knowledge of where the Confucian temple stood.

But as he went he asked, and since the load lay along crowded streets, with the vendors passing back and forth with their baskets and women going out to market, and carriages drawn by horses, and many other vehicles like the one he pulled, and everything pressing against another so that there was no possibility of running, he walked as swiftly as he was able, conscious always of the awkward bumping of his load behind him. To loads upon his back he was used, but not to pulling, and before the walls of the temple were in sight his arms were aching and his hands blistered, for the shafts pressed spots where the hoe did not touch.

The old teacher stepped forth out of the riksha when Wang Lung lowered it as he reached the temple gates, and feeling in the depths of his bosom he drew out a small silver coin and gave it to Wang Lung saying,

"Now I never pay more than this, and there is no use in complaint." And with this he turned away and went into the temple.

Wang Lung had not thought to complain for he had not seen this coin before, and he did not know for how many pence it could be changed. He went to a rice shop near by where money is changed, and the changer gave him for the coin twenty-six pence, and Wang Lung marvelled at the ease with which money comes in the south. But another riksha puller stood near and leaned over as he counted and he said to Wang Lung,

"Only twenty-six. How far did you pull that old head?" And when Wang told him, the man cried out, "Now there is a small-hearted old man! He gave you only half the proper fare. How much did you argue for before you started?"

"I did not argue," said Wang Lung. "He said 'Come' and I came."

The other man looked at Wang Lung pityingly.

"Now there is a country lout for you, pigtail and all!" he called out to the bystanders. "Someone says come and he comes, and he never asks, this idiot born of idiots, 'How much will you give me if I come!' Know this, idiot, only white foreigners can be taken without argument! Their tempers are like quick lime, but when they say 'Come' you may come and trust them, for they are such fools they do not know the proper price of anything, but let the silver run out of their pockets like water." And everyone listening, laughed.

Wang Lung said nothing. It was true that he felt very humble and ignorant in all this crowd of city people, and he pulled his vehicle away without a word in answer.

"Nevertheless, this will feed my children tomorrow," he said to himself stubbornly, and then he remembered that he had the rent of the vehicle to pay at night and that indeed there was not yet half enough to do that.

He had one more passenger during the morning and with this one he argued and agreed upon a price and in the afternoon two more called to him. But at night, when he counted out all his money in his hand he had only a penny above the rent of the riksha, and he went back to his hut in great bitterness, saying to himself that for labor greater than the labor of a day in a harvest field he had earned only one copper penny. Then there came flooding over him the memory of his land. He had not remembered it once during this strange day, but now the thought of it lying back there, far away, it is true, but waiting and his own, filled him with peace, and so he came to his hut.

When he entered there he found that O-lan had for her day's begging received forty small cash, which is less than five pence, and of the boys, the elder had eight cash and the younger thirteen, and with these put together there was enough to pay for the rice in the morning. Only when they put the younger boy's in with all, he howled for his own, and he loved the money he had begged, and slept with it that night in his hand and they could not take it from him until he gave it himself for his own rice.

But the old man had received nothing at all. All day long he had sat by the roadside obediently enough, but he did not beg. He slept and woke and stared at what passed him, and when he grew weary he slept again. And being of the older generation, he could not be reproved. When he saw that his hands were empty he said merely,

"I have ploughed land and I have sown seed and I have reaped harvest and thus have I filled my rice bowl. And I have beyond this begotten a son and son's sons."

And with this he trusted like a child that now he would be fed, seeing that he had a son and grandsons.

XII

NOW after the first sharpness of Wang Lung's hunger was over
and he saw that his children daily had something to eat, and
he knew there was every morning rice to be had, and of his day's
labor and of O-lan's begging there was enough to pay for it, the
strangeness of his life passed, and he began to feel what this city
was, to whose fringes he clung. Running about the streets every
day and all day long he learned to know the city after a fashion,
and he saw this and that of its secret parts. He learned that in the
morning the people he drew in his vehicle, if they were women,
went to the market, and if they were men, they went to the schools
and to the houses of business. But what sort of schools these were
he had no way of knowing, beyond the fact that they were called
such names as "The Great School of Western Learning" or as
"The Great School of China," for he never went beyond the gates,
and if he had gone in, well he knew someone would have come to
ask him what he did out of his place. And what houses of business
they were to which he drew men he did not know, since when he
was paid it was all he knew.

And at night he knew that he drew men to big tea houses and to
places of pleasure, the pleasure that is open and streams out upon
the streets in the sound of music and of gaming with pieces of
ivory and bamboo upon a wooden table, and the pleasure that is
secret and silent and hidden behind walls. But none of these pleasures did Wang Lung know for himself, since his feet crossed no
threshold except that of his own hut, and his road was always

ended at a gate. He lived in the rich city as alien as a rat in a rich man's house that is fed on scraps thrown away, and hides here and there and is never a part of the real life of the house.

So it was that, although a hundred miles are not so far as a thousand, and land road never so far as water road, yet Wang Lung and his wife and children were like foreigners in this southern city. It is true that the people who went about the streets had black hair and eyes as Wang Lung and all his family had, and as all did in the country where Wang Lung was born, and it is true that if one listened to the language of these southerners it could be understood, if with difficulty.

But Anhwei is not Kiangsu. In Anhwei, where Wang Lung was born, the language is slow and deep and it wells from the throat. But in the Kiangsu city where they now lived the people spoke in syllables which splintered from their lips and from the ends of their tongues. And where Wang Lung's fields spread out in slow and leisurely harvest twice a year of wheat and rice and a bit of corn and beans and garlic, here in the farms about the city men urged their land with perpetual stinking fertilizing of human wastes to force the land to a hurried bearing of this vegetable and that besides their rice.

In Wang Lung's country a man, if he had a roll of good wheat bread and a sprig of garlic in it, had a full meal and needed no more. But here the people dabbled with pork balls and bamboo sprouts and chestnuts stewed with chicken and goose giblets and this and that of vegetables, and when an honest man came by smelling of yesterday's garlic, they lifted their noses and cried out, "Now here is a reeking, pig-tailed northerner!" The smell of the garlic would make the very shopkeepers in the cloth shops raise the price of blue cotton cloth as they might raise the price for a foreigner.

But then the little village of sheds clinging to the wall never became a part of the city or of the countryside which stretched beyond, and once when Wang Lung heard a young man haranguing a crowd at the corner of the Confucian temple, where any man may stand, if he have the courage to speak out, and the young man said that China must have a revolution and must rise against the hated foreigners, Wang Lung was alarmed and slunk away feeling that he was the foreigner against whom the young man spoke with such passion. And when on another day he heard another young man speaking—for this city was full of young men speaking—and he said at his street corner that the people of China must unite and must educate themselves in these times, it did not occur to Wang Lung that anyone was speaking to him.

It was only one day when he was on the street of the silk markets looking for a passenger that he learned better than he had known, and that there were those who were more foreign than he in this city. He happened on this day to pass by the door of a shop from whence ladies sometimes came after purchasing silks within, and sometimes thus he secured one who paid him better than most. And on this day someone did come out on him suddenly, a creature the like of whom he had never seen before. He had no idea of whether it was male or female, but it was tall and dressed in a straight black robe of some rough harsh material and there was the skin of a dead animal wrapped about its neck. As he passed, the person, whether male or female, motioned to him sharply to lower the shafts and he did so, and when he stood erect again, dazed at what had befallen him, the person in broken accents directed that he was to go to the Street of Bridges. He began to run hurriedly, scarcely knowing what he did, and once he called to another puller whom he knew casually in the day's work,

"Look at this—what is this I pull?"

And the man shouted back at him,

"A foreigner—a female from America—you are rich—"

But Wang Lung ran as fast as he could for fear of the strange creature behind him, and when he reached the Street of Bridges he was exhausted and dripping with his sweat.

This female stepped out then and said in the same broken accents, "You need not have run yourself to death," and left him with two silver pieces in his palm, which was double the usual fare.

Then Wang Lung knew that this was indeed a foreigner and more foreign yet than he in this city, and that after all people of black hair and black eyes are one sort and people of light hair and light eyes of another sort, and he was no longer after that wholly foreign in the city.

When he went back to the hut that night with the silver he had received still untouched, he told O-lan and she said,

"I have seen them. I always beg of them, for they alone will drop silver rather than copper into my bowl."

But neither Wang Lung nor his wife felt that the foreigner dropped silver because of any goodness of heart but rather because of ignorance and not knowing that copper is more correct to give to beggars than silver.

Nevertheless, through this experience Wang Lung learned what the young men had not taught him, that he belonged to his own kind, who have black hair and black eyes.

Clinging thus to the outskirts of the great, sprawling, opulent city it seemed that at least there could not be any lack of food. Wang Lung and his family had come from a country where if men starve it is because there is no food, since the land cannot bear under a relentless heaven. Silver in the hand was worth little because it could buy nothing where nothing was.

Here in the city there was food everywhere. The cobbled streets of the fish market were lined with great baskets of big silver fish, caught in the night out of the teeming river; with tubs of small shining fish, dipped out of a net cast over a pool; with heaps of yellow crabs, squirming and nipping in peevish astonishment; with writhing eels for gourmands at the feasts. At the grain markets there were such baskets of grain that a man might step into them and sink and smother and none know it who did not see it; white rice and brown and dark yellow wheat and pale gold wheat, and yellow soybeans and red beans and green broad beans and canary-colored millet and grey sesame. And at the meat markets whole hogs hung by their necks, split open the length of their great bodies to show the red meat and the layers of goodly fat, the skin soft and thick and white. And duck shops hung row upon row, over their ceilings and in their doors, the brown baked ducks that had been turned slowly on a spit before coals and the white salted ducks and the strings of duck giblets, and so with the shops that sold geese and pheasant and every kind of fowl.

As for the vegetables, there was everything which the hand of man could coax from the soil; glittering red radishes and white, hollow lotus root and taro, green cabbages and celery, curling bean sprouts and brown chestnuts and garnishes of fragrant cress. There was nothing which the appetite of man might desire that was not to be found upon the streets of the markets of that city. And going hither and thither were the vendors of sweets and fruits and nuts and of hot delicacies of sweet potatoes browned in sweet oils and little delicately spiced balls of pork wrapped in dough and steamed, and sugar cakes made from glutinous rice, and the children of the city ran out to the vendors of these things with their hands full of pennies and they bought and they ate until their skins glistened with sugar and oil.

Yes, one would say that in this city there could be none who starved.

Still, every morning a little after dawn Wang Lung and his family came out of their hut and with their bowls and chop-sticks they made a small group in a long procession of people, each issuing from his hut, shivering in clothes too thin for the damp river fog, walking curved against the chill morning wind to the public kitchens, where for a penny a man may buy a bowl of thin rice gruel. And with all Wang Lung's pulling and running before his riksha and with all O-lan's begging, they never could gain enough to cook rice daily in their own hut. If there was a penny over and above the price of the rice at the kitchens for the poor, they bought a bit of cabbage. But the cabbage was dear at any price, for the two boys must go to hunt for fuel to cook it between the two bricks O-lan had set up for a stove, and this fuel they had to snatch by handfuls as they could from the farmers who carried the loads of reed and grass into the city fuel markets. Sometimes the children were caught and cuffed soundly and one night the elder lad, who was more timid than the younger and more ashamed of what he did, came back with an eye swollen shut from the blow of a farmer's hand. But the younger lad grew adept and indeed more adept at petty thieving than at begging.

To O-lan this was nothing. If the boys could not beg without laughing and play, let them steal to fill their bellies. But Wang Lung, although he had no answer for her, felt his gorge rise at this thievery of his sons, and he did not blame the elder when he was slow at the business. This life in the shadow of the great wall was not the life Wang Lung loved. There was his land waiting for him.

One night he came late and there was in the stew of cabbage a good round piece of pork. It was the first time they had had flesh to eat since they killed their own ox, and Wang Lung's eyes widened.

"You must have begged of a foreigner this day," he said to O-lan. But she, according to her habit, said nothing. Then the younger boy, too young for wisdom and filled with his own pride of cleverness, said,

"I took it—it is mine, this meat. When the butcher looked the other way after he had sliced it off from the big piece upon the counter, I ran under an old woman's arm who had come to buy it and I seized it and ran into an alley and hid in a dry water jar at a back gate until Elder Brother came."

"Now will I not eat this meat!" cried Wang Lung angrily. "We will eat meat that we can buy or beg, but not that which we steal. Beggars we may be but thieves we are not." And he took the meat out of the pot with his two fingers and threw it upon the ground and was heedless of the younger lad's howling.

Then O-lan came forward in her stolid fashion and she picked up the meat and washed it off with a little water and thrust it back into the boiling pot.

"Meat is meat," she said quietly.

Wang Lung said nothing then, but he was angry and afraid in his heart because his sons were growing into thieves here in this city. And although he said nothing when O-lan pulled the tender cooked flesh apart with her chopsticks, and although he said nothing when she gave great pieces of it to the old man and to the boys and even filled the mouth of the girl with it and ate of it herself, he himself would have none of it, contenting himself with the cabbage he had bought. But after the meal was over he took his younger son into the street out of hearing of the woman and there behind a house he took the boy's head under his arm and cuffed it soundly on this side and that, and would not stop for the lad's bellowing.

"There and there and there!" he shouted. "That for a thief."

But to himself he said when he had let the lad go sniveling home,

"We must get back to the land."

XIII

DAY by day beneath the opulence of this city Wang Lung lived in the foundations of poverty upon which it was laid. With the food spilling out of the markets, with the streets of the silk shops flying brilliant banners of black and red and orange silk to announce their wares, with rich men clothed in satin and in velvet, soft-fleshed rich men with their skin covered with garments of silk and their hands like flowers for softness and perfume and the beauty of idleness, with all of these for the regal beauty of the city, in that part where Wang Lung lived there was not food enough to feed savage hunger and not clothes enough to cover bones.

Men labored all day at the baking of breads and cakes for feasts for the rich and children labored from dawn to midnight and slept all greasy and grimed as they were upon rough pallets on the floor and staggered to the ovens next day, and there was not money enough given them to buy a piece of the rich breads they made for others. And men and women labored at the cutting and contriving of heavy furs for the winter and of soft light furs for the spring and at the thick brocaded silks, to cut and shape them into sumptuous robes for the ones who ate of the profusion at the markets, and they themselves snatched a bit of coarse blue cotton cloth and sewed it hastily together to cover their bareness.

Wang Lung, living among these who labored at feasting others, heard strange things of which he took little heed. The older men and women, it is true, said nothing to anyone. Grey-beards pulled rikshas, pushed wheelbarrows of coal and wood to bakeries and palaces, strained their backs until the muscles stood forth like ropes as they pushed and pulled the heavy carts of merchandise over the cobbled roads, ate frugally of their scanty food, slept their brief nights out, and were silent. Their faces were like the face of O-lan, inarticulate, dumb. None knew what was in their minds. If they spoke at all it was of food or of pence. Rarely was the word silver upon their lips because rarely was silver in their hands.

Their faces in repose were twisted as though in anger, only it was not anger. It was the years of straining at loads too heavy for them which had lifted their upper lips to bare their teeth in a seeming snarl, and this labor had set deep wrinkles in the flesh about their eyes and their mouths. They themselves had no idea of what manner of men they were. One of them once, seeing himself in a mirror that passed on a van of household goods had cried out, "There is an ugly fellow!" And when others laughed at him loudly he smiled painfully, never knowing at what they laughed, and looking about hastily to see if he had offended someone.

At home in the small hovels where they lived, around Wang Lung's hovel, heaped one upon another, the women sewed rags together to make a covering for the children they were forever breeding, and they snatched at bits of cabbage from farmers' fields and stole handfuls of rice from the grain markets, and gleaned the year round the grass on the hillsides; and at harvest they followed the reapers like fowls, their eyes piercing and sharp for every dropped grain or stalk. And through these huts passed children; they were born and dead and born again until neither mother or father knew how many had been born or had died, and scarcely knew even how many were living, thinking of them only as mouths to be fed.

These men and these women and these children passed in and out of the markets and the cloth shops and wandered about the countryside that bordered on the city, the men working at this and that for a few pence and the women and children stealing and begging and snatching, and Wang Lung and his woman and his children were among them.

The old men and the old women accepted the life they had. But there came a time when the male children grew to a certain age, before they were old and when they ceased to be children, and then they were filled with discontent. There was talk among the young men, angry, growling talk. And later when they were fully men and married and the dismay of increasing numbers filled their hearts, the scattered anger of their youth became settled into a fierce despair and into a revolt too deep for mere words because all their lives they labored more severely than beasts, and for nothing except a handful of refuse to fill their bellies. Listening to such talk one evening Wang Lung heard for the first time what was on the other side of the great wall to which their rows of huts clung.

It was at the end of one of those days in late winter when for the first time it seems possible that spring may come again. The ground about the huts was still muddy with the melting snow and the water ran into the huts so that each family had hunted here and there for a few bricks upon which to sleep. But with the discomfort of the damp earth there was this night a soft mildness in the air and this mildness made Wang Lung exceedingly restless so that he could not sleep at once as was his wont after he had eaten, so that he went out to the street's edge and stood there idle.

Here his old father habitually sat squatting on his thighs and leaning against the wall and here he sat now, having taken his bowl of food there to sup it, now that the children filled the hut to bursting when they were clamoring. The old man held in one hand the end of a loop of cloth which O-lan had torn from her girdle, and within this loop the girl child staggered to and fro without falling. Thus he spent his days looking after this child who had now grown rebellious at having to be in her mother's bosom as she begged. Besides this, O-lan was again with child and the pressure of the larger child upon her from without was too painful to bear.

Wang Lung watched the child falling and scrambling and falling again and the old man pulling at the loop ends, and standing thus he felt upon his face the mildness of the evening wind and there arose within him a mighty longing for his fields.

"On such a day as this," he said aloud to his father, "the fields should be turned and the wheat cultivated."

"Ah," said the old man tranquilly, "I know what is in your thought. Twice and twice again in my years I have had to do as we did this year and leave the fields and know that there was no seed in them for fresh harvests."

"But you always went back, my father."

"There was the land, my son," said the old man simply.

Well, they also would go back, if not this year, then next, said Wang to his own heart. As long as there was the land! And the thought of it lying there waiting for him, rich with the spring rains, filled him with desire. He went back to the hut and he said roughly to his wife,

"If I had anything to sell I would sell it and go back to the land. Or if it were not for the old head, we would walk though we starved. But how can he and the small child walk a hundred miles? And you, with your burden!"

O-lan had been rinsing the rice bowls with a little water and now she piled them in a corner of the hut and looked up at him from the spot where she squatted.

"There is nothing to sell except the girl," she answered slowly.

Wang Lung's breath caught.

"Now, I would not sell a child!" he said loudly.

"I was sold," she answered very slowly. "I was sold to a great house so that my parents could return to their home."

"And would you sell the child, therefore?"

"If it were only I, she would be killed before she was sold . . . the slave of slaves was I! But a dead girl brings nothing. I would sell this girl for you—to take you back to the land."

"Never would I," said Wang Lung stoutly, "not though I spent my life in this wilderness."

But when he had gone out again the thought, which never alone would have come to him, tempted him against his will. He looked at the small girl, staggering persistently at the end of the loop her grandfather held. She had grown greatly on the food given her each day, and although she had as yet said no word at all, still she was plump as a child will be on slight care enough. Her lips that had been like an old woman's were smiling and red, and as of old she grew merry when he looked at her and she smiled.

"I might have done it," he mused, "if she had not lain in my bosom and smiled like that."

And then he thought again of his land and he cried out passionately,

"Shall I never see it again! With all this labor and begging there is never enough to do more than feed us today."

Then out of the dusk there answered him a voice, a deep burly voice,

"You are not the only one. There are a hundred hundred like you in this city."

The man came up, smoking a short bamboo pipe, and it was the father of the family in the hut next to Wang Lung's hut. He was a man seldom seen in the daylight, for he slept all day and worked at night pulling heavy wagons of merchandise which were too large for the streets by day when other vehicles must continually pass each other. But sometimes Wang Lung saw him come creeping home at dawn, panting and spent, and his great knotty shoulders drooping. Wang Lung passed him thus at dawn as he went out to his own riksha pulling, and sometimes at dusk before the night's work the man came out and stood with the other men who were about to go into their hovels to sleep.

"Well, and is it forever?" asked Wang Lung bitterly.

The man puffed at his pipe thrice and then spat upon the ground. Then he said,

"No, and not forever. When the rich are too rich there are ways, and when the poor are too poor there are ways. Last winter we sold two girls and endured, and this winter, if this one my woman bears is a girl, we will sell again. One slave I have kept—the first. The others it is better to sell than to kill, although there are those who prefer to kill them before they draw breath. This is one of the ways when the poor are too poor. When the rich are too rich there is a way, and if I am not mistaken, that way will come soon." He nodded and pointed with the stem of his pipe to the wall behind them. "Have you seen inside that wall?"

Wang Lung shook his head, staring. The man continued,

"I took one of my slaves in there to sell and I saw it. You would not believe it if I told you how money comes and goes in that house. I will tell you this—even the servants eat with chopsticks of ivory bound with silver, and even the slave women hang jade and pearls in their ears and sew pearls upon their shoes, and when the shoes have a bit of mud upon them or a small rent comes such as you and I would not call a rent, they throw them away, pearls and all!"

The man drew hard on his pipe and Wang Lung listened, his mouth ajar. Over this wall, then, there were indeed such things!

"There is a way when men are too rich," said the man, and he was silent for a time and then as though he had said nothing he added indifferently,

"Well, work again," and was gone into the night.

But Wang Lung that night could not sleep for thinking of silver and gold and pearls on the other side of this wall against which his body rested, his body clad in what he wore day after day, because there was no quilt to cover him and only a mat upon bricks beneath him. And temptation fell on him again to sell the child, so that he said to himself,

"It would be better perhaps that she be sold into a rich house so that she can eat daintily and wear jewels, if it be that she grow up pretty and please a lord." But against his own wish he answered himself and he thought again, "Well, and if I did, she is not worth her weight in gold and rubies. If she bring enough to take us back to the land, where will come enough to buy an ox and a table and a bed and the benches once more? Shall I sell a child that we may starve there instead of here? We have not even seed to put into the land."

And he saw nothing of the way of which the man spoke when he said, "There is a way, when the rich are too rich."

XIV

S PRING seethed in the village of huts. Out to the hills and the grave lands those who had begged now could go to dig the small green weeds, dandelions and shepherd's purse that thrust up feeble new leaves, and it was not necessary as it had been to snatch at vegetables here and there. A swarm of ragged women and children issued forth each day from the huts, and with bits of tin and sharp stones or worn knives, and with baskets made of twisted bamboo twigs or split reeds they searched the countryside and the roadways for the food they could get without begging and without money. And every day O-lan went out with this swarm, O-lan and the two boys.

But men must work on, and Wang Lung worked as he had before, although the lengthening warm days and the sunshine and sudden rains filled everyone with longings and discontents. In the winter they had worked and been silent, enduring stolidly the snow and ice under their bare, straw-sandalled feet, going back at dark to their huts and eating without words such food as the day's labor and begging had brought, falling heavily to sleep, men, women and children, together, to gain that for their bodies which the food was too poor and too scanty to give. Thus it was in Wang Lung's hut and well he knew it must be so in every other.

But with the coming of spring talk began to surge up out of their hearts and to make itself heard on their lips. In the evening when the twilight lingered they gathered out of their huts and talked together, and Wang Lung saw this one and that of the men who had lived near him and whom through the winter he had not known. Had O-lan been one to tell him things he might have heard, for instance, of this one who beat his wife, of that one who had a leprous disease that ate his cheeks out, of that one who was king of a gang of thieves. But she was silent beyond the spare questions and answers she asked and gave, and so Wang Lung stood diffidently on the edge of the circle and listened to the talk.

Most of these ragged men had nothing beyond what they took in the day's labor and begging, and he was always conscious that he was not truly one of them. He owned land and his land was waiting for him. These others thought of how they might tomorrow eat a bit of fish, or of how they might idle a bit, and even how they might gamble a little, a penny or two, since their days were alike all evil and filled with want and a man must play sometimes, though desperate.

But Wang Lung thought of his land and pondered this way and that, with the sickened heart of deferred hope, how he could get back to it. He belonged, not to this scum which clung to the walls of a rich man's house; nor did he belong to the rich man's house. He belonged to the land and he could not live with any fullness until he felt the land under his feet and followed a plow in the springtime and bore a scythe in his hand at harvest. He listened, therefore, apart from the others, because hidden in his heart was the knowledge of the possession of his land, the good wheat land of his fathers, and the strip of rich rice land which he had bought from the great house.

They talked, these men, always and forever of money; of what pence they had paid for a foot of cloth, and of what they had paid for a small fish as long as a man's finger, or of what they could earn in a day, and always at last of what they would do if they had the money which the man over the wall had in his coffers. Every day the talk ended with this:

"And if I had the gold that he has and the silver in my hand that he wears every day in his girdle and if I had the pearls his concubines wear and the rubies his wife wears . . ."

And listening to all the things they would do if they had these things, Wang Lung heard only of how much they would eat and sleep, and of what dainties they would eat that they had never yet tasted, and of how they would gamble in this great tea shop and in that, and of what pretty women they would buy for their lust, and above all, how none would ever work again, even as the rich man behind the wall never worked.

Then Wang Lung cried out suddenly,

"If I had the gold and the silver and the jewels, I would buy land with it, good land, and I would bring forth harvests from the land!"

At this they united in turning on him and in rebuking him,

"Now here is a pig-tailed country bumpkin who understands nothing of city life and of what may be done with money. He would go on working like a slave behind an ox or an ass!" And each one of them felt he was more worthy to have the riches than was Wang Lung, because they knew better how to spend it.

But this scorn did not change the mind of Wang Lung. It only made him say to himself instead of aloud for others to hear,

"Nevertheless, I would put the gold and the silver and the jewels into good rich lands."

And thinking this, he grew more impatient every day for the land that was already his.

Being possessed continually by this thought of his land, Wang Lung saw as in a dream the things that happened about him in the city every day. He accepted this strangeness and that without questioning why anything was, except that in this day this thing came. There was, for an example, the paper that men gave out here and there, and sometimes even to him.

Now Wang Lung had never in his youth or at any time learned the meaning of letters upon paper, and he could not, therefore, make anything out of such paper covered with black marks and pasted upon city gates or upon walls or sold by the handful or even given away. Twice had he had such paper given him.

The first time it was given by a foreigner such as the one he had pulled unwittingly in his riksha one day, only this one who gave him the paper was a man, very tall, and lean as a tree that has been blown by bitter winds. This man had eyes as blue as ice and a hairy face, and when he gave the paper to Wang Lung it was seen that his hands were also hairy and redskinned. He had, moreover, a great nose projecting beyond his cheeks like a prow beyond the sides of a ship and Wang Lung, although frightened to take anything from his hand, was more frightened to refuse, seeing the man's strange eyes and fearful nose. He took what was thrust at him, then, and when he had courage to look at it after the foreigner had passed on, he saw on the paper a picture of a man, white-skinned, who hung upon a crosspiece of wood. The man was without clothes except for a bit about his loins, and to all appearances he was dead, since his head drooped upon his shoulder and his eyes were closed above his bearded lips. Wang Lung looked at the pictured man in horror and with increasing interest. There were characters beneath, but of these he could make nothing.

He carried the picture home at night and showed it to the old man. But he also could not read and they discussed its possible meaning, Wang Lung and the old man and the two boys. The two boys cried out in delight and horror,

"And see the blood streaming out of his side!"

And the old man said,

"Surely this was a very evil man to be thus hung."

But Wang Lung was fearful of the picture and pondered as to why a foreigner had given it to him, whether or not some brother of this foreigner's had not been so treated and the other brethren seeking revenge. He avoided, therefore, the street on which he had met the man and after a few days, when the paper was forgotten, O-lan took it and sewed it into a shoe sole together with other bits of paper she picked up here and there to make the soles firm.

But the next time one handed a paper freely to Wang Lung it was a man of the city, a young man well clothed, who talked loudly as he distributed sheets hither and thither among the crowds who swarm about anything new and strange in a street. This paper bore also a picture of blood and death, but the man who died this time was not white-skinned and hairy but a man like Wang Lung himself, a common fellow, yellow and slight and black of hair and eye and clothed in ragged blue garments. Upon the dead figure a great fat one stood and stabbed the dead figure again and again with a long knife he held. It was a piteous sight and Wang Lung stared at it and longed to make something of the letters underneath. He turned to the man beside him and said,

"Do you know a character or two so that you may tell me the meaning of this dreadful thing?"

And the man said,

"Be still and listen to the young teacher; he tells us all."

And so Wang Lung listened, and what he heard was what he had never heard before.

"The dead man is yourselves," proclaimed the young teacher, "and the murderous one who stabs you when you are dead and do not know it are the rich and the capitalists, who would stab you even after you are dead. You are poor and downtrodden and it is because the rich seize everything."

Now that he was poor Wang Lung knew full well but he had heretofore blamed it on a heaven that would not rain in its season, or having rained, would continue to rain as though rain were an evil habit. When there was rain and sun in proportion so that the seed would sprout in the land and the stalk bear grain, he did not consider himself poor. Therefore he listened in interest to hear further what the rich men had to do with this thing, that heaven would not rain in its season. And at last when the young man had talked on and on but had said nothing of this matter where Wang Lung's interest lay, Wang Lung grew bold and asked,

"Sir, is there any way whereby the rich who oppress us can make it rain so that I can work on the land?"

At this the young man turned on him with scorn and replied,

"Now how ignorant you are, you who still wear your hair in a long tail! No one can make it rain when it will not, but what has this to do with us? If the rich would share with us what they have, rain or not would matter to none, because we would all have money and food."

A great shout went up from those who listened, but Wang Lung turned away unsatisfied. Yes, but there was the land. Money and food are eaten and gone, and if there is not sun and rain in proportion, there is again hunger. Nevertheless, he took willingly the papers the young man gave him, because he remembered that O-lan had never enough paper for the shoe soles, and so he gave them to her when he went home, saying,

"Now there is some stuff for the shoe soles," and he worked as before.

But of the men in the huts with whom he talked at evening there were many who heard eagerly what the young man said, the more eagerly because they knew that over the wall there dwelt a rich man and it seemed a small thing that between them and his riches there was only this layer of bricks, which might be torn down with a few knocks of a stout pole, such as they had, to carry their heavy burdens every day upon their shoulders.

And to the discontent of the spring there was now added the new discontent which the young man and others like him spread abroad in the spirits of the dwellers in the huts, the sense of unjust possession by others of those things which they had not. And as they thought day after day on all these matters and talked of them in the twilight, and above all as day after day their labor brought in no added wage, there arose in the hearts of the young and the strong a tide as irresistible as the tide of the river, swollen with winter snows—the tide of the fullness of savage desire.

But Wang Lung, although he saw this and he heard the talk and felt their anger with a strange unease, desired nothing but his land under his feet again.

Then in this city out of which something new was always springing at him, Wang Lung saw another new thing he did not understand. He saw one day, when he pulled his riksha empty down a street looking for a customer, a man, seized as he stood by a small band of armed soldiers, and when the man protested, the soldiers brandished knives in his face, and while Wang Lung watched in amazement, another was seized and another, and it came to Wang Lung that those who were seized were all common fellows who worked with their hands, and while he stared, yet another man was seized, and this one a man who lived in the hut nearest his own against the wall.

Then Wang Lung perceived suddenly out of his astonishment that all these men were as ignorant as he as to why they were thus being taken, willy nilly, whether they would or not. And Wang Lung thrust his riksha into a side alley and he dropped it and darted into the door of a hot water shop lest he be next and there he hid, crouched low behind the great cauldrons, until the soldiers passed. And then he asked the keeper of the hot water shop the meaning of the thing he had seen, and the man, who was old and shriveled with the steam rising continually about him out of the copper cauldrons of his trade, answered with indifference,

"It is but another war somewhere. Who knows what all this fighting to and fro is about? But so it has been since I was a lad and so will it be after I am dead and well I know it."

"Well, but why do they seize my neighbor, who is as innocent as I who have never heard of this new war?" asked Wang Lung in great consternation. And the old man clattered the lids of his cauldrons and answered,

"These soldiers are going to battle somewhere and they need carriers for their bedding and their guns and their ammunition and so they force laborers like you to do it. But what part are you from? It is no new sight in this city."

"But what then?" urged Wang Lung breathless. "What wage—what return—"

Now the old man was very old and he had no great hope in anything and no interest in anything beyond his cauldrons and he answered carelessly,

"Wage there is none and but two bits of dry bread a day and a sup from a pond, and you may go home when the destination is reached if your two legs can carry you."

"Well, but a man's family—" said Wang Lung, aghast.

"Well, and what do they know or care of that?" said the old man scornfully, peering under the wooden lid of the nearest cauldron to see if the water bubbled yet. A cloud of steam enveloped him and his wrinkled face could scarcely be seen peering into the cauldron. Nevertheless he was kindly, for when he came forth again out of the steam he saw what Wang Lung could not see from where he crouched, that once more the soldiers approached, searching the streets from which now every able-bodied working man had fled.

"Stoop yet more," he said to Wang Lung. "They are come again."

And Wang Lung crouched low behind the cauldrons and the soldiers clattered down the cobbles to the west, and when the sound of their leathern boots was gone Wang Lung darted out and seizing his riksha he ran with it empty to the hut.

Then to O-lan, who had but just returned from the roadside to cook a little of the green stuff she had gathered, he told in broken, panting words what was happening and how nearly he had not escaped, and as he spoke this new horror sprang up in him, the horror that he be dragged to battlefields and not only his old father and his family left alone to starve, but he dying upon a battlefield and his blood spilled out, and nevermore able to see his own land. He looked at O-lan haggardly and he said,

"Now am I truly tempted to sell the little slave and go north to the land."

But she, after listening, mused and said in her plain and unmoved way,

"Wait a few days. There is strange talk about."

Nevertheless, he went out no more in the daylight but he sent the eldest lad to return the riksha to the place from where he hired it and he waited until the night came and he went to the houses of

[111]

merchandise and for half what he had earned before he pulled all night the great wagonloads of boxes, to each wagon a dozen men pulling and straining and groaning. And the boxes were filled with silks and with cottons and with fragrant tobacco, so fragrant that the smell of it leaked through the wood. And there were great jars of oils and of wines.

All night through the dark streets he strained against the ropes, his body naked and streaming with sweating, and his bare feet slipping on the cobbles, slimy and wet as they were with the dampness of the night. Before them to show the way ran a little lad carrying a flaming torch and in the light of this torch the faces and the bodies of the men and the wet stones glistened alike. And Wang Lung came home before dawn, gasping and too broken for food until he had slept. But during the bright day when the soldiers searched the street he slept safely in the furthermost corner of the hut behind a pile of straw O-lan gathered to make a shield for him.

What battles there were or who fought which other one Wang Lung did not know. But with the further coming of spring the city became filled with the unrest of fear. All during the days carriages drawn by horses pulled rich men and their possessions of clothing and satin-covered bedding and their beautiful women and their jewels to the river's edge where ships carried them away to other places, and some went to that other house where firewagons came and went. Wang Lung never went upon the streets in the day, but his sons came back with their eyes wide and bright, crying,

"We saw such an one and such an one, a man as fat and monstrous as a god in a temple, and his body covered with many feet of yellow silk and on his thumb a great gold ring set with green stone like a piece of glass, and his flesh was all bright with oil and eating!"

Or the elder cried,

"And we have seen such boxes and boxes and when I asked what was in them one said, 'There is gold and silver in them, but the rich cannot take all they have away, and some day it will all be

[112]

ours.' Now, what did he mean by this, my father?" And the lad opened his eyes inquisitively to his father.

But when Wang Lung answered shortly, "How should I know what an idle city fellow means?" the lad cried wistfully,

"Oh, I wish we might go even now and get it if it is ours. I should like to taste a cake. I have never tasted a sweet cake with sesame seed sprinkled on the top."

The old man looked up from his dreaming at this and he said as one croons to himself,

"When we had a good harvest we had such cakes at the autumn feast, when the sesame had been threshed and before it was old we kept a little back to make such cakes."

And Wang Lung remembered the cakes that O-lan had once made at the New Year's feast, cakes of rice flour and lard and sugar, and his mouth watered and his heart pained him with longing for that which was passed.

"If we were only back on our land," he muttered.

Then suddenly it seemed to him that not one more day could he lie in this wretched hut, which was not wide enough for him even to stretch his length in behind the pile of straw, nor could he another night strain the hours through, his body bent against a rope cutting into his flesh, and dragging the load over the cobblestones. Each stone he had come to know now as a separate enemy, and he knew each rut by which he might evade a stone and so use an ounce less of his life. There were times in the black nights, especially when it rained and the streets were wet and more wet than usual, that the whole hatred of his heart went out against these stones under his feet, these stones that seemed to cling and to hang to the wheels of his inhuman load.

"Ah, the fair land!" he cried out suddenly and fell to weeping so that the children were frightened and the old man, looking at his son in consternation, twisted his face this way and that under his sparse beard, as a child's face twists when he sees his mother weep.

And again it was O-lan who said in her flat plain voice,

"Yet a little while and we shall see a thing. There is talk everywhere now."

From his hut where Wang Lung lay hid he heard hour after hour the passing of feet, the feet of soldiers marching to battle. Lifting sometimes a very little the mat which stood between them and him, he put one eye to the crack and he saw these feet passing, passing, leather shoes and cloth-covered legs, marching one after the other, pair by pair, score upon score, thousands upon thousands. In the night when he was at his load he saw their faces flickering past him, caught for an instant out of the darkness by the flaming torch ahead. He dared ask nothing concerning them, but he dragged his load doggedly, and he ate hastily his bowl of rice, and slept the day fitfully through in the hut behind the straw. None spoke in those days to any other. The city was shaken with fear and each man did quickly what he had to do and went into his house and shut the door.

There was no more idle talk at twilight about the huts. In the market places the stalls where food had been were now empty. The silk shops drew in their bright banners and closed the fronts of their great shops with thick boards fitting one into the other solidly, so that passing through the city at noon it was as though the people slept.

It was whispered everywhere that the enemy approached and all those who owned anything were afraid. But Wang Lung was not afraid, nor the dwellers in the huts, neither were they afraid. They did not know for one thing who this enemy was, nor had they anything to lose since even their lives were no great loss. If this enemy approached let him approach, seeing that nothing could be worse than it now was with them. But every man went on his own way and none spoke openly to any other.

Then the managers of the houses of merchandise told the laborers who pulled the boxes to and fro from the river's edge that they need come no more, since there were none to buy and sell in these days at the counters, and so Wang Lung stayed in his hut day and night and was idle. At first he was glad, for it seemed his body could never get enough rest and he slept as heavily as a man dead. But if he did not work neither did he earn, and in a few short days what they had of extra pence was gone and again he cast about desperately as to what he could do. And as if it were not enough of evil to befall them, the public kitchens closed their doors also and those who had in this way provided for the poor went into their own houses and shut the doors and there was no food and no work, and no one passing upon the streets of whom anyone could beg.

Then Wang Lung took his girl child into his arms and he sat with her in the hut and he looked at her and said softly,

"Little fool, would you like to go to a great house where there is food and drink and where you may have a whole coat to your body?"

Then she smiled, not understanding anything of what he said, and put up her small hand to touch with wonder his staring eyes and he could not bear it and he cried out to the woman,

"Tell me, and were you beaten in that great house?"

And she answered him flatly and somberly,

"Every day was I beaten."

And he cried again,

"But was it just with a girdle of cloth or was it with bamboo or rope?"

And she answered in the same dead way,

"I was beaten with a leather thong which had been halter for one of the mules, and it hung upon the kitchen wall."

Well he knew that she understood what he was thinking, but he put forth his last hope and he said,

"This child of ours is a pretty little maid, even now. Tell me, were the pretty slaves beaten also?"

And she answered indifferently, as though it were nothing to her this way or that,

"Aye, beaten or carried to a man's bed, as the whim was, and not to one man's only but to any that might desire her that night, and the young lords bickered and bartered with each other for this slave or that and said, 'Then if you tonight, I tomorrow,' and when they were all alike wearied of a slave the men servants bickered and bartered for what the young lords left, and this before a slave was out of childhood—if she were pretty."

Then Wang Lung groaned and held the child to him and said over and over to her softly, "Oh, little fool—oh, poor little fool." But within himself he was crying as a man cries out when he is caught in a rushing flood and cannot stop to think, "There is no other way—there is no other way—"

Then suddenly as he sat there came a noise like the cracking of heaven and every one of them fell unthinking on the ground and hid their faces, for it seemed as though the hideous roar would catch them all up and crush them. And Wang Lung covered the girl child's face with his hand, not knowing what horror might appear to them out of this dreadful din, and the old man called out into Wang Lung's ear, "Now this I have never heard before in all my years," and the two boys yelled with fear.

But O-lan, when silence had fallen as suddenly as it had gone, lifted her head and said, "Now that which I have heard of has come to pass. The enemy has broken in the gates of the city." And before any could answer her there was a shout over the city, a rising shout of human voices, at first faint, as one may hear the wind of a storm approaching, and gathering in a deep howl, louder and more loud as it filled the streets.

Wang Lung sat erect then, on the floor of his hut, and a strange fear crept over his flesh, so that he felt it stirring among the roots of his hair, and everyone sat erect and they all stared at each other waiting for something they knew not. But there was only the noise of the gathering of human beings and each man howling.

Then over the wall and not far from them they heard the sound of a great door creaking upon its hinges and groaning as it opened unwillingly, and suddenly the man who had talked to Wang Lung once at dusk and smoked a short bamboo pipe, thrust his head in at the hut's opening and cried out,

[116]

"Now do you still sit here? The hour has come—the gates of the rich man are open to us!" And as if by magic of some kind O-lan was gone, creeping out under the man's arm as he spoke.

Then Wang Lung rose up, slowly and half dazed, and he set the girl child down and he went out and there before the great iron gates of the rich man's house a multitude of clamoring common people pressed forward, howling together the deep, tigerish howl that he had heard, rising and swelling out of the streets, and he knew that at the gates of all rich men there pressed this howling multitude of men and women who had been starved and imprisoned and now were for the moment free to do as they would. And the great gates were ajar and the people pressed forward so tightly packed together that foot was on foot and body wedged tightly against body so that the whole mass moved together as one. Others hurrying from the back caught Wang Lung and forced him into the crowd so that whether he would or not he was taken forward with them, although he did not himself know what his will was, because he was so amazed at what had come about.

Thus was he swept along over the threshold of the great gates, his feet scarcely touching the ground in the pressure of people, and like the continuous roar of angry beasts there went on all around the howling of the people.

Through court after court he was swept, into the very inner courts, and of those men and women who had lived in the house he saw not one. It was as though here were a palace long dead except that early lilies bloomed among the rocks of the gardens and the golden flowers of the early trees of spring blossomed upon bare branches. But in the rooms food stood upon a table and in the kitchens fire burned. Well this crowd knew the courts of the rich, for they swept past the front courts, where servants and slaves lived and where the kitchens are, into the inner courts, where the lords and ladies have their dainty beds and where stand their lacquered boxes of black and red and gold, their boxes of silken clothing, where carved tables and chairs are, and upon the walls painted scrolls. And upon these treasures the crowd fell,

[117]

seizing at and tearing from each other what was revealed in every newly opened box or closet, so that clothing and bedding and curtains and dishes passed from hand to hand, each hand snatching that which another held, and none stopping to see what he had.

Only Wang Lung in the confusion took nothing. He had never in all his life taken what belonged to another, and not at once could he do it. So he stood in the middle of the crowd at first, dragged this way and that, and then coming somewhat to his senses, he pushed with perseverance toward the edge and found himself at last on the fringe of the multitude, and here he stood, swept along slightly as little whirlpools are at the edge of a pool of current; but still he was able to see where he was.

He was at the back of the innermost court where the ladies of the rich dwell, and the back gate was ajar, that gate which the rich have for centuries kept for their escape in such times, and therefore called the gate of peace. Through this gate doubtless they had all escaped this day and were hidden here and there through the streets, listening to the howling in their courts. But one man, whether because of his size or whether because of his drunken heaviness of sleep, had failed to escape, and this one Wang Lung came upon suddenly in an empty inner room from whence the mob had swept in and out again, so that the man, who had been hidden in a secret place and not been found, now crept out, thinking he was alone, to escape. And thus Wang Lung, always drifting away from the others until he too was alone, came upon him.

He was a great fat fellow, neither old nor young, and he had been lying naked in his bed, doubtless with a pretty woman, for his naked body gaped through a purple satin robe he held about him. The great yellow rolls of his flesh doubled over his breasts and over his belly and in the mountains of his cheeks his eyes were small and sunken as a pig's eyes. When he saw Wang Lung he shook all over and yelled out as though his flesh had been stuck with a knife, so that Wang Lung, weaponless as he was, wondered and could have laughed at the sight. But the fat fellow fell upon

[118]

his knees and knocked his head on the tiles of the floor and he cried forth,

"Save a life—save a life—do not kill me. I have money for you —much money—"

It was this word "money" which suddenly brought to Wang Lung's mind a piercing clarity. Money! Aye, and he needed that! And again it came to him clearly, as a voice speaking, "Money— the child saved—*the land!*"

He cried out suddenly in a harsh voice such as he did not himself know was in his breast,

"Give me the money then!"

And the fat man rose to his knees, sobbing and gibbering, and feeling for the pocket of the robe, and he brought forth his yellow hands dripping with silver and Wang Lung held out the end of his coat and received it. And again he cried out in that strange voice that was like another man's,

"Give me more!"

And again the man's hands came forth dripping with silver and he whimpered,

"Now there is none left and I have nothing but my wretched life," and he fell to weeping, his tears running like oil down his hanging cheeks.

Wang Lung, looking at him as he shivered and wept, suddenly loathed him as he had loathed nothing in his life and he cried out with the loathing surging up in him,

"Out of my sight, lest I kill you for a fat worm!"

This Wang Lung cried, although he was a man so softhearted that he could not kill an ox. And the man ran past him like a cur and was gone.

Then Wang Lung was left alone with the silver. He did not stop to count it, but thrust it into his bosom and went out of the open gate of peace and across the small back streets to his hut. He hugged to his bosom the silver that was yet warm from the other man's body and to himself he said over and over,

"We go back to the land—tomorrow we go back to the land!"

XV

BEFORE a handful of days had passed it seemed to Wang Lung that he had never been away from his land, as indeed, in his heart he never had. With six pieces of the silver he bought good seed from the south, full grains of wheat and of rice and of corn, and for very recklessness of riches he bought seeds the like of which he had never planted before, celery and lotus for his pond and great red radishes that are stewed with pork for a feast dish and small red fragrant beans.

With ten silver pieces he bought an ox from a farmer ploughing in the field, and this before ever he reached his own land. He saw the man ploughing and he stopped and they all stopped, the old man and the children and the woman, eager as they were to reach the house and the land, and they looked at the ox. Wang Lung had been struck with its great strong neck and noticed at once the sturdy pulling of its shoulder against the wooden yoke and he called out,

"That is a worthless ox! What will you sell it for in silver, seeing that I have no animal and am hard put to it and willing to take anything?"

And the farmer called back,

"I would sooner sell my wife than this ox which is but three years old and in its prime," and he ploughed on and would not stop for Wang Lung.

Then it seemed to Wang Lung as if out of all the oxen the world held he must have this one, and he said to O-lan and to his father,

"How is it for an ox?"

And the old man peered and said, "It seems a beast well castrated."

And O-lan said, "It is a year older than he says."

But Wang Lung answered nothing because upon this ox he had set his heart because of its sturdy pulling of the soil and because of its smooth yellow coat and its full dark eye. With this ox he could plough his fields and cultivate them and with this ox tied to his mill he could grind the grain. And he went to the farmer and said,

"I will give you enough to buy another ox and more, but this ox I will have."

At last after bickering and quarrelling and false starts away the farmer yielded for half again the worth of an ox in those parts. But silver was suddenly nothing to Wang Lung when he looked at this ox, and he passed it over to the farmer's hand and he watched while the farmer unyoked the beast, and Wang Lung led it away with a rope through its nostrils, his heart burning with his possession.

When they reached the house they found the door torn away and the thatch from the roof gone and within their hoes and rakes that they had left were gone, so only the bare rafters and the earthen walls remained, and even the earthen walls were worn down with the belated snows and the rains of winter and early spring. But after the first astonishment all this was as nothing to Wang Lung. He went away to the town and he bought a good new plow of hard wood and two rakes and two hoes and mats to cover the roof until they could grow thatch again from the harvest.

Then in the evening he stood in the doorway of his house and looked across the land, his own land, lying loose and fresh from the winter's freezing, and ready for planting. It was full spring and in the shallow pool the frogs croaked drowsily. The bamboos at the corner of the house swayed slowly under a gentle night wind and through the twilight he could see dimly the fringe of trees at the border of the near field. They were peach trees, budded most delicately pink, and willow trees thrusting forth tender green

[121]

leaves. And up from the quiescent, waiting land a faint mist rose, silver as moonlight, and clung about the tree trunks.

At first and for a long time it seemed to Wang Lung that he wished to see no human being but only to be alone on his land. He went to no houses of the village and when they came to him, those who were left of the winter's starving, he was surly with them.

"Which of you tore away my door and which of you have my rake and my hoe and which of you burned my roof in his oven?" Thus he bawled at them.

And they shook their heads, full of virtue; and this one said, "It was your uncle," and that one said, "Nay, with bandits and robbers roving over the land in these evil times of famine and war, how can it be said that this one or that stole anything? Hunger makes thief of any man."

Then Ching, his neighbor, came creeping forth from his house to see Wang Lung and he said,

"Through the winter a band of robbers lived in your house and preyed upon the village and the town as they were able. Your uncle, it is said, knows more of them than an honest man should. But who knows what is true in these days? I would not dare to accuse any man."

This man was nothing but a shadow indeed, so close did his skin stick to his bones and so thin and grey had his hair grown, although he had not yet reached forty-five years of his age. Wang Lung stared at him awhile and then in compassion he said suddenly,

"Now you have fared worse than we and what have you eaten?"

And the man sighed forth in a whisper,

"What have I not eaten? Offal from the streets like dogs when we begged in the town and dead dogs we ate and once before she died my woman brewed some soup from flesh I dared not ask what it was, except that I knew she had not the courage to kill, and if we ate it was something she found. Then she died, having less strength than I to endure, and after she died I gave the girl to a soldier because I could not see her starve and die also." He paused and fell silent and after a time he said, "If I had a little seed I would plant once more, but no seed have I."

"Come here!" cried Wang Lung roughly and dragged him into the house by the hand and he bade the man hold up the ragged tail of his coat and into it Wang Lung poured from the store of seed he had brought from the south. Wheat he gave him and rice and cabbage seed and he said,

"Tomorrow I will come and plough your land with my good ox."

Then Ching began to weep suddenly and Wang Lung rubbed his own eyes and cried out as if he were angry, "Do you think I have forgotten that you gave me that handful of beans?" But Ching could answer nothing, only he walked away weeping and weeping without stop.

It was joy to Wang Lung to find that his uncle was no longer in the village and where he was none knew certainly. Some said he had gone to a city and some said he was in far distant parts with his wife and his son. But there was not one left in his house in the village. The girls, and this Wang Lung heard with stout anger, were sold, the prettiest first, for the price they could bring, but even the last one, who was pock-marked, was sold for a handful of pence to a soldier who was passing through to battle.

Then Wang Lung set himself robustly to the soil and he begrudged even the hours he must spend in the house for food and sleep. He loved rather to take his roll of bread and garlic to the field and stand there eating, planning and thinking, "Here shall I put the black-eyed peas and here the young rice beds." And if he grew too weary in the day he laid himself into a furrow and there with the good warmth of his own land against his flesh, he slept.

And O-lan in the house was not idle. With her own hands she lashed the mats firmly to the rafters and took earth from the fields and mixed it with water and mended the walls of the house, and she built again the oven and filled the holes in the floor that the rain had washed.

Then she went into the town one day with Wang Lung and

[123]

together they bought beds and a table and six benches and a great iron cauldron and then they bought for pleasure a red clay teapot with a black flower marked on it in ink and six bowls to match. Last of all they went into an incense shop and bought a paper god of wealth to hang on the wall over the table in the middle room, and they bought two pewter candlesticks and a pewter incense urn and two red candles to burn before the god, thick red candles of cow's fat and having a slender reed through the middle for wick.

And with this, Wang Lung thought of the two small gods in the temple to the earth and on his way home he went and peered in at them, and they were piteous to behold, their features washed from their faces with rain and the clay of their bodies naked and sticking through the tatters of their paper clothes. None had paid any heed to them in this dreadful year and Wang Lung looked at them grimly and with content and he said aloud, as one might speak to a punished child,

"Thus it is with gods who do evil to men!"

Nevertheless, when the house was itself again, and the pewter candlesticks gleaming and the candles burning in them shining red, and the teapot and the bowls upon the table and the beds in their places with a little bedding once more, and fresh paper pasted over the hole in the room where he slept and a new door hung upon its wooden hinges, Wang Lung was afraid of his happiness. O-lan grew great with the next child; his children tumbled like brown puppies about his threshold and against the southern wall his old father sat and dozed and smiled as he slept; in his fields the young rice sprouted as green as jade and more beautiful, and the young beans lifted their hooded heads from the soil. And out of the silver there was still enough left to feed them until the harvest, if they ate sparingly. Looking at the blue heaven above him and the white clouds driving across it, feeling upon his ploughed fields as upon his own flesh the sun and rain in proportion, Wang Lung muttered unwillingly,

"I must stick a little incense before those two in the small temple. After all, they have power over earth."

XVI

ONE night as Wang Lung lay with his wife he felt a hard lump the size of a man's closed hand between her breasts and he said to her,

"Now what is this thing you have on your body?"

He put his hand to it and he found a cloth-wrapped bundle that was hard yet moved to his touch. She drew back violently at first and then when he laid hold of it to pluck it away from her she yielded and said,

"Well, look at it then, if you must," and she took the string which held it to her neck and broke it and gave him the thing.

It was wrapped in a bit of rag and he tore this away. Then suddenly into his hand fell a heap of jewels and Wang Lung gazed at them stupefied. There were such a heap of jewels as one had never dreamed could be together, jewels red as the inner flesh of watermelons, golden as wheat, green as young leaves in spring, clear as water trickling out of the earth. What the names of them were Wang did not know, having never heard names and seen jewels together in his life. But holding them there in his hand, in the hollow of his brown hard hand, he knew from the gleaming and the glittering in the half-dark room that he held wealth. He held it motionless, drunk with color and shape, speechless, and together he and the woman stared at what he held. At last he whispered to her, breathless,

"Where—where—"

And she whispered back as softly,

"In the rich man's house. It must have been a favorite's treasure. I saw a brick loosened in the wall and I slipped there carelessly so no other soul could see and demand a share. I pulled the brick away, caught the shining, and put them into my sleeve."

"Now how did you know?" he whispered again, filled with admiration, and she answered with the smile on her lips that was never in her eyes,

"Do you think I have not lived in a rich man's house? The rich are always afraid. I saw robbers in a bad year once rush into the gate of the great house and the slaves and the concubines and even the Old Mistress herself ran hither and thither and each had a treasure that she thrust into some secret place already planned. Therefore I knew the meaning of a loosened brick."

And again they fell silent, staring at the wonder of the stones. Then after a long time Wang Lung drew in his breath and said resolutely,

"Now treasure like this one cannot keep. It must be sold and put into safety—into land, for nothing else is safe. If any knew of this we should be dead by the next day and a robber would carry the jewels. They must be put into land this very day or I shall not sleep tonight."

He wrapped the stones in the rag again as he spoke and tied them hard together with the string, and opening his coat to thrust them into his bosom, by chance he saw the woman's face. She was sitting cross-legged upon the bed at its foot and her heavy face that never spoke of anything was moved with a dim yearning of open lips and face thrust forward.

"Well, and now what?" he asked, wondering at her.

"Will you sell them all?" she asked in a hoarse whisper.

"And why not then?" he answered, astonished. "Why should we have jewels like this in an earthen house?"

"I wish I could keep two for myself," she said with such helpless wistfulness, as of one expecting nothing, that he was moved as he might be by one of his children longing for a toy or for a sweet.

"Well, now!" he cried in amazement.

"If I could have two," she went on humbly, "only two small ones—the two small white pearls even . . ."

"Pearls!" he repeated, agape.

"I would keep them—I would not wear them," she said, "only keep them." And she dropped her eyes and fell to twisting a bit of the bedding where a thread was loosened, and she waited patiently as one who scarcely expects an answer.

Then Wang Lung, without comprehending it, looked for an instant into the heart of this dull and faithful creature, who had labored all her life at some task at which she won no reward and who in the great house had seen others wearing jewels which she never even felt in her hand once.

"I could hold them in my hand sometimes," she added, as if she thought to herself.

And he was moved by something he did not understand and he pulled the jewels from his bosom and unwrapped them and handed them to her in silence, and she searched among the glittering colors, her hard brown hand turning over the stones delicately and lingeringly until she found the two smooth white pearls, and these she took, and tying up the others again, she gave them back to him. Then she took the pearls and she tore a bit of the corner of her coat away and wrapped them and hid them between her breasts and was comforted.

But Wang Lung watched her astonished and only half understanding, so that afterwards during the day and on other days he would stop and stare at her and say to himself,

"Well now, that woman of mine, she has those two pearls between her breasts still, I suppose." But he never saw her take them out or look at them and they never spoke of them at all.

As for the other jewels, he pondered this way and that, and at last he decided he would go to the great house and see if there were more land to buy.

To the great house he now went and there was in these days no gateman standing at the gate, twisting the long hairs of his mole, scornful of those who could not enter past him into the House of

Hwang. Instead the great gates were locked and Wang Lung pounded against them with both fists and no one came. Men who passed in the streets looked up and cried out at him,

"Aye, you may pound now and pound again. If the Old Lord is awake he may come and if there is a stray dog of a slave about she may open, if she is inclined to it."

But at last he heard slow footsteps coming across the threshold, slow wandering footsteps that halted and came on by fits, and then he heard the slow drawing of the iron bar that held the gate and the gate creaked and a cracked voice whispered,

"Who is it?"

Then Wang Lung answered loudly, although he was amazed,

"It is I, Wang Lung!"

Then the voice said peevishly,

"Now who is an accursed Wang Lung?"

And Wang Lung perceived by the quality of the curse that it was the Old Lord himself, because he cursed as one accustomed to servants and slaves. Wang Lung answered, therefore, more humbly than before.

"Sir and lord, I am come on a little business, not to disturb your lordship, but to talk a little business with the agent who serves your honor."

Then the Old Lord answered without opening any wider the crack through which he pursed his lips,

"Now curse him, that dog left me many months ago and he is not here."

Wang Lung did not know what to do after this reply. It was impossible to talk of buying land directly to the Old Lord, without a middleman, and yet the jewels hung in his bosom hot as fire, and he wanted to be rid of them and more than that he wanted the land. With the seed he had he could plant as much land again as he had, and he wanted the good land of the House of Hwang.

"I came about a little money," he said hesitatingly.

At once the Old Lord pushed the gates together.

"There is no money in this house," he said more loudly than he

[128]

had yet spoken. "The thief and robber of an agent—and may his mother and his mother's mother be cursed for him—took all that I had. No debts can be paid."

"No—no—" called Wang Lung hastily, "I came to pay out, not to collect debt."

At this there was a shrill scream from a voice Wang Lung had not yet heard and a woman thrust her face suddenly out of the gates.

"Now that is a thing I have not heard for a long time," she said sharply, and Wang Lung saw a handsome, shrewish, high-colored face looking out at him. "Come in," she said briskly and she opened the gate wide enough to admit him and then behind his back, while he stood astonished in the court, she barred them securely again.

The Old Lord stood there coughing and staring, a dirty grey satin robe wrapped about him, from which hung an edge of bedraggled fur. Once it had been a fine garment, as anyone could see, for the satin was still heavy and smooth, although stains and spots covered it, and it was wrinkled as though it had been used as a bedgown. Wang Lung stared back at the Old Lord, curious, yet half-afraid, for all his life he half feared the people in the great house, and it seemed impossible that the Old Lord, of whom he had heard so much, was this old figure, no more dreadful than his old father, and indeed less so for his father was a cleanly and smiling old man, and the Old Lord, who had been fat, was now lean, and his skin hung in folds about him and he was unwashed and unshaven and his hand was yellow and trembled as he passed it over his chin and pulled at his loose old lips.

The woman was clean enough. She had a hard, sharp face, handsome with a sort of hawk's beauty of high bridged nose and keen bright black eyes and pale skin stretched too tightly over her bones, and her cheeks and lips were red and hard. Her black hair was like a mirror for smooth shining blackness, but from her speech one could perceive she was not of the lord's family, but a slave, sharp voiced and bitter tongued. And besides these two, the

[129]

woman and the Old Lord, there was not another person in the court where before men and women and children had run to and fro on their business of caring for the great house.

"Now about money," said the woman sharply. But Wang Lung hesitated. He could not well speak before the Old Lord and this the woman instantly perceived as she perceived everything more quickly than speech could be made about it, and she said to the old man shrilly, "Now off with you!"

And the aged lord, without a word, shambled silently away, his old velvet shoes flapping and off at his heels, coughing as he went. As for Wang Lung, left alone with this woman, he did not know what to say or do. He was stupefied with the silence everywhere. He glanced into the next court and still there was no other person, and about the court he saw heaps of refuse and filth and scattered straw and branches of bamboo trees and dried pine needles and the dead stalks of flowers, as though not for a long time had anyone taken a broom to sweep it.

"Now then, wooden head!" said the woman with exceeding sharpness, and Wang Lung jumped at the sound of her voice, so unexpected was its shrillness. "What is your business? If you have money, let me see it."

"No," said Wang Lung with caution, "I did not say that I had money. I have business."

"Business means money," returned the woman, "either money coming in or money going out, and there is no money to go out of this house."

"Well, but I cannot speak with a woman," objected Wang Lung mildly. He could make nothing of the situation in which he found himself, and he was still staring about him.

"Well, and why not?" retorted the woman with anger. Then she shouted at him suddenly, "Have you not heard, fool, that there is no one here?"

Wang Lung stared at her feebly, unbelieving, and the woman shouted at him again, "I and the Old Lord—there is no one else!"

[130]

"Where then?" asked Wang Lung, too much aghast to make sense in his words.

"Well, and the Old Mistress is dead," retorted the woman. "Have you not heard in the town how bandits swept into the house and how they carried away what they would of the slaves and of the goods? And they hung the Old Lord up by his thumbs and beat him and the Old Mistress they tied in a chair and gagged her and everyone ran. But I stayed. I hid in a gong half full of water under a wooden lid. And when I came out they were gone and the Old Mistress sat dead in her chair, not from any touch they had given her but from fright. Her body was a rotten reed with the opium she smoked and she could not endure the fright."

"And the servants and the slaves?" gasped Wang Lung. "And the gateman?"

"Oh, those," she answered carelessly, "they were gone long ago —all those who had feet to carry them away, for there was no food and no money by the middle of the winter. Indeed," her voice fell to a whisper, "there are many of the men servants among the bandits. I saw that dog of a gateman myself—he was leading the way, although he turned his face aside in the Old Lord's presence, still I knew those three long hairs of his mole. And there were others, for how could any but those who knew the great house find where jewels were hid and the secret treasure stores of things not to be sold? I would not put it beneath the old agent himself, although he would consider it beneath his dignity to appear publicly in the affair, since he is a sort of distant relative of the family."

The woman fell silent and the silence of the courts was heavy as silence is after life has gone. Then she said,

"But all this was not a sudden thing. All during the lifetime of the Old Lord and of his father the fall of this house has been coming. In the last generation the lords ceased to see the land and took the moneys the agents gave them and spent it carelessly as water. And in these generations the strength of the land has gone from them and bit by bit the land has begun to go also."

[131]

"Where are the young lords?" asked Wang Lung, still staring about him, so impossible was it for him to believe these things.

"Hither and thither," said the woman indifferently. "It is good fortune that the two girls were married away before the thing happened. The elder young lord when he heard what had befallen his father and his mother sent a messenger to take the Old Lord, his father, but I persuaded the old head not to go. I said, 'Who will be in the courts, and it is not seemly for me, who am only a woman.' "

She pursed her narrow red lips virtuously as she spoke these words, and cast down her bold eyes, and again she said, when she had paused a little, "Besides, I have been my lord's faithful slave for these several years and I have no other house."

Wang Lung looked at her closely then and turned quickly away. He began to perceive what this was, a woman who clung to an old and dying man because of what last thing she might get from him. He said with contempt,

"Seeing that you are only a slave, how can I do business with you?"

At that she cried out at him, "He will do anything I tell him. I have been more than slave."

Wang Lung pondered over this reply. Well, and there was the land. Others would buy it through this woman if he did not.

"How much land is there left?" he asked her unwillingly, and she saw instantly what his purpose was.

"If you have come to buy land," she said quickly, "there is land to buy. He has a hundred acres to the west and to the south two hundred that he will sell. It is not all in one piece but the plots are large. It can be sold to the last acre."

This she said so readily that Wang Lung perceived she knew everything the old man had left, even to the last foot of land. But still he was unbelieving and not willing to do business with her.

"It is not likely the Old Lord can sell all the land of his family without the agreement of his sons," he demurred.

But the woman met his words eagerly.

"As for that, the sons have told him to sell when he can. The land is where no one of the sons wishes to live and the country is run over with bandits in these days of famine, and they have all said, 'We cannot live in such a place. Let us sell and divide the money.' "

"But into whose hand would I put the money?" asked Wang Lung, still unbelieving.

"Into the Old Lord's hand, and whose else?" replied the woman smoothly. But Wang Lung knew that the Old Lord's hand opened into hers.

He would not, therefore, talk further with her, but turned away saying, "Another day—another day—" and he went to the gate and she followed him, shrieking after him into the street,

"This time tomorrow—this time or this afternoon—all times are alike!"

He went down the street without answer, greatly puzzled and needing to think over what he had heard. He went into the small tea shop and ordered tea of the slavey and when the boy had put it smartly before him and with an impudent gesture had caught and tossed the penny he paid for it, Wang Lung fell to musing. And the more he mused the more monstrous it seemed that the great and rich family, who all his own life and all his father's and grandfather's lives long had been a power and a glory in the town, were now fallen and scattered.

"It comes of their leaving the land," he thought regretfully, and he thought of his own two sons, who were growing like young bamboo shoots in the spring, and he resolved that on this very day he would make them cease playing in the sunshine and he would set them to tasks in the field, where they would early take into their bones and their blood the feel of the soil under their feet, and the feel of the hoe hard in their hands.

But all this time here were these jewels hot and heavy against his body and he was continually afraid. It seemed as though their brilliance must shine through his rags and someone cry out,

"Now here is a poor man carrying an emperor's treasure!"

And he could not rest until they were changed into land. He watched, therefore, until the shopkeeper had a moment of idleness and he called to the man and said,

"Come and drink a bowl at my cost, and tell me the news of the town, since I have been a winter away."

The shopkeeper was always ready for such talk, especially if he drank his own tea at another's cost, and he sat down readily at Wang Lung's table, a small weasel-faced man with a twisted and crossed left eye. His clothes were solid and black with grease down the front of his coat and trousers, for besides tea he sold food also, which he cooked himself, and he was fond of saying, "There is a proverb, 'A good cook has never a clean coat,' " and so he considered himself justly and necessarily filthy. He sat down and began at once,

"Well, and beyond the starving of people, which is no news, the greatest news was the robbery at the House of Hwang."

It was just what Wang Lung hoped to hear and the man went on to tell him of it with relish, describing how the few slaves left had screamed and how they had been carried off and how the concubines that remained had been raped and driven out and some even taken away, so that now none cared to live in that house at all. "None," the man finished, "except the old Lord, who is now wholly the creature of a slave called Cuckoo, who has for many years been in the Old Lord's chamber, while others came and went, because of her cleverness."

"And has this woman command, then?" asked Wang Lung, listening closely.

"For the time she can do anything," replied the man. "And so for the time she closes her hand on everything that can be held and swallows all that can be swallowed. Some day, of course, when the young lords have their affairs settled in other parts they will come back and then she cannot fool them with her talk of a faithful servant to be rewarded, and out she will go. But she has her living made now, although she live to a hundred years."

"And the land?" asked Wang Lung at last, quivering with his eagerness.

"The land?" said the man blankly. To this shopkeeper land meant nothing at all.

"Is it for sale?" said Wang Lung impatiently.

"Oh, the land!" answered the man with indifference, and then as a customer came in he rose and called as he went, "I have heard it is for sale, except the piece where the family are buried for these six generations," and he went his way.

Then Wang Lung rose also, having heard what he came to hear, and he went out and approached again the great gates and the woman came to open to him and he stood without entering and he said to her,

"Tell me first this, will the Old Lord set his own seal to the deeds of sale?"

And the woman answered eagerly, and her eyes were fastened on his,

"He will—he will—on my life!"

Then Wang Lung said to her plainly,

"Will you sell the land for silver or for jewels?"

And her eyes glittered as she spoke and she said,

"I will sell it for jewels!"

XVII

NOW Wang Lung had more land than a man with an ox can plough and harvest, and more harvest than one man can garner, and so he built another small room to his house and he bought an ass and he said to his neighbor, Ching,

"Sell me the little parcel of land that you have and leave your lonely house and come into my house and help me with my land." And Ching did this and was glad to do it.

The heavens rained in season then; and the young rice grew and when the wheat was cut and harvested in heavy sheaves, the two men planted the young rice in the flooded fields, more rice than Wang Lung had ever planted he planted this year, for the rains come in abundance of water, so that lands that were before dry were this year fit for rice. Then when this harvest came he and Ching alone could not harvest it, so great it was, and Wang Lung hired two other men as laborers who lived in the village and they harvested it.

He remembered also the idle young lords of the fallen great house as he worked on the land he had bought from the House of Hwang, and he bade his two sons sharply each morning to come into the fields with him and he set them at what labor their small hands could do, guiding the ox and the ass, and making them, if they could accomplish no great labor, at least to know the heat of the sun on their bodies and the weariness of walking back and forth along the furrows.

But O-lan he would not allow to work in the fields for he was no longer a poor man, but a man who could hire his labor done if he would, seeing that never had the land given forth such harvests as it had this year. He was compelled to build yet another room to the house to store his harvests in, or they would not have had space to walk in the house. And he bought three pigs and a flock of fowls to feed on the grains spilled from the harvests.

Then O-lan worked in the house and made new clothes for each one and new shoes, and she made coverings of flowered cloth stuffed with warm new cotton for every bed, and when all was finished they were rich in clothing and in bedding as they had never been. And once more she laid herself down upon her bed and gave birth again, although still she would have no one with her; even though she could hire whom she chose, she chose to be alone.

This time she was long at labor and when Wang Lung came home at evening he found his father standing at the door and laughing and saying,

"An egg with a double yolk this time!"

And when Wang Lung went into the inner room there was O-lan upon the bed with two new-born children, a boy and a girl as alike as two grains of rice. He laughed boisterously at what she had done and then he thought of a merry thing to say,

"So this is why you bore two jewels in your bosom!"

And he laughed again at what he had thought of to say, and O-lan, seeing how merry he was, smiled her slow, painful smile.

Wang Lung had, therefore, at this time no sorrow of any kind, unless it was this sorrow, that his eldest girl child neither spoke nor did those things which were right for her age, but only smiled her baby smile still when she caught her father's glance. Whether it was the desperate first year of her life or the starving or what it was, month after month went past and Wang Lung waited for the first words to come from her lips, even for his name which the children called him, "da-da." But no sound came, only the sweet, empty smile, and when he looked at her he groaned forth,

"Little fool—my poor little fool—"

And in his heart he cried to himself,

"If I had sold this poor mouse and they found her thus they would have killed her!"

And as if to make amends to the child he made much of her and took her into the field with him sometimes and she followed him silently about, smiling when he spoke and noticed her there.

In these parts, where Wang Lung had lived all his life and his father and his father's father had lived upon the land, there were famines once in five years or so, or if the gods were lenient, once in seven or eight or even ten years. This was because the heavens rained too much or not at all, or because the river to the north, because of rains and winter snows in distant mountains, came swelling into the fields over the dykes which had been builded by men for centuries to confine it.

Time after time men fled from the land and came back to it, but Wang Lung set himself now to build his fortunes so securely that through the bad years to come he need never leave his land again but live on the fruits of the good years, and so subsist until another year came forth. He set himself and the gods helped him and for seven years there were harvests, and every year Wang Lung and his men threshed far more than could be eaten. He hired more laborers each year for his fields until he had six men and he builded a new house behind his old one, a large room behind a court and two small rooms on each side of the court beside the large room. The house he covered with tiles, but the walls were still made of the hard tamped earth from the fields, only he had them brushed with lime and they were white and clean. Into these rooms he and his family moved, and the laborers, with Ching at their head lived in the old house in front.

By this time Wang Lung had thoroughly tried Ching, and he found the man honest and faithful, and he set Ching to be his steward over the men and over the land and he paid him well, two silver pieces a month besides his food. But with all Wang Lung's urging Ching to eat and eat well, the man still put no flesh on his bones, remaining always a small, spare, lean man of great gravity. Nevertheless he labored gladly, pottering silently from dawn until dark, speaking in his feeble voice if there was anything to be said, but happiest and liking it best if there were nothing and he could be silent; and hour after hour he lifted his hoe and let it fall, and at dawn and sunset he would carry to the fields the buckets of water or of manure to put upon the vegetable rows.

But still Wang Lung knew that if any one of the laborers slept too long each day under the date trees or ate more than his share of the beancurd in the common dish or if any bade his wife or child come secretly at harvest time and snatch handfuls of the grain that was being beaten out under the flails, Ching would, at the end of the year when master and man feast together after the harvest, whisper to Wang Lung,

"Such an one and such an one do not ask back for the next year."

And it seemed that the handful of peas and of seed which had passed between these two men made them brothers, except that Wang Lung, who was the younger, took the place of the elder, and Ching never wholly forgot that he was hired and lived in a house which belonged to another.

By the end of the fifth year Wang Lung worked little in his fields himself, having indeed to spend his whole time, so increased were his lands, upon the business and the marketing of his produce, and in directing his workmen. He was greatly hampered by his lack of book knowledge and of the knowledge of the meaning of characters written upon a paper with a camel's-hair brush and ink. Moreover, it was a shame to him when he was in a grain shop where grain was bought and sold again, that when a contract was written for so much and for so much of wheat or rice, he must say humbly to the haughty dealers in the town,

"Sir, and will you read it for me, for I am too stupid."

And it was a shame to him that when he must set his name to the contract another, even a paltry clerk, lifted his eyebrows in scorn and, with his brush pointed on the wet ink block, brushed

[139]

hastily the characters of Wang Lung's name; and greatest shame that when the man called out for a joke,

"Is it the dragon character Lung or the deaf character Lung, or what?" Wang Lung must answer humbly,

"Let it be what you will, for I am too ignorant to know my own name."

It was on such a day one harvest time after he had heard the shout of laughter which went up from the clerks in the grain shop, idle at the noon hour and all listening to anything that went on, and all lads scarcely older than his sons, that he went home angrily over his own land saying to himself,

"Now, not one of these town fools has a foot of land and yet each feels he can laugh a goose cackle at me because I cannot tell the meanings of brush strokes over paper." And then as his indignation wore away, he said in his heart, "It is true that this is a shame to me that I cannot read and write. I will take my eldest son from the fields and he shall go to a school in the town and he shall learn, and when I go into the grain markets he will read and write for me so that there may be an end of this hissing laughter against me, who am a landed man."

This seemed to him well and that very day he called to him his eldest son, a straight tall lad of twelve years now, looking like his mother for his wide face bones and his big hands and feet but with his father's quickness of eye, and when the boy stood before him Wang Lung said,

"Come out of the fields from this day on, for I need a scholar in the family to read the contracts and to write my name so that I shall not be ashamed in the town."

The lad flushed a high dark red and his eyes shone.

"My father," he said, "so have I wished for these last two years that I might do, but I did not dare to ask it."

Then the younger boy when he heard of it came in crying and complaining, a thing he was wont to do, for he was a wordy, noisy lad from the moment he spoke at all, always ready to cry out that his share was less than that of others, and now he whined forth to his father,

"Well, and I shall not work in the fields, either, and it is not fair that my brother can sit at leisure in a seat and learn something and I must work like a hind, who am your son as well as he!"

Then Wang Lung could not bear his noise and he would give him anything if he cried loudly enough for it, and he said hastily,

"Well and well, go the both of you, and if Heaven in its evil take one of you, there will be the other one with knowledge to do the business for me."

Then he sent the mother of his sons into the town to buy cloth to make a long robe for each lad and he went himself to a paper and ink shop and he bought paper and brushes and two ink blocks, although he knew nothing of such things, and being ashamed to say he did not, was dubious at everything the man brought forward to show him. But at last all was prepared and arrangements made to send the boys to a small school near the city gate kept by an old man who had in past years gone up for government examinations and failed. In the central room of his house therefore he had set benches and tables and for a small sum at each feast day in the year he taught boys in the classics, beating them with his large fan, folded, if they were idle or if they could not repeat to him the pages over which they pored from dawn until sunset.

Only in the warm days of spring and summer did the pupils have a respite for then the old man nodded and slept after he had eaten at noon, and the dark small room was filled with the sound of his slumber. Then the lads whispered and played and drew pictures to show each other of this naughty thing and that, and snickered to see a fly buzzing about the old man's hanging, open jaw, and laid wagers with each other as to whether the fly would enter the cavern of his mouth or not. But when the old teacher opened his eyes suddenly—and there was no telling when he would open them as quickly and secretly as though he had not slept—he saw them before they were aware, and then he laid about him with his fan, cracking this skull and that. And hearing the cracks of his stout fan and the cries of the pupils, the neighbors said,

"It is a worthy old teacher, after all." And this is why Wang Lung chose the school for the one where his sons should go to learn.

On the first day when he took them there he walked ahead of them, for it is not meet that father and son walk side by side, and he carried a blue kerchief filled with fresh eggs and these eggs he gave to the old teacher when he arrived. And Wang Lung was awed by the old teacher's great brass spectacles and by his long loose robe of black and by his immense fan, which he held even in winter, and Wang Lung bowed before him and said,

"Sir, here are my two worthless sons. If anything can be driven into their thick brass skulls it is only by beating them, and therefore if you wish to please me, beat them to make them learn." And the two boys stood and stared at the other boys on benches, and these others stared back at the two.

But going home again alone, having left the two lads, Wang Lung's heart was fit to burst with pride and it seemed to him that among all the lads in the room there were none equal to his two lads for tallness and robustness and bright brown faces. Meeting a neighbor coming from the village as he passed through the town gate, he answered the man's inquiry,

"This day I am back from my sons' school." And to the man's surprise he answered with seeming carelessness, "Now I do not need them in the fields and they may as well learn a stomachful of characters."

But to himself he said, passing by,

"It would not surprise me at all if the eldest one should become a prefect with all this learning!"

And from that time on the boys were no longer called Elder and Younger, but they were given school names by the old teacher, and this old man, after inquiring into the occupation of their father, erected two names for the sons; for the eldest, Nung En, and for the second Nung Wen, and the first word of each name signified one whose wealth is from the earth.

XVIII

THUS Wang Lung built the fortunes of his house and when the seventh year came and the great river to the north was too heavy with swollen waters, because of excessive rains and snows in the northwest where its source was, it burst its bounds and came sweeping and flooding all over the lands of that region. But Wang Lung was not afraid. He was not afraid although two-fifths of his land was a lake as deep as a man's shoulders and more.

All through the late spring and early summer the water rose and at last it lay like a great sea, lovely and idle, mirroring cloud and moon and willows and bamboos whose trunks stood submerged. Here and there an earthen house, abandoned by the dwellers, stood up until after days of the water it fell slowly back into the water and the earth. And so it was with all houses that were not, like Wang Lung's, builded upon a hill, and these hills stood up like islands. And men went to and from town by boat and by raft, and there were those who starved as they ever had.

But Wang Lung was not afraid. The grain markets owed him money and his store-rooms were yet filled full with harvests of the last two years and his houses stood high so that the water was a long way off and he had nothing to fear.

But since much of the land could not be planted he was more

idle than he had ever been in his life and being idle and full of good food he grew impatient when he had slept all he could sleep and done all there was to be done. There were, besides, the laborers, whom he hired for a year at a time, and it was foolish for him to work when there were those who ate his rice while they were half idle waiting day after day for the waters to recede. So after he had bade them mend the thatching of the old house and see to the setting of the tiles where the new roof leaked and had commanded them to mend the hoes and the rakes and the plows and to feed the cattle and to buy ducks to herd upon the water and to twist hemp into ropes—all those things which in the old days he did himself when he tilled his land alone—his own hands were empty and he did not know what to do with himself.

Now a man cannot sit all day and stare at a lake of water covering his fields, nor can he eat more than he is able to hold at one time, and when Wang Lung had slept, there was an end to sleeping. The house, as he wandered about it impatiently, was silent, too silent for his vigorous blood. The old man grew very feeble now, half blind and almost wholly deaf, and there was no need of speech with him except to ask if he were warm and fed or if he would drink tea. And it made Wang Lung impatient that the old man could not see how rich his son was and would always mutter if there were tea leaves in his bowl, "A little water is well enough and tea like silver." But there was no telling the old man anything for he forgot it at once and lived drawn into his own world and much of the time he dreamed he was a youth again and in his own fullness and he saw little of what passed him now.

The old man and the elder girl, who never spoke at all but sat beside her grandfather hour after hour, twisting a bit of cloth, folding and re-folding it and smiling at it, these two had nothing to say to a man prosperous and vigorous. When Wang Lung had poured the old man a bowl of tea and had passed his hand over the girl's cheek and received her sweet, empty smile, which passed with such sad swiftness from her face, leaving empty the dim and unshining eyes, there was nothing left. He always turned away from her with a moment's stillness, which was his daughter's mark of sadness on him, and he looked to his two younger children, the boy and the girl whom O-lan had borne together, and who now ran about the threshold merrily.

But a man cannot be satisfied with the foolishness of little children and after a brief time of laughter and teasing they went off to their own games and Wang Lung was alone and filled with restlessness. Then it was that he looked at O-lan, his wife, as a man looks at the woman whose body he knows thoroughly and to satiation and who has lived beside him so closely that there is nothing he does not know of her and nothing new which he may expect or hope from her.

And it seemed to Wang Lung that he looked at O-lan for the first time in his life and he saw for the first time that she was a woman whom no man could call other than she was, a dull and common creature, who plodded in silence without thought of how she appeared to others. He saw for the first time that her hair was rough and brown and unoiled and that her face was large and flat and coarse-skinned, and her features too large altogether and without any sort of beauty or light. Her eyebrows were scattered and the hairs too few, and her lips were too wide, and her hands and feet were large and spreading. Looking at her thus with strange eyes, he cried out at her,

"Now anyone looking at you would say you were the wife of a common fellow and never of one who has land which he hires men to plough!"

It was the first time he had ever spoken of how she seemed to him and she answered with a slow painful gaze. She sat upon a bench threading a long needle in and out of a shoe sole and she stopped and held the needle poised and her mouth gaped open and showed her blackened teeth. Then as if she understood at last that he had looked at her as a man at a woman, a thick red flush crept up over her high cheek bones and she muttered,

"Since those two last ones were born together I have not been well. There is a fire in my vitals."

Now he saw that in her simplicity she thought he accused her because for more than seven years she had not conceived. And he answered more roughly than he meant to do,

"I mean, cannot you buy a little oil for your hair as other women do and make yourself a new coat of black cloth? And those shoes you wear are not fit for a land proprietor's wife, such as you now are."

But she answered nothing, only looked at him humbly and without knowing what she did, and she hid her feet one over the other under the bench on which she sat. Then, although in his heart he was ashamed that he reproached this creature who through all these years had followed him faithfully as a dog, and although he remembered that when he was poor and labored in the fields himself she left her bed even after a child was born and came to help him in the harvest fields, yet he could not stem the irritation in his breast and he went on ruthlessly, although against his inner will,

"I have labored and have grown rich and I would have my wife look less like a hind. And those feet of yours——"

He stopped. It seemed to him that she was altogether hideous, but the most hideous of all were her big feet in their loose cotton cloth shoes, and he looked at them with anger so that she thrust them yet farther under the bench.

And at last she said in a whisper,

"My mother did not bind them, since I was sold so young. But the girl's feet I will bind—the younger girl's feet I will bind."

But he flung himself off because he was ashamed that he was angry at her and angry because she would not be angry in return but only was frightened. And he drew his new black robe on him, saying fretfully,

"Well, and I will go to the tea shop and see if I can hear anything new. There is nothing in my house except fools and a dotard and two children."

His ill-temper grew as he walked to the town because he remembered suddenly that all these new lands of his he could not have bought in a lifetime if O-lan had not seized the handful of jewels from the rich man's house and if she had not given them to him when he commanded her. But when he remembered this he was the more angry and he said as if to answer his own heart rebelliously,

"Well, but she did not know what she did. She seized them for pleasure as a child may seize a handful of red and green sweets, and she would have hidden them forever in her bosom if I had not found it out."

Then he wondered if she still hid the pearls between her breasts. But where before it had been strange and somehow a thing for him to think about sometimes and to picture in his mind, now he thought of it with contempt, for her breasts had grown flabby and pendulous with many children and had no beauty, and pearls between them were foolish and a waste.

Yet all this might have been nothing if Wang Lung were still a poor man or if the water was not spread over his fields. But he had money. There was silver hidden in the walls of his house and there was a sack of silver buried under a tile in the floor of his new house and there was silver wrapped in a cloth in the box in his room where he slept with his wife and silver sewed into the mat under their bed and his girdle was full of silver and he had no lack of it. So that now, instead of its passing from him like life blood draining from a wound, it lay in his girdle burning his fingers when he felt of it, and eager to be spent on this or that, and he began to be careless of it and to think what he could do to enjoy the days of his manhood.

Everything seemed not so good to him as it was before. The tea shop which he used to enter timidly, feeling himself but a common country fellow, now seemed dingy and mean to him. In the old days none knew him there and the tea boys were impudent to him, but now people nudged each other when he came in and he could hear a man whisper to another,

"There is that man Wang from the Wang village, he who bought the land from the House of Hwang that winter the Old Lord died when there was the great famine. He is rich, now."

[147]

And Wang Lung, hearing this, sat down with seeming careless-ness, but his heart swelled with pride at what he was. But on this day when he had reproached his wife even the deference he re-ceived did not please him and he sat gloomily drinking his tea and feeling that nothing was as good in his life as he had believed. And then he thought suddenly to himself,

"Now why should I drink my tea at this shop, whose owner is a cross-eyed weasel and whose earnings are less than the laborer's upon my land, I who have land and whose sons are scholars?"

And he rose up quickly and threw his money on the table and went out before any could speak to him. He wandered forth upon the streets of the town without knowing what it was he wished. Once he passed by a story-teller's booth and for a little while he sat down upon the end of a crowded bench and listened to the man's tale of old days in the Three Kingdoms, when warriors were brave and cunning. But he was still restless and he could not come under the man's spell as the others did and the sound of the little brass gong the man beat wearied him and he stood up again and went on.

Now there was in the town a great tea shop but newly opened and by a man from the south, who understood such business, and Wang Lung had before this passed the place by, filled with horror at the thought of how money was spent there in gambling and in play and in evil women. But now, driven by his unrest from idle-ness and wishing to escape from the reproach of his own heart when he remembered that he had been unjust to his wife, he went toward this place. He was compelled by his restlessness to see or to hear something new. Thus he stepped across the threshold of the new tea shop into the great, glittering room, full of tables and open to the street as it was, and he went in, bold enough in his bearing and trying to be the more bold because his heart was timid and he remembered that only in the last few years was he more than a poor man who had not at any time more than a silver piece or two ahead, and a man who had even labored at pulling a riksha on the streets of a southern city.

At first he did not speak at all in the great tea house but he bought his tea quietly and drank it and looked about him with wonder. This shop was a great hall and the ceiling was set about with gilt and upon the walls there were scrolls hung made of white silk and painted with the figures of women. Now these women Wang Lung looked at secretly and closely and it seemed to him they were women in dreams for none on earth had he seen like them. And the first day he looked at them and drank his tea quickly and went away.

But day after day while the waters held on his land he went to this tea shop and bought tea and sat alone and drank it and stared at the pictures of the beautiful women, and each day he sat longer, since there was nothing for him to do on his land or in his house. So he might have continued for many days on end, for in spite of his silver hidden in a score of places he was still a country-looking fellow and the only one in all that rich tea shop who wore cotton instead of silk and had a braid of hair down his back such as no man in a town will wear. But one evening when he sat drinking and staring from a table near the back of the hall, someone came down from a narrow stair which clung to the furthermost wall and led to the upper floor.

Now this tea shop was the only building in all that town which had an upper floor, except the Western Pagoda, which stood five stories high outside the West Gate. But the pagoda was narrow and more narrow toward the top, while the second floor of the tea shop was as square as that part of the building which stood upon the ground. At night the high singing of women's voices and light laughter floated out of the upper windows and the sweet strumming of lutes struck delicately by the hands of girls. One could hear the music streaming into the streets, especially after midnight, although where Wang Lung sat the clatter and noise of many men drinking tea and the sharp bony click of dice and sparrow dominoes muffled all else.

Thus it was that Wang Lung did not hear behind him on this night the footsteps of a woman creaking upon the narrow stair, and so he started violently when one touched him on the shoulder, not expecting that any would know him here. When he looked up it was into a narrow, handsome, woman's face, the face of Cuckoo, the woman into whose hands he had poured the jewels that day he bought land, and whose hand had held steady the Old Lord's shaking one and helped him to set aright his seal upon the deed of the sale. She laughed when she saw him, and her laughter was a sort of sharp whispering.

"Well, and Wang the farmer!" she said, lingering with malice on the word farmer, "and who would think to see you here!"

It seemed to Wang Lung then that he must prove at any cost to this woman that he was more than a mere country fellow, and he laughed and said too loudly,

"Is not my money as good to spend as another man's? And money I do not lack in these days. I have had good fortune."

Cuckoo stopped at this, her eyes narrow and bright as a snake's eyes, and her voice smooth as oil flowing from a vessel.

"And who has not heard it? And how shall a man better spend the money he has over and above his living than in a place like this, where rich men take their joy and elegant lords gather to take their joy in feasting and pleasure? There is no such wine as ours— have you tasted it, Wang Lung?"

"I have only drunk tea as yet," replied Wang Lung and he was half ashamed. "I have not touched wine or dice."

"Tea!" she exclaimed after him, laughing shrilly. "But we have tiger bone wine and dawn wine and wine of fragrant rice—why need you drink tea?" And as Wang Lung hung his head she said softly and insidiously,

"And I suppose you have not looked at anything else, have you, eh?—No pretty little hands, no sweet-smelling cheeks?"

Wang Lung hung his head yet lower and the red blood rushed into his face and he felt as though everyone near looked at him with mockery and listened to the voice of the woman. But when he took heart to glance about from under his lids, he saw no one paying any heed and the rattling of dice burst out anew and so he said in confusion,

"No—no—I have not—only tea—"

Then the woman laughed again and pointed to the painted silken scrolls and said,

"There they are, their pictures. Choose which one you wish to see and put the silver in my hand and I will place her before you."

"Those!" said Wang Lung, wondering. "I thought they were pictures of dream women, of goddesses in the mountain of Kwen Lwen, such as the story-tellers speak of!"

"So they are dream women," rejoined Cuckoo, with mocking good humor, "but dreams such as a little silver will turn into flesh." And she went on her way, nodding and winking at the servants standing about and motioning to Wang Lung as at one of whom she said, "There is a country bumpkin!"

But Wang Lung sat staring at the pictures with a new interest. Up this narrow stairway then, in the rooms above him, there were these women in flesh and blood, and men went up to them—other men than he, of course, but men! Well, and if he were not the man he was, a good and working man, a man with a wife and sons, which picture would he, pretending as a child pretends that he might do a certain thing, pretending then, which would he pretend to take? And he looked at every painted face closely and with intensity as though each were real. Before this they had all seemed equally beautiful, before this when there had been no question of choosing. But now there were clearly some more beautiful than others, and out of the score and more he chose three most beautiful, and out of the three he chose again and he chose one most beautiful, a small, slender thing, a body light as a bamboo and a little face as pointed as a kitten's face, and one hand clasping the stem of a lotus flower in bud, and the hand as delicate as the tendril of a fern uncurled.

He stared at her and as he stared a heat like wine poured through his veins.

[151]

"She is like a flower on a quince tree," he said suddenly aloud, and hearing his own voice he was alarmed and ashamed and he rose hastily and put down his money and went out and into the darkness that had now fallen and so to his home.

But over the fields and the water the moonlight hung, a net of silver mist, and in his body his blood ran secret and hot and fast.

XIX

NOW if the waters had at this time receded from Wang Lung's land, leaving it wet and smoking under the sun, so that in a few days of summer heat it would need to have been ploughed and harrowed and seed put in, Wang Lung might never have gone again to the great tea shop. Or if a child had fallen ill or the old man had reached suddenly to the end of his days, Wang Lung might have been caught up in the new thing and so forgotten the pointed face upon the scroll and the body of the woman slender as a bamboo.

But the waters lay placid and unmoved except for the slight summer wind that rose at sunset, and the old man dozed and the two boys trudged to school at dawn and were away until evening and in his house Wang Lung was restless and he avoided the eyes of O-lan who looked at him miserably as he went here and there and flung himself down in a chair and rose from it without drinking the tea she poured and without smoking the pipe he had lit. At the end of one long day, more long than any other, in the seventh month, when the twilight lingered murmurous and sweet with the breath of the lake, he stood at the door of his house, and suddenly without a word he turned abruptly and went into his room and put on his new coat, even the coat of black shining cloth, as shining almost as silk, that O-lan made for feast days, and with no word to anyone he went over the narrow paths along the water's edge and through the fields until he came to the darkness of the city gate and through this he went and through the streets until he came to the new tea shop.

There every light was lit, bright oil lamps which are to be bought in the foreign cities of the coast, and men sat under the lights drinking and talking, their robes open to the evening coolness, and everywhere fans moved to and fro and good laughter flowed out like music into the street. All the gayety which Wang Lung had never had from his labor on the land was held here in the walls of this house, where men met to play and never to work.

Wang Lung hesitated upon the threshold and he stood in the bright light which streamed from the open doors. And he might have stood there and gone away, for he was fearful and timid in his heart still, although his blood was rushing through his body fit to burst his veins, but there came out of the shadows on the edge of the light a woman who had been leaning idly against the doorway and it was Cuckoo. She came forward when she saw a man's figure, for it was her business to get custom for the women of the house, but when she saw who it was, she shrugged her shoulders and said,

"Ah, it is only the farmer!"

Wang was stung with the sharp carelessness in her voice, and his sudden anger gave him a courage he had not otherwise, so that he said,

"Well, and may I not come into the house and may I not do as other men?"

And she shrugged herself again and laughed and said,

"If you have the silver that other men have, you may do as they do."

[153]

Then he must show her that he was lordly and rich enough to do as he liked, and he thrust his hand into his girdle and brought it out full of silver and he said to her,

"Is it enough and is it not enough?"

She stared at the handful of silver and said then without further delay,

"Come and say which one you wish."

And Wang Lung, without knowing what he said, muttered forth,

"Well, and I do not know that I want anything." And then his desire overcame him and he whispered, "That little one—that one with the pointed chin and the little small face, a face like a quince blossom for white and pink, and she holds a lotus bud in her hand."

The woman nodded easily and beckoning him she threaded her way between the crowded tables, and Wang Lung followed her at a distance. At first it seemed to him that every man looked up and watched him but when he took courage to see he saw that none paid him any heed, except for one or two who called out, "Is it late enough, then, to go to the women?" and another called, "Here is a lusty fellow who needs must begin early!"

But by this time they were walking up the narrow straight stairway, and this Wang Lung did with difficulty, for it was the first time he had ever climbed steps in a house. Nevertheless, when they reached the top, it was the same as a house on the earth, except that it seemed a mighty way up when he passed a window and looked into the sky. The woman led the way down a close dark hall, then, and she cried as she went,

"Now here is the first man of the night!"

All along the hall doors opened suddenly and here and there girls' heads showed themselves in patches of light, as flowers burst out of their sheaths in the sun, but Cuckoo called cruelly,

"No, not you—and not you—no one had asked for any of you! This one is for the little pink-faced dwarf from Soochow—for Lotus!"

A ripple of sound ran down the hall, indistinct, derisive, and one girl, ruddy as a pomegranate, called out in a big voice,

"And Lotus may have this fellow—he smells of the fields and of garlic!"

This Wang Lung heard, although he disdained to answer, although her words struck him like a dagger thrust because he feared that he looked indeed what he was, a farmer. But he went on stoutly when he remembered the good silver in his girdle, and at last the woman struck a closed door harshly with the flat palm of her hand and went in without waiting and there upon a bed covered with a flowered red quilt, sat a slender girl.

If one had told him there were small hands like these he would not have believed it, hands so small and bones so fine and fingers so pointed with long nails stained the color of lotus buds, deep and rosy. And if one had told him that there could be feet like these, little feet thrust into pink satin shoes no longer than a man's middle finger, and swinging childishly over the bed's edge—if anyone had told him he would not have believed it.

He sat stiffly on the bed beside her, staring at her, and he saw that she was like the picture and having seen the picture he would have known her if he had met her. But most of all her hand was like the painted hand, curling and fine and white as milk. Her two hands lay curling into each other upon the pink and silken lap of her robe, and he would not have dreamed that they were to be touched.

He looked at her as he had looked at the picture and he saw the figure slender as bamboo in its tight short upper coat; he saw the small pointed face set in its painted prettiness above the high collar lined with white fur; he saw the round eyes, the shape of apricots, so that now at last he understood what the story-tellers meant when they sang of the apricot eyes of the beauties of old. And for him she was not flesh and blood but the painted picture of a woman.

Then she lifted that small curling hand and put it upon his shoulder and she passed it slowly down the length of his arm, very slowly. And although he had never felt anything so light, so soft as that touch, although if he had not seen it, he would not have known that it passed, he looked and saw the small hand moving down his arm, and it was as though fire followed it and burned under through his sleeve and into the flesh of his arm, and he watched the hand until it reached the end of his sleeve and then it fell with an instant's practiced hesitation upon his bare wrist and then into the loose hollow of his hard dark hand. And he began to tremble, not knowing how to receive it.

Then he heard laughter, light, quick, tinkling as the silver bell upon a pagoda shaking in the wind, and a little voice like laughter said,

"Oh, and how ignorant you are, you great fellow! Shall we sit here the night through while you stare?"

And at that he seized her hand between both of his, but carefully, because it was like a fragile dry leaf, hot and dry, and he said to her imploringly and not knowing what he said,

"I do not know anything—teach me!"

And she taught him.

Now Wang Lung became sick with the sickness which is greater than any a man can have. He had suffered under labor in the sun and he had suffered under the dry icy winds of the bitter desert and he had suffered from starvation when the fields would not bear and he had suffered from the despair of laboring without hope upon the streets of a southern city. But under none of these did he suffer as he now did under this slight girl's hand.

Every day he went to the tea shop; every evening he waited until she would receive him, and every night he went in to her. Each night he went in and each night again he was the country fellow who knew nothing, trembling at the door, sitting stiffly beside her, waiting for her signal of laughter, and then fevered, filled with a sickened hunger, he followed slavishly, bit by bit, her unfolding, until the moment of crisis, when, like a flower that is ripe for plucking, she was willing that he should grasp her wholly.

Yet never could he grasp her wholly, and this it was which kept him fevered and thirsty, even if she gave him his will of her. When O-lan had come to his house it was health to his flesh and he lusted for her robustly as a beast for its mate and he took her and was satisfied and he forgot her and did his work content. But there was no such content now in his love for this girl, and there was no health in her for him. At night when she would have no more of him, pushing him out of the door petulantly, with her small hands suddenly strong on his shoulders, his silver thrust into her bosom, he went away hungry as he came. It was as though a man, dying of thirst, drank the salt water of the sea which, though it is water, yet dries his blood into thirst and yet greater thirst so that in the end he dies, maddened by his very drinking. He went into her and he had his will of her again and again and he came away unsatisfied.

All during that hot summer Wang Lung loved thus this girl. He knew nothing of her, whence she came or what she was; when they were together he said not a score of words and he scarcely listened to the constant running of her speech, light and interspersed with laughter like a child's. He only watched her face, her hands, the postures of her body, the meaning of her wide sweet eyes, waiting for her. He had never enough of her, and he went back to his house in the dawn, dazed and unsatisfied.

The days were endless. He would not sleep any more upon his bed, making a pretense of heat in the room, and he spread a mat under the bamboos and slept there fitfully, lying awake to stare into the pointed shadows of the bamboo leaves, his breast filled with a sweet sick pain he could not understand.

And if any spoke to him, his wife or his children, or if Ching came to him and said, "The waters will soon recede and what is there we should prepare of seed?" he shouted and said,

"Why do you trouble me?"

And all the time his heart was like to burst because he could not be satiated with this girl.

[157]

Thus as the days went on and he lived only to pass the day until the evening came, he would not look at the grave faces of O-lan and of the children, suddenly sober in their play when he approached, nor even at his old father who peered at him and asked,

"What is this sickness that turns you full of evil temper and your skin as yellow as clay?"

And as these days went past to the night, the girl Lotus did what she would with him. When she laughed at the braid of his hair, although part of every day he spent in braiding and in brushing it, and said, "Now the men of the south do not have these monkey tails!" he went without a word and had it cut off, although neither by laughter nor scorn had anyone been able to persuade him to it before.

When O-lan saw what he had done she burst out in terror,

"You have cut off your life!"

But he shouted at her,

"And shall I look an old-fashioned fool forever? All the young men of the city have their hair cut short."

Yet he was afraid in his heart of what he had done, and yet so he would have cut off his life if the girl Lotus had commanded it or desired it, because she had every beauty which had ever come into his mind to desire in a woman.

His good brown body that he washed but rarely, deeming the clean sweat of his labor washing enough for ordinary times, his body he now began to examine as if it were another man's, and he washed himself every day so that his wife said, troubled,

"You will die with all this washing!"

He bought sweet-smelling soap in the shop, a piece of red scented stuff from foreign parts, and he rubbed it on his flesh, and not for any price would he have eaten a stalk of garlic, although it was a thing he had loved before, lest he stink before her.

And none in his house knew what to make of all these things.

He bought also new stuffs for clothes, and although O-lan had always cut his robes, making them wide and long for good measure and sewing them stoutly this way and that for strength, now he was scornful of her cutting and sewing and he took the stuffs to a tailor in the town and he had his clothes made as the men in the town had theirs, light grey silk for a robe, cut neatly to his body and with little to spare, and over this a black satin sleeveless coat. And he bought the first shoes he had had in his life not made by a woman, and they were black velvet shoes such as the Old Lord had worn flapping at his heels.

But these fine clothes he was ashamed to wear suddenly before O-lan and his children. He kept them folded in sheets of brown oiled paper and he left them at the tea shop with a clerk he had come to know, and for a price the clerk let him go into an inner room secretly and put them on before he went up the stairs. And beyond this he bought a silver ring washed with gold for his finger, and as his hair grew where it had been shaved above his forehead, he smoothed it with a fragrant foreign oil from a small bottle for which he had paid a whole piece of silver.

But O-lan looked at him in astonishment and did not know what to make from all this, except that one day after staring at him for a long time as they ate rice at noon, she said heavily,

"There is that about you which makes me think of one of the lords in the great house."

Wang Lung laughed loudly then and he said,

"And am I always to look like a hind when we have enough and to spare?"

But in his heart he was greatly pleased and for that day he was more kindly with her than he had been for many days.

Now the money, the good silver, went streaming out of his hands. There was not only the price he must pay for his hours with the girl, but there was the pretty demanding of her desires. She would sigh and murmur, as though her heart were half broken with her desire,

"Ah me—ah me!"

And when he whispered, having learned at last to speak in her presence, "What now, my little heart?" she answered, "I have no joy today in you because Black Jade, that one across the hall from me, has a lover who gave her a gold pin for her hair, and I have only this old silver thing, which I have had forever and a day."

And then for his life's sake he could not but whisper to her, pushing aside the smooth black curve of her hair that he might have the delight of seeing her small long-lobed ears,

"And so will I buy a gold pin for the hair of my jewel."

For all these names of love she had taught him, as one teaches new words to a child. She had taught him to say them to her and he could not say them enough for his own heart, even while he stammered them, he whose speech had all his life been only of planting and of harvests and of sun and rain.

Thus the silver came out of the wall and out of the sack, and O-lan, who in the old days might have said to him easily enough, "And why do you take the money from the wall?" now said nothing, only watching him in great misery, knowing well that he was living some life apart from her and apart even from the land, but not knowing what life it was. She had been afraid of him from that day on which he had seen clearly that she had no beauty of hair or of person, and when he had seen her feet were large, and she was afraid to ask him anything because of his anger that was always ready for her now.

There came a day when Wang Lung returned to his house over the fields and he drew near to her as she washed his clothes at the pool. He stood there silent for a while and then he said to her roughly, and he was rough because he was ashamed and would not acknowledge his shame in his heart,

"Where are those pearls you had?"

And she answered timidly, looking up from the edge of the pool and from the clothes she was beating upon a smooth flat stone,

"The pearls? I have them."

And he muttered, not looking at her but at her wrinkled, wet hands,

"There is no use in keeping pearls for nothing."

Then she said slowly,

"I thought one day I might have them set in earrings," and fearing his laughter she said again, "I could have them for the younger girl when she is wed."

And he answered her loudly, hardening his heart,

"Why should that one wear pearls with her skin as black as earth? Pearls are for fair women!" And then after an instant's silence he cried out suddenly, "Give them to me—I have need of them!"

Then slowly she thrust her wet wrinkled hand into her bosom and she drew forth the small package and she gave it to him and watched him as he unwrapped it; and the pearls lay in his hand and they caught softly and fully the light of the sun, and he laughed.

But O-lan returned to the beating of his clothes and when tears dropped slowly and heavily from her eyes she did not put up her hand to wipe them away; only she beat the more steadily with her wooden stick upon the clothes spread over the stone.

XX

AND thus it might have gone forever until all the silver was spent had not that one, Wang Lung's uncle, returned suddenly without explanation of where he had been or of what he had done. He stood in the door as though he had dropped from a cloud, his ragged clothes unbuttoned and girdled loosely as ever about him, and his face as it always was but wrinkled and hardened with the sun and the wind. He grinned widely at them all as they sat about the table at their early morning meal, and Wang Lung sat agape, for he had forgotten that his uncle lived and it was like a dead man returning to see him. The old man his father blinked and stared and did not recognize the one who had come until he called out,

"Well, my Elder Brother and his son and his sons and my sister-in-law."

Then Wang Lung rose, dismayed in his heart but upon the surface of his face and voice courteous,

"Well, my uncle, and have you eaten?"

"No," replied his uncle easily, "but I will eat with you."

He sat himself down, then, and he drew a bowl and chopsticks to him and he helped himself freely to rice and dried salt fish and to salted carrots and to the dried beans that were upon the table. He ate as though he were very hungry and none spoke until he supped down loudly three bowls of the thin rice gruel, cracking quickly between his teeth the bones of the fish and the kernels of the beans. And when he had eaten he said simply and as though it was his right,

"Now I will sleep, for I am without sleep these three nights."

Then when Wang Lung, dazed and not knowing what else to do, led him to his father's bed, his uncle lifted the quilts and felt of the good cloth and of the clean new cotton and he looked at the wooden bedstead and at the good table and at the great wooden chair which Wang Lung had bought for his father's room, and he said,

"Well, and I heard you were rich but I did not know you were as rich as this," and he threw himself upon the bed and drew the quilt about his shoulders, all warm with summer though it was, and everything he used as though it were his own, and he was asleep without further speech.

Wang Lung went back to the middle room in great consternation for he knew very well that now his uncle would never be driven forth again, now that he knew Wang Lung had wherewith to feed him. And Wang Lung thought of this and thought of his uncle's wife with great fear because he saw that they would come to his house and none could stop them.

As he feared so it happened. His uncle stretched himself upon the bed at last after noon had passed and he yawned loudly three times and came out of the room, shrugging the clothes together upon his body, and he said to Wang Lung,

"Now I will fetch my wife and my son. There are the three of us mouths, and in this great house of yours it will never be missed what we eat and the poor clothes we wear."

Wang Lung could do nothing but answer with sullen looks, for it is a shame to a man when he has enough and to spare to drive his own father's brother and son from the house. And Wang Lung knew that if he did this it would be a shame to him in the village where he was now respected because of his prosperity and so he did not dare to say anything. But he commanded the laborers to move altogether into the old house so that the rooms by the gate might be left empty and into these that very day in the evening his uncle came, bringing his wife and his son. And Wang Lung was exceedingly angry and the more angry because he must bury it all in his heart and answer with smiles and welcome his relatives. This, although when he saw the fat smooth face of his uncle's wife he felt fit to burst with his anger and when he saw the scampish, impudent face of his uncle's son, he could scarcely keep his hand down from slapping it. And for three days he did not go into the town because of his anger.

Then when they were all accustomed to what had taken place and when O-lan had said to him, "Cease to be angry. It is a thing to be borne," and Wang Lung saw that his uncle and his uncle's wife and son would be courteous enough for the sake of their food and their shelter, then his thoughts turned more violently than ever to the girl Lotus and he muttered to himself,

"When a man's house is full of wild dogs he must seek peace elsewhere."

And all the old fever and pain burned in him and he was still never satisfied of his love.

Now what O-lan had not seen in her simplicity nor the old man because of the dimness of his age nor Ching because of his friendship, the wife of Wang Lung's uncle saw at once and she cried out, the laughter slanting from her eyes,

"Hah, Wang Lung is seeking to pluck a flower somewhere." And when O-lan looked at her humbly, not understanding, she laughed and said again, "The melon must always be split wide open before you can see the seeds, eh? Well, then, plainly, your man is mad over another woman!"

This Wang Lung heard his uncle's wife say in the court outside his window as he lay dozing and weary in his room one early morning, exhausted with his love. He was quickly awake, and he listened further, aghast at the sharpness of this woman's eyes. The thick voice rumbled on, pouring like oil from her fat throat,

"Well, and I have seen many a man, and when one smooths his hair and buys new clothes and will have his shoes velvet all of a sudden, then there is a new woman and that is sure."

There came a broken sound from O-lan, what it was she said he could not hear, but his uncle's wife said again,

"And it is not to be thought, poor fool, that one woman is enough for any man, and if it is a weary hard-working woman who has worn away her flesh working for him, it is less than enough for him. His fancy runs elsewhere the more quickly, and you, poor fool, have never been fit for a man's fancy and little better than an ox for his labor. And it is not for you to repine when he has money and buys himself another to bring her to his house, for all men are so, and so would my old do-nothing also, except the poor wretch has never had enough silver in his life to feed himself even."

This she said and more, but no more than this did Wang Lung hear upon his bed, for his thought stopped at what she had said. Now suddenly did he see how to satisfy his hunger and his thirst after this girl he loved. He would buy her and bring her to his house and make her his own so that no other man could come in to her and so could he eat and be fed and drink and be satisfied. And he rose up at once from his bed and he went out and motioned secretly to the wife of his uncle and he said, when she had

[164]

followed him outside the gate and under the date tree where none could hear what he had to say,

"I listened and heard what you said in the courts and you are right. I have need of more than that one and why should I not, seeing that I have land to feed us all?"

She answered volubly and eagerly,

"And why not, indeed? So have all men who have prospered. It is only the poor man who must needs drink from one cup." Thus she spoke, knowing what he would say next, and he went on as she had planned,

"But who will negotiate for me and be the middleman? A man cannot go to a woman and say, 'Come to my house.' "

To this she answered instantly,

"Now do you leave this affair in my hands. Only tell me which woman it is and I will manage the affair."

Then Wang Lung answered unwillingly and timidly, for he had never spoken her name aloud before to anyone,

"It is the woman called Lotus."

It seemed to him that everyone must know and have heard of Lotus, forgetting how only a short two summers' moons before he had not known she lived. He was impatient, therefore, when his uncle's wife asked further,

"And where is her home?"

"Now where," he answered with asperity, "where except in the great tea shop on the main street of the town?"

"The one called the House of Flowers?"

"And what other?" Wang Lung retorted.

She mused awhile, fingering her pursed lower lip, and she said at last,

"I do not know anyone there. I shall have to find a way. Who is the keeper of this woman?"

And when he told her it was Cuckoo, who had been slave in the great house, she laughed and said,

"Oh, that one? Is that what she did after the Old Lord died in her bed one night! Well, and it is what she would do."

Then she laughed again, a cackling "Heh—heh—heh—" and she said easily,

"That one! But it is a simple matter, indeed. Everything is plain. That one! From the beginning that one would do anything, even to making a mountain, if she could feel silver enough in her palm for it."

And Wang Lung, hearing this, felt his mouth suddenly dry and parched and his voice came from him in a whisper,

"Silver, then! Silver and gold! Anything to the very price of my land!"

Then from a strange and contrary fever of love Wang Lung would not go again to the great tea house until the affair was arranged. To himself he said,

"If she will not come to my house and be for me only, cut my throat and I will not go near her again."

But when he thought the words, "if she will not come," his heart stood still with fear, so that he continually ran to his uncle's wife saying,

"Now, lack of money shall not close the gate." And he said again, "Have you told Cuckoo that I have silver enough for my will?" and he said, "Tell her she shall do no work of any kind in my house but she shall wear only silken garments and eat shark's fins if she will every day," until at last the fat woman grew impatient and cried out at him, rolling her eyes back and forth,

"Enough and enough! Am I a fool, or is this the first time I have managed a man and a maid? Leave me alone and I will do it. I have said everything many times."

Then there was nothing to do except to gnaw his fingers and to see the house suddenly as Lotus might see it and he hurried O-lan into this and that, sweeping and washing and moving tables and chairs, so that she, poor woman, grew more and more terror-stricken for well she knew by now, although he said nothing, what was to come to her.

Now Wang Lung could not bear to sleep any more with O-lan and he said to himself that with two women in the house there

[166]

must be more rooms and another court and there must be a place where he could go with his love and be separate. So while he waited for his uncle's wife to complete the matter, he called his laborers and commanded them to build another court to the house behind the middle room, and around the court three rooms, one large and two small on either side. And the laborers stared at him, but dared no reply and he would not tell them anything, but he superintended them himself, so that he need not talk with Ching even of what he did. And the men dug the earth from the fields and made the walls and beat them down, and Wang Lung sent to the town and bought tiles for the roof.

Then when the rooms were finished and the earth smoothed and beaten down for a floor, he had bricks bought and the men set them closely together and welded them with lime and there was a good brick floor to the three rooms for Lotus. And Wang Lung bought red cloth to hang at the doors for curtains and he bought a new table and two carved chairs to put on either side and two painted scrolls of pictured hills and water to hang upon the wall behind the table. And he bought a round red lacquered comfit dish with a cover, and in this he put sesame cakes and larded sweets and he put the box on the table. Then he bought a wide and deep carven bed, big enough for a small room in itself, and he bought flowered curtains to hang about it. But in all this he was ashamed to ask O-lan anything, and so in the evenings his uncle's wife came in and she hung the bed curtains and did the things a man is too clumsy for doing.

Then all was finished and there was nothing to do, and a moon of days had passed and the thing was not yet complete. So Wang Lung dallied alone in the little new court he had built for Lotus and he thought of a little pool to make in the center of the court, and he called a laborer and the man dug a pool three feet square and set it about with tiles, and Wang Lung went into the city and bought five gold fish for it. Then he could think of nothing more to be done, and again he waited impatient and fevered.

During all this time he said nothing to anyone except to scold the children if they were filthy at their noses or to roar out at O-lan that she had not brushed her hair for three days and more, so that at last one morning O-lan burst into tears and wept aloud, as he had never seen her weep before, even when they starved, or at any other time. He said harshly, therefore,

"Now what, woman? Cannot I say comb out your horse's tail of hair without this trouble over it?"

But she answered nothing except to say over and over, moaning,

"I have borne you sons—I have borne you sons—"

And he was silenced and uneasy and he muttered to himself for he was ashamed before her and so he let her alone. It was true that before the law he had no complaint against his wife, for she had borne him three good sons and they were alive, and there was no excuse for him except his desire.

Thus it went until one day his uncle's wife came and said,

"The thing is complete. The woman who is keeper for the master of the tea house will do it for a hundred pieces of silver on her palm at one time, and the girl will come for jade earrings and a ring of jade and a ring of gold and two suits of satin clothes and two suits of silk clothes and a dozen pairs of shoes and two silken quilts for her bed."

Of all this Wang Lung heard only this part, "The thing is complete—" and he cried out,

"Let it be done—let it be done—" and he ran into the inner room and he got out silver and poured it into her hands, but secretly still, for he was unwilling that anyone should see the good harvests of so many years go thus, and to his uncle's wife he said, "And for yourself take a good ten pieces of silver."

Then she made a feint of refusal, drawing up her fat body and rolling her head this way and that and crying in a loud whisper,

"No, and I will not. We are one family and you are my son and I am your mother and this I do for you and not for silver." But Wang Lung saw her hand outstretched as she denied, and into it he poured the good silver and he counted it well spent.

Then he bought pork and beef and mandarin fish and bamboo

sprouts and chestnuts, and he bought a snarl of dried birds' nests from the south to brew for soup, and he bought dried shark's fins and every delicacy he knew he bought and then he waited, if that burning, restless impatience within him could be called a waiting.

On a shining glittering fiery day in the eighth moon, which is the last end of summer, she came to his house. From afar Wang Lung saw her coming. She rode in a closed sedan chair of bamboo borne upon men's shoulders and he watched the sedan moving this way and that upon the narrow paths skirting the fields, and behind it followed the figure of Cuckoo. Then for an instant he knew fear and he said to himself,

"What am I taking into my house?"

And scarcely knowing what he did he went quickly into the room where he had slept for these many years with his wife and he shut the door and there in the darkness of the room he waited in confusion until he heard his uncle's wife calling loudly for him to come out, for one was at the gate.

Then abashed and as though he had never seen the girl before he went slowly out, hanging his head over his fine clothes, and his eyes looking here and there, but never ahead. But Cuckoo hailed him merrily,

"Well, and I did not know we would be doing business like this!"

Then she went to the chair which the men had set down and she lifted the curtain and clucked her tongue and she said,

"Come out, my Lotus Flower, here is your house and here your lord."

And Wang Lung was in an agony because he saw upon the faces of the chairmen wide grins of laughter and he thought to himself,

"Now these are loafers from the town streets and they are worthless fellows," and he was angry that he felt his face hot and red and so he would not speak aloud at all.

Then the curtain was lifted and before he knew what he did he looked and he saw sitting in the shadowy recess of the chair,

[169]

painted and cool as a lily, the girl Lotus. He forgot everything, even his anger against the grinning fellows from the town, everything but that he had bought this woman for his own and she had come to his house forever, and he stood stiff and trembling, watching as she rose, graceful as though a wind had passed over a flower. Then as he watched and could not take his eyes away, she took Cuckoo's hand and stepped out, keeping her head bowed and her eyelids dropped as she walked, tottering and swaying upon her little feet, and leaning upon Cuckoo. And as she passed him she did not speak to him, but she whispered only to Cuckoo, faintly,

"Where is my apartment?"

Then his uncle's wife came forward to her other side and between them they led the girl into the court and into the new rooms that Wang Lung had built for her. And of all Wang Lung's house there was none to see her pass, for he had sent the laborers and Ching away for the day to work on a distant field, and O-lan had gone somewhere he knew not and had taken the two little ones with her and the boys were in school and the old man slept against the wall and heard and saw nothing, and as for the poor fool, she saw no one who came and went and knew no face except her father's and her mother's. But when Lotus had gone in Cuckoo drew the curtains after her.

Then after a time Wang Lung's uncle's wife came out, laughing a little maliciously, and she dusted her hands together as though to free them of something that clung to them.

"She reeks of perfume and paint, that one," she said still laughing. "Like a regular bad one she smells." And then she said with a deeper malice, "She is not so young as she looks, my nephew! I will dare to say this, that if she had not been on the edge of an age when men will cease to look at her, it is doubtful whether jade in her ears and gold on her fingers and even silk and satin would have tempted her to the house of a farmer, and even a well-to-do farmer." And then seeing the anger on Wang Lung's face at this too plain speaking she added hastily, "But beautiful she is and I have never seen another more beautiful and it will be

[170]

as sweet as the eight-jeweled rice at a feast after your years with the thick-boned slave from the House of Hwang."

But Wang Lung answered nothing, only he moved here and there through the house and he listened and he could not be still. At last he dared to lift the red curtain and to go into the court he had built for Lotus and then into the darkened room where she was and there he was beside her for the whole day until night.

All this time O-lan had not come near the house. At dawn she had taken a hoe from the wall and she called the children and she took a little cold food wrapped up in a cabbage leaf and she had not returned. But when night came on she entered, silent and earth-stained and dark with weariness, and the children silent behind her, and she said nothing to anyone, but she went into the kitchen and prepared food and set it upon the table as she always did, and she called the old man and put the chopsticks in his hand and she fed the poor fool and then she ate a little with the children. Then when they slept and Wang Lung still sat at the table dreaming she washed herself for sleeping and at last she went into her accustomed room and slept alone upon her bed.

Then did Wang Lung eat and drink of his love night and day. Day after day he went into the room where Lotus lay indolent upon her bed and he sat beside her and watched her at all she did. She never came forth in the heat of the early autumn days, but she lay while the woman Cuckoo bathed her slender body with lukewarm water and rubbed oil into her flesh and perfume and oil into her hair. For Lotus had said wilfully that Cuckoo must stay with her as her servant and she paid her prodigally so that the woman was willing enough to serve one instead of a score, and she and Lotus, her mistress, dwelt apart from the others in the new court that Wang Lung had made.

All day the girl lay in the cool darkness of her room, nibbling sweetmeats and fruits, and wearing nothing but single garments of green summer silk, a little tight coat cut to her waist and wide trousers beneath, and thus Wang Lung found her when he came to her and he ate and drank of his love.

Then at sunset she sent him away with her pretty petulance, and Cuckoo bathed and perfumed her again and put on her fresh clothes, soft white silk against her flesh and peach-colored silk outside, the silken garments that Wang Lung had given, and upon her feet Cuckoo put small embroidered shoes, and then the girl walked into the court and examined the little pool with its five gold fish, and Wang Lung stood and stared at the wonder of what he had. She swayed upon her little feet and to Wang Lung there was nothing so wonderful for beauty in the world as her pointed little feet and her curling helpless hands.

And he ate and drank of his love and he feasted alone and he was satisfied.

XXI

IT WAS not to be supposed that the coming of this one called Lotus and of her serving woman Cuckoo into Wang Lung's house could be accomplished altogether without stir and discord of some sort, since more than one woman under one roof is not for peace. But Wang Lung had not foreseen it. And even though he saw by O-lan's sullen looks and Cuckoo's sharpness that something was amiss, he would not pay heed to it and he was careless of anyone so long as he was still fierce with his desire.

Nevertheless, when day passed into night, and night changed into dawn, Wang Lung saw that it was true the sun rose in the morning, and this woman Lotus was there, and the moon rose in its season and she was there for his hand to grasp when it would, and his thirst of love was somewhat slaked and he saw things he had not seen before.

For one thing, he saw that there was trouble at once between O-lan and Cuckoo. This was an astonishment to him, for he was prepared for O-lan to hate Lotus, having heard many times of such things, and some women will even hang themselves upon a beam with a rope when a man takes a second woman into the house, and others will scold and contrive to make his life worthless for what he has done, and he was glad that O-lan was a silent woman for at least she could not think of words against him. But he had not foreseen that whereas she would be silent of Lotus, her anger would find its vent against Cuckoo.

Now Wang Lung had thought only of Lotus and when she begged him,

"Let me have this woman for my servant, seeing that I am altogether alone in the world, for my father and my mother died when I could not yet talk and my uncle sold me as soon as I was pretty to a life such as I have had, and I have no one."

This she said with her tears, always abundant and ready and glittering in the corners of her pretty eyes, and Wang Lung could have denied her nothing she asked when she looked up at him so. Besides, it was true enough that the girl had no one to serve her, and it was true she would be alone in his house, for it was plain enough and to be expected that O-lan would not serve the second one, and she would not speak to her or notice that she was in the house at all. There was only the wife of his uncle then, and it was against Wang Lung's stomach to have that one peeping and prying and near to Lotus for her to talk to of him, and so Cuckoo was as good as any and he knew no other woman who would come.

But it seemed that O-lan, when she saw Cuckoo, grew angry with a deep und sullen anger that Wang Lung had never seen and did not know was in her. Cuckoo was willing enough to be friends, since she had her pay from Wang Lung, albeit she did not forget that in the great house she had been in the lord's chamber and

[173]

O-lan a kitchen slave and one of many. Nevertheless, she called out to O-lan well enough when first she saw her,

"Well, and my old friend, here we are in a house together again, and you mistress and first wife—my mother—and how things are changed!"

But O-lan only stared at her and when it came into her understanding who it was and what she was, she answered nothing but she put down the jar of water she carried and she went into the middle room where Wang Lung sat between his times of love, and she said to him plainly,

"What is this slave woman doing in our house?"

Wang Lung looked east and west. He would have liked to speak out and to say in a surly voice of master, "It is my house and whoever I say may come in, she shall come in, and who are you to ask?" But he could not because of some shame in him when O-lan was there before him, and his shame made him angry, because when he reasoned it, there was no need for shame and he had done no more than any man may do who has silver to spare.

Still, he could not speak out, and he only looked east and west and feigned to have mislaid his pipe in his garments, and he fumbled in his girdle. But O-lan stood there solidly on her big feet and waited and when he said nothing she asked again plainly in the same words,

"What is this slave woman doing in our house?"

Then Wang Lung, seeing she would have an answer, said feebly, "And what is it to you?"

And O-lan said,

"I bore her haughty looks all during my youth in the great house and her running into the kitchen a score of times a day and crying out 'now tea for the lord'—'now food for the lord'—and it was always this is too hot and that is too cold, and that is badly cooked, and I was too ugly and too slow and too this and too that . . ."

But still Wang Lung did not answer, for he did not know what to say.

Then O-lan waited and when he did not speak, the hot, scanty tears welled slowly into her eyes, and she winked them to hold back the tears, and at last she took the corner of her blue apron and wiped her eyes and she said at last,

"It is a bitter thing in my own house, and I have no mother's house to go back to anywhere."

And when Wang Lung was still silent and answered nothing at all, but he sat down to his pipe and lit it, and he said nothing still, she looked at him piteously and sadly out of her strange dumb eyes that were like a beast's eyes that cannot speak, and then she went away, creeping and feeling for the door because of her tears that blinded her.

Wang Lung watched her as she went and he was glad to be alone, but still he was ashamed and he was still angry that he was ashamed and he said to himself and he muttered the words aloud and restlessly, as though he quarreled with someone,

"Well, and other men are so and I have been good enough to her, and there are men worse than I." And he said at last that O-lan must bear it.

But O-lan was not finished with it, and she went her way silently. In the morning she heated water and presented it to the old man, and to Wang Lung if he were not in the inner court she presented tea, but when Cuckoo went to find hot water for her mistress the cauldron was empty and not all her loud questionings would stir any response from O-lan. Then there was nothing but that Cuckoo must herself boil water for her mistress if she would have it. But then it was time to stir the morning gruel and there was not space in the cauldron for more water and O-lan would go steadily to her cooking, answering nothing to Cuckoo's loud crying,

"And is my delicate lady to lie thirsting and gasping in her bed for a swallow of water in the morning?"

But O-lan would not hear her; only she pushed more grass and straw into the bowels of the oven, spreading it as carefully and as thriftily as ever she had in the old days when one leaf was precious enough because of the fire it would make under food. Then Cuckoo went complaining loudly to Wang Lung and he was angry that his love must be marred by such things and he went to O-lan to reproach her and he shouted at her,

"And cannot you add a dipperful of water to the cauldron in the mornings?"

But she answered with a sullenness deeper than ever upon her face,

"I am not slave of slaves in this house at least."

Then he was angry beyond bearing and he seized O-lan's shoulder and he shook her soundly and he said,

"Do not be yet more of a fool. It is not for the servant but for the mistress."

And she bore his violence and she looked at him and she said simply,

"And to that one you gave my two pearls!"

Then his hand dropped and he was speechless and his anger was gone and he went away ashamed and he said to Cuckoo,

"We will build another stove and I will make another kitchen. The first wife knows nothing of the delicacies which the other one needs for her flower-like body and which you also enjoy. You shall cook what you please in it."

And so he bade the laborers build a little room and an earthen stove in it and he bought a good cauldron. And Cuckoo was pleased because he said, "You shall cook what you please in it."

As for Wang Lung, he said to himself that at last his affairs were settled and his women at peace and he could enjoy his love. And it seemed to him freshly that he could never tire of Lotus and of the way she pouted at him with the lids drooped like lily petals over her great eyes, and at the way laughter gleamed out of her eyes when she glanced up at him.

But after all this matter of the new kitchen became a thorn in his body, for Cuckoo went to the town every day and she bought this and that of expensive foods that are imported from the southern cities. There were foods he had never even heard of: lichee nuts and dried honey dates and curious cakes of rice flour and nuts and red sugar, and horned fish from the sea and many other things. These all cost money more than he liked to give out, but still not so much, he was sure, as Cuckoo told him, and yet he was afraid to say, "You are eating my flesh," for fear she would be offended and angry at him, and it would displease Lotus, and so there was nothing he could do except to put his hand unwillingly to his girdle. And this was a thorn to him day after day, and because there was none to whom he could complain of it, the thorn pierced more deeply continually, and it cooled a little of the fire of love in him for Lotus.

And there was yet another small thorn that sprang from the first, and it was that his uncle's wife, who loved good food, went often into the inner court at meal times, and she grew free there, and Wang Lung was not pleased that out of his house Lotus chose this woman for friend. The three women ate well in the inner courts, and they talked unceasingly, whispering and laughing, and there was something that Lotus liked in the wife of his uncle and the three were happy together, and this Wang Lung did not like.

But still there was nothing to be done, for when he said gently and to coax her,

"Now, Lotus, my flower, do not waste your sweetness on an old fat hag like that one. I need it for my own heart, and she is a deceitful and untrustworthy creature, and I do not like it that she is near you from dawn to sunset."

Lotus was fretful and she answered peevishly, pouting her lips and hanging her head away from him,

"Now I have no one except you and I have no friends and I am used to a merry house and in yours there is no one except the first wife who hates me and these children of yours who are a plague to me, and I have no one."

Then she used her weapons against him and she would not let him into her room that night and she complained and said,

"You do not love me for if you did you would wish me to be happy."

Then Wang Lung was humbled and anxious and he was submissive and he was sorry and he said,

"Let it be only as you wish and forever."

Then she forgave him royally and he was afraid to rebuke her in any way for what she wished to do, and after that when he came to her, Lotus, if she were talking of drinking tea or eating some sweetmeat with his uncle's wife, would bid him wait and was careless with him, and he strode away, angry that she was unwilling for him to come in when this other woman sat there, and his love cooled a little, although he did not know it himself.

He was angry, moreover, that his uncle's wife ate of the rich foods that he had to buy for Lotus and she grew fat and more oily than she had been, but he could say nothing for his uncle's wife was clever and she was courteous to him and flattered him with good words, and rose when he came into the room.

And so his love for Lotus was not whole and perfect as it had been before, absorbing utterly his mind and his body. It was pierced through and through with small angers which were the more sharp because they must be endured and because he could no longer go even to O-lan freely for speech, seeing that now their life was sundered.

Then like a field of thorn springing up from one root and spreading here and there, there was yet more to trouble Wang Lung. One day his father, whom one would say saw nothing at any time so drowsy with age he was, woke suddenly out of his sleeping in the sun and he tottered, leaning on his dragon-headed staff which Wang Lung had bought for him on his seventieth birthday, to the doorway where a curtain hung between the main room and the court where Lotus walked. Now the old man had never noticed the door before nor when the court was built and seemingly he did not know whether anyone had been added to the house or not, and Wang Lung never told him, "I have another woman," for the old man was too deaf to make anything out of a voice if it told him something new and of which he had not thought.

But on this day he saw without reason this doorway and he went to it and drew the curtain, and it happened that it was at an hour of evening when Wang Lung walked with Lotus in the court, and they stood beside the pool and looked at the fish, but Wang Lung looked at Lotus. Then when the old man saw his son standing beside a slender painted girl he cried out in his shrill cracked voice,

"There is a harlot in the house!" and he would not be silent although Wang Lung, fearing lest Lotus grow angry—for this small creature could shriek and scream and beat her hands together if she were angered at all—went forward and led the old man away into the outer court and soothed him, saying,

"Now calm your heart, my father. It is not a harlot but a second woman in the house."

But the old man would not be silent and whether he heard what was said or not no one knew only he shouted over and over, "There is a harlot here!" And he said suddenly, seeing Wang Lung near him, "And I had one woman and my father had one woman and we farmed the land." And again he cried out after a time, "I say it is a harlot!"

And so the old man woke from his aged and fitful sleeping with a sort of cunning hatred against Lotus. He would go to the doorway of her court and shout suddenly into the air,

"Harlot!"

Or he would draw aside the curtain into her court and then spit furiously upon the tiles. And he would hunt small stones and throw them with his feeble arms into the little pool to scare the fish, and in the mean ways of a mischievous child he expressed his anger.

This too made a disturbance in Wang Lung's house, for he was ashamed to rebuke his father, and yet he feared the anger of Lotus, since he had found she had a pretty petulant temper that she loosed easily. And this anxiety to keep his father from angering her was wearisome to him and it was another thing to make of his love a burden to him.

One day he heard a shriek from the inner courts and he ran in for he heard it was the voice of Lotus, and there he found that the two younger children, the boy and the girl born alike, had between them led into the inner court his elder daughter, his poor fool. Now the four other children were constantly curious about this lady who lived in the inner court, but the two elder boys were conscious and shy and knew well enough why she was there and what their father had to do with her, although they never spoke of her unless to each other secretly. But the two younger ones could never be satisfied with their peepings and their exclamations, and sniffing of the perfume she wore and dipping their fingers into the bowls of food that Cuckoo carried away from her rooms after she had eaten.

Lotus complained many times to Wang Lung that his children were a plague to her and she wished there were a way to lock them out so that she need not be plagued with them. But this he was not willing to do, and he answered her in jest,

"Well, and they like to look at a lovely face as much as their father does."

And he did nothing except to forbid them to enter her courts and when he saw them they did not, but when he did not see them they ran in and out secretly. But the elder daughter knew nothing of anything, but only sat in the sun against the wall of the outer court, smiling and playing with her bit of twisted cloth.

On this day, however, the two elder sons being away at school, the two younger children had conceived the notion that the fool must also see the lady in the inner courts, and they had taken her hands and dragged her into the court and she stood before Lotus, who had never seen her and sat and stared at her. Now when the fool saw the bright silk of the coat Lotus wore and the shining jade in her ears, she was moved by some strange joy at the sight and she put out her hands to grasp the bright colors and she laughed aloud, a laugh that was only sound and meaningless. And Lotus was frightened and screamed out, so that Wang Lung came running in, and Lotus shook with her anger and leaped up and down

[180]

on her little feet and shook her finger at the poor laughing girl and cried out,

"I will not stay in this house if that one comes near me, and I was not told that I should have accursed idiots to endure and if I had known it I would not have come—filthy children of yours!" and she pushed the little gaping boy who stood nearest her, clasping his twin sister's hand.

Then the good anger awoke in Wang Lung, for he loved his children, and he said roughly,

"I will not hear my children cursed, no and not by anyone and not even my poor fool, and not by you who have no son in your womb for any man." And he gathered the children together and said to them, "Now go out, my son and my daughter, and come no more to this woman's court, for she does not love you and if she does not love you she does not love your father, either." And to the elder girl he said with great gentleness, "And you, my poor fool, come back to your place in the sun." And she smiled and he took her by the hand and led her away.

For he was most angry of all that Lotus dared to curse this child of his and call her idiot, and a load of fresh pain for the girl fell upon his heart, so that for a day and two days he would not go near Lotus, but he played with the children and he went into the town and he bought a circle of barley candy for his poor fool and he comforted himself with her baby pleasure in the sweet sticky stuff.

And when he went in to Lotus again neither of them said anything that he had not come for two days, but she took special trouble to please him, for when he came his uncle's wife was there drinking tea, and Lotus excused herself and said,

"Now here is my lord come for me and I must be obedient to him for this is my pleasure," and she stood until the woman went away.

Then she went up to Wang Lung and took his hand and drew it to her face and she wooed him. But he, although he loved her again, loved her not so wholly as before, and never again so wholly as he had loved her.

There came a day when summer was ended and the sky in the early morning was clear and cold and blue as sea water and a clean autumn wind blew hard over the land, and Wang Lung woke as from a sleep. He went to the door of his house and he looked over his fields. And he saw that the waters had receded and the land lay shining under the dry cold wind and under the ardent sun.

Then a voice cried out in him, a voice deeper than love cried out in him for his land. And he heard it above every other voice in his life and he tore off the long robe he wore and he stripped off his velvet shoes and his white stockings and he rolled his trousers to his knees and he stood forth robust and eager and he shouted,

"Where is the hoe and where the plow? And where is the seed for the wheat planting? Come, Ching, my friend—come—call the men—I go out to the land!"

XXII

AS HE had been healed of his sickness of heart when he came from the southern city and comforted by the bitterness he had endured there, so now again Wang Lung was healed of his sickness of love by the good dark earth of his fields and he felt the moist soil on his feet and he smelled the earthy fragrance rising up out of the furrows he turned for the wheat. He ordered his laborers hither and thither and they did a mighty day of labor, ploughing here and ploughing there, and Wang Lung stood first behind the oxen and cracked the whip over their backs and saw the deep curl of earth turning as the plow went into the soil, and then he called to Ching and gave him the ropes, and he himself took a hoe and broke up the soil into find loamy stuff, soft as black sugar, and still dark with the wetness of the land upon it. This he did for the sheer joy he had in it and not for any necessity, and when he was weary he lay down upon his land and he slept and the health of the earth spread into his flesh and he was healed of his sickness.

When night came and the sun had gone blazing down without a cloud to dim it, he strode into his house, his body aching and weary and triumphant, and he tore aside the curtain that went into the inner court and there Lotus walked in her silken robes. When she saw him she cried out at the earth upon his clothes and shuddered when he came near her.

But he laughed and he seized her small, curling hands in his soiled ones and he laughed again and said,

"Now you see that your lord is but a farmer and you are a farmer's wife!"

Then she cried out with spirit,

"A farmer's wife am I not, be you what you like!"

And he laughed again and went out from her easily.

He ate his evening rice all stained as he was with the earth and unwillingly he washed himself even before he slept. And washing his body he laughed again, for he washed it now for no woman, and he laughed because he was free.

Then it seemed to Wang Lung as though he had been for a long time away and there were suddenly a multitude of things he had to do. The land clamored for ploughing and planting and day after day he labored at it, and the paleness which the summer of his love had set on his flesh darkened to a deep brown under the sun and his hands, which had peeled off their calloused parts under the idleness of love, hardened again where the hoe pressed and where the plow handles set their mark.

When he came in at noon and at night he ate well of the food which O-lan prepared for him, good rice and cabbage and beancurd, and fresh garlic rolled into wheat bread. When Lotus held her small nose under her hand at his coming and cried out at his reek, he laughed and cared nothing and he breathed out his stout breath at her and she must bear it as she could for he would eat of what he liked. And now that he was full of health again and free of the sickness of his love he could go to her and be finished with her and turn himself to other things.

So these two women took their place in his house: Lotus for his toy and his pleasure and to satisfy his delight in beauty and in smallness and in the joy of her pure sex, and O-lan for his woman of work and the mother who had borne his sons and who kept his house and fed him and his father and his children. And it was a pride to Wang Lung in the village that men mentioned with envy the woman in his inner court; it was as though men spoke of a rare jewel or an expensive toy that was useless except that it was sign and symbol of a man who had passed beyond the necessity of caring only to be fed and clothed and could spend his money on joy if he wished.

And foremost among the men in the village who exclaimed over his prosperity was his uncle, for his uncle in these days was like a dog who fawns and desires to win favor. He said,

"There is my nephew, who keeps such an one for his pleasure as none of us common men have ever seen." And again he said, "And he goes in to his woman, who wears robes of silk and satin like a lady in a great house. I have not seen it, but my woman tells me." And again he said, "My nephew, the son of my brother, is founding a great house and his sons will be the sons of a rich man and they need not work all their lives long."

The men of the village, therefore, looked upon Wang Lung with increasing respect and they talked to him no more as to one of themselves but as to one who lived in a great house, and they came to borrow money of him at interest and to ask his advice concerning the marriage of their sons and daughters, and if any two had a dispute over the boundary of a field, Wang Lung was asked to settle the dispute and his decision was accepted, whatever it was.

Where Wang Lung had been busy with his love, then, he was now satisfied of it and was busied with many things. The rains came in season and the wheat sprouted and grew and the year turned to winter and Wang Lung took his harvests to the markets, for he saved his grain until prices were high, and this time he took with him his eldest son.

Now there is a pride a man has when he sees his eldest son reading aloud the letters upon a paper and putting the brush and ink to paper and writing that which may be read by others, and this pride Wang Lung now had. He stood proudly and saw this happen and he would not laugh when the clerks, who had scorned him before, now cried out,

"Pretty characters the lad makes and he is a clever one!"

No, Wang Lung would not pretend it was anything out of the common that he had a son like this, although when the lad said sharply as he read, "Here is a letter that has the wood radical when it should have the water radical," Wang Lung's heart was fit to burst with pride, so that he was compelled to turn aside and cough and spit upon the floor to save himself. And when a murmur of surprise ran among the clerks at his son's wisdom he called out merely,

"Change it, then! We will not put our name to anything wrongly written."

And he stood proudly and watched while his son took up the brush and changed the mistaken sign.

When it was finished and his son had written his father's name on the deed of sale of the grain and upon the receipt of the moneys, the two walked home together, father and son, and the father said within his heart that now his son was a man and his eldest son, and he must do what was right for his son, and he must see to it that there was a wife chosen and betrothed for his son so that the lad need not go begging into a great house as he had and pick up what was left there and what no one wanted, for his son was the son of a man who was rich and who owned land in his right.

Wang Lung set himself, therefore, to the seeking of a maid who might be his son's wife, and it was no slight task, for he would have no one who was a common and ordinary female. He talked of it one night to Ching, after the two of them had been alone in the middle room, taking account of what must be bought for spring planting and of what they had of their own seed. He talked not as one who expects great help, for he knew Ching was too simple, but still he knew the man was faithful as a good dog is faithful to its master, and it was relief to speak what he thought to such an one.

Ching stood humbly as Wang Lung sat at the table and spoke, for in spite of Wang Lung's urging, he would not, now that Wang Lung had become rich, sit in his presence as though they were equal, and he listened with fixed attention as Wang Lung spoke of his son and of the one he sought, and when Wang Lung was finished, Ching sighed and he said in his hesitant voice that was scarcely more than a whisper,

"And if my poor girl were here and sound you might have her for nothing at all and my gratitude, too, but where she is I do not know, and it may be she is dead and I do not know."

Then Wang Lung thanked him, but he forbore to say what was in his heart, that for his son there must be one far higher than the daughter of such an one as Ching, who although a good man was, besides that, only a common farmer on another's land.

Wang Lung kept his own counsel, therefore, only listening here and there in the tea shop when maids were spoken of, or men prosperous in the town who had daughters for marriage. But to his uncle's wife he said nothing, guarding his purpose from her. For she was well enough when he had need of a woman from a tea house for himself. She was such an one to arrange a matter like that. But for his son he would have no one like his uncle's wife, who could not know anyone he considered fit for his eldest son.

The year deepened into snow and the bitterness of winter and

the New Year's festival came and they ate and drank, and men came to see Wang Lung, not only from the countryside but now from the town also, to wish him fortune, and they said,

"There is no fortune we can wish you greater than you have, sons in your house and women and money and land."

And Wang Lung, dressed in his silken robe with his sons in good robes beside him on either hand, and sweet cakes and watermelon seeds and nuts upon the table, and red paper signs pasted upon his doors everywhere for the new year and coming prosperity, knew that his fortune was good.

But the year turned to spring and the willows grew faintly green and the peach trees budded pink, and Wang Lung had not yet found the one he sought for his son.

Spring came in long, warm days scented with blossoming plum and cherry, and the willow trees sprouted their leaves fully and unfolded them, and the trees were green and the earth was moist and steaming and pregnant with harvest, and the eldest son of Wang Lung changed suddenly and ceased to be a child. He grew moody and petulant and would not eat this and that and he wearied of his books, and Wang Lung was frightened and did not know what to make of it and talked of a doctor.

There was no correction that could be made of the lad at all, for if his father said to him with anything beyond coaxing, "Now eat of the good meat and rice," the lad turned stubborn and melancholy, and if Wang Lung was angry at all, he burst into tears and fled from the room.

Wang Lung was overcome with surprise and he could make nothing of it, so that he went after the lad and he said gently as he was able,

"I am your father and now tell me what is in your heart." But the lad did nothing except sob and shake his head violently.

Moreover, he took a dislike to his old teacher and would not in the mornings rise out of his bed to go to school unless Wang Lung bawled at him or even beat him, and then he went sullenly and sometimes he spent whole days idling about the streets of the

town, and Wang Lung only knew it at night, when the younger boy said spitefully,

"Elder Brother was not in school today."

Wang Lung was angry at his eldest son then and he shouted at him,

"And am I to spend good silver for nothing?"

And in his anger he fell upon the boy with a bamboo and beat him until O-lan, the boy's mother, heard it and rushed in from the kitchen and stood between her son and his father so that the blows rained upon her in spite of Wang Lung's turning this way and that to get at the boy. Now the strange thing was that whereas the boy might burst into weeping at a chance rebuke, he stood these beatings under the bamboo without a sound, his face carven and pale as an image. And Wang Lung could make nothing of it, although he thought of it night and day.

He thought of it one evening thus after he had eaten his night's food, because on that day he had beaten his eldest son for not going to the school, and while he thought, O-lan came into the room. She came in silently and she stood before Wang Lung and he saw she had that which she wished to say. So he said,

"Say on. What is it, mother of my son?"

And she said, "It is useless for you to beat the lad as you do. I have seen this thing come upon the young lords in the courts of the great house, and it came on them with melancholy, and when it came the Old Lord found slaves for them if they had not found any for themselves and the thing passed easily."

"It need not be so," answered Wang Lung in argument. "When I was a lad I had no such melancholy and no such weepings and tempers, and no slaves, either."

O-lan waited and then she answered slowly, "I have not indeed seen it thus except with young lords. You worked on the land. But he is like a young lord and he is idle in the house."

Wang Lung was surprised, after he had pondered a while, for he saw truth in what she said. It was true that when he himself was a lad there was no time for melancholy, for he had to be up at dawn

for the ox and out with the plow and the hoe and at harvest he must needs work until his back broke, and if he wept he could weep for no one heard him, and he could not run away as his son ran away from school, for if he did there was nothing for him to eat on return, and so he was compelled to labor. He remembered all this and he said to himself,

"But my son is not thus. He is more delicate than I was, and his father is rich and mine was poor, and there is no need for his labor, for I have labor in my fields, and besides, one cannot take a scholar such as my son is and set him to the plow."

And he was secretly proud that he had a son like this and so he said to O-lan,

"Well, and if he is like a young lord it is another matter. But I cannot buy a slave for him. I will betroth him and we will marry him early, and there is that to be done."

Then he rose and went into the inner court.

XXIII

NOW Lotus, seeing Wang Lung distraught in her presence and thinking of things other than her beauty, pouted and said,

"If I had known that in a short year you could look at me and not see me, I would have stayed in the tea house." And she turned her head away as she spoke and looked at him out of the corner of her eyes so that he laughed and seized her hand and he put it against his face and smelled of its fragrance and he answered,

"Well, and a man cannot always think of the jewel he has sewn on his coat, but if it were lost he could not bear it. These days I think of my eldest son and of how his blood is restless with desire and he must be wed and I do not know how to find the one he should wed. I am not willing that he marry any of the daughters of the village farmers, nor is it meet, seeing that we bear the common name of Wang. Yet I do not know one in the town well enough to say to him, 'Here is my son and there is your daughter,' and I am loath to go to a professional matchmaker, lest there be some bargain she has made with a man who has a daughter deformed or idiot."

Now Lotus, since the eldest son had grown tall and graceful with young manhood, looked on the lad with favor and she was diverted with what Wang Lung said to her and she replied, musing,

"There was a man who used to come in to me at the great tea house, and he often spoke of his daughter, because he said she was such an one as I, small and fine, but still only a child, and he said, 'And I love you with a strange unease as though you were my daughter; you are too like her, and it troubles me for it is not lawful,' and for this reason, although he loved me best, he went to a great red girl called Pomegranate Flower."

"What sort of man was this?" asked Wang Lung.

"He was a good man and his silver was ready and he did not promise without paying. We all wished him well, for he was not begrudging, and if a girl was weary sometimes he did not bawl out as some did that he had been cheated, but he always said courteously as a prince might, or some might from a learned and noble house, 'Well, and here is the silver, and rest, my child, until love blooms again.' He spoke very prettily to us." And Lotus mused until Wang Lung said hastily to waken her, for he did not like her to think on her old life,

"What was his business, then, with all this silver?"

And she answered,

"I do not know except I think he was master of a grain market, but I will ask Cuckoo who knows everything about men and their money."

Then she clapped her hands and Cuckoo ran in from the kitchen, her high cheeks and nose flushed with the fire, and Lotus asked her,

"Who was that great, large, goodly man who came to me and then to Pomegranate Flower, because I was like his little daughter, so that it troubled him, although he ever loved me best?"

And Cuckoo answered at once, "Ah, and that was Liu, the grain dealer. Ah, he was a good man! He left silver in my palm whenever he saw me."

"Where is his market?" asked Wang Lung, although idly, because it was woman's talk and likely to come to nothing.

"In the Street of the Stone Bridge," said Cuckoo.

Then before she finished the words Wang Lung struck his hands together in delight and he said,

"Now then, that is where I sell my grain, and it is a propitious thing and surely it can be done," and for the first time his interest was awake, because it seemed to him a lucky thing to wed his son to the daughter of the man who bought his grain.

When there was a thing to be done Cuckoo smelled the money in it as a rat smells tallow, and she wiped her hands upon her apron and she said quickly,

"I am ready to serve the master."

Wang Lung was doubtful, and doubting, he looked at her crafty face, but Lotus said gaily,

"And that is true, and Cuckoo shall go and ask the man Liu, and he knows her well and the thing can be done, for Cuckoo is clever enough, and she shall have the matchmaker's fee, if it is well done."

"That will I do!" said Cuckoo heartily and she laughed as she thought of the fee of good silver on her palm, and she untied her apron from her waist and she said busily, "Now and at once will I go, for the meat is ready except for the moment of cooking and the vegetables are washed."

But Wang Lung had not pondered the matter sufficiently and it was not to be decided so quickly as this and he called out,

"No, for I have decided nothing. I must think of the matter for some days and I will tell you what I think."

The women were impatient, Cuckoo for the silver and Lotus because it was a new thing and she would hear something new to amuse her, but Wang Lung went out, saying,

"No, it is my son and I will wait."

And so he might have waited for many days, thinking of this and that, had not one early morning, the lad, his eldest son, come home in the dawn with his face hot and red with wine drinking, and his breath was fetid and his feet unsteady. Wang Lung heard him stumbling in the court and he ran out to see who it was, and the lad was sick and vomited before him, for he was unaccustomed to more than the pale mild wine they made from their own rice fermented, and he fell and lay on the ground in his vomit like a dog.

Wang Lung was frightened and he called for O-lan, and together they lifted the lad up and O-lan washed him and laid him upon the bed in her own room, and before she was finished with him the lad was asleep and heavy as one dead and could answer nothing to what his father asked.

Then Wang Lung went into the room where the two boys slept together, and the younger was yawning and stretching and tying his books into a square cloth to carry to school, and Wang Lung said to him,

"Was your elder brother not in the bed with you last night?"

And the boy answered unwillingly,

"No."

There was some fear in his look and Wang Lung, seeing it, cried out at him roughly,

"Where was he gone?" and when the boy would not answer, he took him by the neck and shook him and cried, "Now tell me all, you small dog!"

The boy was frightened at this, and he broke out sobbing and crying and said between his sobs,

"And Elder Brother said I was not to tell you and he said he

[192]

would pinch me and burn me with a hot needle if I told and if I do not tell he gives me pence."

And Wang Lung, beside himself at this, shouted out,

"Tell what, you who ought to die?"

And the boy looked about him and said desperately, seeing that his father would choke him if he did not answer,

"He has been away three nights altogether, but what he does I do not know, except that he goes with the son of your uncle, our cousin."

Wang Lung loosed his hand then from the boy's neck and he flung him aside and he strode forth into his uncle's rooms, and there he found his uncle's son, hot and red of face with wine, even as his own son, but steadier of foot, for the young man was older and accustomed to the ways of men. Wang Lung shouted at him,

"Where have you led my son?"

And the young man sneered at Wang Lung and he said,

"Ah, that son of my cousin's needs no leading. He can go alone."

But Wang Lung repeated it and this time he thought to himself that he would kill this son of his uncle's now, this impudent scampish face, and he cried in a terrible voice,

"Where has my son been this night?"

Then the young man was frightened at the sound of his voice and he answered sullenly and unwillingly, dropping his impudent eyes,

"He was at the house of the whore who lives in the court that once belonged to the great house."

When Wang Lung heard this he gave a great groan, for the whore was one well known of many men and none went to her except poor and common men, for she was no longer young and she was willing to give much for little. Without stopping for food he went out of his gate and across his fields, and for once he saw nothing of what grew on his land, and noted nothing of how the crop promised, because of the trouble his son had brought to him. He went with his eyes fixed inward, and he went through the gate of the wall about the town, and he went to the house that had been great.

The heavy gates were swung back widely now, and none ever closed them upon their thick iron hinges, for any who would might come and go in these days, and he went in, and the courts and the rooms were filled with common people, who rented the rooms, a family of common people to a room. The place was filthy and the old pines hewed down and those left standing were dying, and the pools in the courts were choked with refuse.

But he saw none of this. He stood in the court of the first house and he called out,

"Where is the woman called Yang, who is a whore?"

There was a woman there who sat on a three-legged stool, sewing at a shoe sole, and she lifted her head and nodded toward a side door opening on the court and she took up her sewing again, as though many times she had been asked this question by men.

Wang Lung went to the door and he beat on it, and a fretful voice answered,

"Now go away, for I am done my business for this night and I must sleep, since I work all night."

But he beat again, and the voice cried out, "Who is it?"

He would not answer, but he beat yet again, for he would go in whether or not, and at last he heard a shuffling and a woman opened the door, a woman none too young and with a weary face and hanging, thick lips, and coarse white paint on her forehead and red paint she had not washed from her mouth and cheeks, and she looked at him and said sharply,

"Now I cannot before tonight and if you like you may come as early as you will then in the night, but now I must sleep."

But Wang Lung broke roughly into her talking, for the sight of her sickened him and the thought of his son here he could not bear, and he said,

"It is not for myself—I do not need such as you. It is for my son."

[194]

And he felt suddenly in his throat a thickening of weeping for his son. Then the woman asked,

"What of your son?"

And Wang Lung answered and his voice trembled,

"He was here last night."

"There were many sons of men here last night," replied the woman, "and I do not know which was yours."

Then Wang Lung said, beseeching her,

"Think and remember a little slight young lad, tall for his years, but not yet a man, and I did not dream he dared to try a woman."

And she, remembering, answered,

"Were there two, and was one a young fellow with his nose turned to the sky at the end and a look in his eye of knowing everything, and his hat over one ear? And the other, as you say, a tall big lad, but eager to be a man!"

And Wang Lung said, "Yes—yes—that is he—that is my son!"

"And what of your son?" said the woman.

Then Wang Lung said earnestly,

"This: if he ever comes again, put him off—say you desire men only—say what you will—but every time you put him off I will give you twice the fee of silver on your palm!"

The woman laughed then and carelessly and she said in sudden good humor,

"And who would not say aye to this, to be paid for not working? And so I say aye also. It is true enough that I desire men and little boys are small pleasure." And she nodded at Wang Lung as she spoke and leered at him and he was sickened at her coarse face and he said hastily,

"So be it, then."

He turned quickly and he walked home, and as he walked he spat and spat again to rid him of his sickness at the memory of the woman.

On this day, therefore, he said to Cuckoo,

"Let it be as you said. Go to the grain merchant and arrange the

[195]

matter. Let the dowry be good but not too great if the girl is suitable and if it can be arranged."

When he had said this to Cuckoo he went back to the room and he sat beside his sleeping son and he brooded, for he saw how fair and young the boy lay there, and he saw the quiet face, asleep and smooth with its youth. Then when he thought of the weary painted woman and her thick lips, his heart swelled with sickness and anger and he sat there muttering to himself.

And as he sat O-lan came in and stood looking at the boy, and she saw the clear sweat standing on his skin and she brought vinegar in warm water and washed the sweat away gently, as they used to wash the young lords in the great house when they drank too heavily. Then seeing the delicate childish face and the drunken sleep that even the washing would not awaken, Wang Lung rose and went in his anger to his uncle's room, and he forgot the brother of his father and he remembered only that this man was father to the idle, impudent young man who had spoiled his own fair son, and he went in and he shouted,

"Now I have harbored an ungrateful nest of snakes and they have bitten me!"

His uncle was sitting leaning over a table eating his breakfast, for he never rose until midday, seeing there was no work he had to do, and he looked up at these words and he said lazily,

"How now?"

Then Wang Lung told him, half-choking, what had happened, but his uncle only laughed and he said,

"Well, and can you keep a boy from becoming a man? And can you keep a young dog from a stray bitch?"

When Wang Lung heard this laughter he remembered in one crowded space of time all that he had endured because of his uncle; how of old his uncle had tried to force him to the selling of his land, and how they lived here, these three, eating and drinking and idle, and how his uncle's wife ate of the expensive foods Cuckoo bought for Lotus, and now how his uncle's son had spoiled his own fair lad, and he bit his tongue between his teeth and he said,

"Now out of my house, you and yours, and no more rice will there be for any of you from this hour, and I will burn the house down rather than have it shelter you, who have no gratitude even in your idleness!"

But his uncle sat where he was and ate on, now from this bowl and now from that, and Wang Lung stood there bursting with his blood, and when he saw his uncle paid no heed to him, he stepped forward with his arm upraised. Then the uncle turned and said,

"Drive me out if you dare."

And when Wang Lung stammered and blustered, not understanding, "Well—and what—well and what—" his uncle opened his coat and showed him what was against its lining.

Then Wang Lung stood still and rigid, for he saw there a false beard of red hair and a length of red cloth, and Wang Lung stared at these things, and the anger went out of him like water and he shook because there was no strength left in him.

Now these things, the red beard and the red length of cloth were sign and symbol of a band of robbers who lived and marauded toward the northwest, and many houses had they burned and women they had carried away, and good farmers they had bound with ropes to the threshold of their own houses and men found them there next day, raving mad if they lived and burnt and crisp as roasted meat if they were dead. And Wang Lung stared and his eyes hung out of his head, and he turned and went away without a word. And as he went he heard his uncle's whispered laughter as he stooped again over his rice bowl.

Now Wang Lung found himself in such a coil as he had never dreamed of. His uncle came and went as before, grinning a little under the sparse and scattered hairs of his grey beard, his robes wrapped and girdled about his body as carelessly as ever, and Wang Lung sweated chilly when he saw him but he dared not speak anything except courteous words for fear of what his uncle might do to him. It was true that during all these years of his prosperity and especially during the years when there were no harvests or only very little and other men had starved with their children, never had bandits come to his house and his lands, although he had many times been afraid and had barred the doors stoutly at night. Until the summer of his love he had dressed himself coarsely and had avoided the appearance of wealth, and when among the villagers he heard stories of marauding he came home and slept fitfully and listened for sounds out of the night.

But the robbers never came to his house and he grew careless and bold and he believed he was protected by heaven and that he was a man of good fortune by destiny, and he grew heedless of everything, even of incense of the gods, since they were good enough to him without, and he thought of nothing except of his own affairs and of his land. And now suddenly he saw why he had been safe and why he would be safe so long as he fed the three of his uncle's house. When he thought of this he sweated heavy cold sweat, and he dared to tell no one what his uncle hid in his bosom.

But to his uncle he said no more of leaving the house, and to his uncle's wife he said with what urging he could muster,

"Eat what you like in the inner courts and here is a bit of silver to spend."

And to his uncle's son he said, although the gorge rose in his throat, yet he said,

"Here is a bit of silver, for young men will play."

But his own son Wang Lung watched and he would not allow him to leave the courts after sundown, although the lad grew angry and flung himself about and slapped the younger children for nothing except his own ill-humor. So was Wang Lung encompassed about with his troubles.

At first Wang Lung could not work for thinking of all the trouble that had befallen him, and he thought of this trouble and that, and he thought, "I could turn my uncle out and I could move inside the city wall where they lock the great gates every night against robbers," but then he remembered that every day he must come to work on his fields, and who could tell what might happen to him as he worked defenseless, even on his own land? Moreover, a man could not live locked in a town and in a house in the town, and he would die if he were cut off from his land. There would surely come a bad year, moreover, and even the town could not withstand robbers, as it had not in the past when the great house fell.

And he could go into the town and go to the court where the magistrate lived and say to him,

"My uncle is one of the Redbeards."

But if he did this, who would believe him, who would believe a man when he told such a thing of his own father's brother? It was more likely that he would be beaten for his unfilial conduct rather than his uncle suffer, and in the end he would go in fear of his life, for if the robbers heard of it, they would kill him for revenge.

Then as if this were not enough Cuckoo came back from the grain merchant and although the affair of the betrothal had gone well, the merchant Liu was not willing that anything should take place now except the exchange of the betrothal papers, for the maid was too young for marriage, being but fourteen years old, and it must wait for another three years. Wang Lung was dismayed at three more years of this lad's anger and idleness and mooning eyes, for he would not go to school now two days out of ten, and Wang Lung shouted at O-lan that night when he ate,

"Let us betroth these other children as soon as we are able, and the sooner the better, and let us marry them as soon as they begin to yearn, for I cannot have this over again three more times!"

And the next morning he had not slept but a little through the night, and he tore off his long robes and kicked off his shoes, and as was his wont when the affairs of his house became too deep for him, he took a hoe and he went out to his fields, and he went through the outer court where the elder girl sat smiling and twisting her bit of cloth through her fingers and smoothing it, and he muttered,

"Well, that poor fool of mine brings me more comfort than all the others put together."

And he went out to his land day after day for many days.

Then the good land did again its healing work and the sun shone on him and healed him and the warm winds of summer wrapped him about with peace. And as if to cure him of the root of his ceaseless thought of his own troubles, there came out of the south one day a small slight cloud. At first it hung on the horizon small and smooth as a mist, except it did not come hither and thither as clouds blown by the wind do, but it stood steady until it spread fanwise up into the air.

The men of the village watched it and talked of it and fear hung over them, for what they feared was this, that locusts had come out of the south to devour what was planted in the fields. Wang Lung stood there also, and he watched, and they gazed and at last a wind blew something to their feet, and one stooped hastily and picked it up and it was a dead locust, dead and lighter than the living hosts behind.

Then Wang Lung forgot everything that troubled him. Women and sons and uncle, he forgot them all, and he rushed among the frightened villagers, and he shouted at them,

"Now for our good land we will fight these enemies from the skies!"

But there were some who shook their heads, hopeless from the start, and these said,

"No, and there is no use in anything. Heaven has ordained that this year we shall starve, and why should we waste ourselves in struggle against it, seeing that in the end we must starve?"

And women went weeping to the town to buy incense to thrust before the earth gods in the little temple, and some went to the big temple in the town, where the gods of heaven were, and thus earth and heaven were worshipped.

But still the locusts spread up into the air and on over the land.

Then Wang Lung called his own laborers and Ching stood silent and ready beside him and there were others of the younger farmers, and with their own hands these set fire to certain fields and they burned the good wheat that stood almost ripe for cutting and they dug wide moats and ran water into them from the wells, and they worked without sleeping. O-lan brought them food and the women brought their men food, and the men ate standing and in the field, gulping it down as beasts do, as they worked night and day.

Then the sky grew black and the air was filled with the deep still roar of many wings beating against each other, and upon the land the locusts fell, flying over this field and leaving it whole, and falling upon that field, and eating it as bare as winter. And men sighed and said, "So Heaven wills," but Wang Lung was furious and he beat the locusts and trampled on them and his men flailed them with flails and the locusts fell into the fires that were kindled and they floated dead upon the waters of the moats that were dug. And many millions of them died, but to those that were left it was nothing.

Nevertheless, for all his fighting Wang Lung had this as his reward: the best of his fields were spared and when the cloud moved on and they could rest themselves, there was still wheat that he could reap and his young rice beds were spared and he was content. Then many of the people ate the roasted bodies of the locusts, but Wang Lung himself would not eat them, for to him they were a filthy thing because of what they had done to his land. But he said nothing when O-lan fried them in oil and when the laborers crunched them between their teeth and the children pulled them apart delicately and tasted them, afraid of their great eyes. But as for himself he would not eat.

Nevertheless, the locusts did this for him. For seven days he thought of nothing but his land, and he was healed of his troubles and his fears, and he said to himself calmly,

"Well, every man has his troubles and I must make shift to live with mine as I can, and my uncle is older than I and he will die, and three years must pass as they can with my son and I shall not kill myself."

And he reaped his wheat and the rains came and the young green rice was set into the flooded fields and again it was summer.

XXIV

ONE day after Wang Lung had said to himself that peace was in his house, his eldest son came to him as he returned at noon from the land, and the lad said,

"Father, if I am to be a scholar, there is no more that this old head in the town can teach me."

Wang Lung had dipped from the cauldron in the kitchen a basin of boiling water and into this he dipped a towel and wrung it and holding it steaming against his face he said,

"Well, and how now?"

The lad hesitated and then he went on,

"If I am to be a scholar, I would like to go to the south to the city and enter a great school where I can learn what is to be learned."

Wang Lung rubbed the towel about his eyes and his ears and with his face all steaming he answered his son sharply, for his body ached with his labor in the fields,

"What nonsense is this? I say you cannot go and I will not be teased about it, for I say you cannot go. You have learning enough for these parts."

And he dipped the cloth in again and wrung it.

But the young man stood there and stared at his father with hatred and he muttered something and Wang Lung was angry for he could not hear what it was, and he bawled at his son,

"Speak out what you have to say!"

Then the young man flared at the noise of his father's voice and he said,

"Well, and I will, then, for go south I will, and I will not stay in this stupid house and be watched like a child, and in this little town which is no better than a village! I will go out and learn something and see other parts."

Wang Lung looked at his son and he looked at himself, and his son stood there in a pale long robe of silver grey linen, thin and cool for the summer's heat, and on his lip were the first black hairs of his manhood, and his skin was smooth and golden and his hands under his long sleeves were soft and fine as a woman's. Then Wang Lung looked at himself and he was thick and stained with earth and he wore only trousers of blue cotton cloth girt about his knees and his waist and his upper body was naked, and one would have said he was his son's servant rather than his father. And this thought made him scornful of the young man's tall fine looks, and he was brutal and angry and he shouted out,

"Now then, get you into the fields and rub a little good earth on yourself lest men take you for a woman, and work a little for the rice you eat!"

And Wang Lung forgot that he had ever had pride in his son's writing and in his cleverness at books, and he flung himself out, stamping his bare feet as he walked and spitting upon the floor coarsely, because the fineness of his son angered him for the moment. And the lad stood and looked at him with hatred, but Wang Lung would not turn back to see what the lad did.

Nevertheless, that night when Wang Lung went into the inner courts and sat beside Lotus as she lay upon the mat on her bed where Cuckoo fanned her as she lay, Lotus said to him idly as of a thing of no account, but only something to say,

"That big lad of yours is pining and desires to go away."

Then Wang Lung, remembering his anger against his son, said sharply,

"Well, and what is it to you? I will not have him in these rooms at his age."

But Lotus made haste to reply, "No—no—it is Cuckoo who says it." And Cuckoo made haste to say, "Anyone can see the thing and a lovely lad he is and too big for idleness and longing."

Wang Lung was led aside by this and he thought only of his anger against his son and he said,

"No, he shall not go. I will not spend my money foolishly." And he would not speak of it any more and Lotus saw he was peevish from some anger, and she sent Cuckoo away and suffered him there alone.

Then for many days there was nothing said and the lad seemed suddenly content again, but he would not go to school any more and this Wang Lung allowed him, for the boy was nearly eighteen and large like his mother in frame of bones, and he read in his own room when his father came into the house and Wang Lung was content and he thought to himself,

"It was a whim of his youth and he does not know what he wants and there are only three years—it may be a little extra silver will make it two, or even one, if the silver is enough. One of these days when the harvests are well over and the winter wheat planted and the beans hoed, I will see to it."

Then Wang Lung forgot his son, for the harvests, except what the locusts had consumed, were fair enough and by now he had gained once more what he had spent on the woman Lotus. His silver was precious to him once more, and at times he marvelled secretly at himself that he had ever spent so freely upon a woman.

Still, there were times when she stirred him sweetly, if not so strongly as at first, and he was proud to own her, although he saw well enough that what his uncle's wife had said was true, that she was none too young for all her smallness of stature, and she never conceived to bear a child for him. But for this he cared nothing, since he had sons and daughters, and he was willing enough to keep her for the pleasure she gave him.

As for Lotus, she grew lovelier as her fullness of years came on, for if before she had had a fault, it was her bird-like thinness that made too sharp the lines of her little pointed face and hollowed too much her temples. But now under the food which Cuckoo cooked for her, and under the idleness of her life with one man only, she became soft and rounded in body, and her face grew full and smooth at the temples, and with her wide eyes and small mouth she looked more than ever like a plump little cat. And she slept and ate and took on her body this soft smooth flesh. If she was no longer the lotus bud, neither was she more than the full-blown flower, and if she was not young, neither did she look old, and youth and age were equally far from her.

With his life placid again and the lad content, Wang Lung might have been satisfied except that one night when he sat late and alone, reckoning on his fingers what he could sell of his corn and what he could sell of his rice, O-lan came softly into the room. This one, with the passing of the years had grown lean and gaunt and the rocklike bones of her face stood forth and her eyes were sunken. If one asked her how she did she said no more than this,

"There is a fire in my vitals."

Her belly was as great as though with child these three years, only there was no birth. But she rose at dawn and she did her work and Wang Lung saw her only as he saw the table or his chair or a tree in the court, never even so keenly as he might see one of the oxen drooping its head or a pig that would not eat. And she did her work alone and spoke no more than she could escape speaking with the wife of Wang Lung's uncle, and she never spoke at all to Cuckoo. Never once had O-lan gone into the inner courts, and rarely, if Lotus came out to walk a little in a place other than her own court, O-lan went into her room and sat until one said, "She is gone." And she said nothing but she worked at her cooking and at the washing at the pool even in the winter when the water was stiff with ice to be broken. But Wang Lung never thought to say,

"Well, and why do you not, with the silver I have to spare, hire a servant or buy a slave?"

It did not occur to him that there was any need of this, although he hired laborers for his fields and to help with the oxen and asses and with the pigs he had, and in the summers when the river flooded, he hired men for the time to herd the ducks and geese he fed upon the waters.

On this evening, then, when he sat alone with only the red candles in the pewter stands alight, she stood before him and looked this way and that, and at last she said,

"I have something to say."

Then he stared at her in surprise and he answered,

"Well, and say on."

And he stared at her and at the shadowed hollows of her face and he thought again how there was no beauty in her and how for many years had he not desired her.

Then she said in a harsh whisper,

"The eldest son goes too often into the inner courts. When you are away he goes."

Now Wang Lung could not at first grasp what she said thus whispering and he leaned forward with his mouth agape and he said,

"What, woman?"

She pointed mutely to her son's room and pursed her thick dry lips at the door of the inner court. But Wang Lung stared at her, robust and unbelieving.

"You dream!" he said finally.

She shook her head at this, and, the difficult speech halting on her lips, she said further,

"My lord, come home unexpectedly." And again, after a silence, "It is better to send him away, even to the south." And then she went to the table and took his bowl of tea and felt of it and spilled the cool tea on the brick floor and filled the bowl again from the hot pot, and as she came she went, silent, and left him sitting there agape.

Well, and this woman, she was jealous he said to himself. Well, and he would not trouble about this, with his lad content and reading every day in his own room, and he rose and laughed and put it away from him, laughing at the small thoughts of women.

But when he went in that night to lie beside Lotus and when he turned upon the bed she complained and was petulant and she pushed him away saying,

"It is hot and you stink and I wish you would wash yourself before you come to lie beside me."

She sat up, then, and pushed her hair fretfully back from her face and she shrugged her shoulders when he would have drawn her to him, and she would not yield to his coaxing. Then he lay still and he remembered that she had yielded unwillingly these many nights, and he had thought it her whim and the heavy hot air of departing summer that depressed her, but now the words of O-lan stood out sharply and he rose up roughly and said,

"Well, sleep alone then, and cut my throat if I care!"

He flung himself out of the room and strode into the middle room of his own house and he put two chairs together and stretched himself on them. But he could not sleep and he rose and went out of his gate and he walked among the bamboos beside the house wall, and there he felt the cool night wind upon his hot flesh, and there was the coolness of coming autumn in it.

Then he remembered this, that Lotus had known of his son's desire to go away, and how had she known? And he remembered that of late his son had said nothing of going away but had been content, and why was he content? And Wang Lung said to his heart, fiercely,

"I will see the thing for myself!"

And he watched the dawn come ruddy out of a mist over his land.

When the dawn was come and the sun showed a gold rim over

the edge of the fields, he went in and he ate, and then he went out to oversee his men as his custom was in times of harvest and planting, and he went here and there over his land, and at last he shouted loudly, so that anyone in his house might hear,

"Now I am going to the piece by the moat of the town and I shall not be back early," and he set his face to the town.

But when he had gone half-way and reached as far as the small temple he sat down beside the road on a hillock of grass that was an old grave, now forgotten, and he plucked a grass and twisted it in his fingers and he meditated. Facing him were the small gods and on the surface of his mind he noted how they stared at him and how of old he had been afraid of them, but now he was careless, having become prosperous and in no need of gods, so that he scarcely saw them. Underneath he thought to himself, over and over,

"Shall I go back?"

Then suddenly he remembered the night before when Lotus had pushed him away, and he was angry because of all he had done for her and he said to himself,

"Well I know that she would not have lasted many years more at the tea house, and in my house she is fed and clothed richly."

Then in the strength of his anger he rose and he strode back to his house by another way and he went secretly into his house and stood at the curtain that hung in the door to the inner court. And listening, he heard the murmuring of a man's voice, and it was the voice of his own son.

Now the anger that arose in Wang Lung's heart was an anger he had not known in all his life before, although as things had prospered with him and as men came to call him rich, he had lost his early timidity of a country fellow, and had grown full of small sudden angers, and he was proud even in the town. But this anger now was the anger of one man against another man who steals away the loved woman, and when Wang Lung remembered that the other man was his own son, he was filled with a vomiting sickness.

[208]

He set his teeth then, and he went out and chose a slim, supple bamboo from the grove and he stripped off the branches, except for a cluster of small branches at the top, thin and hard as cord, and he ripped off the leaves. Then he went in softly and suddenly he tore aside the curtain and there was his son, standing in the court, and looking down at Lotus, who sat on a small stool at the edge of the pool. And Lotus was dressed in her peach-colored silk coat, such as he had never seen her dressed in by the light of the morning.

These two talked together, and the woman laughed lightly and looked at the young man from the corner of her eyes, her head turned aside, and they did not hear Wang Lung. He stood and stared at them, his face whitening and his lips lifted back and snarling from his teeth, and his hands tightened about the bamboo. And still the two did not hear him and would not, except that the woman Cuckoo came out and saw him and shrieked and they saw.

Then Wang Lung leaped forward and he fell on his son, lashing him, and although the lad was taller than he, he was stronger from his labor in the fields and from the robustness of his mature body, and he beat the lad until the blood streamed down. When Lotus screamed and dragged at his arm he shook her off, and when she persisted, screaming, he beat her also and he beat her until she fled and he beat the young man until he stooped cowering to the ground, and covered his torn face in his hands.

Then Wang Lung paused and his breath whistled through his parted lips and the sweat poured down his body until he was drenched and he was weak as though with an illness. He threw down his bamboo and he whispered to the boy, panting,

"Now get you to your room and do not dare to come out of it until I am rid of you, lest I kill you!"

And the boy rose without a word and went out.

Wang Lung sat on the stool where Lotus had sat and he put his head in his hands and closed his eyes and his breath came and went in great gasps. No one drew near him and he sat thus alone until he was quieted and his anger gone.

[209]

Then he rose wearily and he went into the room and Lotus lay there on her bed, weeping aloud, and he went up to her and he turned her over, and she lay looking at him and weeping and there on her face lay the swollen purple mark of his whip.

And he said to her with great sadness,

"So must you ever be a whore and go a-whoring after my own sons!"

And she cried more loudly at this and protested,

"No, but I did not, and the lad was lonely and came in and you may ask Cuckoo if he ever came nearer to my bed than you saw him in the court!"

Then she looked at him frightened and piteous and she reached for his hand and drew it across the welt on her face and she whimpered,

"See what you have done to your Lotus—and there is no man in the world except you, and if it is your son, it is only your son, and what is he to me!"

She looked up at him, her pretty eyes swimming in her clear tears, and he groaned because this woman's beauty was more than he could wish and he loved her when he would not. And it seemed to him suddenly that he could not bear to know what had passed between these two and he wished never to know and it was better for him if he did not. So he groaned again and he went out. He passed his son's room and he called without entering,

"Well, and now put your things in the box and tomorrow go south to what you will and do not come home until I send for you."

Then he went on and there was O-lan sitting sewing on some garment of his, and when he passed she said nothing, and if she had heard the beating and the screaming, she made no sign of it. He went on and out to his fields and into the high sun of noon, and he was spent as with the labor of a whole day.

XXV

WHEN the eldest son was gone Wang Lung felt the house was purged of some surcharge of unrest and it was a relief to him. He said to himself that it was a good thing for the young man to be gone, and now he could look to his other children and see what they were, for what with his own troubles and the land which must be planted and harvested in season whatever might happen elsewhere, he hardly knew what he had for children after this eldest son. He decided, moreover, that he would early take the second lad out of school and he would apprentice him to a trade and not wait for the wildness of young manhood to catch him and make him a plague in the house as the older one had been.

Now the second son of Wang Lung was as unlike the elder as two sons in a house may be. Where the elder was tall and big-boned and ruddy faced as men of the north are and like his mother, this second one was short and slight and yellow-skinned, and there was that in him which reminded Wang Lung of his own father, a crafty, sharp, humorous eye, and a turn for malice if the moment came for it. And Wang Lung said,

"Well, and this boy will make a good merchant and I will take him out of school and see if he can be apprenticed in the grain market. It will be a convenient thing to have a son there where I sell my harvests and he can watch the scales and tip the weight a little in my favor."

Therefore he said to Cuckoo one day,

"Now go and tell the father of my eldest son's betrothed that I have something to say to him. And we should at any rate drink a cup of wine together, seeing that we are to be poured into one bowl, his blood and mine."

Cuckoo went, then, and came back saying,

"He will see you when you wish and if you can come to drink wine this noon it is well, and if you wish it he will come here instead."

But Wang Lung did not wish the town merchant to come to his house because he feared he would have to prepare this and that, and so he washed himself and put on his silk coat and he set out across the fields. He went first to the Street of Bridges, as Cuckoo had told him, and there before a gate which bore the name of Liu he stopped. Not that he knew the word himself, but he guessed the gate, two doors to the right of the bridge, and he asked one who passed and the letter was the letter of Liu. It was a respectable gate built plainly of wood, and Wang Lung struck it with the palm of his hand.

Immediately it opened and a woman servant stood there, wiping her wet hands on her apron as she spoke to ask who he was, and when he answered his name, she stared at him, and led him into the first court where the men lived and she took him into a room and bade him seat himself, and she stared at him again, knowing he was the father of the betrothed of the daughter of the house. Then she went out to call her master.

Wang Lung looked about him carefully, and he rose and felt of the stuffs of the curtains in the doorway, and examined the wood of the plain table, and he was pleased, for there was evidence of good living but not of extreme wealth. He did not want a rich daughter-in-law lest she be haughty and disobedient and cry for this and that of food and clothes and turn aside his son's heart from his parents. Then Wang sat down again and waited.

Suddenly there was a heavy step and a stout elderly man entered and Wang Lung rose and bowed and they both bowed, looking secretly at each other, and they liked each other, each respecting the other for what he was, a man of worth and prosperity. Then they seated themselves and they drank of the hot wine which the servant woman poured out for them, and they talked slowly of crops and prices and what the price would be for rice this year if the harvest were good. And at last Wang Lung said,

"Well, and I have come for a thing and if it is not your wish, let us talk of other things. But if you have need for a servant in your great market, there is my second son, and a sharp one he is, but if you have no need of him, let us talk of other things."

Then the merchant said with great good humor,

"And so I have such need of a sharp young man, if he reads and writes."

Wang Lung answered proudly,

"My sons are both good scholars and they can each tell when a letter is wrongly written, and whether the wood or the water radical is right."

"That is well," said Liu. "Let him come when he will and his wages at first are only his food until he learns the business, and then after a year if he do well, he may have a piece of silver at the end of every moon, and at the end of three years three pieces, and after that he is no longer apprentice, but he may rise as he is able in the business. And besides this wage, there is whatever fee he may extract from this buyer and that seller—this I say nothing about if he is able to get it. And because our two families are united, there is no fee of guaranty I will ask of you for his coming."

Wang Lung rose then, well-pleased, and he laughed and said,

"Now we are friends, and have you no son for my second daughter?"

Then the merchant laughed richly, for he was fat and well-fed, and he said,

"I have a second son of ten whom I have not betrothed yet. How old is the girl?"

Wang Lung laughed again and answered,

"She is ten on her next birthday and she is a pretty flower."

Then the two men laughed together and the merchant said,

"Shall we tie ourselves together with a double rope?"

Then Wang Lung said no more, for it was not a thing that could be discussed face to face beyond this. But after he had bowed and gone away well-pleased, he said to himself, "The thing may be done," and he looked at his young daughter when he came home and she was a pretty child and her mother had bound her feet well, so that she moved about with small graceful steps.

But when Wang Lung looked at her thus closely he saw the marks of tears on her cheeks, and her face was a shade too pale and grave for her years, and he drew her to him by her little hand and he said,

"Now why have you wept?"

Then she hung her head and toyed with a button on her coat and said, shy and half-murmuring,

"Because my mother binds a cloth about my feet more tightly every day and I cannot sleep at night."

"I have not heard you weep," he said, wondering.

"No," she said simply, "my mother said I was not to weep aloud because you are too kind and weak for pain and you might say to leave me as I am, and then my husband would not love me even as you do not love her."

This she said as simply as a child recites a tale, and Wang Lung was stabbed at hearing this, that O-lan had told the child he did not love her who was the child's mother, and he said quickly,

"Well, and today I have heard of a pretty husband for you, and we will see if Cuckoo can arrange the matter."

Then the child smiled and dropped her head, suddenly a maid and no more a child. And Wang Lung said to Cuckoo on that same evening when he was in the inner court,

"Go and see if it can be done."

But he slept uneasily beside Lotus that night and he woke and fell to thinking of his life and of how O-lan had been the first woman he had known and how she had been a faithful servant beside him. And he thought of what the child said, and he was sad, because with all her dimness O-lan had seen the truth in him.

[214]

In the near days after this he sent his second son away into the town and he signed the papers for the second girl's betrothal and the dowry was decided upon and the gifts of clothing and jewelry for her marriage day were fixed. Then Wang Lung rested and he said to his heart,

"Well, and now all my children are provided for, and my poor fool can do nothing but sit in the sun with her bit of cloth and the younger boy I will keep for the land and he shall not go to school, since two can read and it is enough."

He was proud because he had three sons and one was a scholar and one a merchant and one a farmer. He was content, then, and he gave over thinking any more about his children. But whether he would or not there came into his mind the thought of the woman who had borne them for him.

For the first time in his years with her Wang Lung began to think about O-lan. Even in the days of her new-coming he had not thought of her for herself and not further than because she was a woman and the first he had known. And it seemed to him that with this thing and that he had been busy and without time to spare, and only now, when his children were settled and his fields cared for and quiet under the coming of winter, and now, when his life with Lotus was regulated and she was submissive to him since he had beat her, now it seemed to him he had time to think of what he would and he thought of O-lan.

He looked at her, not because she was woman this time, and not that she was ugly and gaunt and yellow-skinned. But he looked at her with some strange remorse, and he saw that she had grown thin and her skin was sere and yellow. She had always been a dark woman, her skin ruddy and brown when she worked in the fields. Yet now for many years she had not gone into the fields except perhaps at harvest time, and not then for two years and more, for he disliked her to go, lest men say,

"And does your wife still work on the land and you rich?"

Nevertheless, he had not thought why she had been willing at last to stay in the house and why she moved slowly and more slowly about, and he remembered, now that he thought of it, that in the mornings sometimes he heard her groaning when she rose from her bed and when she stooped to feed the oven, and only when he asked, "Well, and what is it?" did she cease suddenly. So, looking at her and at the strange swelling she had on her body, he was stricken with remorse, although he did not know why, and he argued with himself,

"Well, and it is not my fault if I have not loved her as one loves a concubine, since men do not." And to himself he said for comfort, "I have not beat her and I have given her silver when she asked for it."

But still he could not forget what the child had said and it pricked him, although he did not know why, seeing that, when he came to argue the matter out, he had always been a good husband to her and better than most.

Because he could not be rid of this unease towards her, then, he kept looking at her as she brought in his food or as she moved about, and when she stooped to sweep the brick floor one day after they had eaten, he saw her face turn grey with some inner pain, and she opened her lips and panted softly, and she put her hand to her belly, although still stooping as though to sweep. He asked her sharply,

"What is it?"

But she averted her face and answered meekly,

"It is only the old pain in my vitals."

Then he stared at her and he said to the younger girl,

"Take the broom and sweep, for your mother is ill." And to O-lan he said more kindly than he had spoken to her in many years, "Go in and lie on your bed, and I will bid the girl bring you hot water. Do not get up."

She obeyed him slowly and without answer, and she went in to her room and he heard her dragging about it, and at last she lay down and moaned softly. Then he sat listening to this moaning until he could not bear it, and he rose and went in to the town to ask where a doctor's shop was.

[216]

He found a shop recommended to him by a clerk in the grain market where his second son now was, and he went to it. There the doctor sat idle over a pot of tea. He was an old man with a long grey beard and brass spectacles large as an owl's eyes over his nose, and he wore a dirty grey robe whose long sleeves covered his hands altogether. When Wang Lung told him what his wife's signs were, he pursed his lips and opened a drawer of the table at which he sat, and he took out a bundle wrapped in a black cloth and he said,

"I will come now."

When they came to O-lan's bed she had fallen into a light sleep and the sweat stood like dew on her upper lip and on her forehead, and the old doctor shook his head to see it. He put forth a hand as dried and yellow as an ape's hand and he felt for her pulse, and then after he had held it for a long time, he shook his head again gravely, saying,

"The spleen is enlarged and the liver diseased. There is a rock as large as a man's head in the womb; the stomach is disintegrated. The heart barely moves and doubtless there are worms in it."

At these words Wang Lung's own heart stopped and he was afraid and he shouted out angrily,

"Well, and give her medicine, can you not?"

O-lan opened her eyes as he spoke and looked at them, not understanding and drowsy with pain. Then the old doctor spoke again,

"It is a difficult case. If you do not wish guarantee of recovery, I will ask for fee ten pieces of silver and I will give you a prescription of herbs and a tiger's heart dried in it and the tooth of a dragon, and these boil together and let her drink the broth. But if you wish complete recovery guaranteed, then five hundred pieces of silver."

Now when O-lan heard the words, "five hundred pieces of silver," she came suddenly out of her languor and she said weakly,

"No, for my life is not worth so much. A good piece of land can be bought for so much."

Then when Wang Lung heard her say this all his old remorse smote him and he answered her fiercely,

"I will have no death in my house and I can pay the silver."

Now when the old doctor heard him say, "I can pay the silver," his eyes shone greedily enough, but he knew the penalty of the law if he did not keep his word and the woman died, and so he said, although with regret,

"Nay, and as I look at the color of the whites of her eyes, I see I was mistaken. Five thousand pieces of silver must I have if I guarantee full recovery."

Then Wang Lung looked at the doctor in silence and in sad understanding. He had not so many pieces of silver in the world unless he sold his land, but he knew that even though he sold his land it was no avail, for it was simply that the doctor said, "The woman will die."

He went out with the doctor, therefore, and he paid him the ten pieces of silver, and when he was gone Wang Lung went into the dark kitchen where O-lan had lived for the most part, and where, now that she was not there, none would see him, and he turned his face to the blackened wall, and he wept.

XXVI

BUT there was no sudden dying of life in O-lan's body. She was scarcely past the middle of her span of years, and her life would not easily pass from her body, so that she lay dying on her bed for many months. All through the long months of winter she lay dying and upon her bed, and for the first time Wang Lung and his children knew what she had been in the house, and how she made comfort for them all and they had not known it.

It seemed now that none knew how to light the grass and keep it burning in the oven, and none knew how to turn a fish in the cauldron without breaking it or burning one side black before the other side was cooked, and none knew whether sesame oil or bean were right for frying this vegetable or that. The filth of the crumbs and dropped food lay under the table and none swept it unless Wang Lung grew impatient with the smell of it and called in a dog from the court to lick it up or shouted at the younger girl to scrape it up and throw it out.

And the youngest lad did this and that to fill his mother's place with the old man his grandfather, who was helpless as a little child now, and Wang Lung could not make the old man understand what had happened that O-lan no longer came to bring him tea and hot water and to help him lie down and stand up, and he was peevish because he called her and she did not come, and he threw his bowl of tea on the ground like a wilful child. At last Wang Lung led him in to O-lan's room and showed him the bed where she lay, and the old man stared out of his filmed and half blind eyes, and he mumbled and wept because he saw dimly that something was wrong.

Only the poor fool knew nothing, and only she smiled and twisted her bit of cloth as she smiled. Yet one had to think of her to bring her into sleep at night and to feed her and to set her in the sun in the day and to lead her in if it rained. All this one of them had to remember. But even Wang Lung himself forgot, and once they left her outside through a whole night, and the next morning the poor wretch was shivering and crying in the early dawn, and Wang Lung was angry and cursed his son and daughter that they had forgotten the poor fool who was their sister. Then he saw that they were but children trying to take their mother's place and not able to do it, and he forbore and after that he saw to the poor fool

[219]

himself night and morning. If it rained or snowed or a bitter wind blew he led her in and he let her sit among the warm ashes that dropped from the kitchen stove.

All during the dark winter months when O-lan lay dying Wang Lung paid no heed to the land. He turned over the winter's work and the men to the government of Ching, and Ching labored faithfully, and night and morning he came to the door of the room where O-lan lay and he asked twice each day thus in his piping whisper how she did. At last Wang Lung could not bear it because every day and every night he could only say,

"Today she drank a little soup from a fowl," or "today she ate a little thin gruel of rice."

So he commanded Ching to ask no more but to do the work well, and it would be enough.

All during the cold dark winter Wang Lung sat often beside O-lan's bed, and if she were cold he lit an earthen pot of charcoal and set it beside her bed for warmth, and she murmured each time faintly,

"It is too expensive."

At last one day when she said this he could not bear it and he burst forth,

"This I cannot bear! I would sell all my land if it could heal you."

She smiled at this and said in gasps, whispering,

"No, and I would not—let you. For I must die—sometime anyway. But the land is there after me."

But he would not talk of her death and he rose and went out when she spoke of it.

Nevertheless because he knew she must die and it was his duty, he went one day into the town to a coffin-maker's shop and he looked at every coffin that stood there ready to be bought, and he chose a good black one made from heavy and hard wood. Then the carpenter, who waited for him to choose, said cunningly,

"If you take two, the price is a third off for the two, and why do you not buy one for yourself and know you are provided?"

"No, for my sons can do it for me," answered Wang Lung, and then he thought of his own father and he had not yet a coffin for the old man and he was struck with the thought and he said again, "But there is my old father and he will die one day soon, weak as he is on his two legs and deaf and half blind, and so I will take the two."

And the man promised to paint the coffins again a good black and send them to Wang Lung's house. So Wang Lung told O-lan what he had done, and she was pleased that he had done it for her, and had provided well for her death.

Thus he sat by her many hours of the day, and they did not talk much for she was faint, and besides there had never been talk between them. Often she forgot where she was as he sat there in stillness and silence, and sometimes she murmured of her childhood, and for the first time Wang Lung saw into her heart, although even now only through such brief words as these,

"I will bring the meats to the door only—and well I know I am ugly and cannot appear before the great lord—" And again she said, panting, "Do not beat me—I will never eat of the dish again —" And she said over and over, "My father—my mother—my father—my mother—" and again and again, "Well I know I am ugly and cannot be loved—"

When she said this Wang Lung could not bear it and he took her hand and he soothed it, a big hard hand, stiff as though it were dead already. And he wondered and grieved at himself most of all because what she said was true, and even when he took her hand, desiring truly that she feel his tenderness towards her, he was ashamed because he could feel no tenderness, no melting of the heart such as Lotus could win from him with a pout of her lips. When he took this stiff dying hand he did not love it, and even his pity was spoiled with repulsion towards it.

But because of this, he was more kind to her and he bought her

[221]

special food and delicate soups made of white fish and the hearts of young cabbages. Moreover, he could not take his pleasure of Lotus, for when he went into her to distract his mind from its despair over this long agony of dying, he could not forget O-lan, and even as he held Lotus, he loosed her, because of O-lan.

There were times when O-lan woke to herself and to what was about her and once she called for Cuckoo, and when in great astonishment Wang Lung summoned the woman, O-lan raised herself trembling upon her arm, and she said plainly enough,

"You may have lived in the courts of the Old Lord, and you were accounted beautiful, but I have been a man's wife and I have borne him sons, and you are still slave."

When Cuckoo would have answered angrily to this, Wang Lung besought her and led her out, saying,

"That one does not know what words mean, now."

When he went back into the room, O-lan still leaned her head upon her arm and she said to him,

"After I am dead that one nor her mistress neither is to come into my room or touch my things, and if they do, I will send my spirit back for a curse." Then she fell into her fitful sleep, and her head dropped upon the pillow.

But one day before the new year broke, she was suddenly better, as a candle flickers brightly at its end, and she was herself as she had not been and she sat up in bed and twisted her hair for herself, and she asked for tea to drink, and when Wang Lung came she said,

"Now the New Year is coming and there are no cakes and no meats ready, and I have thought of a thing. I will not have that slave in my kitchen, but I would have you send for my daughter-in-law, who is betrothed to our eldest son. I have not seen her yet, but when she comes I will tell her what to do."

Wang Lung was pleased at her strength, although he cared nothing for festivities on this year, and he sent Cuckoo in to beseech Liu, the grain merchant, seeing how sad the case was. And after a while Liu was willing when he heard that O-lan would not live the winter out, perhaps, and after all the girl was sixteen and older than some who go to their husband's houses.

But because of O-lan there were no feastings. The maiden came quietly in a sedan chair, except that her mother and an old servant came with her, and her mother went back when she had delivered the maiden to O-lan, but the servant remained for the maiden's use.

Now the children were moved from the room where they had slept and that room was given to the new daughter-in-law, and all was arranged as it should be. Wang Lung did not speak with the maiden, since it was not fitting, but he inclined his head gravely when she bowed, and he was pleased with her, for she knew her duty and she moved about the house quietly with her eyes downcast. Moreover, she was a goodly maid, fair enough, but not too fair so as to be vain over it. She was careful and correct in all her behavior, and she went into O-lan's room and tended her, and this eased Wang Lung of his pain for his wife, because now there was a woman about her bed, and O-lan was very content.

O-lan was content for three days and more and then she thought of another thing and she said to Wang Lung when he came in the morning to see how she did through the night,

"There is another thing before I can die."

To this he replied angrily,

"You cannot speak of dying and please me!"

She smiled slowly then, the same slow smile that ended before it reached her eyes, and she answered,

"Die I must, for I feel it in my vitals waiting, but I will not die before my eldest son comes home and before he weds this good maid who is my daughter-in-law, and well she serves me, holding the hot water basin steadily and knowing when to bathe my face when I sweat in pain. Now I want my son to come home, because I must die, and I want him to wed this maid first, so that I may die easily, knowing your grandson is stirred into life and a great grandson for the old one."

Now these were many words for her at any time, even in health, and she said them more sturdily than she had said anything for many moons, and Wang Lung was cheered at the strength in her voice and with what vigor she desired this, and he would not cross her, although he would have liked more time for a great wedding for his eldest son. He only said heartily to her therefore,

"Well, and we will do this thing, and today I will send a man south and he shall search for my son and bring him home to be wed. And then you must promise me that you will gather your strength again and give over dying and grow well, for the house is like a cave for beasts without you."

This he said to please her and it pleased her, although she did not speak again, but lay back and closed her eyes, smiling a little.

Wang Lung despatched the man, therefore, and told him,

"Tell your young lord that his mother is dying and her spirit cannot rest in ease until she sees him and sees him wed, and if he values me and his mother and his home, he must come back before he draws another breath, for on the third day from now I will have feasts prepared and guests invited and he will be wed."

And as Wang Lung said, so he did. He bade Cuckoo provide a feast as best she could, and she was to call in cooks from the tea shop in town to help her, and he poured silver into her hands and he said,

"Do as it would have been done in the great house at such an hour, and there is more silver than this."

Then he went into the village and invited guests, men and women, everyone whom he knew, and he went into the town and invited whom he knew at the tea shops and at the grain markets and everyone whom he knew. And he said to his uncle,

"Ask whom you will for my son's marriage, any of your friends or any of your son's friends."

This he said because he remembered always who his uncle was and Wang Lung was courteous to his uncle and treated him as an honored guest, and so he had done from the hour when he knew who his uncle was.

[224]

On the night of the day before his marriage, Wang Lung's eldest son came home, and he came striding into the room and Wang Lung forgot all that the young man had troubled him when he was at home. For two years and more had passed since he saw this son of his, and here he was and no longer a lad, but a tall man and a goodly one, with a great square body and high ruddy cheeks and short black hair, shining and oiled. And he wore a long dark red gown of satin such as one finds in the shops of the south, and a short black velvet jacket without sleeves, and Wang Lung's heart burst with pride to see his son, and he forgot everything except this, his goodly son, and he led him to his mother.

Then the young man sat beside his mother's bed and the tears stood in his eyes to see her thus, but he would not say anything except cheerful things such as these, "You look twice as well as they said and years away from death."

But O-lan said simply,

"I will see you wed and then I must die."

Now the maid who was to be wed must not of course be seen by the young man and Lotus took her into the inner court to prepare her for marriage, and none could do this better than Lotus and Cuckoo and the wife of Wang Lung's uncle. These three took the maid and on the morning of her wedding day they washed her clean from head to foot, and bound her feet freshly with new white cloths under her new stockings, and Lotus rubbed into her flesh some fragrant almond oil of her own. Then they dressed her in garments she had brought from her home; white flowered silk next her sweet virgin flesh and then a light coat of sheep's wool of the finest and most curling kind, and then the red satin garments of marriage. And they rubbed lime upon her forehead and with a string tied skilfully they pulled out the hairs of her virginity, the fringe over her brow, and they made her forehead high and smooth and square for her new estate. Then they painted her with powder and with red paint, and with a brush they drew out in two long slender lines her eyebrows, and they set upon her head the bride's crown and the beaded veil, and upon her small feet they put shoes, embroidered, and they painted her fingertips and scented the palms of her hands, and thus they prepared her for marriage. To everything the maid was acquiescent, but reluctant and shy as was proper and correct for her.

Then Wang Lung and his uncle and his father and the guests waited in the middle room and the maid came in supported by her own slave and by the wife of Wang Lung's uncle, and she came in modestly and correctly with her head bowed and she walked as though she were unwilling to wed a man and must be supported to it. This showed her great modesty and Wang Lung was pleased and said to himself that she was a proper maid.

After this Wang Lung's eldest son came in dressed as he had been in his red robe and his black jacket and his hair was smooth and his face fresh shaven. Behind him came his two brothers, and Wang Lung, seeing them, was fit to burst with pride at this procession of his goodly sons, who were to continue after him the life of his body. Now the old man, who had not understood what was happening at all and could hear only the fragments of what was shouted to him, now suddenly he understood, and he cackled out with cracked laughter and he said over and over in his piping old voice,

"There is a marriage and a marriage is children again and grandchildren!"

And he laughed so heartily that the guests all laughed to see his mirth and Wang Lung thought to himself that if only O-lan had been up from her bed it would have been a merry day.

All this time Wang Lung looked secretly and sharply at his son to see if he glanced at the maid, and the young man did glance secretly and from the corner of his eyes, but it was enough, for he grew pleased and merry in his ways and Wang said proudly to himself,

"Well, and I have chosen one he likes for him."

Then the young man and the maid together bowed to the old man and to Wang Lung, and then they went into the room where O-lan lay, and she had caused herself to be dressed in her good black coat and she sat up when they came in and on her face there burned two fiery spots of red, which Wang Lung mistook for health, so that he said loudly, "Now she will be well, yet!"

And the two young persons went up and bowed to her and she patted the bed and said,

"Sit here and drink the wine and eat the rice of your marriage, for I would see it all and this will be your bed of marriage since I am soon to be finished with it and carried away."

Now none would answer her when she spoke thus but the two sat down side by side, shy and in silence of each other, and the wife of Wang Lung's uncle came in fat and important with the occasion, bearing two bowls of hot wine, and the two drank separately, and then mingled the wine of the two bowls and drank again, thus signifying that the two were now one, and they ate rice and mingled the rice and this signified that their life was now one, and thus they were wed. Then they bowed again to O-lan and to Wang Lung and then they went out and together they bowed to the assembled guests.

Then the feasting began and the rooms and the courts were filled with tables and with the smell of cooking and with the sound of laughter, for the guests came from far and wide, those whom Wang Lung had invited and with them many whom Wang Lung had never seen, since it was known he was a rich man and food would never be missed or counted in his house at such a time. And Cuckoo had brought cooks from the town to prepare the feast, for there were to be many delicacies such as cannot be prepared in a farmer's kitchen and the town cooks came bearing great baskets of food ready cooked and only to be heated, and they made much of themselves and flourished their grimy aprons and bustled here and there in their zeal. And everyone ate more and yet more and drank all they were able to hold, and they were all very merry.

O-lan would have all the doors open and the curtains drawn so that she could hear the noise and the laughter and could smell the food, and she said again and again to Wang Lung, who came in often to see how she did,

"And has everyone wine? And is the sweet rice dish in the middle of the feast very hot and have they put full measure of lard and sugar into it and the eight fruits?"

When he assured her that everything was as she wished it, she was content and lay listening.

Then it was over and the guests were gone and night came. And with the silence over the house and with the ebbing of merriment strength passed from O-lan and she grew weary and faint and she called to her the two who had been wed that day and she said,

"Now I am content and this thing in me may do as it will. My son, look to your father and your grandfather, and my daughter, look to your husband and your husband's father and his grandfather and the poor fool in the court, there is she. And you have no duty to any other."

This last she said, meaning Lotus, to whom she had never spoken. Then she seemed to fall into a fitful sleep, although they waited for her to speak further, and once more she roused herself to speak. Yet when she spoke it was as though she did not know they were there or indeed where she was, for she said, muttering and turning her head this way and that and her eyes closed,

"Well, and if I am ugly, still I have borne a son; although I was but a slave there is a son in my house." And again she said, suddenly, "How can that one feed him and care for him as I do? Beauty will not bear a man sons!"

And she forgot them all and lay muttering. Then Wang Lung motioned to them to go away, and he sat beside her while she slept and woke, and he looked at her. And he hated himself because even as she lay dying he saw how wide and ghastly her purpled lips drew back from her teeth. Then as he looked she opened her eyes and it seemed there was some strange mist over them, for she stared at him full and stared again, wondering and fixing her eyes on him, as though she wondered who he was. Suddenly her head dropped off the round pillow where it lay, and she shuddered and was dead.

*   *   *

Once she lay dead it seemed to Wang Lung that he could not bear to be near O-lan, and he called his uncle's wife to wash the body for burial, and when it was finished he would not go in again, but he allowed his uncle's wife and his eldest son and his daughter-in-law to lift the body from the bed and set it into the great coffin he had bought. But to comfort himself he busied himself in going to the town and calling men to seal the coffin according to custom and he went and found a geomancer and asked him for a lucky day for burials. He found a good day three months hence and it was the first good day the geomancer could find, so Wang Lung paid the man and went to the temple in the town and he bargained with the abbot there and rented a space for a coffin for three months, and there was O-lan's coffin brought to rest until the day of burial, for it seemed to Wang Lung he could not bear to have it under his eyes in the house.

Then Wang Lung was scrupulous to do all that should be done for the one dead, so he caused mourning to be made for himself and for his children, and their shoes were made of coarse white cloth, which is the color of mourning, and about their ankles they bound bands of white cloth, and the women in the house bound their hair with white cord.

After this Wang Lung could not bear to sleep in the room where O-lan had died and he took his possessions and moved altogether into the inner court where Lotus lived and he said to his eldest son,

"Go with your wife into that room where your mother lived and died, who conceived and bore you, and beget there your own sons."

So the two moved into it and were content.

Then as though death could not easily leave the house where it had come once, the old man, Wang Lung's father, who had been distraught ever since he saw them putting the stiff dead body of O-lan into the coffin, lay down on his bed one night for sleeping, and when the second daughter came in to him in the morning to bring him his tea, there he lay on his bed, his scattered old beard thrust up into the air, and his head thrown back in death.

She cried out at the sight and ran crying to her father and Wang Lung came in and found the old man so; his light, stiff old body was dry and cold and thin as a gnarled pine tree and he had died hours before, perhaps as soon as he had laid himself upon the bed. Then Wang Lung washed the old man himself and he laid him gently in the coffin he had bought for him and he had it sealed and he said,

"On the same day we will bury these two dead from our house and I will take a good piece of my hill land and we will bury them there together and when I die I will be laid there also."

So he did what he said he would do. When he had sealed the old man's coffin he set it upon two benches in the middle room and there it stood until the appointed day came. And it seemed to Wang Lung that it was a comfort to the old man to be there, even dead, and he felt near to his father in the coffin, for Wang Lung grieved for his father, but not unto death, because his father was very old and full of years, and for many years had been but half alive.

Then on the day appointed by the geomancer in the full of the spring of the year Wang Lung called priests from the Taoist temple and they came dressed in their yellow robes and their long hair knotted on their crowns, and he called priests from the Buddhist temples and they came in their long grey robes, their heads shaven and set with the nine sacred scars, and these priests beat drums and chanted the whole night through for the two who were dead. And whenever they stopped their chanting Wang Lung poured silver into their hands and they took breath again and chanted and did not cease until dawn rose.

Now Wang Lung had chosen a good place in his fields under a date tree upon a hill to set the graves, and Ching had the graves dug and ready and a wall of earth made about the graves, and there was space within the walls for the body of Wang Lung and for each of his sons and their wives, and there was space for sons'

sons, also. This land Wang Lung did not begrudge, even though it was high land and good for wheat, because it was a sign of the establishment of his family upon their own land. Dead and alive they would rest upon their own land.

Then on the appointed day after the priests had finished the night of chanting, Wang Lung dressed himself in a robe of white sackcloth and he gave a robe like it to his uncle and his uncle's son, and to his own sons each a robe, and to his son's wife and to his own two daughters. He called chairs from the town to carry them, for it was not meet that they walk to the place of burial as though he were a poor man and a common fellow. So for the first time he rode on men's shoulders and behind the coffin where O-lan was. But behind his father's coffin his uncle rode first. Even Lotus, who in O-lan's lifetime could not appear before her, now that O-lan was dead, she came riding in a chair in order that before others she might appear dutiful to the first wife of her husband. So for his uncle's wife and for his uncle's son Wang Lung hired chairs also and for all of them he had robes of sackcloth, and even for the poor fool he made a robe and hired a chair and put her in it, although she was sorely bewildered and laughed shrilly when there should have been only weeping.

Then mourning and weeping loudly they went to the graves, the laborers and Ching following and walking and wearing white shoes. And Wang Lung stood beside the two graves. He had caused the coffin of O-lan to be brought from the temple and it was put on the ground to await the old man's burial first. And Wang Lung stood and watched and his grief was hard and dry, and he would not cry out loud as others did, for there were no tears in his eyes, because it seemed to him that what had come about was come about, and there was nothing to be done more than he had done.

But when the earth was covered over and the graves smoothed, he turned away silently and he sent away the chair and he walked home alone with himself. And out of his heaviness there stood out strangely but one clear thought and it was a pain to him, and it was this, that he wished he had not taken the two pearls from O-lan that day when she was washing his clothes at the pool, and he would never bear to see Lotus put them in her ears again.

Thus, thinking heavily, he went on alone and he said to himself,

"There in that land of mine is buried the first good half of my life and more. It is as though half of me were buried there, and now it is a different life in my house."

And suddenly he wept a little, and he dried his eyes with the back of his hand, as a child does.

XXVII

DURING all this time Wang Lung had scarcely thought of what the harvests were, so bgusy had he been with the wedding feasts and funerals in his house, but one day Ching came to him and he said,

"Now that the joy and sorrow are over, I have that to tell you about the land."

"Say on, then," Wang answered. "I have scarcely thought whether I had land or not these days except to bury my dead in."

Ching waited in silence for a few minutes in respect to Wang Lung when he spoke thus, and then he said softly,

"Now may Heaven avert it, but it looks as though there would be such a flood this year as never was, for the water is swelling up over the land, although it is not summer yet, and too early for it to come like this."

But Wang Lung said stoutly,

"I have never had any good from that old man in heaven yet.

Incense or no incense, he is the same in evil. Let us go and see the land." And as he spoke he rose.

Now Ching was a fearful and timid man and however bad the times were he did not dare as Wang Lung did to exclaim against Heaven. He only said "Heaven wills it," and he accepted flood and drought with meekness. Not so Wang Lung. He went out on his land, on this piece and that, and he saw it was as Ching said. All those pieces along the moat, along the waterways, which he had bought from the Old Lord of the House of Hwang, were wet and mucky from the full water oozing up from the bottom, so that the good wheat on this land had turned sickly and yellow.

The moat itself was like a lake and the canals were rivers, swift and curling in small eddies and whirlpools, and even a fool could see that with summer rains not yet come, there would be that year a mighty flood and men and women and children starving again. Then Wang Lung ran hastily here and there over his land and Ching came silently as a shadow behind him, and they estimated together which land could be planted to rice and which land before the young rice could be put on it would already be under water. And looking at the canals brimming already to the edge of their banks, Wang Lung cursed and said,

"Now that old man in heaven will enjoy himself, for he will look down and see people drowned and starving and that is what the accursed one likes."

This he said loudly and angrily so that Ching shivered and said,

"Even so, he is greater than any one of us and do not talk so, my master."

But since he was rich Wang Lung was careless, and he was as angry as he liked and he muttered as he walked homeward to think of the water swelling up over his land and over his good crops.

Then it all came to pass as Wang Lung had foreseen. The river to the north burst its dykes, its furthermost dykes first, and when men saw what had happened, they hurried from this place to that to collect money to mend it, and every man gave as he was able, for it was to the interest of each to keep the river within its bounds. The money they entrusted, then, to the magistrate in the district, a man new and just come. Now this magistrate was a poor man and had not seen so much money in his lifetime before, being only newly risen to his position through the bounty of his father, who had put all the money he had and could borrow to buy this place for his son, so that from it the family might acquire some wealth. When the river burst again the people went howling and clamoring to this magistrate's house, because he had not done what he promised and mended the dykes, and he ran and hid himself because the money he had spent in his own house, even three thousand pieces of silver. And the common people burst into his house howling and demanding his life for what he had done, and when he saw he would be killed he ran and jumped into the water and drowned himself, and thus the people were appeased.

But still the money was gone, and the river burst yet another dyke and another before it was content with the space it had for itself, and then it wore away these walls of earth until none could tell where a dyke had been in that whole country and the river swelled and rolled like a sea over all the good farming land, and the wheat and the young rice were at the bottom of the sea.

One by one the villages were made into islands and men watched the water rising and when it came within two feet of their doorways they bound their tables and beds together and put the doors of their houses upon them for rafts, and they piled what they could of their bedding and their clothes and their women and children on these rafts. And the water rose into the earthen houses and softened the walls and burst them apart and they melted down into the water and were as if they had never been. And then as if water on earth drew water from heaven it rained as though the earth were in drought. Day after day it rained.

Wang Lung sat in his doorway and looked out over the waters that were yet far enough from his house that was built on a high wide hill. But he saw the waters covering his land and he watched lest it cover the new made graves, but it did not, although the waves of the yellow clay-laden water lapped about the dead hungrily.

There were no harvests of any kind that year and everywhere people starved and were hungry and were angry at what had befallen them yet again. Some went south, and some who were bold and angry and cared nothing for what they did joined the robber bands that flourished everywhere in the countryside. These even tried to beleaguer the town so that the townspeople locked the gates of the wall continually except for one small gate called the western water gate, and this was watched by soldiers and locked at night also. And besides those who robbed and those who went south to work and to beg, even as Wang Lung had once gone with his old father and his wife and children, there were others who were old and tired and timid, and who had no sons, like Ching, and these stayed and starved and ate grass and what leaves they could find on high places and many died upon the land and water.

Then Wang Lung saw that a famine such as he had never seen was upon the land, for the water did not recede in time to plant the wheat for winter and there could be no harvest then the next year. And he looked well to his own house and to the spending of money and food, and he quarreled heartily with Cuckoo because for a long time she would still buy meat every day in the town, and he was glad at last, since there must be flood, that the water crept between his house and the town so that she could no longer go to market when she would, for he would not allow the boats to be put forth except when he said, and Ching listened to him and not to Cuckoo, for all her sharpness of tongue.

Wang Lung allowed nothing to be bought and sold after the winter came except what he said, and he husbanded carefully all that they had. Every day he gave out to his daughter-in-law what food was needed in the house for that day, and to Ching he gave out what the laborers should have, although it hurt him to feed idle men, and it hurt him so greatly that at last when winter cold came and the water froze over, he bade the men be gone to the south to beg and to labor until the spring came, when they might return to him. Only to Lotus he gave secretly sugar and oil, because she was not accustomed to hardship. Even on the New Year they did eat but a fish they caught themselves in the lake and a pig they killed from the farm.

Now Wang Lung was not so poor as he wished to seem, for he had good silver hidden away in the walls where his son slept with his wife, though his son and daughter-in-law did not know it, and he had good silver hidden in a jar at the bottom of the lake under his nearest field, and he had some hidden among the roots of the bamboos, and he had grains from the year before which he had not sold at market, and there was no danger of starvation in his house.

But all around him there were people starving, and he remembered the cries of the starving at the gate of the great house once when he passed, and he knew that there were many who hated him well because he had still that which he could eat and feed to his children, and so he kept his gates barred and he let none in whom he did not know. Yet he knew very well that even this could not have saved him in these times of robbers and lawlessness if it had not been for his uncle. Well did Wang Lung know that if it had not been for his uncle's power he would have been robbed and sacked for his food and for his money and for the women in his house. So he was courteous to his uncle and to his uncle's son and to his uncle's wife and the three were like guests in his house and they drank tea before others and dipped first with their chopsticks into the bowls at mealtime.

Now these three saw well enough that Wang Lung was afraid of them and they grew haughty and demanded this and that and complained of what they ate and drank. And especially did the woman complain, for she missed the delicacies she had eaten in the inner courts and she complained to her husband and the three of them complained to Wang Lung.

Now Wang Lung saw that although his uncle himself grew old and lazy and careless and would not have troubled to complain if he had been let alone, yet the young man, his son, and his wife

[236]

goaded him, and one day when Wang Lung stood at the gate he heard these two urging the old man,

"Well, and he has money and food, and let us demand silver of him." And the woman said, "We shall never have such a hold as this again, for he knows that if you were not his uncle and the brother of his father he would be robbed and sacked and his house left empty and a ruin, since you stand next to the head of the Redbeards."

Wang Lung standing there secretly and hearing this grew so angry that his skin was like to burst on him, but he was silent with great effort and he tried to plan what he could do with these three, but he could think of nothing to do. When, therefore, his uncle came to him next day saying, "My good nephew, give me a hand-ful of silver to buy me a pipe and a bit of smoke and my woman is ragged and needs a new coat," he could say nothing but he handed the old man the five pieces of silver from his girdle, although he gnashed his teeth secretly, and it seemed to him that never in the old days when silver was rare with him had it gone from him so unwillingly.

Then before two days were passed his uncle was at him again and again for silver and Wang Lung shouted at last,

"Well, and shall we all starve soon?"

And his uncle laughed and said carelessly,

"You are under a good heaven. There are men less rich than you who hang from the burnt rafters of their houses."

When Wang Lung heard this, cold sweat broke out on him and he gave the silver without a word. And so, although they went without meat in the house, these three must eat meat, and although Wang Lung himself scarcely tasted tobacco, his uncle puffed un-ceasingly at his pipe.

Now Wang Lung's eldest son had been engrossed in his mar-riage and he scarcely saw what happened except that he guarded his wife jealously from the gaze of his cousin so that now these two were no longer friends but enemies. Wang Lung's son scarcely let his wife stir from their room except in the evenings when the other man was gone with his father and during the day he made her stay shut in the room. But when he saw these three doing as they would with his father he grew angry, for he was of a quick temper, and he said,

"If you care more for these three tigers than you do for your son and his wife, the mother of your grandsons, it is a strange thing and we had better set up our house elsewhere."

Wang Lung told him plainly then what he had told no one,

"I hate these three worse than my life and if I could think of a way I would do it. But your uncle is lord of a horde of wild robbers, and if I feed him and coddle him we are safe, and no one can show anger toward them."

Now when the eldest son heard this he stared until his eyes hung out of his head, but when he had thought of it for a while he was more angry than ever and he said,

"How is this for a way? Let us push them all into the water one night. Ching can push the woman for she is fat and soft and helpless, and I will push the young one my cousin, whom I hate enough for he is always peeping at my wife, and you can push the man."

But Wang Lung could not kill; although he would rather have killed his uncle than his ox, he could not kill even when he hated and he said,

"No, and even if I could do this thing, to push my father's brother into the water I would not, for if the other robbers heard of it what should we do, and if he lives we are safe, and if he is gone we are become as other people who have a little and so are in danger in such times as these."

Then the two of them fell silent, each thinking heavily what to do, and the young man saw that his father was right and death was too easy for the trouble and that there must be another way. And Wang Lung spoke aloud at last, musing,

"If there were a way that we could keep them here but make

them harmless and undesiring what a thing it would be, but there is no such magic as this!"

Then the young man struck his two hands together and cried out,

"Well, and you have told me what to do! Let us buy them opium to enjoy, and more opium, and let them have their will of it as rich people do. I will seem to be friends with my cousin again and I will entice him away to the tea house in the town where one can smoke and we can buy it for my uncle and his wife."

But Wang Lung, since he had not thought of the thing first himself, was doubtful.

"It will cost a great deal," he said slowly, "for opium is as dear as jade."

"It is dearer than jade to have them at us like this," the young man argued, "and to endure besides their haughtiness and the young man peeping at my wife."

But Wang Lung would not at once consent, for it was not so easy a thing to do, and it would cost a good bag of silver to do it.

It is doubtful whether the thing would ever have been done and they would have gone as they were until the waters chose to recede had not a thing happened.

This thing was that the son of Wang Lung's uncle cast his eyes upon the second daughter of Wang Lung, who was his cousin and by blood the same as his sister. Now the second daughter of Wang Lung was an exceedingly pretty girl, and she looked like the second son who was a merchant, but with her smallness and lightness, she had not his yellow skin. Her skin was fair and pale as almond flowers and she had a little low nose and thin red lips and her feet were small.

Her cousin laid hold of her one night when she passed alone through the court from the kitchen. He laid hold of her roughly and he pressed his hand into her bosom and she screamed out, and Wang Lung ran out and beat the man about the head, but he was like a dog with a piece of stolen meat that he would not drop, so

[239]

that Wang Lung had to tear his daughter away. Then the man laughed thickly and he said,

"It is only play and is she not my sister? Can a man do any evil with his sister?" But his eyes glittered with lust as he spoke and Wang Lung muttered and pulled the girl away and sent her into her own room.

And Wang Lung told his son that night what had come about, and the young man was grave and he said,

"We must send the maid into the town to the home of her betrothed; even if the merchant Liu says it is a year too evil for wedding we must send her, lest we cannot keep her virgin with this hot tiger in the house."

So Wang Lung did. He went the next day into the town and to the house of the merchant and he said,

"My daughter is thirteen years old and no longer a child and she is fit for marriage."

But Liu was hesitant and he said,

"I have not enough profit this year to begin a family in my house."

Now Wang Lung was ashamed to say, "There is the son of my uncle in the house and he is a tiger," so he said only,

"I would not have the care of this maid upon me, because her mother is dead and she is pretty and is of an age to conceive, and my house is large and full of this and that, and I cannot watch her every hour. Since she is to be your family, let her virginity be guarded here, and let her be wed soon or late as you like."

Then the merchant, being a lenient and kindly man, replied,

"Well, and if this is how it is, let the maid come and I will speak to my son's mother, and she can come and be safe here in the courts with her mother-in-law, and after the next harvest or so, she can be wed."

Thus the matter was settled and Wang Lung was well content, and he went away.

But on his way back to the gate in the wall, where Ching held a boat waiting for him, Wang Lung passed a shop where tobacco and opium are sold, and he went in to buy himself a little shredded tobacco to put in his water pipe in the evenings, and as the clerk had it on the scales, he said half unwillingly to the man,

"And how much is your opium if you have it?"

And the clerk said,

"It is not lawful in these days to sell it over the counter, and we do not sell it so, but if you wish to buy it and have the silver, it is weighed out in the room behind this, an ounce for a silver piece."

Then Wang Lung would not think further what he did, but he said quickly,

"I will take six ounces of it."

XXVIII

THEN after the second daughter was sent away and Wang Lung was free of his anxiety about her, he said to his uncle one day,

"Since you are my father's brother, here is a little better tobacco for you."

And he opened the jar of opium and the stuff was sticky and sweet smelling and Wang Lung's uncle took it and smelled of it, and he laughed and was pleased and he said,

"Well now, I have smoked it a little but not often before this, for it is too dear, but I like it well enough."

And Wang Lung answered him, pretending to be careless,

"It is only a little I bought once for my father when he grew old and could not sleep at night and I found it today unused and I thought, 'There is my father's brother, and why should he not have it before me, who am younger and do not need it yet?' Take it then, and smoke it when you wish or when you have a little pain."

Then Wang Lung's uncle took it greedily, for it was sweet to smell and a thing that only rich men used, and he took it and bought a pipe and he smoked the opium, lying all day upon his bed to do it. And Wang Lung saw to it that there were pipes bought and left here and there and he pretended to smoke himself, but he only took a pipe to his room and left it there cold. His two sons in the house and Lotus he would not allow to touch the opium, saying as his excuse that it was too dear, but he urged it upon his uncle and upon his uncle's wife and son, and the courts were filled with the sweetish smell of the smoke, and the silver for this Wang Lung did not begrudge because it bought him peace.

Now as the winter wore away and the waters began to recede so that Wang Lung could walk abroad over his land it happened one day that his eldest son followed him and said to him proudly,

"There will soon be another mouth in the house and it will be the mouth of your grandson."

Then Wang Lung, when he heard this, turned himself about and he laughed and he rubbed his hands together and said,

"Here is a good day, indeed!"

And he laughed again, and went to find Ching and tell him to go to the town to buy fish and good food and he sent it in to his son's wife and said,

"Eat, make strong the body of my grandson."

All during the spring Wang Lung had the knowledge of this birth to come for his comfort. And when he was busy about other things he thought of it, and when he was troubled he thought of it and it was a comfort to him.

And as the spring grew into summer, the people who had gone away from the floods came back again, one by one and group by group, spent and weary with the winter and glad to be back, although where their houses had been there was nothing now but the yellow mud of the water-soaked land. But out of this mud houses could be fashioned again, and mats bought to roof them, and many

[242]

came to Wang Lung to borrow money, and he loaned it at high interest, seeing how greatly it was in demand, and the security he always said must be land. And with the money they borrowed they planted seed upon the earth that was fat with the richness of the dried water, and when they needed oxen and seed and plows and when they could borrow no more money, some sold land and part of their fields that they might plant what was left. And of these Wang Lung bought land and much land, and he bought it cheaply, since money men must have.

But there were some who would not sell their land, and when they had nothing wherewith to buy seed and plow and oxen, they sold their daughters, and there were those who came to Wang Lung to sell, because it was known he was rich and powerful and a man of good heart.

And he, thinking constantly of the child to come and of others to come from his sons when they were all wed, bought five slaves, two about twelve years of age with big feet and strong bodies, and two younger to wait upon them all and fetch and carry, and one to wait on the person of Lotus, for Cuckoo grew old and since the second girl was gone there had been none other to work in the house. And the five he bought in one day, for he was a man rich enough to do quickly what he decided upon.

Then one day many days later a man came bearing a small delicate maid of seven years or so, wanting to sell her, and Wang Lung said he would not have her at first, for she was so small and weak. But Lotus saw her and fancied her and she said pettishly,

"Now this one I will have because she is so pretty and the other one is coarse and smells like goat's meat and I do not like her."

And Wang Lung looked at the child and saw her pretty frightened eyes and her piteous thinness and he said partly to humor Lotus and partly that he might see the child fed and fattened,

"Let it be so if you wish it."

So he bought the child for twenty pieces of silver and she lived in the inner courts and slept on the foot of the bed where Lotus slept.

Now it seemed to Wang Lung that he could have peace in his house. When the waters receded and summer came and the land was to be planted to good seed, he walked hither and thither and looked at every piece and he discussed with Ching the quality of each piece of soil and what change there should be of crops for the fertility of the land. And whenever he went he took with him his youngest son, who was to be on the land after him, that the lad might learn. And Wang Lung never looked to see how the lad listened and whether he listened or not, for the lad walked with his head downcast and he had a sullen look on his face, and no one knew what he thought.

But Wang Lung did not see what the lad did, only that he walked there in silence behind his father. And when everything was planned Wang Lung went back to his house well content and he said to his own heart,

"I am no longer young and it is not necessary for me to work any more with my hands since I have men on my land and my sons and peace in my house."

Yet when he went into his house there was no peace. Although he had given his son a wife and although he had bought slaves enough to serve them all, and although his uncle and his uncle's wife were given enough opium for their pleasure all day, still there was no peace. And again it was because of his uncle's son and his own eldest son.

It seemed as though Wang Lung's eldest son could never give over his hatred of his cousin or his deep suspicion of his cousin's evil. He had seen well enough with his own eyes in his youth that the man, his cousin, was full of all sorts of evil, and things had come to a pass where Wang Lung's son would not even leave the house to go to the tea shop unless the cousin went also, and he watched the cousin and left only when he left. And he suspected the man of evil with the slaves and even of evil in the inner court with Lotus, although this was idle, for Lotus grew fatter and older every day and had long since given over caring for anything except her foods and her wines and would not have troubled to look at the man had he come near, and she was even glad when Wang Lung came to her less and less with his age.

Now when Wang Lung entered with his youngest son from the fields, his eldest son drew his father aside and he said,

"I will not endure that fellow my cousin in the house any more with his peepings and his lounging about with his robes unbuttoned and his eyes on the slaves." He did not dare to say further what he thought, "And even he dares to peep into the inner courts at your own woman," because he remembered with a sickness in his vitals that he himself had once hung about this woman of his father's, and now seeing her fat and older as she was, he could not dream that he had ever done this thing and he was bitterly ashamed of it and would not for anything have recalled it to his father's memory. So he was silent of that, and mentioned only the slaves.

Wang Lung had come in robustly from the fields and in high humor because the water was off the land and the air dry and warm and because he was pleased with his youngest son that he had gone with him, and he answered, angry at this fresh trouble in his house,

"Well, and you are a foolish child to be forever thinking of this. You have grown fond and too fond of your wife and it is not seemly, for a man ought not to care above all else in the world for his wife whom his parents gave him. It is not meet for a man to love his wife with a foolish and overweening love, as though she were a harlot."

Then the young man was stung with this rebuke of his father against him, for more than anything he feared any who accused him of behavior that was not correct, as though he were common and ignorant, and he answered quickly,

"It is not for my wife. It is because it is unseemly in my father's house."

But Wang Lung did not hear him. He was musing in anger and he said again,

"And am I never to be done with all this trouble in my house

[245]

between male and female? Here am I passing into my age and my blood cools and I am freed at last from lusts and I would have a little peace, and must I endure the lusts and jealousies of my sons?" And then after a little silence, he shouted again, "Well, and what would you have me do?"

Now the young man had waited patiently enough for his father's anger to pass, for he had something to say, and this Wang Lung saw clearly when he shouted, "What would you have me do?" The young man then answered steadily,

"I wish we could leave this house and that we could go into the town and live. It is not meet that we go on living in the country like hinds and we could go and we could leave my uncle and his wife and my cousin here and we could live safely in the town behind the gates."

Wang Lung laughed bitterly and shortly when his son said this, and he threw the desire of the young man aside for something worthless and not to be considered.

"This is my house," he said stoutly, seating himself at the table and drawing his pipe toward him from where it stood, "and you may live in it or not. My house and my land it is, and if it were not for the land we should all starve as the others did, and you could not walk about in your dainty robes idle as a scholar. It is the good land that has made you something better than a farmer's lad."

And Wang Lung rose and tramped about loudly in the middle room and he behaved roughly and he spat upon the floor and acted as a farmer may, because although one side of his heart triumphed in his son's fineness, the other side was robust and scornful of him and this although he knew he was secretly proud of his son, and proud because none who looked at this son could dream that he was but one generation removed from the land itself.

But the eldest son was not ready to give over. He followed his father saying,

"Well, and there is the old great house of the Hwangs. The front part of it is filled with this and that of common people but the inner courts are locked and silent and we could rent them and live there peacefully and you my youngest brother could come to and fro to the land and I would not be angered by this dog, my cousin." And then he persuaded his father and he allowed the tears to come into his eyes and he forced them upon his cheeks and did not wipe them away and he said again, "Well, and I try to be a good son and I do not gamble and smoke opium and I am content with the woman you have given me and I ask a little of you and it is all."

Now whether the tears would have alone moved Wang Lung he did not know, but he was moved by the words of his son when he said "the great house of the Hwangs."

Never had Wang Lung forgotten that once he had gone crawling into that great house and stood ashamed in the presence of those who lived there so that he was frightened of even the gateman, and this had remained a memory of shame to him all his life and he hated it. Through all his life he had the sense that he was held in the eyes of men a little lower than those who lived in the town, and when he had stood before the Old Mistress of the great house, this sense became crisis. So when his son said, "We could live in the great house," the thought leaped into his mind as though he saw it actually before his eyes, "I could sit on that seat where that old one sat and from whence she bade me stand like a serf, and now I could sit there and so call another into my presence." And he mused and he said to himself again, "This I could do if I wished."

And he toyed with the thought and he sat silent and he did not answer his son, but he put tobacco in his pipe and lit it with a spill that stood ready and he smoked and he dreamed of what he could do if he wished. So not because of his son and not because of his uncle's son he dreamed that he could live in the House of Hwang, which was to him forever the great house.

Therefore although he was not willing at first to say that he would go or that he would change anything, yet thereafter he was more than ever displeased with the idleness of his uncle's son, and he watched the man sharply and he saw that it was true he did cast eyes at the maids and Wang Lung muttered and said,

"Now I cannot live with this lustful dog in my house."

And he looked at his uncle and he saw that he grew thin as he smoked his opium and his skin was yellow with opium and he was bent and old and he spat blood when he coughed; and he looked at his uncle's wife and she was a cabbage of a woman who took eagerly to her opium pipe and was satisfied with it and drowsy; and these were little trouble enough now, and the opium had done what Wang Lung wished it would do.

But here was the uncle's son, this man, still unwed, and a wild beast for his desires, and he would not yield to opium easily as the two old ones had done and take out his lusts in dreams. And Wang Lung would not willingly let him wed in the house, because of the spawn he would breed and one like him was enough. Neither would the man work, since there was no need and none to drive him to it, unless the hours he spent away at night could be called work. But even these grew less frequent, for as men returned to the land order came back to the villages and to the town and the robbers withdrew to the hills in the northwest, and the man would not go with them, preferring to live on Wang Lung's bounty. Thus he was a thorn in the household and he hung about everywhere, talking and idling and yawning, and half dressed even at noon.

One day, therefore, when Wang Lung went into the town to see his second son at the grain market he asked him,

"Well, my second son, what say you of the thing your elder brother desires, that we move into the town to the great house if we can rent part of it?"

The second son was grown a young man by now and he had grown smooth and neat and like the other clerks in the shop, although still small of stature and yellow-skinned and with crafty eyes, and he answered smoothly,

"It is an excellent thing and it would suit me well, for then I could wed and have my wife there also and we would all be under one roof as a great family is."

Wang Lung had done nothing toward the wedding of this son, for he was a cool youth and cool-blooded and there had never been any sign of lust in him and Wang Lung had much else to trouble him. Now, however, he said in some shame, for he knew he had not done well by his second son, "I have said to myself this long time that you should be wed, but what with this thing and that I have not had time, and with this last famine and having to avoid all feasting—but now that men may eat again, the thing shall be done."

And he cast about secretly in his mind where he should find a maid. The second son said then,

"Well, and wed I will then, for it is a good thing and better than spending money on a jade when the need comes, and it is right for a man to have sons. But do not get me a wife from a house in town, such as my brother has, for she will talk forever of what was in her father's house and make me spend money and it will be an anger to me."

Wang Lung heard this with astonishment, for he had not known that his daughter-in-law was thus, seeing only that she was a woman careful to be correct in her behavior and fair enough in her looks. But it seemed to him wise talk and he was rejoiced that his son was sharp and clever for the saving of money. This lad he had, indeed, scarcely known at all, for he grew up weak beside the vigor of his elder brother, and except for his piping tales he was not a child or a youth to whom one would pay great heed, so that when he went into the shop, Wang Lung forgot him day after day, except to answer when anyone asked him how many children he had, "I have three sons."

Now he looked at the youth, his second son, and he saw his smooth-cut hair, oiled and flat, and his clean gown of small-patterned grey silk, and he saw the youth's neat movements and steady, secret eyes and he said to himself in his surprise,

"This also is my son!" And aloud he said, "What sort of a maid would you have, then?"

Then the young man answered as smoothly and steadily as if he had the thing planned before,

"I desire a maid from a village, of good landed family and without poor relatives, and one who will bring a good dowry with her, neither plain nor fair to look upon, and a good cook, so that even though there are servants in the kitchen she may watch them. And she must be such an one that if she buys rice it will be enough and not a handful over and if she buys cloth the garment will be well cut so that the scraps of cloth left over should lie in the palm of her hand. Such an one I want."

Now Wang Lung was the more astonished when he heard this talk, for here was a young man whose life he had not seen, even though it was his own son. It was not such blood as this that ran in his own lusty body when he was young, nor in the body of his eldest son; yet he admired the wisdom of the young man and he said laughing,

"Well, and I shall seek such a maid and Ching shall look for her among the villages."

Still laughing, he went away and he went down the street of the great house and he hesitated between the stone lions and then, since there was none to stop him, he went in and the front courts were as he remembered them when he came in to seek the whore whom he feared for his son's sake. The trees were hung with drying clothes and women sat everywhere gossiping as they drove their long needles back and forth through shoe soles they made, and children rolled naked and dusty upon the tiles of the courts and the place reeked with the smell of common people who swarm into the courts of the great when the great are gone. And he looked towards the door where the whore had lived, but the door stood ajar and another lived there now, an old man, and for this Wang Lung was glad and he went on.

Now Wang Lung in the old days when the great family were there would have felt himself one of these common people and against the great, half hating, half fearful of them. But now that he had land and that he had silver hidden safely away, he despised these people who swarmed everywhere, and he said to himself that they were filthy and he picked his way among them with his nose up and breathing lightly because of the stink they made. And he despised them and was against them as though he himself belonged to the great house.

He went back through the courts, although it was for idle curiosity and not because he had decided anything, but still he went on and at the back he found a gate locked into a court and beside it an old woman drowsing, and he looked and he saw that this was the pock-marked wife of the man who had been gateman. This astonished him, and he looked at her, whom he had remembered as buxom and middle-aged, now haggard and wrinkled and white haired, and her teeth were yellow snags loose in her jaws, and looking at her thus he saw in a full moment how many and how swift were the years that had passed since he was a young man coming with his first-born son in his arms, and for the first time in his life Wang Lung felt his age creeping upon him.

Then he said somewhat sadly to the old woman,

"Wake and let me into the gate."

And the old woman started up blinking and licking her dry lips, and she said,

"I am not to open except to such as may rent the whole inner courts."

And Wang Lung said suddenly,

"Well, and so I may, if the place please me."

But he did not tell her who he was, only he went in after her and he remembered the way well and he followed her. There the courts stood in silence; there the little room where he had left his basket; here the long verandas supported by the delicate, red-varnished pillars. He followed her into the great hall itself, and his mind went back how quickly over the years past when he had stood there waiting to wed a slave of the house. There before him was the great carven dais where the old lady had sat, her fragile, tended body wrapped in silvery satin.

And moved by some strange impulse he went forward and he

sat down where she had sat and he put his hand on the table and from the eminence it gave him he looked down on the bleary face of the old hag who blinked at him and waited in silence for what he would do. Then some satisfaction he had longed for all his days without knowing it swelled up in his heart and he struck the table with his hand and he said suddenly,

"This house I will have!"

XXIX

IN THESE days when Wang Lung had decided a thing he could not do it quickly enough. As he grew older her grew impatient to have done with things and to sit in the latter part of the day at peace and idle and to watch the late sun and sleep a little after he had strolled about his land. So he told his eldest son what he had decided and he commanded the young man to arrange the matter, and he sent for his second son to come and help with the moving and on a day when they were ready they moved, first Lotus and Cuckoo and their slaves and goods, and then Wang Lung's eldest son and his wife and their servants and the slaves.

But Wang Lung himself would not go at once, and he kept with him his youngest son. When the moment came for leaving the land whereon he was born he could not do it easily nor so quickly as he had thought and he said to his sons when they urged him,

"Well then, prepare a court for me to use alone and on a day that I wish I will come, and it will be a day before my grandson is born, and when I wish I can come back to my land."

And when they urged him yet again, he said,

"Well, and there is my poor fool and whether to take her with me or not I do not know, but take her I must, for there is no one who will see if she is fed or not unless I do it."

This Wang Lung said in some reproach to the wife of his eldest son, for she would not suffer the poor fool near her, but was finicking and squeamish and she said, "Such an one should not be alive at all, and it is enough to mar the child in me to look at her." And Wang Lung's eldest son remembered the dislike of his wife and so now he was silent and said no more. Then Wang Lung repented his reproach and he said mildly,

"I will come when the maid is found who is to wed the second son, for it is easier to stay here where Ching is until the matter is completed."

The second son, therefore, gave over his urging.

There was left in the house, then, none but the uncle and his wife and son and Ching and the laboring men, besides Wang Lung and his youngest son and the fool. And the uncle and his wife and son moved into the inner courts where Lotus had been and they took it for their own, but this did not grieve Wang Lung unduly, for he saw clearly there were not many days of life left for his uncle and when the idle old man was dead Wang Lung's duty to that generation was over and if the younger man did not do as he was told none would blame Wang Lung if he cast him out. Then Ching moved into the outer rooms and the laborers with him, and Wang Lung and his son and the fool lived in the middle rooms, and Wang Lung hired a stout woman to be servant to them.

And Wang Lung slept and rested himself and took no heed of anything, for he was suddenly very weary and the house was peaceful. There was none to trouble him, for his youngest son was a silent lad who kept out of his father's way and Wang Lung scarcely knew what he was, so silent a lad was he.

But at last Wang Lung stirred himself to bid Ching find a maid for his second son to wed.

Now Ching grew old and withered and lean as a reed, but there was the strength of an old and faithful dog in him yet, although

Wang Lung would no longer let him lift a hoe in his hand or follow the oxen behind the plow. But still he was useful for he watched the labor of others and he stood by when the grain was weighed and measured. So when he heard what Wang Lung wished him to do he washed himself and put on his good blue cotton coat and he went hither and thither to this village and that and he looked at many maidens and at last he came back and he said,

"Now would I liefer have to choose a wife for myself than for your son. But if it were I and I young, there is a maid three villages away, a good, buxom, careful maid with no fault except a ready laugh, and her father is willing and glad to be tied to your family by his daughter. And the dowry is good for these times, and he has land. But I said I could give no promise until you gave it."

It seemed to Wang Lung then that this was good enough and he was anxious to be done with it and so he gave his promise and when the papers were come he set his mark to them, and he was relieved and he said,

"Now there is but one more son and I am finished with all this wedding and marrying and I am glad I am so near my peace."

And when it was done and the wedding day set, he rested and sat in the sun and slept even as his father had done before him.

Then it seemed to Wang Lung that as Ching grew feeble with age and since he himself grew heavy and drowsy with his food and his age and his third son was yet too young for responsibility, that it would be well to rent some of his farthest fields to others in the village. This Wang Lung did, then, and many of the men in the villages near by came to Wang Lung to rent his land and to become his tenants, and the rent was decided upon, half of the harvests to go to Wang Lung because he owned the land, and half to the one who hired because of his labor, and there were other things which each must furnish besides: Wang Lung certain stores of manure and of beancake and of sesame refuse from his oil mill after the sesame was ground, and the tenant to reserve certain crops for the use of Wang Lung's house.

And then, since there was not the need for his management that there had been, Wang Lung went sometimes into the town and slept in the court which he caused to be prepared for him, but when day came he was back upon his land, walking through the gate in the wall about the town as soon as it was open after dawn came. And he smelled the fresh smell of the fields and when he came to his own land he rejoiced in it.

Then as if the gods were kind for the once and had prepared peace for his old age his uncle's son, who grew restless in the house now quiet and without women save for the stout serving woman who was wife to one of the laborers, this uncle's son heard of a war to the north and he said to Wang Lung.

"It is said there is a war to the north of us and I will go and join it for something to do and to see. This I will if you will give me silver to buy more clothes and my bedding and a foreign firestick to put over my shoulder."

Then Wang Lung's heart leaped with pleasure but he hid his pleasure artfully and he demurred in pretense and he said,

"Now you are the only son of my uncle and after you there are none to carry on his body and if you go to war what will happen?"

But the man answered, laughing,

"I am no fool and I will not stand anywhere that my life is in danger. If there is to be a battle I will go away until it is over. I wish for a change and a little travel and to see foreign parts before I am too old to do it."

So Wang Lung gave him the silver readily and this time again the giving was not hard so that he poured the money out into the man's hand and he said to himself,

"If he likes it there is an end to this curse in my house, for there is always a war somewhere in the nation." And again he said to himself, "He may even be killed, if my good fortune holds, for sometimes in wars there are those who die."

He was in high good humor, then, although he concealed it, and

[255]

he comforted his uncle's wife when she wept a little to hear of her son's going, and he gave her more opium and lit her pipe for her and he said,

"Doubtless he will rise to be a military official and honor will come to us all through him."

Then at last there was peace, for there were only the two old sleeping ones in the house in the country besides his own, and in the house in the town the hour drew near for the birth of Wang Lung's grandson.

Now Wang Lung, as this hour grew near, stayed more and more in the house in town and he walked about the courts and he could never have done with musing on what had happened, and he could never have his fill of wonder at this, that here in these courts where the great family of Hwang had once lived now he lived with his wife and his sons and their wives and now a child was to be born of a third generation.

And his heart swelled with him so that nothing was too good for his money to buy and he bought lengths of satin and of silk for them all for it looked ill to see common cotton robes upon the carved chairs and about the carved tables of southern blackwood, and he bought lengths of good blue and black cotton for the slaves so not one of them needed to wear a garment ragged. This he did, and he was pleased when the friends that his eldest son had found in the town came into the courts and proud that they should see all that was.

And Wang Lung took it into his heart to eat dainty foods, and he himself, who once had been well satisfied with good wheaten bread wrapped about a stick of garlic, now that he slept late in the day and did not work with his own hands on the land, now he was not easily pleased with this dish and that, and he tasted winter bamboo and shrimps' roe and southern fish and shellfish from the northern seas and pigeons' eggs and all those things which rich men use to force their lagging appetites. And his sons ate and Lotus also, and Cuckoo, seeing all that had come about, laughed and said,

[256]

"It is like the old days when I was in these courts, only this body of mine is withered and dried now and not fit even for an old lord."

Saying this, she glanced slyly at Wang Lung and laughed again, and he pretended not to hear her lewdness, but he was pleased, nevertheless, that she had compared him to the Old Lord.

So with this idle and luxurious living and rising when they would and sleeping when they would, he waited for his grandson. Then one morning he heard the groans of a woman and he went into the courts of his eldest son and his son met him and said,

"The hour is come, but Cuckoo says it will be long, for the woman is narrowly made and it is a hard birth."

So Wang Lung went back to his own court and he sat down and listened to the cries, and for the first time in many years he was frightened and felt the need of some spirit's aid. He rose and went to the incense shop and he bought incense and he went to the temple in the town where the goddess of mercy dwells in her gilded alcove and he summoned an idling priest and gave him money and bade him thrust the incense before the goddess saying,

"It is ill for me, a man, to do it, but my first grandson is about to be born and it is a heavy labor for the mother, who is a town woman and too narrowly made, and the mother of my son is dead, and there is no woman to thrust in the incense."

Then as he watched the priest thrust it in the ashes of the urn before the goddess he thought with sudden horror, "And what if it be not a grandson but a girl!" and he called out hastily,

"If it is a grandson I will pay for a new red robe for the goddess, but nothing will I do if it is a girl!"

He went out in agitation because he had not thought of this thing, that it might be not a grandson but a girl, and he went and bought more incense, although the day was hot and in the streets the dust was a span's depth, and he went out in spite of this to the small country temple where the two sat who watched over fields and land and he thrust the incense in and lit it and he muttered to the pair,

"We have cared for you, my father and I and my son, and now here comes the fruit of my son's body, and if it is not a son there is nothing more for the two of you."

Then having done all he could, he went back to the courts, very spent, and he sat down at his table and he wished for a slave to bring him tea and for another to bring him a towel dipped and wrung from steaming water to wipe his face, but though he clapped his hands none came. No one heeded him, and there was running to and fro, but he dared to stop no one to ask what sort of a child had been born or even if any had been born. He sat there dusty and spent and no one spoke to him.

Then at last when it seemed to him it must soon be night, so long he had waited, Lotus came in waddling upon her small feet and leaning upon Cuckoo because of her great weight, and she laughed and said loudly,

"Well, and there is a son in the house of your son, and both mother and son are alive. I have seen the child and it is fair and sound."

Then Wang Lung laughed also and he rose and he slapped his hands together and laughed again and he said,

"I have been sitting here like a man with his own first son coming and not knowing what to do of this and that and afraid of everything."

And then when Lotus had gone on to her room and he sat again he fell to musing and he thought to himself,

"Well, and I did not fear like this when that other one bore her first, my son." And he sat silent and musing and he remembered within himself that day and how she had gone alone into the small dark room and how alone she had borne him sons and again sons and daughters and she bore them silently, and how she had come to the fields and worked beside him again. And here was this one, now the wife of his son, who cried like a child with her pains, and who had all the slaves running in the house, and her husband there by her door.

And he remembered as one remembers a dream long past how

O-lan rested from her work a little while and fed the child richly and the white rich milk ran out of her breast and spilled upon the ground. And this seemed too long past ever to have been.

Then his son came in smiling and important and he said loudly,

"The man child is born, my father, and now we must find a woman to nurse him with her breasts, for I will not have my wife's beauty spoiled with the nursing and her strength sapped with it. None of the women of position in the town do so."

And Wang Lung said sadly, although why he was sad he did not know,

"Well, and if it must be so, let it be so, if she cannot nurse her own child."

When the child was a month old Wang Lung's son, its father, gave the birth feast, and to it he invited guests from the town and his wife's father and mother, and all the great of the town. And he had dyed scarlet many hundreds of hens' eggs, and these he gave to every guest and to any who sent guests, and there was feasting and joy through the house, for the child was a goodly fat boy and he had passed his tenth day and lived and this was a fear gone, and they all rejoiced.

And when the birth feast was over Wang Lung's son came to his father and he said,

"Now that there are the three generations in this house, we should have the tablets of ancestors that great families have, and we should set the tablets up to be worshipped at the feast days for we are an established family now."

This pleased Wang Lung greatly, and so he ordered it and so it was carried out, and there in the great hall the row of tablets was set up, his grandfather's name on one and then his father's, and the spaces left empty for Wang Lung's name and his son's when they should die. And Wang Lung's son bought an incense urn and set it before the tablets.

When this was finished Wang Lung remembered the red robe he had promised the goddess of mercy and so he went to the temple to give the money for it.

And then, on his way back, as if the gods cannot bear to give freely and not hide sting somewhere in the gift, one came running from the harvest fields to tell him that Ching lay dying suddenly and had asked if Wang Lung would come to see him die. Wang Lung, hearing the panting runner, cried angrily,

"Now I suppose that accursed pair in the temple are jealous because I gave a red robe to a town goddess and I suppose they do not know they have no power over childbirth and only over land."

And although his noon meal stood ready for him to eat he would not take up his chopsticks, and although Lotus called loudly to him to wait until after the evening sun came he would not stay for her, and he went out. Then when Lotus saw he did not heed her she sent a slave after him with an umbrella of oiled paper, but so fast did Wang Lung run that the stout maid had difficulty in holding the umbrella over his head.

Wang Lung went at once to the room where Ching had been laid and he called out loudly to anyone,

"Now how did all this come about?"

The room was full of laborers crowding about and they answered in confusion and haste,

"He would work himself at the threshing . . ." "We told him not at this age . . ." "There was a laborer who is newly hired . . ." "He could not hold the flail rightly and Ching would show him . . ." "It is labor too hard for an old man . . ."

Then Wang Lung called out in a terrible voice,

"Bring me this laborer!"

And they pushed the man in front before Wang Lung, and he stood there trembling and his bare knees knocking together, a great, ruddy, coarse, country lad, with his teeth sticking out in a shelf over his lower lip and round dull eyes like an ox's eyes. But Wang Lung had no pity on him. He slapped the lad on both his cheeks and he took the umbrella from the slave's hand and he beat the lad about the head, and none dared stop him lest his anger go into his blood and at his age poison him. And the bumpkin stood it humbly, blubbering a little and sucking his teeth.

[260]

Then Ching moaned from the bed where he lay and Wang Lung threw down the umbrella and he cried out,

"Now this one will die while I am beating a fool!"

And he sat down beside Ching and took his hand and held it, and it was as light and dry and small as a withered oak leaf and it was not possible to believe that any blood ran through it, so dry and light and hot it was. But Ching's face, which was pale and yellow every day, was now dark and spotted with his scanty blood, and his half-opened eyes were filmed and blind and his breath came in gusts. Wang Lung leaned down to him and said loudly in his ear,

"Here am I and I will buy you a coffin second to my father's only!"

But Ching's ears were filled with his blood, and if he heard Wang Lung he made no sign, but he only lay there panting and dying and so he died.

When he was dead Wang Lung leaned over him and he wept as he had not wept when his own father died, and he ordered a coffin of the best kind, and he hired priests for the funeral and he walked behind wearing white mourning. He made his eldest son, even, wear white bands on his ankles as though a relative had died, although his son complained and said,

"He was only an upper servant, and it is not suitable so to mourn for a servant."

But Wang Lung compelled him for three days. And if Wang Lung had had his way wholly, he would have buried Ching inside the earthen wall where his father and O-lan were buried. But his sons would not have it and they complained and said,

"Shall our mother and grandfather lie with a servant? And must we also in our time?"

Then Wang Lung, because he could not contend with them and because at his age he would have peace in his house, buried Ching at the entrance to the wall and he was comforted with what he had done, and he said,

"It is meet, for he has ever stood guardian to me against evil."

And he directed his sons that when he himself died he should lie nearest to Ching.

Then less than ever did Wang Lung go to see his lands, because now Ching was gone it stabbed him to go alone and he was weary of labor and his bones ached when he walked over the rough fields alone. So he rented out all his land that he could and men took it eagerly, for it was known to be good land. But Wang Lung would never talk of selling a foot of any piece, and he would only rent it for an agreed price for a year at a time. Thus he felt it all his own and still in his hand.

And he appointed one of the laborers and his wife and children to live in the country house and to care for the two old opium dreamers. Then seeing his youngest son's wistful eyes, he said,

"Well, and you may come with me into the town, and I will take my fool with me too, and she can live in my court where I am. It is too lonely for you now that Ching is gone, and with him gone, I am not sure that they will be kind to the poor fool seeing there will be none to tell if she is beaten or ill fed. And there is no one now to teach you concerning the land, now that Ching is gone."

So Wang Lung took his youngest son and his fool with him and thereafter he came scarcely at all for a long time to the house on his land.

XXX

NOW to Wang Lung it seemed there was nothing left to be desired in his condition, and now he could sit in his chair in the sun beside his fool and he could smoke his water pipe and be at peace since his land was tended and the money from it coming into his hand without care from him.

And so it might have been if it had not been for that eldest son of his who was never content with what was going on well enough but must be looking aside for more. So he came to his father saying,

"There is this and that which we need in this house and we must not think we can be a great family just because we live in these inner courts. There is my younger brother's wedding due in a bare six months and we have not chairs enough to seat the guests and we have not bowls enough nor tables enough nor anything enough in these rooms. It is a shame, moreover, to ask guests to come through the great gates and through all that common swarm with their stinks and their noise, and with my brother wed and his children and mine to come we need those courts also."

Then Wang Lung looked at his son standing there in his handsome raiment and he shut his eyes and drew hard on his pipe and he growled forth,

"Well, and what now and what again?"

The young man saw his father was weary of him but he said stubbornly, and he made his voice a little louder,

"I say we should have the outer courts also and we should have what befits a family with so much money as we have and good land as we have."

Then Wang Lung muttered into his pipe,

"The land is mine and you have never put your hand to it."

"Well, my father," the young man cried out at this, "it was you who would have me a scholar and when I try to be a fitting son to a man of land you scorn me and would make a hind of me and my wife." And the young man turned himself away stormily and made as though he would knock his brains out against a twisted pine tree that stood there in the court.

Wang Lung was frightened at this, lest the young man do himself an injury, since he had been fiery always, and so he called out,

"Do as you like—do as you like—only do not trouble me with it!"

Hearing this, the son went away quickly lest his father change and he went well pleased. As quickly as he was able, then, he bought tables and chairs from Soochow, carved and wrought, and he bought curtains of red silk to hang in the doorways and he bought vases large and small and he bought scrolls to hang on the wall and as many as he could of beautiful women, and he bought curious rocks to make rockeries in the courts such as he had seen in southern parts, and thus he busied himself for many days.

With all this coming and going he had to pass many times through the outer courts, even every day, and he could not pass among the common people without sticking his nose up and he could not bear them, so that the people who lived there laughed at him after he had passed and they said,

"He has forgotten the smell of the manure in the dooryard on his father's farm!"

But still none dared to speak thus as he passed, for he was a rich man's son. When the feast came when rents are decided upon these common people found that the rent for the rooms and the courts where they lived had been greatly raised, because another would pay that much for them, and they had to move away. Then they knew it was Wang Lung's eldest son who had done this, although he was clever and said nothing and did it all by letters to the son of the old Lord Hwang in foreign parts, and this son of the Old Lord cared for nothing except where and how he could get the most money for the old house.

The common people had to move, then, and they moved complaining and cursing because a rich man could do as he would and they packed their tattered possessions and went away swelling with anger and muttering that one day they would come back even as the poor do come back when the rich are too rich.

But all this Wang Lung did not hear, since he was in the inner courts and seldom came forth, since he slept and ate and took his ease as his age came on, and he left the thing in the hands of his eldest son. And his son called carpenters and clever masons and they repaired the rooms and the moon gates between the courts that the common people had ruined with their coarse ways of living, and he built again the pools and he bought flecked and golden fish to put in them. And after it was all finished and made beautiful as far as he knew beauty, he planted lotus and lilies in the pools, and the scarlet-berried bamboo of India and everything he could remember he had seen in southern parts. And his wife came out to see what he had done and the two of them walked about through every court and room and she saw this and that still lacking, and he listened with great heed to all she said that he might do it.

Then people on the streets of the town heard of all that Wang Lung's eldest son did, and they talked of what was being done in the great house, now that a rich man lived there again. And people who had said Wang The Farmer now said Wang The Big Man or Wang The Rich Man.

The money for all these doings had gone out of Wang Lung's hand bit by bit, so that he scarcely knew when it went, for the eldest son came and said,

"I need a hundred pieces of silver here"; or he said, "There is a good gate which needs only an odd bit of silver to mend it as good as new"; or he said, "There is a place where a long table should stand."

And Wang Lung gave him the silver bit by bit, as he sat smoking and resting in his court, for the silver came in easily from the land at every harvest and whenever he needed it, and so he gave it easily. He would not have known how much he gave had not his second son come into his court one morning when the sun was scarcely over the wall and he said,

"My father, is there to be no end to all this pouring out of money and need we live in a palace? So much money lent out at twenty per cent would have brought in many pounds of silver, and what is the use of all these pools and flowering trees that bear no fruit even, and all these idle, blooming lilies?"

Wang Lung saw that these two brothers would quarrel over this yet, and he said hastily, lest he never have any peace,

"Well, and it is all in honor of your wedding."

Then the young man answered, smiling crookedly and without any meaning of mirth,

"It is an odd thing for the wedding to cost ten times as much as the bride. Here is our inheritance, that should be divided among us when you are dead, being spent now for nothing but the pride of my elder brother."

And Wang Lung knew the determination of this second son of his and he knew he would never have done with him if talk began, so he said hastily,

"Well—well—I will have an end to it—I will speak to your brother and I will shut my hand. It is enough. You are right!"

The young man had brought out a paper on which was written a list of all the moneys his brother had spent, and Wang Lung saw the length of the list and he said quickly,

"I have not eaten yet and at my age I am faint in the morning until I eat. Another time for this." And he turned and went into his own room and so dismissed his second son.

But he spoke that same evening to his eldest son, saying,

"Have done with all this painting and polishing. It is enough. We are, after all, country folk."

But the young man answered proudly,

"That we are not. Men in the town are beginning to call us the great family Wang. It is fitting that we live somewhat suitably to that name, and if my brother cannot see beyond the meaning of silver for its own sake, I and my wife, we will uphold the honor of the name."

Now Wang Lung had not known that men so called his house, for as he grew older he went seldom even to the tea shops and no more to the grain markets since there was his second son to do his business there for him, but it pleased him secretly and so he said,

"Well, even great families are from the land and rooted in the land."

[266]

But the young man answered smartly,

"Yes, but they do not stay there. They branch forth and bear flowers and fruits."

Wang Lung would not have his son answering him too easily and quickly like this, so he said,

"I have said what I have said. Have done with pouring out silver. And roots, if they are to bear fruit, must be kept well in the soil of the land."

Then since evening came on, he wished his son would go away out of this court and into his own. He wished the young man to go away and leave him in peace in the twilight and alone. But there was no peace for him with this son of his. This son was willing to obey his father now, for he was satisfied in the rooms and the courts, at least for the time, and he had done what he would do, but he began again,

"Well, let it be enough, but there is another thing."

Then Wang Lung flung his pipe down upon the ground and he shouted,

"Am I never to be in peace?"

And the young man went on stubbornly,

"It is not for myself or for my son. It is for my youngest brother who is your own son. It is not fit that he grow up so ignorant. He should be taught something."

Wang Lung stared at this for it was a new thing. He had long ago settled the life of his youngest son, what it was to be, and he said now,

"There is no need for any more stomachfuls of characters in this house. Two are enough, and he is to be on the land when I am dead."

"Yes, and for this he weeps in the night, and this is why he is so pale and so reedy a lad," answered the eldest son.

Now Wang Lung had never thought to ask his youngest son what he wished to do with his life, since he had decided one son must be on the land, and this that his eldest son had said struck him between the brows and he was silent. He picked up his pipe from the ground slowly and pondered about his third son. He was a lad not like either of his brothers, a lad as silent as his mother, and because he was silent none paid any attention to him.

"Have you heard him say this?" asked Wang Lung of his eldest son, uncertainly.

"Ask him for yourself, my father," replied the young man.

"Well, but one lad must be on the land," said Wang Lung suddenly in argument and his voice was very loud.

"But why, my father?" urged the young man. "You are a man who need not have any sons like serfs. It is not fitting. People will say you have a mean heart. 'There is a man who makes his son into a hind while he lives like a prince.' So people will say."

Now the young man spoke cleverly for he knew that his father cared mightily what people said of him, and he went on,

"We could call a tutor and teach him and we could send him to a southern school and he could learn and since there is I in your house to help you and my second brother in his good trade, let the lad choose what he will."

Then Wang Lung said at last,

"Send him here to me."

After a while the third son came and stood before his father and Wang Lung looked at him to see what he was. And he saw a tall and slender lad, who was neither his father nor his mother, except that he had his mother's gravity and silence. But there was more beauty in him than there had been in his mother, and for beauty alone he had more of it than any of Wang Lung's children except the second girl who had gone to her husband's family and belonged no more to the house of Wang. But across the lad's forehead and almost a mar to his beauty were his two black brows, too heavy and black for his young, pale face, and when he frowned, and he frowned easily, these black brows met, heavy and straight, across his brow.

And Wang Lung stared at his son and after he had seen him well, he said,

[268]

"Your eldest brother says you wish to learn to read."

And the boy said, scarcely stirring his lips,

"Aye."

Wang Lung shook the ash from his pipe and pushed the fresh tobacco in slowly with his thumb.

"Well, and I suppose that means you do not want to work on the land and I shall not have a son on my own land, and I with sons and to spare."

This he said with bitterness, but the boy said nothing. He stood there straight and still in his long white robe of summer linen, and at last Wang Lung was angry at his silence and he shouted at him,

"Why do you not speak? Is it true you do not want to be on the land?"

And again the boy answered only the one word,

"Aye."

And Wang Lung looking at him said to himself at last that these sons of his were too much for him in his old age and they were a care and burden to him and he did not know what to do with them, and he shouted again, feeling himself ill-used by these sons of his,

"What is it to me what you do? Get away from me!"

Then the boy went away swiftly and Wang Lung sat alone and he said to himself that his two girls were better after all than his sons, one, poor fool that she was, never wanted anything more than a bit of any food and her length of cloth to play with, and the other one married and away from his house. And the twilight came down over the court and shut him into it alone.

Nevertheless, as Wang Lung always did when his anger passed, he let his sons have their way, and he called his eldest son and he said,

"Engage a tutor for the third one if he wills it, and let him do as he likes, only I am not to be troubled about it."

And he called his second son and said,

"Since I am not to have a son on the land it is your duty to see to the rents and to the silver that comes in from the land at each harvest. You can weigh and measure and you shall be my steward."

The second son was pleased enough for this meant the money would pass through his hands at least, and he would know what came in and he could complain to his father if more than enough was spent in the house.

Now this second son of his seemed more strange to Wang than any of his sons, for even at the wedding day, which came on, he was careful of the money spent on meats and on wines and he divided the tables carefully, keeping the best meats for his friends in the town who knew the cost of the dishes, and for the tenants and the country people who must be invited he spread tables in the courts, and to these he gave only the second best in meat and wine, since they daily ate coarse fare, and a little better was very good to them.

And the second son watched the money and the gifts that came in, and he gave to the slaves and servants the least that could be given them, so that Cuckoo sneered when into her hand he put a paltry two pieces of silver and she said in the hearing of many,

"Now a truly great family is not so careful of its silver and one can see that this family does not rightly belong in these courts."

The eldest son heard this, and he was ashamed and he was afraid of her tongue and he gave her more silver secretly and he was angry with his second brother. Thus there was trouble between them even on the very wedding day when the guests sat about the tables and when the bride's chair was entering the courts.

And of his own friends the eldest son asked but a few of the least considered to the feast, because he was ashamed of his brother's parsimony and because the bride was but a village maid. He stood aside scornfully, and he said,

"My brother has chosen an earthen pot when he might, from my father's position, have had a cup of jade."

And he was scornful and nodded stiffly when the pair came and bowed before him and his wife as their elder brother and sister.

[270]

And the wife of the eldest son was correct and haughty and bowed only the least that could be considered proper for her position.

Now of all of them who lived in these courts it seemed there was none wholly at peace and comfortable there except the small grandson who had been born to Wang Lung. Even Wang Lung himself, waking within the shadows of the great carved bed where he slept in his own room that was next to the court where Lotus lived, even he woke to dream sometimes that he was back in the simple, dark, earth-walled house where a man could throw his cold tea down where he would not splatter a piece of carven wood, and where a step took him into his own fields.

As for Wang Lung's sons, there was continual unrest, the eldest son lest not enough be spent and they be belittled in the eyes of men and lest the villagers come walking through the great gate when a man from the town was there to call, and so make them ashamed before him; and the second son lest there was waste and money gone; and the youngest son striving to repair the years he had lost as a farmer's son.

But there was one who ran staggering hither and yon and content with his life and it was the son of the eldest son. This small one never thought of any other place than this great house and to him it was neither great nor small but only his house, and here was his mother and here his father and grandfather and all those who lived but to serve him. And from this one did Wang Lung secure peace, and he could never have enough of watching him and laughing at him and picking him up when he fell. He remembered also what his own father had done, and he delighted to take a girdle and put it about the child and walk, holding him thus from falling, and they went from court to court, and the child pointed at the darting fish in the pools and jabbered this and that and snatched the head of a flower and was at his ease in the midst of everything, and only thus did Wang Lung find peace.

Nor was there only this one. The wife of the eldest son was faithful and she conceived and bore and conceived and bore regularly and faithfully, and each child as it was born had its slave. Thus Wang Lung each year saw more children in the courts and more slaves, so that when one said to him, "There is to be another mouth again in the eldest son's court," he only laughed and said,

"Eh—eh—well, there is rice and enough for all since we have the good land."

And he was pleased when his second son's wife bore also in her season, and she gave birth to a girl first as was fitting and it was seemly out of respect to her sister-in-law. Wang Lung, then, in the space of five years had four grandsons and three grand-daughters and the courts were filled with their laughter and their weeping.

Now five years is nothing in a man's life except when he is very young and very old, and if it gave to Wang Lung these others, it took away also that old dreamer, his uncle, whom he had almost forgotten except to see that he and his old wife were fed and clothed and had what they wished of opium.

On the winter of the fifth year it was very cold, more cold than any thirty years before, so that for the first time in Wang Lung's memory the moat froze about the wall of the town and men could walk back and forth on it. A continual icy wind blew also from the northeast and there was nothing, no garment of goatskin or fur, that could keep a man warm. In every room in the great house they burned braziers of charcoal and still it was cold enough to see a man's breath when he blew it out.

Now Wang Lung's uncle and his wife had long since smoked all the flesh off their bones and they lay day in and day out on their beds like two old dry sticks, and there was no warmth in them. And Wang Lung heard his uncle could not sit up even any more in his bed and he spat blood whenever he moved at all, and he went out to see, and he saw there were not many hours left for the old man.

Then Wang Lung bought two coffins of wood good enough but not too good, and he had the coffins taken into the room where his uncle lay that the old man might see them and die in comfort, knowing there was a place for his bones. And his uncle said, his voice a quavering whisper,

"Well, and you are a son to me and more than that wandering one of my own."

And the old woman said, but she was still stouter than the man,

"If I die before that son comes home, promise me you will find a good maid for him, so that he may have sons for us yet." And Wang Lung promised it.

What hour his uncle died Wang Lung did not know, except that he lay dead one evening when the serving woman went in to take a bowl of soup, and Wang Lung buried him on a bitter cold day when the wind blew the snow over the land in clouds, and he put the coffin in the family enclosure beside his father, only a little lower than his father's grave, but above the place where his own was to be.

Then Wang Lung caused mourning to be made for the whole family and they wore the sign of mourning for a year, not because any truly mourned the passing of this old man who had never been anything but a care to them, but because it is fitting so to do in a great family when a relative dies.

Then Wang Lung moved his uncle's wife into the town where she would not be alone, and he gave her a room at the end of a far court for her own, and he told Cuckoo to supervise a slave in the care of her, and the old woman sucked her opium pipe and lay on her bed in great content, sleeping day after day, and her coffin was beside her where she could see it for her comfort.

And Wang Lung marvelled to think that once he had feared her for a great fat blowsy country woman, idle and loud, she who lay there now shriveled and yellow and silent, and as shriveled and yellow as the Old Mistress had been in the fallen House of Hwang.

XXXI

NOW all his life long Wang Lung had heard of war here and there but he had never seen the thing come near except the once that he wintered in the southern city when he was young. It had never come nearer to him than that, although he had often heard men say from the time he was a child, "There is a war to the west this year," or they said, "War is to the east or the northeast."

And to him war was a thing like earth and sky and water and why it was no one knew but only that it was. Now and again he heard men say, "We will go to the wars." This they said when they were about to starve and would rather be soldiers than beggars; and sometimes men said it when they were restless at home as the son of his uncle had said it, but however this was, the war was always away and in a distant place. Then suddenly like a reasonless wind out of heaven the thing came near.

Wang Lung heard of it first from his second son who came home from the market one day for his noon rice and he said to his father,

"The price of grain has risen suddenly, for the war is to the south of us now and nearer every day, and we must hold our stores of grain until later for the price will go higher and higher as the armies come nearer to us and we can sell for a good price."

Wang Lung listened to this as he ate and he said,

"Well, and it is a curious thing and I shall be glad to see a war for what it is, for I have heard of it all my life and never seen it."

To himself then he remembered that once he had been afraid because he would have been seized against his will, but now he was too old for use and besides he was rich and the rich need not fear anything. So he paid no great heed to the matter beyond this and he was not moved by more than a little curiosity and he said to his second son,

"Do as you think well with the grain. It is in your hands."

And in the days to come he played with his grandchildren when he was in the mood, and he slept and ate and smoked and sometimes he went to see his poor fool who sat in a far corner of his court.

Then sweeping out of the northwest like a swarm of locusts there came one day in early summer a horde of men. Wang Lung's small grandson stood at the gate with a man servant to see what passed one fine sunny morning in early spring and when he saw the long ranks of grey-coated men, he ran back to his grandfather and he cried out,

"See what comes, Old One!"

Then Wang Lung went back to the gate with him to humor him, and there the men were filling the street, filling the town, and Wang Lung felt as though air and sunlight had been suddenly cut off because of the numbers of grey men tramping heavily and in unison through the town. Then Wang Lung looked at them closely and he saw that every man held an implement of some sort with a knife sticking out of the end, and the face of every man was wild and fierce and coarse; even though some were only lads, they were so. And Wang Lung drew the child to him hastily when he saw their faces and he murmured,

"Let us go and lock the gate. They are not good men to see, my little heart."

But suddenly, before he could turn, one saw him from among the men and shouted out at him,

"Ho there, my old father's nephew!"

Wang Lung looked up at this call, and he saw the son of his

uncle, and he was clad like the others and dusty and grey, but his face was wilder and more fierce than any. And he laughed harshly and called out to his fellows,

"Here we may stop, my comrades, for this is a rich man and my relative!"

Before Wang Lung could move in his horror, the horde was pouring past him into his own gates and he was powerless in their midst. Into his courts they poured like evil filthy water, filling every corner and crack, and they laid themselves down on the floors and they dipped with their hands in the pools and drank, and they clattered their knives down upon carven tables and they spat where they would and shouted at each other.

Then Wang Lung, in despair over what had happened, ran back with the child to find his eldest son. He went into his son's courts and there his son sat reading a book and he rose when his father entered, and when he heard what Wang Lung gasped forth, he began to groan and he went out.

But when he saw his cousin he did not know whether to curse him or to be courteous to him. But he looked and he groaned forth to his father who was behind him,

"Every man with a knife!"

So he was courteous then and he said,

"Well, my cousin, welcome to your home again."

And the cousin grinned widely and said,

"I have brought a few guests."

"They are welcome, being yours," said Wang Lung's eldest son, "and we will prepare a meal so that they may eat before they go on their way."

Then the cousin said, still grinning,

"Do, but make no haste afterwards, for we will rest a handful of days or a moon or a year or two, for we are to be quartered on the town until the war calls."

Now when Wang Lung and his son heard this they could scarcely conceal their dismay, but still it must be concealed be-

[276]

cause of the knives flashing everywhere through the courts, so they smiled what poor smiles they could muster and they said,

"We are fortunate—we are fortunate—"

And the eldest son pretended he must go to prepare and he took his father's hand and the two of them rushed into the inner court and the eldest son barred the door, and then the two, father and son, stared at each other in consternation, and neither knew what to do.

Then the second son came running and he beat upon the door and when they let him in he fell in and scarcely could save himself in his haste and he panted forth,

"There are soldiers everywhere in every house—even in the houses of the poor—and I came running to say you must not protest, for today a clerk in my shop, and I knew him well—he stood beside me every day at the counter—and he heard and went to his house and there were soldiers in the very room where his wife lay ill, and he protested and they ran a knife through him as though he were made of lard—as smoothly as that—and it came through him clean to the other side! Whatever they wish we must give, but let us only pray that the war move on to other parts before long!"

Then the three of them looked at each other heavily, and thought of their women and of these lusty, hungry men. And the eldest son thought of his goodly, proper wife, and he said,

"We must put the women together in the innermost court and we must watch there day and night and keep the gates barred and the back gate of peace ready to be loosed and opened."

Thus they did. They took the women and the children and they put them all into the inner court where Lotus had lived alone with Cuckoo and her maids, and there in discomfort and crowding they lived. The eldest son and Wang Lung watched the gate day and night and the second son came when he could, and they watched as carefully by night as by day.

But there was that one, the cousin, and because he was a relative none could lawfully keep him out and he beat on the gate and he would come in and he walked about at will, carrying his knife shining and glittering and open in his hand. The eldest son followed him about, his face full of bitterness, but still not daring to say anything, for there was the knife open and glittering, and the cousin looked at this and that and appraised each woman.

He looked at the wife of the eldest son and he laughed his hoarse laugh and he said,

"Well, and it is a proper dainty bit you have, my cousin, a town lady and her feet as small as lotus buds!" And to the wife of the second son he said, "Well, here is a good stout red radish from the country—a piece of sturdy red meat!"

This he said because the woman was fat and ruddy and thick in the bone, but still not uncomely. And whereas the wife of the eldest son shrank away when he looked at her and hid her face behind her sleeve, this one laughed out, good humored and robust as she was, and she answered pertly,

"Well, and some men like a taste of hot radish, or a bite of red meat."

And the cousin answered back, promptly,

"That do I!" and he made as if to seize her hand.

All this time the eldest son was in an agony of shame at this byplay between man and woman who ought not even to speak to each other, and he glanced at his wife because he was ashamed of his cousin and of his sister-in-law before her who had been more gently bred than he, and his cousin saw his timidity before his wife and said with malice,

"Well, and I had rather eat red meat any day than a slice of cold and tasteless fish like this other one!"

At this the wife of the eldest son rose in dignity and withdrew herself into an inner room. Then the cousin laughed coarsely and he said to Lotus, who sat there smoking her water pipe,

"These town women are too finicking, are they not, Old Mistress?" Then he looked at Lotus attentively and he said, "Old Mistress indeed, and if I did not know my cousin Wang Lung were rich I should know by looking at you, such a mountain of flesh you have become, and well you have eaten and how richly! It is only rich men's wives who can look like you!"

Now Lotus was mightily pleased that he called her Old Mistress, because it is a title that only the ladies of great families may have, and she laughed, deep and gurgling, out of her fat throat and she blew the ash out of her pipe and handed the pipe to a slave to fill again, and she said, turning to Cuckoo,

"Well, this coarse fellow has a turn for a joke!"

And as she said this she looked at the cousin out of her eyes coquettishly, although such glances, now that her eyes were no longer large and apricot-shaped in her great cheeks, were less coy than they once were, and seeing the look she gave him, the cousin laughed in uproar and cried out,

"Well, and it is an old bitch, still!" and he laughed again loudly.

And all this time the eldest son stood there in anger and in silence.

Then when the cousin had seen everything he went to see his mother and Wang Lung went with him to show where she was. There she lay on her bed, asleep so her son could hardly wake her, but wake her he did, clapping the thick end of his gun upon the tiles of the floor at her bed's head. Then she woke and stared at him out of a dream, and he said impatiently,

"Here is your son and yet you sleep on!"

She raised herself then in her bed and stared at him again and she said wondering,

"My son—it is my son—" and she looked at him for a long time and at last as though she did not know what else to do she proffered him her opium pipe, as if she could think of no greater good than this, and she said to the slave that tended her, "Prepare some for him."

And he stared back at her and he said,

"No, I will not have it."

Wang Lung stood there beside the bed and he was suddenly afraid lest this man should turn on him and say,

[279]

"What have you done to my mother that she is sere and yellow like this and all her good flesh gone?"

So Wang said hastily himself,

"I wish she were content with less, for it runs into a handful of silver a day for her opium, but at her age we do not dare to cross her and she wants it all." And he sighed as he spoke, and he glanced secretly at his uncle's son, but the man said nothing, only stared to see what his mother had become, and when she fell back and into her sleep again, he rose and clattered forth, using his gun as a stick in his hand.

None of the horde of idle men in the outer courts did Wang Lung and his family hate and fear as they did this cousin of theirs; this, although the men tore at the trees and the flowering shrubs of plum and almond and broke them as they would, and though they crushed the delicate carvings of chairs with their great leathern boots, and though they sullied with their private filth the pools where the flecked and golden fish swam, so that the fish died and floated on the water and rotted there, with their white bellies up-turned.

For the cousin ran in and out as he would and he cast eyes at the slaves and Wang Lung and his sons looked at each other out of their eyes haggard and sunken because they dared not sleep. Then Cuckoo saw it and she said,

"Now there is only one thing to do, he must be given a slave for his pleasure while he is here, or else he will be taking where he should not."

And Wang Lung seized eagerly on what she said because it seemed to him he could not endure his life any more with all the trouble there was in his house, and so he said,

"It is a good thought."

And he bade Cuckoo go and ask the cousin what slave he would have since he had seen them all.

So Cuckoo did, then, and she came back and she said,

[280]

"He says he will have the little pale one who sleeps on the bed of the mistress."

Now this pale slave was called Pear Blossom and the one Wang Lung had bought in a famine year when she was small and piteous and half starved, and because she was delicate always they had petted her and allowed her only to help Cuckoo and to do the lesser things about Lotus, filling her pipe and pouring her tea, and it was thus the cousin had seen her.

When Pear Blossom heard this she cried out as she poured the tea for Lotus, for Cuckoo said it all out before them in the inner court where they sat, and she dropped the pot and it broke into pieces on the tiles and the tea all streamed out, but the maid did not see what she had done. She only threw herself down before Lotus, and she knocked her head on the tiles and she moaned forth,

"Oh, my mistress, not I—not I—I am afraid of him for my life—"

And Lotus was displeased with her and she answered pettishly,

"He is only a man and a man is no more than a man with a maid and they are all alike, and what is this ado?" And she turned to Cuckoo and said, "Take this slave and give her to him."

Then the young maid put her hands together piteously and cried as though she would die of weeping and fear and her little body was all trembling with her fear, and she looked from this face to that, beseeching with her weeping.

Now the sons of Wang Lung could not speak against their father's wife, nor could their wives speak if they did not, nor could the youngest son, but he stood there staring at her, his hands clenched on his bosom and his brows drawn down over his eyes, straight and black. But he did not speak. The children and the slaves looked and were silent, and there was only the sound of this dreadful, frightened weeping of the young girl.

But Wang Lung was made uncomfortable by it, and he looked at the young girl doubtfully, not caring to anger Lotus, but still

[281]

moved, because he had always a soft heart. Then the maid saw his heart in his face and she ran and held his feet with her hands and she bent her head down to his feet and wept on in great sobs. And he looked down at her and saw how small her shoulders were and how they shook and he remembered the great, coarse, wild body of his cousin, now long past his youth, and a distaste for the thing seized him and he said to Cuckoo, his voice mild,

"Well now, it is ill to force the young maid like this."

These words he said mildly enough, but Lotus cried out sharply,

"She is to do as she is told, and I say it is foolish, all this weeping over a small thing that must happen soon or late with all women."

But Wang Lung was indulgent and he said to Lotus,

"Let us see first what else can be done, and let me buy for you another slave if you will, or what you will, but let me see what can be done."

Then Lotus, who had long been minded for a foreign clock and a new ruby ring, was suddenly silent and Wang Lung said to Cuckoo,

"Go and tell my cousin the girl has a vile and incurable disease, but if he will have her with that, then well enough and she shall come to him, but if he fears it as we all do, then tell him we have another and a sound one."

And he cast his eyes over the slaves who stood about and they turned away their faces and giggled and made as if they were ashamed, all except one stout wench, who was already twenty or so, and she said with her face red and laughing,

"Well, and I have heard enough of this thing and I have a mind to try it, if he will have me, and he is not so hideous a man as some."

Then Wang Lung answered in relief,

"Well, go then!"

And Cuckoo said,

"Follow close behind me, for it will happen, I know, that he will seize the fruit nearest to him." And they went out.

But the little maid still clung to Wang Lung's feet, only now she ceased her weeping and lay listening to what took place. And Lotus was still angry with her, and she rose and went into her room without a word. Then Wang Lung raised the maid gently and she stood before him, drooping and pale, and he saw that she had a little, soft, oval face, egg-shaped, exceedingly delicate and pale, and a little pale red mouth. And he said kindly,

"Now keep away from your mistress for a day or two, my child, until she is past her anger, and when that other one comes in, hide, lest he desire you again."

And she lifted her eyes and looked at him full and passionately, and she passed him, silent as a shadow, and was gone.

The cousin lived there for a moon and a half and he had the wench when he would and she conceived by him and boasted in the courts of it. Then suddenly the war called and the horde went away quickly as chaff caught and driven by the wind, and there was nothing left except the filth and destruction they had wrought. And Wang Lung's cousin girded his knife to his waist and he stood before them with his gun over his shoulder and he said mockingly,

"Well, and if I come not back to you I have left you my second self and a grandson for my mother, and it is not every man who can leave a son where he stops for a moon or two, and it is one of the benefits of the soldier's life—his seed springs up behind him and others must tend it!"

And laughing at them all, he went his way with the others.

XXXII

WHEN the soldiers were gone Wang Lung and his two elder sons for once agreed and it was that all trace of what had just passed must be wiped away, and they called in carpenters and masons again, and the men servants cleaned the courts, and the carpenters mended cunningly the broken carvings and tables, and the pools were emptied of their filth and clean fresh water put in, and again the eldest son bought flecked and golden fish and he planted once more the flowering trees and he trimmed the broken branches of the trees that were left. And within a year the place was fresh and flowering again and each son had moved again into his own court and there was order once more everywhere.

The slave who had conceived by the son of Wang Lung's uncle he commanded to wait upon his uncle's wife as long as she lived, which could not be long now, and to put her into the coffin when she died. And it was a matter for joy to Wang Lung that this slave gave birth only to a girl, for if it had been a boy she would have been proud and have claimed a place in the family, but being a girl it was only slave bearing slave, and she was no more than before.

Nevertheless, Wang Lung was just to her as to all, and he said to her that she might have the old woman's room for her own if she liked when the old one was dead, and she could have the bed also, and one room and one bed would not be missed from the sixty rooms in the house. And he gave the slave a little silver, and the woman was content enough except for one thing, and this she told to Wang Lung when he gave her the silver.

"Hold the silver as dowry for me, my master," she said, "and if it is not a trouble to you, wed me to a farmer or to a good poor man. It will be merit to you, and having lived with a man, it is hardship to me to go back to my bed alone."

Then Wang Lung promised easily, and when he promised he was struck with a thought and it was this. Here was he promising a woman to a poor man, and once he had been a poor man come into these very courts for his woman. And he had not for half a lifetime thought of O-lan, and now he thought of her with sadness that was not sorrow but only heaviness of memory and things long gone, so far distant was he from her now. And he said heavily,

"When the old opium dreamer dies, I will find a man for you, then, and it cannot be long."

And Wang Lung did as he said. The woman came to him one morning and said,

"Now redeem your promise, my master, for the old one died in the early morning without waking at all, and I have put her in her coffin."

And Wang Lung thought what man he knew now on his land and he remembered the blubbering lad who had caused Ching's death, and the one whose teeth were a shelf over his lower lip, and he said,

"Well, and he did not mean the thing he did, and he is as good as any and the only one I can think of now."

So he sent for the lad and he came, and he was a man grown now, but still he was rude and still his teeth were as they were. And it was Wang Lung's whim to sit on the raised dais in the great hall and to call the two before him and he said slowly, that he might taste the whole flavor of the strange moment,

"Here, fellow, is this woman, and she is yours if you will have her, and none has known her except the son of my own uncle."

And the man took her gratefully, for she was a stout wench and good-natured, and he was a man too poor to wed except to such an one.

Then Wang Lung came down off the dais and it seemed to him

that now his life was rounded off and he had done all that he said he would in his life and more than he would ever have dreamed he could, and he did not know himself how it had all come about. Only now it seemed to him that peace could truly come to him and he could sleep in the sun. It was time for it, also, for he was close to sixty-five years of his age and his grandsons were like young bamboos about him, three the sons of his eldest son, and the eldest of these nearly ten years old, and two the sons of his second son. Well, and there was the third son to wed one day soon, and with that over there was nothing left to trouble him in his life, and he could be at peace.

But there was no peace. It seemed as though the coming of the soldiers had been like the coming of a swarm of wild bees that leave behind them stings wherever they can. The wife of the eldest son and the wife of the second son who had been courteous enough to each other until they lived in one court together, now had learned to hate each other with a great hatred. It was born in a hundred small quarrels, the quarrels of women whose children must live and play together and fight each other like cats and dogs. Each mother flew to the defense of her child, and cuffed the other's children heartily but spared her own, and her own had always the right in any quarrel, and so the two women were hostile.

And then on that day when the cousin had commended the country wife and laughed at the city wife, that had passed which could not be forgiven. The wife of the eldest son lifted her head haughtily when she passed her sister-in-law and she said aloud one day to her husband as she passed,

"It is a heavy thing to have a woman bold and ill-bred in the family, so that a man may call her red meat and she laugh in his face."

And the second son's wife did not wait but she answered back loudly,

"Now my sister-in-law is jealous because a man called her only a piece of cold fish!"

[286]

And so the two fell to angry looks and hatred, although the elder, being proud of her correctness, would deal only in silent scorn, careful to ignore the other's very presence. But when her children would go out of their own court she called out,

"I would have you stay away from ill-bred children!"

This she called out in the presence of her sister-in-law who stood within sight in the next court, and that one would call out to her own children,

"Do not play with snakes or you will be bitten!"

So the two women hated each other increasingly, and the thing was the more bitter because the two brothers did not love each other well, the elder always being fearful lest his birth and his family seem lowly in the eyes of his wife who was town bred and better born than he, and the younger fearful lest his brother's desire for show and place lead them into wasting their heritage before it was divided. Moreover it was a shame to the elder brother that the second brother knew all the money their father had and what was spent and the money passed through his hands, so that although Wang Lung received and dispensed all the moneys from his lands, still the second brother knew what it was and the elder did not, but must go and ask his father for this and that like a child. So when the two wives hated each other, their hatred spread to the men also and the courts of the two were full of anger and Wang Lung groaned because there was no peace in his house.

Wang Lung had also his own secret trouble with Lotus since the day when he had protected her slave from the son of his uncle. Ever since that day the young maid had been in disfavor with Lotus, and although the girl waited on her silently and slavishly, and stood by her side all day filling her pipe and fetching this and that, and rising in the night at her complaint that she was sleepless and rubbing her legs and her body to soothe her, still Lotus was not satisfied.

And she was jealous of the maid and she sent her from the room when Wang Lung came in and she accused Wang Lung that he looked at the maid. Now Wang Lung had not thought of the girl except as a poor small child who was frightened and he cared as he might care for his poor fool and no more. But when Lotus accused him he took thought to look and he saw it was true that the girl was very pretty and pale as a pear blossom, and seeing this, something stirred in his old blood that had been quiet these ten years and more.

So while he laughed at Lotus saying, "What—are you thinking I am still a-lust, when I do not come into your room thrice a year?" yet he looked sidelong at the girl and he was stirred.

Now Lotus, for all she was ignorant in all ways except the one, in the way of men with women she was learned and she knew that men when they are old will wake once again to a brief youth, and so she was angry with the maid and she talked of selling her to the tea house. But still Lotus loved her comfort and Cuckoo grew old and lazy and the maid was quick and used about the person of Lotus and saw what her mistress needed before she knew it herself, and so Lotus was loath to part with her and yet she would part with her, and in this unaccustomed conflict Lotus was the more angry because of her discomfort and she was more hard than usual to live with. Wang Lung stayed away from her court for many days at a time because her temper was too ill to enjoy. He said to himself that he would wait, thinking it would pass, but meanwhile he thought of the pretty pale young maid more than he himself would believe he did.

Then as though there was not enough trouble with the women of his house all awry, there was Wang Lung's youngest son. Now his youngest son had been so quiet a lad, so bent on his belated books, that none thought of him except as a reedy slender youth with books always under his arm and an old tutor following him about like a dog.

But the lad had lived among the soldiers when they were there and he had listened to their tales of war and plunder and battle, and he listened rapt to it all, saying nothing. Then he begged novels of his old tutor, stories of the wars of the Three Kingdoms and of the brotherhood of bandits who lived in ancient times in a mountain lair, and his head was full of dreams.

So now he went to his father and he said,

"I know what I will do. I will be a soldier and I will go forth to wars."

When Wang Lung heard this, he thought in great dismay that it was the worst thing that could yet happen to him and he cried out with a great voice,

"Now what madness is this, and am I never to have any peace with my sons!" And he argued with the lad and he tried to be gentle and kindly when he saw the lad's black brows gather into a line and he said, "My son, it is said from ancient times that men do not take good iron to make a nail nor a good man to make a soldier, and you are my little son, my best little youngest son, and how shall I sleep at night and you wandering over the earth here and there in a war?"

But the boy was determined and he looked at his father and drew down his black brows and he said only,

"I will go."

Then Wang Lung coaxed him and said,

"Now you may go to any school you like and I will send you to the great schools of the south or even to a foreign school to learn curious things, and you shall go anywhere you like for study if you will not be a soldier. It is a disgrace to a man like me, a man of silver and of land, to have a son who is a soldier." And when the lad was still silent, he coaxed again, and he said, "Tell your old father why you want to be a soldier?"

And the lad said suddenly, and his eyes were alight under his brows,

"There is to be a war such as we have not heard of—there is to be a revolution and fighting and war such as never was, and our land is to be free!"

Wang Lung listened to this in the greatest astonishment he had yet had from his three sons.

"Now what all this stuff is, I do not know," he said wondering.

[289]

"Our land is free already—all our good land is free. I rent it to whom I will and it brings me silver and good grains and you eat and are clothed and are fed with it, and I do not know what freedom you desire more than you have."

But the boy only muttered bitterly,

"You do not understand—you are too old—you understand nothing."

And Wang Lung pondered and he looked at this son of his and he saw the suffering young face, and he thought to himself,

"Now I have given this son everything, even his life. He has everything from me. I have let him leave the land, even, so that I have not a son after me to see to the land, and I have let him read and write although there is no need for it in my family with two already." And he thought and he said to himself further, still staring at the lad, "Everything this son has from me."

Then he looked closely at his son and he saw that he was tall as a man already, though still reedy with youth, and he said, doubtfully, muttering and half-aloud, for he saw no sign of lust in the boy,

"Well, it may be he needs one thing more." And he said aloud then and slowly, "We will wed you soon, my son."

But the boy flashed a look of fire at his father from under his heavy gathered brows and he said scornfully,

"Then I will run away indeed, for to me a woman is not answer to everything as it is to my eldest brother!"

Wang Lung saw at once that he was wrong and so he said hastily to excuse himself,

"No—no—we will not wed you—but I mean, if there is a slave you desire—"

And the boy answered with lofty looks and with dignity, folding his arms on his breast,

"I am not the ordinary young man. I have my dreams. I wish for glory. There are women everywhere." And then as though he remembered something he had forgotten, he suddenly broke from his dignity and his arms dropped and he said in his usual voice,

"Besides, there never were an uglier set of slaves than we have. If I cared—but I do not—well, there is not a beauty in the courts except perhaps the little pale maid who waits on the one in the inner court."

Then Wang knew he spoke of Pear Blossom and he was smitten with a strange jealousy. He suddenly felt himself older than he was —a man old and too thick of girth and with whitening hair, and he saw his son a man slim and young, and it was not for this moment father and son, but two men, one old and one young, and Wang Lung said angrily,

"Now keep off the slaves—I will not have the rotten ways of young lords in my house. We are good stout country folk and people with decent ways, and none of this in my house!"

Then the boy opened his eyes and lifted his black brows and shrugged his shoulders and he said to his father,

"You spoke of it first!" and then he turned away and went out.

Then Wang Lung sat there alone in his room by his table and he felt dreary and alone, and he muttered to himself,

"Well, and I have no peace anywhere in my house."

He was confused with many angers, but, although he could not understand why, this anger stood forth most clearly; his son had looked on a little pale young maid in the house and had found her fair.

XXXIII

WANG LUNG could not cease from his thought of what his youngest son had said of Pear Blossom and he watched the maid incessantly as she came and went and without his knowing it the thought of her filled his mind and he doted on her. But he said nothing to anyone.

One night in the early summer of that year, at the time when the night air is thick and soft with the mists of warmth and fragrance, he sat at rest in his own court alone under a flowering cassia tree and the sweet heavy scent of the cassia flowers filled his nostrils and he sat there and his blood ran full and hot like the blood of a young man. Through the day he had felt his blood so and he had been half of a mind to walk out on his land and feel the good earth under his feet and take off his shoes and his stockings and feel it on his skin.

This he would have done but he was ashamed lest men see him, who was no longer held a farmer within the gates of the town, but a landowner and a rich man. So he wandered restlessly about the courts and he stayed away altogether from the court where Lotus sat in the shade and smoked her water pipe, because well she knew when a man was restless and she had sharp eyes to see what was amiss. He went alone, then, and he had no mind to see either of his two quarreling daughters-in-law, nor even his grandchildren, in whom was his frequent delight.

So the day had passed very long and lonely and his blood was full and coursing under his skin. He could not forget his youngest son, how he had looked standing tall and straight and his black brows drawn together in the gravity of his youth, and he could not forget the maid. And to himself he said,

"I suppose they are of an age—the boy must be well on eighteen and she not over eighteen."

Then he remembered that he himself would before many years be seventy and he was ashamed of his coursing blood, and he thought,

"It would be a good thing to give the maid to the lad," and this he said to himself again and again, and every time he said it the thing stabbed like a thrust on flesh already sore, and he could not but stab and yet he could not but feel the pain.

And so the day passed very long and lonely for him.

When night came he was still alone and he sat in his court alone and there was not one in all his house to whom he could go as friend. And the night air was thick and soft and hot with the smell of the flowers of the cassia tree.

Then as he sat there in the darkness under the tree one passed beside where he was sitting near the gate of his court where the tree stood, and he looked quickly and it was Pear Blossom.

"Pear Blossom!" he called, and his voice came in a whisper.

She stopped suddenly, her head bent in listening.

Then he called again and his voice would scarcely come from his throat,

"Come here to me!"

Then hearing him she crept timidly through the gate and stood before him and he could scarcely see her standing there in the blackness, but he could feel her there and he put out his hand and laid hold of her little coat and he said, half choking,

"Child—!"

There he stopped with the word. He said to himself that he was an old man and it was a disgraceful thing for a man with grandsons and grand-daughters nearer to this child's age than he was, and he fingered her little coat.

Then she, waiting, caught from him the heat of his blood and

[293]

she bent over and slipped, like a flower crumpling upon its stalk, to the ground, and she clasped his feet and lay there. And he said slowly,

"Child—I am an old man—a very old man—"

And she said, and her voice came out of the darkness like the very breath of the cassia tree,

"I like old men—I like old men—they are so kind—"

He said again, tenderly, stooping to her a little,

"A little maid like you should have a tall straight youth—a little maid like you!" And in his heart he added, "Like my son—" but aloud he could not say it, because he might put the thought into her mind, and he could not bear it.

But she said,

"Young men are not kind—they are only fierce."

And hearing her small childish voice quavering up from about his feet his heart welled in a great wave of love for this maid, and he took her and raised her gently, and then he led her into his own court.

When it was done, this love of his age astonished him more than any of his lusts before, for with all his love for Pear Blossom he did not seize upon her as he had seized upon the others whom he had known.

No, he held her gently and he was satisfied to feel her light youth against his heavy old flesh, and he was satisfied merely with the sight of her in the day and with the touch of her fluttering coat against his hand and with the quiet resting of her body near him in the night. And he wondered at the love of old age, which is so fond and so easily satisfied.

As for her, she was a passionless maid and she clung to him as to a father, and to him she was indeed more than half child and scarcely woman.

Now the thing that Wang Lung had done did not quickly come out, for he said nothing at all, and why should he, being master in his own house?

But the eye of Cuckoo marked it first and she saw the maid slipping at dawn out of his court and she laid hold on the girl and laughed, and her old hawk's eyes glittered.

"Well!" she said. "And so it is the Old Lord over again!"

And Wang Lung in his room, hearing her, girded his robe about him quickly and he came out and smiled sheepishly and half proudly and he said muttering,

"Well, and I said she had better take a young lad and she would have the old one!"

"It will be a pretty thing to tell the mistress," Cuckoo said, then, and her eyes sparkled with malice.

"I do not know myself how the thing happened," answered Wang Lung slowly. "I had not meant to add another woman to my courts, and the thing came about of itself." Then when Cuckoo said, "Well, and the mistress must be told," Wang Lung, fearing the anger of Lotus more than anything begged Cuckoo and he said again, "Do you tell her, if you will, and if you can manage it without anger to my face I will give you a handful of money for it."

So Cuckoo, still laughing and shaking her head, promised, and Wang Lung went back to his court and he would not come forth for a while until Cuckoo came back and said,

"The thing is told, and she was angry enough until I reminded her she wanted and has wanted this long time the foreign clock you promised her, and she will have a ruby ring for her hand and a pair so that there will be one on each hand, and she will have other things as she thinks of them and a slave to take Pear Blossom's place, and Pear Blossom is not to come to her any more, and you are not to come soon either, because the sight of you sickens her."

And Wang Lung promised eagerly and he said,

"Get her what she wills and I do not begrudge anything."

And he was pleased that he need not see Lotus soon and until anger was cooled with the fulfillment of her wishes.

There were left yet his three sons, and he was strangely ashamed before them of what he had done. And he said to himself again and again,

"Am I not master in my own house and may I not take my own slave I bought with my silver?"

But he was ashamed, and yet half proud too, as one feels himself who is still lusty and a man when others hold him to be only grandfather. And he waited for his sons to come into his court.

They came one by one, separately, and the second one came first. Now this one when he came talked of the land and of the harvest and of the summer drought which would this year divide the harvest by three. But Wang Lung considered nothing in these days of rain or drought, for if the harvest of the year brought him in little there was silver left from the year before and he kept his courts stuffed with silver and there was money owing to him at the grain markets and he had much money let out at high interest that his second son collected for him, and he looked no more to see how the skies were over his land.

But the second son talked on thus, and as he talked he looked here and there about the rooms with his eyes veiled and secret and Wang Lung knew that he looked for the maid to see if what he had heard was true, and so he called Pear Blossom from where she hid in the bedroom, and he called out,

"Bring me tea, my child, and tea for my son!"

And she came out, and her delicate pale face was rosy as a peach and she hung her head and crept about on her little silent feet, and the second son stared at her as if he had heard but could not believe until now.

But he said nothing at all except that the land was thus and so and this tenant and that must be changed at the end of the year, and the other one, because he smoked opium and would not gather from the land what it could bear. And Wang Lung asked his son how his children did, and he answered they had the hundred days' cough, but it was a slight thing now that the weather was warm.

Thus they talked back and forth, drinking tea, and the second son took his fill of what he saw and he went away, and Wang Lung was eased of his second son.

Then the eldest son came in before the same day was half over and he came in tall and handsome and proud with the years of his maturity, and Wang Lung was afraid of his pride, and he did not call out Pear Blossom at first, but he waited and smoked his pipe. The oldest son sat there then stiff with his pride and his dignity and he asked after the proper manner for his father's health and for his welfare. Then Wang Lung answered quickly and quietly that he was well, and as he looked at his son his fear went out of him.

For he saw his eldest for what he was: a man big in body but afraid of his own town wife and more afraid of not appearing nobly born than of anything. And the robustness of the land that was strong in Wang Lung even when he did not know it swelled up in him, and he was careless again of this eldest son as he had been before, and careless of his proper looks, and he called easily of a sudden to Pear Blossom,

"Come, my child, and pour out tea again for another son of mine!"

This time she came out very cold and still and her small oval face was white as the flower of her name. Her eyes dropped as she came in and she moved stilly and did only what she was told to do and she went quickly out again.

Now the two men had sat silent while she poured the tea, but when she was gone and they lifted their bowls, Wang Lung looked fully into his son's eyes, and he caught there a naked look of admiration, and it was the look of one man who envies another man secretly. Then they drank their tea and the son said at last in a thick, uneven voice,

"I did not believe it was so."

"Why not?" replied Wang Lung tranquilly. "It is my own house."

The son sighed then and after a time he answered,

"You are rich and you may do as you like." And he sighed

again and he said, "Well, I suppose one is not always enough for any man and there comes a day—"

He broke off, but there was in his look the tinge of a man who envies another man against his will, and Wang Lung looked and laughed in himself, for well he knew his eldest son's lusty nature and that not forever would the proper town wife he had hold the leash and some day the man would come forth again.

Then the eldest son said no more but he went his way as a man does who has had a new thought put into his head. And Wang sat and smoked his pipe and he was proud of himself that when he was an old man he had done what he wished.

But it was night before the youngest son came in and he came alone also. Now Wang Lung sat in his middle room in the court and the red candles were lit on the table and he sat there smoking, and Pear Blossom sat silently on the other side of the table from him, and her hands were folded and quiet in her lap. Sometimes she looked at Wang Lung, fully and without coquetry as a child does, and he watched her and was proud of what he had done.

Then suddenly there was his youngest son standing before him, sprung out of the darkness of the court, and no one had seen him enter. But he stood there in some strange crouching way, and without taking thought of it, Wang Lung was reminded in a flash of memory of a young tiger he had once seen the men of the village bring in from the hills where they had caught it, and the beast was tied but he crouched for a spring, and his eyes gleamed, and the lad's eyes gleamed and he fixed them upon his father's face. And those brows of his that were too heavy and too black for his youth, he gathered fierce and black above his eyes. Thus he stood and at last he said in a low and surcharged voice,

"Now I will go for a soldier—I will go for a soldier—"

But he did not look at the girl, only at his father, and Wang Lung, who had not been afraid at all of his eldest son and his second son, was suddenly afraid of this one, whom he had scarcely considered from his birth up.

And Wang Lung stammered and muttered, and would have

spoken, but when he took his pipe from his mouth, no sound came, and he stared at his son. And his son repeated again and again,

"Now I will go—now I will go—"

Suddenly he turned and looked at the girl once, and she looked back at him, shrinking, and she took her two hands and put them over her face so that she could not see him. Then the young man tore his eyes from her and he went in a leap from the room and Wang Lung looked out into the square of the darkness of the door, open into the black summer night, and he was gone and there was silence everywhere.

At last he turned to the girl and he said humbly and gently and with a great sadness and all his pride gone,

"I am too old for you, my heart, and well I know it. I am an old, old man."

But the girl dropped her hands from her face and she cried more passionately than he had ever heard her cry,

"Young men are so cruel—I like old men best!"

When the morning came of the next day Wang Lung's youngest son was gone and where he was gone no one knew.

XXXIV

THEN as autumn flares with the false heat of summer before it dies into the winter, so with the quick love Wang Lung had for Pear Blossom. The brief heat of it passed and passion died out of him; he was fond of her, but passionless.

With the passing of the flame out of him he was suddenly cold with an age and he was an old man. Nevertheless, he was fond of her, and it was a comfort to him that she was in his court and she served him faithfully and with a patience beyond her years, and he was always kind to her with a perfect kindness, and more and more his love for her was the love of father for daughter.

And for his sake she was even kind to his poor fool and this was comfort to him, so that one day he told her what had long been in his mind. Now Wang Lung had thought many times of what would come to his poor fool when he was dead and there was not another one except himself who cared whether she lived or starved, and so he had bought a little bundle of white poisonous stuff at the medicine shop, and he had said to himself that he would give it to his fool to eat when he saw his own death was near. But still he dreaded this more than the hour of his own death, and it was a comfort to him now when he saw Pear Blossom was faithful.

So he called her to him one day and he said,

"There is none other but you to whom I can leave this poor fool of mine when I am gone, and she will live on and on after me, seeing that her mind has no troubles of its own, and she has nothing to kill her and no trouble to worry her. And well I know that no one will think when I am gone to feed her or to bring her out of the rain and the cold of winter nor to set her in the summer sun, and she will be sent out to wander on the street, perhaps—this poor thing who has had care all her life from her mother and from me. Now here is a gate of safety for her in this packet, and when I die, after I am dead, you are to mix it in her rice and let her eat it, that she may follow me where I am. And so shall I be at ease."

But Pear Blossom shrank from the thing he held in his hand and she said in her soft way,

"I can scarcely kill an insect and how could I take this life? No, my lord, but I will take this poor fool for mine because you have been kind to me—kinder than any in all my life, and the only kind one."

And Wang Lung could have wept for what she said because no

[300]

one had ever requited him like this, and his heart clung to her and he said,

"Nevertheless, take it, my child, for there is none I trust as I do you, but even you must die one day—although I cannot say the words—and after you there is none—no, not one—and well I know my sons' wives are too busy with their children and their quarrels and my sons are men and cannot think of such things."

So when she saw his meaning, Pear Blossom took the packet from him and said no more and Wang Lung trusted her and was comforted for the fate of his poor fool.

Then Wang Lung withdrew more and more into his age and he lived much alone except for these two in his courts, his poor fool and Pear Blossom. Sometimes he roused himself a little and he looked at Pear Blossom and he was troubled and said,

"It is too quiet a life for you, my child."

But she always answered gently and in great gratitude,

"It is quiet and safe."

And sometimes he said again,

"I am too old for you, and my fires are ashes."

But she always answered with a great thankfulness,

"You are kind to me and more I do not desire of any man."

Once when she said this Wang Lung was curious and he asked her,

"What was it in your tender years that made you thus fearful of men?"

And looking at her for answer he saw a great terror in her eyes and she covered them with her hands and she whispered,

"Every man I hate except you—I have hated every man, even my father who sold me. I have heard only evil of them and I hate them all."

And he said wondering,

"Now I should have said you had lived quietly and easily in my courts."

"I am filled with loathing," she said, looking away. "I am filled with loathing and I hate them all. I hate all young men."

And she would say nothing more, and he mused on it, and he did not know whether Lotus had filled her with tales of her life and had threatened her, or whether Cuckoo had frightened her with lewdness, or whether something had befallen her secretly that she would not tell him, or what it was.

But he sighed and gave over his questions, because above everything now he would have peace, and he wished only to sit in his court near these two.

So Wang Lung sat, and so his age came on him day by day and year by year, and he slept fitfully in the sun as his father had done, and he said to himself that his life was finished and he was satisfied with it.

Sometimes, but seldom, he went into the other courts and sometimes, but more seldom, he saw Lotus, and she never mentioned the maid he had taken, but she greeted him well enough and she was old too and satisfied with the food and the wine she loved and with the silver she had for the asking. She and Cuckoo sat together now after these many years as friends and no longer as mistress and servant, and they talked of this and that, and most of all of the old days with men and they whispered together of things they would not speak aloud, and they ate and drank and slept, and woke to gossip again before eating and drinking.

And when Wang Lung went, and it was very seldom, into his sons' courts, they treated him courteously and they ran to get tea for him and he asked to see the last child and he asked many times, for he forgot easily,

"How many grandchildren have I now?"

And one answered him readily,

"Eleven sons and eight daughters have your sons together."

And he, chuckling and laughing, said back,

"Add two each year, and I know the number, is it so?"

Then he would sit a little while and look at the children gathering around him to stare. His grandsons were tall lads now, and he looked at them, peering at them to see what they were, and he muttered to himself,

"Now that one has the look of his great-grandfather and there is a small merchant Liu, and here is myself when young."

And he asked them,

"Do you go to school?"

"Yes, grandfather," they answered in a scattered chorus, and he said again,

"Do you study the Four Books?"

Then they laughed with clear young scorn at a man so old as this and they said,

"No, grandfather, and no one studies the Four Books since the Revolution."

And he answered, musing,

"Ah, I have heard of a revolution, but I have been too busy in my life to attend to it. There was always the land."

But the lads snickered at this, and at last Wang Lung rose, feeling himself after all but a guest in his sons' courts.

Then after a time he went no more to see his sons, but sometimes he would ask Cuckoo,

"And are my two daughters-in-law at peace after all these years?"

And Cuckoo spat upon the ground and she said,

"Those? They are at peace like two cats eyeing each other. But the eldest son wearies of his wife's complaints of this and that— too proper a woman for a man, she is, and always talking of what they did in the house of her father, and she wearies a man. There is talk of his taking another. He goes often to the tea shops."

"Ah?" said Wang Lung.

But when he would have thought of it his interest in the matter waned and before he knew it he was thinking of his tea and that the young spring wind blew cold upon his shoulders.

And another time he said to Cuckoo,

"Does any ever hear from that youngest son of mine where he is gone this long time?"

And Cuckoo answered, for there was nothing she did not know in these courts,

"He does not write a letter, but now and then one comes from the south and it is said he is a military official and great enough in a thing they call a revolution there, but what it is I do not know— perhaps some sort of business."

And again Wang Lung said, "Ah?"

And he would have thought of it, but the evening was falling and his bones ached in the air left raw and chill when the sun withdrew. For his mind now went where it would and he could not hold it long to any one thing. And the needs of his old body for food and for hot tea were more keen than for anything. But at night when he was cold, Pear Blossom lay warm and young against him and he was comforted in his age with her warmth in his bed.

Thus spring wore on again and again and vaguely and more vaguely as these years passed he felt it coming. But still one thing remained to him and it was his love for his land. He had gone away from it and he had set up his house in a town and he was rich. But his roots were in his land and although he forgot it for many months together, when spring came each year he must go out on to the land; and now although he could no longer hold a plow or do anything but see another drive the plow through the earth, still he must needs go and he went. Sometimes he took a servant and his bed and he slept again in the old earthen house and in the old bed where he had begotten children and where O-lan had died. When he woke in the dawn he went out and with his trembling hands he reached and plucked a bit of budding willow and a spray of peach bloom and held them all day in his hand.

Thus he wandered one day in a late spring, near summer, and he went over his fields a little way and he came to the enclosed place upon a low hill where he had buried his dead. He stood trembling on his staff and he looked at the graves and he remembered them every one. They were more clear to him now than the sons who lived in his own house, more clear to him than anyone except his poor fool and except Pear Blossom. And his mind went back many years and he saw it all clearly, even his little second daughter of whom he had heard nothing for longer than he could remember, and he saw her a pretty maid as she had been in his house, her lips as thin and red as a shred of silk—and she was to him like these who lay here in the land. Then he mused and he thought suddenly,

"Well, and I shall be the next."

Then he went into the enclosure and he looked carefully and he saw the place where he would lie below his father and his uncle and above Ching and not far from O-lan. And he stared at the bit of earth where he was to lie and he saw himself in it and back in his own land forever. And he muttered,

"I must see to the coffin."

This thought he held fast and painfully in his mind and he went back to the town and he sent for his eldest son, and he said,

"There is something I have to say."

"Then say on," answered the son, "I am here."

But when Wang Lung would have said he suddenly could not remember what it was, and the tears stood in his eyes because he had held the matter so painfully in his mind and now it had slipped wilfully away from him. So he called Pear Blossom and he said to her,

"Child, what was it I wanted to say?"

And Pear Blossom answered gently,

"Where were you this day?"

"I was upon the land," Wang Lung replied, waiting, his eyes fixed on her face.

And she asked gently again,

"On what piece of land?"

Then suddenly the thing flew into his mind again and he cried, laughing out of his wet eyes,

"Well, and I do remember. My son, I have chosen my place in

[305]

the earth, and it is below my father and his brother and above your mother and next to Ching, and I would see my coffin before I die."

Then Wang Lung's eldest son cried out dutifully and properly,

"Do not say that word, my father, but I will do as you say."

Then his son bought a carven coffin hewn from a great log of fragrant wood which is used to bury the dead in and for nothing else because that wood is as lasting as iron, and more lasting than human bones, and Wang Lung was comforted.

And he had the coffin brought into his room and he looked at it every day.

Then all of a sudden he thought of something and he said,

"Well, and I would have it moved out to the earthen house and there I will live out my few days and there I will die."

And when they saw how he had set his heart they did what he wished and he went back to the house on his land, he and Pear Blossom and the fool, and what servants they needed; and Wang Lung took up his abode again on his land, and he left the house in the town to the family he had founded.

Spring passed and summer passed into harvest and in the hot autumn sun before winter comes Wang Lung sat where his father had sat against the wall. And he thought no more about anything now except his food and his drink and his land. But of his land he thought no more what harvest it would bring or what seed would be planted or of anything except of the land itself, and he stooped sometimes and gathered some of the earth up in his hand and he sat thus and held it in his hand, and it seemed full of life between his fingers. And he was content, holding it thus, and he thought of it fitfully and of his good coffin that was there; and the kind earth waited without haste until he came to it.

His sons were proper enough to him and they came to him every day or at most once in two days, and they sent him delicate food fit for his age, but he liked best to have one stir up meal in hot water and sup it as his father had done.

Sometimes he complained a little of his sons if they came not every day and he said to Pear Blossom, who was always near him,

"Well, and what are they so busy about?"

But if Pear Blossom said, "They are in the prime of life and now they have many affairs. Your eldest son has been made an officer in the town among the rich men, and he has a new wife, and your second son is setting up a great grain market for himself." Wang Lung listened to her, but he could not comprehend all this and he forgot it as soon as he looked out over his land.

But one day he saw clearly for a little while. It was a day on which his two sons had come and after they had greeted him courteously they went out and they walked about the house on to the land. Now Wang Lung followed them silently, and they stood, and he came up to them slowly, and they did not hear the sound of his footsteps nor the sound of his staff on the soft earth, and Wang Lung heard his second son say in his mincing voice,

"This field we will sell and this one, and we will divide the money between us evenly. Your share I will borrow at good interest, for now with the railroad straight through I can ship rice to the sea and I . . ."

But the old man heard only these words, "sell the land," and he cried out and he could not keep his voice from breaking and trembling with his anger,

"Now, evil, idle sons—sell the land?" He choked and would have fallen, and they caught him and held him up, and he began to weep.

Then they soothed him and they said, soothing him,

"No—no—we will never sell the land—"

"It is the end of a family—when they begin to sell the land," he said brokenly. "Out of the land we came and into it we must go— and if you will hold your land you can live—no one can rob you of land—"

And the old man let his scanty tears dry upon his cheeks and

they made salty stains there. And he stooped and took up a handful of the soil and he held it and he muttered,

"If you sell the land, it is the end."

And his two sons held him, one on either side, each holding his
arm, and he held tight in his hand the warm loose earth. And they
soothed him and they said over and over, the eldest son and the
second son,

"Rest assured, our father, rest assured. The land is not to be
sold."

But over the old man's head they looked at each other and
smiled.

THE STORY OF
The Good Earth

ABOUT a book that has had a career such as that of *The Good Earth,* legends grow up, some of which are not true. The issue of this Standard Edition seems a good occasion to trace the record and set the facts straight.

This was not Pearl Buck's first novel. One was in finished manuscript and was destroyed when a revolutionary mob looted her house in Nanking in March, 1927. Several white people were killed that day, and she barely escaped with her life and nothing else but the old clothing she wore while she lay hidden for fourteen hours. She never tried to re-create that first novel. "I console myself by thinking it probably was not any good," she says. "At any rate, it was a lot of work—gone for nothing."

Her first published book was *East Wind: West Wind*, which came out on April 30, 1930. It was this manuscript, not *The Good Earth*, that had been rejected by many American publishers, having been offered by the novelist's agent, David Lloyd, for forty-seven weeks before the John Day Company, as he puts it, "decided to plump for it." In England, after three declinations, it readily found its imprint, though only after being overtaken by *The Good Earth*, which was the first of the author's books published abroad. The only publisher in the world who ever rejected *The Good Earth* ruefully tells the story on himself. It happened that one of his staff was in New York and learned directly from us of our enthusiasm for the book. Proofs were sent to the publisher in Lon-

[309]

don and promptly declined, the decision resting, it is understood, on the old ground that people did not want to read about China.

The Good Earth came to us simply because we had taken a chance on the author's first slight book. Our instant belief that this second one was a great book is shown by the words we wrote to go on the jacket, before we knew the opinion of others. We have never seen reason to change one of these words, which read:

> The reader soon becomes unaware of distinctions of race, of period, of locale. These people are born, play, toil, suffer, and dream as all humans have done, under whatever sun, on whatever patch of our common earth. Wang Lung, rising from humble farmer to wealthy landowner, gloried in the soil he worked, held it above his family, even above his gods. But between the kindly soil and him were interposed flood and drought, pestilence and revolution. We see him first on his wedding day, and through him and his children, trace the whole cycle of life, its terrors, its passions, its persistent ambitions and its meagre rewards.
>
> Worthy of a place on the short shelf of mighty novels of the soil.

One of the first to see the proofs was the veteran publisher, Mitchell Kennerley, who said, "A work of genius—I predict a popular and distinguished success." Then recognition came from the Book-of-the-Month Club, and most vocally from Dorothy Canfield, who wrote, "To find such a book gave me a thrill of delight. A rare, fine sterling piece of work." Chosen as the Book of the Month for March, 1931, and published on the second day of that month, the book had almost unanimous approval by reviewers. It leaped to the best-seller list where it stayed for twenty-one months, a record made up to that time by no other book since *Quo Vadis*, thirty-five years earlier.

Among the many praises, perhaps the one that did most to drive the book through the crust of literary choice into the ken of the great average reading public was that of Will Rogers. Will was then writing his amazing daily paragraphs that stood in boxes on the front pages of newspapers. One fine day, in one of these boxes, he said that *The Good Earth* was "not only the greatest book about a people ever written, but the best book of our generation." Demand increased at once all over the country.

The Good Earth won for its author, in May, 1932, the Pulitzer Prize for the best novel of its year by an American author, and in November, 1935, the William Dean Howells Medal. In presenting the latter, Robert Grant said, "The donor of this gold medal provided that it should be given every fifth year in recognition of the most distinguished work of American fiction published during that period. The first recipient of one of these gold medals was Mary E. Wilkins Freeman in November 1925. The second was Willa Cather. . . . For the third time the medal is to be awarded to a woman, a choice acquiesced in by the four Academicians serving as the Committee, three of whom are men, and approved by a majority of the members of the American Academy of Arts and Letters.

"It is to honor those who can write so convincingly of people, whether in the tragedy or comedy of human life, that the puppets cease to be puppets, and live and move and have their being, that this memorial to William Dean Howells was endowed. Because she has done this so unerringly and with such an artistic sense of values, I am commissioned to bestow upon the author of *The Good Earth* this medal of gold for the five year period just ended."

In responding the author laid stress on her gratitude to her own country. She said:

"I find here, surely more than in any other country in the world, opportunity for a writer, unknown and obscure, with no influence of any kind, without money or particular friends, to come into recognition, to find generous praise and welcome and many friends. No one could have had more unpromising beginnings than I—to write of subjects so foreign, to live so far. And yet, at every step I have found open to the writer one opportunity after another. . . . When I remember the little distant poor room in which I began to write, and when I look about me today in your presence, I cannot but feel a great humility and gratitude for opportunity so freely given, and so richly rewarded, in America."

In January, 1936, she was elected a member of the National Institute of Arts and Letters.

In 1938 she received the Nobel Prize for Literature, the first American woman to be so honored. The award was made not for *The Good Earth* only, as is sometimes mistakenly said, but for the body of her work, which was reviewed at length in an address at the ceremonies in Stockholm, by Per Hallstrom, secretary of the Swedish Academy.

But such honors were of less importance than the influence of the book itself upon its period. *The Good Earth* opened a new Old World to the people of America and of other lands. Not only through its own pages, and those of later books by its author, but also through those of many fine books by other authors, the life of the Chinese people has been made clear and understandable. Lewis Gannett has said, "Nobody thought a book on China would sell until Pearl Buck did one." Since 1931 writers, publishers, and the editors of magazines have faced Chinese topics with new confidence. This new understanding of China has expressed itself in many practical ways of friendship and sympathy and in vast projects of relief and reconstruction.

We do not mean to stress too much the influence of a single book. For just about one hundred years American interest in China had been growing, largely through the activities of business-men and missionaries, and to some extent of diplomats. There had been in Europe as well as in America scholarly and aesthetic concern with Chinese philosophy, poetry, and art, a highly developed literature in these fields, and magnificent collections in the museums. In American homes, especially along the sea coasts from which our traders had sailed, were many Chinese things, ranging from mere curios made for tourists to beautiful objects of art.

But to the general public the Chinese as a person was unknown. He had been first the "heathen Chinee," peculiar "for ways that are dark and tricks that are vain." He was the laundryman, the cook, and the restaurant keeper, the queer denizen of an exotic Chinatown. He was the picturesque envoy, Li Hung Chang. He was the villain of Sax Rohmer or the shrewd detective Charlie Chan. He was the seriocomic sage of "Confucius say . . ." Now he and his wife and sons and all his relations quite suddenly became people just like ourselves, no longer strange or mysterious. We knew them for what they are and liked them well.

This impact of *The Good Earth* was magnified by the screen. The Theatre Guild staged a play by Owen and Donald Davis based on the book. While this play had no great success, it in turn became the basis of a motion picture that was shown throughout the world. Millions who never read the book came to know its people through the film. This process still goes on. Although the picture no longer appears in the regular theaters in the United States, it does appear constantly in other countries, and a shortened version is in steady use in American schools, churches, clubs, and film councils.

To a certain sort of chauvinistic Chinese all this has not been pleasing. Traditionally Chinese intellectuals have been remote from the people. These "two-and-one-half percent," as they have been called—for that is their ratio to the vast population of China —consider themselves the actual representative Chinese. They did not relish the idea that in foreign eyes the peasant was now the real Chinese. Wise and genuine intellectuals, of whom Lin Yutang was a notable and early example, hailed *The Good Earth* as true and valuable. But lesser men went about telling foreigners wistfully that the book did not correctly portray their country. This had little effect other than to expose the fact that these intellectuals, many of them trained in foreign universities, did not really know their own people. Amusing incidents occurred while the motion picture was being shot in China. Bureaucrats were anxious that the Chinese farmer should not appear old-fashioned. They urged the producers to have him plow his fields not with the faithful water buffalo but with a modern tractor. An editorial in a Nanking newspaper wailed that in spite of official efforts it was feared that some of the women in the film would appear in soiled garments. There were devoted attempts to persuade the director that all younger women should wear flowers over their ears. It has been rumored, though never confirmed, that through sabotage many of the sequences shot in China were ruined by acid poured into the cans and had to be remade on artificial location in Hollywood.

Not only the film but the widespread use of reprint editions enlarged the influence of the book. After it was by way of becoming a classic, we agreed on a policy of granting nonexclusive reprint rights for any edition at any price. This was by the author's wish. She said, "I am always glad when any of my books can be put into an inexpensive edition, because I like to think that any people who might wish to read them can do so. Surely books ought to be within the reach of everybody." So it came about that the book could be bought in any of a number of editions at various prices, from twenty-five cents up. The first reprint contract was made with Grosset and Dunlap, the next with the Modern Library. Beginning in 1936 P. F. Collier issued six-volume sets of the author's novels, sold by subscription in areas not reached by bookstores. In these sets *The Good Earth* has been a constant unit, with the other titles changing from set to set.

When Robert De Graff first conceived the plan of Pocket Books, he wished to test it by a local campaign using one book as a sample. The author and the publishers were glad to have *The Good Earth* used for this test. They have always been proud that its success added something to the founding of an enterprise which has taken twenty-five-cent books to millions of readers.

From the outset the obvious idea of an illustrated edition was resisted. We felt that readers had already formed their own mental pictures of Wang Lung, O-lan, and the other characters and did not want to disturb these by an artist's concepts. When the film was made, we did not permit the usual "motion-picture edition" with still photographs from the film—particularly because the actors, though able, did not have Chinese features. In 1947, however, the World Publishing Company wished to include the book in its illustrated Living Library, edited by Carl Van Doren. We agreed, with the stipulation that the illustrations were not to try to portray the faces or forms of the main characters. The artist, Howard Willard, knew China well, and he conveyed the scenes and atmosphere of the story with great skill. In his introduction to this edition Mr. Van Doren called *The Good Earth* "the most widely known novel of recent times, a true people's book of all the peoples." He made the point that this book came out in a decade of world depression when people "saw that the complex systems of their lives had broken down, it might be forever so far as they knew" and that Wang Lung's passionate clinging to his land met with sympathetic understanding in every country. "It is clear," he said, "that *The Good Earth* must be remembered and honored as the great novel of that world depression. It is a lasting part of the history of the time . . . it is a universal story told with the music of a fitting style which makes it universal art."

Reprint editions and the motion picture indeed carried the story to many parts of the world. Even more pervasive have been the translations. In addition to the thirty or more languages for which translations have been authorized, there have been an unknown number of others. Pirated editions came out promptly in Chinese; sometimes there was competition between three or more differing versions, one of them being a condensation of the bare story for the hasty Chinese reader. Japanese translations, made without permission under the Japanese-American treaty that then prevailed, sold in vast numbers. One of these was issued, according to the Japanese custom, under the name of a famous translator, although the actual work of it was done by an obscure hack. The latter, some time later, wrote to the author asking her to intercede for him, claiming that he had not been paid a fair share—and this in spite of the fact that she had not received one yen of royalty!

There are editions in several India vernaculars and in at least three of the languages of the Soviet Union. There is one in the Ibo language of Nigeria. We do not know how many unauthorized translations there may be in the vernacular languages of India, Africa, and other lands. There still come letters from remote places, written in broken English, by men and women who want to say that through this book they have come to know and love the people of China.

Such were, and are, the ever widening circles that started in that little distant attic room in which the book was written. To a publisher it is a matter of humble pride that his acceptance of a slender manuscript by an unknown person far across the seas should have been of help. The author had been told that no one wanted to read about China. At that time of her life she could write only about China. She knew nothing else well. She was planning, therefore, to make a living as a teacher, even though she knew that she must write, somehow. The acceptance of *East Wind: West Wind* changed all her plans. She tells how it was. She had in that year (1929) left China for a hurried business trip to America. "While we were there a letter was forwarded to me from China, whither it had been sent by my agent, saying that the John Day Company had made an acceptable offer for the book and would I cable concerning certain matters. At the instant of receiving this letter I happened to be but a few hours from New York; I had so completely forgotten the whole matter that I had neglected to tell the agency of my change of continents. When I could, therefore, I went to New York and to the John Day offices. . . . So runs the slight story of *East Wind: West Wind*. The book is of value to me chiefly because it gave me confidence to go on writing, since now I had found a publisher who could be interested in what I wrote, even though I could write only about China."

Returning to Nanking, she climbed to the attic room and wrote *The Good Earth*, typing it twice herself, in three months.

THE JOHN DAY COMPANY

August 1, 1949

SONS

I

WANG LUNG lay dying. He lay dying in his small, dark, old earthen house in the midst of his fields, in the room where he had slept as a young man, upon the very bed where he had lain on his marriage night. The room was less even than one of the kitchens in that great town house, which was his also, where his sons and their sons now lived. But he was content to die here in the midst of his lands, in this old house of his fathers, in this room with its rude, unpainted table and benches, under his blue cotton bed curtains, since die he must.

For Wang Lung knew that his time had come to die, and he looked at his two sons who were beside him and he knew they waited for him to die, and his hour was come. They had hired good physicians to come from the town, and these came with their needles and their herbs and they felt his pulse long and looked at his tongue, but in the end they gathered their medicines together to depart and they said,

"His age is on him and none can avert his destined death."

Then Wang Lung heard those two sons of his whisper together, who had come to stay with him in this earthen house until he died, and they thought him sunken in sleep, but he heard them, and they said staring at each other solemnly,

"We must send south for his other son, our brother."

And the second son answered, "Yes, and we must send at once, for who knows where he is wandering under that general he serves?"

3

And hearing this, Wang Lung knew they prepared for his funeral.

Beside his bed stood his coffin which his sons had bought for him and placed there for his comfort. It was a huge thing, hewn of a great tree of ironwood, and it crowded the small room, so that who came and went must circle and press about it. The price of this coffin was nearly six hundred pieces of silver, but even Wang the Second had not begrudged the spending, although usually money passed through his fingers so slowly it seldom came out so much as it went in. No, his sons did not begrudge the silver, for Wang Lung took a vast comfort in this fine coffin of his, and every now and then, when he felt able, he stretched out his feeble yellow hand to feel the black, polished wood. Inside there was an inner coffin also, planed to smoothness like yellow satin, and the two fitted into each other like a man's soul into his body. It was a coffin to comfort any man.

But for all this Wang Lung did not slip off into death so easily as his old father had done. It was true his soul was ready to start on its way half a score of times, but every time his strong old body rebelled that it must be left behind, its day ended, and when the struggle began between these two, Wang Lung was frightened at the warring he felt in himself. He had ever been more body than soul and he had been a stout and lusty man in his time, and he could not lightly let his body go, and when he felt his soul stealing away he was afraid, and he cried out in a hoarse gasping voice, wordlessly as a child cries.

Whenever he cried out thus, his young concubine, Pear Blossom, who sat by him day and night, reached out and soothed his old hand with her young hand, and his two sons hastened forward to comfort him with the tales of the funeral

4

they would give him, and they told him over and over all they planned to do. The eldest son stooped his great, satin-clad body to the small, shriveled, old, dying man, and he shouted into his ear, "We will have a procession more than a mile long, and we shall all be there to mourn you, your wives weeping and mourning as they should, and your sons and your sons' sons, in white hempen garments of woe, and all the villagers and the tenants from your land! And your soul's sedan shall go first and in it the picture we have had an artist draw of you, and after it is to come your great, splendid coffin, wherein you will lie like an emperor in the new robes we have waiting for you, and we have rented embroidered cloths of scarlet and of gold to be spread over your coffin as it is carried through the streets of the town for all to see!"

Thus he shouted until his face was red and he was breathless, for he was a very fat man, and when he stood erect again to pant more easily, Wang Lung's second son took up the tale. He was a small, yellow, crafty man, and his voice came out of him through his nose and piping and small, and he said,

"There will come the priests also, who shall chant your soul into paradise, and there will come all the hired mourners and the bearers in red and yellow robes who shall carry the things we have prepared for you to use when you are a shade. We have two paper and reed houses standing ready in the great hall, and one house is like this and one like the town house, and they are filled with furniture and with servants and slaves and a sedan chair and a horse, and all you need. They are so well made and so made of paper of every hue that when we have burnt them at your grave and sent them after you, I swear I believe there will be no other shade so fine as yours, and all these things are to be carried in the procession for everyone to see, and we pray for a fair day for the funeral!"

5

Then the old man was vastly cheered and he gasped out, "I suppose—the whole town—will be there!"

"The whole town, indeed!" cried his eldest son loudly, and he flung out his big, soft, pale hand in a large gesture. "The streets will be lined on either side with all the people who come to see, for there has not been such a funeral, no, not since the great House of Hwang was at its height!"

"Ah—" said Wang Lung, and he was so comforted that once more he forgot to die, and he dropped into one of his sudden, light slumbers.

But even this comfort could not go on forever, and there came an hour in the early dawn of the sixth day of the old man's dying when it ended. The two sons were wearied with their waiting for the hour, for they were not accustomed to the hardships of a cramped house like this where they had not lived since they were young, and, exhausted with their father's long dying, they had gone to bed in the small inner court he had built long ago in the days when he took his first concubine, Lotus, in the days when he was in his prime. They told Pear Blossom when they went at the beginning of the night that she was to call them if their father began his dying again suddenly, and they went to their rest. There upon the bed which Wang Lung had once thought so fine and where he had loved so passionately, his eldest son now lay down and he complained because the bed was hard and rickety with age, and he complained because the room was dark and close now that the season was spring. But once down he slept heavily and loudly, and his short breath caught in his thick throat. As for Wang the Second, he lay upon a small bamboo couch that stood against the wall and he slept lightly and softly as a cat sleeps.

But Pear Blossom did not sleep at all. She sat the night through in the still way she had, motionless upon a little

bamboo stool so low that as she sat beside the bed her face
was near the old man's, and she held his dried old palm between her own soft palms. She was young enough in years to
be Wang Lung's daughter; yet she did not look young, either,
for she had the strangest look of patience on her face, and all
she did was done with the most perfect, tutored patience,
which is not like youth. Thus she sat beside the old man who
had been very kind to her and more like her father than any
she had ever known, and she did not weep. She looked at his
dying face steadfastly hour after hour, as he slept a sleep as
still and nearly as deep as death.

Suddenly at that small hour when it is blackest night and
just before dawn breaks, Wang Lung opened his eyes, and he
felt so weak that it seemed to him his soul was out of his
body already. He rolled his eyes a little and he saw his Pear
Blossom sitting there. He was so weak he began to be afraid,
and he said whispering, his breath caught in his throat and
fluttering through his teeth, "Child—is this—*death?*"

She saw him in his terror and she said quietly and aloud
and in her natural voice,

"No, no, my lord—you are better, you are not dying!"

"You—are sure?" he whispered again, comforted with her
natural voice, and he fixed his glazing eyes upon her face.

Then Pear Blossom, seeing what must come, felt her heart
begin to beat hard and quick, and she rose and bent over him
and she said in her same, soft, usual voice,

"Have I ever deceived you, my lord? See, your hand I hold
feels so warm and strong—I think you are growing better
every moment. You are so well, my lord! You need not be
afraid—no, fear nothing—you are better—you are better—"

So she soothed him steadily on, saying over and over how
well he was and holding his hand close and warm, and he
lay smiling up at her, his eyes dimming and fixing, his lips

7

stiffening, his ears straining to catch her steady voice. Then when she saw he was dying indeed, she leaned down close to him and she lifted her voice clear and high and she called,

"You are better—you are better! No death, my lord—it is not death!"

Thus she comforted him and even as he gathered his last heart beats together at the sound of her voice, he died. But he could not die peacefully. No, although he died comforted, yet when his soul tore itself out of him, his choked body gave a great leap as though of anger and his arms and legs flung themselves out and so strongly that his bony old hand jerked upward and struck Pear Blossom as she leaned over him. It struck her full in the face and with a blow so sharp she put her hand to her cheek and she murmured,

"The only blow you ever gave me, my lord!"

But he gave her no answer. Then she looked down and saw him lying all askew and as she looked his last breath went out of him in a gust and he was still. She straightened his old limbs then, touching him lightly and delicately, and she smoothed his quilts decently over him. With her tender fingers she closed his staring eyes that saw her no more, and she gazed for an instant at the smile, still on his face, which had come when she told him he was not dying.

When she finished all this, she knew she must go and call his sons. But she sat down upon the low stool again. Well she knew she must call his sons. But she took the hand that had struck her and she held it and bowed her head upon it and she wept a few silent tears while she was yet alone. But hers was a strange heart, sad in its very nature, and she could never weep and ease it as other women do, for her tears never brought her comfort. . . . She did not sit long, therefore, but rose and went and called the two brothers, and she said,

"You need not hasten yourself, for he is dead already."

8

But they answered her call and they did hasten themselves and they came out, the elder with his satin under robes all rumpled with sleep and his hair awry, and they went at once to their father. There he lay as Pear Blossom had straightened him, and these two sons of his stared at him as though they had never seen him before and as though they were half afraid of him now. Then the eldest son said, whispering as though there were some stranger in the room,

"Did he die easily or hardly?"

And Pear Blossom answered in her quiet way,

"He died without knowing he did."

Then the second son said,

"He lies as if he slept and were not dead at all."

When these two sons had stared for a while at their dead father they seemed filled with some vague and confused fear, because he lay there so helpless for them to gaze upon, and Pear Blossom divined their fear and she said gently,

"There is much to be done for him yet."

Then the two men started and they were glad to be reminded of living things again, and the elder smoothed his robes over himself hastily and passed his hand over his face and he said huskily,

"True—true—we must be about his funeral—" and they hastened away, glad to be out of that house where their father lay dead.

II

Now before Wang Lung had died one day he commanded his sons that his body was to be left in its coffin in the earthen house until he was buried in his land. But when his sons came to this time of preparation for his funeral they found it very irksome to come and to go so far from their house in the town, and when they thought of the forty and nine days which must pass before the burial, it seemed to them they could not obey their father, now that he was dead. And indeed it was a trouble to them in many ways, for the priests from the town temple complained because they must come so far to chant, and even the men who came to wash and to dress Wang Lung's body and to put his silken burial robes on him and to lift him into his coffin and seal it, demanded a double fee and they asked so much that Wang the Second was in horror.

The two brothers looked at each other, then, over the old man's coffin, and they each thought the same thing, that the dead man could say no more. So they called the tenants and told them to carry Wang Lung into the courts where he had lived in the town house, and Pear Blossom, although she spoke against it, could not prevail with them. When she saw her words useless, she said quietly,

"I thought the poor fool and I would never go to that town house again, but if he goes we must go with him," and she took this fool, who was Wang Lung's eldest daughter and a woman grown in years, but still the same foolish child she had been all her life, and they followed behind Wang Lung's coffin as it went along the country road, and the fool went laughing because the day was fair and warm with spring and the sun shone so brightly.

Thus did Pear Blossom go yet again to the court where she had lived once with Wang Lung alive, and it was to this court that Wang Lung had taken her on a certain day when his blood ran full and free even in his age, and he was lonely in his great house. But the court was silent now, and on every door in the great house the red paper signs had been torn off to show that death was here, and upon the great gates open to the street white paper was pasted for a sign of death. And Pear Blossom lived and slept beside the dead.

One day as she thus waited with Wang Lung in his coffin, a serving maid came to the door of the court and by her Lotus, Wang Lung's first concubine, sent word that she must come and pay her respects to her dead lord. Pear Blossom must return a courteous word, and so she did, although she hated Lotus who had been her old mistress, and she rose and waited, moving a candle here or there as it burned about the coffin.

It was the first time Pear Blossom had seen Lotus since that day when Lotus knew what Wang Lung had done and she sent word to him that she wished never to see Pear Blossom again because she was so angry that he had taken into his own court a girl who had been her slave since childhood. She was so jealous and angry that she pretended not to know if Pear Blossom lived or died. But the truth was she was curious, and now that Wang Lung was dead she had told Cuckoo, her servant,

"Well, if that old man is dead, she and I have no more to quarrel over and I will go and see what she is like now." Thus filled with her curiosity she had waddled out of her court, leaning upon her slaves, and she chose an hour when it was still too early for the priests to be there chanting by the coffin.

Thus she came into the room where Pear Blossom stood waiting, and she had brought candles and incense for decency's sake, and she commanded one of her slaves to light these before the coffin. But while the slave did this, Lotus could not keep her eyes from Pear Blossom and she stared avidly to see how Pear Blossom had changed and to see how old she looked. Yes, although Lotus wore white shoes of mourning upon her feet and robes of mourning, her face did not mourn and she cried to Pear Blossom,

11

"Well, and you are the same small pale thing you ever were, and you are not changed. I do not know what he ever saw in you!" And she took comfort in this, that Pear Blossom was so small and colorless and without any bold beauty.

Then Pear Blossom stood by the coffin, her head hanging, and she stayed silent, but such a loathing filled her heart that she frightened herself and she was humbled by the knowledge that she could be so evil and hate even her old mistress like this. But Lotus was not one who could keep her old wandering mind even on hatred, and after she had stared her fill at Pear Blossom, she looked at the coffin and muttered,

"A pretty heap of silver his sons paid for that, I'll swear!" And she rose heavily and went and felt of the wood to appraise it.

But Pear Blossom could not bear this coarse touch upon the thing she watched so tenderly and she cried out suddenly and sharply,

"Do not touch him!" And she clenched her little hands on her bosom and drew her lower lip between her teeth.

At this Lotus laughed and she cried out, "What—do you still feel so toward him?" And she laughed in easy scorn, and she sat awhile and watched the candles burn and sputter, and wearying of this soon, she rose and went out into the court to go away. But looking everywhere in her curiosity, she saw the poor fool sitting there in a patch of sunlight, and she called out,

"What—is that thing still alive?"

Pear Blossom went and stood beside the fool at this, and her loathing filled her heart still, so that she could scarcely bear it, and when Lotus was gone, she went and found a cloth and she wiped again and again the place on Wang Lung's coffin where Lotus had put her hand, and she gave the fool a little sweet cake, and the fool took it merrily, since she had not expected it, and she ate it with cries of joy. And Pear Blossom watched her sadly for a while and at last she said, sighing,

"You are all I have left of the only one who was ever kind to me or saw me for more than slave." But the fool only ate her cake, for she neither spoke nor understood any who spoke to her.

So Pear Blossom waited the days out until the funeral, and those days were very silent in the courts except for the hours when the priests chanted, for not even Wang Lung's sons came near him unless they must for some duty. They were all somewhat uneasy and afraid in that whole house because of the earthy spirits a dead man has, and since Wang Lung had been so strong and lusty a man, it could not be expected that these seven spirits of his would leave him easily. Nor did they, for the house seemed full of new and strange sounds, and servant maids cried out that they felt chill winds seize them at night in their beds and toss their hair askew, or they heard mischievous rattling at their lattices, or a pot would be knocked out of a cook's hand, or a bowl drop from a slave's hand as she stood to serve.

When the sons and their wives heard such servants' talk they pretended to smile at it for foolishness of ignorance, but they were uneasy, too, and when Lotus heard these tales she called out,

"He was ever a wilful old man!"

But Cuckoo said, "Let a dead man have his way, mistress, and speak well of him until he is under ground!"

Only Pear Blossom was not afraid, and she lived alone with Wang Lung now as she had when he was living. Only when she saw the yellow-robed priests did she rise and go to her room and there she sat and listened to their mournful chanting and to the slow beating of their drums.

13

Little by little were the seven earthy spirits of the dead man released, and every seven days the head priest went to the sons of Wang Lung and said,

"There is another spirit gone out of him." And the sons rewarded him with silver every time he came and said this.

Thus the days passed, seven times seven, and the day drew near for the funeral.

Now the whole town knew what day the geomancer had appointed for the funeral of so great a man as Wang Lung and on that day in the full spring of the year and close upon summer, mothers hastened their children at the morning meal so they would not dally and be too late to see all that was to be seen, and men in their fields left off farming for the day, and in the shops the clerks and the apprentices in trades plotted to see how they could stand and see the procession pass for this funeral. For everyone in that whole countryside knew Wang Lung and how he had been poor once and a man on the land like any other and how he grew rich and founded a house and left his sons rich. Every poor man longed to see the funeral because it was a thing to ponder on that a man as poor as himself had died rich, and it was a cause for secret hope in every poor man. Every rich man would see the sight because they knew the sons of Wang Lung were left rich, and so must every rich man pay his respects to this great old dead man.

But in Wang Lung's own house that day there were confusion and noise, for it was no easy thing to have so vast a funeral set forth in order, and Wang the Eldest was distracted with all he had to do, and since he was the head of the house, he must have oversight of all, of hundreds of people and mourning fitted to each as was his station, and the hiring of the sedan chairs for the ladies and children. He was distracted and yet he was proud of his importance and that all came running to him and bawling to ask what to do in this and that, and being agitated so that the sweat ran down his face like in mid-summer, his rolling eye fell upon his second brother who stood calmly there, and this coolness angered Wang the Eldest in the midst of his heat, and he cried out,

"You leave all to me and you cannot even see that your own wife and children are dressed and sober-faced."

At this Wang the Second answered with a secret sneer, and very smoothly,

"Why should anyone do anything when you can be pleased only with what you do yourself? Well we know, my wife and I, that nothing else will please you and your lady, and we do desire to please you first!"

So even at his funeral Wang Lung's sons bickered together, but this was partly because they were both secretly distraught because their other brother had not come home yet and each blamed the other for the delay, the elder son that his second brother had not given the messenger money enough if he had to travel far to find the one he sought, and the second because his elder brother had delayed in sending the messenger for a day or two.

There was only one peaceful in all that great house on this day and it was Pear Blossom. She sat in her mourning robes of a white hempen cloth that were lesser in degree of mourning only to those that Lotus wore and she sat quietly and waited beside Wang Lung. She had robed herself early and she had dressed the fool in mourning, too, although that poor creature had no notion of what this was all about and laughed continuously and was disturbed by the strange garments she wore so that she tried to pull them off. But Pear Blossom gave her a cake to eat and saw to it that she had her strip of red cloth to play with and so she soothed her.

15

As for Lotus, she was never in such a pother as she was this day, for she could not sit in the usual sedan, being so mountainous as she was now, and she tried this chair and that as it was brought to her and she was shrieking that none would do and she did not know why they made chairs so small and narrow now-a-days, and she wept and was beside herself for fear she would not be able to join in the procession of so great a dead man as her husband. When she saw the fool all dressed in mourning she fixed her anger there and she cried out in complaint to Wang the Eldest,

"What—is that thing to go, too?" And she complained that the fool ought to be left behind on such a public day.

But Pear Blossom said softly and positively,

"No, my lord said I was never to leave this poor child of his and this was the command he laid on me. I can quiet her for she listens to me and is used to me and we will trouble no one."

Then Wang the Eldest let the matter pass because he was so torn with many things to be done, and with the knowledge that hundreds of people waited for the day to begin; and seeing his anxiety, the chair bearers seized the chance of necessity and they demanded more money than they ought to have and the men who carried the coffin complained that it was so heavy and so far to the family burial place, and tenants and idlers from the town flooded into the courts and stood about everywhere useless and gaping to see what could be seen. To all this was added another thing and it was that Wang the Eldest's lady was continually upbraiding him and complaining that things were not managed well, so that in the midst of all this Wang the Eldest ran about and sweated as he had not in many a day, and although he shouted until he was hoarse no one heeded him greatly.

Whether they would ever have finished the funeral that

16

day or not none knows, except the most opportune thing happened, and this was that suddenly Wang the Third came in from the south. At this very last moment he came in and they all stared to see what he had become, for he had been away from home ten years and they had not seen him since that day when Wang Lung took Pear Blossom to himself. No, he had left in the strangest passion on that day and he had never come home again. He left a wild, tall, angry lad, his black brows drawn down over his eyes, and he left hating his father. Now he came back a man, the tallest of the three brothers and so changed that if it had not been for his two black brows frowning as ever and his mouth still surly, they would not have known him.

He came striding into the gate in his soldier's garb, but it was not the garb of a common soldier either. The coat and the trousers were of a fine dark cloth and there were gilded buttons on his coat and he had a sword girdled to his leather belt. Behind him marched four soldiers with guns over their shoulders, all good enough men except for one who had a harelip; yet he, too, was stout and strong as any in body.

When these came marching through the great gate a silence fell over the confusion and the noise and every face turned to see this Wang the Third, and everyone was silent because he looked so fierce and so used to command. He went with firm long steps through the crowd of tenants and priests and idlers who pressed everywhere to see all that could be seen, and he said in a loud voice,

"Where are my brothers?"

Now one had already run to tell the two brothers that their other brother was here and so they came out not knowing how to receive him, whether respectfully, or as a younger brother who was a runaway. But when they saw this third brother clad as he was and the four fierce soldiers behind him motionless at his command, they were quickly courteous, and as courteous as they would have been to a stranger. They bowed and sighed heavily at the sadness of the day. Then Wang the Third bowed also deeply and properly to his elder brothers, and he looked to the right and to the left and he said,

"Where is my father?"

Then the two brothers led him into the inner court where Wang Lung lay in his coffin under the scarlet coverings embroidered in gold, and Wang the Third commanded his soldiers to stay in the court and he went alone into the room. When Pear Blossom heard the clatter of leathern shoes upon the stones she took one hasty look to see who came and she saw and turned herself away quickly with her face to the wall and she stood thus turned away.

But if Wang the Third saw her at all or marked who she was he made no sign of it. He bowed before the coffin and he called for the hempen robes that had been prepared for him, although when he drew them on they were too short for him, for his brothers had not thought him so tall a fellow as he was. Nevertheless, he drew the robes on and he lit two fresh candles he had bought and he called for fresh meats to be brought as a sacrifice before his father's coffin.

When all these things were ready he bowed himself to the ground before his father three times, and he cried out very properly, "Ah, my father!" But Pear Blossom kept her face steadfastly to the wall and she did not turn herself once to see what went on.

When Wang the Third had finished his duty he rose and said in his swift short way, "Let us proceed if affairs are ready!"

Then it was the strangest thing that where there had been so much confusion and noise and men bawling here and there at each other, now there were silence and willingness to obey, and it seemed that the very presence of Wang the Third and of his four soldiers was power, for when the chair bearers began again their complaint that they were making to Wang the Eldest in such surly tones, their voices grew pleading and mild and their words reasonable. Even so Wang the Third drew his brows together and stared at the men so that their voices grew faint and died away and when he said, "Do your work and be sure you shall be justly treated in this house!" they fell silent and went to the chairs as though there were some magic in soldiers and guns.

Each man went to his place and at last the great coffin was carried out into the courts and hempen ropes were put about it and under it and poles like young trees slipped through the ropes and the bearers put their shoulders under the poles. There also was the sedan for Wang Lung's spirit and in it they had placed certain possessions of his, the pipe he smoked for many years and a garment he had worn and the picture they had hired an artist to paint of him after he was ill, since he had never such a likeness made before. True, the picture did not look like Wang Lung and it was only a picture of some old sage or other, but still the artist did his best and he brushed in great whiskers and eyebrows and many wrinkles such as old men do have sometimes.

So the procession started, and now the women began their weeping and wailing and loudest of all was Lotus. She pulled her hair awry and she had a new white kerchief and put it to her eyes, to one and to the other, and she cried out in great sobs,

"Ah, he who was my support is gone—is gone—"

And all along the streets people stood thick and pressed together to see Wang Lung pass this last time, and when they saw Lotus they murmured and approved the sight and they said,

19

"She is a very proper woman and she mourns a good man gone." And some marvelled to see so large and fat a lady weeping so stoutly and with such a clamor and they said, "How rich he was to have her able to eat herself to such a size as this!" And they envied Wang Lung his possessions.

As for the wives of the sons of Wang Lung, they wept each according to her nature. The lady of Wang the Eldest wept decently and as much as she should, touching her eyes from time to time with her kerchief and it was not right that she weep as much as Lotus. The concubine her husband had, who was a pretty plump girl newly wed a year or so before, looked at this lady and wept when she wept. But the country wife of Wang the Second forgot to weep for it was the first time she had ever been carried through the streets of the town like this on men's shoulders and she could not weep for staring about her at all the hundreds of faces of men and women and children standing pressed against the walls and crowded into doorways, and if she remembered and put her hand to her eyes she peeped through and saw and forgot again.

Now it has been said from ancient times that all women who weep may be divided into three sorts. There are those who lift up their voices and their tears flow and this may be called crying; there are those who utter loud lamentations but whose tears do not flow and this may be called howling; there are those whose tears flow but who utter no sound and this may be called weeping. Of all those women who followed Wang Lung in his coffin, his wives and his sons' wives and his maid servants and his slaves and his hired mourners, there was only one who wept and it was Pear Blossom. She sat in her sedan and she pulled the curtain down so no one could see her, and there she wept silently and without a sound. Even when the mighty funeral was over and Wang Lung was in his land and covered with it, when the houses and servants and beasts of paper and reed had been burned to ashes, when the incense was lit and smouldering and his sons had made their obeisances and the mourners had howled their due time out and been paid, when all was finished and the earth heaped high over the new grave, then when no one wept because it was over and there was no use in any more weeping, even then Pear Blossom wept on in her silent way.

Nor would she go back to the town house. She went to the earthen house and when Wang the Eldest urged her to return with them to the town house and live with the family, at least until the inheritance was divided, she shook her head and she said,

"No, I lived here with him longest and I have been most happy here and he left me this poor child to care for. She will be irksome to the First Lady if we go back there, and that one does not love me either, and so we two will stay on here in my lord's old house. You are not to trouble about us. When I need anything I will ask you for it, but I can need only a very little and we shall be safe here with the old tenant and his wife and I can take care of your sister thus, and so fulfil my lord's command he laid on me."

"Well, if you so wish it, then," said Wang the Eldest as though he were unwilling.

Yet he was pleased, too, for his lady had spoken against the fool that she was such a thing as ought not to be about the courts, especially where there were women bearing children, and now that Wang Lung was gone it was true that Lotus might be more cruel than she dared to be when he was alive, and so trouble come forth. So he let Pear Blossom have her way, and she took the fool by the hand and led her to that earthen house where she had nourished Wang Lung in his age. She lived there and cared for the fool and she went only so far away as Wang Lung's grave.

Yes, thereafter she was the only one who went often to Wang Lung, for if Lotus came it was only at such few seasons as a widow must in decency go to her husband's place of burial and she took care to go at such hours as people were about to see how dutiful she was. But Pear Blossom went secretly and often and whenever her heart grew too full and lonely, and she took care to go when no one was near, at times when people were secure in their houses and asleep in the night, or if they were busy and away in their fields. At such lonely times she took the fool and went to Wang Lung's grave.

But she did not weep aloud there. No, she leaned her head down on his grave and if she did weep a little sometimes she made no sound except to whisper a time or two,

"Ah, my lord and my father, and the only father I ever had!"

III

Now although this mighty old man of the land was dead and in his grave he could not be forgotten yet, for he was due the three years of mourning which sons must give their father. The eldest son of Wang Lung, who was now head of the family, took the greatest care that everything should be done decently and as it should be, and when he was not sure of how this was, he went to ask his wife. For Wang the Eldest had been a country lad in his childhood and he had grown up in the midst of fields and villages before his father grew rich enough by a lucky chance and his own cleverness to buy this great town house for them all. Now when he went to his wife secretly for her counsel she answered coldly, as though she despised him somewhat for what he did not know, and yet she answered him carefully, too, for she cared enough not to be ashamed in this house,

"If the tablet where his soul lives for the time is set up in the great hall, then prepare the sacrificial food in bowls before it and let our mourning all be made thus—"

And she told him how everything should be and Wang the Eldest listened and then went out from her and gave the commands as his own. Thus the garments of second mourning were arranged for them all and cloth bought and tailors hired. For a hundred days the three sons were to wear white shoes and afterwards they might wear pale grey ones or of some such lifeless hue. But they were not to wear any silk garments, neither the sons of Wang Lung nor his wives, until the full three years were over and the final tablet for the resting place of Wang Lung's soul was made and inscribed and set in its true place among the tablets of his father and his grandfather.

Thus Wang the Eldest commanded and the mourning garments for each man and woman and grandson were prepared as he said. He made his voice very loud and lordly now whenever he spoke, since he was head of this house, and he took as his right the highest seat in any room where he sat with his brothers. His two brothers listened, the second one with his small narrow mouth awry as though he smiled inwardly, for he felt himself secretly always wiser than this elder brother of his, because it was to the second son that Wang Lung in his lifetime had entrusted the stewardship of the lands, and he alone knew how many tenants there were and how much money could be expected each season from the fields, and such knowledge gave him power over his brothers, at least in his own mind. But Wang the Third listened to the commands of his elder brother as one does who has learned to hear commands when it is needful to hear them, but still

23

as one whose heart is not in what he does and as though he were eager to be away.

The truth was that each of these three brothers longed for the hour when the inheritance was to be divided, for they were agreed it must be divided, since each had in his inner heart a purpose for which he wished to have his own given him, and neither Wang the Second nor Wang the Third would have been willing for the lands to be wholly in the power of their elder brother, so that they must be dependent on him. Each brother longed in his own way, the eldest because he wanted to know how much he would have and if it would be enough or not for his household and his two wives and for his many children and for his secret pleasures he could not deny himself. The second brother longed because he had great grain markets and he had money loaned out and he wanted his inheritance free so that he could enlarge himself in his making of money. As for the third brother, he was so strange and silent that no one knew what he wished and that dark face of his never told anything at all. But he was restless and it could be seen at least that he was eager to be away, although what he would do with his inheritance no one knew and no one dared to ask. He was the youngest of the three but they were all afraid of him and every servant, man and maid, leaped twice as quickly when he called out to them as they did for anyone else, and they went slowest of all for Wang the Eldest, for all his loud and lordly voice.

Now Wang Lung had been the last to die in his generation, so long and lustily had he held to life, and there was no one left of his time except a cousin of his, a wandering rascally soldier, and the brothers did not know where he was, for he was only a small captain in some wandering horde that was but half soldier and more than half robber and turning to whatever general paid them best, or to none if it suited them better to rob alone. The three brothers were glad enough not to know where this cousin of their father's was unless they could know he was dead.

But, since they had no other older relative, by common law they must ask some worthy man among their neighbors to come in to divide the inheritance before an assembly of honest and good citizens. And as they talked together one evening as to who this should be, Wang the Second said,

"There is none nearer us and more to be trusted, my elder brother, than Liu, the grain merchant, under whom I had my apprenticeship as a clerk, and whose daughter is your lady. Let us ask him to divide our inheritance, for he is a man whom all hold just, and rich enough so that he will not be envious for himself."

When Wang the Eldest heard this he was displeased secretly because he had not thought of it first and he answered weightily,

"I wish you would not be so quick to speak, brother, because I was just about to say let us invite the father of the mother of my sons to do it for us. But since you have said it, let it be and we will ask him. Nevertheless, I was just on the point of saying so myself, and you are always too quick and speaking out of your place in the family."

At this rebuke the elder brother stared hard at Wang the Second and breathed heavily with his thick lips pursed, and Wang the Second drew his mouth down as though he could have laughed but did not. Then Wang the Eldest looked away hastily and he said to his younger brother,

"And how does it seem to you, my little younger brother?"

But Wang the Third looked up in his haughty half-dreaming way, and he said,

"It is nothing to me! But whatever you do, do it quickly."

Wang the Eldest rose then as though he would make all

haste, although as he came into these middle years of his life he could not make haste without confusion, and if he even walked quickly his feet and hands seemed too many for him.

But the matter was arranged at last and Liu the merchant was willing, for he had respected Wang Lung for a shrewd man. The brothers invited also such of the neighbors as were high enough for them and they invited certain high men of the town who were both rich and stable in their position, and these men gathered on the appointed day in the great hall of Wang Lung's house, and each took his seat according to his rank.

Then Wang the Second, when Liu the merchant called upon him to give an account of all the lands and moneys to be divided, rose and gave the paper on which all was written into the hands of Wang the Eldest and Wang the Eldest gave it to Liu the merchant and Liu received it. First he opened it and put his great brass spectacles across his nose and he muttered the account over to himself, and they all waited in silence until he had done. Then he read it over again aloud, so that all the men sitting there in that great hall knew that Wang Lung when he died had been lord over a mighty number of acres of land, in all more than eight hundred acres, and seldom had anyone in those parts ever heard of so much going under the name of one man and scarcely under one family, even, and surely not under any since the time of the great Hwang family's height. Wang the Second knew it all, and he would not look surprised, but the others could not but let their wonder leak out, however much they held their faces straight and calm for propriety. Only Wang the Third seemed not to care and he sat as he always did, as though his mind were elsewhere and he were waiting impatiently for this to be done and over so that he might go away where his heart was.

Besides all this land there were the two houses which were

Wang Lung's, the farm house in the fields and this great old town house that he bought from the dying lord of the House of Hwang, when that house had fallen into decay and its sons scattered. And besides houses and lands, there were sums of money lent here and there and sums of money in the grain business and there were bags of money lying idle and hidden, so that the money itself was half as much as the value of the lands.

But there were certain claims to be decided before all this inheritance could be divided between the brothers and, besides certain small claims to a few tenants and some tradesmen, the chiefest were those of the two concubines that Wang Lung had taken in his lifetime: Lotus, whom he took out of a tea house for her beauty and for his passion and for the satisfaction of his maturity when his country wife palled upon his flesh, and Pear Blossom, who had been a slave in his own house when he took her to comfort his old age. There were these two, and neither of them was true wife and both but concubines, and a concubine cannot be reproached overmuch if she choose to seek another when her master is dead if she is not too old. Still, the three brothers knew that if these did not wish to go out then they must be fed and clothed and they had the right to remain in the house of the family so long as they lived. Lotus indeed could not go out to another man, seeing how old and fat she was, and she would be glad to stay snugly in her court. So it was that now when the merchant Liu called for her, she rose out of a seat near the door, and she leaned on two slaves and wiping her eyes with her sleeves, she said in a very mournful voice,

"Ah, he that fed me is gone, and how can I think of another and where can I go? I am in my age now, and I need but a little to feed me and to clothe me and give me a little wine and tobacco to lighten my sad heart, and the sons of my lord are generous!"

Then the merchant Liu, who was so good a man he thought all others good, too, looked at her kindly and he never remembered who she was nor that he had ever seen her anything except a good man's wife, and he said with respect,

"You speak well and becomingly, for the one gone was a kind master, and so I have heard from all. Well, I will decree thus, then; you are to be given twenty pieces of silver a month and you may live on in your courts and you are to have your servants and slaves and your food and some pieces of cloth yearly besides."

But when Lotus heard this, and she listened to catch every word, she rolled her eyes from one son to the other and she clasped her hands piteously and she set up a piercing wail and she said,

"But twenty? What—but twenty? It will scarcely buy me my sweetmeats I need because I have so small a little appetite and I have never eaten coarse and common foods!"

At this the old merchant drew off his spectacles and he stared at her astonished and he said sternly,

"Twenty pieces a month is more than many a whole family has, and half would be generous enough in most houses and not poor houses, either, when the master is dead!"

Then Lotus began to cry in good earnest and there was no pretence in her now and she cried for Wang Lung as she had never done yet and she cried,

"Would that you had not left me, indeed, my lord! I am cast aside and you have gone into the far places and you cannot save me!"

Now the wife of Wang the Eldest stood behind a curtain near and she drew it aside now and made signs to her husband that this behavior was indecent before all these goodly people

28

here, and she was in such an agony that Wang the Eldest
fidgeted on his chair and tried not to see her and yet he must
see her, and at last he rose and called out loudly above the
din that Lotus made,

"Sir, let her have a little more so that we can get on!"

But Wang the Second could not bear this and he rose in his
place and called out,

"If it is to be more, then let my elder brother give it from
his share, for it is true that twenty pieces are enough and
more than enough, even with all her gaming!"

This he said, because as she grew older Lotus grew fond
to passion of gaming and what time she did not eat or sleep
she gamed. But the wife of Wang the Eldest grew the more
indignant and she made violent signs to her husband that he
must refuse to do this and she whispered loudly,

"No, the shares must be given to the widows before the
inheritance is divided. What is she more to us than to them?"

Now here was a pother and the old peaceful merchant
looked in dismay from one to the other, and Lotus would
not cease her din for one moment, so that all the men were
distracted with such confusion. So it would have gone on for
longer except that Wang the Third was outraged and he rose
suddenly and stamped his hard leathern shoes upon the tiles
and he shouted,

"I will give it! What is a little silver? I am weary of this!"

Now this seemed a good way out of the trouble, and the
lady of Wang the Eldest said,

"He can do it, for he is a lone man. He has no sons to
think of as we have."

And Wang the Second smiled and shrugged himself a little
and smiled his secret smile as one who says to himself, "Well,
it is no affair of mine if a man is too foolish to defend his
own!"

But the old merchant was very glad and he sighed and took out his kerchief and wiped his face, for he was a man who lived in a quiet house, and he was not used to such as Lotus. As for Lotus, she might have held to her din for a while longer except there was something so fierce about this third son of Wang Lung's that she thought better of it. So she ceased her noise suddenly and sat down, well pleased with herself, and although she tried to keep her mouth drawn down and grieved, she forgot very soon and she stared freely at all the men, and she took watermelon seeds from a plate a slave held for her and cracked them between her teeth that were strong and white and sound still in spite of her age. And she was at her ease.

Thus it was decided for Lotus. Then the old merchant looked about and he said,

"Where is the second concubine? I see her name is written here."

Now this was Pear Blossom and not one of them had looked to see whether she was here or not and they looked now about the great hall and they sent slaves into the women's courts, but she was not anywhere in that house. Then Wang the Eldest remembered he had forgot to summon her at all, and he sent for her in great haste and they waited an hour or so until she could come and they drank tea and waited and walked about, and at last she came with a maid servant to the door of the hall. But when she looked in and saw all the men she would not go in, and when she saw that soldier she went into the court again, and at last the old merchant went out to her there. He looked at her kindly and not full in the face so as to dismay her, and he saw how young she still was, a young woman still and very pale and pretty, and he said,

"Lady, you are so young that none can blame you if your life is not over yet, and there is plenty of silver to give you a good sum and you may go to your home again and marry a good man or do as you will."

But she, being all unprepared for such words, thought she was being sent out somewhere and she did not understand and she cried out, her voice fluttering and weak with her fright,

"Oh, sir, I have no home and I have no one at all except my dead lord's fool and he left her to me and we have nowhere to go! Oh, sir, I thought we could live on in the earthen house and we eat very little and we need only cotton clothes for I shall never wear silk again, now that my lord is dead, not so long as I live, and we will not trouble anyone in the great house!"

The old merchant went back into the hall then and he asked the eldest brother, wondering,

"Who is this fool of whom she speaks?"

And Wang the Eldest answered, hesitating, "It is but a poor thing, a sister of ours, who was never right from her childhood, and my father and mother did not let her starve or suffer as some do to these creatures to hasten their end and so she has lived on to this day. My father commanded this woman of his to care for her, and if she will not wed again let some silver be given her and let her do as she wishes, for she is very mild and it is true she will trouble no one."

At this Lotus called out suddenly, "Yes, but she need not have much, because she has ever been but a slave in this house and used to the coarsest fare and cotton clothes until my old lord made himself silly in his old age about her white face, and doubtless she wheedled him to it, too—and as for that fool the sooner she is dead the better!"

This Lotus called out and when Wang the Third heard it he stared at her so terribly that she faltered and turned her head away from his black eyes, and then he shouted out,

31

"Let this one be given the same as the old one and I will give it!"

But Lotus demurred, and although she did not dare to say it loudly, she muttered,

"It is not meet that elder and younger be treated as one and equal—and she my own slave!"

So she muttered and it seemed she might fall to her old noise again, and the old merchant seeing this said with all haste,

"True—true—so I decree twenty-five pieces to the elder lady and twenty to the younger—" And he went out and said to Pear Blossom, "Go back to your house and be at peace again, lady, because you are to do as you will and you shall have twenty silver pieces a month for your own."

Then Pear Blossom thanked him prettily and with all her heart and her little pale mouth quivered and she was trembling because she had not known what would happen to her and it was a relief to know she might live on as she had and be safe.

With these claims ended, then, and the decision made, the rest was not hard and the old merchant went on and he was about to divide lands and houses and silver equally into four parts to give two parts to Wang the Eldest as head of the house, and one part to Wang the Second and one part to Wang the Third when suddenly this third son spoke out,

"Give me no houses and lands! I had enough of the land when I was a lad and my father would have me be a farmer. I am not wed, and what do I want with a house! Give me my share in silver, my brothers, or else if I must have house and land, then do you, my brothers, buy them from me and give me silver!"

Now the two older brothers were struck dazed when they heard this, for whoever heard of a man who wanted his whole inheritance in silver, which can escape a man so easily and leave no trace behind, and will not have house and land, which can remain to him for a possession? The elder brother said gravely,

"But, my brother, no good man in this whole world goes unwed all his life and sooner or later we will find you a woman, since our father is gone, whose duty it was to do it, and you will want house and land then."

Then the second brother said very plainly, "Whatever you do with your share of the land we will not buy it from you, for there has been trouble in many a family because one has taken his inheritance in silver and spent it all and then has come howling back, crying out that he is defrauded of lands and inheritance, and the silver is gone then and no proof that it ever was beyond a bit of paper that could be written by anyone, or else men's bare words, and these are no proof. No, and if the man himself does not do this, his sons will and their sons' sons and it means strife into the generations. I say the land must be divided. If you wish it I will see to your lands for you and send you the silver they bring to you every year, but you shall not have your inheritance in silver."

Now the wisdom of this struck everyone, so that although the soldier said again, muttering it, "I will have no house nor land!" no one paid heed to him this time except that the old merchant said curiously,

"What would you do with so much silver?"

To this the soldier answered in his harsh voice, "I have a cause!"

But not one of them knew what he meant and after a time the old merchant decreed that the silver and the lands should be divided and if he truly did not wish a share in this fine town house he might have the old earthen house in the country, which was worth little indeed, seeing it was made out of

33

the earth of the fields at the slight cost of a little labor. He decreed beyond this that the two elder brothers should have a sum ready, too, for Wang the Third's marriage, as it was the duty of elder brothers to the younger, if the father was dead.

Wang the Third sat in silence and heard all this and when it was decided at last and all divided fairly and according to law the sons of Wang Lung gave a feast to those who had sat to hear the division, but they still did not make merry or wear silk, because the time of their mourning was not yet over.

Thus were the fields upon which Wang Lung had spent his whole life divided and the land belonged now to his sons and no more to him, except that small part where he lay, and this was all he owned. Yet out of this small secret place the clay of his blood and bones melted and flowed out to join with all the depths of the land; his sons did as they pleased with the surface of the earth but he lay deep within it and he had his portion still and no one could take it from him.

IV

Now Wang the Third could scarcely wait for the inheritance to be divided, and as soon as it was finished he made ready with his four men and they prepared to go out again to those parts from which he had come. When Wang the Eldest saw this haste he was astonished and he said,

"What—and will you not wait even until the three years of mourning are over for our father before you set out on your business again?"

"How can I wait three more years?" returned the soldier passionately, and he turned his fierce and hungry eyes to his brother as he spoke. "So far as I am away from you and this house, men will not know what I do nor is there one to care if he did know!"

At this Wang the Eldest looked curiously at his brother and he said with some passing wonder,

"What thing is it that presses you so?"

Then Wang the Third stayed himself in the act of girdling his sword to his leather belt. He looked at his elder brother and saw him, a great soft man, his face full and hung with fat, and his lips thick and pouting, and all his body clothed in soft pale flesh, and he held his fingers apart, and his hands were soft as a woman's with his fat, the nails long and white and the palms pink and soft and thick. When Wang the Third saw all this he turned his eyes away again and he said in contempt,

"If I told you you would not understand. It is enough if I say I must return quickly, for there are those who wait for me to lead them. It is enough if I say I have men under my command ready to do my bidding."

"And are you paid well for it?" asked Wang the Eldest, wondering and not perceiving his brother's scorn, since he held himself to be a goodly man.

"Sometimes I am and sometimes I am not," said the soldier.

But Wang the Eldest could not think of anyone's doing a thing for which he was not paid and so he said on,

"It is a strange business which does not pay its men. If a general commanded me and paid me nothing I would change to another general if I were a soldier like you and a captain with men under me."

But the soldier did not answer. He had a thing in his mind to do before he left and he went and found his second brother and he said to him privately,

"You are not to forget to pay that younger lady of my

35

father's her full share. Before you send me my silver take the extra five pieces every month out of it."

The second brother opened his narrow eyes at this and since he was one who did not easily understand the giving away of such sums he said,

"Why do you give her so much?"

The soldier replied in some strange haste, "She has that fool to care for, too."

And he seemed to have more to say but he would not say it and while his four soldiers tied his possessions together in a bundle he was very restless. He was so restless he walked out to the city gate and he looked out toward where his father's lands had lain and where the earthen house was that was his own now, for all he did not want it, and he muttered once,

"I might go and see it once, since it is mine."

But he took his breath deeply again and he shook his head and he went back to the town house. Then he led out his four men and he went quickly and he was glad to be gone, as though there were some power over him here yet from his old father, and he was one who would have no power over him of any kind.

So did the other two sons yearn also to be free of their father. The eldest son longed to have the three years of mourning past and he longed to put the old man's tablet away into the little loft over the great hall where the other tablets were kept, because so long as it stood where it did every day in the hall it seemed as though Wang Lung were watching these sons of his. Yes, there his spirit was, seated in the tablet, watching his sons, and his eldest son longed to be free to live for his pleasure and to spend his father's money as he would. But he could not, so long as that tablet was there, put his hand freely into his girdle and take his pleasure where he would, and there were these years of mourning to be passed, when it is not decent for a son to be too merry. Thus upon this idle man, whose mind was ever running upon secret pleasures, the old man still laid his restraining power.

As for the second son, he had his schemes too, and he longed to turn certain of the fields into money because he had a plan to enlarge his grain business and buy over some of the markets of Liu the merchant who grew old and whose son was a scholar and did not love his father's shops, and with so large a business Wang the Second could ship grain out of that region and even to foreign countries near by. But it is scarcely seemly to do such great things while mourning is yet going on, and so Wang the Second could but possess himself in patience and wait and say little except to ask his brother as though idly,

"When these days of mourning are over what will you do with your land—sell it or what?"

And the elder brother replied with seeming carelessness, "Well, I do not know yet. I have scarcely thought, but I suppose I must keep enough to feed us, seeing I have no business as you have and at my age I can scarcely begin a new thing."

"But land will be a trouble to you," said his brother. "If you are a landlord you must see to the tenants and you must go yourself to weigh out grain and there are many very wearisome such things for a landlord to do if he is to make his living at all. As for me, I did these things for my father, but I cannot do them for you, for I have my own affairs now. I shall sell all but the very best land and invest the silver at high interest and we will see who will get rich the more quickly, you or I."

Now Wang the Eldest heard this with the greatest envy for he knew he needed a great deal of money and more than he had, and he said weakly,

"Well, I shall see, and it may be I will sell more than I thought I would, perhaps, and put the money out at interest with yours, but we shall see."

But without knowing it when they talked of selling the land they dropped their voices low as though they were afraid the old man in the land might hear them still.

Thus these two waited with impatience for the three years to be over. And Lotus waited, too, and grumbled as she waited, because it was not fitting for her to wear silk these three years and she must wear her mourning faithfully and she groaned because she was so weary of the cotton things she wore and she could not go out to feasts and be merry with her friends except secretly. For Lotus in her age had begun to make merry with some five or six old ladies in other well-to-do houses and these old ladies went about in their sedans from this house to that to game and to feast and to gossip. None of them had any cares now that they could not bear children any more and if their lords lived they had turned to younger women.

Among these old ladies Lotus complained often of Wang Lung and she said,

"I gave that man the best of my youth and Cuckoo will tell you how great a beauty I was so that you may know it is true, and I gave it all to him. I lived in his old earthen house and never saw the town until he was rich enough to come here and to buy this house. And I did not complain; no, I held myself ready for his pleasure at any moment, and yet all this was not enough for him. As soon as I was old at all he took to himself a slave of my own, a poor pale thing I kept out of pity for she was so weak she was little use to me, and now that he is dead I have only these few paltry bits of silver for my pains!"

Then this old lady or that would commiserate her, and

each pretended she did not know that Lotus had been only a singing girl out of a tea house, and one would cry out,

"Ah, so it is with all men, and as soon as our beauty is gone they look about for another, even though they used our beauty heedlessly until it was gone! So it is with us all!"

And they all agreed upon these two things, that all men were wicked and selfish and they themselves were most to be pitied of all women because they had sacrificed themselves so wholly, and when they were agreed upon these things and each had shown how her lord was the worst, they fell with relish to their eating and then with zest to their gaming, and so Lotus spent her life. And since it is a servant's due to have what her mistress earns at gaming, or else a share in it, Cuckoo was zealous to urge her on to such a life.

But still Lotus longed for the days of her mourning to be over so she could take off her cotton robes and wear silks again and forget that Wang Lung had lived. Yes, except for the certain times when she must for decency's sake go to his grave and weep and when the family went to burn paper and incense to his shade, she did not think of him except when she must draw on those mourning robes in the morning and take them off at night, and she longed to be rid of this so she need not think of him at all.

There was only Pear Blossom who was in no haste, and she went as she always did and mourned by that grave in the land. When no one was by to see her she went and mourned there.

Now while the two brothers waited they must live on together in this great house, they and their wives and children, and it was not easy living because of the hostility of their wives to each other. The wives of Wang the Eldest and Wang the Second hated each other so heartily that the two men were distracted by them, for the two women could not keep their

39

anger to themselves, but each must pour it forth to her husband, when she had him alone.

The wife of Wang the Eldest said to him in her proper, pompous way, "It is a strange thing I can never have the decent respect which is my due in this house to which you brought me. I thought while the old man lived I must endure it because he was so coarse and ignorant a person that I was shamed before my sons when they saw what they had for a grandfather. Yet I bore it all because it was right for me so to do. But now he is dead and you are the head of the family, and if he did not see what your brother's wife is and how she treats me, and he did not see it because he was so ignorant and unlearned, you are the head and you see it and still you do nothing to teach that woman her place. I am set at naught by her every day, a coarse, country woman and irreligious, too."

Then Wang the Eldest groaned in himself and he said with what patience he could muster,

"What does she say to you?"

"It is not only in what she says," the lady replied in her chill way, and when she talked her lips scarcely moved and her voice did not rise or fall. "It is in all she does and is. When I come into a room where she is she pretends to be at some task from which she cannot rise and give me place, and she is so red and loud I cannot bear her if she speaks at all, no, not even if I see her pass, even."

"Well, and I can scarcely go to my brother and say, 'Your wife is too red and too loud and the mother of my sons will not have her so,'" replied Wang the Eldest, wagging his head and feeling for his tobacco pipe in the girdle under his robe. He felt he had said a very good thing and he dared to smile a little.

Now the lady was not one who was ever quick to answer and the truth was she could not answer many times as quickly as she longed to do, and one reason she hated her sister-in-law was because the country wife had a sharp witty tongue, although it was coarse, too, and before the townswoman could finish a speech she set out to make slowly and with dignity, the country wife had with some roll of her eyes and with some quick word interspersed put to naught the townswoman and made her seem absurd so that when the slaves and servants who stood by heard it they had to turn away quickly to hide their smiles. But sometimes a young maid turned too late and her laughter burst out of her with a great squeak before she could stop herself and then others must needs laugh as though at the noise she made, and the townswoman was so angry she hated the country wife with all her heart. So when Wang the Eldest said what he did, she looked at him sharply to see if he made sport of her too, and there he sat in a reed chair he had for his ease, and there he was smiling his soft smile, and she drew herself up very hard and she sat erect and chill upon the stiff wooden chair she always chose, and she dropped the lids over her eyes and made her mouth very small and tight and she said,

"I know very well you despise me, too, my lord! Ever since you brought home that common creature you have despised me, and I wish I had never left my father's house. Yes, and I wish now I could give myself to the gods and enter myself a nun somewhere and so I would if it were not for my children. I have given myself to building up this house of yours to make it more than a mere farmer's house, but you give me no thanks."

She wiped her eyes with her sleeves carefully as she said this, and she rose and went into her room and soon Wang the Eldest heard her reciting aloud some Buddhist prayer. For this lady of late years had recourse to nuns and to priests and she had grown very scrupulous in her duty to the gods

41

and she spent much time in prayers and chants and the nuns came often to teach her. She made a parade, too, of being able to eat but a very little meat, although she had not taken the strict vows, and she did all this in a rich man's house where there is no need for such worship as a poor man must give to the gods for safety's sake.

So now, as she always did when she was angered, she began to pray aloud in her room and when Wang the Eldest heard it he rubbed his hand ruefully over his head and he sighed, for it was true this lady of his had never forgiven him that he had come to the taking of a second woman into his house, a pretty, simple girl he saw on the street one day at a poor man's door. She had sat on a little stool beside a tub washing clothes, and she was so young and pretty he looked at her twice and thrice as he passed, and he passed again and again. Her father was glad enough to let her go to so goodly a rich man and Wang the Eldest paid him well. But she was so simple that now he knew all she was Wang the Eldest did sometimes wonder how it was he had longed for her as he had, for she was so simple that she feared his lady very much and had no temper at all of her own, and sometimes when Wang the Eldest called for her to come to his room at night she even hung her head and faltered,

"But will my lady let me tonight?"

And sometimes when he saw how timid she was Wang the Eldest grew angry and vowed he would take a good, robust, ill-tempered wench next who would not fear his lady as they all did. But sometimes he groaned and thought to himself that after all it was better so, because at least he had peace between his two women, seeing that the younger one obeyed her mistress abjectly and would not so much as look at him if the lady were by.

Nevertheless, although this somewhat satisfied the lady, still

42

she never ceased to reproach Wang the Eldest, first that he had taken any other woman at all, and then if he must, that he had taken so poor a thing. As for Wang the Eldest, he bore with his lady and he loved the girl still sometimes for her pretty childish face, and he seemed to love her most whenever his lady spoke most bitterly against her, so that he managed by stealth and by schemes to get the girl who was his own. He would answer when she feared to come to him,

"You may come freely for she is too weary to be troubled by me tonight."

It was true enough that his lady was a woman of a chill heart and she was glad when her days of child-bearing were over. Then Wang the Eldest gave her the respect that was her due and he deferred to her by day in everything and so did the girl, but by night the girl came to him, and so he had peace with his two wives in his house.

Still the quarrel with the sister-in-law was not so easily settled, and the wife of Wang the Second was at her husband too, and she said,

"I am sick to death of that white-faced thing who is your brother's wife, and if you do not something to separate our courts from theirs, I shall take my revenge one day and bawl in the streets against her, and that will make her die of shame she is so puling and so fearful lest one does not bow deep enough every time she comes in. I am as good as she is and better, and I am glad I am not like her and that you are not like that great fat fool, even though he be the elder brother over you!"

Now Wang the Second and his wife agreed very well. He was small and yellow and quiet and he liked her because she was ruddy and large and had a lusty heart, and he liked her because she was shrewd and a good wife in the house and she spent money hardly and although her father had been a farmer and she was never used to fine living, now that she could have it she did not crave it as some women would have. She ate coarse food by choice and wore cotton rather than silk, and her only faults were a tongue too ready for gossip and that she liked to chatter with the servants.

It was true she could never be called a lady since she liked to wash and to rub and work with her own hands. Yet since she was so she did not need so many servants and she had only a country maid or two whom she treated as friends, and this was another thing her sister-in-law held against her, that she could not treat a servant properly but must look on them all as her equals, and so bring the family to shame. For servants talk to servants, and the elder wife had heard the maids in her sister-in-law's house boast about their mistress and how much more generous she was than the other and how she gave them bits of dainties left over and bits of stuffs for shoes, if she were in such a mood.

It was true the lady was hard with her servants, but so she was with all and she was hard with herself, too, and she never came forth as the other one did, who ran anywhere with her garments faded and worn and her hair awry and her shoes soiled and turned under at the heel, although her feet were none too small, either. Neither had the lady ever sat as the country wife did, who suckled her child where she sat or stood, with her bosom all out.

Indeed, the greatest quarrel these two ever had was because of this suckling, and the quarrel drove the two brothers at last to find a way of peace. It happened on a certain day that the lady went to the gate to enter her sedan, for it was the birthday of a god who had a temple in the town, and she went to make an offering. As she passed into the street there was the country wife at the gate with her bosom all bare like a slave's, and she was suckling her youngest child and talking to a

44

vendor from whom she bought a fish for the noon meal of the day.

It was a hideous coarse sight and the lady could not bear it, and she set herself to reproach her sister-in-law bitterly, and she began,

"Truly it is a very shameful sight to see one who should be lady in a great house do such a thing as I would scarcely allow a slave of mine—"

But her slow and sedate tongue could not match the other's, and the country wife shouted out,

"Who does not know that children must be suckled and I am not ashamed I have sons to suckle and two breasts to suckle them at!"

And instead of buttoning her coat decently she shifted her child triumphantly and suckled it at her other breast. Then hearing her loud voice a crowd began to gather to see the fray and women ran out of their kitchens and out of their courts, wiping their hands as they ran, and farmers who passed set their baskets down awhile to enjoy the quarrel.

But when the lady saw these brown and common faces she could not bear it and she sent the sedan away for the day and tottered into her own courts, all her pleasure spoiled. Now the country wife had never seen such squeamishness as this, for she had always seen children suckled wherever their mothers happened to be, for who can say when a child will cry for this and that and the breast is the only way it will be quieted? So she stood and abused her sister-in-law in such merry ways that the crowd roared with laughter and was in high good humor at the play.

Then a slave of the lady's who stood by, curious, went and told her mistress faithfully all that the country wife said and she whispered,

"Lady, she says you are so high that you make my lord go

45

in terror for his life and he does not even dare to love his little concubine unless you say he may and then only so long as you say, and all the crowd laughed!"

The lady turned pale at this and she sat down suddenly on a chair beside the table in the chief room and waited and the slave ran and came back again and said breathlessly,

"Now she is saying you care more for priests and nuns than you do for your children and it is well known what such as they are for secret evil!"

At such vileness as this the lady rose and she could not bear it and she told the slave she was to command the gateman to come to her at once. So the slave ran out again in pleasure and excitement, for it was not every day there was such an ado as this, and she brought the gateman in. He was a gnarled old laborer who had once been on Wang Lung's land and because he was so old and trusty and he had no son to feed him when he grew old he had been allowed to see to the gates. He went fearful of this lady as they all did and he stood bowing and hanging his head before her and she said in her majestic way,

"Since my lord is at his tea house now and knows not of all this unseemly commotion and since his brother is not here either to control his house, I must do my duty and I will not have the common people on the streets gaping like this at our house and you are to shut the gates. If my sister-in-law is shut out, let her be shut out, and if she asks you who told you to shut the gates say I did, and you must obey me."

The old man bowed again and went out speechless and did as he was commanded. Now the country wife was still there and she enjoyed it mightily when the crowd laughed at her and she did not see the gates closing slowly behind her until they were closed almost to a crack. Then the old gateman put his lips to the crack and he whispered hoarsely,

46

"Hist—mistress!"

She turned then and saw what was happening and she made a rush and pushed the gates and ran through, her child still at her breast, and she shrieked at the old man,

"Who told you to lock me out, you old dog?"

And the old man answered humbly, "The lady did, and she said I was to lock you out because she would not have such a din here at her gates. But I called to you so you would know."

"And they are her gates, are they, and I am to be locked out of my own house, am I?" And shrieking thus the country wife bounced into her sister-in-law's courts.

But the lady had foreseen this and so she had gone into her own rooms and barred the door and she had fallen to her prayers, and although the country wife knocked and beat mightily upon the door, she had no satisfaction and all she heard was the steady, monotonous drone of prayers.

Nevertheless, be sure the two brothers heard of it that night each from his own wife, and when they met in the street the next morning on their way to the tea house they looked at each other wanly, and the second brother said, his face in a wry smile,

"Our wives will drive us into enmity yet and we cannot afford to be enemies. We had better divide them. You take the courts you are in and the gate that is upon the main street shall be your gate. I will stay in my own courts and open a gate to the side street and that will be my gate, and so can we pursue our lives peacefully. If that third brother of ours ever comes home to live he may have the courts where our father lived and if the first concubine is dead then hers where she is adjoining it."

Now Wang the Eldest had been told many times in the night by his lady every word of what had passed and he was so pressed by his lady that this time he swore to her he

47

would not be mild and yielding; no, this time he would do what was fitting for the head of the house to do when the mistress of the house is so outraged as this by one who is her inferior and ought to pay her deference. So now when he heard what his younger brother said he remembered how hard pressed he had been in the night, and he said feebly in reproach,

"But your wife did very wrong to speak of my lady as she did before the common crowd and it is not enough to let it pass so easily. You should beat her a time or two. I must insist you beat her a time or two."

Then Wang the Second let his little sharp eyes twinkle and he coaxed his brother and he said,

"We are men, you and I, my brother, and we know what women are and how ignorant and simple the best of them are. Men cannot concern themselves in the affairs of women and we understand each other, my elder brother, we men. It is true that my wife behaved like a fool and she is a country woman and nothing better. Tell your lady I said so and that I send my apologies for my wife. Apologies cost nothing. Then let us separate our women and children and we will have peace, my brother, and we can meet in the tea house and discuss the affairs we have together and at home we will live separately."

"But—but—" said Wang the Eldest, stammering, for he could not think so fast and so smoothly as this.

Then Wang the Second was clever and he saw immediately that his brother did not know how he was to satisfy his lady and so he said quickly,

"See, my elder brother, say it thus to your lady: 'I have cut my younger brother's house off from us and you shall never be troubled again. Thus have I punished them.'"

48

The elder brother was pleased, then, and he laughed and rubbed his fat pale hands together and he said,

"See to it—see to it!"

And Wang the Second said, "I will call masons this very day."

So each man satisfied his wife. The younger one told his wife,

"You shall not be troubled by that prudish, proud towns-woman any more. I have told my elder brother I will not live under the same roof with her. No, I will be master in my own house and we will divide ourselves, and I will not be under his heel any more, and you not at her beck and call."

And the elder one went to his lady and said in a loud voice, "I have managed it all and I have punished them very well. You can rest your heart. I said to my brother, I said, 'You shall be cut off from my house, you and your wife, and your children, and we will take the courts we have by the great gate, and you must cut a little side gate on to the alley toward the east, and your woman is not to trouble my lady any more. If that one of yours wishes to hang about at her door suckling her children like a sow does her pigs in the street, at least it will not disgrace us!' So have I done, mother of my sons, and rest yourself, for you need not see her any more."

Thus each man satisfied his wife, so that each woman thought herself triumphant and the other altogether van-quished. Then the two brothers were better friends than they had ever been and each felt himself a very clever fellow and one who understood women. They were in high good humor with themselves and with each other and they longed for the days of mourning to be over soon so that they might set a day to meet at the tea house and plan the selling of such land as they wished to sell.

So the three years passed in this varied waiting and the

49

time came when the mourning for Wang Lung could be ended. A day for this was chosen from the almanac and the name of that day had the proper letter in it for such a day, and Wang the Eldest prepared everything for the rites of the release from mourning. He talked with his lady and again she knew all that was fitting and she told him and he did it.

The sons and the sons' wives and all who were near to Wang Lung and had worn mourning these three years dressed themselves in gay silks and the women put on some hue of red. Then over these they put the hempen robes they had worn and they went outside the great gate, as the custom was in those parts, and there a heap of spirit money in gold and silver had been made and priests stood ready and they lit the paper. Then by the light of the flames they who wore mourning for Wang Lung took it off and stood manifest in the gay robes they wore underneath.

When the rites were complete, they went into the house and each congratulated all that the days of sorrow were over, and they bowed to the new tablet that had been made for Wang Lung, for the old one was burned, and they put wine and sacrifices of cooked meats before the tablet. Now this new tablet was the permanent tablet and it was made, as such are, of a very fine hard wood and it was set into a little wooden casket to hold it. When it was made and varnished with very costly varnish of black, the sons of Wang Lung searched for the most learned man in the town to inscribe it for them with the name and the spirit of Wang Lung.

There was none more learned than the son of the old Confucian scholar who had once been their teacher, a man who had gone up in his youth to the imperial examinations. True, he had failed, but still he was more learned than those who had not gone at all, and he had given all his learning to his son and this son was a scholar too. When he was invited to so honorable a task as this, therefore, he came swinging his robes as he walked and setting his feet out as scholars do, and he wore his spectacles low upon the end of his nose. When he was come he seated himself at the table before the tablet, having first bowed as many times as he ought to it, and then, pushing back his long sleeves and pointing his brush of camel's hair very fine and sharp, he began to write. Brush and ink slab and ink and all were new, for so they must be at such a task, and thus he inscribed. When he came to the last letter of the inscription he paused for a time before he wrote the very end, and he waited and closed his eyes and meditated so that he might catch the whole spirit of Wang Lung in the last touch of the last word.

And after he had meditated awhile it came to him thus: "Wang Lung, whose riches of body and soul were of the earth." When he thought of this it seemed to him that he had caught the essence of Wang Lung's being, so that his very soul would be held fast, and he dipped his brush in red and set the last stroke upon the tablet.

Thus was it finished, and Wang the Eldest took his father's tablet and carried it carefully in both his hands and they all went together and set the tablet in that small upper room where the other tablets were, the tablets of the two old farmers who had been Wang Lung's father and grandfather. Here their tablets were in this rich house, and they would never have dreamed when they were alive of having tablets such as only rich people have, and if they thought at all of themselves when they would be dead, it was only to suppose their names would be written upon a bit of paper by some fellow a little learned and pasted to the earthen wall of the house in the fields and so stay until it wore away after a while. But when Wang Lung had moved into this town house he had tablets made for his two ancestors as though they had lived

51

here, too, although whether their spirits were there or not, no one could know.

Here then was Wang Lung's tablet put also, and when his sons had done all that should be done they shut the door and came away, and they were glad in their secret hearts.

Now it was the proper time to invite guests and to feast and to be merry, and Lotus put on robes of a bright blue flowered silk, too bright for so huge and old a creature, but no one corrected her, knowing what she was, and they all feasted. And as they feasted they laughed together and drank wine and Wang the Eldest shouted again and again, for he loved a great merry gathering,

"Drink to the bottom of your cups—let the bottom be seen!"

And he drank so often that the dark red came up from the wine in him and flushed his cheeks and eyes. Then his lady, who was apart with the women in another court, heard he was about to be drunken and she sent her maid out to him to say, "It is scarcely seemly to be drunken yet and at such a feast as this." So he recalled himself.

But even Wang the Second was cheerful this day and did not begrudge anything. He took opportunity to speak secretly with some of the guests to see if any wished to buy more land than he had, and he spread it about here and there secretly that he had some good land to part with, and thus the day passed, and each brother was satisfied because he broke the bond under which he had been to the old man who lay in the earth.

There was one who did not feast among them and Pear Blossom sent her excuse saying, "The one I care for is a little less well than usual and I beg to be excused." So, since no one missed her, Wang the Eldest sent word she was to be excused if she liked from the feasting and she alone did not take off her mourning that day, nor the white shoes she wore nor the white cord that bound her hair where it was coiled. Neither did she take these signs of sadness from the fool either. While the others feasted she did what she loved to do. She took the fool by the hand and led her to Wang Lung's grave and they sat down. Then while the fool played, content to be near the one who cared for her, Pear Blossom sat and looked over the land, and there it was spread in its small green fields laid edgewise and crosswise and fitted into each other for as many miles as her eyes could reach. Here and there a spot of blue stood or moved where some farmer bent over his spring wheat. So had Wang Lung once bent also over the fruit of his earth when it had been his turn to have it for his own, and Pear Blossom remembered how in his old age he had dwelled on those years before she was born and how he loved to tell her of them and of how he had been used to plough this field and plant that one.

So did this time pass and so did this day pass for the family of Wang Lung. But his third son did not come home even for such a day. No, wherever he was he remained there and he busied himself in some life of his own and apart from them all.

V

Now as the branches of some great old tree spring out from the stout trunk and strain away from that trunk and from each other, straining and spreading each upon its own way, although their root is the same, so it was with the three sons of Wang Lung, and the strongest and most wilful of the three was Wang the Third, Wang Lung's youngest son, who was a soldier in a southern province.

On the day when Wang the Third had received the news

that his father lay dying he was standing in front of a temple outside the city where his general lived, for there was a piece of bare ground before that temple, and he marched his soldiers to and fro and he taught them feints and postures of war. So he was doing when his brothers' messenger came running and panting and, breathless with the importance of the message he bore, gasped forth,

"Sir, and our third young lord—your father, the old lord—lies dying!"

Now Wang the Third had had no dealing with his father at all since the day he had run away from home in a mighty fit of anger because his father took into his own court, when he was already a very old man, a certain young maid who had been reared in the house, who was Pear Blossom, and Wang the Third had not known he loved her until he heard what his father had done. That same night he ran into his father's court, for he had brooded the whole day since he heard, and he was so surcharged with his brooding that he dashed into the room where his father sat with the maid. Yes, he dashed into that room out of the hot darkness of a summer's night and there she sat, still and pale, and he knew surely he could have loved her. Then such a sea of anger rose in him against his father that he could not bound it, for he was given to anger, and he knew if he stayed to let it swell it must have burst his heart, and he flung himself out of his father's house that very night, and because he had always longed to adventure forth and to be a hero under some banner of war, he spent the silver he had by him and went south as far as he could and took service under a general famous at that time in a rebellion. And Wang the Third was so tall and strong and fierce a youth and his face so dark and angry and his lips hard and pressed over his great white teeth, that the general had marked him at once and wanted him near himself and he had raised Wang the Third up very quickly and much more quickly than usual. This was partly because he was so silent and changeless a young man that the general came to trust him and partly because Wang the Third had such a fierce and angry temper that when it was roused he did not fear to kill nor to risk being killed, and there are not many men so brave as this to be hired. Besides this, there was a war or two and war is a time when soldiers may rise rapidly and so it was with Wang the Third, for as men above him were killed or displaced the general gave him higher and higher office until from a common soldier he had risen to be a captain over many men, and so he had been when he set out for his father's house.

When Wang the Third heard what the messenger had to say he sent his men away and he walked alone over the fields and the messenger walked a distance behind him. It was a day in early spring, such a day as his father Wang Lung had been used to stir himself and go out and look over his land and on such a day he would take his hoe and turn over the earth between the rows of his wheat. There, although there were no signs of new life to any other eye than his, to his eye there was a swelling and a change, the promise of a new harvest out of the earth. Now he was dead, and Wang the Third could not imagine death on such a day.

For in his own way did Wang the Third feel the spring also. Where his father had gone out restless to his land Wang the Third grew restless, too, and every spring he turned his mind to a plan he had, and it was to leave the old general and set out upon a war of his own and entice such men as would to come under the banner he would set up for himself. Every spring it seemed to him a thing he could do and at last a thing that he must do, and as year after year he planned how he could do it, it grew into his dream and his ambition, and so great had it grown that in this very spring he had said to himself he must set out on it, and he could not any longer endure the life he led under the old general.

For the truth was that Wang the Third was very bitter against the old general. When he had first come to the banner under which he served, the general was one of those who led in a rebellion against a wicked ruler and he had been still young enough then so he could talk of revolution and how fine a thing it was and how all brave men must fight for a good right cause, and he had a great rolling voice and words slipped easily from his tongue and he had a trick of moving men beyond what he felt himself, although those who heard him did not know this.

When Wang the Third had first heard these fair words he was very moved, for his was a simple heart, and he swore to himself he would stand by such a general as this in so good a cause, and his deep heart was filled with the purpose.

It astonished him, therefore, when the rebellion was successful and the general came back from his wars and took this rich river valley for his place to live, to see this man, who had been a hero in wars, settle himself with zest to these things he now did, and Wang the Third could not forgive him that he had forgotten himself like this, and in the strangest way it seemed to Wang the Third he had been robbed or defrauded somehow of something, although he did not know what, either, and it was out of this bitterness the thought had first come that he would leave this general he had once served with all his heart in war, and that he would pursue alone his own path.

For in these years power had passed out of the old general and he grew idle and he lived off the land and went no more out to any wars. He let himself grow huge in flesh and he ate the richest meats every day and drank wines from foreign countries that do eat out a man's belly they are so fiery, and he talked no more of war but all his talk was of how this cook had made such a sauce upon a fish caught out of the sea, and of how that cook could pepper a dish to suit a king, and when he had eaten all he could eat then the only other game he knew was women and he had fifty wives and more and it was his humor to have women of every sort, so that he had even a strange woman with a very white skin and leaf-colored eyes and hair like hemp, whom he had bought for a price somewhere. But he was afraid of her, too, because she had so much discontent in her that she was festering with some bitterness and she would mutter to herself in her own strange tongue as though she cast a spell. But still it amused the old general and it was a thing to boast of that he could have such a one, even, among his women.

Under a general like this the captains grew weak and careless also and they caroused and drank and lived off the people and all the people hated the general and his men very heartily. But the young men and the brave grew rest-less and stifled with inaction and when Wang the Third held himself above them all and lived his plain way and would not even look at women, these young men turned to him, one after the other, this handful and that, this brotherhood and that, and they said among themselves,

"Is it he who can lead us out?"

And they turned their eyes to him expectantly.

There was but one thing that held Wang the Third back from his dream now and it was that he had no money, for after he left his father's house he had no more except the paltry bit he received at the end of each month from the old general, and often he did not have even that, for sometimes the general had not enough to pay his men, since he needed so much himself and fifty women in a man's house are rapacious and they vie with one another in their jewels and their garments and in what they can secure by tears and coquetry out of an old man who is their lord.

So it seemed to Wang the Third he could never do what he hoped unless he became a robber for a while and his men a robber band, as many like him have done, and when he had robbed for a time until he had enough, he could wait for a lucky war and make terms with some state army or other somewhere and demand to be pardoned and received into the state again.

But it was against his stomach to be a robber, too, for his father had been an honest man and not such a man as falls easily into robbery in any famine or time of war, and Wang the Third might have struggled on for more years yet and waited for a chance, for now he had dreamed so long that it had come to be a certainty in him that heaven itself had marked out his destiny for him even as he dreamed and he had but to wait until his hour came and he could seize it.

The one thing which made it well-nigh impossible for him to wait, for he was not a man of patient temper, was that his soul had come to loathe this southern country where he lived and he longed to be out of it and away to his own north. He was a man of the north and there were days when he could scarcely swallow one more time the endless white rice these southerners loved and he longed to set his great hard white teeth into a stiff sheet of unleavened wheaten bread rolled about a garlic stalk. Yes, he made his own voice harsher and louder even than its nature was because he hated so heartily the smooth oiled courtesies of these southern men, who were so smooth they must be tricky since it is against nature to be always gentle, and he thought all clever men must have hollow hearts. Yes, he scowled at them often and was angry with them often because he longed to be in his own country again where men grew tall as men ought to be and not little apes as these southerners were, and where men's speech was scant and plain and their hearts stern and straight. And because Wang the Third had so evil a temper men were afraid of him and they feared his black brows' frowning and his surly mouth and because of these and his white long teeth, they made a nickname for him and they called him Wang the Tiger.

Often in the night in the small room he had for his own Wang the Tiger would roll upon his hard and narrow bed and seek for a plan and a way to do what he dreamed. Well he knew if his old father died he would have his inheritance. But his father would not die, and gnashing his teeth Wang the Tiger muttered often into the night,

"The old man will live clean through my own prime and it will be too late for me to grow great if he does not die soon! How perverse an old man is he that he will not die!"

So at last in this spring he had come to the place where, however unwilling he was to do it, yet he had made up his mind he must turn robber rather than wait on and scarcely had he made up his mind when the news came of his father's dying. . . . Now having this news he walked back across the fields, his heart swelling and pounding in his bosom because he saw the way that was set out before him clear and plain for him to follow, and it was so great a comfort he need not be a robber that he could have shouted had he not been so silent a man by nature. Yes, far above every other thought was this; he had not been mistaken in his destiny and with his inheritance he would have all he needed, and heaven guarded him. Yes, far above every other thought was this; now he could take the first step out upon that upward and endless road of his destiny, for he knew he was destined to be great.

But none saw this exultation upon his face. None ever saw anything upon that fierce changeless face of his; his mother had given to him her steadfast eye and her firm mouth and her look of something rocklike in the very substance of which his flesh was made. He said nothing therefore but he went to his room and prepared himself for the long journey north, and he told off four trusty men whom he commanded to come with him. When his scanty preparations were made, he marched to the great old house in that city which the general had taken for his own use and he sent a guard in to announce him, and the guard came back and called out that he was to enter. Then Wang the Tiger marched in, bidding his men wait at the door, and he went into the room where the old general sat finishing his noon meal.

The old man sat crouching over his food as he ate and two of his wives stood to serve him. He was unwashed and unshaven and his coat was loose upon him and not buttoned, for he loved now as he grew old to go unwashed and un-shaven and careless of his looks as he had when he was young, for he had been in his day a very low and common working man except that he would not work and fell to robbery and then he rose out of robbery at a turn of some war or other. But he was a genial merry old man, too, very reckless in all he said, and he always welcomed Wang the Tiger, and respected him because he did those things he was too indolent to do himself now in his fat old age.

So now when Wang the Tiger came in and made his obeisance and said, "One came today to say my father is dying and my brothers wait for me to come to bury him," the old general leaned back easily and said, "Go, my son, and do your duty to your father and then come back to me." Then he fumbled in his girdle and wrenched at it and brought out a handful of money and he said, "Here is a largesse for you and do not deal too hardly with yourself on your travels."

And he leaned far back in his chair and called out suddenly he had something in a hollow tooth, and one of his wives plucked a long slender silver pin from her hair and gave it to him and he busied himself and forgot Wang the Tiger.

So had Wang the Tiger gone back to his father's house, and with his impatience seething in him, he waited until the inheritance was divided and he could hasten away again. But he would not set out upon his plan until the years of mourning were over. No, he was a scrupulous man, and he chose his duty to do it if he could, and he waited, therefore. But it was easy for him to wait now, for his dream was sure at last, and he spent the three years in perfecting every means and in saving his silver and in choosing and watching what men he hoped would follow him.

Of his father he thought no more since he had what he needed, except as the branch may think of the trunk from which it sprang. Wang the Tiger had no more thought of his father than that, for he was a man whose usual thoughts ran deep and narrow and there was room in him for only one thing at a time, and in his heart space but for one person. That person now was himself, and he had no dream except his one dream.

Yet that dream had enlarged itself this much. In those days when he was idle in his brothers' courts he saw something his brothers had that he had not and he envied them this one possession. He did not envy them their women nor their houses nor goods nor all the prosperous airs they had nor the bows men gave them everywhere. No, he envied them only this, and it was the sons they had. He stared at

61

all those lads of his brothers', and he watched them as they played and quarrelled and clamored, and it came to him suddenly for the first time in his life that he wished he had a son of his own, too. Yes, it would be a very good thing for a lord of war to have a son of his own, for no blood is wholly loyal to a man except his own, and he wished he had a son.

But when he had thought of it for a while, he put the wish away again, at least for the present, for it was not the hour now for him to pause for a woman. He had a distaste for women and it seemed to him no woman could be aught but a hindrance to him at this beginning of his venture. Nor would he have any common woman he could leave and not count a wife, for if he took a woman for the hope of a son, he wanted true son from true wife. He put his hope away for a while, then, and he let it lie in his heart and deep in the future.

VI

Now while Wang the Tiger was preparing to go forth out of the south and for himself at last, there was a certain day when Wang the Second said to his elder brother,

"If you have the leisure tomorrow morning come with me to the tea house on the Street of the Purple Stones and let us talk together of two things."

When Wang the Eldest heard his brother say this he wondered to himself, for he knew the land must be talked about but he did not know what else, and so he said,

"I will surely come, but what other thing is there to talk about?"

"I have a strange letter from that third brother of ours," replied Wang the Second. "He makes us an offer for as many

sons as we can spare, because he sets out on some great
endeavor, and he needs men of his own blood about him,
because he has no sons of his own."

"Our sons!" repeated Wang the Eldest astounded and his
great mouth ajar with his astonishment and his eyes staring
at his brother.

Wang the Second nodded his head. "I do not know what
he will do with them," he said, "but come tomorrow and we
will talk." And he made as though to pass on his way, for
he had stopped his brother upon the street as he came back
from his grain market.

But Wang the Eldest could not finish with anything so
quickly and he had always time and to spare for anything
that came up, and so he said, being in a mood to be merry
these days now that he had come into his own,

"It is easy enough for a man to have sons of his own! We
must find him a wife, Brother!"

And he narrowed his two eyes and made his face sly as
though he were about to say a good piece of wit. But Wang
the Second seeing this smiled a very little and he said in
his wintry way,

"We are not all so easy with women as you are, Elder
Brother!"

And he walked on as he spoke, for he was not minded to
let Wang the Eldest begin upon his loose talk now when
they stood there in the street and people passing to and fro
and ready to stop and listen to any tale.

The next morning, therefore, the two brothers met at the
tea house and they found a table in a corner where they
might look out and see anything there was to be seen but
where men could not easily hear what they had to say to
each other and there they took their places, and Wang the
Eldest sat in the inner seat, which was the higher place and

his own by right. Then he shouted for the serving man of that house and when he came Wang the Eldest ordered this and that of food, some sweet hot cakes and some light sorts of salty meat such as men eat in the morning to tempt their stomachs, and a jug of hot wine and some other meats that men eat to send the wine down so that its heat will not rise and they be drunken early in the day, and he ordered on of such things as struck his fancy, for he was a man who loved good food. Wang the Second sat and listened and at last he fidgeted in his seat and was in an agony for he did not know whether or not he would have to pay his share of all this and at last he called out sharply,

"If all these meats and foods are for me, Brother, then I will not have them, because I am an abstemious man and my appetite is small and especially in the morning."

But Wang the Eldest said largely,

"You are my guest for today and you need not mind for I will pay."

So he set his brother at rest, and when the meats were come, Wang the Second did his best to eat all he could, seeing he was a guest, for it was a trick of his he could not keep from, that although he had plenty of money he could not keep from saving all he could and especially if it was something for which he had not paid anything. Where other men gave their old garments and any unwanted thing to servants he could not bear to do it, but must take them secretly to a pawnshop keeper and get a little out of it. So when he was a guest he must needs stuff himself as best he could, although he was a spare man with a lean belly. But he forced himself and ate all he could so that he was not hungry for a day or two afterward, and it was strange for he did not need to do it either.

Yet so he did this morning and while the brothers ate

they did not talk at all but ate on and when they waited for the servant to bring a new dish they sat in silence and looked about the room where they sat, for it is a thing very ill for a man's appetite if he begin to discuss some matter of business while he eats, and it closes his stomach against its food.

Now although they did not know it, this was the very tea house to which their father Wang Lung had once come and where he had found Lotus, the singing girl whom he took for his concubine. To Wang Lung it had seemed a place of wonder, and a magic and beautiful house with its paintings of pretty women on silken scrolls hung upon the walls. But to these two sons of his it was a very usual place and they never dreamed of what it had been to their father, or how he had come in timidly and half ashamed as a farmer among townsmen. No, the two sons sat here in their silken robes and they looked about them at their ease and men knew who they were and made haste to rise and bow to them if the brothers looked their way, and servants made haste to wait on them and the master of the house came himself with the serving man who carried the jugs of heated wine and he said,

"This wine is from jars newly opened and I broke their clay seals with my own hand for you, sirs." And he asked again and again if all were to their liking.

Yes, so it was with these sons of Wang Lung, although in a far corner there still hung that silk scroll upon which Lotus was painted, a slight girl with a lotus bud in her little hand. Once Wang Lung had looked at it with his heart beating hard in his bosom and his mind all confusion, but now he was gone and Lotus was what she was, and the scroll hung here grimed with smoke and specked with flies' filth and no one ever looked at it or thought to ask, "Who is that beauty hanging hidden in the corner?" No, and these

65

two men who were Wang Lung's sons never dreamed it was Lotus or that she could ever have looked like that.

They sat here now respected of all and ate on, and although Wang the Second did his best yet he could not keep up eating so long as his elder brother did. For when Wang the Second had eaten all and more than he could Wang the Eldest ate on robustly and he drank his wine and smacked his full lips over its flavor and ate again until the sweat stood out on him and his face was as though it had been oiled. Then when even he had done the best he could he sat back in his seat and the serving man brought towels wrung out of boiling water and the two men wiped their heads and necks and hands and arms, and the serving man took away the broken meats that were left and the dregs of wine and he wiped the bones and bits of food from the table and he brought fresh green tea, and so the two men were ready to talk together.

By now it was mid-morning and the house was filled with men like themselves who had come out of their homes to eat in peace away from their women and children, and having eaten to talk with friends and sup tea together and to hear the latest news. For there can be no peace for any man in his house where women and children are, since women shriek and call and children are bawling and weeping, for so their nature is. But here in this house it was a peaceful place with the busy hum of men's voices rising everywhere in good talk. In the midst of all this peace, then, Wang the Second drew a letter out of his narrow bosom and he drew the paper from the envelope and laid it upon the table before his brother.

Wang the Eldest took it up and he cleared his throat and coughed loudly and he read it muttering the letters to himself as he read. When the scanty words of common greeting

66

were written, Wang the Tiger wrote on, and his letters looked like him because they were straight and black and he brushed them boldly upon the paper,

"Send me every ounce of silver you can, for I need all. If you will lend me silver, I will repay it at a high interest on the day when I achieve what I set out to do. If you have sons over seventeen send them to me also. I will raise them up and raise them higher than you dream, for I need men of my own blood about me that I can trust in my great venture. Send me the silver and send me your sons, since I have no son of my own."

Wang the Eldest read these words and he looked at his brother and his brother looked at him. Then Wang the Eldest said, wondering,

"Did he ever tell you at all what he did beyond that he was in an army with some southern general? It is strange he does not tell us what he will do with our sons. Men do not have sons to cast out like that into something they do not know."

They sat for a while in silence and drank their tea, and each thought with doubt that it was a wild thing to send sons out not knowing where and yet each thought jealously of the words, "I will raise your sons high," and each thought to himself that since he had a son or two old enough he might after all spare a son on the chance. Then Wang the Second said cautiously,

"You have sons who are more than seventeen."

And Wang the Eldest answered, "Yes, I have two over seventeen, and I could send the second son, and I have not thought what I would do with any of them, they grow up so easily in a house like mine. The eldest must not go out, since he is next to me in the family, but I could send the second one."

Then Wang the Second said, "My eldest is a girl, and the one after her is a son, and that one could go, I suppose, since your eldest son is at home to carry on the name."

Each man sat and mused over his children then and thought what he had and what worth their lives could be to him. Wang the Eldest had six children by his lady, but of these two were dead in childhood, and he had one by his concubine, but his concubine was ripe to give birth again in a month or two, and of these children he had every one was sound except the third son whom a slave had dropped when he was but a few months old, so that his back grew twisted in a knot on his shoulders, and his head was too large for him and it set into this knot like a turtle's head into its shell. Wang the Eldest had called a doctor or two to see it and he had even promised a robe to a certain goddess in the temple if she would cure the child, although in usual times he did not believe in such things. But it was all useless, for the child would carry his burden until he died, and the only pleasure his father had out of it was that he made the goddess go without her robe, since she would not do anything for him.

As for Wang the Second, he had five children in all, and three were sons, the eldest and youngest being girls. But his wife was in her prime yet and the line of his children was not ended either, doubtless, for she was so robust a woman she would bear on into her middle age.

So it was true that out of all these children a son or two could be spared out of so many, and thus each man thought when he had meditated awhile. At last Wang the Second looked up and he said,

"How shall I answer our brother?"

The elder brother hesitated then, for he was not a man to decide anything quickly for himself, having leaned for many years upon the decisions of his lady and said what she told him to say, and this Wang the Second knew and he said cunningly,

"Shall I say we will send a son apiece and I will send as much silver as I am able?"

And Wang the Eldest was glad to have it said thus and he answered, "Yes, do so, my brother, and let us decide it. I will send a son gladly, after all, because my house seems so full sometimes with brats squalling and the big ones bickering that I do swear I have not a moment's peace. I will send my second one and you your eldest, and then if anything untoward comes, there is my eldest son left to carry our name on."

So it was decided and the two drank tea for a while. Then when they were rested they began to talk of the lands, and of what they would sell. Now to both of these men as they sat and whispered together came a strong memory and it was of a certain day when they had first spoken of selling the land, and their father Wang Lung was in his age and they did not know he had strength enough to come creeping out after them to hear what they said as they stood in a certain field near the earthen house. But he did come and when he heard them say "sell the land" he had cried out in mighty anger,

"Now, evil, idle sons—sell the land?"

And he had been so angry he would have fallen if they had not held him up on either side, and he kept muttering over and over, "No—no—we will never sell the land—" and to soothe him, for he was too aged to be so angry, they had promised him they would never sell it. Yet even as they promised they smiled at each other over his nodding old head, foreseeing this very day when they would come together for this very purpose.

Eager as they were, therefore, upon this day, to heap up

69

money now, the memory was still strong in them of the old man in the land so that they could not speak as easily of selling the land as they had thought they could, and each was held back in his own heart by some caution that perhaps the old man was right after all, and each resolved to himself that he would not at once sell all; no, hard times must come and if business grew bad they would still have enough land to feed themselves. For in such times as these none could be sure what day a war might come near or a robber chief seize the countryside for a time or some curse or other fall upon the people, and it was better to have something that they could not lose. Yet they were both greedy after high interest from the silver that land will bring when it is sold, and so they were torn between their desires. Therefore when Wang the Second said,

"What lands of yours will you sell?" Wang the Eldest replied with a caution that sat strangely upon him,

"After all, I have not a business as you have, and there is nothing I can do except to be a landlord, and so I must not sell more than enough to bring me in ready cash to use, and I must not sell all."

Then Wang the Second said, "Let us go out to our lands and see all we have and where it is and how it lies, the distant and scattered pieces also. For our old father was so greedy for land that in his middle years he would buy it anywhere when it was cheap in a famine year, and we have lands all over the countryside, and some fields but a few paces in size. If you are to be landlord, it will be easier for you to have yours near together and so easy to control."

This seemed good and reasonable to them both, and so they rose, after Wang the Eldest had paid out his money for the food they had eaten and the wines, and something over and above for the serving man. They went out then,

Wang the Eldest first, and as they went men rose here and there in the room to bow and let it be known to all that they were acquainted with these two great men of the town. As for the two brothers, the eldest nodded freely and easily to all and smiled, for he loved this homage; but the younger one went with his eyes downcast and he nodded a little and very swiftly and he looked at no one, as though he feared if he were too friendly one might stop him and draw him aside and ask to borrow money of him.

So the two brothers went out to their land, and the younger one set his steps slow to match the pace of his elder brother, who was fat and heavy and unused to walking. At the city gate he was weary already and so they hailed two men who stood there with donkeys saddled and for hire, and the brothers bestrode these beasts and went out the gate.

That whole day did these two brothers spend upon their land, stopping at a wayside inn to eat at noon, and they went far and wide to every scattered field and they eyed the land sharply and saw what the tenants did. And the tenants were humble before them and anxious, since these were their new landlords, and Wang the Second marked every piece it was best to sell. All the lands that were their third brother's they so marked for sale, except the little that was about the earthen house. But with common accord the two brothers did not go near that house, no, nor near to that high hillock under a great date tree, where their father lay.

At the end of the day they drew near again to the city upon their weary beasts, and at the gate they dismounted and paid the men the price they had agreed upon. The men were weary too, having run behind the beasts all day, and they begged for a little more than the price, having run so far and so long that their shoes were worn somewhat the worse. Wang the

71

Eldest would have given it but Wang the Second would not and he said,

"No, I have given you your just due, and it is not my business what happens to your shoes."

And he walked away as he said it and would pay no heed to the muttered curses of the men. So the two brothers came to their own house and as they parted they looked at each other as men do who have a common purpose, and Wang the Second said,

"If you are willing, let us send our sons this day seven days, and I will take them there myself."

Wang the Eldest nodded then and walked wearily into his own gate for he had never done such a day's work as this in his whole life, and he thought to himself that a landlord's life was very hard.

VII

On the appointed day, therefore, Wang the Second said to his elder brother,

"If it be that your second son is ready, then mine is too, and I will take them tomorrow at dawn and go to that southern city where our brother is, and present them to him and he may do as he likes with them."

Then Wang the Eldest that same day when he was idle called his second son to him and he looked at the boy well to see what he was and how he would be for the purpose for which he was destined. The lad came when he was called and stood before his father waiting. He was a lad small in stature and very fragile and delicate in his looks, not beautiful either, and very timid and easily afraid, and his hands were always trembling and moist in the palms. He stood before his

72

father now, twisting his trembling hands together without knowing he did, and his head hung down but every now and again he looked up quickly and cornerwise at his father and then hung his head down again.

Wang the Eldest stared at him awhile, seeing him for the first time alone and out of his place among the other children, and he said suddenly, half musing,

"It would have been better if you had been the eldest and the eldest in your place, for he is better framed than you are to be a general, and you look so weak I do not know whether you can stick on a horse or not."

At this the lad fell suddenly to his knees and he forked his quivering fingers together and he implored his father,

"Oh, my father, I do hate the very thought of being a soldier and I thought I would be a scholar for I love my books so! Oh, my father, let me stay home with you and my mother, and I will not even ask to go away to a school—no, I will read and study as best I can alone, and I will never trouble you for anything if you will not send me away to be a soldier!"

Now although Wang the Eldest would have sworn he had said nothing at all about this matter, still the thing had leaked out somehow, and the truth of it was that Wang the Eldest could keep nothing to himself. He was such a man that without his knowing it every time some thought came to him or he laid some secret plan his very puffs and sighs and his half sentences and his portentous looks betrayed him. He would have sworn he had told no one, but he had told his eldest son and he had told his concubine in the night and he had told his wife last, coming to her, indeed, perforce, to have her approval. He put the matter so well to her, too, that the lady thought her son would step into being a general at once and she was willing, although she felt, after all, it was no more than he was fit for as her son. But the eldest son who was a clever lad and knew more than anyone dreamed he did, because he had such a finicking languid air and he seemed to see nothing, had tormented his younger brother and had sneered at him and said,

"You are to be made into a common soldier to follow that wild uncle of ours!"

Now this younger lad of Wang the Eldest's was indeed such a one that he could never even see a fowl killed without running somewhere to vomit, and he could scarcely bear to eat flesh at all he had such a puny stomach, and when he heard his brother say this he was beside himself with fear and he did not know what to do. He could not believe it and he was sleepless the whole night and he could do nothing, either, except to wait until he was called, and so he had thrown himself before his father to beg for mercy.

But when Wang the Eldest saw his son kneeling and begging like this he was angry, for he was a man who could be mulish and full of temper when he knew he had power, and he cried out, stamping his foot upon the tiled floor,

"You shall go, for this is such a chance as we cannot refuse, and your cousin is going too, and you ought to be glad to go! When I was young I would have rejoiced at such a chance and it did not come. No, I was sent south to nothing at all and even there I stayed but a little time because my mother died and my father bade me come home. And I never dreamed of disobeying him; I would not have dreamed of it! No, I had no such chance to grow great through an uncle's high position!"

And then Wang the Eldest sighed suddenly, because there came to him this thought, that if he had been given such a chance as this his son had, how great he could have grown by now and how noble he would have looked in a soldier's gilded coat and bestride a great high horse of war, for so he imagined generals did look, and he saw himself a great huge man as a general ought to be. Then he sighed again and he looked at this little wretched son of his and he said,

"I would have liked a better son than you to send, it is true, but I have not one old enough except you, and the eldest cannot leave home, for he is my chiefest heir and next to me in the family, and your younger brother is hunchback and the next but a child. You must go, then, and all your weeping is no help to you, either, for you must go." And he rose and went out of the room quickly so that he need not be troubled any more by this son of his.

But the son of Wang the Second was no such lad as this. He was a merry boisterous boy who had had smallpox when he was three years old from too strong a pox his mother had pushed into his nose with her thumb to make him safe against the disease, and he had kept his pocks all his years until now he was called by everyone, "Pocks" instead of his name, even by his own parents. When Wang the Second had called to him and said, "Get your clothes into a bundle because tomorrow you go south with me, for I shall give you to your soldier uncle," he capered and ran about in glee because he was one who was always ready to see what was new and he loved to make a boast of what he had seen.

But his mother looked up from a pot she stirred upon some coals in a little earthen stove there by the kitchen door, and since she had not heard of the thing before she cried out in her loud way,

"What do you spend good silver to go south for?"

Wang the Second told her then and she listened and stirred, but her eyes were fastened sharply meantime upon a maid who cleaned a fowl there and she watched lest the maid take

75

the liver or the unlaid eggs secretly and so she heard only the last of what her husband said, and it was this,

"It will be a venture and I do not know what he means by raising the lad up, but there are other sons to put into the business, and we have only this one old enough. Besides, my brother sends one."

When his wife heard these last words, she brought her mind to the thing and she said at once,

"Well, and if their sons are to be raised to a high position we must send ours, or else I shall be forever hearing my sister-in-law talk of her son who is a military hero. It is true this son of ours ought to be doing something he is so big and so full of his clownish tricks. And as you say, we have the others for the shop."

So Wang the Second the very next day took these two lads each with his garments, but the son of Wang the Eldest had his in a good pigskin box and he was fastidious. Although his eyes were still red with weeping, and he delayed to see that his man servant carried it properly with the top uppermost so that his books should not be all askew within. But the son of Wang the Second owned no book, and he had his few clothes tied into a large blue cotton kerchief and he carried this himself, and he ran as he went and shouted aloud over everything he saw. It was a clear bright day in spring and the streets of the town were full of the first produce of the fields and everyone was busy buying and selling. To this lad it was a good year and a bright day and he was setting forth on a journey which he had never done before, and his mother had cooked him a dish he loved to eat that morning, and so he was very merry. But the other lad walked along decorously and slowly and in silence and he hung his head down and he scarcely looked at his cousin, and from time to time he wet his pale lips as though they were very dry.

76

Thus Wang the Second walked with the two lads and he mused on his own affairs, for he was never one to pay heed to children, and so they came to the north of the town where the place was to mount the fire wagon, and Wang the Second paid money and they mounted. Then the son of Wang the Eldest was put to much shame because his uncle had bought the cheapest places that could be bought, thinking it good enough for two lads, and so this youth found he must go into a carriage where very common people sat, who reeked of garlic, and their cotton clothes were unwashed and smelled of poverty, and here was he in his good blue silk gown and he must sit among them. But he did not dare to complain for he was afraid of his uncle's secret scorn, so he could only take his place and put his box between him and the common farmer fellow that sat next, and he looked piteously at his servant who must leave him now, but still he did not dare to say anything.

But Wang the Second and his son looked little better than any because Wang the Second had put on himself a cotton robe that morning when he rose, for it seemed to him he had better not look too fine before his third brother, lest he seem richer than he would seem. As for his son, he did not own a silk robe yet and his stout cotton clothes were stitched by his mother and cut full and loose and long for him to grow to fit. And Wang the Second looked at his nephew and said in his wry way,

"It is ill to travel all day in such fine clothes as you wear. You had better take off that silk robe of yours and fold it and put it into your box, and sit in your under garments and so spare your best."

The boy muttered then, "But I have better than this, and it is what I wear every day at home." Nevertheless, he did not dare to disobey and so he rose and did what his uncle said.

Thus they went all that day by land, and Wang the Second stared at the fields and the towns through which they passed, appraising all he saw, and his son cried out at every new thing, and he longed to taste the fresh cakes of every vendor when they stopped, only his father would not have it. But the other lad sat pale and timorous, and he was sick because the carriage went so fast, and he leaned his head upon his pigskin box and said nothing all day, and he shook his head even at food.

Then they went by sea also two days in a small and crowded ship, and thus at last they came to the town where they must find the one they sought, and when they came out of the ship and were upon land again, Wang the Second hired rikshas, and put the two lads into one and he took one himself. The puller of the lads complained bitterly of his double burden, but Wang the Second explained to him they were but young lads and not men yet, and one of them pale and thin and less than usual because of his seasickness, and at last by haggling and paying a little more, but not so much as another vehicle cost, the puller was somewhat willing. And the rikshas came to the name of the house and street which Wang the Second gave them, and when they stopped, he drew the letter out of his bosom and he compared the letters written over the gate with those in the letter and they were the same.

He came out of his riksha then and he bade the two lads come out of theirs, and after he had haggled awhile with the pullers, because the place was not so far as they had said, and he paid them a little less than the price agreed upon at first, he took the box at one end and the two lads took it at the other end, and they started to walk through the great gate, on either side of which stood two stone lions.

But there was a soldier standing there beside one of the lions and he cried out,

78

"What, do you think you can come through this gate as you please?" And he took the gun off his shoulder and pounded its butt upon the stones and he was so fierce and rude in his looks that the three stood dazed, and the son of Wang the Eldest began to tremble, and even the pocked lad looked grave for a moment, because he had never stood so near a gun before.

Then Wang the Second hastened to draw his brother's letter out of his bosom and he gave it to the soldier to see and he said,

"We are the three mentioned here and this is our proof."

But the soldier could not read and so he shouted for another soldier and he came and after he had stared awhile at them and heard their whole tale he took the letter. Yet he could not read either, and after he had looked at it he took it inside somewhere. After a long time he came back and he pointed inside with his thumb and he said,

"It is true enough—they are relatives of the captain and they are to go in."

So they picked up the box again and they went in and past the stone lions, although the man with the gun looked after them as though he were unwilling and very doubtful still. Nevertheless they followed the other soldier and he led them through ten courts or so, every court filled with soldiers who idled there, some eating and some drinking, and some sitting naked in the sun to pick the vermin out of their clothes, and some lying asleep and snoring, and thus they went on to an inner house and there in its central room sat Wang the Tiger. He sat there at the table waiting for them and he wore good dark clothes of some rough foreign stuff and they were fastened with buttons of brass upon which were stamped a sign.

When he saw these relatives of his come in he rose quickly

and shouted to the soldiers who served him to bring wine and meats and he bowed to his brother, and Wang the Second bowed also, and bade the two lads bow, and they all seated themselves according to rank, Wang the Second in the highest seat and then Wang the Tiger, and the two lads in side seats below them. Then a serving man brought the wine and poured it out, and when this was done Wang the Tiger looked at the lads and he said in his sudden, harsh way,

"That ruddy one looks stout enough but I am not sure what wisdom he has behind that pocked face. He looks a clown. I hope he is not a clown, Elder Brother, because I do not like too much laughter. He is yours?—I see a smack of his mother in him. As for the other one—is that the best my eldest brother can do?"

When he said this the pale lad hung his head deeper than ever and it could be seen that a light chill sweat stood out on his upper lip and he took his hand and wiped it furtively away, looking doggedly down all the time he did this. But Wang the Tiger continued to stare at them steadily with his hard black stare, until even the pocked lad who was always so ready did not know where to look, so that he turned his eyes this way and that and moved his feet and gnawed his fingernail. Then Wang the Second said in apology,

"It is true they are but two poor things, my brother, and we are grieved that we had none more meet for your kindness. But my elder brother's eldest son is chiefest heir, and the one after this one is a hunchback, and this pocked one is my eldest and my next but a child, and so these two are the best we have for the time."

Then Wang the Tiger, having seen what they were, told a soldier to lead the lads into a side room and let them eat their meat there, and they were not to come again unless he called for them. The soldier led them away then, but the son of

Wang the Eldest cast piteous looks back at his uncle and Wang the Tiger seeing him waver like this called,

"Why do you linger?"

Then the lad stopped and said in his feeble way, "But am I not to have my box?"

Wang the Tiger looked then and saw the fine pigskin box beside the door and he said with some measure of contempt,

"Take it, but it will be no use to you for you shall strip off those robes and get into the good stout clothes that soldiers wear. Men cannot fight in silk robes!"

The lad turned clay-colored at this and went without a word and the two brothers were left alone.

For a long time Wang the Tiger sat in silence, for he was never one to make talk for courtesy's sake, and at last Wang the Second asked him,

"What is it of which you think so deeply? Is it something about our sons?"

Then Wang the Tiger said slowly, "No, except I thought how that most men so old as I am have sons of their own growing up and it must be a very comforting sight to a man."

"Why, so might you have them if you had wed soon enough," said Wang the Second, smiling a little. "But we did not know where you were for so long and my father did not know either and he could not wed you as he would have. But my brother and I will do it willingly, and the money for it is there when you need it for such a thing."

But Wang the Tiger put the thought from him resolutely and he said,

"No, it will seem strange to you, but I do not stomach a woman. It is a strange thing but I have never seen a woman—" and he broke off there for the serving man came in with meats, and the brothers said no more.

When they had eaten and the dishes were taken away again

and tea was brought Wang the Second made ready to ask what thing it was that Wang the Tiger wished to do with all his silver and with these lads, but he did not know how to begin to ask it, and before he had decided on a skilful way, Wang the Tiger said suddenly,

"We are brothers. You and I understand each other. I depend on you!"

And Wang the Second drank some tea and then he said cautiously and mildly,

"Depend upon me you may, since we are brothers, but I should like to know what your plan is so that I can know what I am to do for you."

Then Wang the Tiger leaned forward and he said in a great whisper and his words rushed out fast and his breath was like a hot wind blowing into Wang the Second's ear,

"I have loyal men about me, a good hundred and more, and they are all weary of this old general! I am weary, too, and I long for my own country and I never want to see one of these little yellow southern men again. Yes, I have loyal men! At my sign they will march out with me in the dead of a certain night. We will make for the north where the mountains are, and we will march to the far north before we entrench ourselves to make a war of revolution if this old general comes after us. But he may not stir—he is so old and so sunken in his eating and drinking and his women, except that among my hundred are his best and strongest men, men not of the south but out of fiercer, braver tribes!"

Now Wang the Second had always been a small and peaceful man, a merchant, and while he knew there was always a war somewhere he had had nothing to do with wars except once when in a revolution soldiers had been quartered in his father's house, and he knew nothing of how war is begun or waged except that if it is waged too near the prices of grain are high and if it is distant then prices fall again. He had never been so near a war as this, even in his own family was this war! His narrow mouth gaped and his small eyes widened and he whispered back, "But what can I do to help in this, who am so peaceful a man as I am?"

"This!" said Wang the Tiger and his whisper was the grating of iron upon iron. "I must have much silver, all my own, and I must borrow of you and at the least interest you will give me until I can establish myself!"

"But what security?" said Wang the Second, breathless.

"This!" said Wang the Tiger again. "You are to lend me what I need and what the land will bring until I can gather a mighty army and I will establish myself somewhere north of our own region and I will make myself lord of that whole territory! Then when I am lord I will enlarge myself and my lands, and I shall grow greater and more great with every war I wage until—" He paused and seemed to look off into some distant age, into some distant country, as though he saw it plain before him, and Wang the Second waited and then could not wait.

"Until what?" he said.

Wang the Tiger rose suddenly to his feet. "Until there is none greater than I in this whole nation!" he said, and now his whisper was like a shout.

"What will you be then?" asked Wang the Second astounded.

"I shall be what I will!" cried Wang the Tiger, and his black brows flew up over his eyes suddenly and sharply and he smote the table with the flat of his hand so that Wang the Second leaped at the crack, and the two men stared at each other.

Now all this was the strangest thing of which Wang the Second had ever heard. He was not a man who could dream great dreams and his greatest dream was to sit down at night with his books of accounts and look over what he had sold that year and plan in what safe sure ways he could enlarge himself the next year in his markets. Now, therefore, he sat and stared at this brother of his and he saw him tall and black and strange and his eyes shining like a tiger's eyes, and those straight black brows like banners above his eyes. Thus staring Wang the Second was lifted out of himself so that he was afraid of his brother and he did not dare to say anything to thwart him for there was a look in the man's eyes that was half crazed and it was so mighty a look that even Wang the Second could feel in his pinched heart the power of this man, his brother. Still he was cautious, though, and still he could not forget his habit of caution, and so he coughed dryly and said in his little dry voice,

"But what is there in all this for me and for us all and what security if I lend my silver to you?"

And Wang the Tiger answered with majesty, and he brought his eyes back to rest upon his brother,

"Do you think I will forget my own when I have raised myself up and are not you my brothers and your sons my brothers' sons? Did you ever hear of a mighty lord of war who did not raise up all his house as he rose? Is it nothing to you to be the brother of—*a king?*"

And he gazed down into his brother's eyes, and Wang the Second suddenly half believed this brother of his, although unwillingly too, for all this was the strangest tale he had ever heard, and he said in his sensible way,

"At least I will give you what is your own and I will lend you what I can spare, if it be that indeed you can rise like this, for doubtless there are many who do not rise so high as they think they can. At least you shall have your own."

Then some fire went suddenly out of Wang the Tiger's

eyes and he sat down and he pressed his lips together straight and hard and he said,

"You are cautious, I see!"

His voice was so hard and cold that Wang the Second was a little afraid and he said to excuse himself,

"But I have a family and many little children and the mother of my sons is not old yet and she is exceedingly fertile, and I have all these to plan and care for. You are unwed yet and you do not know what it is to have so many depending on you for everything, and food and clothing costing more every year!"

Wang the Tiger shrugged himself and he turned away, and he said as if carelessly,

"I do not, indeed, but hear me! Every month I will send my trusty man to you and you will know him by his harelip. You are to give him as much money as he is able to carry. Sell my lands as quickly and as well as you are able, for I shall need a thousand pieces of silver a month."

"A thousand!" cried Wang the Second, and his voice was cracked and his eyes idiotic in his surprise. "But how can you spend it?"

"There are a hundred men to be fed and clothes and arms to be bought. I must buy guns before I can increase my army if I cannot capture them quickly enough," said Wang the Tiger speaking very fast. Then suddenly he was angry. "You are not to ask me this and that!" he roared, smiting the table again. "I know what I must do and I must have silver until I can establish myself and be lord over a territory! Then I can tax the people, as I will. But now I must have silver. Stand by me and you shall have a certain reward. Fail me—and I can forget you are my blood!"

When he said these last words he thrust his face very near to his brother's and Wang the Second, looking into those fierce eyes hooded beneath the heavy black brows, drew back hastily and coughed and said, "Well, and of course I will do it. I am your brother. But when will you begin?"

"When can you sell my parcel of land?" asked Wang the Tiger.

"The wheat harvest will come before many months," said Wang the Second slowly, musing as he spoke and hesitating, for he was dazed with all he had heard.

"Then men will have money," returned Wang the Tiger, "and you can sell something before rice is put in, doubtless."

Now this was true enough and Wang the Second did not dare to oppose this strange brother of his at all for he was afraid of him, and he knew he must manage the thing somehow. So he rose and said,

"If there is such haste as this I must return at once and see what I can do, for harvests are quickly spent and then men think themselves poor again and hard-worked with what land they have to plant and more land will seem too much for them."

So he would not stay at all for he wanted to be away out of this place where there were such fierce men and guns and weapons of war everywhere. He stayed only to go into the next room where the lads had been sent and they were sitting on a bench before a small unpainted table upon which food was placed. It was the broken meats of what Wang the Tiger had put before his brother, but it was good enough for these lads, and Wang the Second's son stuffed it into his mouth very willingly, his bowl to his lips. But the other lad was dainty and accustomed to better than what was left over after others had eaten, and he sat and picked a little rice up with his chopsticks and did not touch the meats. Then Wang the Second felt some strange unwillingness to leave these lads and especially his own, and he had a doubt for a moment as to whether it was not a hazard he should not have taken for his son. But the thing was begun now and he could not undo what was begun, so he merely said,

"I return, and my only command on you both is that you are to obey your uncle in every single point, for you are his now, and he is a fierce and impatient man and he will not bear anything from you. But if you are obedient and will do all he says, you may rise to what you do not know. There is some destiny written for your uncle."

Then he turned quickly and went away, for he could not help it that his heart was a little heavy to leave his son, more than he could have thought it would be, and to ease it he muttered to himself,

"Well, such a chance does not come to every lad, and if it is chance it is a fair one. He will not be a common soldier after all, but an official of some sort if the thing succeeds."

And he determined he would do well and do all he could to make it succeed; at least for his son's sake he would do all he could.

But the pale lad who was Wang the Eldest's son began to weep when he saw his uncle go and he wept aloud, and Wang the Second hurried away. Yet the sound of that weeping pursued him, and he made haste to reach the gate where the lions were, so that he could hear it no more.

VIII

Now began this strange enterprise which, if Wang Lung's soul had not been in some far country, could have made his body rise out of that land of his where he slept, because in his lifetime he had hated above anything else war and soldiers, and here was his good land being sold for such a cause. But he slept there and he slept on and there was no one to stay these sons of his in what they did; no, there was no one except Pear Blossom and she did not for a long time know what they did. These two elder sons feared her for her faithfulness to their father and so they hid their plans from her.

For when Wang the Second had come back to his house he told Wang the Eldest to come to the tea house where they could talk in peace and there over their bowls of tea they talked. But this time Wang the Second chose a secret hidden corner where two walls came together without any window or door in either wall, and they sat so they could see who came near and they bent their heads over the table and talked in whispers and hints and broken words. Thus Wang the Second told his brother what Wang the Tiger planned, and whereas now he was come back to his own house again and into the common ways of his usual life the plan of the soldier had seemed more and more a dream and an impossible dream, the eldest brother seized on it as he listened as a thing wonderful but easy to do, too. The truth was that this huge and child-like man grew excited as the plan unfolded before him, for he saw himself raised above his highest fancy—brother to a king! He was a man of little learning and less wisdom and besides one who loved to see plays and he had seen many old plays which tell of the deeds of ancient and fabled heroes, who were at first but common men and then by the skill of their arms and by their wit and guile, they rose high enough to found dynasties. Now he saw himself the brother of such an one, and more than that, the elder brother of such an one, and his eyes glistened and he whispered hoarsely,

"I always said our brother was like no other lad! It was I who besought our father to take him out of the fields and hire a tutor for him and teach him what he ought to know as a landlord's son. Doubtless my brother will not forget what his eldest brother did for him, and how if it had not been for me he would have been but a hind on my father's land!"

And he looked down pleased with himself, and he smoothed over his great belly the rich purple satin robe he wore, and he thought of his second son and how the family would all rise, and he himself would be perhaps a nobleman; doubtless he would be made a nobleman when his brother was a king. There were stories of such things in the books he had read and he had seen these things in the playhouse. Then Wang the Second, who had been more and more dubious as he came back to himself, and indeed the fierce enterprise seemed very far from this quiet town, when he saw the mind of his elder brother flying into the future he grew jealous and his very caution made him greedy and he thought to himself,

"I must be careful lest haply there is a little in what my younger brother dreams, and lest perhaps he does even succeed in a tenth part of what he dreams. I must be ready to share his success with him and I must not draw back too far," and he said aloud, "Well, but I have to furnish him the silver and without me he could do nothing. He must have what he needs until he can establish himself, and how I am to get so much I do not know. After all, I am but a little rich man, and scarcely counted rich by those who are lords of wealth. The first few months I can get it by selling his land, and then we can sell some land, you and I. But what shall we do if he is not established by that time?"

"I will help him—I will help him—" said the elder brother hastily and he could not at this moment bear to think that anyone should do more for this younger brother than he did.

The two men rose then in the haste of their common greed and Wang the Second said,

"Let us go out to the lands once more and this time we will sell!"

Now this time, also, when the two brothers went out to the land they remembered Pear Blossom and they did not go near that earthen house. No, they bestrode two donkeys that stood among many at the city gate to be hired by their masters and thus they went out along the narrow paths between the fields, and the donkey keepers, who were young lads, ran after them and beat the donkeys upon the thighs and shrieked at them to urge them on, and they went to the north and away from that house and that bit of land. The beast that Wang the Second rode went willingly enough, but the other swayed upon its delicate feet beneath the mighty weight of Wang the Eldest, for this man grew fatter every month, and it was plain that in another ten years or so he would be a marvel in the town and the countryside, seeing that now, when he was but turned his forty-fifth year, he was so round and full about his middle and his cheeks hanging and thick as haunches. So they must wait a little for the burdened beast, but still they went well enough, and in that one day they visited all the tenants which were on the lands that had been marked before for sale. And Wang the Second inquired of every man if he would buy the land he worked and if he would then when, and how soon he could pay for it.

Now it so happened that it had been decided, since Wang the Tiger wished for silver, that they would give him the largest single piece of land and it was the farthest from the town and tilled now under one farmer, a prosperous good man, who had begun humbly enough as a laborer upon Wang Lung's own land and he had married a slave out of the town house, a strong, honest, noisy woman, who worked hard while she bore her children and she drove her husband to work harder too than he would have, left alone. They had prospered, and each year they rented more of Wang Lung's land until they had a number of acres under them and they had to hire men to help with the labor of it. But still they themselves worked, for they were a saving, thrifty pair.

To this man the two brothers came this day and Wang the Eldest asked him saying,

"We have more land than we wish and we need silver to venture in other affairs, and if you want to buy these pieces you till, well enough and we will sell them to you."

Then the farmer's round, ox-like eyes opened and he let his mouth go agape under the shelf of his teeth and he said, his voice hissing and spitting against his teeth when he spoke, for so his way was and he could not help it,

"I did not dream your house was ready to sell its land already, seeing how fastened to the land the old man your father was!"

Then Wang the Eldest drew down his thick mouth and he looked very grave and he said,

"For all his love of it he has left us a very heavy burden to bear. We have his two concubines to care for, and neither of them is our mother, and the elder one loves her good wines and her fine foods and she must have her gaming every day, and she is not clever enough to win at it every day either. Money from the lands comes in slowly and it is dependent upon the whims of Heaven. And such a house as we have must spend money generously, for it would be unseemly of us and unworthy of us as our father's sons if we let our family look poor and mean and poorer than when he was alive. So we must take some of the land for our livelihood."

But Wang the Second had fidgeted and coughed and frowned while his brother made this ponderous speech and it seemed to him his brother was little better than a fool, for if it is seen that one is eager to sell his goods, the price goes down. He made haste to say now in his turn,

"But there are many who inquire after our land to buy it because it is well known in these parts that the lands our father bought are good and the best in this countryside. If you do not want the land you hire, then let us know quickly, for there are others who wait for it."

Now this shelf-toothed farmer loved the land he tilled, and he knew it every foot and how each bit lay, how that field sloped, and how this one must be ditched if he was to secure the harvest. Much good manure had he put into the land, too, not only the excrements of his own beasts and of his household, but he had labored and gone into the town and carried out for this long distance buckets of the town's waste. He had risen often and early in the morning to do this. Now he thought of all those stinking loads he had carried and of all his labor gone into these fields, and it seemed to him an ill thing indeed if now it were all to pass to another man. So he said hesitating,

"Well, I had not thought of owning the land myself yet. I thought in my son's time perhaps it might be ready to sell. But if it is to be sold now I will think what I can do and I will tell you tomorrow when I have thought of it. But what is your price?"

The two brothers looked at each other then and Wang the Second said quickly before the elder brother could speak, for he feared that one would say too little,

"The price is just and fair; fifty pieces of silver for a field the size of the sixth of an acre."

Now this was a high price and too much for land so far from town as this and it was more than could be paid for it, and they all knew this, but still it was a start to the bargain. Then the farmer said,

"Such a price I cannot pay, poor as I am, but I will tell you tomorrow when I have thought."

Then Wang the Eldest grew too anxious for the money and he said,

"A little more or less will not spoil the bargain!"

But Wang the Second cast him an angry look and he plucked his brother by the sleeve lest he say more foolishness yet and he led him to go away again. But the farmer called after them,

"I will come tomorrow when I have thought!"

This he said, although what he meant was that he must talk with his wife, but it would seem very small in a man if he said he held what his wife thought to be of any account, and so he put it thus to save his own pride.

When the next day came after he had talked with his wife in the night he went to the town where the two brothers lived, and there he bickered and bargained with them and he bargained as once Wang Lung had in that very house for the land that house owned, a house now scattered and dispersed of which only these bricks and stones were left. But a price was agreed upon at last, a third less than Wang the Second had said, and this was fair enough and the farmer was willing because it was a price his wife had mentioned he might take if so be he could get the land for no less. When the land was thus sold, the farmer said,

"How will you have the purchase money, in silver or in grain?"

And Wang the Second said quickly, "Half in silver and the rest in grain."

This he said thinking if he took the grain he could sell it a time or two and turn a little extra silver on it and it would not be robbing his brother either, since it was no one's affair save his own if the grain were turned a time or two and the profit was due him for all this labor. But the farmer said,

"I cannot muster so much silver. I will give you a third in silver and a third in grain now and the last third I promise from next year's harvest."

Then Wang the Elder rolled his eyes in his lordly way and he stamped his foot and shifted his chair where he sat with them in the great hall and he said,

"But how can you tell what the skies will be next year and what rains will come and how will we know what we are to have?"

But the farmer stood there very humble before these rich townsmen, who were his landlords, and he sucked his teeth before he spoke and then he said patiently,

"We on the land are at the mercy of heaven always, and if you cannot share the risk you must take the land again as security."

So it was settled at last, and on the third day the farmer brought the silver, not all at once but in three times, each time with a roll of it wrapped in a blue cloth and hidden in his bosom. Each time he took the silver out slowly and his face drew together as though he were in some pain and he put the silver down on the table hardly, as though he did it with sorrow, and so he did, for into this silver had gone so many years of his life, so many pounds of his flesh, so much of the strength of his sinew. He had collected from every place where he had hid his little stores of gain and he had borrowed all he could, and he could not even have had this except by bitter, frugal living.

But the two brothers saw only the silver and when they had set their seal upon the receipt of it and the farmer had sighed and gone away, Wang the Eldest cried with contempt,

"Well, and the farming folk always cry out and make such

an ado because they live so hard and have so little. But any of us would be willing to gain silver like this man has been able to do, and it has not been hard for him, I dare say! If they can heap it up like this from the land, I swear I shall press harder upon my tenants after this!"

And he pushed back his long silken sleeves and smoothed his soft pale hands and he took up the silver and let it slip through his fat fingers that were dimpled at the knuckles as a woman's are. But Wang the Second took up the money and Wang the Eldest watched him unwillingly as he did it, and Wang the Second counted it swiftly and skilfully into tens once more, although it had been well counted already. Into tens he counted it all and wrapped it up neatly as clerks do in some sheets of paper he had. Wang the Eldest stared at it unwilling to see it go and at last he said longingly,

"Need we send it all to him?"

"We need send it," said Wang the Second coldly, seeing his brother's greed. "We must send it now or his venture fails. And I must take the grain and sell it and be ready for the day when his trusty man comes."

But he did not tell his brother he would turn the grain over a time or two, and Wang the Eldest did not know these tricks a merchant has, and so he could only sit and sigh to see the silver go away. When his brother was gone he sat on awhile, feeling melancholy, and poor as though he had been robbed.

Now Pear Blossom might never have heard of all this that went on, for Wang the Second was cunning beyond all and he never hinted of anything he did, no, not even when at the proper time he took to her the allowance of silver that was hers. Twenty-five pieces he took to her every month as Wang the Tiger had said he must, and the first time he did it she said in her soft voice,

95

"But where does this five come from, for I know only twenty was given to me, and I do not need even so much, only for this poor child of my lord's. But this five I have not heard of."

To this Wang the Second replied,

"Take it, for my younger brother said you were to have it and it comes from his share."

But when Pear Blossom heard this she counted out five pieces with all speed, her small hands trembling, and she pushed the money to one side as though she feared it might burn her, and she said,

"I will not have it—no, I will have nothing except my due!"

At first Wang the Second had thought he would press her, but then he remembered what a risk he ran when he loaned money for this venture of his brother's, and he remembered all the trouble he had for which he received no pay, and he remembered all the possibility there was that the venture might fail. When he thought of all this he scraped up the silver she had set aside and he put it carefully into the bosom of his robe and he said in his small, quiet voice,

"Well, it may be better so, since the other and the elder has as much, and it is true you should have a little less. I will tell my brother."

But seeing what her temper was he forebore to say the very house she lived in belonged to that third son, for it suited them all to have her live there with the fool. He went away, then, and he never said more to Pear Blossom than this, and except for such casual meetings for some purpose or other, Pear Blossom did not see the family in the great town house. Sometimes, it is true, she saw Wang the Eldest pass at the turn of the season, in the spring when he came out to measure the seed for his tenants as a landlord must, although he did but stand by very high and important while some agent he had hired measured it. Or he came out sometimes before the harvest to appraise what the fields had, so that he could know whether or not his tenants lied to him when they cried out as they always did of this and that and what a bad year it had been for them and how much or how little it had rained.

So he came and went a few times a year, and each time he was sweating and hot and ill-tempered with his labor, and he grunted his greeting to Pear Blossom if he saw her, and although she bowed decorously if she saw him, she did not speak if she could help it, because he grew such a great blowsy man and he had a way of leering his eyes secretly at women.

Nevertheless, seeing him come and go, she supposed that the land was as it had always been, and that Wang the Second saw to his lands and the third brother's, and no one thought to tell her anything. She was not indeed one with whom it was easy to gossip, because she was still and distant in her manner to all except children, so that, although she was gentle, yet there was that about her that made people fear her, too. She had no friends at all except that of late she had acquainted herself with some nuns who lived in a nunnery not far away, a quiet house built of grey bricks, and set behind a green willow hedge. These nuns she received gladly when they came to teach her their patient doctrines, and she listened to them and brooded upon them after the nuns were gone, for she longed to learn enough to pray for Wang Lung's soul.

So might she never have known about the selling of the land except that in that very year when the farmer had bought the first parcel of land the little hunchbacked son of Wang the Eldest followed his father at a distance, so that the man did not know it, when he came out to the harvest fields.

Now this lad was the strangest little lad and he was not like any of the children in the courts of the great house. His mother had disliked him from the hour he was born for some reason that none knew, perhaps because he was less ruddy and good to see than her other children or perhaps because she was weary then of child-bearing and weary of him before he was born. But because of her dislike she had given him at once to a slave to suckle and this slave did not love him either because they had taken her child away from her for his sake, and she said he had an eye too wise for his age, that looked evil in his baby face. She said he was full of malice, too, and that he bit her wilfully when he suckled, and once she screeched as she held him to her breast and she dropped him upon the tiles of the court where she sat under a shade tree with him, and when they came to see what was amiss she said he had bit her until she bled, and she held her breast out for them to see, and it was true it did bleed.

From that time on this lad grew hunched, and it was as though all his strength of growing went into this great knot he carried on his shoulders, and everyone named him Hunchback and by that name did even his parents call him. Seeing what a poor thing he was and that there were other sons there was no trouble taken over him and he did not have to learn his letters or do anything at all, and he learned early to stay out of men's sight, and especially out of the sight of other children, who mocked him cruelly for the burden he bore. He prowled about the streets or he walked far out in the countryside alone, limping as he walked, and carrying that great load of his upon his back.

On this harvest day he had followed his father unseen and he kept out of his father's sight, for well he knew his father's ill temper on such days as he must go to his land, and he followed him out as far as the earthen house. But Wang the Eldest passed on to his fields, and the hunchback stayed to see who it was that sat at the door of the house.

Now it was only Wang Lung's poor fool, and she sat there

in the sun as she always did, but she was a woman grown in body now and more than that for she was nearly forty years old and there were white streaks in her hair. But she was still the same poor child and she sat there grimacing and folding her bit of cloth, and the hunchback wondered at her, for he had never seen her before, and in his malicious way he began to mock her and make grimaces, too, and he snapped his fingers so loudly under her nose that the poor thing shrieked in fear.

Then Pear Blossom came running out to see what went wrong and when the lad saw her he ran limping and hobbling into the pointed shadows of the bamboo grove, and from there he peered out like a little savage beast. But Pear Blossom saw who it was and she smiled her gentle sad smile and she drew out of her bosom a small sweet cake, for she carried such cakes with her to coax the fool sometimes when she grew stubborn suddenly from some strange caprice and was unwilling to obey. This cake she held out to the hunchback, and he stared at her first and at last he crept out and seized the cake and stuffed it all into his mouth at once. Then enticing the child she got him to come and sit beside her upon a bench at the door and when she saw how this poor lad sat himself down all askew and how small and weary his face looked under the great burden on his back, and his eyes so deep and sorrowful she did not know whether he was man or child except he was so small, she reached out her arm and she laid it about his crooked body, and she said in her pitying soft way,

"Tell me, little brother, if you are the son of my lord's son or not, for I have heard he had one like you."

Then the child shook her arm off sullenly and nodded and made as if he would go away again. But she coaxed him and gave him another cake and she smiled at him and said,

"I do believe you have a look about your mouth like my dead lord's, and he lies now under that date tree there. I miss him so sorely that I wish you would come here often because you have some look of his."

This was the very first time that anyone had ever said such a thing to the hunchback before, to wish him there, for he was used, even though he was a rich man's son, to have his brothers push him aside and to have the very servants careless of him and serve him last because they knew his mother did not care for him. Now he stared at her piteously and his lips began to quiver and suddenly he wept, although he did not know why he did, and he cried out in his weeping,

"I wish you would not make me weep so—I do not know why I weep so—"

Then Pear Blossom soothed him with her arm about that knotty back of his and although he could not have said so, the lad felt it was the sweetest touch he had ever had upon him and he was soothed without knowing why or how he was. But Pear Blossom did not pity him too long. No, she looked at him as though his back were straight and strong as other lads' are, and after this day the hunchback came often to the earthen house, for no one cared where he went or what he did. Day after day he came, until his very soul was knit to Pear Blossom. She was skilful with him, too, and she made as though she leaned on him and needed his help to care for the fool, and since no one had ever looked to the lad for help of any sort before, he grew quiet and gentle and much of his evil spirit went out of him as the months went on.

If it had not been for this lad, then, Pear Blossom might never have known how the land was being sold away. Nor did the lad know he told her, for he talked to her of everything as it came into his mind and he prattled of this and that and he said, one day,

"I have a brother who will be a great soldier. Some day my uncle is to be a great general, and my brother is with him learning how to be a soldier. My uncle is to be a very king some day, and then my brother will be his chief captain, for I heard my mother telling it so."

Pear Blossom was sitting on the bench by the door when the lad said this, and she looked away over the fields and she said in her quiet voice,

"Is your uncle so great, then?" She paused awhile and then she said again, "But I wish he were not a soldier because it is so cruel a thing to be!"

But the lad cried, boasting a little, "Yes, he is to be the greatest general and I think a soldier, if he is a brave, good hero, is the most magical thing a man can be. And we are all to be great with him. Every month my father and my second uncle send my soldier uncle silver against the time he will be great and a hideous great harelipped man comes for the silver. But some day we are to have it all back again, for I heard my father tell my mother so."

Now when Pear Blossom heard this a small strange doubt came into her mind and she pondered a little and then she said gently as though it were a matter of no account and as though she asked from idle curiosity,

"And where does so much silver come from, I wonder? Does your second uncle loan it from his shop?"

And the lad answered innocently and proud of his knowledge,

"No, they sell the land that was my grandfather's, and I see the farmers come in every day or so and they take a roll out of their bosoms and unwrap it and there the silver is, shining like stars when it falls upon the table in my father's room. I have seen it more times than a few and they do not mind if I am standing by because I am of such little worth."

Then Pear Blossom rose so quickly that the little lad looked at her wondering, for she moved usually very softly, and she checked herself then and said to him in the gentlest way,

"I have only just thought of something I must do. Will you look after my poor fool for me while I am gone? There is no one whom I trust as I do you."

This the lad was proud to do for her now and he forgot what he had said and he sat there proudly holding a bit of the fool's coat in his hand while Pear Blossom made ready to go. So he sat and Pear Blossom saw him thus when she had drawn a dark coat about her and had set forth in all haste across the fields. There was that in these two poor creatures, that even now stayed her a moment to look back at them, and it drew her heart out and curved her lips into a smile of sad tenderness. But she hastened on, for if she looked at these two with love, and she loved no one else now, there was such an anger in her heart as must out, and if it were a quiet anger, seeing her anger was always so and she could have no other kind, still it was a firm anger, too, and she could not rest until she went and found the brothers and found out what they truly did with the good lands they had from their father, even the land he had bid them keep for the generations to come in his family.

She hastened through the fields upon the narrow foot paths and she was alone and there was no one to be seen in these byways except here and there in the distance the figure of a man in his blue cotton work garments bending over his land. Seeing these her eyes filled with tears as they often did now and too easily in these days, for she remembered how Wang Lung used to go about on these very paths and how he loved the earth so that he would stop sometimes and pick up a handful of it and turn it over in his fingers, and how he would never lease it longer than a year because he would keep it his own—and here were these sons of his selling it away from him!

For although Wang Lung was dead, he lived on for Pear Blossom and, to her, his soul was always hovering about these fields and she felt he surely knew it if they were sold. Yes, whenever a small chill breeze smote her suddenly on the face by day or by night, or a little whirling wind wheeled along the roadway, such winds as others fear because these winds are so strange it is said they must be souls flying past, Pear Blossom lifted her face and smiled when such a wind smote her, and this because she believed it might be the soul of the old man who had been like a father to her and dearer than the father who sold her to him.

So with this feeling of his presence, she hastened through the land and it lay fair and fruitful before her, for there had been no famine these five years, and there would be none this year either, and the fields lay tended and fruitful and waving with the tall wheat which was still too green for harvest. She passed by such a field now and a little wind rose out of the grain and rippled it so that it bent silvery and smooth as though a hand had brushed over it and she smiled and wondered what wind it was and lingered an instant in her purpose until the wind sank into the grain again and left it still.

When she came to the town and to the gate where the vendors spread their stores of fruits she bent her head and kept her eyes steadfastly upon the ground and she did not once look up to meet the eyes of anyone. No one paid heed to her, either, for she was so small and slight and not young as she had once been, and clad as she was in her dark robe and her face without powder or red paint, she was not one for men to see above any other woman. Thus she went. If any had looked at her tranquil pale face he would not have dreamed that a good deep anger burned in her and that she was going bent on bitter reproof, and brave for the hour.

When she reached the great gate of the town house she passed through it without calling out she was come. The old gateman sat there on the threshold nodding, his jaw ajar and showing the only three teeth he had scattered here and there in his mouth, and he gave a start as she passed, but he knew her and he nodded again. She went as she had planned straight to the house of Wang the Eldest, for although she disliked him heartily, she had more hope of moving him than the greedy heart of Wang the Second. She knew, too, that Wang the Eldest was seldom purposely unkind and she knew that if he were foolish, yet he had a kind, loose heart sometimes, too, and he could be kind if it did not trouble him too much at the moment. But she feared the cold narrow eyes of the second son.

She entered the first courts and a slave was there idling, a pretty girl who had slipped out to catch the eye of a young serving man who waited in the court for something, and Pear Blossom said to the slave in her courteous way,

"Child, tell your mistress I am come for something if she will see me."

Now the lady of Wang the Eldest had been somewhat friendly to Pear Blossom after Wang Lung died, and far more friendly than she had ever been to Lotus, because Lotus was so coarse and so free with what she said, and Pear Blossom never spoke in such ways. Of latter times when they had met at some common family day of ceremony the lady used even to say to Pear Blossom,

"You and I, after all, are nearer to each other than to these others, for the eyes of our hearts are finer and more delicate."

And of late she had said, "Come and talk with me sometimes about the things the nuns and priests say of the gods. You and I are the only devout ones in this house."

This she said when she had heard that Pear Blossom listened to the nuns from that nunnery not far from the earthen house. So Pear Blossom asked for her now, and the pretty slave came out soon, her eyes creeping here and there to see if the young serving man were still there or not, and she said,

"My lady says you are to come and sit down in the great hall and she will come as soon as she finishes the round of prayers she is making on her rosary that she has vowed to make every morning."

So Pear Blossom went in and sat down in a side seat in the great hall.

Now it happened that on this day Wang the Eldest had risen very late for he had been to a feast the night before in a certain fine inn in the town. It had been a noble feast with the best of wines and behind every guest's chair a pretty singing girl was hired to pour out his wine for him and to sing and to prattle and to do anything else the guest to whom she was appointed might like her to do. Wang the Eldest had eaten mightily and had drunk more than he usually did, and his singing girl had been the prettiest little lisping maid, not more than seventeen years old, but still so wise in her coquetry that she might have been a woman used to men for ten years and more. But Wang the Eldest had drunk so well that even this morning he did not remember all that had happened the night before, and he came into the hall smiling and yawning and stretching himself, not seeing that anyone was there before him. Indeed the truth was his eyes were slow to see anything this morning, because he was smiling and thinking inwardly of the little maid and how she had slipped her small cool fingers into his coat against his neck to tease him when he played with her. And, thinking of this he said to himself that he would ask his friend who had been host where this maid lived and to what public house she belonged and he would seek her out and see what she was.

Thus yawning loudly he stretched his arms above his head and then he slapped his thighs to waken himself and he came sauntering into the great hall clad only in his silken undergarments and his feet were bare and thrust into silken slippers. Then his eye fell suddenly on Pear Blossom. Yes, she stood there straight and quiet as a shadow in her grey robe, but trembling because she loathed this man so much. He was so astonished to see her there that he let his arms drop suddenly and he broke off his yawn unfinished and stared to see her. Then seeing it was really she he coughed in embarrassment and said courteously enough,

"I was not told anyone was here. Does my lady know you are here?"

"Yes, I sent one to tell her," said Pear Blossom, and as she spoke she bowed. Then she hesitated and she thought to herself, "It is better if I do speak now and speak out what I have to say to him alone." And she began to speak quickly and more quickly than her wont was, the words hurrying and pressing upon each other, "But I have come to see the Eldest Lord. I am so distressed—I cannot believe it. My own lord said, 'The land is not to be sold.' And you are selling it—I know you are selling it!"

And Pear Blossom felt a rare slow red come up into her cheeks and she was suddenly so angry she could scarcely keep from weeping. She bit her lips and lifted her eyes and looked at Wang the Eldest, although she loathed him so she could scarcely bear to do it, and even while she did it for Wang Lung's sake, she could not but see how fat and yellow and loathly this man's neck was where he had left his coat unbuttoned, and how the flesh hung pouched under his eyes, and how his lips puffed out full and thick and pale. Then when

106

he saw her eyes steadfastly upon him he was confused for he feared very much the anger of women and he turned away and made as though he must button up his coat for decency's sake. He said hastily over his shoulder,

"But you have heard an idle tale—but you have had a dream!"

Then Pear Blossom said more violently than anyone had ever heard her say anything,

"No, I do not dream—I had it from the lips of one who spoke the truth!" She would not tell where she had heard it lest the man beat his poor hunched son, so she held back the name of the lad but she went on, "I do marvel at my lord's sons that you disobey him like this. Although I am weak and worthless I must speak and I will tell you this, my lord will avenge himself! He is not so far away as you think, and his soul hovers over his land still, and when he sees it gone he will have ways to avenge himself upon sons who do not obey their father!"

Now she said this in such a strange way and her eyes grew so large and earnest and her soft voice so chill and low that a vague fear fell upon Wang the Eldest, and indeed he was a man easily afraid in spite of his great body. No one could have persuaded him to go alone among grave lands at night and he believed secretly the many tales told about spirits; although he laughed falsely and loudly, still secretly he did believe. So when Pear Blossom spoke thus he said hastily,

"There has been only a little sold—only a little of what belonged to my younger brother, and he needs the silver and a soldier cannot want land. I promise you no more shall be sold."

At this Pear Blossom opened her mouth to speak but before her voice could come the lady of Wang the Eldest entered and she was plaintive this morning and vexed with her lord because she had heard him come in drunken and talking of some maid or other he had seen. She saw him now and cast him a scornful look so that he made haste to smile and nod negligently as though naught were amiss, yet watching secretly too, and he was secretly glad Pear Blossom was here, for his lady was too proud to speak her full mind if he were not alone. He grew voluble and made a great fuss to feel the teapot on the table to see if it were hot and he said,

"Ah, here is the mother of my sons, and is this tea hot enough for you? I have not eaten yet and was but now on my way to the tea house for a sup of tea there, and I will go my way and not disturb you—well I know ladies have that to say to each other which is not for us men to hear—" and laughing falsely and hollowly and uneasy beneath his wife's haughty silence and the stiff looks she threw at him, he bowed and made such haste away that his flesh shook on him.

The lady said nothing at all while he was there but she seated herself and held her back straight and away from the chair, for she would never lean at all, and she waited for him to be gone. Indeed she did look a very perfect lady, for she wore a smooth satin coat of a blue grey hue, and her hair was combed and coiled and smooth with oil although it was scarcely mid-day yet and at an hour when most ladies do not do more than turn upon their beds and reach out a hand for their first drink of tea.

When she had seen her lord gone, she heaved a sigh and she said solemnly,

"There is no one who knows what my life is with that man! I gave him my youth and my beauty, and I never complained however often I had to bear, even after I had three sons, even after he went and took to himself a common daughter of the people, a maid such as I might have hired for a servant. No,

I have borne with him in all he did, although I am wholly unused to such low ways as he has."

She sighed and Pear Blossom saw that for all her pretences she was truly sad, and she said to divert her,

"Well we all know how good a wife you are and I have heard the nuns say you do learn the good rites more quickly than any lay sister they have ever taught."

"Do they say so?" cried the lady greatly pleased, and she began to talk of what prayers she said and how many times a day and how some time she would take the vow against all meat eating, and how it behooved all of us who are mortal to think gravely of the future, since there are but heaven and hell for final resting places for all souls until the bitter round of life begins again, and the good have their reward and the evil theirs also.

So she prattled on and Pear Blossom did but half listen and with the other half of her heart she wondered heavily if she could believe what the man said when he promised to sell no more land, and it was hard for her to believe he could be true. And suddenly she was very weary and she took the moment when the lady was silent for an instant to sup tea, and she rose and said gently,

"Lady, I do not know what your lord tells you of his affairs, but if you can bring to his mind sometimes what his father's last command was, that the land was not to be sold, I pray you will do it. My own lord labored all his life to bring together these lands that his sons of a hundred generations might rest upon a sure foundation, and it is surely not well that already in this generation they should be sold. I beg your help, lady!"

Now this lady had indeed not heard how much of the land was sold, but she would pretend there was nothing she did not know and so she said with great certainty,

"You need not fear that I will let my lord do anything that is unseemly. If land is sold it is only the distant bit that belongs to the third brother, because he has schemes to be a general, and to raise us all up, and he needs silver more than land."

Now when Pear Blossom heard this same thing said over again she was somewhat reassured and she thought it must be true, if it were thus said again, and so she took her leave a little comforted. She bowed and said her farewells in her soft still way, giving every deference to the lady so that she left her complacent and pleased with herself. And Pear Blossom returned to the earthen house.

But Wang the Eldest saw his brother in the tea house to which he went and Wang the Second was there eating his noon meal, and he dropped himself down heavily beside the table where his brother sat alone and he said pettishly,

"It does seem as though men can never be free from the nagging of women, and as if I had not enough of it in my own house that last woman of our father's must come and tell me she hears a rumor of the land being sold and she clamors to get me to promise it is not to be sold!"

Then Wang the Second looked at his brother, and his smooth thin face curved into its slight smile and he said,

"What do you care what such an one says? Let her say! She is the least in my father's house and she has no authority of any kind. Pay no heed to her and if she mentions land to you, talk to her of anything except the land. Mention this and that to her but let her see you pay her no heed because she has no power to do anything. She should be glad she is fed every month and allowed to live on in that house."

The serving man came at this moment with the account, and Wang the Second looked at it sharply and cast it up in his mind and found it correct. He took the few coins out then that were needed, and he paid the money out slowly as though he did protest that the charge should not have been wrong somehow. Then he bowed a little to his brother and went away, and Wang the Eldest stayed on alone.

In spite of what his brother said he felt some melancholy sitting with him and he wondered with a touch of fear what Pear Blossom had meant when she said the old man was not far away even though he was dead. And as he thought he grew very uneasy so that at last he called to the serving man and he ordered a rare and dainty dish of crabs to divert himself and make him able to forget what did not please him.

IX

TWICE and thrice did Wang the Tiger send his trusty harelipped man to his brothers and twice and thrice did the man bring back silver to his captain. He carried it on his back and wrapped in blue cloth as if it were some poor possession of his own and he was clad in a coarse blue coat and trousers and he was barefoot except for rough straw sandals. No one on the road seeing this man plod along in the dust with his load in a bundle on his back would have dreamed that he carried rounds of silver there or that he was anything more than some common fellow, although if anyone had taken thought to look more closely than usual he would have seen that the man sweated strangely under so small a load as he had. But no one looked at him as closely as this, since he was so poorly clad and his face was common and coarse and like a hundred others to be seen in a day except for his split lip, and if anyone stared at him a moment it was only to wonder at this hideous lip of his and at the two teeth he had growing out of the roots of his nose.

Thus safely the trusty man brought the silver to his captain, and when Wang the Tiger had enough buried under his tent to last him three months until he could establish himself, he set the day for his going forth for himself. He gave his own secret signal and the word ran among the men who were ready to go with him and on a certain day after the cutting of the rice harvest and before the cold came down out of the north, on a certain night when there was no moon until dawn and then but a warped thing hung crookedly in the sky, these men crept out each from his bed where he slept and they left the banner of the old general under whom they served.

A hundred men in all so crept forth on that dark night, and every man rose in utter silence and rolled his quilt and tied it upon his back and took up his gun if he had one, and he took his neighbor's also if he could do it without waking the man, although this was not easy for by custom every man slept with his gun under his body in such a way that if any-one moved to take it from him he was awakened and could cry out. This was because a gun was so precious a thing and it could be sold for a heap of silver and sometimes men stole a gun to sell if they lost too heavily at gambling or if they were unpaid for many months when there was no war on, and no looting, and so no silver coming in. Yes, if a soldier lost his gun it was a grievous thing, for guns are brought from very distant and foreign parts of the world. On this night, therefore, the men who crept forth took what they could, but they did not get in all more than twenty guns or so beyond their own, because the soldiers all slept so warily. Still, twenty was good and they could enlarge their number by twenty men.

All these hundred soldiers were the stoutest men and the

best that had fought under the old general, his bravest and most daring, his most ruthless and experienced among the younger soldiers he had. They were very few from the south and nearly all were come from wild inner provinces where men are bold and lawless and not afraid of dealing death. Such men were the more easily caught by the proud looks and the tall straight body of Wang the Tiger, and they admired his silences and his sudden angers and his ferocity, and they admired him the more because there was nothing now to worship in the fat old general who grew so fat he could not even climb his horse any more unless two men hoisted and heaved his legs over the saddle. Yes, there was not anything to fire a young man in such as he and so they were ready to desert him and to follow a new hero.

Each man with his gun then and each with his horse if he had one rose in the dead of that night at the signal, and the signal was when any man felt three light strokes upon his right cheek he was to rise instantly and buckle on his belt with his ammunition and take up what he had for a gun, and mount his horse or come on foot if he had not one, to a certain spot in a shallow valley that lay in the top of a mountain five miles away. There was an old temple there, deserted except for an aged hermit, dazed in his head, who lived among the ruins, and poor shelter though this was, it would shelter them until Wang the Tiger could shape them into an army and lead them on to the place he would choose.

Now Wang the Tiger had already prepared everything there and days before he had sent out the trusty man and his pocked nephew and they had wines set in the temple in jars and some live pigs and fowls and even three fat oxen penned into an empty cell where some priest had lived once. These Wang the Tiger had bought from farmers round about, and he was an honorable man and paid for all he took, and he would not, as some soldiers do, take what the poor have and pay nothing for it. No, he had his trusty man pay close to the full value and so the beasts were driven up the mountain to that temple and the pocked lad stayed there to watch them.

The trusty man had bought three great iron cauldrons, too, and he carried them up the mountain one by one over his head, and he set them on little ovens he built out of the old bricks of the ruined temple. But more than this he did not buy, for Wang the Tiger had it in his mind to go quickly away from this place and as quickly as he could to the north to some fastness there where he would be safe from the old general. Not that he wanted to go near the northern capital, either, lest he have to contend too soon with the state soldiers who come out sometimes against such lords of war as Wang the Tiger had it in his mind to be. Still, he feared neither of these very much, for the old general's wrath was short-lived these days, and as for the state it was a time when one dynasty ended and no new dynasty had come up to take its place, and so the state was weak and robbers flourished and lords of war strove heartily together for highest place and there was nothing to restrain them.

To this temple, then, did Wang the Tiger come on that dark night and he took with him the pale son of Wang the Eldest, and it was a puzzle to him often to know what he would do with this timorous, down-cast youth. The pocked youth had rejoiced in the adventure and he had gone out merrily enough to do what he was told, but this other one hid himself out of sight and now when Wang the Tiger roared at him to follow him he crept shivering behind his uncle, and when Wang the Tiger flashed the light of his flaming torch on him he could see the lad was all of a sweat and Wang the Tiger shouted at him in scorn,

"How is it you sweat when you do nothing?"

But he did not stay to hear if there were any answer. He strode on through the night and the lad's faltering footsteps followed.

There at the pass at the top of the mountain which led to the ruined temple Wang the Tiger set himself down upon a rock and he sent the lad into the temple to help with the food. He stayed there alone and he waited to see who would come to his banner that night out of all who had promised. Then men came in pairs and singly and in eights and tens, and Wang the Tiger rejoiced to see each one, and he called out to each,

"Ha, you are come!" and he called out, "Ha, you noble good fellows!"

Whenever he heard footsteps of those who came to join him as they came up the ruined stone steps of the temple path he took the smouldering torch he held in his hand and he blew it into flame and let its light fall over the faces and he exulted to see this good man he knew and that among those who came. Thus the one hundred assembled themselves, and Wang the Tiger told them off, and when all had come that he knew would come he commanded that the oxen be killed and the fowls and the pigs too. Then the men set themselves heartily to such a task, for they had not eaten very good meat in many a day. Some lit the ovens and set them roaring and some fetched water from a mountain stream that ran near there, and others killed the beasts and skinned them and hewed them in pieces. But when they had plucked the fowls they stuck them upon spits of green wood that were forked branches the men hacked from the trees about the temple, and these fowls they roasted whole before the fires.

Then when all was ready they spread the feast upon the stone terrace in front of the temple, a ruined terrace where the weeds were forcing the old stones apart. In the center was a great old iron urn, higher than a man is tall, but even it was crumbling into red dust it was so old. By this time it was day and the newly risen sun streamed down upon the men and the cool sharp mountain air made them famished, and they all crowded laughing and eager about the smoking food. And everyone ate and was filled full, and there was joy everywhere because it seemed to all that a new and better day was beginning for them under this new leader, young and brave, and he would take them into new lands where there were food and women and all the plenty a lusty man needs.

When they had satisfied their first hunger and before they fell to again they broke the clay seals of the wine jars and into each man's bowl he carried they poured out wine, and they drank and laughed and shouted and they cried out to each other to drink to this and to that, and most of all to their new leader.

Out of the shadows of the bamboo thicket the poor dazed hermit watched them beside himself with wonder, and he muttered to himself, thinking they were devils. He stared to see them eat and drink so lustily and the water ran out of his mouth when he saw them tearing the smoking meats apart. But he did not dare to come out for he did not know what devils they were come suddenly like this into the quiet valley where none but himself had lived these thirty years alone, tending a bit of land to feed himself. And as he stared, one of the soldiers, being stuffed with food and drowsy with wine, threw away the thigh bone of an ox he chewed upon and it fell at the edge of the thicket. Then the hermit put forth his scrawny hand and seized it and drew it silently into the shadows and he put the bone to his own mouth and sucked and gnawed it, and he trembled strangely for he had not eaten meat all these years and he had forgotten the flavor of

116

it and how good it was. And he could not but suck and mumble at the bone, although he groaned within himself as he did it, knowing through all his daze that for him this was a sin.

Then when they had eaten all they could and the remnants were strewed about the court, Wang the Tiger rose with a sharp swift leap and he leaped upon a monstrous old stone turtle that stood to one side and a little above the terrace at the base of a great old juniper tree. This turtle had once marked some famous grave place and it had borne on its back one past day a high stone tablet extolling the virtues of the one dead, but the tree in its indomitable growing had pushed this tablet aside so that at last it fell and now it lay split upon the ground with its letters rubbed away by wind and rain, while the tree grew on.

Upon this turtle Wang the Tiger leaped and he stood and looked down upon all his own men. He stood proudly with his hand upon the hilt of his sword and one foot thrust forward upon the turtle's head, and he looked at them in his arrogance, his black brows drawn down, and his eyes glittering and piercing. And as he looked on these men who were his, his heart swelled and swelled until it seemed his body would burst with it, and he thought to himself,

"These are my own men—sworn to follow me. My hour is come!" And aloud he cried and his proud voice rang through those silent woods and echoed in the ruined courts of the temple, and he said, "Good brothers! This is who I am! I am a man humble as yourselves. My father farmed the land and I am from the land. But there was a destiny for me beyond the tilling of the fields and I ran away when I was but a lad and I joined the soldiers of the revolution under the old general.

"Good brothers! At first I dreamed of noble wars against

117

a corrupt ruler, for so the old general said his wars were. But his victory was too easy, and he became what we know he is, and I could not longer serve under such an one. Now, seeing that the revolution he led had no such fruition as I dreamed, and seeing as I do how the times are corrupt and every man fights for himself, it came to me as my destiny that I must call for all good fellows who were restless and unpaid under the old general, and that I must lead these forth to hew out for ourselves a place to be our own, free from corruption. I do not need to tell you that there are no honorable rulers, and the people cry out under the cruelties and oppressions of those who ought to treat them as fathers treat their sons. This has been so from the old days, even five hundred years ago, when good brave fellows banded together to punish the rich and to protect the poor. So shall we do also! I call on you, brave and good fellows, to follow where I go! Let us swear to live and to die together!"

There he stood, shouting this out in his great deep voice, his eyes shining and darting here and there over the men who squatted on the stones before him, his brows now drawn, now springing up like flags unfurled, lighting and changing from instant to instant the look upon his face. When he had finished speaking, every man leaped to his feet and a mighty shout went up from them,

"We swear! A thousand thousand years to our captain!"

Then one man who was more waggish than the others cried out in a squeaky high voice,

"I say he looks like a black-browed tiger, I say!"

And so Wang the Tiger did look, he was so slender and long and he moved so smoothly and his face was narrow at the chin and wide at the cheek bones and very high, and his eyes were wild and watchful and shining, and there above them were his long black brows, pressing down and shadowing his eyes so that when he drew them down his eyes seemed peering and shining out of some cavern. When he lifted his brows up his eyes seemed to spring out from under them and his whole face opened suddenly as though a tiger sprang forth.

Then all the men laughed fiercely and they took up the cry and they shouted,

"Ha, the Tiger, the Black-browed Tiger!"

As for the poor dazed hermit, he did not know what to make of all this shouting of tigers through the valley, and it was true there were tigers roaming in these hills, and he feared them more than anything. Now when he heard these great shouts he looked here and there in his thicket and he ran and hid himself in a small wretched room at the back of the temple where he slept, and he drew the rude bar across the door and he crept into his bed and pulled the ragged quilt over his head and there he lay shivering and weeping and wishing he had not tasted the meat.

Now Wang the Tiger had all a tiger's caution, too, and he knew that his venture was but barely begun and he must take thought of what was ahead of him. He let the men sleep for a while until the wine they had drunk was worn away and the fumes passed off from them, and while they slept he called out three of his men whom he knew to be clever tricky fellows and he told them to disguise themselves. One he bade strip himself except for his ragged inner trousers, and he bade him smear mud and filth on himself as a beggar does and go begging in the villages near the town where the old general was encamped, and he was to hear and to see what he could and to find out whether the old general was making ready to give chase or not. The other two he told to go into a market town and buy at some pawnshop a farmer's garments and his baskets and pole and they were to buy produce and carry it into the city and loiter and see what men said and if any talked of what had happened and of what might happen now that the old general's best men had run away from him. At the mouth to the pass Wang the Tiger set his trusty hare-lipped man to watch and to search the countryside with his keen eyes, and if he saw any movements of more than a few men anywhere he was to run without delay and bring the word to his captain.

When this was done and these men gone and the others had slept away their wine, Wang the Tiger took stock of all he had. He set down with a brush upon paper the number of his men and how many guns he had and how much ammunition and what the clothing of the men was and what their shoes were, whether good for a long march or not. He commanded his men to file past him and he looked closely at every one, and he found he had a hundred and eight good lusty men, not counting his two lads, and not one among them was too old and only a few were diseased, beyond sore eyes or the itch or such small things that anyone may have and these cannot be counted illness. Now as his men went past him slowly thus, they gaped and stared at the marks he made upon the paper, for not more than a scant two or three of them could read or write, and they were more in awe at Wang the Tiger than ever, because besides the skill at arms he had this wisdom also, that he could brush marks upon a piece of paper and he could look at them again and see meaning there.

And Wang the Tiger found he had besides his men a hundred and twenty-two guns and every man had his belt full of ammunition, and besides this Wang the Tiger had eighteen boxes of bullets he had taken secretly from the general's store to which he had had access. These he had sent one by one and his trusty man had brought them here and stored them behind the crumbling old Buddha in the temple, because there the roof was best and leaked least, and the Buddha sheltered them from rains driving in the gaping doors.

As for clothing, the soldiers had what they wore and it was enough until winter winds came and each man had his quilt to sleep in.

Wang the Tiger was well pleased at all he had and there was enough left of food to feed them three days more, and it was his plan then to march out by night as quickly as he could to his new territories in the north. Even if he had not loathed these southern lands he would have marched to another place, because the old general was so indolent that for ten years and more he had not moved from this place and he lived upon the people taxing them heavily beyond what they could afford to pay, and he took shares of their grain, too, and this he had done until the people were poor and there was nothing more to be had from them, and so Wang the Tiger must seek fresher lands.

Neither was it in his purpose to fight a battle with the old general over this stretch of over-taxed land, and he planned he would move on to the regions near his own home, for there were hills there to the northwest where he might shelter his men, and if he were pursued too hotly he could retreat into the more inaccessible parts, into those places where mountains are fierce and wild and the people are savage, and even lords of war seldom go there save at such times when they are driven into robbery and retreat. Not that he thought of retreat now; no, it seemed to Wang the Tiger that his way lay open before him, and he had only to be fearless and press on and make his name great in the land, and he set no defines to his greatness.

Then the ones whom he had sent out came back and one said,

"The news is everywhere that the old hive of bees has divided and a new swarm has come out and everywhere people are frightened because they say they are sucked so dry and they say the land cannot feed two hordes."

And the one who was the beggar said, "I hung about the very old camp and I smeared mud and filth on my face, so that no one could see what I was, and I listened and watched as I whined for alms, and the whole camp is astir and the old general is shouting and screeching and ordering this and that and taking it back again and saying something else, and he is all askew with his confusion and anger and his face is all purple and swollen. I dared so much as that, even, and I went close to see him, and he shouted out and I heard him, 'I did not dream that black-browed devil could do a turn like this, and I trusted him with everything. Yes, and people do say the northerners are more honest than we! I wish I had him skewered here upon my gun, the cursed thief and son of a thief!' And he cries out every word or two that his men are to take up arms and pursue us and give battle!"

The man paused and chuckled and he was that same fellow who loved to joke in his squeaky way, and now he said, and his voice went squeaking higher and higher and he grinned through his mud,

"But I did not see a single soldier move at all!"

Then Wang the Tiger smiled a little and grimly and he knew he had nothing to fear, for those men had gone unpaid for nearly a year and they stayed on only because they could be idle and yet fed. But if they were to fight they must be paid before they would do it and Wang the Tiger knew that when it came to such a point the old general would not pay them and so in a day or two his anger would cool and he would shrug himself and go back to his women, and his soldiers would sleep in the sun and wake to eat and sleep again.

As for Wang the Tiger, he set his face to the north and he knew he need fear no one.

X

THREE days did Wang the Tiger allow his men to feast and they ate all they could and they drank the jars of wine down to the very lees. When they were fed as they had not been in many months and stuffed and full with their feeding, and when they had slept until they could sleep no more they rose up strong and quarrelsome and lusty. Now all these years Wang the Tiger had lived among soldiers and he had learned well how men are and he knew how to manage strong, common, ignorant fellows, how to watch their moods and make use of these and how to seem to give liberty and yet hold all he could within the leash of his own will. So when he heard his men fall easily into quarreling and when they threatened each other over nothing at all or over nothing more serious than that one fell over another's outstretched legs as he tried to sleep, and when he saw how some began to think of women and long after them, he knew the hour was come when some new hard thing must be begun.

Then he sprang upon the old stone turtle again and he crossed his arms on his breast and he cried out,

"Tonight when the sun is gone behind the edge of the flat fields at the foot of the mountain we must start upon the journey to our own lands! Let every man take heed to himself, and if he has it still in his mind to return to easy feeding and sleeping under the old general let him return now and I will not kill him. But if, having set out with me tonight, any man turns back from the oath we have sworn, then I will stick him through with my sword!"

When he said these last words Wang the Tiger drew out his sword as swiftly as a flash of lightning plays across a cloud, and he thrust it straight out at the listening men and they were so startled they fell back one upon the other and they looked at each other in terror. Wang the Tiger stood waiting and staring and as he waited there were five among the older men who looked doubtfully at each other and at that sharp glittering sword he held thrust at them, and without a word they rose and crept away and down the mountain and they were seen no more. Wang the Tiger watched them go, and he held his sword out still motionless and shining, and he shouted,

"Is there any other one?"

There was a great silence over the men and not one moved for a time. Then suddenly a slight stooped figure stirred on the edge of the crowd and it made haste to creep away, and it was the son of Wang the Eldest. But when Wang the Tiger saw who it was he roared out,

"Not you, you young fool! Your father has given you to me, and you are not free!"

And he sheathed his sword as he spoke and he muttered with contempt as he did it, "I would not dip this good blade into such pale blood. No, I will whip you soundly, as one whips a child!" And he waited until the lad stood still again, his head hanging down as he always held it.

Then Wang the Tiger said in his usual voice,

"Let it be so then. See to your guns and tie your shoes fast upon your feet and gird yourselves, for tonight we make a mighty march. We will sleep by day and march by night so that men will not know we are moving through the country-side. But every time we come into the territory of a lord of war I will tell you what his name is, and if any ask you who we are you must say, 'We are a wandering band who come to join the lord of these lands.'"

Thus it came about that when the sun fell and there was yet a little light of day but the stars were out too, without a moon, the men filed raggedly to the pass, each man girded and with his bundle on his back and his gun in his hand. But Wang the Tiger had the extra guns given only to the men he knew best and whom he could trust for there were many among these men of his who were untried as yet and he could spare a man better than a gun. Such as had horses led them down the mountain and at the foot of the mountain before they set out on the highway to the north Wang the Tiger paused and he said in his harsh way,

"Not one of you is to stop except where I say and we will make no long stop until dawn at a village which I shall choose. There you may eat and drink and I will pay for it."

So saying he leaped upon his own horse, a high red beast with thick bones and long curled hair that had come from the plains of Mongolia, very strong and tireless. It had need so to be this night, for under him Wang the Tiger had put many pounds of silver he carried, and what he could not take he had given to his trusty man to carry and to certain others in lesser amounts, so that if one yielded to a temptation such as may assail any man, no great quantity would be lost. But strong as his beast was Wang the Tiger would not let it go at its full best. No, he was kind at heart and he held his horse reined in and kept it walking, mindful of those men who had no horses and must walk. On either side of him, also, rode his two nephews and he had bought asses for them, and the short legs of the asses could not match his own horse's stride. Some thirty odd of his men were on horses and the rest afoot, and Wang the Tiger divided his horsemen and put half before and half behind and the walking men between.

So through the silent night did they march, mile after mile, stopping now and then when Wang the Tiger shouted that they might rest for a little time and moving again when he gave the command. And his men were sturdy and uncomplaining and they followed him well, for they hoped much from him. Wang the Tiger was pleased with them, too, and he swore to himself that if they did not fail him neither would he fail them and in the days when he was great he would raise up every one of these first followers of his. Thus watching them and thinking of them as dependent upon him and trustful of him, even as children are in those who care for them, there arose in Wang the Tiger's heart a tenderness toward these men of his, for he was a man who could be thus tender secretly, and he was kind to his men and he let them rest a little longer now and then when they threw themselves upon some grassy plot of land, or under juniper trees such as are planted about graves.

Thus they marched for more than twenty nights, and by day they rested in such villages as Wang the Tiger appointed. But before they came to any village he took care to inquire who the lord of that territory was, and if any asked who this horde was and where they went, Wang the Tiger had his answer ready and smooth upon his tongue.

At every village, though, the people set up a mighty lamentation when they saw them coming, not knowing how long such wandering soldiers would stay or what they would eat or what women they might desire. But Wang the Tiger in these first days had very high purposes and he held the leash tightly over his men, and the more tightly because he had so strange a coldness in his own heart against women that he was the more impatient if other men were full of their heat, and he said,

"We are not robbers nor bandits and I am no robber chief! No, I shall hew out for myself a better road than that to greatness and we will win by skill of arms and by honorable means and not by preying upon the people. What you need you are to buy and I will pay for it. You are to have your wage every month. But you shall not touch any woman unless it be such as are willing and accustomed to men for money and their living, and go to them only when you must. Take care for yourselves that you do not go to those who are too cheap and who carry a vile death in them and strew it about. Keep yourselves from such. But if I hear that any man of mine has taken unlawfully a virtuous wife or a virgin daughter, that man will I kill before he has time even to say what he has done!"

Now when Wang the Tiger spoke like this every man of his stopped to hear and to think for there were those eyes of his glittering under his brows and well these men knew that for all his good heart their captain did not fear to kill a man. The young men murmured with admiration, for indeed Wang the Tiger was in these days their hero, and they called out, "Ha, the Tiger—Ha, the Black-browed Tiger!" So they marched on or they stayed at his command and every man obeyed Wang the Tiger or hid it very well if he did not.

There were many reasons why Wang the Tiger had chosen to settle upon lands not too far from his home, and among them was that he would be near to his brothers and so certain of the revenue they would give him for a time until he could establish taxes for himself, and he would be spared the danger of losing his silver by robbery along the way until it was brought to him. Moreover, if he met a reverse very sudden and great, such as is possible sometimes to any man if Heaven turns against him, he could disappear among his own folk, and his family was so great and rich he would be safe. Therefore he shaped his way steadfastly toward the town where his brothers lived.

But on the day before they came into sight of the town walls, Wang the Tiger grew impatient with his men for they lagged at marching and when night came and he commanded them to set out they were slow to move and Wang the Tiger heard some of them muttering and complaining, and one said,

"Well, now, and there are better things than glory and I do not know if we did well to come after a wild fierce fellow like this!" And another said, "It is better to have time to sleep and to have no need for wearing one's legs to the knee, even though there be less to eat!"

The truth was these men were very weary for they were not used to marching so steadfastly, for in these later years the old general had lived so softly his laxness had spread throughout his men. And knowing well how fickle ignorant men are, Wang the Tiger cursed them in his heart that now when they were nearing their northern lands they could fall into complaining. He forgot that while he had been rejoicing in this north and filled with content that he could buy hard-baked bread and sniff the good stout garlic again, these were still strange things to his men. His trusty man said to him secretly one midnight as they rested under a juniper tree,

"It is time we let them rest somewhere three days or so on end and time to feast them and give them a bit of extra silver."

Wang the Tiger leaped to his feet and he shouted,

"Show me the man who talks of straggling, and I will put a shot into his back!"

But the trusty harelipped man drew Wang the Tiger aside and he whispered peaceably,

"No, now, my captain, do not talk thus. Cease your anger. These soldiers are only children at heart, and they will show such strength as you would not believe true if they have the hope of some little joy ahead, even a small reward such as a dish of meat or a jug of new wine or a day's leisure to gamble. They are as simple as this, as easily pleased and quickly sad. The eyes of their minds are not open as yours are, my captain, so that they can remember to see what is more than a day ahead."

Now while this trusty man pleaded thus he stood in a patch of faint moonlight, for the moon had been new and now was full again as they marched, and he was very hideous to see in this light. But Wang the Tiger had tried him so often and knew him to be true and sensible, and he no longer saw the man's split lip, but he saw only his good common brown face and his faithful humble eyes, and he trusted him. Yes, Wang the Tiger trusted this man, although he did not know who he was, for the man never said anything of himself, and if he were very hard pressed he said only,

"I am native to a very far place and if I told you what place you would not know the name it is so far."

But it was rumored that he had committed a crime. It was said he had had a beautiful wife, a pretty girl who could not bear his looks, and she had taken a lover, and this man had found the pair together and he killed them and fled. Whether the tale was true or not none knew, but true it was that this man had attached himself to Wang the Tiger at first for no other reason except that the young man was so fierce and beautiful, and because of his very beauty a marvel to this poor, hideous fellow. And Wang the Tiger felt this love in the man, and he valued him above all others, because the man followed him for no reason of gain or position, but because of this strange love that asked for no return except to be near him. So he leaned on the man's loyalty, and he always heard what he had to say. Now he knew the man was again right, and so Wang the Tiger went to where his men lay outstretched and weary and in silence under the juniper trees, and he said more kindly than his wont was,

"Good brothers, we are hard upon my own town, and near to the village where I was born, and I know every road and path in these parts. You have been brave and tireless all these weary days and nights, and now I shall prepare your reward. I will lead you into the villages round about my own hamlet, but not into that one place, because the folk there are our own, and I would not offend them. And I will have cattle bought and killed and pigs also, and ducks and geese roasted, and you shall eat your fill. Wine you shall have, too, and the best wine in this country is made here, and it is a heady bright wine and the fumes rise quickly. And every man shall have three pieces of silver for his reward."

Then the men were cheered and they rose and they laughed and shouldered their guns and they marched that same night to the town and they passed it and Wang the Tiger led them to the hamlets beyond his own. There he halted and he chose four small hamlets and quartered his men in them. But he did not quarter them there arrogantly as some lords of war will. No, he went himself from village to village first in the early dawn when smoke was beginning to steal out of the open doors, as fires were lit for the first meal, and he sought the village heads and he said courteously,

"Silver I will pay for everything and no man of mine is to look at a woman not free to him. You must take twenty-five men."

But in spite of all his courtesy the village elders were distressed because they had had lords of war promise them before this and yet pay nothing and they looked askance out of their eyes at Wang the Tiger and they stroked such beards as they had and murmured together in their doorways, and at last they asked for some earnest of Wang the Tiger's good faith.

Then Wang the Tiger took out his silver liberally, for these were countrymen of his, and he left an earnest in the hand of every village elder and he said to his own men privately before he left them,

"You are to bear in mind that these folk were friends of my father and this is my own land and the people who see you see me. Speak courteously and take nothing without pay, and if any man of mine looks at a woman who is not public, I will kill him!"

Seeing how fierce he was his men promised him loudly and with many good sound curses on themselves if they failed to do what he said. Then when they were all quartered and food was being prepared for them and he paid out enough silver to change the sour looks of the villagers to smiles, when all was done he looked at his two nephews and he said to them with rough good humor, for indeed it was pleasant to him to be in his own country,

"Well, lads, your fathers will be glad to see you, I swear, and for these seven days I will rest too, for our war lies just ahead."

And he turned his horse toward the south and he passed by the earthen house without stopping for he did not pass near on purpose, and his two nephews followed him on their asses. So they drew near to the town and they went through the old gates again and came to the house. And for the first time in all these months a pale cheer was upon the face of the son of Wang the Eldest and he made a little haste toward his home.

SEVEN days and seven nights did Wang the Tiger stay in the great house in the town and his brothers feasted him and treated him as an honored guest. Four days and four nights he stayed in the courts of his elder brother and Wang the Eldest did all he could to win his younger brother's favor. But all he knew to do was to give him those things he himself counted pleasure, and so he feasted Wang the Tiger every night and he took him to the tea houses where there are singing girls and players on the lute, and he took him to playhouses. Yet it did seem as if Wang the Eldest gave himself pleasure more than he did his brother, for Wang the Tiger was a strange man. He would not eat more than he needed to stay his hunger and then he stopped and sat on in silence while others ate, and he would not drink more than he liked.

Yes, he sat on at feast tables where men made merry and ate and drank until they sweated and must needs take off this robe and that garment and some even went out and vomited what they had eaten so as to have the pleasure of eating more. But Wang the Tiger would not be tempted, no, not by the finest soups nor the most delicate flesh of sea serpents that are sold very dearly because they are so rare and hard to catch, nor would sweets tempt him nor anything made from fruits nor lotus seeds candied, nor honey nor any of those things which men will usually eat, however filled their bellies be.

And although he went with his elder brother to those tea houses where men go to play and toy with women, he sat stiff and sober and his sword hung from his belt and he would not unloose it and he watched everything with those black eyes of his. If he did not seem displeased neither was he pleased and he seemed to see no singing girl above another in beauty of voice or face, although there were more than one or two who noted him and yearned over his dark strength and his good looks so that they made every effort and they went and put their little hands on him even and they drew out their glances long and sweet and languid and fastened upon him. But he sat on as he was, rigid and unmoved and staring at all alike, and his lips were as surly as ever, and if he ever did say anything it was not the things to which pretty women are accustomed, but he would say,

"This singing is like the cackling of jays to me!" And once when a little soft creature, painted and pouting, looked straight to him and sang her little warble, he shouted out, "I am weary of all this!" and he rose and went away and Wang the Eldest had to follow him although it went against him sore to leave so good a play.

The truth was that Wang the Tiger had from his mother his scanty sparing tricks of speech so that he never said anything he need not say and his speech when it came was so bitter and true that after a time or two men feared it when his lips so much as moved.

Thus he spoke one day when the lady of Wang the Eldest was of a mind to come and urge him a little and say a good word or two for her second son. She came into the room where Wang the Tiger sat drinking tea one afternoon and Wang the Eldest sat by a small table drinking wine. She came in with mincing steps and with much modesty and very proper downcast looks, and she bowed and simpered and did not so much as look at the men, although when he saw her come in Wang the Eldest wiped his face hurriedly and poured out a bowl of tea for himself instead of the wine he had there hot in a pewter jug.

She came in plaintively and tottering on her little feet and

133

she sat down in a lower seat than her right was although Wang the Tiger rose, too, and motioned her to sit higher. But the lady said, and she made her voice weak and delicate as she did now-a-days unless she forgot herself or grew angry,

"No, I know my place, Brother-in-law, and I am but a weak and worthless woman. If ever I forget it, my lord takes pains to make me remember again, seeing that he holds so many women better and more worthy than I."

This she said and she cast an oblique look at Wang the Eldest so that he broke into a light sweat and murmured in a feeble way,

"Now, lady, when did I ever—"

And he began to cast over in his mind if there had been any special thing he had done of late of which she could have heard adversely. It was true he had found and sought the singing girl who was young and coy and who had pleased him so well at a feast one night, and he had begun to visit her and to pay her a regular sum and he had thoughts of establishing her somewhere in the town on a bounty as men do when they do not care to add the trouble of a new woman to their courts, yet desire her enough to keep her for themselves for a time at least. But this thing he had not yet accomplished, for the girl's mother lived and she was such a greedy old hag that she would not come down to Wang the Eldest's price for her daughter. So he thought his lady could not have heard of it before the thing was done and he wiped his face with his sleeve again and looked away from her and drank his tea heavily in loud sips.

But the lady was not thinking of him this time and she went on without heeding his muttering and she said,

"I have said to myself that humble as I am and a mere woman, yet I am my son's mother and I ought to come and thank my brother-in-law for what you have done for our

134

worthless second son, and though my thanks can be nothing to one like you yet it is my pleasure to do what I ought and so I do it spite of every burden and slight I have to bear."

Here she cast another of her looks at her lord and he scratched his head and looked at her foolishly and was all in a sweat again because he did not know what she was about to say and being so fat he sweat at nothing at all. But she went on,

"So here be my thanks, Brother-in-law, and worthless though they are they come from a sincere heart. As for my son, I will say that if there is a lad worthy of your kindness he is that one and he is the kindest, best and gentlest lad and such a wise head as he has! I am his mother and although it is said mothers see the best always in their children, still I will say again that we gave you the best son we have, my lord and I."

All this time Wang the Tiger had sat and stared at her as his way was when anyone spoke, and he stared so strangely one could not know whether he heard what was said or not, except when his answer came, and it came now, brutal and blunt,

"If that is so, Sister-in-law, then I am sorry for my brother and you. He is the timidest, weakest lad I ever did see and his gall is no larger than the gall in a white hen. I wish you could have given me your eldest son. He is a good wilful lad and I could break him and make him into something of a good wilful man, obedient to me and none other. But this second son of yours is always weeping and it is like carrying a leaking dipper with me everywhere. There is no breaking him for he has nothing in him and so no making him, either. No, both my brothers' lads disappoint me, for your lad is so soft and timid his brains are washed out in tears, and the other one is good and lusty and rough enough for the life but he is thoughtless and he loves his laughter and he is a clown, and I do not know how high a clown can go. It is an evil thing for me that I have no son of my own to use now when I need him."

Now what the lady might have said to such a speech as this none knows, but Wang the Eldest was trembling for he knew no one had ever spoken to her so plainly as this before, and the high red was flooding into her face and she opened her lips to make sharp answer. But before her voice could shape the words, her eldest son came out suddenly from behind a curtain where he was listening and he cried out eagerly,

"Oh, let me go, my mother—I want to go!"

There he stood before them all, eager and beautiful in his youth, and he looked quickly from one face to the other. He wore a bright blue gown the color of a peacock's feathers, such as young lords love to wear, and shoes of foreign leather, and he had a jade ring on his finger and his hair was cut in the newest fashion and smoothed back with fragrant oil. He was pale as young men in rich houses are pale who never need to labor or be burned by the sun, and his hands were soft as a woman's hands. Yet there was something very lusty in his looks too, for all his beauty and paleness, and he had a good, impatient eye. Nor did he move languidly when he forgot himself and forgot that it was the fashion for young men about town to be languid and careless of anything. No, he could be as he was now, his languor all laid aside, when he was full of the flame of a desire.

But his mother cried out sharply,

"Now this is the greatest nonsense I ever heard, for you are the eldest son and after your father the head of the house, and how can we let you go to wars and perhaps even go to a battle and be killed? We have spared nothing at all for you and we have sent you to every school in this town and hired scholars to teach you, and we have loved you too well to send you south to a school even, and how can we let you go to war?" Then seeing that Wang the Eldest sat there silent and hanging his head she said sharply, "My lord, am I to take this whole burden on myself, too?"

Then Wang the Eldest said feebly,

"Your mother is right, my son. She is always right, and we cannot spare you to such hazard."

But the young man, although he was nearly nineteen years old, began to stamp his feet and to weep and to storm and he ran and beat his head against the door lintel and he cried out,

"I shall poison myself if I cannot do what I like!"

Then his parents rose up in great dismay and the lady cried out that the young lord's servant was to be sent for, and when the man came running in terror, she cried to him,

"Take the child to some place for play and divert him and see if this anger can go out of him!"

And Wang the Eldest made haste to take a good handful of silver out of his girdle and he pressed it upon his son and said,

"Take it, my son, and go and buy yourself something you like or use it for a game or whatever you like."

At first the lad pushed the silver away and made as if he would not have such consolation, but the man servant coaxed and besought him, so that after a while the youth took the silver as though very unwillingly, and then flinging himself about and crying out that he would go, and he would go with his uncle, he suffered himself to be led away.

When it was over the lady sank upon a chair and she sighed piteously and she gasped,

"He has always had such—a spirit—we have not known

how to do with him—he is much harder to teach than the one we gave you!"

Now Wang the Tiger had sat gravely and watched all that passed, and now he said,

"It is easier to teach where there is a will than where there is nothing. I could make that lad if I had him and all this storming is because he has not been taught."

But the lady had been too put about to endure more and she would not bear it to have it said her sons were not well taught. So she rose in her majestic way and she said, and she bowed,

"Doubtless you have much to say to each other," and she went out.

Then Wang the Tiger looked at his eldest brother with a grim pity and they said nothing for a time, only Wang the Eldest began to drink his wine again, but not with any zest now, and his fat face was mournful. At last he said more thoughtfully than he usually spoke, and he sighed heavily before he spoke,

"There is a thing that is a riddle to me and it is this, that a woman can be so yielding and delicate and pliant to man's will when she is young and when her years come on her she grows another person altogether and is so scolding and troublesome and devoid of all reason as to keep a man dazed. I swear sometimes I will keep off all women, for I do believe my second one will learn of the first one, and they are all so." And he looked at his brother with a strange envy and with eyes as sorrowful as a great child's and he said sadly, "You are fortunate and more fortunate than I; you are free of women and you are free of land. Twice bound I am. I am bound by this accursed land my father left me. If I do not attend to it we have nothing from it, for these accursed country folk are all robbers and leagued against the landlord, however just and good he be. And as for my steward—who has ever heard of an honest man who was a steward?" He drew down his thick mouth plaintively and he sighed again and looked again at his brother and said, "Yes, you are fortunate. You have no land and you are bound to no woman at all."

And Wang the Tiger replied in greatest scorn,

"I do not know any women at all."

And he was glad when the four days were gone and he could go to the courts of Wang the Second.

Now when Wang the Tiger came into his second brother's house he could not but marvel to see how different it was from the other's, and how full of high good humor, in spite of bickering and quarreling among the children, too. And all the noise and good humor swelled and centered about Wang the Second's country wife. She was a noisy, boisterous creature and whenever she spoke her voice rang through the house she was so ruddy and loud. Yet, although she lost her temper a score of times a day and knocked this child's head against that one's or flung her arm out, with its sleeve forever rolled above her elbow, and slapped some child's cheek with a crack so that the house was full of roaring and bawling from morning until night and every servant was as loud as the mistress, yet she was fond too, in her rough way, and she would seize a child who passed and nuzzle her nose into his fat neck. And while she could be so saving of money, yet when a child came crying for a penny to buy a lump of candy or a bowl of some hot sweet stuff from a passing vendor or a stick of haws dipped in sugar or some such thing children love, she always reached into her deep bosom and fumbled out a penny. Through this noisy lusty house Wang the Second moved quiet and serene and filled with his secret plans, and he was always well pleased with them all and he and his wife lived content with each other.

For the first time Wang the Tiger in these days laid aside for the present his plans of glory and while his men rested and feasted he lived in his brother's house and there was something here in Wang the Second's house that he liked. He saw why his pocked nephew came out of this home merry and laughing and how the other one was always timid and fearful and he felt the content between Wang the Second and his wife and he felt the content the children had too, although they were not washed often nor did any servant take heed of them beyond seeing them fed by day and put into some bed or other at night. But every child was merry out of all the crew, and Wang the Tiger watched them everywhere with some strange moving in his heart. There was one boy of five years or so and Wang the Tiger watched him most, for he was the roundest, fairest boy and Wang the Tiger yearned for him somehow. But when he reached his hand out diffidently to the child, or found a penny and held it to him, the boy was suddenly grave and put his finger in his mouth and stared at Wang the Tiger's grave looks, and ran away, shaking his head. And Wang the Tiger was as pained by this refusal as though the boy were a man, although he tried to smile and make it nothing.

Thus Wang the Tiger waited for these seven days to pass, and his rare idleness made him more thoughtful than he usually was, and seeing these two houses full of children he felt afresh his lack that he had no son to be knit to him. And he thought on and a little about women, for this was the first time he had lived freely in a house where there were wives and maid servants and young slaves running here and there, and there was some strange sweet stir in him sometimes when he saw a slender maid with her back turned

140

to him at some task she had and he could remember once Pear Blossom had looked so about these very courts, where he had been a lad. But when the maid turned and he saw her face his old confusion fell on him, and the truth was there had been in that youth of his such a sealing of his fountains that at the sight of any woman's face there was some stopping in his heart and he turned himself away.

Still in his idleness and with this faint stir in him too, he was restless and one afternoon he told himself he would go and pay his respects to Lotus, for it was in Lotus's courts he used most often to see Pear Blossom in those old days, and he had a secret fancy to see the rooms again and the court. He went then to Lotus, having first sent his servant to announce his coming, and Lotus rose from the table where she sat gaming with her friends, the old ladies of other houses. But he would not sit long. No, he cast his eyes about this room, and he remembered it, and then he wished he had not come and he rose and was restless again and would not stay. But Lotus did not understand his brooding looks and she cried out,

"Stay, for I have sugared ginger in a jar and I have sweetened lotus root and such things as young men love! I have not forgotten what young men are like, no, for all I am so old and fat, I do remember how you all are!"

And she laid her hand on his arm and she laughed her thick laugh and leered at him. Then he loathed her suddenly and he stiffened himself and bowed and made his excuses again and he went away quickly. But he heard the cackling laughter of the old women as they gamed and it followed him through the courts.

Yet even as he went his remembrance made him more restless and he said to harden himself that his life was very far from here now and he must be on his way, and as soon as he

141

had visited once his father's grave as it was his duty to do and especially before he went on with his venture, he would be away once more and out of these courts.

So on the next morning, the sixth day, he said to Wang the Second,

"I will not stay longer than to burn a little incense at my father's grave, else my men will be growing lax and lazy and there is a long fierce road ahead. What have you to say of the moneys I need?"

And Wang the Second said,

"Nothing except that I will give you every month what we have agreed."

But Wang the Tiger cried impatiently, "Be sure I will return you one day all you lend me! Now I go to my father's grave. Do you, then, see that the two lads are ready for me and that they are not drunken or overfed tonight for we set forth at dawn tomorrow!" And he went away, half wishing he need not take his elder brother's son again, but not knowing how to refuse, lest it breed jealousy. And as he went he took a little incense from a store kept in the house and he went out to his father's grave.

Now these two, father and son, had been very far apart when they lived, and even Wang the Tiger's childhood had been bitter because his father had said he must stay on the land, and Wang the Tiger had grown up hating the land. He hated it now and as he drew near to the earthen house which was his he hated it; although it had been his childhood home, he did not love it because it had been a prison to him once and he had thought he would never be free of it. He did not go near it, but he circled around and drew near through a small grove of trees to the hillock where were set the graves of the family.

As he drew near with his swift steps he heard a low soft

142

sound as though one wept and when he heard it he wondered who could weep at that grave, for he knew Lotus was gaming and well he knew it could not be she. He softened his striding then, and he drew near, and he peered through the trees. There was the strangest sight he had ever seen. Pear Blossom leaned her head upon his father's grave and she sat crouched in the grass in the way that women have when they weep and think no one near and they can weep on uncomforted. Not far from her sat his sister, the fool, whom he had not seen these many years and now although her hair was nearly white and her face shrunken and small she sat in a spot of autumn sunlight and played at a bit of red cloth, folding and refolding it and smiling to see the sun on it so red. And holding to her coat faithfully, as a child does who has been bid to do something for one he loves, sat a small, twisted, hunched boy. He had his face turned sorrowfully to the weeping woman and his mouth was all puckered and he was near to weeping, too, for her sake.

Wang the Tiger stood there, stricken motionless with his surprise, and he listened to Pear Blossom mourning on in that soft low way she had as though the weeping came from some innermost part of her, and suddenly he could not bear it. No, all his old anger fell once more against his father, and he could not bear it. He dropped the incense there where he stood and he turned and walked quickly away, breathing heavily in great sighs as he went, although he did not know he did.

He rushed back over the land and he only knew he must be away from this place, this land—this woman—he must be at his own business. He walked back through the hard autumn sunlight, falling brilliant and clear across the fields, but he saw none of it and noted no beauty.

143

At dawn he was up and on his red horse and the horse was curveting and impatient in the chill air and his hoofs thudded heavily upon the cobbled street and the pocked lad, well fed with all he had eaten for his morning meal, was on his ass and they rode around to the gate of Wang the Eldest to fetch that other lad. But before they could wait at all a man servant came running out of the gate and he cried as he ran somewhere,

"What a thing of evil is this—what a curse upon this house!" And he ran his way somewhere.

Then Wang the Tiger felt his impatience rise in him and he shouted out,

"What curse is it? Curse it is that the sun is near the horizon and I am not on my way yet!"

But the man did not look back. Then Wang the Tiger cursed very heartily and he cried to the pocked lad,

"That cursed lad your cousin is nothing but a burden to me and never will be else! Go and find him and tell him he is to come or I will not have him!"

The pocked lad slid down at once from his small old ass and ran in and more slowly Wang the Tiger came down from his horse and went to the gate and gave the reins over to the gateman to hold for him. But before he could go further the lad was out again, white as a spirit and breathing as fast as though he had run around the town walls. He gasped out between his breaths,

"He will never come again—he is hung and dead!"

"What do you say, you small monkey!" shouted Wang the Tiger and he leaped and ran into his brother's house.

There was confusion indeed and men and women and servants and all were gathered about something in the court, and above the din and shouting a woman's loud shrieks were heard, and it was the lad's mother who so cried. But Wang

144

the Tiger pushed them aside and in the center of the crowd was Wang the Eldest. His fat face was yellow as old tallow and all shaken with tears, and he held supported in his arms the body of his second son. The lad lay there outstretched in the court, under the bright morning sky, dead, and his head hung back over his father's arm. He had hanged himself with his girdle upon the beam in the room where he slept with his elder brother, and the brother had not known it until he woke in the morning, for he slept hard after wine at some merrymaking the night before. When he woke in the pale dawn and saw the slight form dangling he thought at first it was a garment and he wondered why it hung there but when he looked again he screamed and so woke the house.

Then Wang the Tiger, when one had told him this tale and a score of others helped in the telling, stood and looked down on this dead son with the strangest feeling, and he pitied this lad for a while as he never had when the lad was alive. He was so very small and slight now he was dead. And Wang the Eldest looked up and saw his brother there and he blubbered,

"I never dreamed this child of mine would choose death to going with you! You must have treated him very ill to make him hate you like this! Well for you that you are my brother, or I would—I would—"

"No, Brother," said Wang the Tiger more gently than he was used to speak, "I did not treat him ill. He even had an ass to ride when others older than he walked. But neither did I dream he was brave enough to die. I might have made something of him after all if I had known he had in him the power to die!"

He stood and stared awhile. But bustle began suddenly when the serving man who had run somewhere returned with a geomancer and with priests and their drums and with all

145

those whose duty it is to come with such an untoward death, and in the commotion Wang the Tiger went away and waited in a room alone.

But when he had waited and done all that he should do as brother in so sad a house he mounted his horse and he rode away. And as he went he was sadder than he had been and he was compelled to harden himself and to remember again and again how he had never beaten the lad or treated him ill in any way and none could have known he had this despair in him to take his own life, and Wang the Tiger told himself it was so destined by heaven and not any man could have averted this thing, for so the life of everyone is wholly with heaven. Thus he forced himself to forget the pale lad and how he had looked when his head lay over his father's arm, and Wang the Tiger said to himself,

"Even sons are not all blessing, it may be."

When he had comforted himself like this he was better, and he called heartily to the pocked lad,

"Come, lad, there is a long road before us and we must set out upon it!"

XII

THEN Wang the Tiger struck his horse with the braided leathern whip he carried and he let the beast have its full way and the horse sped over the countryside as though it were winged. It was a day fit to start upon so high a venture as Wang the Tiger's, for the sky was cloudless and the wind blew keen and cool and full of vigor and it turned the trees this way and that and wrenched at them and whipped the late leaves from their branches and it stirred the dust in the roadways and whirled itself over the shorn grain lands. In Wang the Tiger's heart a recklessness rose like the very wind itself and he purposely took his way far from the earthen house and he made a wide circle from the place where Pear Blossom lived and he said to his own heart,

"All the past is finished and I look forward to my greatness and to my glory!"

So the day began and the sun rose full and enormous and glittering over the edge of the fields, but he looked at it unblinking, and it seemed to him that heaven itself set its seal upon him in such a day as this and he would achieve his greatness, for greatness was his destiny.

Early in the morning he came to the hamlets where his men were, and his trusty harelipped man came out to meet him and he said,

"It is very well, my captain, that you have come, for the men are rested and full of food and they are chafing to be on to more freedom."

"Round them out, then, when they have had their morning meal," shouted Wang the Tiger, "and let us be on our way and half way to our own lands by tomorrow."

Now during these days that Wang the Tiger had been in the house of Wang the Second he had been thinking much of what lands he should take for his own rule and he had talked with his brother who was cautious and wise, and it seemed to them that the lands just over into the borders of the next province were very good lands for the purpose and the best to be had. These regions were far enough from Wang the Tiger's home so that if dire need came he would not be taking from those who were his own people and yet near enough so that if he were vanquished in a war he could take refuge among his own. Moreover, it was near enough so that the silver he would need until he was established could be brought to him easily and without too great risk of robbers. As for the lands themselves, they were famous good lands where the famine did not strike too often, and some of the lands were high and some were low, and there were mountains to serve for retreat and hiding. There was besides all this a certain highway that was a passage between the north and south for travellers coming to and fro, and such travellers could very well be taxed also for revenues and the right to pass that way. There were two or three large towns too, and a small city, so that Wang the Tiger need not be wholly dependent upon the people who tilled the earth. These lands had another value also, and it was that they sent out the best grain to the markets for wine and the people were not very poor.

There was but one hindrance to all these goods, and it was that there was already a lord of war over that region and Wang the Tiger must first drive him out if he was to prosper to the utmost, for there is no region rich enough to maintain two lords of war. Now what this lord was or who he was or how strong he was were things Wang the Tiger did not know, for he could not find out anything sure from his brothers except that they had heard him called the Leopard, because he had such a strange slanting forehead sloping back into his head as leopards' foreheads do, and he ruled the people harshly, so that they hated him.

Therefore Wang the Tiger knew he must go secretly to those lands and not in any bold array. No, he must go stealthily, separating his men into small bands so that they would not look more dangerous than bands of deserting soldiers, and he would seek out some retreat in a mountain and from that vantage he would search out the country with his trusty men and see what sort of a lord of war he had to fight and from whom he must take the lands he felt were already his by destiny.

As he planned, so he did. When his men were gathered out of the hamlets and when he had seen each man fed and warmed with good wine against the chill winds that contended with the heat of the mounting sun, when he had taken care that all was paid for and he had asked the villagers, "Did my men do anything in your houses they should not?" and had heard them answer volubly, "No, they did not, and we wish all soldiers were like yours," then Wang the Tiger was well pleased and he drew his men far out beyond the villages and he told them as they stood about him of the lands to which he would lead them and he said,

"There are the best lands anywhere and there is only one lord to fight against. There is such heady wine, too, in that land, as you have never tasted before!"

When the men heard this they shouted with joy and they clamored,

"Take us there, our captain—we have longed for such lands!"

Then Wang the Tiger answered them, smiling his grim smile,

"It is not so easy as this, for we must search out the strength of the lord who holds it. If his men are too many for us, we must seek ways of winning them away from him, and every man of you must be a spy to see and to hear. Nor must anyone know why we are come or we are undone. I will go myself first to see where we can make our camp, and my trusty hare-lipped man shall stay at the border at a hamlet there called the Valley of Peace. He will stay at an inn there that I have heard of, and it is the very last inn on the street and there is a wine flag hanging out of the door. He is to wait for you and give you the name of the place I shall set for us to gather. Now you are to break up into threes and fives and sevens and saunter as though you were runaways, and if any man asks you where you go, ask him where the Leopard is for you come to join him. To everyone I will give three pieces of silver for food until we meet. But there is one thing I say to every man. If it comes to my ears that any man has injured a humble man or looked at a woman not free to him I shall not ask what man it is but I will kill two men for every such man I hear about."

Then one man called out, "But, my captain, are we never to be free to do the things soldiers may?"

And Wang the Tiger shouted at him, "When I give the command you are free! But you have not fought for me yet, and shall you have the rewards of battle when there has been no battle?"

The man was silent then and he was afraid, for Wang the Tiger was known to be very sudden in his tempers and swift with his sword and he was not a man whom one could move with a witty word or a merry saying fitly spoken. Yet he was known to be just, too, and these men who followed him were good enough and they knew what was fair. It was true they had not fought yet and they were willing to wait so long as they were fed and sheltered and paid.

Then Wang the Tiger watched them as they scattered into groups and when they were so scattered, he paid them from the store he had, and with the pocked lad on his ass and the harelipped trusty man upon a mule Wang the Tiger had bought for him at a hamlet, the three started alone toward the northwest.

When Wang the Tiger came to the border of that region of which he had heard he forced his red horse up a large, tall grave of some rich man's that stood there, and from this vantage he looked out over the land. It was the fairest land he had ever seen and it spread itself out before him, rolling in little low hills and in wide shallow valleys that were already faintly green with the newly sprouted winter wheat. To the northwest the hills rose suddenly into jagged mountains full of cliffs cut clearly against the bright sky of the day. The houses of the people of that land were scattered in small villages and hamlets, good earthen houses not fallen into decay, and many had the roofs newly thatched with straw from that year's harvest. There were even a few houses of brick and tile. In every dooryard near enough for him to see there were ricks of straw and he could hear the distant cackling of hens that had laid their eggs, and now and again the wind blew to him where he stood fragments of some song a farmer sang as he cultivated his fields. It was a very fair land and his heart leaped to see how fair it was. But he had no mind to go through clad as he was in a soldier's garb and on his red horse and let a rumor of war loose too early upon the people. No, he looked and he planned out for himself a winding way to the mountains where he could hide himself and his men and seek out the strength of his enemy before any could even know he was come.

At the foot of the low hill upon which this tall grave and many other graves were, was a little village, the border village of which he had told his men. It stretched out its few furlongs of one street, and Wang the Tiger turned his horse there and he rode through it, with the pair behind him. It was at that time of the morning when farmers return to their own hamlets, and the village tea house was full of farmers drinking tea or supping up bowls of noodles made from wheaten flour or buckwheat. They had their baskets emptied from the markets piled on the ground beside them as they ate, and they looked up in wonder when they heard the clattering of hoofs upon the street and they stared with jaws ajar as Wang the Tiger passed. He looked back at them, too, to see what sort of men they were, and he was very pleased to see how goodly they were, how brawny and brown and hearty and how well fed and he said to himself freshly he had chosen his lands very well if it could breed such men as these. But, save that he looked at them, he went with unusual modesty and as one goes who passes through a place a guest and going on to some other far place.

At the end of the street there was the wine shop he had heard of and he told the pair to wait outside, and he halted his horse and dismounted and he pushed aside the curtain at the door and went into the shop. There was no one there for it was a very small place with but a table or so for guests, and Wang the Tiger sat down and slapped the table with his hand. A lad came running out then and seeing how fierce a man was there he ran back to his father, who was the keeper of the shop, and the man came out and wiped the table with his torn apron and he said, courteously,

"My lord guest, what will you have for wine?"

"What have you?" returned Wang the Tiger.

The shop keeper answered him, "We have the fresh sorghum wine made in these parts. It is the best wine and shipped over the whole earth, I suppose, even to the emperor in the capital."

At this Wang the Tiger laughed in some scorn and he said,

"Have you not heard in this little village that we have no emperor these days?"

At this a great look of terror came over the man's face and he said in a whisper,

"No, and I had not heard it! When did he die? Or was his throne taken by violence, and if it was, who is our new emperor?"

And Wang the Tiger marvelled that there could be a man so ignorant as this and he replied with some slight scorn,

"We have no new emperor these days at all."

"Then who rules us?" said the man in consternation as at some new disaster newly fallen on him unawares.

"It is a time of striving," said Wang the Tiger. "There are many rulers and it is not known which can seize the highest seat. It is such a time as any man may use to rise to glory."

This he said, and the ambition that was the greatest part of him soared up suddenly and he cried to his own heart, "And why may not that one be I?" But he said nothing aloud; he only sat and waited for his wine beside the small unpainted table.

Then the man when he had fetched the jug of wine came back and it could be seen from his sober face that he was much troubled and he said to Wang the Tiger,

"It is a very evil thing to have no emperor, for this is to have a body without a head and this means wild movements everywhere and none to guide us all. It is an ill thing you have told me, my lord guest, and I wish you had not told me for now I shall not be able to forget it. Humble as I am, I shall not be able to forget it, and however peaceful our village is I shall be afraid every day for the next."

And with downcast looks the man poured the warm wine into a bowl. But Wang the Tiger did not answer for he had his thoughts elsewhere than on this humble soul, and as for him he was glad it was such an hour as it was. He poured out the wine and drank it down quickly. It spread through his blood, hot and strong, and he felt it mount to his cheeks and fume through his head. He did not drink above a few bowls of it then, but he paid for it and for a bowl more and this he took out to his trusty harelipped man. The man was very grateful for it, too, and he took the bowl in both his hands and supped as best he could, lapping it somewhat as a dog does to taste it and then throwing his head back and pouring it down his throat because his upper lip was so little use to him, divided as it was.

Then Wang the Tiger went back into the shop and he said to the keeper,

"And who rules you here in this region?"

The man looked east and west at this but there was no one near and so he said in a low voice,

"It is a robber chief who is called the Leopard. He is the cruellest bitter fellow. Every one of us must pay a tax to him or he comes sweeping down on us with all his ne'er-do-wells, he and his men like a flock of evil crows to pick us clean. Well do we all wish we could be rid of him!"

"But is there no one to contend with him?" asked Wang the Tiger, and he sat down as though it were a small careless thing he said and of no importance to him. And to seem more careless he said, "Bring me a pot of mild green tea. The wine stays like fire in my throat."

And as the man fetched the tea he answered Wang the Tiger, "Not one to contend, my lord guest. We would complain of him to those above if it were of use so to do. Once we did go to our county court and the highest magistrate in our region lives there. We told him our case and we asked him to send his soldiers out and to borrow soldiers from the one yet above him and see if together they could not drive out this fellow who oppresses us. But, sir, when those soldiers came they were such cruel men and they so lived in our houses and took our daughters and so ate their fill of what they would and did not pay us that they grew to be a burden we could not bear. No, and besides this they were such cowards that they ran at the very smell of a battle and the robbers grew all the more arrogant. So we went then and begged the magistrate to take his soldiers off from us again and he did at last. But it was a very bitter thing at best, for many of the soldiers went and took service under the robbers, giving as excuse that they had not been paid for long and they must eat, and we

154

were worse off than before for a soldier has a gun to take with him where he goes. And as if it were not enough, that magistrate of ours who lives in the county seat there sent out his tax gatherers and put a heavy tax upon us all, on men on the lands and on keepers of shops, too, because he said the state had been put to such a cost to protect us that we must pay them for it. Well enough we knew he and his opium pipe were the state, and so since that time we have never asked for any help, choosing rather to pay so much and so much to the Leopard every feast day and so keep him in bounds. It is well enough while we have no famine and we have had so many good years now that heaven will surely send us a bad year soon, and there must be many bad years in store for us. Then I do not know how we shall do."

To all of this long tale Wang the Tiger listened carefully as he drank his tea. Then he asked again,

"Where does this Leopard live?"

Then the wine shop keeper took Wang the Tiger by the sleeve and he led him to a small window at the east of the shop and he pointed with his crooked forefinger, stained with wines, and he said,

"There is a mountain yonder with two crests and it is called the Double Dragon Mountain. Between the two crests is a valley and in that valley is the robbers' lair."

Now this was what Wang the Tiger waited to hear and so he affected the more negligence of it and he said carelessly, smoothing his hard mouth with his hand,

"Well, I shall stay away from that mountain then. And now I must be on the way to my home northward. Here is the silver I owe you. As for the wine, it is as you say it is, a very good bright heady wine."

Then Wang the Tiger went out and he mounted his horse again and with the two behind him he rode round about so as not to pass any more villages. He rode over the tops of circling hills and through lonely places although he was never far from men either, because that place was so well tilled and so full of hamlets and villages. But he kept his eyes fixed on that double-crested mountain and he guided his horse to the south of it to a certain other lower mountain he saw that was partly wooded with pine trees.

All through that day they rode in silence, for no one spoke to Wang the Tiger if he did not speak first, unless there were some very pressing thing to be said. Once the lad began to sing a little under his breath, because he was such an one as found silence wearisome, but Wang the Tiger hushed him sternly, for he was in no mood for any merry noise.

At the end of the afternoon but before the sun was set they came to the foot of that wooded mountain toward which they had been many hours riding, and Wang the Tiger dismounted from his weary horse and began to climb some rude stone steps that led upward. These he followed and the pair behind him also, their beasts stumbling over the stones, and as they went the mountain grew wilder and there were cliffs over which the road led and streams burst forth here and there between the rocks and the trees, and the grasses grew thick and deep. The mosses upon the stones also were soft and showed but little sign of the passage of human feet except in the very center, as though only one or two persons ever passed this way. When the sun was set they had reached the end of this mountain road and it ended at a temple built of rough stone and set with its back to the cliff so that indeed this cliff was its innermost wall. The temple was very nearly hidden by trees but it could be seen because its faded red walls gleamed out in the setting sun. It was but a small temple, old and ruinous, and its gates were closed.

Wang the Tiger went up to it and for a while he stood with

his ear pressed against the closed gate. But he heard nothing and so he beat upon it with the handle of his leathern whip. No one came for a long time and then he beat very furiously and with anger. At last the door opened a little and the face of a shorn and shaven priest looked out, a very old and shriveled face. And Wang the Tiger said,

"We seek for shelter here tonight," and as he spoke his voice rang out hard and sharp and clear in that quiet place.

But the priest opened the door a very little more and he answered in a little piping voice,

"Are there no inns and tea houses in the villages? We be but a scant handful of men who have left the world and have but the poorest of food without any meat and we drink only water." And his old knees shook in his robes when he looked at Wang the Tiger.

But Wang the Tiger pushed his way in through the gates and past that old priest and he called to his lad and the trusty man,

"Here is the very place for which we seek!"

He went in then without any heed at all to the priests. He went into the temple through the main hall where the gods were, and they were like the temple, very aged and their gilt peeling from their clay bodies. But Wang the Tiger did not even look at them. He passed them and went into the inner side houses where the priests lived, and he chose out a small room for himself better than the others and cleaned not too many days ago. Here he ungirdled his sword, and the trusty man went hither and thither and found food and drink for him, although it was only a little rice and cabbage.

But that night as Wang the Tiger laid himself down upon the bed in the room he had chosen he heard a deep, low wailing come out of the hall where the gods were and he rose and went out to see what it was. There the five old

157

priests of the temple were and the two little acolytes they had who were farmers' sons left there for some prayer answered. They all knelt and wailed to the Buddha who sat leaning on his fat belly in the center of the hall and as they wailed they prayed the god to save them. A torch burned there and the flame flew this way and that in the night winds and in the light of the flying flame these knelt and prayed aloud.

Now Wang the Tiger stood and looked at them and listened to them and he found that they prayed to be protected against him and they cried,

"Save us—save us from the robber!"

When he heard this Wang the Tiger shouted out heartily and the priests leaped to hear his sudden voice and they stumbled to their feet entangled in their robes with their haste, all except one old priest who was the abbot of that temple and he fell flat on his face, thinking his last hour was come. But Wang the Tiger shouted,

"I shall not hurt you, you old baldheads! Look, I have silver to spare, and why should you be afraid of me?" And as he spoke he opened his girdle purse and he showed them the silver he carried there and it was true there was more silver in it than they had ever seen and he said on, "Beyond this I have more silver and I want nothing of you except shelter for a little while such as any man may claim in his need from a temple."

The sight of this silver did comfort the priests very much and they looked at one another and they said among themselves,

"He is some military captain or other who has killed a man he should not have killed, or who has lost his general's favor and so he must hide for a little time. We have heard of such."

As for Wang the Tiger he let them think what they would

and he smiled his slight and mirthless smile, and he went back to his bed.

The next day at dawn Wang the Tiger rose and he went out to the gate of the temple. It was a morning of mists and the clouds filled the valleys and covered this mountain top from every other and he was alone and hid from the world. Nevertheless, the chill in the air reminded him that winter must soon come and he had much to do before snows set in, for his men depended on him for food and shelter and for clothing against the cold. So he went into the temple again and he went into a kitchen where his trusty man and the lad slept. They had covered themselves with straw and they still slept and the breath whistled through the man's split lip. They slept fast enough, although already an acolyte was feeding straw carefully into the mouth of the brick oven and from under the wooden lid of the iron cauldron on the bricks a bubble of steam leaked out. When the acolyte saw Wang the Tiger he shrank back and hid himself.

But Wang the Tiger paid no heed to him. He shouted to his trusty man and seized him and shook him, and bade him rise and eat and get gone to the inn, lest some of the men pass that morning. Then did the trusty man stagger up out of his sleep rubbing his two hands over his face and yawning hideously. But he shuffled into his clothes and he dipped a bowl into the simmering cauldron and supped some of the scalding sorghum gruel the acolyte brewed there. Away he went down the mountain, then, a goodly enough man if one saw only his back and not his face, and Wang the Tiger watched him go and valued him for his faithfulness.

Then as Wang the Tiger waited that day for his men to gather to him in this lonely place, he planned what he would do and whom he would choose for his trusty men to be his helpers and take counsel with him. He portioned out cer-

159

tain labor to certain numbers of men also, to these to be spies, and to these to forage for food and to others to gather fuel and to others cooking and the mending and cleaning of weapons, to each man his share in their common life. And he thought that he must remember to keep a hard hand over them all, and to reward them only where reward was due and he would order all under his complete command. Life and death should be in his own hand.

Beyond this he planned how each day he would spend certain hours training his men in feints and postures of war so that when his times of struggle came they would be ready. He dared not waste his bullets for the guns at practice, seeing he had not many beyond his need yet. But he would teach them what he could.

So he waited restless in that still mountain top and before the day was ended there were fifty and more men who had found their way to him again and by the end of the next day nearly fifty more. The few left never came and it seemed they had deserted to some other cause. Wang the Tiger waited two more days but they did not come, and he grieved, not because of the men but because with each he had lost a good gun and a belt of bullets.

Now when the old priests saw this horde of men gathering into their peaceful temple they were beside themselves and they did not know what to do. But Wang the Tiger comforted them and he said over and over,

"You shall be paid for everything and you need not fear."

But the old abbot answered in his feeble way, for he was very aged and the flesh upon his bones was dried and shriveled with his age,

"It is not only that we fear no return, but there are things for which silver makes no restoration. This has been a very quiet place and its very name is The Temple of Holy Peace.

We few have lived out of the world these many years in this place. Now here are all your lusty hungry men and peace is gone with their coming. They crowd into the hall where the gods are and they spew their spittle everywhere and they stand anywhere, even before a god himself, and pass their water as they please and they are coarse and wild in all they do."

Then Wang the Tiger said, "It is easier for you to move yourselves and your gods than for me to change such things in my men, for they are soldiers. Move your gods then into the innermost hall and I will tell them that to that one place they shall not go. So may you be at peace."

Thus the old abbot did, then, seeing that there was no other way, and they moved every god on its pedestal, except the gilt Buddha who was too large and they feared if he fell he would burst into pieces and bring disaster upon them all. The soldiers lived in the hall with him then and the priests covered his face with a piece of cloth so that he might not see and be angered by what sins they could not avoid.

Then Wang the Tiger chose out from his men the three he would have as his trusty men. First he took the harelipped man and after him two others, one nicknamed the Hawk, because he had a very curious hooked nose in the middle of his thin face and a narrow, down-drooping mouth, and one nicknamed the Pig Butcher. The Pig Butcher was a great thick fat red man, and his face was large and flat and his features smashed upon it as though a hand had smeared him in the making. But he was a lusty fellow, and it was true enough he had once been a pig butcher, but he had killed a neighbor in a brawl and he would often bemoan it and say, "If I had been eating my rice and had chopsticks in my hand I could never have killed him. But he quarreled with me when I had my chopping knife in my hand and the thing seemed to fly out of its own accord." Nevertheless, the man having died of his bleeding, the Pig Butcher had need to run away to save himself from the court. He had one strange skill. Coarse and thick as he was, he had swift and delicate speed in his hand so that if he took a pair of chopsticks he could pluck the flies out of the air as they flew, one by one he plucked them, and many times his fellows would bid him to do this for them to see and they roared with laughter to see such skill. With this exactness he could prick a man as delicately and spill his blood out neatly and swiftly, too.

Now these three men were very canny men, although not one could read or write. But for such a life as theirs they needed no learning in books, nor did they dream such learning could be useful to them. Wang the Tiger called them to his room when he had chosen them and he said,

"I shall look to you as my three trusty men above the others to watch them and to see if any betrays me or fails in what I have commanded. Be sure you shall have a reward on the day when I rise to glory."

Then he sent the Hawk out and the Pig Butcher too, and he kept only the harelipped trusty man and to him he said with great sternness,

"You I set above those other two and it is your duty to see if they, too, fail me in loyalty."

Then he called the three together again and he said, "As for me, I shall kill anyone whose loyalty is even brought to question. I will kill him so swiftly that the next breath he had planned as a thing of course shall be left half taken and hanging in the air."

Then his harelipped man answered peaceably, "You need not fear me, my captain. Your own right hand shall betray you before I do so."

Then the other two swore eagerly also, and the Hawk said loudest of all,

"Shall I forget you took me as a common soldier and raised me up?" This he said, for he had his own hopes in him, too.

Then the three made their obeisances before Wang the Tiger to show their humility and their faithfulness, and when this was over Wang the Tiger chose out certain tricky clever men and he sent them out through the land everywhere to spy out what the news was about his enemy. He commanded,

"Make all haste and find out what you can so that we can establish ourselves before the great cold begins. Find out how many men follow the Leopard and if you come upon any of them talk to them and test their loyalty to him and see if they can be bribed away or not. I will bribe everyone I can because your lives are more precious to me than silver, and I shall not waste one life if I can buy a man instead."

Then these men took off their soldiers' garb and they wore their old ragged inner garments and Wang the Tiger gave them money to buy what they might need of common upper clothes. They went down the mountain then and into the villages and the pawnshops and bought the old worn clothes that farmers and common men pawn for a few pence and never redeem again they are so poor. Thus clad the men wandered all through that countryside. They idled at inns and at tables where men gamed to pass the time away and they stayed at wayside shops and everywhere they listened. Then they came back and told everything to Wang the Tiger.

Now what these men told was the same that Wang the Tiger had heard in the wine shop and it was that the people of these lands hated and feared this robber chief, the Leopard, because every year he demanded more of them if he was not to come and lay waste their houses and fields. His excuse was that each year he had a greater horde of men to feed and he beat off other robbers from the common people and for this he ought to be paid. It was true that his band grew very large and larger every year because every idler in that whole region who did not wish to work and all who had committed some crime fled to the lair in the Double Dragon Mountain and joined the Leopard's banner. If they were good fellows and brave they were very welcome and if they were weak and cowards they were kept to serve the others. There were even some women who went there, bold women whose husbands were dead and who did not care for fame, good or ill, and some men when they went took their wives with them, and some women were captives and held for the men's pleasure. And it was true, too, that the Leopard did hold off other robber chiefs from this whole region.

But in spite of this the people hated him and they were unwilling to give him anything. Yet whether they wished it or not they gave, for they had no weapons. In olden days they might have risen with forks and scythes and knives and such simple tools, but now that the robbers had foreign guns, these were of no avail; nor was any courage or anger of avail against so leaping a death as this.

When Wang the Tiger asked his spies how many men followed the Leopard he had strange answers, for some said they had heard five hundred and others said two or three thousand and others said more than ten thousand. He could not find out what the truth was and he only knew that it was more by many than the men he had. This gave him much to ponder upon and he saw that he must use guile and keep his guns until the last sharp battle and he must avoid even this if he could. So he pondered as he sat and listened to what his spies said, and he let them say on freely, knowing that an ignorant man tells most when he does not know it. And the man who loved to be merry, the same one who had named his captain the Black-browed Tiger, said, making his little weak voice high and boasting,

"As for me, I am so fearless I pushed my way in to the largest town which is the seat of this whole county and I listened there and they are afraid there, too. Every year this Leopard makes a demand at the feast days and the merchants must give him a vast heap of silver or he says he will attack the town itself. And I said to the fellow who told me, and he was a vendor of pork balls, the very best I ever did eat—they have rare pigs here, my captain, and they put garlic into their meats, and I am glad if we stay here—and I said, 'But why does your magistrate not send his soldiers out to fight and do battle with this robber for the people's sake?' And that maker of pork balls—he was a good fellow too, and he gave a bit of a broken ball more than I paid for—and he said, 'That magistrate of ours sits sunken in his opium and he is afraid of his own shadow and the general he keeps for his army has never been to war at all and he does not know how to hold a gun—a little fuming, fussy fellow he is who cares more how his soup is brewed than what happens to us! As for that magistrate you should see the guards he keeps about him and he pays them more and more lest they turn against him or be bribed by someone and he spends out money like one pours tea on the ground out of a cold pot. And with all this he is so afraid he shivers and shakes if the Leopard's name is even mentioned and he moans to be free and yet does not make a stir of his hand and every year he pays out more to the Leopard to keep him off.' So this vendor told me and when I had eaten the pork and saw he was in no mind to give me more even if I paid for one more, I went on and I talked with a beggar who sat picking the lice out of his garments in a sunny spot between two walls. He was a wise old

165

man, too, who begged all his life in the streets of that town. He was the cleverest old man and he bit off the head of every louse he pinched and he crunched them. He was well fed, I swear, with all the lice he had! And he said when we had talked of many things that the magistrate this year seemed more of a mind to do something because those higher had heard how he let a robber rule in his regions and there were many who craved his place and they are bringing an accusation against him at the higher court that he does not do his duty and if he must come down there are a dozen who will strive for his place, because these regions are so good and full of revenue. And the people grieve over this, too, for they say, 'Well, we have fed this old wolf and he is not so greedy as he was and if a new one comes in ravenous he must be fed from the very start again.'"

Thus Wang the Tiger let his men talk as they would and they did as ignorant men will, telling all they heard and guffawing and making merry, for they were full of high hopes and they had faith in their captain, and everyone was fed and pleased with the land and with the hamlets they had passed through. For although the people had to feed these two, the Leopard and the magistrate, still they had enough left to feed themselves well enough, too, for it was such a goodly land and much was left them. And Wang the Tiger let them talk, and if much they said was no worth, still they often let fall something he wanted to know and he could sift the wheat from the chaff, for he was much wiser than they.

As this fellow ceased his piping, Wang the Tiger laid hold on the last thing he had said, that the magistrate feared lest he lose his place and he thought deeply on this, and it seemed to him that here was the secret of the whole venture, and through this weak old man he might seize the power over these lands. The more he listened to his men the more sure he grew that the Leopard was not so strong as he had thought, and after a time he made up his mind that he would send a spy to the very strongholds of the robbers' lair and see what men were there and all the Leopard had for strength.

He looked about his men as they sat that night at their evening meal, sitting on their haunches and every man with a roll of hard bread to gnaw and a bowl of grain gruel to sup, and for a time he could not decide which of them to send and none seemed clever and wise enough. Then his eye fell on his nephew, the lad he kept near him, and he was at this instant gorging himself, his cheeks puffed and full with food. Wang the Tiger did but walk away to his own room and the lad followed him instantly as it was his duty to do, and Wang the Tiger bade him close the door and stand to hear what he said, and he said,

"Are you brave enough for a certain thing I shall tell you?"

And the lad said sturdily, still chewing his great mouthful, "Try me, my uncle, and see!"

And Wang the Tiger said, "I will try you. You are to take a little sling such as lads use to kill birds and you are to go to that double-crested mountain and go about evening time and pretend you have lost your way and are afraid of the wild beasts on the mountain, and you are to go crying at the gates of the lair. When they let you in then say you are a farmer's son from the valley beyond and you came up the mountain to look for birds and you did not see how swiftly the night came down and you are lost and beg a night's shelter from this temple. If they will not let you stay then beg them at least for a guide to the pass and use your eyes—see everything and see how many men there are and how many guns and what the Leopard is like and tell me everything. Can you be so brave as this?"

Wang the Tiger fixed his two black eyes on the youth and

167

he saw the lad's ruddy face turn pale so that the pocks stood out like scars on the skin, but he spoke up well enough and he said, although somewhat breathless,

"I can do it."

"I have never asked you anything," said Wang the Tiger sternly, "but perhaps your clownishness can be of some use now. If you are lost and do not use your wits or if you betray yourself it is your own fault. But you have that merry, silly face and I know you look more simple than you are, and so I have chosen you. But play the part of a simple witless lad and you are safe enough. If you are caught—can you be brave enough to die and be silent?"

Then the good red came surging back into the boy's face and he stood there sturdy and strong in his coarse clothes of blue cotton, and he said,

"Try me, my captain!"

Then Wang the Tiger was pleased with him and he said, "Brave lad! It is the test and if you do well you are worthy to move higher." And he smiled a little as he stared at the boy and his heart that so seldom moved at anything except his gusts of anger now moved a little toward this boy, yet not for the boy's sake either for he did not love him, but it moved with some vague yearning and he wished again he might have a son of his own; not like this lad, either, but a strong, true, grave son of his own.

So he bade the boy put on such clothes as a farmer's son wears and girdle a towel about his waist and he had him put on old worn shoes on his bare feet, for he had a long way to go and rough rocks to clamber over. The lad made a little sling then such as all boys have and made out of the small forked branch of a tree and when it was made he ran lightly down the mountainside and he disappeared into the woods.

Then during the two days he was gone Wang the Tiger

ordered his men as he planned he would and he apportioned out the work to them all so that none could be idle and mischievous. He sent his trusty men out into the countryside to buy food and he sent them separately and they bought meat and grains in small quantities so that none might suspect they bought for a hundred men.

When the evening of the second day was come Wang the Tiger went out and he looked down the rocky steps to see if the lad was come. Deep in his heart he feared for the lad and when he thought of him perhaps cruelly dead he found some strange compassion and remorse in his heart and as night came on and the new moon rose he looked toward the Double Dragon Mountain and he thought to himself,

"I should have sent a man I could spare, perhaps, and not my own brother's son. If he is cruelly dead, how shall I meet my brother? Yet I could only trust my own blood, too."

He watched on after his men slept and the moon came clear of the mountains and swung high in the heavens, but still the lad did not come. At last the night wind grew very chill and Wang the Tiger went in and his heart was heavy because he found what he had not known before, that he would miss the lad a little if he never came back, because he had such merry tricky ways and he could not be angered.

But in the small late hours of the night as he lay awake he heard a little beating on the gate and he rose himself and in haste and he went out. There the lad was when Wang the Tiger had drawn away the wooden bar, and he looked very weary and spent but still good humored. He came limping in and his trousers were torn from his thigh and blood had streamed down his leg and dried. But he was still in high humor.

"I am back, Uncle," he cried in a spent small voice, and

169

Wang the Tiger laughed suddenly and silently in the way he had if he were truly pleased and he said roughly,

"What have you done to your thigh?"

But the lad answered lightly, "It is nothing."

Then Wang the Tiger made one of the few jokes he ever made in his life, because he was so pleased, and he said,

"I hope the Leopard did not claw it!"

The lad laughed aloud at this for he knew his uncle meant it for laughter, and he sat down on the step into the temple and he said,

"No, he did not. I fell upon a briary tree, for the moss is damp with dew and slippery, and the tree scratched me like this. I am starving, Uncle!"

"Come and eat then," said Wang the Tiger, "eat and drink and sleep before I hear your tale."

And he told the lad to come into the hall and sit down and he roared out for a soldier to bring food and drink for the once to serve this lad. But the noise of it woke this man and that and one after the other waked and they came crowding into the court lit by the light of the high moon and they all wanted to hear what the lad had seen. Then Wang the Tiger, seeing how after the lad had eaten and drunk, that he was so important and excited with the success of his venture that he was far from sleep, and seeing that dawn was now near, he said,

"Tell it all now, then, and afterwards go to your sleep."

So the boy sat on the altar before the Buddha whose face was covered and he said,

"Well, and I went and I went, and that mountain is twice as high as this one, Uncle, and the lair is in a valley round as a bowl at the top, and I wish we could have it for ours when we take the region. They have houses and everything there like a little village. And I did what you said, Uncle. I went

crying and limping to the gates at night with my dead birds
in my bosom, and some of the birds on that mountain are the
strangest, brightest hue. One I struck was bright yellow all
over like gold and I have it yet, it was so pretty—" and as he
spoke he drew out of his bosom a yellow bird and it hung in
his hand soft and dead and like a handful of limp gold there.
Wang the Tiger was in all haste to hear the lad's tale and he
chafed at this childishness of a dead bird, but he restrained
himself and let the lad tell his tale in his own way, and so the
lad went on and he laid his bird carefully on the altar beside
him and he looked from one face to another of the men who
listened to him, and beside him flared the torch Wang the
Tiger had caused to be lit and thrust into the ashes of the incense urn on that altar, and the lad said,

"Well, and when they heard the beating on the gate they
came from within and first they opened a very narrow crack
and peered to see who it was. And I cried piteously and said,
'I am far from my home—I have wandered too far and the
night has come down on me and I am afraid of the beasts of
the wood and let me come into this temple!' Then the one
who opened shut the gate again and he ran and asked someone and I cried on and moaned as piteously as I could," and
here the lad moaned to show them all what he did and
all the men roared with laughter and admired him and here
and there one called out,

"The little monkey—the little pocked devil!"

The lad grinned all over his pocked face with delight and
he told on and he said,

"They let me in at last and I was so simple as I could be and
after I had eaten wheaten bread and a bowl of gruel I pretended to be frightened and to know where I was and I began
to cry, 'I want to go to my home. I am afraid here because
you are the robbers and I am afraid of the Leopard!' and I

ran to the gate and wanted to be let out and I said, 'I would liefer be among wild beasts after all!'

"Then they all laughed because I was so simple and they comforted me and said, 'Do you think we will hurt a lad? Wait until morning and you may go your way in peace.' So I ceased my shivering and crying after a while and I pretended to be more at ease and they asked me where I had come from and I told them the name of a village I had heard was on the other side of the mountain. Then they asked me what I had heard about them and I said I had heard they were very heroic, fearless men and their leader not a man, but a man's body with a leopard's head on it, and I said, 'I would like to see him, but I would be afraid, too, to see such a sight.' They all laughed at me, then, and one said, 'Come and I will show you him,' and he led me to a window and I looked in out of the darkness and there were torches burning inside, and there the chief sat. He is truly a curious and monstrous fellow, Uncle, and his head is wide at the top and slopes at the brow so that he does look like a leopard, and he sat drinking with a young woman. She was very fierce, too, and still she was pretty, but fierce, and they drank together from a jug of wine. First he drank and then she drank."

"How many men were there in that place and what their guns?" asked Wang the Tiger.

"Oh, many men, Uncle," said the lad earnestly. "Three times our number of fighting men and many serving men and there are women and there are little children running every-where and some lads like me. I asked one of them who his father was and he said he did not know because they had no separate fathers there and they only knew their mothers but not their fathers. And that is a strange thing, too. All the fight-ing men have guns but the serving men have only sickles and knives and such homely things. But at the head of the cliffs about the lair they have great heaps of round rocks piled to roll down upon any who attack them, and there is only one pass into that lair, for there are cliffs everywhere about it and guards always at the pass. Only the guard slept when I came by and I crept past him. He slept so that I might have taken his gun for it lay there on the rock beside him and he snored so that I might have taken it. But I did not, though I was tempted, for they might have thought I was not what I seemed."

"Did the fighting men seem large and brave?" asked Wang the Tiger again.

"Brave enough," replied the lad. "Some are big and some small, but they talked among themselves after they had eaten and they paid no heed to me for I stayed with the lads after a while, and I heard them complain against the Leopard because he would not divide the spoils according to their law, and he kept so much for himself and he was greedy with all the pretty women and he would not let the other men have them until he was tired of them. He did not share as brothers should share, they said, and he held himself too high, although he was born a common fellow, and he cannot read and write, and they are weary of his highness."

Now this pleased Wang the Tiger greatly when he heard it and he mused on as the lad told his story of this and that and what he had to eat and how clever he was and Wang the Tiger mused and planned, and after a while he saw that the lad had told all and only repeated his words and searched his brain for a last thing so that he might keep the attention and the admiration of the men as long as he could. Then Wang the Tiger rose and he commended the lad and bade him go to sleep now and he told the men to be at their tasks for it was dawn, and the torch was burned down and its flickering flame pale in the light of the rising sun.

He went into his room, then, and he called his trusty men to him and he said,

"I have mused and planned and I believe I can do this thing without losing a life or a gun, and we must avoid battle, since they are so many more than we are in that lair. The thing to do when one kills a centipede is to crush its head and then its hundred legs are in confusion and they run hither and thither against each other and they are harmless. We will kill the poisonous head of this robber band thus."

The men stared astounded at such boldness and the Pig Butcher said in his loud coarse way,

"Captain, it sounds well, but you must first catch the centipede before you can cut off its head!"

"So shall I," returned Wang the Tiger, "and here is my plan. You are to help me. We are to garb ourselves very fine and bravely as heroes do, and we will go to the magistrate of this region and say we are braves and wandering soldiers and that we seek for service under him, secret service as a private guard, and we will give as our pledge that we will kill the Leopard for him. He is anxious now for his seat and he will be eager for our help. Here is the plan. I will tell him he is to pretend truce with the robbers and invite the Leopard and the next to him to a mighty feast. Then when the moment comes, and he can mark it by a wine cup dropped from his hand and shattered, you and I will rush from where we are hidden and fall upon the robbers and kill them. I will have our men scattered through the town secretly everywhere and they shall fall upon such of the smaller robbers as will not come to my banner. So we will kill this centipede's head and it is not a thing hard to do."

Now all of them saw this thing was feasible and they were struck with admiration and they agreed heartily to it. After they had talked a little more of how it would be managed,

Wang the Tiger dismissed them and he called his men into the temple hall. He sent his trusty men to see that the priests were not near where they could hear him and then he told his gathered men what his plan was. When they heard it they shouted loudly,

"Good! Good! Ha, the Black-browed Tiger!"

And Wang the Tiger heard them as he stood there beneath the veiled god and although he said nothing and he was very proud and silent and aloof, yet there surged up in him such a deep pleasure in his power that he lowered his eyes and stood there grave among his men. When they were still once more and waited to hear what else he might tell them, he said,

"You are to eat and drink well, and then garb yourselves as commonly as you can, but still as soldiers, and take your guns and scatter yourselves through the city only not too far from the magistrate's court. When I send out my shrill whistle you are to come. But wait the number of days until I call." And he turned to his trusty harelipped man and he said, "Pay every man five pieces of silver for wine and lodging and the food he needs."

This was done and every man was content. Then Wang the Tiger called his three trusty men to him and they dressed themselves bravely and concealed short swords in their garments and they took up their guns and they all went away together.

As for the priests, they rejoiced very much to see these wild fellows go. But when Wang the Tiger saw them rejoicing he said,

"Do not rejoice too soon, for we may come back. But if we can find a better place we will not." He paid them well, nevertheless, and above what he owed he gave them a sum and he said to the abbot, "Mend your roofs and repair your house and buy yourselves each a new robe."

175

The priests were overjoyed at such generosity and the old abbot was somewhat ashamed and he said,

"You are a good man after all, and I shall pray before the gods for you and how else can I reward you?"

To this Wang the Tiger answered, "No, do not trouble yourself with gods, for I have never had faith in them very much. But if in after days you hear of one called the Tiger, then speak well of him and say the Tiger treated you well."

The old abbot stared and stammered in a daze and he said he would, he would! And he held the silver clasped preciously against his bosom in his two hands.

XIII

STRAIGHT to the city did Wang the Tiger lead his trusty men and when they were come to it then straight to the gates of the magistrate's court they went. When Wang the Tiger was come to the gate he said boldly to the guards that leaned idly against the stone lions there,

"Let me in, for I have something private to say to the magistrate."

Now the guard at the gate demurred, for Wang the Tiger did not show any silver at all, and when Wang the Tiger saw the man's unwillingness he shouted once and his trusty men leaped forward and pointed their guns at the man's breast. He turned green-skinned and fell back and so they passed through, making their shoes clatter upon the stones of the court. There were those idling about the gates who had seen what happened and not one dared to move against them. Then Wang the Tiger cried roughly and fiercely and he drew his black brows down over his eyes,

"Where is the magistrate?"

But not a man moved and when Wang the Tiger saw he grew suddenly angry and he took his gun and pricked the man nearest him in the belly, and the man leaped in terror and cried out,

"I will take you to him—I will take you to him!" And he ran pattering ahead, and Wang the Tiger laughed silently to see his terror.

So they followed him and they passed through court after court. But Wang the Tiger did not look east or west. He kept his face straight and furious and his trusty men did the same thing as much as they could. At last they came to an innermost court, very beautiful and set out with a pool and a terrace of peonies and some old pine trees. But the lattices of the rooms upon it were drawn down and there was silence everywhere. The man who led them halted on the threshold and coughed and a servant came then to the lattice and he said,

"What do you wish? Our lord sleeps."

But Wang the Tiger shouted out loudly, and his voice seemed to crash about him in that quiet court,

"Wake him, then, for I have something of greatest importance to tell him. He must wake, for it concerns his very seat!"

The servant stared at them uncertainly, but he saw how full of authority was Wang the Tiger's look, and he surmised these men must be messengers from some higher court. He went in then and shook the sleeping old magistrate and the old man woke out of his dream and he rose and washed himself and put on his robes and he went and sat down in his hall and he told the servant to bring them in. Then Wang the Tiger went in boldly and loudly and he made a proper obeisance before the old magistrate, but still he did not bow too deeply nor full of reverence.

The old magistrate was full of terror at the fierceness of

177

these men before him and he rose in haste and invited them to be seated and he had cakes and wine and fruits brought. And he spoke the usual courteous words that are spoken to a guest, and Wang the Tiger returned the scantest courtesy that he could. At last when these rites were over he said plainly,

"We have heard from those above that you, most honorable, are oppressed by robber bands and we are come to offer our good arms and our skill to help you be rid of them."

Now all this time the old magistrate had been wondering and trembling and when he heard this he said in his cracked and quavering voice,

"It is true I am so plagued, and I am not a man of arms myself, but a scholar, and I do not know how to deal with such men. It is true I have a general I hire, but he is paid by the state so much whatever he does, and he does not like a battle, either, and the people of this region are so wilful and foolish that in a battle we do not know whether or not they would take the side of the robbers against the state even, they are so easily angered by a little rightful tax. But who are you, and what your honored surnames, and where the place where your ancestors resided?"

But Wang the Tiger said no more than this, "We are wandering braves, and we offer our arms where they are needed. We have heard this land is ridden by a pest of robbers and we have a plan, if you will hire us."

Now whether or not the old magistrate would in common times have listened to strangers like this none can tell, but it was true that at this time he was very fearful lest his living be taken from him and he had no son and he could not at his age hope for another living. He had an old wife and a hundred lesser relatives of one sort and another all dependent on him and his place, and in his helpless age his enemies grew strong and greedy, and so he grasped at anything that might

178

deliver him out of his troubles. He lent his ear now, having sent away his servants, except a few for guard, and Wang the Tiger told his plan, and when he had heard it he seized eagerly upon it. There was only one thing he feared and it was that if they failed and did not kill the Leopard, the robbers would take very bitter revenge. But when Wang the Tiger saw what the old man feared he said carelessly,

"I can kill a leopard as easily as a cat, and I can cut off his head and let the blood drip, and my hand will not falter. I swear it!"

And the old magistrate mused and thought how old he was and how his own soldiers were weak and cowardly and it seemed to him there was no other chance for him but this. And he said,

"I see no other way."

Then he called his servants back and he bade them bring meats and wines and prepare a feast and he treated Wang the Tiger and his trusty men as honored guests. Wang the Tiger waited then and he planned with the old magistrate and they laid every part of their plan very well, and as they planned they did in the next few days.

The old magistrate sent emissaries to the robbers' lair and he told them to say he was growing old and he was leaving his post and another would come to take his place. But before he left he wished to make sure that no enmity stayed after him and he wished the Leopard and his chiefs would come and dine and feast with them and he would recommend them to the new magistrate. When the robbers heard this they were wary, but Wang the Tiger had thought of this, also, and he told the magistrate to spread rumors everywhere that he was going away. The robbers asked among the common people, therefore, and they heard the same story. So they believed it, then, and they felt it would be a good thing if the new magistrate could be influenced in their favor and fear them and pay the sums they demanded and it would spare them battle. They accepted the truce the old magistrate held out to them, and they sent word they would come upon a certain night when the moon was dark.

Now it happened that on that day rains fell and the night was dark and full of mists and winds, but the robbers held to their word and they came in their best robes and with their weapons sharp and clean and bright, and every man held his sword drawn and glittering in his hand. The courts were filled with the guard they brought and some stood out in the streets about the gates to guard against treachery. But the old magistrate did his part very well, and if his withered old knees shook in his robes, still he kept his face peaceful and his voice courteous, and he caused all weapons among his own men to be put aside, and when the robbers saw no weapons except their own they were more at ease.

The old magistrate had caused the best sort of feast to be prepared by his own cooks and this feast was to be spread forth for the chiefs in the innermost hall but the robber guards were to be fed in the courts. Now when all was ready the old magistrate led the chiefs to the hall of feasting, and he assigned the seat of honor to the Leopard, and after many refusals and bows of courtesy the Leopard took it, and the old magistrate sat in the host's seat. But he had taken care before to have it near a door, for he planned when the moment came for him to throw down his wine bowl as a signal that he would escape and hide until all was over.

So the feast began, and at first the Leopard drank cautiously and glowered if any of his chiefs drank too easily. But the wine was very good, the best good wine of all that region, and the meats that were brought in were cunningly seasoned to make men thirsty, and they were such meats as

the robbers had never tasted who knew only their rough coarse
fare. Such hot and delicate dishes they had not dreamed of,
for they were from birth but coarse fellows and unused to
any dainties. At last their reserve gave way and they ate and
drank fully and recklessly, and so their guards did also in the
courts, and the more easily they, since they were not even so
wise as their chiefs.

Now Wang the Tiger and his trusty men watched from a
curtain round a latticed window near the door through which
they were to charge. Every man held his sword drawn and
ready and they listened for the crash of the porcelain wine
bowl which was to be their sign. There came a moment when
the feast had lasted three hours or more, and it was a moment when the wine flowed at its freest, and the servants
bustled here and there and the robbers were full of meat and
wine and heavy with all they had in their bellies. Suddenly
the old magistrate began to tremble and his face turned ashy
and he faltered out,

"The strangest pain has struck my heart!"

He lifted his wine bowl in all haste but his hand shook so
that the delicate thing seemed to shiver out of his hand and
fell upon the tiles and he staggered up and out of the door.

Then before they could draw a breath in surprise, Wang the
Tiger blew his whistle and he shouted once to his men and
they charged through the door upon the robber chiefs and
each trusty man sprang upon the one whom Wang the Tiger
had already appointed to him. But the Leopard Wang the
Tiger kept for himself to kill.

Now the servants had been told that when they heard the
shout they were to bar every door, and when the Leopard saw
this he leaped to his feet and dashed to the door through which
the old magistrate had staggered. But Wang the Tiger sprang
upon him and pinned his arms, and the Leopard had but a

short sword he had plucked as he leaped, and not his own sword, and he was helpless. Each man thus fell upon his enemy and the room was full of cries and curses and struggling men and no trusty man looked to see what any other did, until he had killed the one appointed to him. But some robbers were easily killed because they were fumbling and drunken, and as each trusty man killed his enemy he went to Wang the Tiger to see how he did and to help him.

Now the Leopard was no mean enemy and although he was half drunken he was so swift with his flying feet and he could kick and fence so well that Wang the Tiger could not end him with a single sword thrust. But he would not have help for he wanted this glory and he struggled with the Leopard. And indeed when he saw how bravely this man fought and how desperately with only the poor weapon he had snatched, Wang the Tiger was moved to admiration, as a brave man is even against a foe if he be brave also, and he was sorry he must kill the man. But still he must, and so he drove the Leopard into a corner with his flying sword, and the man was too full fed and too drunken to do his best. Moreover, it was hopeless for the Leopard who had taught himself all he knew, and Wang the Tiger had been taught in an army and he knew the skill of weapons and every sort of feint and posture. The moment came then when the Leopard could not defend himself quickly enough and Wang the Tiger drove his sword into the man's vitals and twisted it strongly once and blood and water rushed out. But as the Leopard sank and died he gave Wang the Tiger such a look that Wang the Tiger never did forget it his whole life long it was so wild and fierce. And the man did indeed look like a leopard, for his eyes were not black as are the eyes of common mortals, but they were pale and yellow as amber. When Wang the Tiger saw him still at last and lying dead and his yellow eyes staring he said to himself that this was a true Leopard, for besides his eyes, his head was wide at the top and sloped back in the strangest, beast-like way. The trusty men gathered then to praise their captain, but Wang the Tiger held his bloody sword, forgetful of it, and he stared down at the dead man still, and he said sorrowfully,

"I wish I need not have killed him, for he was a fierce, brave man and he had the look of a hero in his eyes."

But even as he stood and looked sadly at what he had had to do, the Pig Butcher shouted out that the Leopard's heart was not yet cold, and before any knew what he was about he had stretched out his hand and taken a bowl from the table and with the swift delicate skill that was lodged so curiously in his coarse hand he cut a stroke into the Leopard's left breast and he pinched the ribs together and the Leopard's heart leaped out of the cleft and the Pig Butcher caught it in the bowl. It was true the heart was not cold and it quivered a time or two there in the bowl and the Pig Butcher stretched out the bowl in his hand to Wang the Tiger and he called out in a loud, merry way,

"Take it and eat it, my captain, for from old times it has been said the heart of a brave foe eaten warm makes one's own heart twice as brave!"

But Wang the Tiger would not. He turned away and he said, haughtily,

"I do not need it." And his eye fell on the floor near the chair where the Leopard had sat to feast and he saw the Leopard's sword glittering there. He went and picked it up. It was a fine steel sword such as cannot be made this day, so keen that it could cut through a bolt of silk and so cold it could divide a cloud in two. Wang the Tiger tried it upon the robe of a robber who lay dead there and it melted through to the man's bone even before he pressed it at all. And Wang the Tiger said,

"This sword alone will I take for my share. I have never seen a sword like this."

Just then he heard a gagging noise and it was his pocked lad who had stood staring at the Pig Butcher, and he was suddenly sick and vomited at what he saw. And Wang the Tiger hearing it said kindly, for he knew it was the first time the lad had seen men killed,

"You have done well not to be sick before this. Go out into the cool court."

But the lad would not, and he stood his ground sturdily and Wang the Tiger was pleased at this and he said,

"If I am Tiger, you are fit to be a Tiger's cub, I swear!"

And the lad was so pleased he grinned, and his teeth shone out of his white sick face.

When Wang the Tiger had thus done what he promised he would he went out into the courts to see what his men had done with the lesser robbers. It was a cloudy dark night, and the shapes of his men were but a little more solid and dark than the night. They waited and he commanded that torches be lit, and when they were flaring he saw that only a few men lay dead and he was pleased, for he had commanded that men were not to be wantonly killed and that they were to have the chance to choose if they would change their banner or not, if they were brave.

But Wang the Tiger's work was not done yet. He was determined to storm the lair now that it was weakest and before the robbers who were left had any time to reinforce themselves. He did not stay even to see the old magistrate, but he sent word saying, "I will not claim a reward until I have stamped out this nest of snakes." And he called to his men

184

and they went through the dark night across the fields to the Double Dragon Mountain.

Now Wang the Tiger's men did not follow him very willingly for they had fought already this night and the march was a good three miles or so and they must perhaps fight again and many of them had hoped to be allowed to loot in the city as a reward for their battle. They complained to him then saying,

"We fought for you and we risked our lives and you have not let us take any booty either. We have never served under so hard a master for we have never heard that soldiers must fight and have no booty; no, and not so much as touch a maid, either, and we have held ourselves off until we fought for you, and still you give us no freedom."

At first Wang the Tiger would not answer this but he could not bear it when he heard several of them muttering together and he knew he must be cruel and hard or they would betray him. So he turned on them and slashed his fine sword whistling through the air and he roared at them,

"I have killed the Leopard and I will kill any and all of you and care nothing. Do you have no wisdom at all? Can we despoil the very place which we hope to be ours and turn the people against us with hatred the very first night? No more of these cursed words! When we come to the lair you may loot anything and take it all, except that you are not to force a woman against her will."

Then his men were cowed and one said timidly, "But, captain, we were only joking." And another said, half wondering, "But, captain, it was not I who complained, and if we do loot the lair where are we to live, for I thought we were to have the lair."

Then Wang the Tiger answered sullenly, for he was still angry,

"We are no robber band and I am no common robber chief. I have a better plan if you will but trust me and not be fools. That lair shall be burned to the ground and the curse of those robbers shall pass from this countryside, so that men need fear them no more."

Then his men were more astonished than ever, even his trusty men, and they said, one speaking for all,

"But what shall we be, then?"

"We shall be men of battle, but not robbers," answered Wang the Tiger very harshly. "We will have no lair. We shall live in the city and in the magistrate's own courts and we shall be his private army and we need fear no one for we shall be under the name of the state."

Then the men fell silent in very awe of the cleverness of this leader of theirs, and their evil humor passed from them like a wind. They laughed aloud and they trusted to him, and they mounted the steps eagerly that led to the pass to the lair, and about them the fogs wreathed and curled in those mountains, and their torches smoked in the cold mists.

They came suddenly to the mouth of the pass and a guard was there so astonished he could not run, and one of the men, being very merry, ran him through with his sword before he could speak. Wang the Tiger saw this but he did not reprove his man for once, because it was but one he killed, and it is true that a captain cannot hold ignorant and wild men too closely in check, lest they turn and rend him. So he let the man lie dead and they went on to the gates of the lair.

Now this lair was indeed like a village and it had a wall of rock hewn out of the mountain and welded together with clay and lime so that it was very strong and there were great iron-bound gates set into the wall. Wang the Tiger beat upon those gates, but they were locked fast and strong, and no answer came. When he beat again and still no answer came, he knew that those within had heard of what had befallen their leader, and doubtless some of the robbers had run back and warned the others, and either they had fled from the lair or they had entrenched themselves within the houses and prepared for attack.

Then Wang the Tiger bade his men prepare fresh torches out of the dried autumn grass that was about the lair and they set fire to these torches of twisted grass and they burned a hole in the wooden part of one of the gates, and when the hole was big enough one slipped through it and unbarred the gates swiftly. They all went in then, and Wang the Tiger led the way.

But the lair was as still as death. Wang the Tiger stood to listen and there was not a sound. Then he gave the command that every man was to blow his torch to flame and the houses were to be set on fire. Every man ran to the task and they yelled and screeched as the thatched roofs of the houses caught fire and as the whole lair began to burn suddenly people began to run out of the houses as ants will run out of a hill. Men, women, and little children streamed out and they ran cowering here and there and Wang the Tiger's men began to stab them as they ran until Wang the Tiger shouted that they were to be allowed to escape, but that the men might go in and take their goods.

So Wang the Tiger's men rushed into such houses as were not too ablaze and they began to drag out booty of silken pieces and yards of cloth and garments and anything they could carry. Some found gold and silver and some found jars of wine and food and they began to eat and drink gluttonously and some in their eagerness perished in the very flames they themselves had lit. Then Wang the Tiger seeing how childish they were sent his trusty men to see that they did not come to harm and so not many perished.

187

As for Wang the Tiger, he stood apart and watched it all, and he kept his brother's son near him and he would not let the lad loot anything. He said,

"No, lad, we are not robbers and you are my own blood and we do not rob. These are common, ignorant fellows and I must let them have their way once in a time or they will not serve me loyally, and it is better to let them loose here. I must use them for my tools—they are my means to greatness. But you are not like them."

So he kept the lad by him, and it was very well he did, for the strangest thing happened. As Wang the Tiger stood there leaning on his gun and watching the flaming houses that were beginning already to smoke and to smoulder, the lad suddenly gave a great scream. Wang the Tiger whirled and he saw from above a sword descending down upon him. Instantly he lifted his sword up and met it and the blade slipped down the smooth sword and it fell a little on his hand, but so little it was scarcely a wound, and fell to the ground.

But Wang the Tiger leaped into the darkness, swifter than a tiger, and he laid hold on someone and he dragged it out into the light of the fires, and it was a woman. He stood there confounded, holding her by the arm he had caught, and the lad cried out,

"It is the woman I saw drinking with the Leopard!"

But before Wang the Tiger could say a word, the woman had twisted and writhed and turned herself, and when she found he held her fast and beyond her strength to free herself, she threw back her head and she spat full into Wang the Tiger's eyes. Now he had never had such a thing happen to him before and it was such a filthy, hateful thing that he lifted his hand and slapped her upon the cheek as one slaps a wilful child, and his hard hand left the marks of his fingers there purple upon her cheek, and he shouted,

"That for you, you tigress!"

This he said without thinking what he said and she shouted back at him viciously,

"I wish I had killed you, you accursed—I meant to kill you!"

And he said grimly holding her fast still,

"Well I know you did, and if it had not been for my pocked lad here I would have lain dead this instant with my skull cleft!" And he called to some of his men to bring a rope from somewhere and bind her and they bound her to a tree there by the gate until he could know what to do with her.

Now they bound her very tightly and she struggled and chafed and cut her flesh but she could not so much as loosen herself, and as she struggled she cursed them all and especially Wang the Tiger with such curses as are seldom heard anywhere they were so rich and vile. Wang the Tiger stood and watched while the men bound her and when she was safely tied and tight and the men had gone to their pleasure again, he walked back and forth then in front of her and every time he passed he looked at her. Each time he looked more steadfastly and with more wonder, and he saw she was young and that she had a hard, bright, beautiful face, her lips thin and red and her forehead high and smooth and her eyes bright and sharp and angry. It was a face narrow and bright as a fox's face. Yes, it was beautiful, even now when she had it twisted with hate for him every time he passed her and each time he passed she cursed him and spat at him.

But he paid no heed to her. He only stared at her as he went in his silent way and after a time as the night wore on to dawn she grew weary for they had tied her so tightly that she was in much pain and at last she could not bear it. At first she did not curse and only spat, and after a while she suffered so she did not spit either and at last she said, panting and licking her lips,

"Loosen me even a little, for I am in such pain!"

But Wang the Tiger did not heed this, either, and he only smiled hardly, for he thought it was a trick of hers. She begged him thus every time he came near her but he would not answer. At last one time he came past and her head hung down and she was silent. Still he would not go near her, for he would not be spit on again and he thought she feigned sleep or faintness. But when she did not move for several times he passed, he sent the lad to her, and the lad went and took her by the chin and turned her face up, and it was true she had fainted.

Then Wang the Tiger went to her and he looked at her closely, and he saw that she was fairer than he had even seen her to be in the dim and flickering light of dying fires. She was not more than five and twenty, and she did not look a common farmer's daughter or a common woman and he could not but wonder who she was and how she came to be here and where the Leopard had found such a one. He called a soldier then to come and cut her down and he had her trussed still, but more lightly and not hung against a tree. He bade them lay her on the ground and there she lay and she did not come to herself until it was dawn and the sunlight was beginning to creep through the morning mists.

Then at this hour Wang the Tiger called his men and he said,

"The time is up. We have other things to do than this."

His men ceased their quarrelling over booty slowly and they gathered at his call for he made his voice very loud and fierce and he held his gun cocked and ready for any who would not obey him, and he said, when his men were come, "Collect every gun and all the ammunition there is, for these are mine. I claim these as my share."

When his men had done this, Wang the Tiger counted the guns and there were a hundred and twenty guns and a goodly amount of ammunition, too. But some of the guns were old and rusty and of little value, and these Wang the Tiger, because they were of such ancient and clumsy design, kept to one side to throw away as soon as he could find better.

Then in the midst of the ruined and smoking lair his men tied their booty into bundles, some large and some small, and Wang the Tiger counted over the guns they had found and these he gave to the more trustworthy men to guard. At last he turned to the woman who was tied. She had come to herself and she lay on the ground, her eyes open. When Wang the Tiger looked at her she stared back at him angrily and he said to her harshly,

"Who are you and where is your home that I may send you there?"

But she would not answer him one word. She spat at him for answer and her face was like an angry cat's. This enraged Wang the Tiger greatly, so he called out to two of his men,

"Put a pole through her bonds and carry her to the magistrate's court and throw her into the gaol there. Perhaps she will tell then who she is!"

The men obeyed him and they thrust the pole ruthlessly through the ropes and carried the ends of the poles on their shoulders, and she swung there.

As for Wang the Tiger, when all was ready, the sun was clear of the mountain tops and he walked ahead of his men down the pass. From the lair a feeble cloud of smoke still rose, but Wang the Tiger did not turn to look at it once.

Thus they marched along the road through the country to the city once more. Many a man passing this strange throng

191

looked cornerwise out of his eyes, and especially at the woman trussed to the pole, her head hanging down and her fox-like face pale as ashes. Every man wondered, but not one dared to ask of what had happened, lest he be drawn into some desperate brawl or other, and they were afraid and each went about his business and kept his eyes down after he had glanced a time or two. It was full day and the sun was streaming over the fields when at last Wang the Tiger and his men reached the city gates.

But when he was in the darkness of the passage through the city wall his harelipped trusty man came and led him aside behind a tree that stood there by the gate, and he whispered to Wang the Tiger, hissing with the earnestness of what he had to say,

"I have this to say that I must say, my captain. It is better not to have anything to do with this woman. She has a fox's face and fox eyes and women like this are only half human and the other half fox, and they have a very magic wickedness. Let me put my knife in her deeply and so end her!"

Now Wang the Tiger had very often heard the tales of things that women who are half fox will do, but he was so bold and fearless in himself that he laughed loudly now and he said,

"I am afraid of no man and no spirit and this is only a woman!" And he brushed the man away and went to the head of his throng again.

But the harelipped trusty man followed behind him muttering, and he muttered,

"But this is a woman and more evil than a man, and she is a fox and more evil than a woman."

XIV

WHEN Wang the Tiger came into the same courts where the night before he had done such a deed, and his men followed after him with haphazard steps because they were so weary, they found those courts cleaned and all as they had been before. All the dead had been taken away and the blood wiped and washed away with water. Every guard and servant stood in his place, and they were frightened and careful when Wang the Tiger came through the gates, and he came as arrogant as a king and everyone hastened to make obeisance before him.

But he held himself straight and haughty and he strode through the courts and the halls, pride magnificent upon his dark face. Well he knew he held this whole region now in the hollow of his hand. He turned to a guard who stood there and he shouted,

"Take this trussed woman and put her somewhere in the court gaol! Guard her and see that she is fed and not treated ill, for she is my prisoner and when I wish I will decide what her punishment is to be."

He stood and watched then while the men carried her away on the pole. She was exhausted and her face was as white as tallow. Even her lips that had been so red were white now, too, and her eyes were as black as inkstone in her paleness and she gasped for her every breath. But she still could turn those great fierce black eyes to Wang the Tiger and when she saw him watch her she twisted her face in a grimace against him, but her mouth was dry. And Wang the Tiger was astounded, for he had never seen such a woman as this, and he puzzled what he would ever do with her, for she never could be let go free so full of hatred as this, and so strong in her revengefulness.

But he put the matter from him for this while and he went in before the old magistrate. Now the old magistrate had been waiting since before dawn, and he sat there in his full robes and he had ordered foods prepared of the finest kind. When he saw Wang the Tiger come in he was all of a twitter and in great confusion, because though he was grateful for what Wang the Tiger had done, yet he knew such a man would not serve another for nothing, and he dreaded to hear what reward Wang the Tiger would ask, lest it be so great that he was more burdened than he had been by the Leopard.

So he waited in dreadful uncertainty, and when it was announced to him that Wang the Tiger was come and when he saw Wang the Tiger come in with the great measured strides such as a hero uses, the old magistrate was so confused with his fears that he did not know what to do with his hands and feet and without his knowing it they trembled and moved as though they had a life of their own apart from him. But he invited Wang the Tiger to be seated, and Wang the Tiger made the proper courteous replies, and when the rites of courtesy were over and Wang the Tiger had bowed and bowed but not too deeply, either, and the old magistrate had ordered tea and wines and meats to be brought, they sat down at last and they made a little idle talk.

But the moment came when the thing that had been done could not be avoided longer, and looking east and west and gazing every which way except at Wang the Tiger, the old magistrate opened his mouth to speak. Nor did Wang the Tiger help him, for the power was now his, and he knew very well the condition in the old magistrate's heart and he did no more than fix his steadfast eyes on the nervous old man, because he knew he frightened him thus, and the knowledge gave pleasure to Wang the Tiger because of the malice in him. At last the old magistrate began in his hurried feeble old voice, very soft and whispering and low,

"Be sure I never can forget what you did last night and I can never thank you enough that I am rid of the pest under which I have suffered all these years and my old age can be peaceful now. And what shall I say to you who have delivered me, and how shall I reward you, who are more to me than a son? And how reward your noble men? Ask what you will, even to my very seat, and it is yours."

And he waited trembling and biting his forefinger. Wang the Tiger sat calm and waiting until the old magistrate was done and then he replied decently,

"I do not ask anything at all. From my youth I have been against all wicked and evil men, and what I did I did to rid the people from a pest."

Then he sat silent and waited again, and now it was the magistrate's turn and he said,

"You have the heart of a hero and I did not dream there were such as you in these days. But still I cannot close my eyes in peace even when I am dead if I do not give you thanks in some certain way, and so speak and say what will please you best."

Thus they talked back and forth and with each speech spoken in turn and very properly and courteously they came nearer to the point at last, and then Wang the Tiger made it known in winding words that he was minded to open the ranks of his men to all of the Leopard's old followers who wished to change their banner. At this the old magistrate was filled with fright and he grasped the sides of his carved chair and he rose to his feet and said,

"But are you minded to be a robber chief in his place then?"

And to himself he said that if this were so then was he undone indeed, for this strange tall black-browed fellow, who had come to him from nowhere, was fiercer to see than even the Leopard had been and he was more clever. At least the Leopard had been known to all, and it was known how much he would demand; and thinking thus the old magistrate began to groan aloud a little without knowing that he did. But Wang the Tiger spoke out straightly and he said,

"You need not fear. I have no mind to be a robber. My father was an honorable man who owned land and I have my own inheritance from him. I am not poor so that I need to rob for anything. Moreover, my two older brothers are rich and proper men. If I carve out my future way to greatness it will be by my own skill at war and by no such low trickery as robbers use. No, this is my reward and all I ask of you. Let me stay here with my men in your courts and appoint me as your own chief general in your army you have here. I and my men will come as part of your retinue, and I will protect you from robbers and I will protect your people, also. You can feed us and give us certain revenues that are our due, and you can give me the shelter of the name of the state."

Now the old magistrate listened to this in bewilderment and he said feebly,

"But what shall I do with the general I have already? I shall be torn between you, for he will not go down lightly from his post."

To this Wang the Tiger made brave answer,

"Let us fight it out as honorable men do, and if he wins, I will go away and let him have my men and my guns. If I win, he is to go away and leave me his."

Then the magistrate, groaning and sighing, for he was a scholar and a follower of sages, and he loved peace, sent out and called for his general to come in. And after a while the man came, a little pompous round-bellied man who wore war garments of a foreign sort, and he grew a little sparse beard and he brushed his scanty eyebrows up and did his little best to look fierce and brave. He dragged a long sword at his heels as he came in and he came stamping his feet down hard at each step. When he bowed, he bowed from his waist and he tried to be very ferocious.

Then halting and sweating, the old magistrate somehow made known to him what the matter was and Wang the Tiger sat there coldly and he looked away and seemed to think of other things. At last the old magistrate was silent and he hung his head and he wished himself dead and he thought to himself that he would soon be dead between these two, for he had always thought his own general fierce enough since the man had a hot swift little temper of his own, but Wang the Tiger was far swifter and deeper in his anger, as any man could see who looked at that face of his.

Now the little pot-bellied general was angry enough at what he heard and he laid his little fat hand on his sword and made as though he would dart at Wang the Tiger. But Wang the Tiger saw the movement almost before it was made, although at the time he had been staring seemingly into the peony terrace in the court, and he drew his wide lips back from his white teeth and pulled down his heavy black brows and folded his arms across his breast and he stared so heavily at the little general and with such a dire look, that the little man faltered and thought better of what he did and swallowed his anger as best he could. And indeed he was not a fool. He saw his day was over, for he did not dare to measure himself against Wang the Tiger. He said at last to the old magistrate,

"I have thought for a long time that I ought to return to my old father, for I am his only son and he grows very old. But I have never been free to go because my duties here at your honored court have been so arduous and continuous.

197

Besides this filial duty that is mine there is the illness in my belly, which seizes me every now and again. You know of this illness, my lord, and how because of it I have not been able to go as I have so longed to do against those robbers and all these years I have chafed at my inability which Heaven itself put upon me. So now I gladly retire to my old village home to do what I should for my old father and to nurse also my increasing illness."

This he said and he bowed very stiffly and the old magistrate rose and bowed also and he murmured,

"Be sure you shall be well rewarded for all your faithful years."

And the magistrate looked after the little general regretfully as he withdrew and he sighed and he thought to himself that after all he had been a very easy man of war and if he had not put down the robbers still he was not hard to have in the courts except when his little tempers flew up over some small question of meat and drink and these were easily settled. And then the old magistrate stole a look at Wang the Tiger and he was very ill at ease because Wang the Tiger looked young and harsh and very fierce and ill-tempered. But he only said in his peaceable way,

"Now you have the reward you wish. You may have the courts the old general had as soon as he is gone, and you may take the soldiers. But there is one thing more. What shall I say to those above me when it is known I have changed my general, and what even if the old general goes to complain of me?"

But Wang the Tiger was clever and he answered at once, "It will all bring glory to you. Tell them you hired a brave and he put down the robbers and you have retained the brave as a private guard. Then do you force the general—and I will put my force behind yours—to write and ask that he be

198

allowed to retire and he must name me in his place, and so shall the glory be yours, that you hired me and through me you routed the robbers."

Then, although unwillingly, the old magistrate saw this was no mean plan and he began to be somewhat cheered except that he was still afraid of Wang the Tiger and he feared his ruthlessness lest it ever be turned against himself. But Wang the Tiger let him be afraid, for this suited him, and he smiled his cold smile.

Now did Wang the Tiger settle himself into those courts, for the winter was come down out of the north. He was well pleased with all he had done, for his men were fed and clothed and his revenues began to come in and he could buy them winter garments and they were all warm and fed.

When he had arranged everything for them and the deep of the winter drew on and the days passed each other in regular procession, Wang the Tiger bethought himself suddenly one idle day of the woman he had still in the gaol. He smiled to himself harshly when he thought of her and he shouted to the guard at his door,

"Go and fetch that woman out of the gaol I sent there some sixty days or so ago! I had forgot that I have not fixed her punishment and she tried to kill me." Then he laughed silently and said again, "She is tamed by now, I dare swear!"

So he waited in some pleasure and interest to see how tamed she would be. He sat alone in a hall of his own and beside him was a large iron brazier of coals. Outside the snow of deep winter fell heavily and the court was filled with the snow and it hung thickly on every branch and tree, for there was no wind on that day, only a very bitter, silent cold, frozen with the dampness of the falling snow. But Wang the Tiger waited idle and warm beside the brazier of coals, and he was wrapped well in a sheepskin robe, and a tigerskin was thrown across the back of his chair to keep the chill away.

It was nearly an hour before he heard a commotion in the silent court and he looked toward the door. The guard was coming with his prisoner, but he had two other guards to help him. Even so she twisted this way and that and she strained against the ropes that bound her. But the guards forced her into the door and in the struggling the snow swept in with them. When they had her fast at last and standing before Wang the Tiger, the guard said in apology,

"General, forgive me because so long a time has passed before I could obey your command. But we have had to force this young hag every step. She lay naked in her bed in the gaol and we could not go in for decency's sake, for we are respectable men with wives of our own, and so the other women in the gaol had to force her clothes upon her. She bit and scratched and fought against them but at last they had enough on her so that we could go in and tie her and drag her out. She is mad—it must be she is mad. We have never seen a woman like this. There are those in the gaol who say even that she is not a woman but a fox changed into a woman for some evil purpose of the devils."

But the young woman shook back her streaming hair when she heard this. Her hair had been cut short once, but now it was grown nearly to her shoulders. She screamed forth,

"I am not mad unless it be with hate against *him!*" and she cursed and she thrust her chin out at Wang the Tiger and she spat at him and would have spat on him except that he drew back hastily and the guards seeing her purpose jerked her back so that her spittle fell hissing upon the hot coals of the brazier. At this the guard stared and he said again with conviction,

"You see she is mad, my general!"

200

But Wang the Tiger said nothing. He only fastened his eyes on this strange wild creature, and he listened to her speech, for even when she cursed it was not the speech of a common or ignorant woman. He looked at her closely and he saw that although she was slender and now gaunt to thinness, she was still handsome and haughty, and she did not look like a thick country wench. Yet her feet were big and they looked as though they had never been bound, and this was not as it should in those parts for a woman who came from a good family. He could make nothing of her, therefore, with all these contradictions, and he only stared on at her and he watched her fine black brows twisting above her angry eyes and her thin pouting lips drawn back from her smooth white teeth, and as he watched it came to him that she was the most beautiful woman he had ever seen. Yes, even with her face pale and pinched and angry she was beautiful. So at last he said slowly,

"I have never known you at all. Why should you hate me?"

And the woman answered passionately, and she had a clear, piercing voice, "You killed my lord and I will not rest until I have revenged him. Though you kill me I will hold my dead eyes open until I am revenged for him!"

At this the guard was horrified and he lifted his sword and he cried, outraged, "To whom do you speak, vixen?" And he would have smote her across the mouth with the flat of his sword except that Wang the Tiger made a sign that she was not to be touched. Then Wang the Tiger said in his still way,

"Was the Leopard your master?"

And she cried in the same piercing, passionate voice, "Yes!"

Then Wang the Tiger leaned forward indolently and he said quietly and very scornfully,

"I have killed him. Now you have a new master, and it is I."

At this the young woman lunged forward as if she would have fallen upon him and killed him if she could and the two guards struggled with her, and Wang the Tiger watched them. When they had her fast again so she could not move, the sweat poured down her temples and she was gasping and half weeping, but she stood and fixed her furious eyes on Wang the Tiger's face. Then he met her eyes and stared at her and she stared back at him in defiance, and as though she did not fear him and would not look away and as if she had determined to down his look before she lowered her own bold eyes. But Wang the Tiger only stared on indomitably and without any anger visible, and with a mighty and calm patience and for all his depth of anger he had a power of such strong patience if he were not angry.

As for the woman, she stared on for a long time. But at last, although he still stared unmoved, her eyelids fluttered and she gave a cry and turned and she said to the guards,

"Oh, take me away to the gaol again!" And she would not look at him any more.

Then Wang the Tiger, smiling in the mirthless way he had, said to her,

"You see, I said you have a new master."

But she would not answer him anything. She stood suddenly drooping and she parted her lips and panted a little, and at last he told the guards to take her away again and this time she went without any struggle, glad to go away from him.

Then Wang the Tiger was all the more curious to know who she was and he was very curious to know how she came to be in the robbers' lair and he had it in his mind to know her story. So when the guard came back shaking his head and saying, "I have had wild ones in my hand in my day, but not like this tigress," Wang the Tiger said to him,

"Tell the chief of the gaol that I must know who she is and why she was in the lair."

"She will not answer any question," said the guard. "No, she says nothing. The only change in her was that at first she would not eat but now she eats ravenously, yet not as though she were hungry but as though she ate to be strong for a purpose. But she will not tell anyone who she is. The women are curious and they have tried every cunning way to question her but she will not tell. Torture may force it from her, but even then I do not know, for she is so fierce and bitter a thing. Do you order torture, my general?"

Wang the Tiger thought for a while, then and at last he set his teeth together and he said, "If there is no other way, let it be by torture. She is to obey me. But it is not to be torture to her death." And after a while he said again, "And break none of her bones and do not mar her skin."

At the end of the day the guard came to him once more to make report and he said in consternation, "My general, high above me, it is not possible to make that woman say anything so long as we must torture her so gently as to break no bones and not mar her skin. She laughs at us."

Then Wang the Tiger looked at him gloomily and he said, "Let her be for the time then. And give her meats and some wine to eat and to drink." And he put the matter into the recesses of his mind, until he could think what to do with her.

Then while he waited for a thought to come to him, Wang the Tiger sent his trusty harelipped man southward to his old home and he bade the man tell his brothers all that had befallen him and how great his success was and how he had won it and lost but a few men, and how he had entrenched himself in his region. He warned the man, however, saying,

"You are not to boast too much of what I have done, for this small place and this little county seat is but the first step up the high mountain of glory before me, and you must not let my brothers think I am as high as I plan to go, or they will come hanging on me and beg me to foist up this son of theirs or that and I want no more of their sons, no, even though I have not the son of my own I wish I had. Tell them the small measure of my success, and tell it so that they will be encouraged to give me the moneys I need still, for I have five thousand men now to feed and clothe, and they eat like wolves. But tell them I have begun and I shall go on until I have this province in my rule and after that more provinces. There is no boundary to my way."

To all this the trusty man gave his promise, and he went his way south dressed as a poor pilgrim who goes to worship at some distant temple.

As for Wang the Tiger he set himself then to the settling of his men and it was true he had every right to take pride in what he had done. He had established himself honorably and not as a common robber chief and he was established in the magistrate's court and as part of the government of that country. And everywhere by river and lake his fame went forth through that region and everywhere people spoke of the Tiger, and when he opened his lists for anyone to take service under him, as he now did, men flocked to his banners. But he chose them carefully and he rejected the old and unfit and such as looked weak or half blind or imbecile, and he paid off such of the state soldiers as did not seem able or strong, and there were many of these who had been in the army merely to have food to eat. Thus Wang the Tiger gathered to himself a mighty army of nearly eight thousand men, all young and strong and fit for war.

He took the hundred he had in the beginning, except the few who had been killed in the brawl with the robbers or who had been burned in the lair, and these he raised into captains and sergeants over the new men. But when all this was done, Wang the Tiger did not, as many men in his place would have done, sit in idleness and ease to eat and drink. No, he made himself rise early, even in the winter, and he taught and trained his men and he forced them to learn every skill of war and battle that he knew himself, and how to feint and to attack and to ambush, and how to retreat without loss. Everything he could he made up his mind he would teach them, for he had no purpose to stay forever in this small court of a county magistrate. No, his dreams were swelling in him, and he let them grow as great as they would.

XV

Now the two elder brothers of Wang the Tiger had been waiting with hearty impatience to hear how he did with his venture, but each brother showed it in his own way. Wang the Eldest, since his son had hanged himself, pretended to have no more interest in his brother, and he mourned his son whenever he thought of him. His lady did, also, but her mourning found comfort in complaining against her husband and she said, often,

"I said from the first he ought not to go. I said from the first that it was an ill thing for a family like ours to send so good a son for a soldier. It is a low common life, and I said so."

At first Wang the Eldest had been foolish enough to make answer to her and to say,

"Now, lady, I did not know you were unwilling, and it seemed to me you were ready enough, the more because he was to be no common soldier but my brother would raise him as he raised himself."

But this lady had made up her mind as to what she had said, and she cried out vehemently,

"You never do know what I say because your mind is always on something else—some woman or other, I suppose! I said plainly and often that he ought not to go—and what is your brother but a common soldier? If you had listened to me, our son would have been living and well today and he was our best son and framed to be a scholar. But I am never listened to in my own house!"

She sighed and made a piteous face and Wang the Eldest looked east and west and he was very uneasy to have called this storm on himself and he did not answer a word, hoping that the force of her anger would spend itself more quickly thus. The truth was that now her son was dead the lady continually moaned that he had been her best son after all, although when he lived she scolded him too, and found fault with him, and thought her eldest son the best by much. But now the eldest was not good enough for her in anything and so the dead son seemed better. There was that third and hunchbacked one, but she never asked for him after she heard he liked to live with Pear Blossom, as he now did wholly, and she said if anyone spoke of him,

"He is not strong and the country air is good for him."

She sent a little present to Pear Blossom sometimes in lieu of thanks, some small, useless thing or other, a little bowl of flowered pottery or a bit of cheap cloth only partly silk but brave in show or color, such as Pear Blossom never wore. But Pear Blossom always thanked her prettily, whatever the gift, and sent back fresh eggs or some produce of the land, careful always to return something and so owe nothing. Then she took the cloth and gave it to the fool, or she made a gay coat or shoes to please the poor thing, and she gave the pottery bowl to the hunchback if he liked it, or to the farmer's wife who lived there in the earthen house, if she fancied the flowery town stuff more than her own blue and white ware.

As for Wang the Second he waited in his own way to hear what his younger brother did, and he listened secretly here and there and he heard rumors that the robber chief to the north of them had been killed by a new young brave, but he did not know if it were true or not or if the brave were his brother or not. So he waited and saved his money until the trusty man came, and he sold Wang the Tiger's lands when he could do it prudently, and he put the money out at very high interest, and if he turned the money over a time or two more than he told anyone, this he considered his just wage for all the trouble he had for his brother, and he did no injury to his brother thus, for no one else would have done as well as he did for Wang the Tiger.

But on the day when the harelipped trusty man stood upon the threshold, Wang the Second could scarcely wait to hear his tale, and with an unused eagerness upon his face he drew the trusty man into his own room and poured tea out for him, and then the trusty man told what he had to say, and Wang the Second heard it through to the end without a word.

When it was finished, and the trusty man told it exactly and well and he ended as Wang the Tiger had told him to end, saying,

"Your brother and my general says we are not to be hasty and say he has climbed his mountain because this is but his first step and he holds but a small county seat and he dreams of provinces."

Then Wang the Second drew his breath in a little and he asked,

"But do you think he is sure enough so that I can safely risk my own silver on him?"

Then the trusty man answered, "Your brother is a very clever man and many a man would have been content to settle into the robbers' lair and maraud the region and so rise somewhat high. But your brother is too wise for that, knowing that a robber must turn respectable before he can be a king, and so he has the power of state behind him. Yes, although it is only a small magistrate's seat, still it is the state and he is a state's general, and when he goes out to fight with other lords of war and when he finds a cause of quarrel with someone as he will when the spring comes, then he can go out as one with authority and not as rebel."

Such caution as this pleased Wang the Second very much, and so he said with more than usual heartiness, the hour being near to noon,

"Come out and eat and drink with us, if you will bear our common meal," and he took the man with him and set him at their family table.

Then when Wang the Second's wife saw the trusty man she cried a greeting to him in her hearty way and she said,

"What news of my little pocked son?"

The trusty man rose to his feet then and answered that her son was very well and he did well and the general was minded to raise him up, doubtless, for he kept him always about his person. But before he could say a word, the woman shouted that he was to sit and not stand in courtesy. So when he had sat down again he thought to tell them about how the lad had gone to the robbers' lair and how tricky he was and how neatly he had done what he had to do. But he stopped himself, because he knew that women are so strange and their tempers are uncertain, and mothers are the strangest of all, for they see fears and harms about their children where there are no such things. He contented himself with silence, therefore, when he had said enough to please her.

In a few minutes she had forgotten all she asked, for she was busy about many things, and she bustled here and there fetching bowls and setting them out on the table, and she held a babe at her breast as she worked. The child suckled tranquilly, while with her free arm she was zealous in dipping out food to the guest and to her husband and to the clamoring, hungry children who did not eat at the table, but stood at the door or on the street with their bowls and chopsticks, and when their bowls were empty they came running in for fresh rice and vegetables and meats.

When the meal was over and they had finished their tea after they ate, Wang the Second took the trusty man to his elder brother's gate, and there he bade the man wait until he could call his brother out and then they would go to a tea house to talk. But he told the man not to show himself lest the lady see him and they would need to go and hear her talk for a time. And so saying Wang the Second went inside and through a court or two to his elder brother's own rooms, and there he found him lying fast asleep on a couch beside a brazier of red coals, snoring after his noon meal.

But when Wang the Eldest felt his brother's light touch on his arm he started out of his sleep with a snort, and after being dazed for a while he understood what was wanted and he struggled up and drew on the fur robes he had laid aside, and he followed his brother softly so that he would not be heard. No one saw them go out except his pretty concubine who thrust her head out of a door to see who passed, and Wang the Eldest held up his hand as a sign of silence, and she let him go, for if she were timid and fearful of the lady, she was a kind, mild creature, too, and she could lie kindly and she would say she had not seen him, if she were asked.

They went together to the tea house and there the trusty man told his story over again, and Wang the Eldest groaned in his heart that he had not a son to give his younger brother, and he was jealous that his second brother's son did so well. But he kept it to himself for once, and he only spoke well to the man and he agreed to all his brother said in the matter of moneys to be sent back, and he waited until he reached his home again.

Then suddenly it seemed as though his heart overflowed with jealousy and he went and sought out his eldest son. The young man lay in the curtained bed in his own room, and he lay there idle and flushed and reading a loose lascivious tale called *The Three Fair Women,* and he started when he saw his father come in and he hid the book under his robe. But his father did not even see it he was so full of what he had come to say and began in haste,

"Son, do you still wish to go to be with your uncle and rise with him to a high place?"

But the young man had outgrown that moment in his life and now he yawned delicately, and his mouth was as pretty and pink as a girl's when he opened it thus and he looked at his father and smiled idly and he said,

"Was I ever so foolish as to want to go for a soldier?"

"But you will not be a soldier," urged his father anxiously. "You will be from the first much higher than soldier, and next your uncle." Then he lowered his voice, coaxing his son, "Your uncle is a general already and he has established himself by the wisest guile I ever heard of, and the worst is over."

But the young man shook his head wilfully, and Wang the Eldest, half angered and half helpless, looked at his son lying there on his bed. Some truthful sight came to this man at this instant, and he saw his son for what he was, a young man dainty and fastidious and idle, without any single ambition for anything except his pleasure, and his only fear that he was not better dressed and less in fashion than other young men whom he knew. Yes, Wang the Eldest saw his son lying on the silken quilts of his bed, and the young man wore silk to his very skin, and he had satin shoes on his feet and his skin was like a beauty's skin, oiled and perfumed, and his hair was perfumed and smoothed with some foreign oil also. For the young man studied to make his body beautiful in every way, and well nigh he worshipped it for its softness and beauty, and his reward was that there were many who praised him for it among those whom he played with at night in gaming houses and playhouses. Yes, he was a young lord in a rich man's house, as anyone could see, and none would have dreamed that his grandfather was one Wang Lung, a farmer, and a man of the earth. For this one instant did Wang the Eldest see his eldest son, although he was a man muddled and confused with many small things, and he was frightened for his son and he cried out in a high voice very different from his usual rolling tones,

"I am afraid for you, my son! I am afraid you will come to no good end!" Then he cried out more sharply than he ever had to this son of his, "I say you shall go and hew out some sort of a way of life and not grow old here in idle slothful pleasure!" And he wished in a sort of fright, which he did not understand in himself, that they had seized on the moment of the lad's ambition. But it was too late; the moment was gone.

When the young man heard the unwonted sound of his father's voice he cried out half afraid, half petulant, sitting up suddenly in his bed,

"Where is my mother? I will go and ask my mother if she will have me go or not, and I will see if she is so anxious to be rid of me!"

But Wang the Eldest, hearing this, fell back into himself again, and he said hastily and peaceably,

"We-well—let be—you shall do as you please since you are my eldest!"

And the cloud descended upon him again and the moment of clarity was gone. He sighed and thought to himself that it was true that young lords could not be as other common youths were, and he said to himself that it was true his brother's wife was a very common woman, and doubtless his pocked son was little better than a servant to his uncle. So Wang the Eldest consoled himself vaguely and he shuffled as he went out from his son's room. As for the young man, he lay back on his silk-covered pillow again, and he clasped his hands under his head and smiled his indolent smile, and after a while he felt for the book he had hidden and took it out and began to read it ardently once more, for it was a naughty, zestful book that a friend of his had commended to him.

But Wang the Eldest could not forget his vague despondency and it hung on him still so that for the first time his life did not seem so good to him as he thought it was. It was a very sore thing to him that when he had seen the trusty man gone again, his pilgrim's wallet filled with silver and his belt stiff with silver about his waist, and his bundle filled with it so that he could hardly heave the thing to his back, that he could not think of anything Wang the Tiger could do for him yet, and it seemed a sore thing to him and his life very weary because he had no son to whom he could look for glory and he had nothing but this land that he hated and yet did not dare to part with altogether. His lady even saw his despondency and in his extremity he told her some of his trouble, and she had taught him so well that in his secret heart he did believe her wiser than himself, although he would have denied it stoutly if anyone had asked him if he did. But this time she gave him no help, for when he tried to tell her how great his younger brother had become she laughed shrilly and with scorn and she said,

"A general at a small county seat is no great lord of war, my poor old man, and you are silly to be so envious of him! When he is lord of war in the province it will be time enough to tell off our younger son to him, and more likely it will be your smallest son who is only a suckling now at the other's breast!"

So Wang the Eldest sat silent then and for a time he did not go out as zestfully as he had to his pleasure places, and not even talk with his many friends seemed the worth it had before. No, he sat alone and he was not one to sit thus either, for he was a man who liked to be where there were people running to and fro in a commotion of some sort or other, even though it were but household bustle and servants bickering with a vendor and children crying and quarreling and the usual uproar of daily living. He liked even this better than to sit alone.

But now he sat alone because he was wretched and he did not know why he was except that for the first time it came to him that he was not so young as he was once and his age was creeping on him unawares, and it seemed to him he had not found the good in life he might have found and he was not so great as he should have been. Chiefest of all his vague miseries was one not vague, and it was the land he had from his father. It was a curse to him for it was his only livelihood and he must give it some oversight or he would have nothing to eat, he and his children and his wives and servants, and it seemed to him as though there were some vile magic in that land, and it was always seed time and he must go out to it or time to fertilize and he must see to it or it was harvest and he must stand in the hot sun and measure out grain or it was time to collect his rents; and there was all the hateful round of the land, forcing him to labor when he was by nature a man of leisure and a lord. Yes, even though he had an agent, there was some shrewdness in this man, even against his will, that made his gorge rise to think the agent grew rich at his expense, so that although he hated it he dragged himself each season to the place where he could oversee what was done.

He sat now in his own room and now under a tree in the court outside it if the winter sun were warm enough and he groaned to think how he must go out year after year or the robbers who rented his land from him would give him nothing. Yes, they were forever howling, "Ah, we have had floods this year," and "Ah, we have such a drought as never was," or else it was, "This is the year for locusts," and they and his agent had a hundred tricks against him who was their landlord, and for the weariness of his strife with them he blamed and he loathed the land. He longed for the day when Wang the Tiger would be great enough so that his elder brother need no longer go out in heat and cold; he longed for the day when he could say, "I am brother to Wang the Tiger," and it would suffice. Once it had seemed much that men had come to call him Wang the Landlord, for this was his name now, and it had seemed an honorable good name until this moment.

The truth was this that Wang the Landlord found it very hard because all his life so long as his father Wang Lung had lived he had received money freely from him enough to pay for all he needed, and he never labored over its coming. But after the inheritance was divided he labored more than he ever had and yet with all this labor to which he was unaccustomed he had not all the silver he needed, and his sons and wives never seemed to care how he labored.

No, his sons would wear the very best and they must have this fur in the winter and that dainty light fur to line their robes in the spring and autumn and all kinds of silks each in its season, and it was a hardship fit to break their hearts if they must wear a coat a little too long or a little wider in the cut than was this year's fashion, for they feared more than anything the laughter of the young town dandies who were their companions. So with the eldest son, and now the fourth son was learning this also. Although he was but thirteen years old, he must have his little robes cut thus and so and a ring on his finger and his hair scented and oiled too, and a maid to serve him only and a man to take him out; and because he was his mother's darling and she feared for him at the hands of evil spirits, he wore a gold ring in one ear, too, to deceive the gods and make them think him a girl and worthless.

As for his lady, Wang the Landlord could never persuade her that there was less silver in the house than there had once been and if he said when she wanted a sum of him, "But I have not so much to give you and I can only give you fifty pieces now," she would cry out, "I have promised it to the temple for a new roof over a certain god, and if I do not give it I shall lose my dignity. Indeed you have it, for I know you spend money like water on wining and gaming and on all those low women I know you have and I am the only one in this whole house who looks to the things of the soul and to gods. Some day I may have to pray your soul out of hell, and you will be sorry I had not the silver then!"

So Wang the Landlord had somehow to find the silver, although he hated it very much to see his good money going into the hands of the smooth and secret priests whom he hated and did not trust, and of whom he heard certain very evil things. Yet he could never be sure, either, that they had not some knowledge of magic and he could never be sure, although he pretended disbelief in gods as things fit only for women, that there was not some power in them too, and this was another confusion in him.

The truth was that this lady of his was so deep now in her intimacy with gods and temples and all such things that she grew very holy and she spent many hours in going to this god and that, and it gave her the greatest pleasure to pass into a temple gate leaning as a great lady does upon her maids, and as she came in to see the priests of the temple and even the abbot come to her obsequious and bowing and full of flattery and full of talk that she was a favorite of the gods and a lay nun, and very near the Way.

When they talked thus she simpered and smiled and cast her eyes down and deprecated, but before she well knew what she did oftentimes she had promised them this and that and a sum of money more than she really wished to give. But the priests took care to give her full praise and they put her name up in many places as an example to all devout persons, and one temple even presented her with a wooden ensign painted vermilion red and there were gilt letters on it signifying how this lady was so devout and good a follower of the gods. This ensign was hung in a lesser hall of the temple, but where many might see it. After this she was the more proud and holy and devout in her looks, and she studied to sit calmly always and to fold her hands and often she went holding her rosary and muttering the syllables of her prayer while others gossiped or talked idly. Therefore being so holy she was very hard with her husband and she would have what silver she needed to keep up the name she had.

When Wang the Landlord's younger wife saw what the

lady had she wanted her little share, too, not for the gods, although the girl learned to prate of them to please the lady, but still she wanted her silver. And Wang the Landlord could not think what she did with it, because she did not dress herself in fine flowered silks or buy jewels and gold things for her dress and hair. Yet the money went from her quickly, too, and Wang the Landlord did not complain lest the girl go and weep before the lady, and the lady reproach him that since he had taken such an one he ought to pay her something. For these two women liked each other in some strange cool way, and they stood together against their husband if they wanted something for themselves.

One day Wang the Landlord did find out the truth, however, for he saw his younger wife slip out to a side gate and take something from her bosom and give it to one who stood there, and Wang the Landlord peered and he saw the man was her old father. Then was Wang the Landlord very bitter and he thought to himself,

"So I am feeding that old rascal and his family, too!"

And he went into his own room and sat and sighed and was very bitter for a while and he groaned to himself. But it was no use, and he could do nothing for if she chose to give what she had from her husband to her father and not to spend it on sweetmeats and clothing and such things as most women love, she had this right, except that a woman ought to cleave first to the house of her husband. But Wang the Landlord did not feel he could contend with her and he let it pass.

And Wang the Landlord was the more torn in himself, for he could not control his own desires, even though he did now honestly try for the first time in his life when he was nearly fifty years old, to spend less for his love of women. But he had his weakness with him yet, and he could not bear to be thought a niggard among them when his fancy fixed itself.

Besides these two women in his house, he had the singing girl established as a transient wife by common agreement in another part of the city. But she was a pretty leech, and although he had finished with her soon, she held him by her threats of killing herself and of loving him above all the world, and she cried on his bosom and fixed her little sharp fingers into the deep flesh on his neck and she hung to him so that he did not know what to do with her.

With her she had her old mother also, a vile hag, and she in her turn screeched out,

"How can you cast off my daughter who has given you all? How would she live now, seeing that she has not been in a playhouse all these years you have had her and her voice is gone and others have taken her place? No, I will defend her and I will take her case to the magistrate if you cast her off!"

This frightened Wang the Landlord very much, for he feared the laughter of the town against him if they heard all this old woman's ribald talk that she would vent against him in court if she could, so that he fumbled hastily for what silver he had. When the two women saw he was afraid, they plotted and made every opportunity they could for storm and weeping, knowing that when they did, he would pay them in haste. And the strangest thing of all was that with so many troubles, this great fat weak man still could not keep himself free, but must still be overcome with his desires at a feast somewhere and pay a new little singing girl he saw, even though when he came home and was himself on the next day, he groaned at his own folly and cursed his own fulsome heart.

But now, pondering all this during these weeks of his despondency he grew frightened at his own zestlessness, and he did not even care to eat so much as he had, and when he found his appetite for food waning he was frightened lest he die too soon, and he said to himself that he must rid himself of some of his troubles. And he determined that he would sell a good large share of his land and live on the silver, and he thought to himself secretly that he would spend what was his and his sons must care for themselves if there was not enough left for their lifetime. And it seemed to him suddenly that it was a vain thing for a man to stint himself for those who live on after him. He rose wilfully then and he went to his second brother and he said,

"I am not fitted for the cares of a landlord's life, for I am a city man, a man of leisure. No, I cannot with my increasing weight and years go out at seed time and harvest, and if I do one day I shall drop dead with the heat or the cold. I have not lived with common people, either, and they cheat me before I know it and out of all my land and my labor. Now this I ask of you. Act as my agent and sell a good half of my lands for me now and let me have the money as I need it, and what I do not need put out at interest for me, and let me be free of this accursed land. The other half I will keep to leave to my sons. But there is not one of them who will help me with it now, and when I say to my eldest son that he is to go for me sometimes to the land he is always pressed with a meeting with some friend or he has a headache and we shall starve if we continue as we are now. Only the tenants grow rich from the land."

Then Wang the Second looked at this brother of his, and he despised him in his heart, but he said smoothly,

"I am your brother, and I will not take any commission at all for selling it and I will sell it for you to anyone who bids highest for it. But you must say what your lowest price is for each lot."

But Wang the Landlord was very eager to be finished with his land and he said quickly,

"You are my brother and sell it for what you think fair. Shall I not trust my own brother?"

He went away then in high good humor because he was rid of half of his burden and he could go his way for a time and wait for silver to come into his hands as he longed to do again. But he did not tell his lady what he had done, because she might cry out against him that he had given them over into the other's hand, and she would say that if he wished to sell, he ought to sell it himself to some among the many rich men with whom he feasted and with whom he seemed in such deep friendship, and Wang the Landlord did not wish to do this, for in his heart, for all his bluster, he trusted his brother's wit more than he did his own. And now having done this, his heart rose again and he could eat once more, and once more his life seemed good enough to him and he thought to himself there were others more troubled than he, and he was ardent again.

Now Wang the Second grew more content than ever for he had all in his own hands. He planned that he would buy the best of his brother's lands for himself. It was true that he paid a fair price for them, for he was not a dishonest man as men are reckoned, and indeed he told his elder brother that he bought a little of the best land to keep it in the family. But how much of the land he bought Wang the Landlord did not know, for Wang the Second had him sign the deeds when he was somewhat drunken and he did not look to see what name was on it, but being full of the good humor of drunkenness his brother seemed excellent to him and wholly to be trusted. He would not have been willing had he known to see so much of his land pass into Wang the Second's keeping, perhaps, and so Wang the Second made much of the poorer pieces he sold to tenants or to whom it was who wished to buy. And it was true that Wang the Second did sell much land thus. But

Wang Lung had been very wise in his day and he bought far more good land than any other kind, and so when all the business was over Wang the Second had in his own personal possession and for his sons the best and the choicest of all his father's land, for he had so bought the best of his younger brother's inheritance also. And with all this land he planned he would supply much of the grain to his own markets and increase his stores of silver and gold, and he grew powerful in the town and in that region, and men called him Wang the Merchant.

But unless he knew it no one would have dreamed this small meager man was so rich, for Wang the Merchant still ate the plain spare bit of food he always did and he took no new wife into his house as most men will when they are rich, for show if for nothing else, and he wore the same sort of small patterned silk gown of a dark slate grey that he had always worn. In his house they added no new furniture, and in his courts there was no flower nor any waste thing, and what had been there before now was dead, for his wife was thrifty and raised flocks of fowls and these ran in and out of the rooms to pick up bits of food the children dropped, and they ran about the courts and plucked every grass blade and green leaf, so that the courts were bare except for a few old pines, and the earth grew hard and packed.

Nor would Wang the Merchant let his sons be spendthrift nor idle. No, he planned for each one, and each had a few years of schooling to learn to read and write and to count skilfully upon the abacus. But he would not let them stay long enough to be held scholars in any wise, for scholars will not labor at anything, and he planned apprenticeships for them and they were to come into his business. The pocked one he considered his younger brother's, and the next one he planned to make his steward on the land, but the others he apprenticed when their time came and when each was twelve years old.

In the earthen house Pear Blossom lived on with the two children and every day of her life was like the one before it, and she asked no more than that it should be so always. She grieved no more for the land, for if she did not see the elder she saw the younger son of her dead lord come out before harvest time to estimate the growth of grain and to see the seed weighed off and all such things. Yes, and she heard, too, how Wang the Merchant, for all he was a townsman, was sharper as landlord than his brother even, for he knew to a ten catty weight what a field still standing in green grain would give, and his narrow little eyes were always sharp to see if a tenant pressed his foot secretly against the side of a load to weigh it down or if he poured water into the rice or the wheat to make it swell. His years in the grain market had taught him everything that country people do to cheat the merchant and the townsman, for they are enemies by nature. But if Pear Blossom asked whether any ever saw him angry when he found out a trick, the answer always came with unwilling admiration that he was never angry. No, he was only implacable and calm and more clever than any of them, and the nickname he had in that whole countryside was this, "He Who Wins in Every Bargain."

It was a scornful name and full of hatred, and all the country people hated Wang the Merchant very heartily. But he did not care and he was even pleased to know what they called him, and he knew because an angry farm wife shouted it at him once with curses when he saw her sink a great round stone into the heart of a basket of grain about to be weighed, and she had done it when she thought his back was turned.

More than a time or two did a farm woman curse him, for

a bitter-tongued woman is bolder than any man, and if a man were discovered in a trick he looked sullen or sheepish as his nature was, but a woman would curse and she would cry out after him,

"How is it that in one generation you forget how your father and your mother toiled on the land even as we do and they starved too, as we must, when you grind our blood and bones as you do now?"

Wang the Landlord had grown afraid sometimes when the people grew bitter, for he knew the rich may well fear the poor, who seem so patient and humble and who can be so bold and ruthless when they turn to rend whom they hate. But Wang the Merchant feared nothing, and it was nothing to him even when one day Pear Blossom saw him pass and she called to him and came out and said,

"If so be, sir, my lord's son, that you can be a little less exact with the people, I should be glad. They labor very hard and they are poor and like children in ignorance, oftentimes. It goes against my heart to hear the cruel things they say, sometimes, about my lord's sons."

But Wang the Merchant only smiled and went his way. It was nothing to him what any said or did, so long as he had his full profits. His was the power and he feared nothing, for he felt himself secure in his riches.

XVI

Now the winter wore on very long and cold in those parts and in the time of bitter winds and in the fury of wind-driven snows Wang the Tiger could but stay on in the magistrate's courts in the place that was now his and wait for the spring to come. He entrenched himself in his place and he steadily demanded from the magistrate this tax and that for his eight thousand soldiers. Yes, there was even a tax put on all land for his benefit and it was called the tax for the protection of the people by the state soldiery, but this soldiery was really Wang the Tiger's own private army, and he taught them and trained them and made them ready to enlarge his power for him when he saw the moment was come. Every farmer in that whole region paid something on every field he had and he paid it out for Wang the Tiger; and because the robbers were gone and the lair burned and they need not fear the Leopard any more, the common folk were full of praise for Wang the Tiger and they were ready to pay him well, but still they did not know how well this was.

There were other taxes also that Wang the Tiger had the magistrate lay for him, some on shops and markets, and every traveller who came through that town, which was a pass between north and south, paid a tax and every merchant paid a tax on the goods he took back and forth for sale and barter, and so the money poured steadily and secretly into Wang the Tiger's stores. He was sharp enough, too, to see that it did not touch too many hands in passing, knowing that no hand in this world will readily release as much silver as it grasps. He appointed his own trusty men to see to the collecting of it and although these spoke smoothly to all and he commanded them so to speak, yet he gave them the power over anyone they found taking more than his share, and he told each trusty man that he would punish them himself if they failed him. He was safer than most from treachery for everyone feared him for a ruthless man. Yet they knew him to be just, too, and they knew he did not kill any man carelessly or for mere pleasure.

But as Wang the Tiger waited for the winter to be gone

he chafed very much in spite of his success, for this life in the magistrate's courtyards did not suit him. No, and there were none who could be his friends, for he would not bring himself to intimacy with any, knowing that as long as people feared him he could hold his place the more easily among them; besides, he was one who did not by nature love to take part in feasting and friendship, and he lived alone except for his pocked nephew whom he kept near him always lest he need something, and his trusty harelipped man who was his chief guard.

The truth was that now the magistrate was so old and given to his opium pipe, everything ran slackly about him and his courts were filled with cliques and jealousies and crowded with underlings and underlings' relatives who sought an easy way to live. This man turned against that, and there were deep angers and revenges and quarrels continually. But if these were brought to the old magistrate's ears he turned himself to his opium or he thought of something else, for well he knew he could not settle everything, and he lived alone with his old wife in an inner court and he only came out when he must. But he tried to do his state duty still, and every audience day at dawn he rose and put on his official robes and he went into his audience hall and ascended the dais there and sat down in the chair from whence he heard his cases.

He did his poor best, too, for he was a good and kind man at heart, and he supposed he meted out justice to such as came before him there. But he did not know that every suppliant who came before him had paid his way through from the very gateman at the gates, so that any man who had not silver enough for high and low could not hope even to reach that audience hall, and the very councillors who stood in the presence of the magistrate had each received his share. Nor did the old magistrate know he leaned so heavily on these councillors of his. No, for he was old and easily confused and often he did not catch the point of a case and he was ashamed to say he did not, or he dozed somewhat toward the end of the hour, and did not hear what was said, and he was afraid to ask again, lest men think him not able. So he turned naturally to his councillors who never failed to flatter him and when they said, "Ah, this man is evil and that man has the right of it," the old magistrate would agree hastily and say—"It is what I thought—it is what I thought," and when they cried out, "Such an one ought to be well beaten because he is so lawless," the old magistrate would quaver forth, "Yes—yes, let him be beaten!"

Now in these idle days Wang the Tiger often went to the audience hall to see and to hear and to pass the time away, and when he went he sat to one side and his trusty men and his pocked nephew stood about him as a guard. Thus he heard and saw all this injustice. At first he said to himself that he would pay no heed to any of these things, for he was a lord of war and these civil affairs were no business of his, and he would spend his care on his soldiers, seeing that they did not share in the loose, idle life of the courts, and many a time when he saw that which made him angry in the audience hall he went out and was furious with his soldiers and forced them to marches and to practices of war, whatever the winds were that day, and so he relieved his heart of the pressure of its anger.

But he was a man just at heart and when he saw the injustice go on time after time he could not bear it at last, and he grew surcharged with anger against some of the councillors who had the ear of the magistrate, and especially against the chief councillor. Yet he knew it was no use to say anything to the weak old man. But still, when he had sat sometimes

and listened to cases and when he had seen injustice done
a hundred times, he grew so pent in himself that he would
rise and stride away and he muttered to himself many times,

"If spring does not come quickly I shall kill someone against
my will!"

As for the councillors, they did not love him, either, because
he secured so much revenue and they mocked him for a
coarsely bred fellow and one beneath them in polish and
learning.

Now Wang the Tiger's anger burst forth one day in a
sudden way that he himself had not expected, and it began
with a small matter enough, even as a mighty storm will
begin sometimes with only a little wind and a handful of
ragged cloud.

It happened on a certain day before the new year, when
men are out everywhere to collect debts and those who owe
hide as best they may so that they cannot be found until the
first day of the new year when debts cannot be collected from
anyone, that the old magistrate had his last audience day of
the old year and he sat upon his dais. On that day Wang
the Tiger had been very restless because he was so idle. He
would not game because he did not want his soldiers to see
him at it and feel the more free themselves to do it, and he
could not read overmuch because novels and tales weaken
a man, they are so full of dreams and the stuffs of love, and
he was not scholar enough for the old philosophies. Therefore being sleepless also, he rose and went with his guard
and sat awhile in the audience room to see who would come
that day. But in his heart he was pent and impatient for the
spring, and especially because the last ten days had been so
cold and so filled with a downpour of constant rain that his
men cried out against being taken out of their quarters.

There he sat, and it seemed to him that his was the dreariest life, and there was not one soul to care if he lived or died, and so he sat, listless and glowering in his usual place. Presently he saw a certain rich man come in whom he knew, having seen him here before. This man was a usurer of the town, a smooth-faced, fat man, with very small, smooth, yellow hands that he flourished with a sort of evil grace as he spoke, and he continually pushed back his long silken sleeves from his hands before he waved them. Many times Wang the Tiger had watched his hands and seen how small they were and how soft and full and how pointed the finger tips were with their long nails, and he had watched the man's hands when he did not hear what he said, even.

But today the usurer came in with a poor farmer and the farmer was very frightened and ill at ease, and he threw himself before the magistrate with his face to the ground, and remained there speechless, begging for mercy. Then the usurer told his case and it was that he had loaned a sum of money to this farmer, and had accepted his land as security. This was two years ago, and now the money with its interest had mounted above the worth of the land.

"Yet in spite of this," the usurer cried, and he pushed back his silken sleeves and moved his smooth hands and made his voice rich and reproachful, and he was very unctuous, "in spite of this, O honored magistrate, he will not move from his land!" And the man rolled his little eyes around in indignation at this wicked farmer.

But the farmer said nothing at all. He continued to kneel there with his face bent and leaning upon his two hands forked together. At last the old magistrate asked him,

"Why did you borrow and why do you not pay?"

Then the farmer looked up a little and he fixed his eyes on the magistrate's footstool, and he continued to kneel, and he said anxiously,

228

"Sir, I am a very common man and poor, and I do not know how to speak to such as you, honored Sir. I am very common and I have never spoken to one higher than the head in our village, and I do not know how to speak here, and yet I have no one to speak for me, seeing that I am so poor."

Then the old magistrate said kindly enough,

"You need not fear—only speak on."

Then the farmer after opening his lips a time or two soundlessly began to speak, but still he did not lift his eyes at all, and it could be seen that his spare body was shivering in his patched and ragged clothes from which the old wadding stuck forth out of the holes like old sheep's wool. His feet were bare and thrust only into shoes woven out of reeds and these had now fallen from his feet, so that his hard and horny toes rested stiffly upon the damp stone floor. But he did not seem to feel this, and he began in a weak voice and he said,

"Sir, I had a little land from my fathers. It is very poor land and it has never fed us full. But my parents died early and there were only I and my wife, and if we starved we did it and that was all. But she bore a child, a son, and then after years another, a girl. When they were little it was still not so hard. But they grew and we had to wed the son and his wife had a child. Sir, think of it, the land was not enough for my wife and me and now we have these. The girl was long too young to be wed and I had her to feed somehow. Two years ago I had a chance to betroth her to an old man in a village near us, for his wife was dead and he needed one to mend his household. But I had to give her a wedding garment. Sir, I had nothing so I borrowed a little money— only ten pieces of silver, to most men nothing, but to me very much and more than I had. I borrowed it from this usurer.

In less than a year the ten pieces had grown into twenty of its own accord, for I had no more than the ten to spend. Now in two years it is forty. Sir, how can dead silver grow like that? There is only my land. He says go, but where shall I go? Let him come and drive me off, I say. There is nothing else than this."

When the man had finished saying this he remained perfectly silent. Wang the Tiger stared at him and it was the strangest thing that he could not keep his eyes from the man's feet. The farmer's face was drawn and sallow and told of his life and of his never being full fed since he was born. But his feet told the whole tale. There was something eloquent in this man's two bare feet, knotted and gnarled in the toes, and the soles like the dried hide of a water buffalo. Yes, looking at the man's feet Wang the Tiger felt something welling up in him. Nevertheless, he waited to see what the old magistrate would say.

Now this usurer was a man of the town and well known and he had feasted with the magistrate many times and he kept the good will of the court with him because he paid silver to high and low in every case he had and he had many. The magistrate hesitated, therefore, although it could be seen he was somewhat moved, too. At last he turned to his chief councillor, a man near his own age but strong and straight for his years, and his face was smooth and handsome still, although his scanty whiskers that grew in three parts from his cheeks and chin were white. The magistrate asked this man,

"What do you say, my brother?"

This man smoothed his few white whiskers then and he said slowly as though he pondered justice, but the memory of silver was warm on his palm,

"It cannot be gainsaid that this farmer did borrow money

230

and he has not returned it, and money borrowed must run into interest and this is according to the law. The usurer lives by his loaned moneys as a farmer does by his land. If the farmer rented his land out and received no rent he would complain and his complaint would be just. Yet this is only what the usurer has done. It is just, therefore, that he be paid his due."

The old magistrate listened to this carefully, nodding his head from time to time, and it could be seen he was moved by it, too. But now suddenly the farmer lifted his eyes and for the first time he looked in a kind of daze from one face to the other. Yet Wang the Tiger did not see his face or how his eyes looked. He only saw the man's two old bare feet curl upon each other in an agony, and suddenly he could not bear it. His immense anger rushed forth and he stood up. He clapped his hands together hard and he roared in a great voice,

"I say the poor man shall have his land!"

When all the people gathered in the court heard this roar come out of Wang the Tiger every head turned toward him, and the trusty men Wang the Tiger had, leaped to him and stood with their guns pointed fiercely and seeing them every-one shrank back· and kept silent. But Wang the Tiger felt his anger released now and he could not stay it if he would and he pointed his finger at the usurer and stabbed it through the air again and again as he spoke and he shouted in a great voice, his black brows darting now up, now down above his eyes,

"Again and again have I seen this fat, biting insect here with some tale like this and he has greased his way in with silver to high and low! I am weary of him! Away with him!" And he turned to his guard and shouted, "After him with your guns!"

Now when the people heard this they thought Wang the Tiger had gone suddenly mad and everyone turned and ran for his life. Yes, and swiftest of all to run was the fat usurer and he reached the gate ahead of them all and he went through it with a squeak like a rat that barely escapes. He was so swift and he knew so well the winding alleys that although the trusty men pursued him he was gone and they could not find him, and when they had run so far they could only draw themselves up and look at each other with blank faces and pant awhile. And after they had looked a little more they went back through the hubbub that had risen now in the streets.

When they reached the court again there was an uproar indeed, for Wang the Tiger seeing what he had begun, grew reckless and he called his soldiers and cried out,

"Clear me these courts of everyone—all these cursed sucking worms and all their dirty women and children!"

And his soldiers fell with zest to doing what he said and the people ran out of the courts like rats from a burning house. Yes, in less than an hour there was not a soul there except Wang the Tiger and his own men, and in the magistrate's own courts the old magistrate and his lady and their few personal servants. These Wang the Tiger had commanded were not to be touched.

When Wang the Tiger had done all this, and it had been done in such a burst of rage as he had seldom had in his life before, although he was given to such angers, too, he went into his own room and he sat down by the table and leaned on it and breathed heavily for a while. And he poured himself out some tea and drank it slowly. After a time he saw that he had set a pattern for himself this day that he must follow out somehow. But the more he thought the more he did not regret it, for now he felt free in his heart of all his despondency and gloom, and he felt light and brave and free and when his harelipped man stole in to see what he needed and his pocked lad brought in a jug of wine for him, he cried out to them, laughing his silent laugh as he did,

"Well, at least I have cleared out a serpent's nest this day!"

When the people of that town heard of the rebellion in the court there were many who were pleased for they had known what corruption was there, and while some were afraid and waited to see what Wang the Tiger would do next, there were many who came clamoring about the court gates and they cried out that there should be a time of feasting set and that the prisoners ought to be freed out of the gaol so that everyone could rejoice together.

But the one who had benefited most by the uproar, and it was the poor farmer, was not among that crowd. No, although he had been delivered this once he could not believe that any good fortune could be in store for him, and when he heard the usurer had escaped, he groaned and fled back to his land, and he went to his house and crept into his bed and if anyone came to ask his wife or children where he was they said he had gone away somewhere and they did not know where he was.

When Wang the Tiger heard what the people demanded he remembered that there were in the gaol some dozen or so of men whom he had seen thrown in for one unjust cause or another and they were hopeless of coming out, for most of them were poor and had not money enough to secure their freedom. And so he was willing and he told his trusty men to free the people in the gaol, and he called out to his men that they were to have three days of feasting, and he sent for the cooks of the magistrate's court and he had them come into his presence and he said to them loudly,

"Prepare the best dishes of your native parts, the hot peppery dishes and the fish dishes to go with wine, and everything with which we can make merry."

He ordered good wines, too, and strings of firecrackers and rockets and all such things as please the people. And everyone was glad.

But just before the trusty men went to fulfil his command concerning those in the gaol Wang the Tiger suddenly thought of something, and it was that woman who was in the gaol, too. He had wanted her out a score of times during this winter, but each time he had not known what to do with her either, so he had contented himself with commanding that she be well fed and not chained as some were. Now when he thought of the prisoners free, he thought of her and he thought to himself,

"But how can I free her?"

And he wanted her free and yet he wanted her not so free that she could go away, and he was astonished at himself when he found he cared whether she came or went. He was astonished at his own heart, and being bewildered, he called his harelipped trusty man secretly into the room where he slept and he said,

"But what of that woman we had from the lair?"

Then the trusty man answered gravely, "Yes, there is she, and I wish you would let me tell the Pig Butcher to put a knife to her throat in a way he has so that little blood flows."

But Wang the Tiger looked away and he said, slowly,

"She is only a woman." And he waited awhile and said, "At least I will see her again, and then I can know what I ought to do."

The trusty man looked very downcast at this, but he said nothing and went away, and as he went Wang the Tiger called after him that the woman was to be brought at once to him in the hall of justice where he would go to wait for her.

He went into the hall of justice then and stepped up on the dais into the old magistrate's seat out of some strange impulse of vanity he had, and he thought he would like to have the woman see him there in the great carven seat raised as it was above the other seats, and there was no one to say him nay, for the magistrate did not come out of his own rooms yet, having sent word he was ill of a flux. There Wang the Tiger sat very stiff and haughty and he kept his face smooth and proud as a hero's ought to be.

At last she came in between two guards, and she wore a plain cotton coat and trousers of some dull blue common stuff. But this common garb was not what had changed her. She had eaten well, and the gauntness of her body was changed to a fulness that was still slender. Pretty she could never be because her face was too marked for prettiness, but she was very bold and beautiful. She came in steadily and freely and she stood before Wang the Tiger, quiet and waiting.

He looked at her in greatest astonishment, for he had not dreamed of a change like this, and he said to the guards,

"Why is she so still now, seeing how mad she was before?"

And they shook their heads and moved their shoulders and said, "We do not know, except that when she went out from our captain last time she went broken and weak as though some evil spirit had passed from her, and she has been like this ever since."

"Why did you not tell me?" said Wang the Tiger in a low voice. "I would have had her freed."

The guards were astonished at this and they said to excuse themselves,

"Sir, how could we know that our general cared what came to her? We waited for your commands."

Then words flew of their own accord to the tip of Wang the Tiger's tongue and he all but cried them out, "But I do care!" He did but barely stop them for how could he say such a thing out before all these guards and before this woman?

"Loose her from those bonds!" he shouted suddenly.

Without a word they loosed her and she stood free and they all waited to see what she would do, and Wang the Tiger waited also. She stood there as though she were still bound and she did not move. Then Wang the Tiger called out to her sharply,

"You are free—you may go where you will!"

But she answered, "Where shall I go, seeing I have no home anywhere?"

And saying this, she lifted up her head and looked at Wang the Tiger with a sudden seeming simplicity.

At that look the sealed fountain in Wang the Tiger was unstopped and such a passion rushed out into his blood that he began to tremble within his soldier's clothes. Now it was his eyes that dropped before hers. Now she was stronger than he. The room was filled with the air of this passion that had been stopped so long and men stirred uneasily and stared at each other. Suddenly Wang the Tiger remembered they were there and he roared at them,

"Get you gone, every one of you, and stand outside the door!"

They went away then, crestfallen, for they saw well enough what had befallen their general, even that which may befall any man, high or low. They went out then, and waited upon the threshold.

When there were none but these two left in the hall, Wang the Tiger leaned forward out of his carven seat and he said in a hard, hoarse voice,

"Woman, you are free. Choose where you will go and I will send one to take you there."

And she answered simply, with all the boldness gone out of her, except that she could look at him in the eyes while she said it,

"I have chosen already. I am your bondswoman."

XVII

IF Wang the Tiger had been a coarse and common man and without feeling for what was lawful and decent he might have taken this woman, since she had no father or brother or any man to stand for her, and he might have done as he liked with her. But that hour in his youth which had been like a blow upon his heart made him fastidious still and it made his pleasure more keen to think he could wait, with all his passion, until he could have her as a wife. Moreover, he wanted her as wife, for mingled with all his personal passion for her, which fell more deeply on him hour by hour, was the craving also to have a son by her, his son, his first-born son, and only a true wife can bear a man his true son. Yes, half of the exultation of his secret longing for her was this, to think what a son they would form between them, he with his power and great tall body and all he had to bestow, and she with her fox-like beauty and her spirit of fearlessness. To Wang the Tiger when he dreamed of it, it seemed his son lived already.

In great haste, then, he called his harelipped trusty man and he bade him thus,

"Go to my brothers and tell them I want my share of the silver that was left to me when I should want to wed. I need it now for my marriage, for I have set my will upon this woman. Tell them to give me a thousand pieces of silver, for I have presents to give her and my men must have a very great feast on such a day and I must buy myself a new robe fit for the day. But if he gives you eight hundred, come back with it, and do not delay for the rest. And bid my brothers come and see the marriage, too, they and all they care to bring with them."

The trusty man listened to this in greatest consternation, and his lower jaw hung hideously and he stammered forth in an agony,

"Oh, my general—oh, my captain—to that fox! But take her for a day—a time—not wed—"

"Be silent, fool!" Wang the Tiger roared at him then, starting up from his seat at the man. "Did I ask your counsel? I will order you beaten like a common criminal!"

The man hung his head then silent, but tears rose into his eyes and he went on his errand very heavily, for he felt the woman would bring his master nothing but evil and he muttered many times as he went along the road,

"Yes, and I have seen these fox women! Yes, and my general will never believe any evil I tell him! These fox women do always fasten themselves on the best men—it is always so!"

Thus he went along the road, his feet stirring the dust that lay thick through the dry winter days, and men passing him stared at him curious because of his muttering and because of his tears that rolled down his cheeks sometimes without his knowing it, and when they saw he paid no heed to anything except what was in his own heart, they set him down as mad, and gave him the wider half of the road.

But when this trusty man came with his message to Wang the Merchant, that one was for once startled out of his secret calm and he looked up from his table where he sat casting up accounts, for the trusty man, finding him not at his house, had come straight to his grain shop, and there he was at his desk in a corner behind the counters. He looked up and said in agitation, his pen arrested in his hand,

"But how can I suddenly withdraw so much money from the places where I have it loaned out? My brother ought to tell me when he is betrothed and so give me warning of a year or two. Such haste is scarcely decent in a wedding!"

Now Wang the Tiger knew his brother and how loath he was to part with money and so he had also told his trusty man before he went,

"If my brother delays you are to press him to the point and tell him plainly I will have the money if I have to come and fetch it myself. I will carry this thing through in three days after you return, and you are not to be away more than five. There is need for haste, for I do not know how long it will be before I have an army march down on me from above, for I cannot hope to remain unnoticed when the provincial ruler hears what I did in these courts. He will send men against me, even, and there can be no feasting and wedding on a battlefield."

Now it was true enough that what Wang the Tiger had done by violence he must expect to be heard in the courts above him and it was true that he might be punished. But there was a deeper truth than this, and it was that Wang the Tiger was so hungry for this woman he could not wait for her longer than he must, and he knew he was useless as a warrior until he could have her safely for himself, and so set his mind free for something else. Therefore he had urged his trusty man and he grew fierce in his urging and he added,

"Well I know that merchant brother of mine will howl that he has his money where he cannot get it. You are not to heed him. Tell him I have my sword still, and the very swift and fine sword that I took from the Leopard when I killed him!"

But the trusty man kept this threat as a last resort and he did not use it up at the first, and not until Wang the Merchant seemed about to delay on another score, and it was that it was a shame to the family to wed into it a woman who had no family and no home, and had been a trollop, perhaps, as such women are. But the trusty man did not tell him it was a woman out of a robbers' lair. No, although he was sorely tempted to tell it and tempted to hold back the woman by any means, yet he knew Wang the Tiger well enough to know he would have what he set himself to have, and so he used his threat.

Then Wang the Merchant had to scour about and get what silver he could, and he was in great distress of mind that he was compelled to call in money suddenly like this and lose its interest, and he went very gloomily to his elder brother and said,

"The sum of money due our younger brother for his marriage he calls for now, and he is going to wed some trollop or other whom we have never heard of! He is more like you than me, after all."

Wang the Landlord scratched his head at this and cast about for an answer, and then decided on peace, and he said,

"It is a strange thing, for I thought he would call upon us when he felt the need and when he was established, and ask us to betroth him properly, since our father is dead who should have done it for him. Yes, I had a maid or two in mind even." And in his heart he thought that surely he would have chosen a maid better than anyone else, seeing he knew women so well, and all the best maids, at least by hearsay, who were in the town.

240

But Wang the Merchant had been driven very irritable with the exigency and he sneered and said,

"Be sure you have a maid or two in mind! But that is nothing to me. The thing is what can you give of this thousand he wants, for I have no such great amount of cash to take out of my girdle suddenly like this!"

Wang the Elder stared heavily at his brother, then, and he sat staring with his hands on his fat knees, and he said huskily,

"You know all I have. I never have any ready silver. Sell a piece of my land again."

Then Wang the Merchant groaned a little, for it was not a good time to sell before the New Year, and he had counted on the harvests of wheat to which the land was all planted. But after he had gone back to his shop and had fingered his abacus awhile and cast up his loss and profit, he found it would pay him to sell more land rather than to draw his money out of the places of high interest where he had it, and so he sold a fair field, and when he let it be known, many came to buy of him. He sold the land for a thousand pieces and a little odd sum over, but he gave the trusty man only nine hundred pieces, and held back the rest, lest Wang the Tiger demand more.

But the trusty man was a simple fellow, and he remembered that his master told him he was not to delay for a hundred pieces or so, and he went away with what he had. And Wang the Merchant hastened to put out at interest what had not been asked for, and he was a little comforted that he had saved this much, at any rate.

There was but one untoward thing in this transaction he made, and it was that when he sold the land he sold a piece or two not far from the earthen house, and Pear Blossom happened to be out on the threshing floor in front of the house.

When she saw the knot of men gathered about the field, she shaded her eyes with her hand and looked through the sunshine and she knew what was being done. She hastened then to Wang the Merchant's side and motioned him back a little from the others, and she opened her eyes with reproach and said to him,

"Again do you sell the land?"

But Wang the Merchant would not be troubled with her when he had so much else to trouble him, and he said bluntly,

"My younger brother is to be wed, and there is no other provision for the sum that is rightfully his for such a purpose except to sell a piece."

Then Pear Blossom shrank back in the strangest way and she said no more. No, she went slowly back to the house, and from that day on her life narrowed itself yet more, and what time she did not spend in caring for the two children, as she called them always, she spent assiduously in listening to the nuns who came to visit her, and she besought them now to come every day. Yes, even in the morning, when it is ill luck to see a nun, and many will spit upon a nun if she cross their path before noon, because it is so ill an omen, Pear Blossom welcomed them always.

Eagerly she foreswore eating any more meat her life long, and it was not hard for her, either, because she had always shrunk so from taking any life at all. Yes, she was such an one that even on a hot summer's night she would close the lattices so that the moths would not fly in and burn themselves in the candle flames, and this she counted as the saving of life. Her greatest prayer was that the fool might die before her so that she need never use the packet of white poison that Wang Lung had left to her to use if she must.

She learned of these nuns and far into the night she told off her prayers and she had always wrapped about her wrist the little rosary of beads of fragrant wood. This was all her life.

Now after the trusty man had gone, Wang the Merchant and Wang the Landlord consulted together as to whether they ought or not to go to their brother's wedding. They each longed to share such success as he had had, but the trusty man had made much of the need for haste lest a battle be made by those above, and so the brothers were afraid, also, because they did not know how strong Wang the Tiger was and whether, if he lost, he would be heavily punished and they perhaps entangled in the punishment because they were his brothers. Wang the Landlord longed especially to go and see what sort of a woman his younger brother had, for the trusty man told enough to whet his interest. But when his lady heard of the affair she said gravely,

"It is a very strange and unusual thing to have such a brawl as we have heard. No, if he is punished by those above him in the state, then we may be all punished, for I have often heard it told that if a man commits a crime of rebellion against the state, his family may be killed even to the very ninth-removed cousin."

It was true that in the past such punishments were made, when kings and emperors strove to sweep the country clean of crimes, and Wang the Landlord had seen such things told in plays and he had heard of them in story tellers' booths, where he loved to pass time away, so that now, although he was too high for such low pastimes and dared not join a common crowd in such a place, he still listened eagerly if a passing story teller came into the tea house to tell his tale. Now, remembering, he turned yellow with fright and he went to Wang the Merchant and said,

"We had better have some sort of a signed paper saying

243

our brother was an unfilial son so that we have cast him out of our house, so that if he fails in a battle or is punished we will not be entangled with him, we and our sons." And he thought to himself at that moment that he was glad his son had not wanted to go, after all, and he took pleasure in pitying his brother and saying, "I do feel for you with your own son in such a danger!"

Now although Wang the Merchant merely smiled, yet when he had thought awhile it seemed to him a good, cautious thing to do. So he wrote a paper saying how and in what ways Wang the Third, nicknamed the Tiger, had been unfilial and no longer belonged to the house, and he had his elder brother sign it first and then he signed it and he took it to the magistrate's court and paid a sum of money to have it secretly stamped. Then he took the deed and put it safely away where none might find it unless he needed it.

Thus the two brothers felt safe, and they looked at each other when they met in the tea house one morning, and Wang the Landlord said,

"Why should we not go and feast merrily now, seeing we are safe?"

But before they could consider it, for they were not men who at their age could take a journey easily, there came a rumor over that whole region, told from mouth to mouth, and it was that the ruler of the province had heard with great wrath that some small country upstart, half robber, half runaway soldier from an old southern general, had seized the seat of government in one of the counties, and an army was to be sent against him to capture him. This ruler was responsible to those yet higher than he, and if he did not manage this affair he would be blamed.

When this rumor came filtering through from wayside inn and tea house, and be sure there were those who ran with pleasure to tell it to the two brothers, then Wang the Landlord and Wang the Merchant gave up their plan speedily, and each stayed close in his house for a time, and each was glad he had not boasted too soon that he had a brother in a high place, and it was a comfort to them to think of the paper, signed and stamped at court. If anyone spoke of their third brother before them Wang the Landlord said loudly,

"He has been wild and runaway all his days!"

And Wang the Merchant drew his meager lips together and said,

"Let him do what he likes, for it does not concern us and he is scarcely our brother."

Wang the Tiger was in the midst of his wedding feast when this rumor reached him also, and in the midst of three days of mighty feasting throughout the courts. He had ordered the killing of cows and pigs and fowls, and he ordered everything to be paid for as it was taken to be killed. Although he was so strong in this region now that he could have taken what he liked without price and none would have dared to withstand him, yet because he was a just man he paid for all.

This justice moved the common people toward him very much so that they praised him to each other and man said to man,

"There could be far worse than this lord of war who rules over us. He is strong enough to keep robbers away and he does not rob us himself, beyond the taxes, and I do not see that we could ask for more than this under heaven."

But still at this time they did not come out too openly for him yet, because they had heard the rumor also, and they waited to see if he could be victorious or not, for if he lost they would be blamed if they had showed loyalty to him.

But if he gained then they could take courage to come out for him.

Still they had let Wang the Tiger take what he needed for the feast, although it taxed the people much to feed so many at a time, and he would have the best for once, and he had better than the best even for himself and his bride and his trusty men and the women who cared for the bride. These women were some half score of those about the courts, the wife of the gaoler and of such harmless persons who do not care who is over them and they came creeping back to their places the next day after the overthrow, ready to swear loyalty to anyone who fed them. And Wang the Tiger would have these women properly about his bride, for he was very careful toward her and did not go near her for the days before he married her; no, although he could not sleep at times in the night for thinking of her and wondering who she was and burning for her. But stronger than this was the feeling he had for her to make her the mother of his son, and it seemed to him it was his duty to his son to be careful in all he did.

Different indeed was she from Pear Blossom, and because of that early image of a woman set into his memory he had always thought, if he thought, that he would like mild, pale women best. But now he did not care, and he said to himself wildly that he did not care who she was nor what, so that he had her and had her sealed to him forever through their son.

During those days no one came near him for anything, for his trusty men saw that he was wholly given over to his desire. But they consulted together secretly, for they had heard the rumor and they put their strength to hastening the wedding, so that it could be over and their leader slaked and ready to be himself and lead them on when the need came.

More quickly, then, than Wang the Tiger even could hope,

the feasts were prepared and the wife of the gaol keeper stood for the woman and the courts were thrown open to all such as cared to come and see and feast. But few men of the city came and fewer women, because they were afraid. Only the homeless ones and such as live nowhere and have nothing to lose came in as any may come in to a marriage and ate heartily and stared their fill at the strange bride. But when they went in to fetch the old magistrate and bring him to a seat of honor on such a day, as Wang the Tiger had commanded should be done, he sent out word that he grieved he could not come for he had a flux and could not rise from his bed.

As for Wang the Tiger, throughout that day of his wedding he moved in a dream and he scarcely knew what he did except that the hours of the day moved so slowly that he did not know what to do with himself. It seemed to him that every breath he drew lasted an hour and that the sun would never crawl up the sky to noon, and when it had, that it would stay forever. He could not be merry as men are at their weddings, for he had never been merry, and now he sat as silent as ever, and there was not one to joke at his expense. He thirsted exceedingly all that day, and he drank much wine, but he could eat nothing, for he was as full as though he had eaten a mighty meal.

But into the courts of feasting men and women and the crowds of poor and ragged and the dogs from the streets came in by scores to feast and to eat and to pick the bones that were left, and in his own room Wang the Tiger sat silent and half smiling as in a dream and so the day wore on at last to night.

Then when the women had prepared the bride for the bed he went into her room and she was there. It was the first woman he had ever known. Yes, this was a curious, unheard-of thing, that a man could come to be more than thirty years old and be a soldier and a runaway from his father's house since he was eighteen, and never had he gone near a woman, so sealed his heart had been.

But that fountain was flowing free, now, and naught could ever seal it again, and seeing this woman sitting there on the bed, he drew his breath in sharply, and she hearing it, lifted her eyes and looked at him fully.

So he went to her and he found her silent but passionate and frank upon her marriage bed, and he loved her mightily from that hour, and since he had known no other, she seemed to him faultless.

Once in the middle of the night he turned to her and he said in a husky whisper,

"I do not even know who you are."

And she answered calmly, "What does it matter except that I am here? But some time I will tell you."

And he let it pass, content for the time, for they were neither of them usual folk, and both their lives were not such as are commonly lived.

But the trusty men did not let Wang the Tiger have more than the night, and the next morning at dawn they waited for him, and they saw him come out of his door, calm and refreshed from his marriage chamber. Then the harelipped man said, bowing,

"Sir, and honored, we did not tell you yesterday since it was a day of joy, but we have heard rumors from the north and the provincial ruler has heard that you have seized the government and comes down against you."

And the Hawk said in his turn, "I heard it from a beggar who came from that way and he said he passed ten thousand men upon the way marching down upon us."

248

And the Pig Butcher added his tale, stammering through his thick lips in his haste to speak as he had been told,

"I—I also heard it—when I went out to the market to see how they stick their pigs in this city and a butcher told me."

But Wang the Tiger was all softened and at ease and for the first time he could not bring himself to think of war and he smiled in his slight way and said,

"I can trust my men, and let them come." And he sat down to drink a little tea before he ate and he sat at a table beside a window and it was broad day and a thought came to him suddenly, and it was this, that there is a night at the end of every day, and he seemed to know it for the first time, now, so meaningless had all other nights of his life been except this one night.

But there was one who heard what his trusty men said, and she stood by the curtain and looked through a crack of it, and she saw they were dismayed to see their leader sunk in some pleasing thought of his own. When Wang the Tiger rose and went out of the room to go to the one where food was eaten, she called clearly to the harelipped man and she said,

"Tell me all you have heard."

He was very loath to talk to a woman of what was none of her affair, and he muttered and made as if he had nothing to tell until she said imperiously,

"Do not play the fool with me, who have seen blood and fighting and battle and retreat these five years since I was grown! Tell me!"

Then wondering and abashed before her bold eyes fixed on his and not dropped as the eyes of women usually are, especially when they are newly wed and should be full of shame, he told her as though she had been a man what they all feared and how they were in danger because more men marched against them than they had, and many of their men were untried in their loyalty if a battle came. She sent him away quickly then saying he must beg Wang the Tiger to come to her.

He came as he had never come to any summons, smiling more softly than anyone had ever seen him smile. She sat down upon the bed and he sat down beside her and took up the end of her sleeve and fingered it and he was more abashed in her presence than she was in his and he kept his eyes down, smiling.

But she began to speak swiftly in her clear, somewhat piercing voice,

"I am not a woman such as will stand in your way if there is a battle to be fought and they tell me an army marches against you."

"Who told you?" he answered. "I will not trouble myself for three days. I have given myself three days."

"But if they come nearer in three days?"

"An army cannot come two hundred miles in three days."

"How can you know what day they started?"

"The tale could not have reached the provincial seat in so short a time."

"It could have!" she said swiftly.

Now here was a strange thing. These two, a man and a woman, could sit and talk of something far from love and yet Wang the Tiger was as knit to her as he had been in the night. He was amazed that a woman could talk like this for he had never talked with one before and he had always thought them pretty children in tall bodies, and one reason why he feared them was because he did not know what they knew nor what to say to them. He was so made that even with a woman paid for he could not rush to her as a common soldier does, and half his diffidence with women was because he feared the speech he must make with them. But here he sat and talked with this woman as easily as though she were a man and he listened to her when she said on,

"You have fewer men than the provincial army has, and when a warrior finds his army smaller than his enemy's then he must use guile."

At this he made his silent laugh and said in his gruff way,

"Well I know that, or I would not have had you for mine now."

She dropped her eyes quickly at this as though to veil something that might show itself in them and she bit the edge of her lower lip and she answered,

"The simplest guile is to kill a man, but one must catch him first. The same simple guile will not do now."

Then Wang the Tiger answered with pride, "I will pit my men against thrice their number of state soldiers. I have trained them and taught them this whole winter and hardened them with boxing and running and fencing and with all feints of war and none of them is afraid to die. Moreover, it is known what state soldiers are, and they will always turn to the strongest side, and doubtless the soldiers of this province are not better paid than any others like them."

Then she said with some impatience, and she drew her sleeve out of his fingers as she spoke,

"Still you have no plan! Hear me—I have a plan made while we talked. There is the old magistrate you have guarded in his court. Use him as a hostage of a kind."

Now she spoke so earnestly and soberly that Wang the Tiger listened to her, yet was amazed that he did, for he was not a man who often took counsel with others, thinking himself sufficient for anything. But he listened and she said,

"Take your soldiers out and take him also and force him and tell him what he is to say, that he shall say what you command. Let him go out to meet the provincial general with a trusty man on either side of him who will hear what he says, and if he does not say what you have told him, let them have their swords ready and plunge them into his bowels, and that shall be a sign for battle. But he has a gall no larger than a hen's. He will say what he is told, and let him say that nothing has been done without his consent, that the rumor of a rebellion is only because his own old general rebelled and if it had not been for you who delivered him the seals of state would have been stolen and his own life gone."

Now this seemed excellent good guile to Wang the Tiger, and he listened with his eyes fastened on her face as she spoke. He saw the whole plan there before him and he rose and laughed noiselessly to think what she was and he went out to do what she had said, and she came close behind him. He commanded a trusty man to go and fetch the old magistrate out and bring him to the hall of audience. Then the woman had a fancy and it was that they would go and sit in the audience room, he and she together, and let the old magistrate come before them, and Wang the Tiger was willing because they must frighten the old man thoroughly. So they sat themselves down on the dais, Wang the Tiger in a carven chair, and the woman beside him in another chair.

Soon the old magistrate came tottering in between two soldiers, and he came out trembling and his robe thrown about him anyhow. He looked half dazed about the hall, and he saw not one face he knew. No, even those servants of his who had returned looked away when he came in and found this excuse and that to go away on some other business. There were only the faces of soldiers about the walls of the hall, and every man had his gun and every man was loyal to Wang the Tiger. Then he looked up, his old lips trembling and blue, his mouth open, and he peered up and there sat

Wang the Tiger with his two brows drawn down, fierce and murderous to see, and beside him a strange woman whom the old magistrate had never seen or heard of and he could not think where such an one as she had come from. He stood trembling and timid and ready to die because such an end to his life had come to him as this, who was a man of peace and had been a Confucian scholar in his day.

Then Wang the Tiger shouted in his rough and bitter way, with little courtesy,

"You are in my hand now and you must follow my commands if you would live on here! We march against the army of the province tomorrow, and you are to go with us, and when we meet the army you are to go first with my two trusty men and meet the general who comes against me. Tell him that you have chosen me your lord of war and that I saved you from a rebellion in your own courts and I stay here by your choice. My two trusty men will be there to hear all you say; if one word goes wrong it is your end and your last word. But if you speak well and as I tell you, you may return here and you may take your old place again upon this dais, and I will save your face for you and it need not be known whose is the power here in these courts, for I have no mind to be a petty magistrate, nor will I have another here in your place, so long as you do what I command."

What then could the weak old man do but give his promise and he said, groaning,

"I am caught on the end of your spear. Let it be as you say. I am an old man and I have no son, and what does my life matter to me?"

And he turned and went away shuffling and groaning as he went to his court where his old wife was, who never came out at all. It was true he had no sons, for the two children she had given him died before they could speak.

Now whether the thing could have been done as Wang the Tiger planned or not none knows, but again his destiny helped him. It was now full spring and over the land the willows budded again and the peach trees burst into swift bloom, and while farmers stripped off their winter coats and worked bare backed in the fields again, rejoicing in the mild winds and the warm gentle sun upon their clogged flesh, the lords of war awoke also, and the restlessness of spring filled the countryside. And the lords of war awoke quarrelsome and full of lust of war against each other and old troubles were burnished and made new and old differences sharpened, and every man grew ambitious to achieve some new place for himself while the fresh spring lasted.

Now the chief seat of government of the nation at this time was in the hands of a weak, unready man, and there were many lords of war who cast longing eyes at that seat and thought how easy it would be to seize it. Many counted over such as stood in the way and some banded together and consulted as to how they could take the power of the nation and unseat this unstable and ignorant man whom others had put there, and how they could place their own choice there to serve their own purpose.

Among these lords of war Wang the Tiger was still one of the very least and he was scarcely known among the great ones except as when men of battle gossip among themselves at some meeting or feast, and one might say,

"Did you hear of the captain who split himself off from his old general and has set himself up in such and such a province? He is a good brave, it is said, and he is called the Tiger because of his angers and fierceness and his two black brows."

Thus the chief lord of war in the province where Wang the Tiger now was had heard of him and he had heard how

254

Wang the Tiger had routed the Leopard and had approved the deed. Now this chief lord was one of the great lords of war of the nation and he was one of those who had it in his mind to unseat the weak ruler if he could, and if he could not put himself on the seat at least to put his man there, so that the revenues of the nation would come to his own hands.

During this spring, therefore, when restlessness rose everywhere, strange flowers of ambitions blossomed. There were proclamations pasted on city gates and on walls and all such places where people pass, and these proclamations were sent out by the lord of war of that province. He said that since the ruler was so evil and the people greatly oppressed, he could not endure such crimes as these before heaven. Although he was weak and witless, yet must he come forth to save the people. Having so written, he prepared for war.

As for the people, since few of them could either read or write, they did not know this their savior, but they groaned aloud because fresh taxes were put upon their lands and upon their harvests and upon their carts and in the towns upon shops and goods. If they groaned aloud or complained, there were those minions of the lord of war who heard them and cried out,

"How ungrateful a people are you, who will not pay even for your own salvation! And who else should pay for the soldiers who are to fight for you and make you safe?"

So the people paid what they must, however unwillingly, fearing if they did not either the wrath of the lord they had or of a new lord who might come in and conquer them and devour them afresh, being rapacious with his victory.

Having determined on this war, therefore, the lord of the province was eager to marshal to him every small captain and general, so when he heard of the rebellion Wang the Tiger had made, he said to the civil ruler of the province,

"Do not bear too heavily down upon that little new general whose name is Wang the Tiger, because I hear he is a good angry fierce fellow and I want such as he is under my ensign. This whole nation will divide itself, perhaps this spring, and if not this year then next or next, and the lords of the north will declare against the lords of the south. Let this man be treated gently then."

Now although it is said that lords of war should be subservient in a nation to the civil governors of the people, it is a thing known and proved that the power goes always to the armed man and the man with weapons, and how can a weaponless man, even though he has the right, oppose a man of war in the same region with him, who has soldiers to his command?

Thus it was that destiny helped Wang the Tiger in that spring. For when the armies of state came marching against him, Wang the Tiger led his men out and he sent the old magistrate ahead in his sedan and he ambushed many good strong men near in case of treachery. When they came to a meeting place the old magistrate came out of his sedan and stumbling through the dust of the country road, he went, dressed in his magistrate's robes, and leaning upon the two trusty men. The general who had been sent from the state came to meet him, and after the rites of courtesy had been observed, the old man said in his faltering way,

"You have it wrongly, my lord. This Wang the Tiger is no robber but my own captain and my new young general who protects my court and he saved me from a rebellion in my own retinue."

Now although the general did not believe this, having heard the truth from his spies, and although no one believed it, still he had his orders that Wang the Tiger was not to be offended and that he was not to lose a man in a brawl so little as this when every gun was needed for the greater war. When he heard what the old magistrate said, therefore, he only rebuked him slightly saying,

"You should have sent word of this before because we have been at an expense to bring men to punish what I thought was a rebel. There shall be a fine imposed on you to pay for the expense of an idle errand and it is ten thousand pieces of silver."

When Wang the Tiger heard that this was all he exulted very much and he led his men back in triumph again. And he imposed in his turn a tax beyond what was usual upon all the salt in that place and in less than twice thirty days he had the ten thousand pieces and some over, for that place had much salt and it was even sent out to other places and some said to other countries, too.

When this was over Wang the Tiger was more strong than ever in his power and he had not lost a man, either. It seemed to him that for this honor was due to his woman and he honored her for her wisdom.

Yet he still did not know who or what she was. Passion was still his chief pastime with her, but he wondered sometimes what her story was. Yet if he asked her she always put him off, saying,

"It is a long tale, and I will tell you some day in a winter when there can be no war. But now it is spring and time for battle and for enlarging your self, and not for idle talk."

And she put him off restlessly, her eyes bright and hard.

Then Wang the Tiger knew the woman was right, for over all the country the news came winged that there was to be such a war that spring among the lords of war as had not been in ten years of wars, and the people were dismayed, not knowing from what point the war would strike them, hearing of it coming here or coming there. Yet there was the land to till and they tilled it, and in the cities the merchants had their shops and men must live and children be fed. So the people went on about their lives, and if they groaned at a coming terror, they did their work while they waited to see what would happen to them.

In his region all the eyes of the people were turned to Wang the Tiger, for his rule over them was now open and established and they knew the taxes went through his hands. Although the old magistrate was still there for a show of state, he was an old image and everything was decided by Wang the Tiger. Yes, Wang the Tiger even sat at the magistrate's right hand in the audience hall, and the old magistrate looked to him when the judgment moment came, and the money that used to be paid to the councillors now went into Wang the Tiger's hand and to his trusty men. But Wang the Tiger was still himself, for if he took from the rich, if a poor man came and he knew it, he would let him speak for himself freely. There were many poor who praised him. But all the people turned to Wang the Tiger in this spring to see what he would do, for they knew if he joined in the great war they must pay the soldiers he would need and buy his guns.

As for Wang the Tiger, he had considered the matter well, alone and with his woman and also with his trusty men, but he was still puzzled as to what was best for him. The lord of war of the province had sent out commands to every little separate general and captain and small lord of war and said,

"Follow under my ensign with your men, for now is the hour when we can all rise up a step or two in the tide of war."

But Wang the Tiger did not know whether to come at his call or not, because he could not see which side would win. If he cast in his name with the losing side he would set himself back and perhaps ruin himself, seeing he was so newly risen up. So he took thought for himself and he thought and he sent out his spies to see and to hear and to find out what was the stronger and the winning side, and he said while they were out he would delay and declare himself for no one, and he would wait until the war was fought nearly to an end and the victory plain and then he would make haste to declare himself, and so on the last swelling wave he might ride with others to its crest, and not lose a man or gun, either. He sent out his spies, then, and waited.

In the night he talked about it with his woman, for their love and his ambition were linked in the strangest way, and when he had slaked his thirst and lay at his ease he talked with her as he had never done to anyone in his life. He poured out to her every plan he had and he ended every dream with this saying,

"Thus will I do, and when you give me a son, he will be the meaning for it all."

But she never answered this hope of his and when he pressed on it, she grew restless and spoke of some everyday thing and again and again she said,

"Have you your plans ready and made for the last battle?" and she said often, "Guile is the best warfare, and the best battle is the one at the end when victory is sure and swift."

And Wang the Tiger never noticed any coldness in her at all, he was so hot himself.

All through that spring he waited therefore, although waiting chafed him in usual times, and he could never have borne it now if he had not had this woman new to him and there at his hand. Summer came on and the wheat was cut and all through the valleys the sound of the flails beat all day into the still, hot sunshine. In the fields where the wheat had stood the sorghum cane grew tall and rank and put forth its tassels and while Wang the Tiger waited, wars sprang up everywhere, and this general and that in the south banded together for the moment like generals of the north, and still Wang the Tiger waited. And he hoped greatly that the generals of the south would not win, for it went against some gorge in him to link himself ever again with those little dark and stunted men. It went against him so much that he brooded sometimes, and said to himself sullenly that if the south won he would go and hide in his mountains for a while and wait for a new turn of war.

But he did not wait in complete idleness. He trained his men with fresh zeal and he enlarged his army once more, and enrolled in it many good young fellows who came to him and over the new ones he set the old and other soldiers, and his army swelled to ten thousand men, and to pay for this he added somewhat to his taxes on wine and on salt and on travelling merchants.

His only trouble at this time was that he had not enough guns, and he saw he must do one of two things; either he must get guns by guile, or he must conquer some little near captain and take his guns and ammunition. Now this was because guns were very hard to find, being foreign things and brought in from foreign parts, and Wang the Tiger had not thought of this when he had chosen his region an inland region, and he had no coastal port he controlled, and other ports were guarded so that he could not hope to smuggle guns through them. Moreover, he knew no foreign tongue, nor had he any near him who did, and so he had no way yet to deal with the foreign merchants, and so it seemed to him that after all he must have a little battle somewhere, for many of his men were without guns.

One night he told this to his woman, and she took a sudden interest and put her mind to it, for often she could be listless and paid no heed to him at all. Now when she put her mind to it she said very soon,

"But I thought you said you had a brother who is a merchant!"

"I do have such a one," said Wang the Tiger, wondering, "but he is a grain merchant and not a merchant for guns."

"Yes, but you see nothing!" she cried at him, in the impatient, high way she had. "If he is a merchant and deals with sea coasts, he can buy guns and smuggle them in his goods somehow. I do not know how, but there must be a way."

Now Wang the Tiger thought this over awhile and again it seemed to him this was the cleverest woman, and he made a plan on what she had said. The next day he called his pocked nephew to him, grown tall in this past year, and he kept the youth by him continually for small special things he needed to have done, and he said,

"Go to your father and pretend you are home for a visit and nothing more but when you are alone with him tell him I need three thousand guns and I am hampered sorely because I have not them. Men grow everywhere, but not guns for them, and they are useless to me without each man his gun. Tell him he is a merchant and one who deals with the sea coast and he can think of a way for me. I send you, because the thing must be kept secret, and you are my own blood."

The youth was glad enough to go, and he promised secrecy eagerly, and he was proud with his mission. And again Wang the Tiger waited, but he still received men under his ensign, only he chose his men carefully and tested each as to whether or not he feared to die.

XVIII

THE lad went winding his way homeward, then, over the countryside. He had taken off his soldier's garb and had put on the clothing of a farmer's son and with these coarse blue garments and his face brown and pocked he looked nothing but a country lad, and fit grandson for Wang Lung. He rode upon his old white ass, with a ragged coat folded under him for a saddle, and he kicked the ass under the belly with his bare feet to hasten it sometimes. No one who saw him riding thus and often half asleep under the hot sun of summer would have dreamed that he carried a message that was to bring three thousand guns into that peaceful country. But when he did not sleep he sang his song of soldiers and war, for he loved to sing, and when he did this a farmer would look up at him uneasily from his work in the fields and stare after the youth, and once a farmer shouted after him,

"A curse on you to be singing a soldier's ditty—do you want to bring the black crows around us again?"

But the youth was gay and careless and he spat here and there in the dust of the road to show how careless he was, and to show he would go on singing if he wished to sing. The truth was he did not know any other songs than these, having been so long among reckless and fighting men, and it cannot be expected that soldiers will sing the same songs that farmers sing in their quiet fields.

On the third day at noon he came to his home and as he slid off his ass at the place where the side street parted from the main street, there was his eldest cousin lounging along and he stared and stopped in a yawn he was making and said, in greeting,

"Well, and are you a general yet?"

Then the pocked lad called back quickly and wittily,

"No, but I have taken at least the first degree!"

This he said to mock his cousin a little because everyone knew how Wang the Landlord and his lady had always talked a great deal of how they would make a scholar of this son and how next season he was to go up for examination at such and such a seat of learning and so become a great man. But the season went and the year passed into another, and he never went. Now the pocked youth knew this cousin of his was on his way not to any school but to some tea house, being just up, doubtless, from his bed, and languid after the night he had had somewhere. But the son of Wang the Landlord was dainty and scornful and he surveyed his cousin and said,

"At least being a first degree general has not put a silk coat on your back!"

And he walked on without waiting to hear any answer, swaying himself as he walked so that his own silk robes, the color of the green of a willow tree newly leaved, swayed also with his lordly steps. But the pocked youth grinned and stuck his tongue out toward his cousin's back, and went to his own door.

When he stepped into the court of his own home all was as it ever was. It was time for the noon meal, and the door was open into the house and he saw his father sitting down alone to the table to eat and the children ran anywhere and ate as they always did, and his mother stood at the door with her bowl to her lips and her chopsticks pushing the food into her mouth and as she chewed she chattered to a neighbor woman, who had come in to borrow something, about a salt fish that a cat had stolen the night before, although it was hung high on a beam, too. When she saw the son she shouted at him,

"Well, you are back in time to eat, and you could not have struck it better!" and she went on with her chatter.

The youth grinned at her but he said nothing except to call her name out, and he went inside and his father nodded to him, a little surprised, and the son called his name dutifully and then went and found himself a bowl and a pair of chopsticks and filled his bowl from the food on the table and then went to one side and sat down edgewise on his seat as sons should do if they sit in the presence of those above them.

When they had eaten, the father poured a little tea into his rice bowl, but sparingly, for he was sparing in all he did, and he drank it down in small, meager sips, and then he said to his son,

"Do you bring any word?"

And the son said, "Yes, I do, but I cannot tell you here." This he said because his brothers and sisters crowded around him and stared at him silently, since he was strange to them, and they listened eagerly for any word he might say.

By now the mother was back also to fill her bowl again, for she was a very hearty one to eat and ate a long time after her husband was finished and gone, and she stared too at her son and said,

"You have grown a good ten inches, I swear! And why have you a ragged coat like that on? Does your uncle give you no better? What do they feed you to make you grow like that—good meat and wine, I swear!"

And the lad grinned again and said, "I have good clothes but I did not wear them this time, and we eat meat every day."

At this Wang the Merchant was aghast and he cried with unwonted interest,

"What—does my brother give his soldiers meat every day?"

The lad hastened to say, "No, but now only because he

prepares them for a war and he wants them fierce and full of blood. But I have meat because I do not live with the common soldiers and I may eat what my uncle and his woman leave in their bowls—I and the trusty men."

At this his mother said avidly, "Tell me about that woman of his! It was a strange thing he did not ask us to the wedding."

"He did," said Wang the Merchant hastily, seeing no end to this talk if it began. "Yes, he did ask us, but I said we would not go. It would have cost a pile of silver and you would have wanted new clothes and this and that for a show if you had gone."

To this the woman said with much spirit and in a loud voice,

"Well, and you old miser, I never go anywhere and—"

But Wang the Merchant cleared his throat and said to his son,

"Come with me for there is no peace here," and he rose and brushed his children aside, but not ungently, and he went out and his son followed him.

Wang the Merchant walked ahead of his son down the street to a small tea house where he did not often go, and he chose a table in a quiet corner. But the house was almost empty, for it was an hour when there were not many guests, for farmers had sold their loads and gone home, and city guests had not come in for the afternoon's talk. There in peace then did Wang the Merchant's son tell him his mission.

Wang the Merchant listened very closely to it all and he said not a word until his son had said his say, and when it was over he did not let his face change. No, where Wang the Landlord would have been astonished and rolled his eyes and sworn it was a thing impossible to do, Wang the Merchant had by now grown so secretly rich that nothing was impossible to him and if he ever hesitated, it was to see if the thing would benefit him or not when done. He had his money in all sorts of places and men borrowed of him for everything they could. He had even his money in Buddhist temples, loaned to priests on security of temple lands, for in these days the people were not devout as they had been, and only women and usually old women, too, were the ones to heed the gods, and many temples grew poor and left off their flourishing estate. And Wang the Merchant had his money in ships upon the rivers and upon the seas, and he had money in a railway, and he had a very good sum in a brothel in the city, although he was never a guest at his own brothel, and his elder brother never dreamed that when he went to play at that great new house opened but a year or so ago, that it was his own brother's house. But it was a business that brought good return, and Wang the Merchant reckoned on the common nature of men.

Thus his money flowed out in a hundred secret channels, and if he had recalled it suddenly, thousands would have suffered. Yet he ate no more than he ever did and no better, and he did not game as any man will who has more than he can eat and wear, nor did he let his sons wear silk coats, and seeing him and how he lived, none would have dreamed how rich he was. Therefore he could think of three thousand foreign guns and not be astounded as Wang the Landlord would have been. Yes, looking at those two brothers, if one had met them together in the street, one would have said that Wang the Landlord was the very rich one, for he spent his money so easily and he was so monstrous fat and rolling in his silk and satin robes and his furs and his sons all silk clad too, except the little hunchback who lived with Pear Blossom and grew to quiet manhood there beside her, forgotten day after day.

So Wang the Merchant pondered for a time in silence, and he said at last,

"Did my brother say what security I am to have for so much money as this to buy these guns? I ought to have good security, seeing that it is against the law to buy them."

And the youth said, "He said, 'Tell my brother he must take all the land I have left for security if he cannot trust my word until I can collect revenue to pay for them. I have my hand over all revenues in this region, but I cannot give out a vast sum at once and not make my men suffer.'"

"I do not want more land," said Wang the Merchant, reflecting, "and this has been a hard year here, near to famine, and land is cheap. All he has left will not be enough. His wedding fee ate deep into the lands."

Then the youth said earnestly, and his little bright black eyes shone in his face he was so earnest,

"Father, it is true my uncle is a very great man. You should see how everyone fears him! But he is a good man too, for he does not kill only to kill. Even the ruler of the province fears him. He is not afraid of anything—no, who but he would have dared to marry a woman whom everybody calls a fox! And if you give him these guns it will mean more power to him than ever."

Now the words of his own son cannot move a father too much, but still there was some truth in this and the thing that decided Wang the Merchant was that it would pay him well to have a brother who was a powerful lord of war. Yes, if the time of a great war came on such as was rumored in these years and if the war moved here—and who can tell how a war will move?—his great possessions might be seized and despoiled, if not by enemy soldiers, then perhaps by the lawless poor. For Wang the Merchant now had his wealth no more in lands, and the lands he had were as nothing beside his houses and shops and money-lending business, and such wealth may be taken away so quickly in a time when men are free to despoil, that in a few days a rich man may be made poor if he has no secret power from somewhere to help him and protect him, in a sudden need such as may come at any time.

So he thought to himself that these guns might be a protection for him, too, one day, and he thought a while longer of how he could purchase them and how smuggle them in. This he could do, for he now owned two small ships of his own to carry rice to an outer country near by. It was against the law to send rice out in this way, and he had to do it secretly, but he made a great profit on it and it paid him to give bribes, for the rulers were lax, and if they were paid, they overlooked his two little ships which he kept small on purpose, and vented their anger and zeal for law upon foreign ships or again upon some others that did not bring them any good.

And Wang the Merchant thought of his two ships coming back empty sometimes from that other country or else only half loaded with cotton stuffs and foreign knick-knacks, and he thought he could manage easily enough to smuggle foreign guns among those wares, and if he were caught he would put money out here and there and he would give his two captains something to close their mouths and make silence worth while for all. Yes, he could do this. Then he said to his son, looking about first to see that none was near, no guest or officious servant, and he spoke through his teeth without moving his lips and very softly,

"I can get the guns to the coast and even to a certain point where the railway runs nearest my brother, but how can I get them to him over a day and more of dry land and no way of travel except by foot or beast's back?"

Now Wang the Tiger had not said anything of this to the youth, so he could only scratch his head foolishly and stare at his father and he said,

"I must go back and ask him that."

And Wang the Merchant said, "Tell him I will manage to put the guns into goods of another sort and marked with other names and put them at a point, and then he must get them somehow from there."

So with this the lad went back to his uncle, and he went the very next day. But that night he slept in his own home and his mother cooked him a dish he loved of little steamed loaves of bread with garlic and pork inside, a very dainty dish. He ate himself full of these and what were left he thrust into his bosom to eat on the way. Then seated upon his ass he wound his way back again to Wang the Tiger.

XIX

THERE happened during the next month a thing such as Wang the Tiger in his arrogance would not have believed true if he had been told. The fever of war spread over that whole region when it was known that great lords above waged a war and split the country into two parts. In that fever little war-like spirits arose everywhere, and men who were idle and without work or those who would not work and lovers of any adventure and sons who did not love their parents and gamesters who lost in their gambling and every little discontented man seized on this time to come out and make a showing of some sort.

In this very region where Wang the Tiger now ruled in the name of the old magistrate, these rebellious men joined themselves into bands and they gave themselves the name of

The Yellow Turbans, because they wore strips of yellow about their heads, and they began to prey upon the country. At first they did it in small timid ways, exacting from some farmer food as they passed or they went into a village inn and ate and went on without paying or only partly paying for their meal, showing such fierce looks and raising their voices so high and quarrelsome that the innkeeper was afraid to make an ado and so swallowed his loss as best he could.

But these Yellow Turbans grew bolder as their numbers swelled, and they began to long for guns, for their only guns were the few that runaway soldiers among them had. They grew more bold, therefore, in their marauding among the common people, although they still did not come near any large towns or cities, but kept themselves to small villages and hamlets. At last some of the more courageous among the farmers came to Wang the Tiger and told him and they made report of how the marauders grew bold because they were unchecked and they would come in the night to rob and if they did not find all they liked they would kill a household of farming folk and think nothing of the deed. But Wang the Tiger did not know whether to believe the tale or not, for when he sent spies out to ask other farmers, there were weak ones who were afraid to tell and they denied the whole matter, and so Wang the Tiger for a time did nothing, thinking lightly of it when his whole mind was set on the right moment to declare himself in the great war.

But the time of the great heat of summer came on and many armies marched through to the south and there were some of these soldiers who were lured away to the robber band and the robbers grew greatly in numbers and daring. At this season of the year also the sorghum cane grew very high in those parts and it made a very perfect hiding place for robbers and they grew so bold and it came to such a pass that people did not dare to travel off the highway except in a large number together.

Now whether Wang the Tiger would have believed how bad it was or not cannot be said, for he was somewhat at the mercy of his men and he must believe what his spies and his own trusty men thought and they overpraised him and made him think none would dare to stand before him. But one day there came in from the country to the west two brothers, two farmers, and they carried a hempen bag with them. They would not open this bag for anyone to see, and they said steadfastly to all questions asked them,

"This bag is for the general."

And supposing they brought a gift to Wang the Tiger, the guards let them through the gates and they went to the hall of audience and there Wang the Tiger sat, for it was the hour when he often did so. When the two brothers came before him they made their obeisances, and then without a further word they opened the hempen bag and took from it two pairs of hands, one the hands of a very old woman, worn and hard with work and the dark skin cracked and dry, and the other the hands of an old man calloused in the palms with the holding of the handle of a plow. These hands the two brothers held up by the stumps where the blood now was black and dried. Then the elder of the brothers, a very earnest, angry man of middle age, his face square and honest, said,

"These are the hands of our old parents and they lie dead! Two days ago the robbers marauded in our hamlet and when my old father cried out that he had nothing they cut off his two hands, and when my old mother bravely cursed them they cut off hers also. We two brothers were in the fields but our wives escaped and came screaming to us and we ran back with our forks. But the robbers were gone, for there had been no great band of them, only eight or ten, and our parents were old. Yet not one in the village dared to lift his hand to help them lest they suffer at some later time. Sir, we let you have the revenues and we pay you a heavy tax over and above what we must pay the state, and we pay on land and on salt and on all we buy and sell and we do it to be protected from robbers. What will you do?"

And they held up the worn, stiff old hands of their parents.

Now Wang the Tiger did not, as many a man in his place would have done, grow angry at such bold speech. No, he was astounded at the tale, and he grew angry, not because the farmers had dared to tell him, but that such a thing could be in his regions. He shouted out for his captains and they came in, one by one as they were found here and there, until there were some fifty of them in the hall.

Then Wang the Tiger himself picked up the dead hands from where they lay helplessly upon the tiled floor and he showed them to all and he said,

"These are the hands of good farming folk who were marauded and robbed in the daytime when their sons worked in the fields! Who goes first against these marauders?"

The captains stared and the sight roused them and they were roused to think that robbers dared to rob in lands belonging to them and they muttered together and said here and there,

"Shall we let this go on in a land where we have the first right?"—"Shall these accursed thieves grow great in our own lands?" and they cried out, "Let us go against them!"

Wang the Tiger turned then to the two brothers and he said, "Return to your homes in peace and confidence. Tomorrow these will go out and I shall not rest until I find out who the head of these robbers is and deal with him as I dealt with the Leopard!"

Then the younger brother spoke, and he said, "Most Gracious, we think there is no head yet and they wander in little bands separate from one another except as their name links them, and they look for one strong man to hold them together."

"If this is so," said Wang the Tiger, "it will be the easier to scatter them."

"But not to stamp them out," said the older brother bluntly.

Then the two farmer brothers waited on there as though they had more to say and did not know how to say it, and at last after being impatient for a while in himself because they did not go, Wang the Tiger perceived they mistrusted him and he grew somewhat angry and said,

"Do you doubt that I am strong enough who killed the Leopard, a mighty robber in his day and he lived on you more than twenty years?"

The two brothers looked at each other and the elder one swallowed his spittle and said slowly,

"Most Gracious, it is not that. But we have something to say to you in private."

Wang the Tiger turned to the captains who still stood about and he shouted to them to be gone and prepare their men. When they were all gone except the one or two whom Wang the Tiger always kept about him, the elder brother fell on his face and he knocked his head three times upon the tiles and he said,

"Do not, Most Gracious, be very angry. We are poor men and when we ask a favor we can but ask it and we have no money to pay bribes to insure it."

And Wang the Tiger said in surprise, "What is it? I do not ask for bribes if you ask a thing I can do."

The man answered humbly, "When we came here today our village brothers tried to hold us back because they said

273

if we brought the soldiers it would be worse than the robbers for they demand so much and we are poor men who must work if we eat. The robbers come and go, but the soldiers live on in our houses and look at our maids and eat what we keep for the winter and we dare not oppose them because they have weapons. Most Gracious, if your soldiers are to come like this, then keep them, and we will suffer what we must."

Now Wang the Tiger was a good man and he was furious when he heard this and he rose and shouted for his captains to come again, and when they came back in twos and threes he roared at them and made his face very black and he drew his brows down at them and he said,

"This region I rule over is small enough so that the men can go out and be back the third day and so they shall do! Every man of mine shall be away no more than three days and if any quarters himself upon the people I will have him killed! If they overcome the robbers and rout them I will reward them with silver and food and wine but I am no robber chief and I have no robber band!" And he glared at the captains in so fierce a way that they promised him hastily.

Thus Wang the Tiger did, and he sent the brothers away with his promise and they took the hands of their parents and put them reverently into the hempen bag again, so that the old pair might be buried whole and with all their parts, and they returned to their village full of the praises of Wang the Tiger.

But when Wang the Tiger had sent the brothers away and took time to think what he had promised, he was in some dismay to find where his kind heart had carried him, and he sat in his own room very sober, for he had no mind to lose his good men and his guns in a brawl with robbers. He knew, too, that there must be some in his army such as are in every army, who are idle and looking for a better place, and these might even be enticed away to the robbers and take their guns with them. So he sat there brooding and thinking he had been too hasty and too moved by the token the brothers brought.

And as he sat there, a messenger came with a letter and it was from his brother, Wang the Merchant. Wang the Tiger tore the end and took the letter out and read it and there in devious, winding words, his brother told him that the guns were come and would be left at a certain place on a certain day, and they were hidden in bags of grain brought for making flour in the great northern mills.

Now Wang the Tiger was in as great a puzzle as he ever had been for he had to fetch the guns somehow and yet his men were scattering over the countryside against robbers. He sat awhile and cursed the day to himself, and as he sat the woman he loved came in. She was unusually gentle and languid as she walked, for it was the middle day of the great heat of summer, and she wore only a white silk coat and trousers, and she had unbuttoned the collar of her coat at the throat, so that her neck showed out, very soft and full and paler than her face.

Now Wang the Tiger for all his cursing and trouble saw her and he was caught and held at the sight of her pretty throat and he held his trouble back for an instant and he longed to lay his fingers there upon her pale neck, and he waited until she came near. She did come near and leaned upon the table and she said to him, looking at the letter he still held,

"Is there anything wrong with you that you look so black and angry?" Then she waited and laughed a little, a small high laugh, and she said, "I hope it is not I, for I would be afraid you might kill me with such black looks as you have now!"

Wang the Tiger held the letter out to her saying nothing, but his eyes fixed upon her bare throat and upon the smoothness of the turn it made into her bosom. He had come to such a pass with this woman that even in this short time he told her everything. She took the letter and read it, and he could take thought to be proud that she could read and he deemed her beautiful beyond anything as she bent over the letter, her thin, sharply marked lips moving a little as she read. Her hair was smooth now and oiled and knotted at her neck into a little net of black silk thread, and in her ears were hung gold rings.

She read the letter and then put it into its envelope again, and laid it on the edge of the table, and Wang the Tiger watched her quick light hands, thin and quick, as she did this, and then he said,

"I do not know how to get those bags of grain. I must get them by some guile or force."

"That is not hard," said the woman smoothly. "Guile and force are easy. I have a plan already in my head, made as I read the letter. You need only to send a band of your men as though they were robbers, the robbers that men tell of now-a-days, and let them seem to rob the grain for themselves, and who will know you have anything to do with it?"

Now Wang the Tiger laughed his noiseless laugh when she said this because it seemed to him so wise a plan and he drew her to him, for he was alone in the room and the guards went outside the door whenever she came, and he satisfied himself with his hard hands on her soft flesh, and he said,

"There has never been a woman so wise as you! When I killed the Leopard that day how I blessed myself in that deed!"

And after he had satisfied himself he went out and called
for the Hawk and he said,

"The guns we need are at a place about thirty miles from
here, where the two railroads cross, and they are in bags of
grain as though to be transshipped there to the northern mills.
But take five hundred men and arm yourselves and dress yourselves like some breed of robbers and go there and seize those
bags and seem to carry them away to a lair. But have carts
and asses ready at a near place and bring the bags here, grain
and all."

Now the Hawk was a clever man and he trusted to his wits
and to guile, whereas the Pig Butcher trusted to his two great
fists that were as large as earthen bowls, and a wily deed like
this pleased him, and so he bowed. Then Wang the Tiger
said further,

"When all the guns are here, be sure I shall reward you
and every soldier shall have a reward measured to what he
has done."

Then when this was done Wang the Tiger went back into
his room. The woman was gone, but he sat back in his armchair of carved wood, which had a woven reed seat for coolness, and he unfastened his girdle and his coat at the throat,
for the day grew to a monstrous heat, and he sat and rested
himself and thought of her throat and the turn it made into
her bosom and he marvelled that flesh could be so soft as hers,
and how skin could be so smooth.

Not once did he note that the letter his brother had written
was gone, for the woman had taken it and thrust it deep into
the bosom of her robe, where not even his hands had reached
it.

Now when the Hawk had been gone for a half a day Wang
the Tiger walked alone in the cool of the night before he went
in to sleep, and he walked in the court near a side gate that

was open to the street, a small street where few people passed, and those only by day. And as he walked he heard a cricket cheep. At first he paid no heed to it, because he had so much to dream of. But the cricket cheeped on, and at last he heard it and it came to him that this was not the time of the year for a cricket and so out of idle curiosity he looked to see where it was hid. It came from the gate and as he looked out into the gathering dusk he saw someone crouched and shapeless by the gate. He put his hand to his sword and stepped forward and there in the gathering dusk he saw his nephew's pocked face turned palely toward him and the lad whispered breathlessly,

"No sound, my uncle! Do not tell your lady I am here. But come into the street when you can and I will wait for you at the first forks. I have something to tell you and it must not wait."

The youth was off like a shadow then, but Wang the Tiger would not wait, since he was alone, and he went after the shadow, and came first to the spot. Then he saw his nephew come sliding along in the darkness of the walls, and he said in great astonishment,

"What ails you that you come creeping along like a beaten dog?"

And the youth whispered, "Hush—I have been sent to a place far from here—if your lady saw me here and she is such a clever one I do not know who she has watching me—she said she would kill me if I told, and it is not the first time she has threatened me!"

When Wang the Tiger heard this he was too astonished to speak. He lifted the lad half off his feet and dragged him into the darkness of an alley and he commanded him to speak. Then the lad put his mouth to Wang the Tiger's ear and he said,

"Your woman sent me with this letter to someone, but I do not know to whom, for I have not torn it open. She asked me if I could read and I said no, how could I, being country bred, and she gave me this letter, then, and told me to give it to a certain man who would meet me at the tea house in the north suburb tonight and she gave me a piece of silver for it."

He thrust his hand into his bosom and brought out a letter and Wang the Tiger seized it without a word. Without a word he strode through the alley to a small street where an old man opened a little solitary shop to sell hot water, and there, by the flickering light of the small bean oil lamp that was hung upon a nail on the wall, Wang the Tiger tore open the letter and read it. And as he read he saw plainly there was a plot. She—his woman—had told someone of his guns! Yes, he could see she had met someone and told him, and here in the letter she laid a last command. She wrote,

"When you have the guns and are gathered, I will come."

Now when Wang the Tiger read this it was as though the earth he stood upon whirled out from under his feet, and as though the heavens came down to crush him. He had loved this woman so heartily and so well that he never dreamed she could betray him. He had forgot every warning his trusty harelipped man gave him, and he never saw the man's downcast looks these days, and he loved the woman to such a point that he longed exceedingly for but one more thing, and it was that she would give him a son. Yes, he asked her again and again and with what ardor, every time, whether she had conceived or not. He had so loved her he did not dream she could withstand him in her heart. At this very hour he had been waiting, even, to go to his love; waiting for the night.

Now he saw she had never loved him. She could plot like this at the very hour when he waited for the turn of war and his own great step forward. She could plot like this and lie all night in his bed and pretend sorrow when he asked concerning his son. He was suddenly so angry he could not draw his breath. That old black anger of his rose in him blacker than he had ever known it to come. His heart beat and roared in his ears, his eyes blurred, and his brows knitted themselves until they pained him.

His nephew had followed him and stood in the shadow by the door. But Wang the Tiger flung him aside, without a word, and never seeing that in the strength of his anger he threw the lad down cruelly upon the sharp stones of the road.

He strode back to his courts on the wings of his anger and as he went he took his sword out of its sheath, the Leopard's fine steel sword, and he wiped it upon his thigh as he walked.

He went straight into the room where the woman lay in her bed, and she had not drawn the curtain because of the heat. There she lay, and the full moon of that night had risen over the wall of the court and its light fell upon her as she lay upon the bed. She lay naked for coolness and her hands were flung out and one lay curling and half open upon the edge of the bed.

But Wang the Tiger did not wait. Although he saw how fair she was and fair as an image of alabaster in the moonlight, and underneath his rage he knew there was a pain in him worse than death, he did not stay. For the moment he remembered wilfully how she had tricked him and how she would have betrayed him, and in this strength he lifted up his sword and he drove it down smoothly and cleanly into her throat, upturned as her head hung over her pillow. He twisted it sharply once, and then he brought it out and wiped it on the silken coverlid.

There came a single sound from her lips but the blood choked it so he did not know what she said and she did not move except that the instant his sword was in her throat, her arms and legs flew up and her eyes burst open. Then she died.

But Wang the Tiger would not stop to think what he had done. No, he strode out into the court and he shouted, and his men came running, and he threw his commands at them harsh and sure in his anger. He had to go now without a moment's delay to the succor of the Hawk and see if he could not reach the guns before the robbers did. All his men left he took with him except two hundred whom he left under the captaincy of his harelipped man and he led the others out himself.

As he passed through the gate he saw the old man who watched there come out of his bed yawning and dazed at all the sudden commotion and Wang the Tiger shouted at him as he rode by on his horse,

"There is something in my room where I sleep! Go and carry it out and fling it into a canal or some pond! See to it before I return!"

And Wang the Tiger rode on very high and proud and nursing his anger. But inside his breast it was as though his heart dripped blood secretly into his vitals and however he brooded and blew upon the flame of his anger, his heart dripped steadily and secretly within. And he groaned restlessly of a sudden, although none heard it in the dull thudding of horses' feet upon the dusty road. Neither did Wang the Tiger himself know that he groaned over and over again.

All over that countryside did Wang the Tiger roam with his men that night and the next day, seeking the Hawk, and the sun beat down upon them for the day came windless. But Wang the Tiger would not let his men rest because he had that within himself which could not rest and toward the evening upon the highway that ran north and south he met the

Hawk at the head of his band of walking soldiers. At first Wang the Tiger could not be sure if these were his own men for the Hawk had done what he had been told to do, and he had told his men to wear their ragged inner garments and tie a towel about their heads and Wang the Tiger had need to wait until they came near to see who they were.

But at last Wang the Tiger saw these were indeed his own men. He dismounted then from his red horse and sat down under a date tree that was there beside the road, for he was exceedingly spent from within, and he waited for the Hawk to come near. The more he waited the more afraid he grew that his anger might die down, and he forced himself to remember, with a furious pain, how he had been deceived. But the secret of his pain and anger was that although the woman was dead, yet he still loved her; although he was glad he had killed her, yet he longed for her with passion.

This angry pain made him very surly and when the Hawk was come Wang the Tiger growled at him, scarcely lifting his eyes, and his eyes nearly hidden under his brows,

"Well, I will swear you have not the guns!"

But the Hawk had a voluble good tongue of his own in that peaked face of his and he had a very ready and proud temper and this temper made him brave and he answered with heat, and without any courteous words,

"How did I know the robbers would have been told of the guns? They had been told by some spy or other and they went before us. How can I help it if they were told before you told me?" And as he spoke he threw his gun upon the ground and folded his arms on his bosom and he stared mutinously at his general, to show he would not be put down.

Then Wang the Tiger, seeing justice still, rose wearily from the grass where he sat and he stood under the date tree and leaned against its rough trunk, and he unbuckled his belt and drew it more tightly about him before he spoke. But at last he said wearily and with a great bitterness,

"I suppose all my good guns are gone, then. I shall have to fight the robbers for them. Well, if we must fight we will!" He shook himself impatiently and spat and roused himself and went on with more vigor, "Let us go and find them and press hard on them, and if half of you lie dead after the fray, why, then you are dead and I cannot help it! My guns I must have and if a gun costs me ten men or so, why, I will find ten men more for every gun and the gun is worth it!"

Then he mounted his horse again and held the beast hard when it danced to and fro with impatience that it was taken from the succulent grass that was there, and the Hawk stood there moodily watching and at last he said,

"I know well enough where the robbers are. They are gathering together in the old lair and I can swear they have the guns with them. Who their leader is I do not know, but they have been busy for a few days now, and have given the countryside peace while they gathered together, as though they were ready to choose a leader."

Now Wang the Tiger knew well who their leader was to have been but he said no more except to give his men orders to march against that lair and he said,

"We will go there and you are to fire at them. When the firing is over, I will parley and every man who brings a gun may join my ranks. For every gun you see and pick up and bring to me you shall have a piece of silver." And so saying, he mounted his horse once more.

Once more Wang the Tiger rode over the winding valley paths and over the low foothills until he came to the double-crested mountain, and his men came raggedly behind him. The farming folk looked up from their fields and wondered and the soldiers shouted,

"We go against the robbers!"

To this sometimes farmers made answer back heartily, "A good deed!" But more there were who said nothing and they looked sourly at the soldiers as they tramped into their fields of grain and cabbages and melons, because they did not believe that any good could come of soldiers, they were so weary of them.

Once more did Wang the Tiger ascend the foothills and at the base of the double-crested mountain where the pass wound up between cliffs, he dismounted and led his horse and so did all his men who rode. But he paid no heed to them. He walked along as though he were alone, his body bent to the mountain, and he thought of the woman and how strangely he had come to love her and he loved her still so that he was weeping in himself and he could scarcely see the mosses of the steps. But he would not repent that he had killed her. No, in spite of his love he understood in some dim part of him that such a woman who could deceive him so perfectly as she had when she accepted with smile and with frankness his passion, such a woman could only be true if she were dead, and he muttered to himself,

"She was a fox, after all."

So he led his men steadfastly up that mountain and when he was near to the head of the pass he sent the Hawk and fifty men ahead to see what was in the lair, and he waited in the shade of a cluster of pine trees, for the sun beat down exceedingly hot. In less than an hour the Hawk came back and he said he had circled about the place and he gave report: "They are all unready for they are building up the lair again."

"Did you see anyone above another?" said Wang the Tiger.

"No, I did not," answered the Hawk. "I crept so close I could even hear what they said. They are very ignorant and unlearned in robbery for the pass is not guarded, and there they are quarreling among themselves for the houses least ruined."

This was good news, and Wang the Tiger shouted to his men and at their head he ran swiftly up the pass and as he ran he gave great shouts and he commanded his men to rush into the lair and kill at least a robber apiece, and then stop so that he could parley.

So they did, and Wang the Tiger stood to one side and his men rushed in and shot off a round and everywhere the robbers dropped dead and writhing and crying bitterness as they died or lay dying. It was true they were all unprepared and thinking only of their houses and of how they would establish themselves, and there must have been three or five thousand of them gathered in that lair, like ants in a mound, all piling earthen walls and carrying timbers and straw for roofs and planning for future greatness. When they were surprised like this every man dropped what he did and ran hither and thither and Wang the Tiger saw there was not one to tell them what to do and that they had no certain leader. For the first time some slight weak ray of solace came into Wang the Tiger's heart, for well he knew who would have marshalled them, and it came to him that sooner or later he would have had to fight against the woman he loved and better to kill her as he did.

When he thought of this his old belief in his destiny rose in him once more and he shouted to his men in his lordly way and commanded them to stand and he cried out to the robbers who were not shot,

"I am Wang the Tiger who rules this region, and I will not brook robbers! I am not afraid to kill and not afraid to die. I will kill every one of you if you think to join others against me! Yet I am a merciful man too, and I will make a way out for those of you who are honorable men. I return to my encampment now in the county seat. Within the next three days I will accept into my ranks any man of you who comes with a gun, and if he brings two guns he shall have a free gift of silver for the extra gun he has."

When he had shouted this out, Wang the Tiger called to his men sharply and they all went clattering down the pass again. Only he made certain of this, that some of his men went down backward and that they kept their guns upon the pass, lest there come a shot or two from some bolder robber. But the truth was those robbers were very ignorant men. They had fallen in with the plot of the woman who had been the Leopard's, and they went eagerly to fetch the guns, yet few of them knew how to hold a gun, and those few only runaway soldiers, and they did not dare to fire upon Wang the Tiger lest it be nothing but twisting a tiger's whiskers and he come rushing back upon them, and destroy them all.

There was complete silence in that mountain and not a sound came from the lair, and as Wang the Tiger went on his way there was only the slight rise and fall of the winds in the pines and a bird calling in a tree. And he led his men down the pass. Back through the fields he led them and as he went the soldiers said everywhere in exultation to the farming folk,

"Three days and the robbers will be gone, we swear!"

Some of the folk were glad and thankful, but most of them were guarded in their looks and words and waited to see what Wang the Tiger would want of them, for they had never heard of a lord of war who did anything for a countryside without asking much in return for all he did.

Then Wang the Tiger went back to his own courts and he gave his soldiers each a fee of silver coins and he ordered wine of a good enough quality to be given to every man, enough to comfort him but not to make him drunken. And he had a few kinds of special meats for them. Then he waited for the three days to pass.

One by one or in pairs or in fives and eights and tens the robbers began to come straggling into that city from everywhere, bringing guns with them. Seldom did any man bring two guns, for if he had laid his hand on more than one gun he brought with him a younger friend or a brother or some other one, for truly many of these men were in need and without food enough to eat and they were glad to seek sure service under a leader somewhere.

Wang the Tiger commanded that every sound man not too old be received into his army, and from such as he did not want he took the guns and paid them something. But to such men as he received he gave food and good clothing.

When the three days were over he allowed three more days of mercy and after these three more, and men came in day after day until the courts and the soldiers' camps were bursting and Wang the Tiger was forced to quarter his men into the houses of that town. Sometimes a man who was the father of a family would come to complain that his house was crowded and his family squeezed into a room or two. But if he came and Wang the Tiger saw he was young or that he was bumptious in his complaining, then Wang the Tiger threatened him and said,

"Can you help it? Bear it then! Or would you rather have robbers in the region to despoil you?"

But if the one who complained were an old man or if he came courteously and spoke gently, then Wang the Tiger was courteous, too, and he gave him some silver or a gift of some sort, and said courteously,

"It is only for a short time, for I shall march to the war soon. I shall not rest content always with so small a county seat for my capital."

And he said everywhere to all, and he said with some savage bitterness because he had no woman of his own any more and it galled him in some secret unknown way to think of any man with any woman,

"If any soldier of mine looks on a woman forbidden, tell me, and he is dead!" And he quartered the new soldiers in the houses nearest him, and he threatened them heartily if they did so much as look at a good woman.

To every soldier also Wang the Tiger paid what he promised him. Yes, although he was now hard pressed for silver, since nearly four thousand new men had joined him from the robbers and he had only two thousand and odd out of the three thousand guns he had his brother buy for him, yet he paid every man and kept them all content. But he knew he could not always do this unless he could think of some new tax, for he was now drawing upon his own secret stores, and this was a dangerous thing for a lord of war to do, lest if he be suddenly put down, and must retreat somewhere for a time, he has nothing then to feed to his men. And Wang the Tiger set himself to think of some new tax.

Now the spies that Wang the Tiger had sent out began to gather in again at this time, for the summer was coming to an end, and they all brought the same news, and it was that the southern generals were repulsed once more and again the north was victorious. This Wang the Tiger believed the more readily because during the last few weeks he had not been hard pressed as he had been before by the provincial general to send his forces out to battle for him.

So Wang the Tiger made haste, then, and he sent his nephew and his trusty harelipped man and they took his letter to the capital of the province and he wrote a courteous letter regretting he had been so long putting down the robbers

288

in that land, but now he was ready to join his forces to the north against the south, and he sent gifts.

But his destiny helped him very cleverly again, for on that very day when the pair reached the capital with this letter, truce was sworn and the rebels went south to recover themselves, and the northern armies were given their days of looting for booty as a reward of their victory. So when the general of that province received Wang the Tiger's allegiance he sent back a courteous acceptance, but he said that this war was over and the autumn come. Yet doubtless there would be other wars and spring would come again, and Wang the Tiger was to hold himself ready for such a time.

This was the answer the pair took back to Wang the Tiger and he received it and was well content, for his name he knew would be among those of the victorious generals, and he had not lost a man and not a gun, and he had his great army whole.

XX

THEN the golden winds of autumn blew clear out of the west and over the land once more, and the farmers reaped their harvests and the full moon swung once more to its height and the people rejoiced in the coming of the mid-autumn festival and they made ready to give thanks to the gods for these goods, that there had been no great famine and only a crop or two scarce, that the robbers had been put down once again, and that wars had not come near their region.

And Wang the Tiger took account of himself where he was and how much he had achieved and he found he was better this year than last. Yes, he now had twenty thousand soldiers under him quartered in the town and in its suburbs and he had altogether nearly twelve thousand guns. Moreover, he was now known and reckoned among the lords of war, for the weak and unready ruler whom the war had left still sitting in his place had sent out a proclamation of gratitude to all those generals who had helped him to remain when the generals of the south had tried to end his government, and Wang the Tiger's name was among the others to whom he gave thanks and titles. It is true that the title given to Wang the Tiger was not high and it sounded longer and better than it was, but still it was a title, and for this honor he had not entered a battle or lost a gun.

There remained to him this one great difficulty and it was that at the time for the feast, when it is a time of reckoning for all who lend or borrow, Wang the Merchant sent word that he must receive the money for the guns, for others pressed him for payment. Then Wang the Tiger grew quarrelsome and he parleyed with his brother and sent a man to say that this time he would not pay for the whole of the guns he had lost and he said to his brother through this messenger,

"You should have warned your agents not to turn the guns to the first who came for them."

To this Wang the Merchant answered with reason,

"But how did I know that the ones who brought my own letter for proof and used your name for a sign were not your men?"

This Wang the Tiger could not answer, but he had the power of his armies to use for an argument and so he said back again in great anger,

"I will pay half the loss and no more and if you do not agree to this I will pay nothing, and I do not need to do in these days what I do not wish to do."

Then Wang the Merchant, being a man prudent and full of philosophy if he could not mend a thing, agreed to it and he bore his half well enough because he could raise the certain rentals he had and he put the interest up somewhat in a place or two where he knew he could not be refused and so he did not hurt himself.

But Wang the Tiger at first scarcely knew how to get the sum that he must pay, because he needed so much for his vast army that although a stream of silver ran into his hands every month and even every day yet it all ran out again, too. He called his trusty men into his own room and said to them in private,

"Is there any revenue we could have which we do not have now?"

And his trusty men scratched their heads to warm up their brains and they looked at each other and here and there and they could not think of anything. The harelipped man said,

"If we make the revenues too heavy on foods and goods the people must have every day they may turn against us."

This Wang the Tiger knew was true, for so the common people have done always if they are too pressed and must turn or else starve, and although Wang the Tiger was by now very well entrenched in that region, still he was not great enough to be wholly careless of the people. So he must think of something new and at last he thought of a chief industry in that town and of a tax he could put upon it, and it was the tax of a copper coin or two on every wine jar made in that region.

Now the wine jars of that region were famous, and they were made of a very fine pottery clay and glazed blue and when the wine was poured into them a seal of the same clay was put over the mouth and stamped with a sign, and that sign was known everywhere for a sign of good wine in a good jar. When Wang the Tiger thought of this he slapped his thigh and shouted out,

"The pottery makers grow richer every year, and why should we not make them share a tax with the others?"

All the trusty men agreed to it as a very good thought, and so Wang the Tiger laid the tax that very day. He laid it courteously and he sent word for the heads of the business and told them he protected them for he protected the sorghum lands where the cane grew for their wine, and if he did not there would be no wine for their jars, and he said he needed money to protect the lands, and his soldiers must be fed and armed and paid. But behind all this courtesy were the glittering weapons of his thousands and although the pottery makers met together secretly and grew very angry and talked of a hundred ways and of rebelling and of many things, they knew in the end they could not refuse for Wang the Tiger could do what he liked and there were many worse than he, and this they knew.

They were willing, then, since they must be, and Wang the Tiger sent his trusty men to estimate what the output of the jars was and every month there was a good full sum of silver given to Wang the Tiger, and in three months or so he paid Wang the Merchant. Then, since the pottery makers were used by this time to the tax, Wang the Tiger let it come on into his hands and he did not say the need for it was not so sharp as it had been. Indeed he did need all he could secure, for he had a long road yet before the end of his ambition was come, and he was restless with his ambition and he busied himself in many things.

Then when he took thought and saw that he could not take much more from the people of his lands and keep them content, he cried to himself that he was too great for so small a place and in the next spring time he must enlarge himself far beyond the confines he now had, for this region was so small that if a great famine came, such as might come any year under the cruelty of heaven, he would be undone. He had been protected thus far by his good destiny, for there had been no vast famine yet since he came to this place, and only small ones in this place and that.

Then the winter drew on when there can be no war and Wang the Tiger entrenched himself warmly. He saw to it that so long as the rain and the winds did not beat too bitterly nor the snow fall too deeply, his men went out every day for training and exercise. He himself trained the best and cleverest, and these taught the others. Especially did Wang the Tiger take stock of his guns. Every month he had them counted before his eyes and tallied with his account, both in number and kind, of what he had, and he continually told his men that if there was at any time a gun not there by its tally, he would shoot a man or two or three to keep the proportion what it was. Not one dared to disobey him. More than ever they feared him, for they all knew by now that he had killed even the woman he loved. He could be so angry even as that, and they all dreaded his anger, and leaped if he so much as twisted his black brows together.

Then winter came down out of the bitter north and the dark days came when Wang the Tiger could not go out nor force his men out and he faced at last what he knew was waiting for him and that against which he had been so busy. He was idle and he was alone.

Now did he wish he were like other men who turn eagerly to gambling or to the drinking of wine or to feasting or to the seeking out of some woman to divert them from any trouble they may have. But Wang the Tiger was not so. He had eaten plain food and liked it better than a feast, and the thought of any woman sickened him. Once and twice he tried to game, but he had not the temper for it. He was not quick at dice or at seizing a chance and when he lost he grew angry and felt for his sword and those who gamed with him were alarmed when they saw his brows begin to twist and his mouth grow more surly than it was and when they saw his big hand fly to his hilt, and they made haste to let him win every time. But this wearied Wang the Tiger, too, and he cried out,

"It is a fool's game, as I ever said it was!" and he flung himself away furious because he was not diverted nor eased at all.

Worse than the day was the night that must come and he hated it more than the day, for he slept alone and he must sleep alone. Now this loneliness by day and by night was not a good thing for such a man as Wang the Tiger for he had a heavy bitter heart that did not see mirth as some do, who have even more to bear than he, and the lonely sleep was not good either, for he had a strong and craving body. Still there was not a soul whom he could take for friend.

It was true that the old magistrate lived still in a side court with his old wife who was now dying of a consumption, and he was in his way a good and learned old man. But he was so unused to men like Wang the Tiger and so frightened that he could only fork his two old hands together and make haste to say whenever Wang the Tiger spoke to him,

"Yes, Honored—yes, General!"

And Wang the Tiger was wearied of this after a while and scowled at the old scholar so fearsomely that he turned the color of clay and he scuttled out of the rooms as soon as he dared, his faded robes dragging on his thin old body.

Yet Wang the Tiger held back his impatience, too, for he was a just man and he knew the old magistrate did the best he could and often he sent him away quickly before his impatience grew too high lest he might grow angry and do

294

damage to the old man and his hand fly out before he meant it to do so.

There were his trusty men also, three good and true warriors, and the Hawk was indeed a very good warrior and better than a thousand common soldiers in his cleverness of guile. Still he was but an ignorant man and he could only talk of the ways there are to hold a weapon and the ways there are of sparring with fists and of kicking with the right foot and the left in a circle before the enemy can recover himself, and such ways and feints of battle, and when he had told these over and over and told how he had done this and done so in some fight or other he had had somewhere, he had told all he knew and Wang the Tiger wearied of him even while he valued him.

There was that Pig Butcher and he was very able with his great, nimble fists and his thick body that he could throw against a gate and crush it in, yet he was but heavy, stammering company on a winter's night. And there was the trusty harelipped man, the truest best soul although no great warrior, either, and best when sent on some message, and his hissing and spitting when he talked could be no pleasure. Nor would Wang the Tiger stoop to talk with his nephew who was a generation beneath him, nor would he descend to feasting and carousing with his own soldiers, for he knew that if a leader does this and if he lets himself be common and play among his own men and lets them see him weak and drunken, on the day of battle they will not reverence him or hear his command, and indeed Wang the Tiger took great care never to appear before his own men unless he wore his full accoutrements of war and unless he had his sharp sword he had used in such a way that now he loved and hated it too. Yet it was so keen a blade that he could never find its mate in the world, and he used to take it out and look at it and muse sometimes when he was alone and think how if he brought it down upon a cloud even it would cut it in two. Her throat had been as soft as that and so the blade had done that night.

But even if Wang the Tiger had had friends in the day there must come the night at the end of every day and he must be alone then perforce and he lay upon his bed alone, and the nights in winter are very long and black.

Through such long black nights must Wang the Tiger lie alone and sometimes he lit a taper candle and read his old books he had loved as a lad and which had first turned his mind to soldiering, the stories of the three kingdoms and of the robbers that bordered a great lake, and he read many doughty tales like these. But he could not read forever. The candle burned down to the end of its reed wick, and he grew cold and he must lie alone at last in the black and bitter night.

Then, although every night he put off this hour, yet the hour came when he remembered the woman he loved and he mourned for her. But he did not in all his mourning wish her living again, for he knew and he steadfastly told himself that she could never have been one whom he could have trusted and the sweetness of his love had been that he had opened his whole heart to her. No, dead he could trust her, but if she had been alive and he had prevented and pardoned her, still he would have been afraid of her always. The fear would have divided him, so that only half his heart would have gone on in his cause and he would never have risen to be great.

So he told himself in the night. Yet he pondered painfully on this, that the Leopard, who had been but an ignorant fellow, risen but a little above his robber band, could have so won the love of the woman, who was no common woman, that even though he were dead, yet did she cleave to him and even against her living love she clave to the dead man still.

For Wang the Tiger could not believe she had never loved him. No, he remembered over and over with hunger when he thought of it how frank she had been and passionate upon this very bed where he now lay. He would not believe that such passion had sprung up where no love was. And he grew wretched and weak and felt that somehow he must be a lesser man, for all his pride and place, than the Leopard he had killed, because his living hold upon the woman had been less than the memory of the dead man in her. He could not understand all this, but only he felt it must be so.

And feeling himself less of a man than he thought, his life stretched ahead of him long and meaningless and he doubted himself that he could ever be great and if he did then for what use, seeing he had no son for whom to achieve greatness, and it would all die with him and what he had go to others. He did not love his brothers or his brothers' sons enough to struggle in war and guile for them. And he groaned to himself in the dark and silent room and he groaned out,

"When I killed her I killed two, and the other was the son I might have had!"

Then he remembered again and he always saw her now as she looked when she lay dead, her strong fair throat pierced and the bright blood gushing out. When he saw her thus again and again, he could not bear it, and suddenly he could not lie any longer on this bed, no, although it had been washed and painted freshly and the blood stains were gone and the pillow was new, and although no one had ever mentioned to him what had happened there nor had he ever known where they took her body. He rose from the bed and he wrapped his quilts about him and sat miserable and shivering upon a chair, until the feeble dawn came and showed pale and chill through his lattices.

So the winter nights wore on the same, night after night,

and at last Wang the Tiger cried out to himself that this could not be, for these sad and lonely nights were making him less than a man and they were sucking the ambition out of him. He grew afraid for himself because nothing seemed good to him any more and he was impatient with all who came near, and most of all did he grow impatient with his nephew and he said bitterly,

"This is the best I have, this grinning pocked ape, son of a tradesman—this is nearest I have to my own son!"

At last when it seemed he must go mad a turn came in his own spirit and it came to him one night that the woman even though dead was ruining him as surely as she would have done if she had been alive and gone the way she planned. And suddenly he hardened himself and it seemed he spoke to her own ghost to defy her and he said in his own heart,

"Cannot any woman have sons, and do I not desire a son more than any mere woman? I will have a son. I will take a woman or two or three until I have a son. I have been a fool that I do always cling so to one woman—first to a woman I never even knew beyond a few scattered words such as a man may speak to a slave in his father's house and I went sore for that woman nearly ten years, and then there was the one I had to kill. Shall I never be rid of her too and shall I go sore for her another ten years and be too old to beget a son then? No, I shall be as other men are and I will see if I cannot make myself free as other men do and take a woman and leave her again when I please."

On that very day he called his trusty harelipped man to him and he called him into his own private room and he said,

"I have need of a woman, any woman of a decent kind, and go and tell my brothers that my wife is dead and tell them to find me something since I am busy with the wars that must come in the spring time and I do not care to deviate my thoughts from the wars."

The harelipped man went gladly on this errand then, for he had seen with jealous eyes at least a little of what his general suffered and had guessed the cause, and he thought this good cure.

As for Wang the Tiger, he could but wait to see what time would bring and what his two brothers would do for him, and while he waited he forced himself to plan his wars and to think how he would enlarge himself. And he schemed how to weary himself into sleep at night.

XXI

B Y winding ways, lest men mark his harelip and wonder at his frequent coming, the trusty man came to the town and thence to the great house where the Brothers Wang lived. He asked and found that Wang the Merchant was at this hour, which was nearly noon, in his counting house, and there the trusty man went at once to give his message. Wang the Merchant sat in his own part of the counting house, a small dark room which gave off the main market, and he was fingering an abacus and reckoning certain profits he had made on a ship's load of wheat. He looked up and listened to the trusty man's tale, and when he had heard he said, astounded, his little eyes staring, and his meager mouth pursed,

"Now I can get even silver more easily for him than I can get a woman. How should I know where to turn for a woman? It is an ill thing he has lost the one he had."

The trusty man, sitting cornerwise upon a lowly seat to show he felt his place, answered humbly saying,

"All I ask, my master's brother, is that you find a sort of woman who will not trouble our general and make him love her. He has a strange deep heart and he so fixes himself on one thing that it is a madness with him. So he loved this woman who died and he has not forgotten her yet, no, although months have passed he does not forget her and such constancy in a man is not good for his health."

"How did she die?" asked Wang the Merchant curiously.

But the trusty man was very faithful and discreet and he stopped himself as he was about to answer, because he bethought himself that when men are outside the ranks of soldiers and not acquainted with war-like things, they grow squeamish and they cannot bear killing and dying as soldiers must, whose trade it is to kill and be killed if they cannot save themselves by guile. So he said simply,

"She died of a sudden flow of blood," and Wang the Merchant let it be at that.

Then he sent the trusty man away, first bidding a clerk to take him to some small inn and feed him with rice and pork, and after they were gone Wang the Merchant sat and mused and he thought to himself,

"Well, and here is a time when that older brother of mine will know more than I, for if he knows anything at all it is women, and what woman do I know except the one I have?"

Then Wang the Merchant rose to go out and find his brother, Wang the Landlord, and he took from a nail in the wall his grey silk robe that he wore when he went out but took off in his counting house to spare it wear, and he went to his brother's house and he asked the gateman to know if his master were at home that day. The gateman would have led him in, but Wang the Merchant would wait, and the gateman went in and asked a slave and the slave replied that he was at a certain gaming house. When Wang the Merchant heard this he went to that piece, choosing his way as delicately as a cat over the cobbled street, because it had snowed in the night and the day was so cold that even yet the snow lay there, and there was only a little path in the middle made by vendors and those who must go out for a living or as his brother did, for pleasure.

He came to the gaming house and he asked a clerk and heard that his brother was within at a certain door, and Wang the Merchant went to it and opened it and found Wang the Landlord there gaming with certain of his friends in a small room made hot with a brazier of coals.

When Wang the Landlord saw his brother's head come in at the door he was secretly glad to be disturbed and called away, for he was not over-skilled at gaming, since he had learned the thing late in life. Wang Lung, his father, would not have let a son of his gamble in city gaming houses if he had known it. But Wang the Landlord's son was quick and able enough because he had gamed all his life long, and even the second son had been able to gain a little pile of silver at any game he had a share in.

So when Wang the Landlord saw his brother's head come in at the partly opened door he rose readily and said in haste to his friends,

"I must stop, for my brother needs me for something," and he took up his fur coat he had laid aside in the heat of the room and went out to where Wang the Merchant waited. But he did not say he was glad he had come, because he was too proud to tell that he lost at gaming, since a clever man should win. He only said,

"Have you something to say to me?"

Wang the Merchant answered in his scanty way, "Let us go where we can talk, if there is such a place in this house."

Then Wang the Landlord led the way to a place where

there were tables for tea drinking, and they chose a lonely table set a little apart from the others, and there the two brothers seated themselves, and Wang the Merchant waited while Wang the Landlord ordered tea and then wine and then bethinking himself of the hour, he ordered some meats and dishes of food. At last the serving man was gone, and Wang the Merchant began forthright,

"That younger brother of ours wants a wife, for his woman is dead and he has sent to us this time. I thought here is a thing you can manage better than I."

This Wang the Merchant said drawing down his lips in a secret smile. But Wang the Landlord did not see it. He laughed out loud and his fat cheeks shook and he said,

"Well, and if I know anything at all it is such things, and you are right but it would not do to say it before my lady, though!"

And he laughed and looked sidewise out of his eyes as men will when they talk of these matters. But Wang the Merchant would not joke with him and he waited. Wang the Landlord sobered himself then and he said, further,

"But this comes at a very good time, for I have been looking over the maids of this town for my son, and I know all the likely maids. I have a plan now to betroth the eldest one of my sons to a maid nineteen years of age, a daughter of the younger brother of the magistrate—a very good, honorable maid, and my son's mother has seen some of the samples of her embroidery and handiwork. She is not pretty but very honorable. The only trouble is my son has some silly thought of choosing a wife for himself—he has heard of such new ways in the south.

"But I tell him it is not known here to do such things, and besides he can choose others he likes. As for that poor hunch-

302

back, his mother wants a priest in the family, and it seems a pity to waste a good straight son in such a way—"

But Wang the Merchant was not interested in all these doings of his brother's family, for it is known as a matter of course that every son must be wed sooner or later and his own sons also, but he did not waste his time on such things, deeming them women's duty, and he had put it all into his wife's hands, saying only that such maids as came into his house must be virtuous and stout and hard working. So he broke in now with impatience,

"But are any of the maids you saw fit for our brother, and are their fathers willing to have them go into a house to wife one already wed as he has been?"

But Wang the Landlord would not hasten himself over such a dainty job as this and he let his memory linger upon the maids, this one and that, and on all he knew from what he had heard of them and he said,

"There is a very good maid, not too young, whose father is a scholar and he has made her into something of a scholar, too, he having no son and needing to teach someone what he knew. She is what they call now-a-days a new woman, such as have learning and do not bind their feet, and because she is strange in this way, her marriage has been delayed, because men have not dared to take a woman like this for their sons, lest a trouble come out of it. But I hear there are many like her in the south, and it is only because this is a small old city, doubtless, that men here do not know what to make of her. She goes on the street even and I have seen her once and she went very decorously and did not stare about her, either. With all her learning she is not so hideous as might be feared, and if she is not very young yet she cannot be more than twenty-five or six. Do you think my brother would fancy such a one who is not like a usual woman?"

To this Wang the Merchant answered with reserve, "But do you think she will make a good housewife and be useful to him? He reads and writes himself as well as many a man does, and if he did not he could hire it done for him by some scholar. I do not see that he needs all this learning in a wife."

Then Wang the Landlord, who had been dipping food into his bowl busily, the serving man having come to and fro many times with dishes, paused and held his porcelain spoon in mid-air full of a soup and he cried,

"He can hire a servant too, I swear, or a jade, and it is not all in what a woman can do that makes her a good wife. The chief thing is whether or not she fits a man's fancy or not, especially if he is one like my brother who will not seek out other women. Sometimes I think it would be a pleasant thing to tickle a man if his wife could sit and read poetry to him or some tale of love as he lies on his bed to sleep."

But this was distasteful to Wang the Merchant and he picked delicately at a dish of pigeons stewed with chestnuts and thrust his chopsticks carefully between the bones to find the bit he relished and he said,

"I would rather fit my fancy to a woman careful in the house and who had children and who could save money."

Then Wang the Landlord grew suddenly angry in the wilful way he had even since his childhood and his great full face turned a dark red and Wang the Merchant saw they would never agree on this, and it was not a thing to waste his day upon, for women are but women, whoever they may be otherwise, and one will serve the final purpose of a man as well as another, so he said quickly,

"Ah, well, and that brother of ours is not poor, and let us choose two wives for him then. Do you choose the one you think best, and we will wed him to her first, and then awhile later send him the one I choose, and if he likes one better than the other let him, but two are not many for such a man as he in his position."

Thus they compromised, and Wang the Landlord was pleased that the one he chose was to be the wife, although when he thought, it seemed no more than his due, for no man could lie with two wives on his wedding night, and, after all, he was the eldest son in this family and the head. So they agreed and then parted and Wang the Landlord went bustling to do his part and Wang the Merchant went back to his house to find his wife and talk with her.

When he reached his home she was at the gate standing in the snowy street, her hands wrapped in her apron to warm them, but ever and again she brought them out to probe the crops of fowls that a vendor had there to sell. The snow had made such fowls cheaper than usual since they could not find their own food and she wished to add a hen or two to her stock and as Wang the Merchant came near she did not look up but continued to peer at the fowls. But Wang the Merchant said to her as he passed, to go into the house,

"Have done, woman, come here."

Then she made haste and chose two hens and after quarreling over their weight upon the scales to which the vendor hung them by their legs tied together, they agreed upon the price and she came into the house and thrust the hens under a chair and then sat down cornerwise on it to hear what her husband had to say to her and he said in his dry, scanty way,

"That younger brother of mine wants a wife, for his has died suddenly. I know nothing of women, but you have had your eyes hanging out these two years looking for wives for our sons. Is there one we could send there?"

His wife answered readily, for she delighted in all such things as birth and death and marriage and her constant talk was of these,

305

"There is a very good maid who lived next door to me in my own village, and she is so good I have often wished that she were young enough for our eldest. She is the pleasantest-tempered maid, and very saving, and she has no fault at all except that her teeth grew black even when she was a child from some worm that ate them away, it is said, and now they drop out sometimes. But she is ashamed of this and keeps her lips drawn down to hide them, so they are not easily seen, and because of this she talks very little and very low. Her father is not poor either, and he owns land, and he will be glad to have her wed so well, I know, seeing that she is already a little beyond the age."

Then Wang the Merchant said dryly, "If she cannot talk much that will be worth something. See to it, and after the wedding we will send her." And he told his wife that two women were to be chosen, and she said loudly,

"Well, I feel sorry for him if he has to have one of your brother's choosing for what does he know except lewd women, and I vow if his lady has anything to do with it she will choose a nunnish creature, for I hear now she is so daft over priests and nuns she would have the whole house praying and mumming. It is well enough, I say, to go to the temple once in a way if there is someone sick of a fever or if a woman is childless or something, but I daresay the gods are like all of us, and we do not love best the people who are for ever troubling us and calling at us for this and that!"

And she spat on the floor and rubbed the place with her foot, and forgetting the hens under her chair, she thrust her feet back and struck them and they set up a mighty squawking, so that Wang the Merchant rose and called out impatiently,

"I never saw such a house! Must we have hens everywhere?"

And when she reached under hastily to drag the fowls out

and explain how the price for them was less than usual now, he broke in to what she began to say and said,

"Let be—let be—I must go back to my markets. Attend to the thing and this day two months or so we will call her. Only keep all the costs well in mind for the law does not require that we pay over again for my brother's wedding."

Thus the thing was done and the two maids were betrothed and the deeds drawn up and Wang the Merchant entered the costs carefully into his counting books, and that day month was the day set for the wedding.

Now the day was near the end of the old year, and Wang the Tiger when he had been told of it, made ready to go to his brothers' house to wed once more. He had no heart to do the thing and yet he had determined he would and so he gave over any thought or wavering and he made ready his three trusty men he appointed to watch in his stead, and he left his nephew to be messenger if any trouble should rise while he was gone.

When he had done this he made a feint of asking permission of the old magistrate to leave for five days and six days for the journey to come and to go, and the old magistrate made haste to give his permission. And Wang the Tiger took precaution to tell the old magistrate that he left his army and his trusty men, lest there be some vague hope of rising against him somehow. Then clothing himself in his next best garments and taking his best with him in a roll upon his saddle, Wang the Tiger went south to his home, taking with him a small guard of fifty armed men, for he was a man of such courage that he did not, as many lords of war do, surround himself with hundreds of inner and outer guards.

Through the wintry country Wang the Tiger rode, stopping at village inns by night, and riding on again over the frozen earthen roads. There was no sign yet of spring, and the land lay grey and harsh, and the houses made of the grey clay and thatched with the grey straw, seemed but part of the land. Even the people, bitten with the winds and dust of the northern winter were grey of the same hue, and Wang the Tiger felt no joy rise in his heart these three days, as he rode toward his father's home.

When he was come he went to his elder brother's house, since there he was to be wed, and when he had given them brief greeting he said abruptly that before he wed he would do his duty and go to do reverence at his father's grave. And this they all approved, and especially Wang the Landlord's lady, for it was a decent, proper thing to do, seeing that Wang the Tiger had been so long away, and he had not shared in the regular times that the family paid such respect to their dead.

But Wang the Tiger, although he knew his duty and when he could he did it, now performed it partly because he was restless and dreary in himself, and he did not know why he was either. But he could not bear to sit in his brother's house idle, and he could not bear his brother's unctuous pleasure at the coming wedding, and he was oppressed in himself and he must needs think of some excuse to be out and away from them all, because this house did not seem his home.

He sent a soldier then to buy the paper money and the incense and all such things as are useful to the dead and with these he went out of the city with the men at his horse's heels, their guns on their shoulders. He took a little faint comfort to see how people stared at him on the street and although he held his face stiff and stared ahead seeming to see and to hear nothing, still he heard his soldiers shout out roughly,

"Way for the general, way for our lord!" And as he saw the common people shrink back against the walls and into the gateways he was a little comforted because he was so great to them, and he held himself erect in his state and pomp.

Thus he came to the graves under the date tree which by now had grown knotted and gnarled, although when Wang Lung had first chosen that place to lay his dead, it was a smooth young tree. Now other date trees had sprung from it, and Wang the Tiger, having dismounted while he was yet a long way off to show his respect, came slowly to these trees and one of the soldiers stood and held the red horse, and Wang the Tiger walked slowly and stately in his reverence until he came to the grave of his father. There he made obeisance three times, and the soldiers who carried the money and the incense came forward and arranged it, the most at Wang Lung's grave and the next at the grave of Wang Lung's father and the next at the grave of Wang Lung's brother, and the least at O-lan's grave, whom Wang the Tiger could remember but dimly as his mother.

Then Wang the Tiger went forward again in his slow and stately way and he lit the incense and the paper and he knelt and knocked his head the number of times he should before every grave and when this was finished he stood motionless and meditated, while the fire burned and the silver and the gold paper turned to ash and the incense smouldered sharp and fragrant upon the wintry air of that day. There was no sunshine and no wind, a grey chill day such as may bring snow, and the warm slight smoke of the incense curled clearly in the chill air. The soldiers waited in completest silence while their general communed as long as he wished with his father and at last Wang the Tiger turned away and walked to his horse and mounted it and went back along the path he had come.

But while he meditated he had not thought at all of his father Wang Lung. He thought of himself and of how when

309

he lay dead there would not be one to come and do him reverence as son to father, and when he thought of this it seemed well to him that he was to be wed and he bore a little better the dreariness he had in his soul for the hope of a son.

Now the path on which Wang the Tiger rode skirted the threshold of the earthen house and passed by the edge of the threshing floor that was its door yard, and the noise of the soldiers roused the hunchback youth who lived there with Pear Blossom and he came hobbling out as quickly as he could and stood staring. He did not know Wang the Tiger at all, or even that this was his uncle, and so he only stood there by the path and stared. For all he was now nearly sixteen years old and soon to be a man, he stood scarcely taller than a child of six or seven, and his back rose curved like a hood behind his head and Wang the Tiger was astonished at the sight of him and he asked, drawing his horse back,

"Who are you who live here in my earthen house?"

Then the lad knew him, for he had heard he had an uncle who was a general and he often dreamed of him and wondered what he was like, and now he cried out, yearningly,

"Are you my uncle?"

Then Wang the Tiger remembered, and he said slowly, still staring down at the lad's upturned face,

"Yes, I have heard somewhere that my brother had a brat like you. Strange, for we are all so straight and strong and so was my father, too, the straightest, strongest old man, even in his age."

Then the lad answered simply, as though it were a thing to which he were long used, and he stared avidly at the soldiers as he said it, and at the high red horse,

"But I was dropped." Then he stretched out his hand toward Wang the Tiger's gun and he peered up out of his strange aged face and his little, sad sunken eyes, and he said eagerly,

"I have never held one of those foreign guns in my hand and I would like to hold it for a moment's time."

When he stretched up his hand thus, a little dried, wrinkled hand like an old man's, out of a sudden pity for this poor warped lad Wang the Tiger handed him down his own gun to feel and to look at. And as he waited for the lad to have his fill of it, one came to the door. It was Pear Blossom. Wang the Tiger knew her instantly, for she had not changed much except to grow thinner even than she had been, and her face, always pale and egg-shaped, was now covered with fine thread-like wrinkles drawn lightly into the pale skin. But her hair was as smooth and black as ever. Then Wang the Tiger bowed very stiffly and deeply but without descending from his horse, and Pear Blossom gave a little bow and would have turned quickly away except that Wang the Tiger called out,

"Is the fool still living and well?"

And Pear Blossom answered in her soft small voice, "She is well."

And Wang the Tiger asked again,

"Do you have your full due every month?"

And she answered again in the same voice, "I thank you, I have all my due," and she held her head down as she spoke and looked at the beaten ground of the threshing floor and this time when she had answered him she went swiftly away and he was left staring at the empty doorway.

Then he said suddenly to the lad,

"Why does she wear a robe that is like a nun's?" for he had seen without knowing he did that Pear Blossom's grey robes were crossed at her throat as a nun's are.

The lad answered, scarcely thinking of what he said, so longing and fixed was his heart upon the gun as he fingered it and smoothed its wood,

"When the fool is dead she will go into the nunnery near

here and be a nun. She eats no meat at all now and she knows many prayers by heart and she is a lay nun already. But she will not leave the world and cut off her hair until the fool dies, because my grandfather left her the fool."

Wang the Tiger heard this and he was silent a moment in some vague pain and at last he said pityingly to the lad,

"What will you do then, you poor hunched ape?"

And the lad made answer, "When she goes into the nunnery I am to be a priest in the temple because I am so young I must live for a long time and she cannot wait for me to die, too. But if I am a priest I can be fed and if I am ill and I am often ill with this thing I carry on me, then she can come and tend me, since we are kin." This the boy said carelessly. Then his voice changed and grew half sobbing with some passion, and he looked up at Wang the Tiger and cried out, "Yes, I am to be a priest—but, oh, I wish that I were straight and then I would be a soldier—if you would have me, Uncle!"

There was such fire in his sunken dark eyes that Wang the Tiger was moved by it, and he answered sorrowfully, for he was a merciful man at heart,

"I would have you gladly, you poor thing, but shaped as you are, what can you be now but a priest!"

And the lad hung his head out of its strange socket and he said in a small, low voice,

"I know it."

Without another word he handed the gun back to Wang the Tiger and he turned and limped away across the threshing floor. And Wang the Tiger went on his way to his marriage.

This was a strange marriage to Wang the Tiger. He was in no burning haste this time, and day and night were alike to him. He went through it all silently and decorously as he did everything he had to do unless a rage came over him.

But now love and rage seemed forever equally far from his dead heart, and the red-robed figure of the bride was like some dim, distant figure with which he had nothing at all to do. So also the guests, and so the figures of his brothers and their wives and children, and the monstrous fat figure of Lotus, leaning on Cuckoo. Yet he looked at her once, too, for she panted as she breathed she was so heavy with her flesh and Wang the Tiger could hear this thick gusty breathing as he stood to bow to his elder brothers and to those who sponsored the woman and to the guests and to all those to whom he must bow in ceremony.

But when the wedding feast was brought he scarcely tasted this dish or that, and when Wang the Landlord began his jokes, since there should be merriment even at a man's second wedding, and when a guest took up the laughter, it died away into feebleness and silence before Wang the Tiger's grave face. He said nothing at all at his own wedding feast except that when the wine was brought he took up the bowl quickly as though he were thirsty. But when he had tasted it he set the bowl down again and he said harshly,

"If I had known the wine would be no better than this I would have brought a jar of the wine of my own region."

After the days of wedding were over, he mounted his red horse and went away and he did not cast one look behind at the bride and her serving maid who came behind him in a mule cart, with the curtains drawn. No, he rode on as seeming solitary as he had been when he came, his soldiers at his heels, and the cart lumbering behind them. Thus Wang the Tiger brought his bride to his own regions, and in a month or two and a little more the second woman came under her father's care, and her he received also, since one or two were the same to him.

Then the New Year drew on and its festivals and these

313

passed, and it was the time when spring first begins to stir in the earth, although no sign of it could yet be seen in any leaf upon a tree. Yet there were signs, too, for the snow, if it came on a chill grey day, did not lie but melted in the sudden heat of a warm wind that blew fitfully out of the south, and the wheat plants in the fields, while they did not yet grow, took on a fresher green, and everywhere farmers stirred themselves out of their winter idleness and looked to their hoes and their rakes and fed their oxen a little better to prepare them for labor. By the roadsides the weeds began to send up shoots and children roamed everywhere with their knives and pointed bits of wood and tin if they had not knives, to dig the fresh green stuff for food.

So also did the lords of war bestir themselves in their winter quarters and soldiers stretched their full-fed bodies and wearied of their gaming and brawling and idling about towns where they were entrenched and they stirred themselves to wonder what their fortunes could be in the new wars of the spring, and every soldier dreamed a little and hoped that one above him might be killed and give him place.

So also did Wang the Tiger dream of what he would do. Yes, he had a scheme, and it was a good one, and now he could put himself to it for it seemed to him that his gnawing, nagging love was dead. Or, if not dead, then buried somewhere, and whenever he was troubled by its memory he went deliberately to one of those two wives of his, and if his flesh lagged, he drank wine deeply to rouse it.

And being a very just man, he showed no favor to one wife above the other, although they were very different, too, the one learned and neat and pleasing in a plain and quiet way, and the other somewhat uncouth, but still a woman of virtue and of good heart. Her greatest fault was her black-ened teeth, and that she had a very foul breath if one came near her. But even so Wang the Tiger was fortunate in that they did not quarrel, these two women. Yet doubtless his justice helped this, for he was scrupulous and he went to them each in turn, and the truth was they were the same to him and alike nothing.

But he need no longer lie alone unless he wished. Still, he never grew familiar with either woman, and he always went in to them haughtily and for a set purpose and he made no speech with them and there was no frankness as there had been between him and the one dead and he never gave himself freely.

Sometimes he pondered on this difference that a man may feel toward women, and when he did he told himself bitterly that the one dead had never been truly frank with him, no, not even when she seemed as free as a harlot, for all the time she hugged her design against him in her heart. When he thought of this Wang the Tiger sealed his heart again and calmed his flesh with his two wives. And he had this for a hope and for a fresh light to his ambition, and it was that from one of the twain surely he might have his son at last. In this hope Wang the Tiger encouraged his dreams of glory once more and he swore that in this very year in this very spring he would go forth to a great war somewhere and win for himself power and wide territories, and he saw the victory already his own.

XXII

THEN as spring blossomed and the white cherry trees and the pale pink peach blooms lay like light clouds over the green land, Wang the Tiger took counsel with his trusty men as to war and they waited for two things. The first was to see how the war would renew itself between the lords of north and south, for the truce they had made the year before was very slight and tenuous and it was but a truce of the winter when it is not convenient to do battle in wind and snow and mud. Aside from this, the lords of north and south so differed in their nature, the one being large in body and slow and fierce, and the other little tricky men, good in guile and ambush, that with such difference in temper and even in blood and language, it was not easy for them to agree upon long truce. The other thing for which Wang the Tiger waited and his trusty men with him was for the return of the many spies he sent out early in the year. And while they waited Wang the Tiger took counsel with his trusty men as to what territory they might attach to what they had and so enlarge the region.

Now they took counsel together in the great room which Wang the Tiger used for his own and there they sat, each according to his rank, and the Hawk said,

"North we cannot go, for we are in allegiance with the north."

And the Pig Butcher said loudly, for it was his way to speak whatever the Hawk said, like a rude echo, for he did not like to be thought less wise than the Hawk, and yet he himself could not think easily of a new thing to say,

"Yes, but even so, it is a very poor and meager land there, and the pigs are so accursed and so thin they are no use butchering. I have seen those pigs and I swear their backs are sharp as curved scythes, and a sow's pigs can be counted before ever she gives them birth. It is not a country anyone wants to wage a war to gain."

But Wang the Tiger said slowly,

"Yet south we cannot go, for if we do we will strike my own and my father's folk, and a man cannot tax his own people freely and with an easy mind."

Now the harelipped man spoke little and never until the others had their say out, and now he said in his turn,

"There is a region where my native land once was, but it is nothing to me now, and it is to the southeast of this, between here and the sea, a very rich country, and one end of it lies against the sea. There is a whole county spread out edgewise along a river there that flows to the sea, too, and it is a good country, full of fields and it has a low ridge of hills, and the river is full of fish. The county seat is the only large town, but there are many villages and market towns and the people are thrifty and do well."

Wang the Tiger heard this and he said,

"Yes, but such a good place is not likely to be without its lord of war. Who is it?"

Then the trusty man named the name of one who had once been a robber chief and the very year before this one had thrown in his lot with the south. When he heard this name, Wang the Tiger decided swiftly that he would go against this robber chief, and he remembered to this day how he hated the men of the south and how tasteless their soft rice and peppered meats had been and there was nothing for a man to set his good teeth down upon to chew it, and he remembered the hateful years of his youth and he cried out,

"The very place and the very man, for it will enlarge me and it will count in the general wars, as well!"

As swiftly as this was the thing decided and Wang the Tiger shouted to a serving man to bring wine and they all drank and Wang the Tiger gave his commands that the soldiers were to be prepared for movement and they were to march to the new lands as soon as the first spies returned to tell of what the great war was to be this year. Then the trusty men rose to take their leave and to fulfill these commands, but the Hawk lingered after the others went away, and he

317

leaned and whispered into Wang the Tiger's ear, and his voice was hoarse and his breath hot upon Wang the Tiger's cheek, and he said,

"We must let the soldiers have the usual days of looting after the battle, for they mutter among themselves and they complain that you hold them in so tight and they do not have the privileges under your banner that other lords of war give. They will not fight if they cannot loot."

Then Wang the Tiger gnawed the stiff black hair he had let grow these days about his lips and he said very unwillingly, for he knew the Hawk was right,

"Well, then, tell them they are to have the three days when the victory is ours, but no more."

The Hawk went away well pleased, but Wang the Tiger sat sullen for a while, for the truth was he hated this looting of the people, and yet what else could he do, seeing that soldiers will not risk their lives to fight without this reward? So, although he agreed to it, he was ill at ease for a time, for he could not but see in his mind the picture of the suffering of those people, and he cursed himself for a man too soft for the trade he had chosen. And he forced himself to be hard and he told himself that after all it must be the rich who lose most, since the poor have nothing of worth to anyone, and the rich can bear it. But he was ashamed he was so weak and not for anything would he have had a man of his know he shrank from seeing pain, lest he be despised.

Then the spies returned, one after the other, and each in his turn reported to their general, and they said that although no war as yet was broken forth, yet the lords of north and of south were buying weapons from outer countries and war must come, for everywhere armies were being enlarged and strengthened. Now when Wang the Tiger heard this he decided that he would begin without delay upon his own private war, and on that very day he commanded his men to assemble themselves upon a field outside the city gates, for there was so vast a number they could not gather together inside, and he rode there upon his high red horse with his bodyguard behind him, and to his right his pocked nephew sat, no longer upon an ass, but now upon a good horse, for Wang the Tiger had given him a position there. And Wang the Tiger held himself erect and exceedingly proud, and his men all stared at him in silence, for indeed he was such a warrior as is not often seen in the world for great good looks and heavy fierce brows and on his lips the hair he had let newly grow made him look older than his forty years. Thus before them he sat motionless and he let them stare at him awhile, and suddenly he lifted his voice out in a shout and he called to all his men,

"Soldiers and heroes! Tomorrow six days and we will march to the southeast and we will take that region. It is a rich and fertile land bordering upon a river and the sea, and what I gain there I will share with you. You are to divide under my two trusty men, and the Hawk will lead from the east and the Pig Butcher from the west. I myself with my picked five thousand men will wait to the north and when you have attacked from two sides and hold the city fast, which is the center to the region, I will rush in and close and crush the last resistance. There is a lord of war there, but he is only a robber, and well you have shown me how you can deal with robbers, my good fellows!"

Then he added, but very unwillingly although he had hardened himself for it, "If you are victorious you are to have freedom in that city for three days. But on the dawn of the fourth day your freedom ends. He who does not answer the call of the bugles I shall cause to be blown for a sign to you, him will I kill. I am not afraid to die and not afraid to kill. These are my commands. You have them!"

Then the men shouted out and they stirred restlessly and as soon as Wang the Tiger had gone away they grew very eager and greedy and anxious to be off and every man looked to his weapons and cleaned and sharpened all and he counted the bullets he had. At that time many a man bartered with others for bullets, and those who were weak in their desire for wine or for a turn at a wench paid over their bullets as far as they dared for that for which they yearned.

On the dawn of the sixth day Wang the Tiger led his mighty army out of the city. Yet great as it was he left a small half behind, and he went to the old magistrate who now lay on his bed and never rose from it he grew so weak, and Wang the Tiger told the old man that he left the army to protect him and his court. The magistrate thanked him in his feeble courteous way, but well he knew the army was left a guard upon him still. And the harelipped man was its head, and it was a hard place, for the soldiers were discontented to be left behind, and Wang the Tiger was compelled to promise them a dole of extra silver if they did well and guarded faithfully and he promised them that the next war would be theirs. So they were content a little, or at least less discontent.

Then at the head of his army Wang the Tiger went out, and he caused it to be told among the city people that he went to wage war again for them against an encroaching enemy from the south, and the people were afraid and eager to please him, and the guild of merchants there gave him a sum for a gift, and many from the city followed the army as they left the city that day and they stayed to see Wang the Tiger's ensign set up and the sacrifice made to it of a killed pig and incense so that good fortune might attend the war.

When this was over Wang the Tiger went on in good

earnest and he had not only his men and their weapons to wage the war, but he had brought a goodly sum of silver, too, for he was too clever a general to plunge at once into battle, and he would parley and wait and see how silver could be used, and at least if silver was useless at first in the end it might serve something and buy over some important man to open the gates of the city to them.

It was now the middle of spring and the wheat was two feet high or so over miles of that countryside and ready to head, and Wang the Tiger cast his eyes far and wide over that green land as he rode. He had a pride in its beauty and fruitfulness for it was his own to rule and he loved it as a king may love his realm. Yet he was wise and with all his eye for its beauty he could keep his wits sharp for some new place to fix a tax to maintain this vast army he now had and for his private store he must increase, also.

Thus he passed out of his own region, and when he had come far enough south so that he came to groves of pomegranate trees and saw them putting out from their gnarled grey branches the tiny flame-colored new leaves that come late and after all other trees are leaved, he knew he was in the new lands. He looked everywhere then to see what these were, and everywhere he saw fruitful, nurtured fields, and well fed beasts and fat children and he rejoiced at it all. But as he passed with his men the folk upon the lands looked up at them and scowled to see them and women who had been the moment before talking and laughing in their gossip together grew silent and pale and stared and many a mother put her hand over her child's eyes. And if the soldiers burst into some song of war as they did often when they marched, then men in the fields cursed aloud to hear the quiet air broken like this. The very dogs rushed furiously out of the villages to nip the strangers, but when they saw so vast a horde they were dismayed and shrank away with their tails curled under their bellies. Every now and again an ox broke loose from where it was tied and fled as fast as it could because of the noise of so many men passing, and sometimes if it were yoked it ran plow and all and the farmer plowman after it. Then the soldiers guffawed loudly, but Wang the Tiger if he saw it stopped courteously until the man had his beast in hand again.

In the towns and hamlets also the people were silent and stricken when the soldiers came pushing through the gates clamoring and laughing and hungry for tea and wine and bread and meat, and shop keepers scowled over their counters because they feared their wares gone and they not paid for them, so that some drew the wooden doors over their open shops as though the night were come. But Wang the Tiger had early given command that nothing should be seized without payment and he had given his men money for such things as they needed to eat and to drink. Yet well he knew that the best general cannot control so many thousands of lawless men, and although he had told his captains he would hold them responsible, yet he knew no small amount of evil must surely be done, and he could only shout, "If I hear of it I will kill you!" and he trusted that the men would subdue themselves somewhat, and he did not try to hear everything.

But Wang the Tiger planned this way to control his men to some degree. When they came to a town he made them stay in a suburb and he went with only a few hundred first and he sought the richest merchant in that place. When he had found him he commanded him to gather together the other merchants and he waited in the richest merchant's shop. When they were all there before him very fearful and courteous, then Wang the Tiger was courteous, too, and he said,

"Do not fear that I shall be extortionate and take more than I ought. It is true I have many thousands of men in the suburb,

322

but give me only a fair amount for my expense on this march and I will lead my men on and we will not stay here but the night."

Then the merchants, all pale and fearful, would put forward the spokesman they had chosen and he would stammer forth a sum, but Wang the Tiger knew well it was the lowest they could name, and he would smile coolly but he drew down his brows while he smiled, and he said,

"I see the fine shops you have, the oil shops and the grain markets and the silks and the cloths and I see your people how well they are fed and clothed and how good your streets are. Do you cry your town so small and poor as this? You shame yourselves by such a sum!"

Thus courteously he would force their sum upward, and he never threatened them coarsely as some lords of war do and cry out that he would set his soldiers free in the town if he did not get so much and so much. No, Wang the Tiger used only fair means, for he always said that these men must live too and they ought not to be asked for more than in reason they ought to be able to give. And the end of it and the fruit of his courtesy was that he had that for which he asked and the merchants were glad to be rid of him so easily and rid of his horde.

Thus Wang the Tiger marched his men to the southeast where the sea was and each time he stopped in a town he had a sum of money the merchants gave him and at dawn he went on and the people were glad. But in poor hamlets or small villages Wang the Tiger did not ask for anything unless it were a little food, and the least he could take.

Seven days and seven nights did Wang the Tiger thus lead his men and at the end of those days he was even somewhat enriched by the sums of money he had had, and his men were all in great high heart and well fed and very hopeful.

At the end of the seven days he was within less than a day's journey of the city he planned to take as the heart to this whole region and he rode to a low hill from where he could see it. There that city lay like a treasure encircled by its wall, and set into the rolling green fields, and Wang the Tiger's heart leaped to see it so beautiful and under so fair a sky. There the river ran also, as he had heard it did, and the south gate of the city touched the river, so the city seemed like a jewel hung upon a silver chain. In greatest haste then did Wang the Tiger send his messengers to that city guarded with a thousand men, and he declared to the lord of war who held that city that he who was Wang the Tiger had come down out of the north and he came to save the people from a robber and if the robber would not withdraw peacefully and for a sum to be named then must Wang the Tiger march against the city with his tens of thousands upon thousands of brave armed men.

Now the lord of war in that place was a very doughty old robber and he was so black and hideous a man that the people had nicknamed him after the fearful black god who stands in the entrance halls of temples to be guardian there, so the lord of war was called Liu the Gate God. When he heard the boldness of this message that Wang the Tiger had sent he fell into a mighty rage and he bellowed with his wrath awhile before he could give an answer, and when he could, he answered thus:

"Go back and tell your master that he may fight if he wishes. Who fears him? I have never heard of this little dog who calls himself Wang the Tiger!"

The messengers returned then and repeated this faithfully to Wang the Tiger and he was mightily angry in his turn and he was secretly hurt that the lord of war said he had never heard the name of Wang the Tiger, and he wondered within himself if he were less than he thought. But outwardly he ground his teeth together in his black beard and he called to his men and they marched against the city that very day and encamped themselves all about it. But the gates were locked against them so that they could not go in, and Wang the Tiger bade his men quarter themselves until dawn, and he had a row of tents put up around the city moat so that his men could watch to see what the enemy did and bring him the news.

Now at dawn Wang the Tiger rose very early and he roused his guard and all his men were called by the blowing of bugles and drums and when they were assembled Wang the Tiger gave his commands that they were to be ready for battle when he called, even though it might be that they waited for a month or two. Then with his guard he went to a hill that was to the east of the city and there was an old pagoda there and he climbed up into it and his men he left below to guard him and to terrify the few old priests that were in a temple there, and he saw that while the city was not large, perhaps with not more than fifty thousand souls or so, still the houses were well built and the roofs were of a dark tile and piled upon each other like scales upon a fish's back. He went down then and back to his men and he led them across the moat, but as he did so, a shower of shots dropped from the high city wall, and Wang the Tiger withdrew again in haste.

Wang the Tiger could do no more then but wait, and he took counsel with his captains and these counselled a siege, for a siege is surer than a battle, since people must eat. This seemed a good thing to Wang the Tiger also, because his men must of a certainty be killed if he attacked the city now, and the gates were so strong, and the great beams so joined together with plates of iron, that Wang the Tiger did not know how to prevail against them. Moreover, if they guarded the locked gates so that no food could go in day after day, after a month or two the enemy must be weakened and submit, whereas if they fought now the enemy would be strong and well fed, and it could not be said certainly where the victory would turn. Thus Wang the Tiger reasoned and it seemed to him the better thing to wait until he could do battle and be sure of victory.

Therefore he ordered his soldiers to guard that whole city wall, but to stand back from it far enough so that shots could not reach them but would fall harmlessly into the moat. The soldiers did so encircle the walls and no one could come out or go in, and the soldiers fed on the produce of the land about there and they ate the fowls and the vegetables and the fruits and the grains that the farmers had, and since they paid something for all they took, the farmers did not join against them, and Wang the Tiger's army fared very well. The summer came on in its season and the land was good and the season was prosperous, for it was in these parts a year neither dry nor wet, although it was rumored that toward the west no rains had fallen behind the mountains and there would be famine in that place. When Wang the Tiger heard this, he said to himself that again his good destiny was over him that there was plenty here for him.

Thus a month passed and more and Wang the Tiger waited day after day in his tent and no one came out of that locked city. And he waited twenty more days and he grew very impatient and so did his men also, but the foe was doughty still, and if they went across the moat shots still popped out from the city wall. Wang the Tiger wondered very much and he said in his anger,

"What can they have left to eat that anyone has yet the strength to hold his weapon?"

And the Hawk, who stood by, spat in admiration of so good and brave an enemy and wiping his mouth on his hand he said,

"They must by now have eaten the dogs and the cats and the beasts of every kind and even the rats to be caught in their houses."

Thus the days passed and there came no sign out of the besieged city until the end of the second month of summer. Then as Wang the Tiger went out one morning as he did every day to see if there were any smallest change, he saw a white flag waved above the north gate where he was encamped. And in great haste and excitement he bade a man of his raise a white flag, too, and he exulted for he thought the end was come.

Then the north gate opened a little, and only wide enough to let one man through and it was shut and they could hear the scraping of the iron bars. And Wang the Tiger watched breathless on the other side of the moat where his camp was, and he saw a young man walking slowly toward him, carrying a white flag upon a bamboo pole. Then Wang the Tiger called to his men to stand in line, and he took his place just behind and they waited for the man, and he came near and he called out when he could be heard,

"I come to talk of peace and we will pay you a sum and all we have if you will go away in peace."

Then Wang the Tiger laughed his noiseless laugh and he said, sneering,

"Do you think I have come so far for money alone? I can get money in my own regions. No! Your lord of war must surrender to me for I need this city and this region and it shall be part of my own."

Then the young man leaned upon his pole and he looked

at Wang the Tiger with a look of death and he entreated, saying,

"Have mercy and take your men away!" And he fell on his face before Wang the Tiger.

But Wang the Tiger felt his anger begin to creep up in him as he always did when he was opposed and he was roused and he shouted,

"I will never go away until the land is mine!"

Then the young man rose and he threw back his head proudly and he said,

"Then stay, and spend your life here, for we can bear it!" and without another word he turned back toward the gate.

Then Wang the Tiger felt his old black anger come up in him and he said to himself that he was amazed that an importunate enemy should send so discourteous a messenger, who had not even performed any rites of courtesy, and to himself he thought that this was the most impudent young man he had ever seen, and the more he thought the more angry he grew and suddenly and before he knew it clearly himself he was furious and he called to a soldier,

"Lift me your gun and shoot that fellow!"

The soldier obeyed instantly and he shot very well for the young man fell face down upon a narrow bridge that crossed the moat and his flag fell into the water and the pole floated idly upon the surface of the moat and the whiteness of the flag was sullied with the muddy stream. Then Wang the Tiger commanded his men to run forward and fetch the young man, and they did, running swiftly lest a shot come down from the wall, but not one did come, and Wang the Tiger marvelled a little and wondered what this might mean. But he wondered still more when the young man lay before him dead and fast turning the hue of death, for this young man was not starving at all. No, when Wang the Tiger

328

ordered his clothes to be stripped from him so that he might see his flesh, there the young man lay, not fat but still filled out well so that it could be seen he had been fed with something.

Then was Wang the Tiger somewhat dashed at the sight and he was discouraged for the moment and he cried,

"If this fellow is as fat as he is, what have they to eat that they can last so well against me?" And he cursed and said, "Well, and I can spend my life at this as well as they can!"

Because he was so angry from this day he commanded his soldiers to make themselves easy and to take their comfort, and thereafter when he saw them taking food or goods from the people in the suburbs about that city or from farming folk here and there, he did not stop them as he once would have, and when a farmer came to complain or any came to swear against a soldier that he had come into a private house and done what he should not, Wang the Tiger said sullenly,

"You are an accursed lot, you people, and I believe you are sending food secretly into this city or else how can they be so long fed?"

But the farmers swore they were not and many times one would say piteously,

"What do we care what lord is over us, and do you think we love this old robber who has kept us half starved with his taxes? Sir, if you will only treat us with mercy and keep your men back fom evil, we will even be glad to have you in his place."

But Wang the Tiger grew surly as the summer wore on, and he cursed the heat and the myriads of flies that breeded upon the piles of filth the many soldiers must make, and the mosquitoes that came out of the stagnant moat, and he thought with impatience of the city where his own courts were and where his two wives waited for him, and all his anger made him not so kind as he had been and his men grew very law-less and he let them be so.

There came one night in the time of the great heat, a very hot bright moonlight night and Wang the Tiger walked out-side his tent for coolness, for he could not sleep. He walked alone except for his bodyguard who strolled yawning and half asleep behind him as he walked to and fro. And Wang stared as he ever did at the walls of the city and they stood high and black in the moonlight and it seemed unconquerable to him. And as he stared he grew very angry again, and indeed his anger was never cooled in these days, and he swore to himself very bitterly that he would make every man and woman and even the children in the city suffer for all the discomfort of this war he was waging. At that moment he saw a moving spot upon the blackness of the wall, a spot more black and moving downward. He stared and stood still. At first he could not believe he saw it but the longer he stood and stared the more he could see that there was something small and dark moving like a crab among the vines and the dry small trees that clung to that old wall. At last he saw that it was a man. Yes, the man reached the bottom and he dropped and came out into the moonlight and Wang the Tiger saw that he waved a white cloth.

Then Wang the Tiger commanded that one go to meet him bearing a white flag also, and he commanded that the man be brought to him and he stood and waited there and he strained his sight to see what this man was. When the man was come he threw himself at Wang the Tiger's feet and beat his head on the ground to beg for mercy. But Wang the Tiger shouted,

"Stand him on his feet and let me see him!"

Two soldiers came forward then and lifted the man and Wang the Tiger stared and as he stared he grew so angry

330

that he felt a thickness in his throat, for this man was not yet starved. No, gaunt he was and very thin and black, but he was not starved and Wang the Tiger bellowed,

"Are you come to surrender the city?"

And the man said, "No, the chief will not surrender yet for he still has food, and we who are about him have some food given us every day. The people starve, it is true, but we can let them, and we are able to hold out yet awhile and we hope for help from the south for we have let a man over the wall secretly to go for it."

At this Wang the Tiger felt very insecure and he said doubtfully, holding back his anger as best he could,

"Why have you come if not to surrender?"

And the man said sullenly, "I do come only for my own sake. The general under whom I serve has used me very ill. Yes, he is only a coarse and hateful creature, wild and untutored, and I am a man of gentle blood. My father was even a scholar and I am used to courtesy. He has put me to great shame before my own soldiers. Now a man may forgive much, but he can never forgive being put to shame and it is insult not only to me but to my ancestors for whom I stand in these times, and his ancestors were, if he knows them at all, such as would be held serfs by mine."

"But how could he put you to such shame as this?" asked Wang the Tiger, and he was secretly much astonished at this turn.

And the man answered with a sullen passion, "He belittled me for the way I held my gun and this is my greatest skill and I can fell what I aim for without a miss."

Then a light began to come over Wang the Tiger, for well he knew that laughter and belittling can breed the bitterest hatred in a man's heart even against a friend, and a man will do anything for revenge if shame is put on him, especially if he be a high proud fellow such as this man was in his looks. And Wang the Tiger said plainly,

"Tell me what your price is."

Then the man looked about him and here were the soldiers of Wang the Tiger's bodyguard, listening and their mouths ajar, and he bent and whispered,

"Let me go into your tent with you where I can speak out."

Then Wang the Tiger turned and strode into his tent and he commanded the man to be brought there and he left no more soldiers with him than five or six or so to guard against possible treachery from this man. But there was no treachery in this one, only revenge, and so Wang the Tiger found, for the man said,

"I am so filled with hatred and rage that I am willing to climb back over the wall and open the gate to you and I ask only one thing, that you will take me under your own banners and the few men who follow me whom I do not hate, and protect us, lest if the robber is not killed, I shall be sought for and killed, for he is a bitter enemy."

But Wang the Tiger would not have such generous help free and unrewarded with no more than this, and so he said, looking hard at the man as he stood before him between the two soldiers who held him,

"You are a very proper man not to bear insult and no good fellow will. I am glad to have so good and brave a man with me. Go back, then, and tell your fellows and all the soldiers that I will take them under my own banners, all who surrender themselves and their guns, and not one of them shall be killed. As for you, you shall be a captain in my army, and I will give you two hundred pieces of silver and five pieces to every man with his gun that you bring also."

Then the man's twisted face lightened and he cried warmly,

"You are such a general as I have been searching for all my life long, and I will surely open the gate to you at the moment when the sun is at its zenith on this very day now dawning!"

With this the man turned abruptly and went back and Wang the Tiger rose and went out of his tent and watched the man as he climbed nimbly and skilfully over the wall, catching hold of the roots and the gnarled trees as a monkey might, and so he climbed and disappeared over the wall.

By now the sun rose like a copper rim over the edge of the fields and Wang the Tiger commanded his men to be roused but quietly and without any noise lest some enemy see a commotion and suspect a new plan. But many of the men knew already that one had come out of the city and they had risen in the night and made ready without lighting a single torch. And indeed the light of the moon had been so bright that it was like a pale sun and the men could see such things even as how their triggers were set and where a string should pass through the eyelet of a shoe. By full sunrise every man was in his place and Wang the Tiger gave orders that to each meat should be given to eat and a full deep drink of wine to make his heart warm and brave, and thus fed and comforted the soldiers waited for the drum to beat that would send them forward.

Then as the sun rose high and full and beat down with a breathless heat upon the plain where the city lay, Wang the Tiger shouted from where he stood and his men gathered as they had been told to do in six long lines and when they heard their general shout every man shouted also, and the noise ran like an echo among them. And as they shouted every man lifted his weapon in his hands, each man a gun and a knife, and they all ran forward. Some crossed the moat by the bridge, but many ran across the shallow moat and clambered dripping up the further bank and they pressed against the city wall and clustered about the north gate. But the captains would not let Wang the Tiger stand too near the front, for they did not know at this last moment whether the man would be true or not or whether there would be treachery. Yet Wang the Tiger trusted the man because he knew that revenge is the surest sort of hatred.

Thus they waited, and not a sound came out of that city, and there was no sound of guns upon the city wall. Then as the sun swung upwards into its place in the zenith, Wang the Tiger stood stiff and watching, and he saw that great iron gate swing a little and one stooped and peered and there was a little crack of light along its top. He shouted once, and they rushed forward and Wang the Tiger with them and they pressed against the gate and burst it wide and they poured into the streets of that city like water freed from a dam, and the siege was ended.

Then Wang the Tiger did not stand a moment, but he commanded to be led instantly to the palace where the robber chief lived, and he shouted and roared at his men that they were not free yet and not until he had found the old chief. Then swiftly because of the haste of their greed his men hurried him to that palace, asking as they went and laying ruthless hold on any terrified man they saw. But when Wang the Tiger entered the courts of that palace with a great flourish of drums and bugles it was empty, for the robber chief had fled. How he had known of the betrayal could not be said, but as Wang the Tiger's men had poured into the north gate the old robber and his loyal followers escaped out of the south gate and were fleeing across the countryside. Wang the Tiger hearing this from soldiers who had not gone with him rushed upon the south wall of the city and looked out and far in the distance he could see but a flying cloud of dust. He was in two minds for a while whether or

334

not to pursue it, but it came to him that he had what he wanted and it was the city and the key to this region, and what did a robber and his few men mean?

So he went down then and back into the deserted palace, and there the many soldiers of the enemy who were left came to do obeisance and to beg his protection. He was pleased to see their number, for they came to him as he sat in the chief hall, and they came in tens and in twenties, the thinnest, most haggard men he had ever seen except in famine years. But they had their weapons and when they knelt before him and held out their hands to show their submission, Wang the Tiger accepted them and ordered that every man be fed as much as he was able to eat and that he be given five pieces of silver. But when the man who had betrayed the robber chief came in at the head of his company Wang the Tiger gave him the two hundred pieces of silver he had promised him and he gave it with his own hands and he commanded that captain's garb be brought and given to the man, too. Thus did Wang the Tiger remember what the man had done for him, and he rewarded him and took him into his own ranks.

When this was all finished then Wang the Tiger knew that the time had come when he must redeem his promise to his men, for he had held them as long as he could and they would not be longer held. And Wang the Tiger gave the command for their freedom, wishing he need not while he did. It was a strange thing that now that he had what he wanted his anger against the people was gone, and he shrank from making them suffer. Yet he must keep his word, too, to his men, and when he had given them their freedom for three days he shut himself into the palace and closed the gates and he was alone except for his bodyguard. Yet even these hundred men or so were very restless and demanded their turn, and at last Wang the Tiger had to tell them off and call others back in their place, and when these others came in with their eyes all red and lustful and their faces dark and flushed so that they could not subdue their wild looks, Wang the Tiger turned his eyes away and he would not think of what was going on in that city. When his nephew, whom he kept always by him, grew curious to go out and see what was to be seen, Wang the Tiger burst out on him, glad of one on whom he could with reason fix his anger, and he roared, "Shall my own blood go ravening out like these coarse and common men?"

And he would not let the young man move out of his sight, and kept him busy about his person fetching this or that to eat or to drink or some change he must have in his garments, and when weak cries came through even into the fast closed courts, Wang the Tiger was more imperious and more angry than ever with his nephew, so that the youth was kept all in a sweat with his uncle's temper, and he did not dare to answer him a word.

The truth was that Wang the Tiger could not be cruel unless he was angry, and indeed this was a weakness in a lord of war that he could only kill in anger, whose means to glory is death, and he knew it was his weakness that he could not kill coldly or carelessly or for a cause. And he thought it weakness that he could not keep his anger against the people and he told himself he ought still to hate them because they had been so dull and stubborn and had not thought of a way to open the gates to him. Yet when his soldiers came sheepishly to ask for their food, he cried at them in a confusion of fury and pain,

"What, must I feed you even when you loot?"

To this they made answer, "There is not a handful of grain in this whole city and we cannot eat gold and silver and silks.

These we find but no food, for the farmers are still afraid to come in with their produce."

And Wang the Tiger suffered and was sullen because he saw that what they said was true and he could not but order them fed, although when he did, he shouted in his surliest tones. But once he heard a hearty rude fellow cry coarsely,

"Yes, and the wenches are all so thin they are like plucked fowls and there is no pleasure in them at all!"

Then suddenly Wang the Tiger could not bear his life and he went away into a room by himself and he sat and groaned for a while before he could harden himself again. But he did harden himself once more. He thought of the fair lands and he thought how he had enlarged his power and how he had in this war more than doubled the country over which he ruled, and he told himself that it was his trade and his means of greatness and last and best he thought of the two women he had and how from one of them surely his son would be born, and he cried to his own heart,

"Cannot I for that one bear that others should somewhat suffer for three little days?"

Thus he hardened himself for the three days and he held himself to his promised word.

But on the dawn of the fourth day he rose up early from his restless bed and he ordered signals given and horns blown everywhere and it was a sign to all his soldiers that their looting was over and they must come back to his commands. And because he rose up that morning more than usually fierce and black in his looks and his black brows darted up and down over his eyes, none dared to disobey him.

No, none except one. As Wang the Tiger strode out of the gate that had been fast locked these three days he heard a feeble crying in an alley near by, and being made oversensitive to these cries now, he turned his long steps there to see

337

what it was. In that alley he saw a soldier of his on his way
back to the ranks, but he had seen an old woman pass and
on her finger was a thin, gold ring, a poor, small, worthless
thing, too, for the old woman was only some working wife,
and she could not have any great good thing. But the soldier
had been overcome with a sudden desire for the last bit of
gold and he wrenched at the old woman's hand and she cried
out at him, wailing,

"It has been on my finger nigh upon thirty years and how
can I loose it now?"

And the soldier was in such haste, for the bugle was blowing, that there before his own eyes Wang the Tiger saw the
man whip out his knife and cut off the old woman's finger
clean, and her poor scanty blood had still strength enough
to spurt out in a feeble stream. Then Wang the Tiger gave
a great roaring curse, for the soldier had not seen him he was
in such haste, and Wang the Tiger sprang at the soldier and
he drew out his keen blade as he sprang and drove it straight
through the man's body. Yes, although it was his own man
Wang the Tiger did it, because his anger came up in him so
to see this wretched, starved creature dealt with as she had
been before his very eyes. The soldier fell without a sigh and
his own blood gushed out in a hearty, red stream. As for the
old woman she was terrified at such fierceness, even if it was
to succor her, and she wrapped her smarting stump in her old
apron and ran and hid herself somewhere and Wang the Tiger
did not see her again.

He wiped his sword on the soldier's coat, then, and he
turned away lest he repent what he had done, and it was useless to repent, since the man was dead. He stayed only to
command one of his guards to take the dead man's gun.

Then Wang the Tiger went through that city and he was
astonished beyond any measure to see the few wretched people

338

there were and how they came crawling out into their doorways and sat listless on the benches upon their thresholds, too
weak to lift their heads even to look at Wang the Tiger as he
came striding along in the bright sunshine of autumn, and
his guards glittering and clattering behind him. No, they sat
there as though they were dead, so dull and still they were,
and some strange shame and astonishment was in Wang the
Tiger's heart so that he did not stay to talk with any man.
He held his head very high and he pretended he did not see
the people and only the shops. There were many goods in
these shops such as he had not seen before, since this city was
on the river to the south, and the river ran to the sea, and such
goods could be brought in. Yes, Wang the Tiger saw many
curious foreign things he had not seen before, but they were
carelessly placed now and covered with dust as though no one
had come to buy for a long time.

But two things he did not see in this city. He saw no food
anywhere for sale, and the market place was empty and silent
and there were no vendors or hucksters in the streets such as
make busy any town and city, and he saw no little children.
At first he did not notice how quiet the streets were and then
he noticed and wondered for the reason of the quietness and
then it came to him that he missed the noisy voices and
laughter of the children with which every house is filled in
usual times, and he missed their darting and running upon
the streets. And suddenly he could not bear to look at the
thin dark dull faces of the men and women who were left.
He had done no more than any lord of war may do, and it
could not be counted to him for a crime, since there was no
other way in which he could rise.

But Wang the Tiger was truly too merciful a man for his
trade and he turned and went back to his courts because he
could not bear to see this city now his, and he was cast down

and ill humored and he swore at his soldiers and he roared at them to be out of his way, for he could not endure at all the sound of their loud, satisfied laughter and the sight of their satiate glittering eyes, and he looked with rage upon the gold rings they had on their fingers and the foreign watches they had hung on them and many such things they had taken. Yes, he even saw gold rings on the fingers of his two trusty men, upon the Hawk's hard hand a ring of gold, and a jade ring upon the thumb of the Pig Butcher, that was so large and coarse a thumb the ring stuck half way upon the joint and would go no further. But still he wore it so. Seeing all this Wang the Tiger felt very far and separate from all these men and muttered to himself that they were low and beast-like fellows and he was lonely to the depths of his being and he went and sat alone in his room in mighty ill humor and bellowed for the smallest cause if anyone came near him.

But when he had sat thus a day or two and his soldiers, seeing how angry he was, were frightened and calmed themselves somewhat, Wang the Tiger hardened himself once more and he told himself that such were the ways of war and he had chosen this way of life and heaven had destined him as he was, and he must finish what he had begun. So he rose and washed himself, for he had sat these three days unwashed and unshaven, he was so angry, and he clothed himself freshly, and he sent a messenger to the magistrate of the city that he must come and submit himself. Then Wang the Tiger went into the guest hall of this palace and sat down there and waited for the man to come.

In an hour or two the magistrate came with what haste he could muster and he came in leaning on two men, a very ghastly, pale figure of a man he looked. But he bowed to Wang the Tiger and waited and Wang the Tiger saw this man was well born and a scholar by his gentle looks. He rose therefore and bowed in return and he motioned that the magistrate was to be seated. Then Wang the Tiger was seated too and he could but sit and stare at this other, for the magistrate's face and his hands were the strangest and most dreadful color, and it was the hue of a liver that has been dried for a day or two, and he was so thin one would have said his skin was glued to his bones.

Then Wang the Tiger cried out suddenly in the midst of his wonderment, "What—did you starve too?"

And the man answered simply, "Yes, since my people did also, and it is not the first time."

"But the man they sent out to make truce the first time was fed well enough," said Wang the Tiger.

"Yes, but they fed him specially from the first," answered the magistrate, "so that if you would not make truce you would see they had stores left to eat and could hold out longer."

Then Wang the Tiger could not but approve such good guile as this and he cried out in wonder and admiration of it, and he said,

"But the captain who came out was well fed, too!"

The magistrate answered simply, "They fed the soldiers best and to the last the best they could. But the people starved and many hundreds of them are dead. All the weak and the very old and the young are dead."

And Wang the Tiger heaved a sigh and said, "It is true I saw no babes anywhere." And he stared awhile at the magistrate and then he forced himself to say what he must and he said, "Submit yourself to me now, for I have won the right to take that other lord of war's place over you and over this whole region over which he ruled. I am the ruler now and I add this to my dominion I have already to the north. The revenues shall come into my hand now, and I will demand of

341

you a certain sum fixed and beyond that a proportion of revenues every month."

This Wang the Tiger said with some few courteous words afterwards, for he was not devoid of such courtesy. The magistrate answered in his weak and hollow voice, moving his dry lips over teeth that seemed too large and white for his drawn mouth,

"We are in your power. Only give us a month or two to recover ourselves." Then he waited awhile and he said again with great bitterness, "What is it to us who rules over us if we can only have peace and if we can only pursue our business and have a livelihood and nurture our children? I swear I and my people are willing to pay you in all reason if you will only be strong enough to keep off other lords of war and let us live secure in our generation."

This was all Wang the Tiger cared to know, and now his merciful heart smote him to hear the man's feeble, breathy voice and he cried out to his soldiers,

"Bring in food and wine and feed him and the men with him!" And when he had seen this done, he called his trusty men to him and he commanded again, "Go out now into the countryside and take soldiers and compel the farmers to come in with their grains and their produce so that the people may buy and eat and recover themselves again after this very bitter war."

So did Wang the Tiger show his justice to all the people and the magistrate thanked him, and he was moved with his gratitude. Then Wang the Tiger saw how courteous and gently born and reared this magistrate was for even half starved as he was and his eyes glittered at the food that was set on a table before him, he restrained himself and he dallied and delayed, his trembling hands clasped tightly together, until all the polite and courteous things were said that should be said from guest to host and until Wang the Tiger could seat himself in the host's place. Then the poor man fell upon the food, and still he tried to hold himself back and in very pity Wang the Tiger at last made excuse that he had some affair to which he must go. He went away then and let the man eat alone, for his underlings ate separately, and afterwards Wang the Tiger heard his men say in wonder that the dishes and bowls needed no washing so clean the starving men had licked them.

Then Wang the Tiger took the sweetest pleasure in seeing the markets of that city fill again and in seeing the food begin to lie in vendors' baskets along the sides of the streets and on the counters, and he thought he could see day by day that men and women grew fatter and the dark livid hue left their faces and they won back their clear and golden color of health. All through the winter Wang the Tiger lived in that city, arranging for his revenues and shaping affairs anew, and he rejoiced when children began to be born and women suckled babes again, and the sight stirred some deep in his own heart that he did not understand, except that a longing fell on him to return to his own courts and for the first time he wondered concerning his own two women. And he planned to return to his own house at the end of that year.

Now when Wang the Tiger had finished his siege of the city the spies whom he kept out in other parts had come to him and told him that there was a great war waging between north and south and again they came and said the north had won that war once more. Then Wang the Tiger made haste and he sent a band of men bearing gifts of silver and of silks and he wrote a letter to the general of the province. This letter Wang the Tiger wrote himself, for he was a little vain of his learning, since few lords of war are learned, and he set on it his own great red seal that he had now he was grown great.

In the letter he told how he had fought against a southern general and had defeated him and had taken this region that ran by this river for the north.

Then the general sent back a very good answer, full of praise for Wang the Tiger's success, and he gave him a very fine new title, and all he asked was that a certain sum be sent him every year for the provincial army. Then Wang the Tiger, since he knew he was not strong enough yet to refuse, promised the sum, and thus he established himself in the state.

As the end of the year drew near and Wang the Tiger took stock of his position, he found he had more than doubled his territories, and except for the mountainous parts which were bare, the lands were good and fertile producing both wheat and rice in measure, and besides this, salt and oils of peanuts and sesame and beans. Now, moreover, he had his own way to the sea and he could bring in much he needed and he could be free of Wang the Merchant his brother, when he wanted guns.

For Wang the Tiger longed very much to have great foreign guns, and the longing came to him especially because among the things the old robber chief had left were two very strange, huge guns such as Wang the Tiger had never seen before. They were of a very good iron without bubbles or holes of any sort in it, and so smooth that some clever ironsmith must have shaped them. These guns were heavy, too, so heavy that more than twenty men must put forth their utmost strength to lift them up at all.

And Wang the Tiger was very curious about these guns and he longed to see how to fire them, but no one knew how to do it, nor could they find any bullets for them. But at last two round iron balls were found hid in an old storehouse, and it came to Wang the Tiger that these were for the great guns, and he was in great delight and he had one of the guns taken out into an open spot in front of an old temple which had a waste place behind it. At first no one would come forward to try the gun, but Wang the Tiger offered a very good reward of silver, and at last the captain who had betrayed the city came forward, wanting the reward and hoping to gain favor, and he had seen the guns fired once, and he set all in readiness and very cleverly he fastened a torch on to the end of a long pole and set fire to the gun from a distance. When they saw the smoke begin they all ran a long way off and waited, and the gun blew off its great charge and the earth shook and the very heavens roared and smoke and fire streamed out, so that even Wang the Tiger was staggered and his heart stopped for an instant's fear. But when it was over they all looked and there the old temple lay in a heap of dusty ruins. Then Wang the Tiger laughed his noiseless laugh, and he was struck with delight at so good a toy as this and so fine a weapon of war, and he cried out,

"If I had had a gun like this there would have been no siege for I would have blown the city gates in!" And he thought a moment and he asked the captain, "But why did not your old chief turn them upon us?"

To this the captain said, "We did not think of it. These two guns he captured from another lord of war with whom I was once also, and they were brought here but never fired, and we did not know these balls were here and we did not think of these guns as weapons at all, so long they have stood here in the entrance court."

But Wang the Tiger treasured these great guns very much and he planned he would buy more balls for them and he had them brought and set where he could often see them.

When he had taken stock of all he had done, Wang the Tiger was well pleased with himself and he prepared to return to his home. He left a good large army in that city led by his own old men, and the newest men and the new captain he took back with him. After some pondering, he left in highest command in this city two whom he could trust. He left the Hawk and he left his nephew, who was grown now into a goodly young man, not tall but broad and strong and not ill to look at except for his pocked face which would be marred like that even when he lay dead of old age. It seemed to Wang the Tiger a good pair to leave, for the young man was too young to take command alone, and the Hawk could not be wholly trusted. So Wang the Tiger set them together and he told the young man secretly,

"If you believe he thinks of any treachery, send a messenger to me on wings by night and by day."

The youth promised, his eyes merry with his joy to be lifted up so high and left alone, and Wang the Tiger could go and be at ease, for a man can trust those of his own blood. Then having done all well and made all secure, Wang the Tiger returned victorious to his own home.

As for the people of that city they set themselves steadfastly again to build up once more what had been destroyed. Once more they filled their shops and set to work their looms to make silk and cotton cloths, and they bought and sold and they never talked except of such renewal, for what was passed, had passed, and Heaven lays its destiny upon all.

XXIII

WANG THE TIGER made haste on his homeward journey, although he said it was to see if his army were peaceful as he had left it. And he truly thought this was the chief reason, for he did not understand himself that he made haste for a deeper cause than this and it was to see if he had any son born to him or not. He had been away from his house close upon ten months out of a year, and although he had twice received letters from his learned wife in that time they were such very proper letters and full of such respect, that the sheet was full of these words, and little else said except that all was well enough.

But the moment he stepped into his own courts trium, phantly, he saw at a glance that Heaven was over him still and his good destiny still held, for there in the sunny court, where the south sun shone warm and there was no wind, sat his two wives, and each held a babe, and each babe was dressed in scarlet from head to foot, and upon their doddering little heads were crownless scarlet caps. The unlearned wife had sewed a row of small gold Buddhas upon her child's cap, but the learned wife, because she was so learned, did not believe in these tokens of good fortune, and she had embroidered flowers upon her child's cap. Except for this, there seemed no difference in the pair of children, and Wang the Tiger blinked at them amazed, for he had not thought of two. He stammered out,

"What—what—"

Then the learned wife rose, for she was quick and graceful in speech and she spoke prettily always, very smoothly and throwing in a learned phrase or a line from some old poem or classic, and she made a show of her shining white teeth as she spoke, and she said, smiling,

"These are the babes we have borne for you while you were away, and they are strong and sound from head to foot," and she held up her own for Wang the Tiger to see.

But the other wife would not have it held back that she had borne a son, for the learned wife's was a daughter, and she rose too and made haste to say, although she spoke seldom

347

because of her blackened teeth and the gaps where she had none, and now she held her lips close and she said,

"Mine is the son, my lord, and the other is a girl."

But Wang the Tiger said nothing at all. Indeed he could not speak for he had not known all it would be to have something of his own making belong to him like this. He stood and stared for a while speechless at these two minute creatures who seemed not to see him at all. No, they looked placidly at him as though he had always been there like a tree or a bit of the wall. They winked and blinked at the sunlight and the boy sneezed overloudly for his size so that Wang the Tiger was yet more astonished at such a gust coming out of so small a fragment. But the girl child only opened her mouth as a kitten does, and yawned very widely, and her father stared at her while she did. He had never held a child in his arms, and he did not touch these two. Nor did he know what to say to these two women at such a time, seeing that his speech had always been of warlike things. He could only smile somewhat fixedly, therefore, even while the men who were with him exclaimed in joy and admiration at the son their general had, and when he heard these exclamations he muttered out of his deep pleasure,

"Well, and I suppose women will breed!" and he went hastily into his apartments, being too full of joy for his own comfort.

There he washed and ate and he changed his stiff garments of war for a silk robe of a deep dark blue, and when it was all finished it was evening. Then he sat down by the brazier of coals, for the night came on quiet and chill with frost and there Wang the Tiger sat alone and reflected on all that had come about.

It seemed to him that destiny favored him at every point, and so favored there was nothing to which he could now

348

attain. Now that he had a son his ambition took on meaning and what he did, he did for a purpose. As he thought his heart swelled in him, and he forgot every sorrow and loneliness he ever had, and he shouted suddenly into the stillness of the room,

"I will make a true warrior out of that son of mine!" and he rose and slapped his hand against his thigh in his pleasure.

He strode about the room then for a while, smiling without knowing he did, and he thought what a comfortable thing it was to have a son of his own, and he thought how now he need depend no more on his brothers' sons, for there was his own son to continue his life after him and to increase his domains of war. Then another thought came to him and it was that he also had a daughter. He spent a little time then wondering what he would do with her, and he stood by the latticed window and fingered the hairs of his beard, and thought of his daughter with reticence because she was a girl and at last he said to himself in some doubt,

"I suppose I can wed her to some good warrior when the time comes, and it is all that I can do for her."

From this day on Wang the Tiger saw a new purpose in those two women of his, for from them he saw springing yet more sons, true and loyal sons who would never betray him as might another who had not his own blood in him. No longer did he use those two women to free his own heart and flesh. His heart was freed at the first sight of his son, and of his flesh he hoped for his sons, trusty soldiers to stand beside him and support him when he grew old and weak. So he went regularly to his two wives, and not more to one than the other, for all their secret gentle striving for his favor, and he was very well content with them each in her own way, for he sought from them equally but the one thing, and he did not hope for more from the one than from the other. It troubled him no more that he did not love a woman, now that he had his son.

Thus the winter passed in content. The New Year festival came and passed also, and Wang the Tiger made more merriment than usual because the year had been so good, and he rewarded all his men with wine and meats and with a bounty of silver. To each man he gave also such small things as they craved, tobacco, a towel, a pair of socks, and other small things. To his wives also he made a bounty and at the festival the whole house was very merry. There was but one untoward thing and it came after the feast day, so that no joy was curtailed. This was that the old magistrate died one night in his sleep. Whether he took too much opium, being heavy with his sleep, or whether the bitter cold overcame him in his drugged heaviness, could not be known. But the matter was reported to Wang the Tiger and he ordered a good coffin and all to be done for the gentle old man, and the very next day after it was all finished and the coffin ready to be sent to his old home, for the magistrate had not been native to the province, one came again to tell that his old wife had taken what was left of her husband's opium and so followed him of her own will. Nor could any grieve, for she was old and sickly and she never came out of her own courts, and Wang the Tiger had never seen her in his life. He ordered another coffin, therefore, and when all was ready he sent them with three serving men to be taken to their own city in the next province. Then Wang the Tiger sent report in proper form to those above who should know of it, and he sent his trusty harelipped man with the letter and with him some soldiers, and Wang the Tiger said secretly to the trusty man,

"There are things not to be said except by mouth to ear, and so I have not written this. But if the chance comes to you

350

let it be known that I must have a say in who shall be the civil magistrate here."

The trusty man nodded his head at this and Wang the Tiger was content. In such confused times as these he did not fear the hasty coming of any governor, and he could rule very well himself. So he forgot the matter and he took for his own wives the innermost rooms where the old magistrate had lived and soon he had forgot that any had ever lived here except himself and his own.

The year drew on then to spring again, and Wang the Tiger made up his mind, since he had been so fortunate this year in everything and he had good reports from his new lands and the silver flowed in regularly from all his many revenues so that his soldiers were paid and content and loud in his praise, that he would return for the spring festival to his father's house and pass the feast day with his brothers. It was a fitting thing for a great house to do, the more especially as it is a season when the sons should repair their father's grave. Wang the Tiger, moreover, had a little reckoning yet to do with his second brother, and he was ready now to be free of such borrowing, and he wished to be free. Therefore Wang the Tiger sent some soldiers to tell his elder brothers, with all decent courtesies, that he and his wives and his children and their servants would come by the feast day. To this the two brothers, Wang the Landlord and Wang the Merchant, returned very courteous words of welcome.

When all was ready, then, Wang the Tiger mounted his high red horse and at the head of his guard rode forth. But this time they must needs ride slowly for there were the mule carts where the two women rode and other mule carts for the maid servants. And Wang the Tiger did ride slowly and he was proud to do it for such a cause. Riding thus at the head of his cavalcade, his women and his children, he took his place in the generations. Never did his lands look so fair to him nor so prosperous as they did in this time of bursting spring, of budding willow and unfolding peach blossoms. And seeing the faint tinge of green and peach in every valley and upon every hillside, and seeing the deep brown of moist earth turned to the spring sunshine, he remembered suddenly his father and how every spring he loved to pluck a sprig of willow and a sprig of blooming peach and carry them in his hand or put them above the door of the earthen house, and thinking of his father and of his own son, Wang the Tiger felt his place in the long line of life, and he was never any more separate as he had once been, nor alone. For the first time he forgave his father wholly for certain deep angers he had against him as a youth. Nor did he know he forgave. He only knew that some bitterness left in him since his angry boyhood slipped out of him and was blown away as though on a healthy wind, and he was peaceful with himself, at last.

So Wang the Tiger came to his father's house and he came in triumph and not so much as youngest son and youngest brother, but as a man in his own right by what he had achieved and by the son he had begotten. And they all felt his achievement, and his brothers met him and welcomed him very nearly as though he were a guest, and his brothers' wives contended with each other as to who should be most voluble and ready in her welcome.

The truth of it was that the lady of Wang the Landlord and the wife of Wang the Merchant had struggled with each other as to who should house Wang the Tiger and his family. The lady took it as a matter of course and her right that they should come to her lord's house, for now as Wang the Tiger's fame began to be known she felt it would be an honorable thing to have him as guest and she said,

"It will be fitting, for we chose his wife for him, a very

learned and pleasant lady, and she can scarcely be at home with your brother's wife, who is so ignorant. Let her keep the lesser wife if she wishes, but we must have our brother and his lady here. He may be moved by one of our sons or he may be able to do us some great good. At the very least he will not be subject to her hints and desires!"

But the wife of Wang the Merchant said to him importunately and often, and she would not give up her wish at all,

"How can our brother's woman know how to feed such a number, and she only used to feeding nuns and priests with their poor vegetable stuffs?"

There came to be such anger that these two women quarreled face to face over the matter, and, seeing the coming and the going and hearing the loud talk that grew more loud as the festival day drew near, and seeing that nothing could be decided and that each wife for pride's sake would not give up a smallest point, the two husbands met together in their old trysting place in the tea house, for they were united as they never could have been otherwise by the enmity of their two wives. There they consulted together and Wang the Merchant, who had made his plan, said to his brother,

"Let it be as you say, but what do you think if we put our brother and his retinue into that court our father left empty? True, it belongs to his wife Lotus, but she is so very old now and uses it not at all since she has given up gaming, and if we put them there we can divide the expense between us, and this we can use as a reason to our two ladies and so have peace again."

Now once Wang the Landlord would have wished to use some way he had thought of alone, but as he grew older and so monstrous in his girth he grew exceedingly slothful and he was drowsy much of the day, and he would do anything to avoid trouble. This plan then seemed very good to

353

him, and he wanted to have his powerful younger brother's favor, but still he did not care so much if his second brother did not have more than he. In his growing indolence he had passed the time when he loved guests as he once did, and he was glad not to have those in his house now to whom he must be courteous in season and out of season and so weary himself. He agreed willingly, therefore, and each man went home to his wife and told her the plan. It was a very good compromise for all, for none lost her way altogether, and each determined secretly to seem to be the one responsible for their comfort, and yet each was pleased that the vast cost of wines and feasts and bounty for serving men and women would be halved, and to all of them this was a sound reason enough.

Then those old courts where Wang Lung had lived in the years of his later middle life were swept and garnished and made clean. It was true that Lotus never went into them, and the serving maids sat in them sometimes but that was all. Lotus was grown very huge and old now, and Cuckoo was her only companion except her slaves, for as she grew old Lotus's eyes were filmed and she could not even see at last to cast dice in gaming or to see what the numbers were in any of the games of chance she loved. One by one the old crones who had used to come to her died, or were bed-ridden, and only Lotus lived on, alone with those who served her.

Her slaves she used very bitterly, and as her eyes failed her tongue grew cruelly sharp, so that the brothers had to pay maid servants very high wages or they could not bear her tongue. As for the slaves who were bought and could not leave if they liked, two of them killed themselves, one of them swallowing her poor glass earrings and the other hanging herself on a beam in one of the kitchens where she worked, rather than endure longer Lotus's cruelties. For Lotus would not only wield her tongue coarsely, shrieking out such words as maids cannot bear to hear, but she would nip them cruelly. Her fat old fingers, that were so useless in the strange beauty they still kept and they were smooth and beautiful when all other beauty had faded from her, those old fingers could nip and pinch a young girl's arm until the blood came purple under the skin, and sometimes when this did not satisfy her, Lotus would take the coals out of her pipe and press them into tender young flesh. There was not one whom she did not treat thus if she could except Cuckoo, and she feared Cuckoo, and leaned upon her for everything.

For Cuckoo was what she ever was. In her age, and she was very old now also, she seemed to grow more thin and dry and withered and yet she had a strength in her old frame that was almost what it had been in youth. Her eyes were sharp and her tongue harsh and her face, although wrinkled all over, was still red. She was greedy, too, as ever she had been, and if she guarded her mistress against the thievery of other serving women, she herself thieved most hardily from Lotus. Now that Lotus's eyes were filmed, Cuckoo took what she liked from Lotus and she swelled her own private store, and Lotus, being so old, forgot what jewels she had and what fur garments and what garments of satin and silk, and so she did not know what Cuckoo took. If by chance she remembered and cried out for something of a sudden, Cuckoo diverted her if she could, and if Lotus was perverse and would not forget, Cuckoo went and fetched the thing from her own boxes and gave it to Lotus. But when, after fingering it a time or two Lotus forgot again, Cuckoo took it and kept it once more.

Nor did a slave or serving woman dare complain, for

355

Cuckoo was the real mistress there, and even the brothers deferred to her, for they knew they could find no one to take her place and they dared not anger her. When therefore Cuckoo said Lotus had given her this or that, the maids were silent, for they knew well that if they complained, Cuckoo was so bitter and evil she could have put poison into a bowl of food and thought nothing of it, and sometimes she would boast of all the skill she had in poisoning to keep them afraid. As for Lotus, she leaned on Cuckoo for everything, as she grew blind, and now because of the mighty weight of her flesh she walked no more except from her bed to the great chair of carved black wood where she sat a little while after noon and then back to her bed again. Even so she must be supported by four slaves and more, for those pretty little feet of hers which had once been Wang Lung's pride and pleasure were nothing but stumps beneath the great and monstrous body which in other days had been slender as a bamboo and passionately beloved by Wang Lung.

When one day Lotus heard the commotion in the courts next hers and when she asked and heard that Wang the Tiger was coming with his women and children to pass the feast day and worship at his father's grave with his brothers, she grew petulant and she said,

"I cannot have brats here! I have always hated brats!"

This was true for she was a childless woman and had always some strange hatred against little children, and especially when she passed her time of such fruitage. Then Wang the Landlord who had come in with his brother, soothed her and he said,

"No, no, we will open the other gate so that he need not come near you at all."

Then Lotus cried again in her old, querulous way,

"I forget what son he was of that old man of mine! Was

356

he the one who used to stare at that pale slave I once had and he ran away when that silly old man of mine took her for himself?"

Then both brothers looked at each other aghast and they were astonished at this tale and had never heard it, and Wang the Merchant said hastily, for Lotus was now very free and obscene in her old age and talked of her early life so that neither brother allowed his children to come near her for she did not know decency from indecency and all her old life would come bubbling to the surface of her lips sometimes, and he said,

"We know nothing of this. Our brother is now a famous lord of war and he will ill brook such talk as this against his honor."

But Lotus when she heard this laughed and she spat upon the tile floor and she cried out,

"Oh, and you men are so full of your honor but we women know what poor stuff your honor is made of!" And she listened for Cuckoo to laugh also, and she cried out, "Eh, Cuckoo?" and Cuckoo, who was never far away, gave her thin shrill cackle of laughter, for she was pleased to see these two middle-aged men, each grave and important in his own way, put to such confusion. As for the two brothers, they hurried away to direct the serving men in all that must be done.

When all was ready Wang the Tiger came with his house, and he took up his abode in these days in the court where his father had lived. It was empty for him, now, and swept at last of every presence except his own and his son's and he could forget that anyone had ever lived there except himself and his son.

Then the festival came to this whole house, the festival of spring, and everyone laid aside his private grudge for the

357

once; even the wives of the two elder brothers, when they came together in the family, were formal and courteous with each other. Everything was done in its proper order and in the way it should be done, and there were certain duties at this time which the sons of Wang Lung had toward their father.

It happened that two days before the festival day was Wang Lung's birthday. Wherever he was, on this day he was ninety years old, and since his sons were together they determined to perform their whole filial duty and Wang the Tiger was very ready because since he had his own son his anger against his father had gone of its own accord and he was left ready and eager to take his place in the line of father and son and father and son.

On this birthday of Wang Lung's, therefore, his sons invited many guests and a great feast was prepared, such a feast as they would have made if their father had been with them, and there was rejoicing and congratulation and there was every dish such as is proper at a birthday feast. And they had Wang Lung's tablet there and made obeisance to it and they did him honor on his birthday.

On the same day Wang the Landlord hired priests and he spared no money and each son gave his share, and the priests chanted all their chants for Wang Lung's spirit to give it rest and joy in the happy courts where it now was, and they decked the hall with their sacred emblems and signs, and for half a day the courts were filled with the rise and the fall of their chanting voices and the dull thick sound of the wooden sticks upon their drums of wood.

All this did Wang Lung's sons do in his memory. Beyond this they and their wives and their sons went out to the place where the graves of their fathers were, and Wang Lung's sons saw to it that every grave was made straight and smooth and heaped high with fresh earth. Each grave was shaped to a point and upon the point a clod of earth was put, and white paper cut cunningly into long strips was fastened beneath the clod and streamed in the sweet spring wind of that day. And Wang Lung's sons bowed to the earth before his grave and they set incense to burn, and they brought their sons to bow, and proudest of them all was Wang the Tiger, for he took his own fair son and he bowed the child's little head, too, and he was knit to his fathers and to his brothers through this child, his son.

And as they went home again they saw that over the whole countryside, wherever there were fathers' graves and grandfathers' graves, there were sons who did what they had done for Wang Lung this day, for it was a day of remembrance. Then Wang the Landlord was more moved than he usually was, and he said,

"Let us do this more regularly than we have in past years, for we have but ten more years and our father will be a hundred years old, and then he will have been born again into another body in this world, and we cannot feast his birthday, for it will be a new birth and he will be unknown to us."

And Wang the Tiger, grave in his fatherhood, said, "Yes, we ought so to do for him as we hope our sons will do for us when we are where he is now."

And they went homewards in silence and gravity, each feeling his kinship to the others more than was wont with any of them.

After these duties were over, they all set themselves to the merriment of the festival, and when the day of the festival came to evening the air was unexpectedly warm and sweet and a little slender perfect moon hung in the sky, clear and pale as amber. On this night they all gathered in the court where

359

Lotus lived, for she had that day turned plaintive all of a sudden and she said,

"I am a lonely old woman and they never come near me nor hold me as one of this house at all!"

And she moaned and wept tears out of her blind old eyes so that Cuckoo went and told the brothers, and they yielded to her because this day their hearts were unexpectedly tender toward their father and what had been his. Instead, therefore, of feasting in the courts of Wang the Landlord, where his lady would have had the family gather, they went to the court where Lotus lived. It was a large and beautiful court, too, with pomegranate trees brought from the south in one corner, and in the center was a small octagonal pool where the new little moon shone reflected. There they all ate cakes and drank wine, and the children rejoiced in the moon's light and they ran everywhere hiding in and out of the shadows and running out again to seize a cake or sup a little wine. They all ate their fill of the steamed delicacies and cakes suitable to this festival, some stuffed with pork chopped fine, and some with brown sugar and very dainty. There was so much that even the slaves ate freely and the servants filched and ate behind doors or when they went on a pretense to fetch more wine. Nor was it missed what they took, or if the mistresses' sharp eyes noted it, at least for once nothing was said, so that no reproof might mar the night.

And as they ate and drank, Wang the Landlord's eldest son, who was a very pretty musician, played upon a flute, and his next brother, a lad with nimble, delicate fingers, played upon a harp whose strings he struck lightly with two slender bamboo sticks, and they played ancient songs to the spring, and sang a plaint or two of some dead maiden's to the moon. When they played so well together, their mother was very proud, and she commended them often and cried loudly as soon as one song was finished,

"Play something else, my sons, for it is pretty to play like this under the new moon!" And she was proud of their slender, lovely looks.

But the wife of Wang the Merchant, whose sons were plainly taught and who knew no toying with music, yawned and talked aloud to this one and to that one, but most of all to the wife she had chosen for Wang the Tiger. She made very much of this one and she was pointed in her ignoring of the learned wife; she scarcely glanced at Wang the Tiger's daughter, but she could never be done with smelling and nuzzling the boy child, and one might have thought it all due to her that the child was a boy.

But still there was nothing open said, although the lady darted looks of displeasure at her sister-in-law and that one caught them all and took delight in pretending she did not. But no one else seemed to see, and Wang the Landlord roused himself and he ordered the servants to bring the tables for the night's feast into the courts, and they did. Then everyone set himself to the real food, and the serving men brought in one dainty dish after another, for Wang the Landlord gave this feast to them, and he had outdone himself in ordering it. There were many dishes that Wang the Merchant and Wang the Tiger had never even heard of, such as ducks' tongues stewed with spices and ducks' feet with the dainty black skin peeled from them, and there were many such fine dishes that tickled the tongue very well.

Of all those who ate and drank heartily that night none ate and drank more heartily than Lotus, and the more she ate the more she was moved with merriment. She sat in her great carved chair and there was a slave beside her to put some of every dish into her bowl, but sometimes she would

361

dip for herself, and a slave guided her hand then and she dipped her porcelain spoon into the dish and put it eagerly to her trembling old mouth and supped it loudly. Meats and all she ate, for she had her teeth all strong and sound still.

Then as she grew more merry she paused sometimes in her eating to tell a lewd coarse tale or two that made the young men laugh as much as they dared but they dared not laugh too much before their elders. But she listened for their choking and bursting laughter, and was encouraged to other tales. Wang the Landlord himself could scarcely keep his face decent except that his lady sat there stiff and silent and he could look at her and be grave. But the ruddy wife of Wang the Merchant guffawed loudly and the more loudly when she saw that her sister-in-law would not laugh at all. Even Wang the Landlord's second wife bit her lips, and while she would not laugh because her lady did not, still she was fain to hold her sleeve across her face and smile behind it.

But Lotus grew so free at last when she listened and heard men laugh that for shame's sake she must be silenced, and so the two older brothers plied her with wines to make her drowsy and the more since they feared she would say some very lewd thing about Wang the Tiger and anger him, and they feared his anger. Because of this tongue of Lotus's they had not urged Pear Blossom to come to the family feast, and when she answered the messenger they sent that she could ill leave her charges, they let her be, deeming it were best to rouse no memories in Lotus.

Thus the night passed happily and midnight came and the moon swung high, and soft clouds came up and seemed to swing the moon here and there. The babes were asleep in their mothers' bosoms, for the youngest in every family sought long ago his mother's breasts, except the youngest of

Wang the Landlord's lady, who was by now a proud and slender girl of thirteen, grave because she was betrothed not long ago. But Wang the Landlord's second wife was a warm mother, and she had two in her arms, one a child of a year and more, and the other newly born but a little over a month, for Wang the Landlord still liked her. As for Wang the Tiger's wives, each held her own, and his little son slept with his head thrown back over his mother's arm and the moonlight fell full on his face, and Wang the Tiger looked often at that small sleeping face.

But after midnight the merriment waned, and the sons of Wang the Landlord slipped away one by one, for they had other pleasures waiting, and it wearied them to sit long with elderly folk. They went easily and carelessly, and the second son of Wang the Merchant looked longingly after them, but he dared not go because he feared his father. The servants also grew weary and longed for their rest, and they withdrew and leaned in this doorway and that, yawning mightily, and muttering to each other,

"Their children waked at dawn and we had to tend them and now the old ones feast to midnight and we must tend them still! Will they never let us sleep?"

But at last they did separate, but not before Wang the Landlord was drunken, and his lady called for his serving men to come and let him lean upon them and so go to his bed. Even Wang the Tiger was nearer drunken than he had ever been, but he could walk into his own court. Only Wang the Merchant was as smooth and neat as ever, and his wrinkled yellow face was scarcely changed at all, and not red even, for he was one of those who grow more pale and quiet as he drinks more deeply.

But of them all not one had eaten and drunk as Lotus had, and indeed, old as she was now and nearly seventy-eight years old, she had eaten and drunk too well. In the middle hours between midnight and dawn she moaned and was very restless, for the wine she had drunk seemed to come up in her and heat her to a mighty fever and all the meats and oily dishes she had eaten lay heavy in her as stone. She turned her head this way and that upon her pillow and was ill at ease and called out for one thing and another, but nothing eased her. Then suddenly she gave a strange hoarse scream and Cuckoo ran to her, and when she heard Cuckoo call out, Lotus muttered something and stared out of her filmed eyes and tossed her arms and legs and was suddenly still. Then her fat old face grew dark and purple and her body rigid and stiff, and she began to draw her breath in quick, stammering gusts, loud enough to be heard in the next court. Wang the Tiger would have heard her if he had not been somewhat drunken and so sleeping more heavily than his wont.

But his learned wife slept lightly always and she heard the cry and rose and came in. She had some slight knowledge of old medicines from her father, who was a physician, and now she drew aside the curtain and the light of earliest dawn fell upon Lotus's frightful face. Then the learned woman cried out, aghast,

"It is the old lady's end come on her if we cannot purge her of her wines and meats!"

She called for hot water and for ginger and for all the medicines she knew and she tried them all. But it was no use, for Lotus was deaf to all calls and entreaties now, and her teeth were so locked that even when they forced her blackened lips apart, her teeth were locked inside. It was the strangest thing that in an old body like this her teeth should still be sound and white and good, and they lost her her life now, for if there had been a hole somewhere or a gap

364

where a tooth was gone, they would have poured the medicine in somehow, and Cuckoo could even have taken a mouthful and spurted it in with her own lips. But the sound whole teeth were fast and locked.

So Lotus lay breathing and snorting through half the next day, and suddenly, without ever knowing this was her end, she died. The purple of her face faded away and she turned as pale and as yellow as old wax. Thus did the feasting time end in this death.

Then the two elder brothers saw to the making of her coffin, but they had to let her lie a day or so, for the coffin had to be built twice as big as common, and there was none to be found made ready that was broad enough.

And while they waited Cuckoo truly mourned this creature she had tended all these years. Yes, she truly mourned her, even though she went about and collected all she could of the things that were Lotus's still, opening this box and that and taking all of any value, and she sent her stores out secretly through a hidden back gate, so that at last when Lotus was put into her coffin those who served her marvelled that she had scarcely a coat fit to be buried in and they wondered what she had done with the good sum of silver she had as Wang Lung's widow, seeing she had not gamed it away of late years. Yet for all her thieving Cuckoo mourned for Lotus, and she wiped a few scanty tears away, which if they were few were the only tears she had ever shed for anyone, and when the coffin was filled with lime, for Lotus had begun to stink very soon, and when the lid was sealed down and it was carried out the gate to the temple where it was to lie until a day of burial was chosen, Cuckoo walked after the coffin and hurried her old feet to keep in sight of it until it was put into the empty room of the temple among many other coffins already there. Then she turned away and went to some place of her own she had somewhere, and came no more to the house of Wang, and she mourned Lotus truly and as truly as she was able.

Before the ten allotted days were past Wang the Tiger was weary of his brothers and their sons and the hour of close kinship they had felt in the festival was gone. But he sat the days out and he watched the coming and going of his brothers' sons as he went to this house and to that sometimes and it seemed to him that these sons were but poor weak fellows and promised no great good. The two younger sons of Wang the Merchant looked no higher than to be clerks and they had no ambition except to idle over a counter and laugh and gossip with the other clerks if their father was not by to see them at it, and even the younger one who was but twelve years old was apprenticed in a shop and spent his every moment that he dared in tossing pennies with the urchins on the street who gathered at the shop door to wait for him, and because he was the master's son none dared to say anything against him nor to refuse him a handful of pennies if he clamored for them out of the shop's till, although they all kept a sharp eye out to see if the lad's father came so that he might run back to his place while Wang the Merchant passed. And Wang the Tiger saw that this brother of his was so engrossed in his money making that he never saw his sons at all, nor thought of how they would one day spend as eagerly what he so eagerly gathered together, nor that they only endured their clerking until he died and left them free so that they need not work.

And Wang the Tiger saw the sons of his elder brother, how finicking and dandyish they were, and how they must have everything that touched them soft and fine, cool silk in summer, and warm soft furs in winter. Nor would they eat well and robustly as young men ought to do, but they dallied with their food and complained of this because it was too sweet and of that because it was too sour and salt, and they pushed one bowl after another away from them, and the slaves were kept hurrying hither and thither for them.

All this Wang the Tiger saw with anger that it was so. One night he walked alone in the court that had been his father's and he heard the sound of a woman's giggling laugh. Suddenly a little girl, who was child of some servant or other, ran past the round gate of his court, and she was frightened and breathless and when she saw Wang the Tiger there she stooped to scuttle past him. But he laid hold of her little arm suddenly and shouted at her,

"What woman laughed?"

The child shrank away terrified at his glittering eyes, but he had fast hold of her and she could not twist herself free, and she cast down her eyes and stammered,

"The young lord took my sister aside."

Then Wang the Tiger asked sternly,

"Where?"

The child pointed to the back of the next court to an empty room that Lotus had used as a granary, but now it was empty and locked loosely with a great hasp. Then Wang the Tiger dropped the child's arm and she ran like a rabbit, but he strode to that place where she pointed and he saw the hasp was wide enough so that the doors stood apart from each other nearly a foot, and a slender young body could easily pass through. He stood there in the night and listened, and he heard a woman's laughter, tittering and giggling, and he heard some voice whisper words he could not catch but he heard them come hot and breathless from the man's throat. Then his old sickness against passion rose in him and he was about to beat upon that door except that he stayed himself in the act and he thought with scorn,

"What business is it of mine that there is still such a thing in this same house?"

And he went back weary and sickened to his court. But some strange power even in his disgust made him restless and he walked about the court and while he waited the moon rose late. Soon out of that inner empty room he saw a young slave slip between the hasped doors and she smoothed her hair and he saw her smiling there in the light of the moon and she glanced about her swiftly and went swiftly and soundlessly in her cloth shoes across the tiled empty court which had been Lotus's. Only once she stopped under the pomegranate tree and it was to fasten her loosened girdle.

And after a time, and all this time Wang the Tiger had stood motionless, his heart throbbing with some sort of disgust that was half sick and half sweet, he saw a young man come sauntering by and he sauntered as though he were out to see the night and nothing more. Then Wang the Tiger shouted suddenly,

"Who is it?"

There answered a very pleasant voice, idle and light,

"It is I, Uncle!"

Wang the Tiger saw it was indeed his elder brother's eldest son, and some gorge rose in Wang the Tiger's heart and he could have sprung upon the young man because he told himself he hated lewdness so bitterly, and most of all he hated it in his own blood and he could not bear it. But he held his hands hard to his sides, for well he knew one cannot kill a brother's son and well he knew his own temper that if he let it come up he could not stop it where he would. So he only gave a great snort and he turned blindly away into his room and he grunted to himself,

368

"I must get me out of these courts where one of my brothers is a miser and the other a rake! I cannot breathe this air, for I am a man of freedom and of battle and I cannot keep my angers bottled in me as men must who live like this with women in courts!" And he wished suddenly with some strange desire that there was a need for him to kill someone and shed blood in a cause so that he could free his heart of a charge it had which he could not understand.

Then to calm himself he forced his thoughts to his little son and he crept into the room where the child slept in his mother's bed, and he looked down upon the child. The woman slept heavily as country women will and her mouth was open and her breath came out very foul so that even as he bent over his little son Wang the Tiger was fain to cover his nostrils under his hand. But the child slept serene and still, and looking at his quiet face grave in sleep, Wang the Tiger swore that his son should not be like any of these. No, this boy should be hardened from his youth up and reared to be a great soldier and he should be taught every sort of skill and he should be made into a man.

On the very next day, therefore, Wang the Tiger took his two wives and his children and all those who had come with him and they made their farewells, after they had feasted together with their kinsmen. But in spite of the farewell feasting it seemed to Wang the Tiger that he was the less near to his two brothers, after all, for this visit, and when he saw his elder brother, sleepy and peaceful and sunken in his flesh, and how his heavy eyes never lightened except at some lewdness, and when he saw his second brother, and how his face grew more narrow and his eyes more secret as his age came, it seemed to him they were like men who were blind and deaf and dumb because they did not see what they were or what they had made their sons.

But he said nothing. He sat glowering and silent and he dwelt with a mighty pride upon the thought of his own son, and the man into which he would shape him.

So they parted, and on the surface all was smooth and courteous and they bowed deeply to each other and the elder brothers and their ladies and serving men and maids came out to the street and they called a hundred good wishes. But Wang the Tiger said to himself that he would not soon come back to his father's house.

With the greatest content, therefore, did Wang the Tiger return to his own lands and the lands seemed the best he had ever seen and the people the sturdiest and best and his house was home, and all his men welcomed him and they fired firecrackers at his coming and there were smiles of welcome everywhere when he swung himself down from his red horse and a score of soldiers idling about the courts leaped forward to catch the bridle as he tossed it aside, and it pleased Wang the Tiger to see them do it.

He set himself therefore as the spring widened, and everywhere spread into early summer, to round his men afresh and train them again day after day. He sent out his spies again and he sent out men to see how his newly taken lands were, and he sent his trusty man everywhere to bring him revenues and he sent guards fully armed to bring the treasure to him safely, for in these days it was far more than one man could carry in a sack upon his shoulders as once he had.

But in the evenings when the day was over and he sat in his court alone in the warm spring night, at such times when there are many men whose hearts grow wayward and yearn for some love or other beside what they have tried, Wang the Tiger yearned after his son. Then he had the child brought to him continually, although he did not know how to play with any child, not even his son. He commanded the nurse to seat herself where he could see the child, and he sat and stared at every movement the boy made and at every transient look that flickered across his face. When the boy learned to walk Wang the Tiger could scarcely contain himself for pleasure and when he was alone at night and no one to see him in the courts he took the girdle that the nurse passed around the child's waist and he held it and walked round and round while the boy staggered and panted in the loop of the girdle.

If any had asked Wang the Tiger what he thought while he stared at his son, he would have been in the greatest confusion, for he did not know himself. Only he felt swelling up in him great dreams of power and glory and sometimes out of his fullness he pondered on how in these times a man could rise to any power and place if he had might enough and could make men afraid of him, for there was no emperor and no dynasty in these times, and anyone might struggle and shape events if he would. And feeling this in himself Wang the Tiger would mutter into his beard,

"And such a man am I!"

Now there came a strange thing out of this love Wang the Tiger had for his son and it was that when Wang the Tiger's learned wife heard how he had his son brought to him every day, she dressed her daughter in bright new garments one day and she brought her in all fresh and pink and she had put little silver bracelets upon the child's wrists and tied her black hair with pink bits of yarn, and she forced the child upon her father's attention thus. When Wang the Tiger was embarrassed and turned his eyes aside not knowing what he ought to say, the mother said in her pleasant voice,

"This little daughter of ours craves your notice, too, and she is no whit less strong and fair than your son."

Wang the Tiger was somewhat taken aback with this

woman's courage for he did not know her at all, except in
the darkness of the nights in her turn, and so he could mutter
out of courtesy,

"She is fair enough for a girl."

But the child's mother was not satisfied with this, for he
scarcely looked at her daughter, and she pressed on and said,

"No, my husband, at least look at her, for she is no usual
child. She walked three months before the boy did and talks
now as though she were four instead of two and under. I
have come to ask for a favor to me that you will give her
learning also and share your goods with her as you do with
your son."

To this Wang the Tiger said in astonishment,

"How can I make a soldier out of a girl?"

Then in her steadfast, pleasant way the mother said,

"If not a soldier, then some skill in a school, for there are
many such in these times, my husband."

Suddenly Wang the Tiger heard that she called him by
that name that no woman ever had, and she did not call him
"my lord" as other women would, and he was embarrassed
and out of his confusion he looked at the child because he
could think of nothing to say. Then he saw that truly this
girl was a very enticing little one, very round and fat and
she had a tiny red mouth that she moved in smiles, and her
eyes were large and black and her hands were fat and the
nails very perfect and complete. He saw them because her
mother had stained the nails red as women will do sometimes
for children very loved. The child's feet were cased in little
pink silk shoes and the mother held them both in her one
hand while the other she passed about the child's middle as
she leaped up and down upon her mother's hand. When the
mother saw him looking at the girl babe she said gently,

"I shall not bind her feet, and let us send her to a school

and make such a woman out of her as there are here and there in these days."

"But who will wed such a maid?" cried Wang the Tiger astonished.

To this the mother replied tranquilly, "Such a maid can wed whom she likes, I believe."

Wang the Tiger took some thought at this and he looked at the woman. He had never looked at her before, deeming it enough if she served his purpose, and now as he looked he saw for the first time that she had a wise good face and a manner which made her seem composed and able to do what she liked, and when he looked at her she did not fear him and she looked back at him without giggling or drawing her mouth down as the other wife might have done. And he thought to himself in some wonder,

"This woman is more clever than I thought and I have not seen her very well before," and aloud he said courteously and he rose as he spoke, "When the time comes I will not say nay to you if it seems a wise thing."

Now it was a curious thing that she who had been so composed always and had lived content so far as Wang the Tiger knew or cared, now when she saw this new courtesy in the man seemed moved in some strange way. The color came dull and red into her cheeks and she looked at him earnestly and in silence and with yearning creeping into her eyes. But Wang the Tiger, seeing her change thus, felt the old repulsion against women well into his heart and his tongue was locked and he turned away and muttered that he had forgot something he had to do that hour, and he went away quickly, shaken in himself, and he did not like her when she looked at him in such a way.

But the fruit of the hour was that sometimes if the mother sent a slave with the girl at the time when he called for his son to be brought so that the the two came together, Wang the Tiger did not send the girl away. At first he feared the mother might return and make a custom of talking with him, but when he saw she did not, he let the girl be there for a while and he stared at her, for her sex made him shy of her even though she was but a child staggering hither and thither. Still she was a winning thing and he watched her often and laughed silently at her tempers and her broken words. His son was large and grave and not given to laughter, but this girl was small and quick and full of merriment and her eyes were forever seeking her father's, and if she were not watched she abused her brother and snatched what he had away from him, being so quick. Without knowing it Wang the Tiger came to notice her in a certain fashion, and he knew her for his child among others if he saw a slave holding her at the gate in a crowd to see what went by upon the street, and sometimes he even stopped to touch her hand and see her flash her eyes at him to smile.

Then going into his house when she had thus smiled, he was content and at last he felt no more alone but a man among his own, both women and children.

XXIV

Now Wang the Tiger had it always in his mind that he must enlarge his place and his position for his son's sake, and so he told himself often and he planned how he would do it, where he would creep in and make the victory at the end of some common war, how he would push southward of his river and seize the next county or two in a famine year when the people were pressed by drought or flood. But it happened that for a few years there was no great common war, and one weak and unready man after another came and went upon the central seat of government and if there was no sure peace still there was no great outburst of war, either, nor such a time as a lord of war could take to come out too boldly.

For a second thing, it seemed to Wang the Tiger that he could not as he once had done put his whole heart into his ambitions for enlarging himself, for there was this son of his to plan for and to tend, and after that were all his soldiers and the matters of the domain, for none had ever come to take the old magistrate's place. Once or twice a name had been sent to Wang the Tiger but he had always rejected it quickly because it suited him better to be alone, and now as his son grew out of babyhood into his childhood Wang the Tiger thought sometimes that if he could put the state off for a few more years it would be a very good thing for himself to be the magistrate there when he was too old to be a warrior and when his son could take his place at the head of the army. But he kept this plan secret in himself for it was too soon yet to tell it forth. And indeed, the boy was now only six years old. But Wang the Tiger was in such haste for him to grow into a man that while sometimes the years went fast, yet at other times he thought they would never pass at all, and looking at his son he did not see him for the little lad he was, but for the young man, the young warrior, he would have him be, and without knowing it he forced the child in many ways.

When his son was but six years old Wang the Tiger took him away from his mother and out of the courts of the women, and brought him into his own courts to live with him. This he did so that the boy would not be made soft by women's caresses and women's talk and ways, but partly he did it because he was in such haste for the boy's constant companionship. At first the boy was shy and lost with his father and he wandered about with a look of fright in his eyes and when Wang the Tiger made a mighty effort and put out his hand to draw the child near the boy stood stiff and withdrawn and barely suffered his father, and Wang the Tiger felt the child's fear and he yearned over the child, but he was speechless because he did not know what to say, and he could only let the lad go again. At first it had been Wang the Tiger's purpose to cut the child's life off clean from the mother and from the life of any woman, for he had only soldiers to serve him, but soon it could be seen that so clean a cut was beyond the endurance of so small and childish a heart. The boy did not complain at all. He was a grave and silent lad, patient to endure what he must, but he was never joyful. He sat by his father when his father called to him so to do, and he was dutiful to stand at once when his father came into the room where he was, and he read his books with his old tutor who came every day to teach him, but he never spoke more than he must.

One night Wang the Tiger watched him thus at his night meal, and the lad felt his father watching him and he bent his head over his bowl very low and made as though he ate, but he could not swallow. Then Wang the Tiger grew angry for indeed he had done everything he could think of for this child of his and that very day he had taken the lad with him to review his armies, and he set the lad across his saddle in front of him as he rode, and his heart swelled as the men cried out to the little general, as they called him. The lad had smiled faintly, and had turned his head away until Wang the Tiger forced him saying,

"Hold your head high—they are your men—your soldiers, my son! You shall lead them out one day to war!"

Thus forced the boy held up his head somewhat, but his

cheeks were a burning dark red, and when Wang the Tiger leaned over he saw the boy did not look at the men at all, but looked far off into the fields beyond the grounds where the armies marched and when Wang the Tiger asked him what he saw he lifted his finger and pointed at a little sunburned naked lad in the next field who lay across a water buffalo's back, staring at the brave show of soldiers, and the boy said,

"I would like to be that boy and lie on the buffalo's back."

Wang the Tiger was not pleased at such a common, low wish as this and he said sternly,

"Well, and I think my son might wish higher than to be a cowherd!"

And he bade the boy harshly that he was to look at the army and see how they marched and wheeled and how they held their guns aloft to charge, and the boy obediently did what his father said, and did not again look at the little herd.

But Wang the Tiger had been troubled the whole day for what his son had wished and now he looked at the child and he saw him bend his head lower and lower and he saw the boy could not swallow because he was weeping. Then Wang the Tiger was stricken with fear that his son was in some pain, and he rose and went to the child and took his hand and he cried out,

"Are you in a fever or something?"

But the small hand was cool and moist and the boy shook his head, and he would answer nothing for a long time even though Wang the Tiger forced him and he called for his harelipped trusty man at last to help him with his son. When the man was come Wang the Tiger was so torn with his anxiety and his fear and some anger, too, because the child was so stubborn, that he shouted to the man,

377

"Take this young fool out and see what you can find wrong with him!"

By now the boy sobbed desperately and he had put his head down on his arms to sob and hide his face, and Wang the Tiger sat there angry and near to weeping himself and his face worked and he pulled at his beard. Then the trusty man lifted the child in his arms and took him away somewhere and Wang the Tiger waited in agony for a while, staring at the boy's untasted bowl. When the man came back again but without the child, Wang the Tiger roared at him,

"Speak out and tell me all!"

Then half hesitating the man answered,

"There is no illness in him at all, and he only cannot eat because he is so lonely. He has never lived alone before and without a child and he longs for his mother and for his sisters."

"But at his age he cannot play and idle his time away and with women," said Wang the Tiger, half beside himself, and he tore at his beard and twisted himself in his seat.

"No," said the man calmly, for he knew his master's temper and did not fear him, "but he might return sometimes to see his mother, or his sister might come a few times to play, since they are both but children still, and by such means the parting might be eased for the lad, else he will be ill."

Then Wang the Tiger sat silent awhile and he sat and suffered such mortal jealousy as he had never suffered before since that woman whom he had killed came back to torture him because she had loved the dead robber better than him. But now it was jealousy because his son did not love him wholly and longed for others than his father, and Wang the Tiger suffered because while he found his joy and pride in his son, his son was not content with even so great a love, nor did he value it, and for all he was surrounded with his father's love, he yearned for a woman. And Wang the Tiger

378

said to himself violently that he hated all women and he
rose out of his seat passionately and he shouted at the trusty
man saying,

"Let him go then, if he is such a weakling! What do I care
what he does if he is to be a son, after all, such as my brothers
have?"

But the trusty man answered gently,

"My general, you forget he is only a little child."

And Wang the Tiger sat down again and groaned awhile
and said, "Well, did I not tell you let him go?"

Thereafter once in five days or so the boy went into his
mother's court, and every time he went Wang the Tiger sat
and gnawed his beard until the boy came back and then he
questioned him this way and that as to what he had seen and
heard, and he said,

"What were they doing there?"

And the boy made answer always, half startled by the
passion in his father's eyes, "Nothing, my father."

But Wang the Tiger would persist and he cried, "Were
they gaming or sewing or what? Women do not sit at nothing unless they gossip, and that is something, too!"

Then the boy put his mind to it and he knit his brows and
made painstaking, slow answer,

"My mother cut out a little coat for my youngest sister out
of some red flowered cloth, and my eldest sister, whose mother
is not mine, sat and read a book to show how well she could
do it. I like her better than my other sisters, because she
understands when I speak to her and does not laugh at
nothing as they do. She has very big eyes and her hair comes
below her waist when it is braided now. But she never reads
very long. She is restless and she likes to talk."

This pleased Wang the Tiger and he said with pleasure,

"So all women are and they are given to talking about nothing!"

It was the strangest jealousy in Wang the Tiger's heart, for it drew him still further away from those others of his own household and he went more and more seldom to either of his wives. And indeed it looked as time went on as if this lad was to be his only son, for Wang the Tiger's learned wife had never any more children than the one daughter, and the ignorant wife had two daughters, some years apart, and it came to be, that whether Wang the Tiger was not hot in his blood and had no great taste for women, or whether the love of his son made him content, he went at last no more to the courts of his wives. Partly it was some strange shame in him that after his son came to sleep in his room with him he was ashamed for the lad's sake to rise and go out at night to a woman. No, as time went on Wang the Tiger did not, as many lords of war do when they grow rich and strong, fill their courts with feasting and with women. His treasure he poured into guns and more guns and soldiers, except the certain sum he laid by and increased steadily against the time when some disaster might befall him, and he lived sternly and simply and alone except for his son.

Sometimes, and it was the only woman who ever came into their courts, Wang the Tiger let his eldest daughter come in to play with his son, her brother. The first time or two her mother brought her there and she sat for a moment or so. But Wang the Tiger was very ill at ease to have her there, the more because he felt this woman reproached him for something or even that she yearned for something from him, and suffered under some loss he did not understand, and so he rose and went away with a few courteous words to explain his going. At last it seemed she ceased to expect anything from him and he saw her no more, and a slave brought the girl in to play at the rare times when she came.

But in a year or two even the girl came no more, and the mother sent word that she took her daughter to some school for learning, and Wang the Tiger was glad, because the girl came into the austere courts where he lived and she disturbed him because she wore so bright a coat and because she thrust a red pomegranate flower into her hair or a white jasmine that was very fragrant and she loved best of all to put a spray of cassia flowers into her braid, and Wang the Tiger could not bear cassia flowers, because the scent was so sweet and hot and he hated such scent. She was too merry, too, and wilful and domineering and all the things he hated in a woman, and he hated most of all the light and laughter in his son's eyes and the smiles upon his lips when his sister came. She alone could stir him into gayety and to running and play about the court.

Then Wang the Tiger felt his heart close in possession about his son and his heart closed against his daughter, and the faint impulse he had felt toward her when she had been a babe was gone now that she grew into a slender girl, and into the promise of a woman, and he was glad when her mother prepared to send her away and he gave silver freely and readily and he did not begrudge it at all, for now he had his son to himself.

He made haste before his son could be lonely again to fill his life full with many things and he said to his son,

"Son, we are men, you and I, and now cease to go into your mother's courts except at those times when it is fitting to pay respect to her, for it is a very subtle easy way to waste a life with women, even with mother or sister, for they are still but women and still ignorant and foolish. I would have you learn every sort of soldier's skill, now, both old and new. My trusty men can teach you all you need to know of old, the Pig Butcher how to use fist and foot, and the harelipped one how to wield sword and staff. And for the new ways I have heard of and never seen, I have sent to the coast and hired a new tutor for you, who learned his ways of war in foreign countries, and he knows every sort of foreign weapon and way of war. He is to teach you first and what time besides he has left he is to teach our army."

The boy answered nothing but he stood as his wont was when his father spoke to him and he received his father's words in perfect silence. And Wang the Tiger looking at the boy's face tenderly saw no sign of anything he felt there, and he waited awhile and when the lad did not speak but only to say,

"May I leave the room if it is your will?" Wang the Tiger nodded his head and sighed without knowing why he did, or even that he sighed.

Thus Wang the Tiger taught and admonished his son and he saw to it that every hour of the boy's life, beyond eating and sleeping, was filled with some learning or other. He made the boy rise early and practice his feints of war with the trusty men and when he had finished and had eaten his early meal he spent the morning with his books and when he had eaten again the new young tutor took him for the afternoon and taught him every kind of thing.

Now this new tutor was a young man such as Wang the Tiger had never seen before. He wore western clothes of war and spectacles upon his nose, and he had a very straight, swift body. He could run and leap and fence, and he knew how to set fire to all kinds of foreign weapons of war. Some he held in his hand and threw and they burst into flames, and some he fired like a gun with hand on a trigger, and there were many other kinds. And Wang the Tiger sat by as his son learned all these ways of war, and although the Tiger would not have said it, he learned of many things he himself had never even seen or heard of, and it came to him that it was a small thing to have been so proud of those two old foreign guns, and the only great guns he had. Yes, he saw he knew very little even of war, since there was more to know than he had dreamed, and now he would often sit far into the night talking to his son's new tutor, and he learned of all sorts of clever ways of killing, the death from the air that drops down upon men, and the death that is in the bowels of the sea and comes up to kill, and the death that can fly more miles than men can see and drop and burst upon an enemy. Wang the Tiger listened to this in greatest wonder and he said,

"I see the people of the outer countries are very clever at killing and I did not know it."

Then he began to ponder it all and one day he said to the tutor,

"I have a good rich territory in my hand and we do not have a complete famine more than once in ten or fifteen years, and I have a little silver put together. Now I see I have been too satisfied with my men, and I see that if my son is to learn all these new ways of war he must have an army skilled in such things, too. I will buy some of these machines that are used for war now-a-days in outer countries, and you shall teach my men and shape an army fit for my son when he comes to it."

The young man smiled his quick and flashing smile and he was very willing and he said,

"I have tried to teach your men, but the discourteous truth is that they are a very ragged straggling lot and too content to eat and drink. If you will buy some new machines and if you will set hours of the day when they shall march and learn, I will see if they are to be shaped."

Now Wang the Tiger was displeased secretly at such discourteous truth, for he had put many days of his life into teaching his men, and he said stiffly,

"You must teach my son first."

"I will teach him until he is fifteen," said the young tutor, "and then if you will permit me to advise one so high as you, I will say he should be sent to a school of war in the south."

"What, can men learn war in a school?" said Wang the Tiger wondering.

"There is such a school," replied the young tutor, "and such as come out of it are captains at once in the state's army."

But Wang the Tiger grew haughty at this and he said, "My son has no need to go and search for some little captain's place in the state army as though he had not an army of his own," and after a while Wang the Tiger said again, "Besides, I doubt if any good thing can come out of the south. I served under a southern general in my youth and he was an idle, lustful creature, and his soldiers little monkeys of men."

The tutor, seeing Wang the Tiger was displeased, smiled and took his departure and Wang the Tiger sat on and he thought of his son and it seemed to him that surely he had done everything for his son that could be done. And he searched his heart painfully to remember his youth and he remembered that he had longed once for a horse of his own. The very next day therefore he bought a little black horse for his son, a strong good beast from the plains of Mongolia, and he bought it from a horse dealer whom he knew.

But when he gave it to the boy, and he called him out to see what he had for him, and there the little black horse stood in the court, a red saddle of new leather upon his back, and a red bridle studded with brass, and the groom who held the horse and whose sole duty was to tend it from this day on had in his hand a new whip of red braided leather. Wang the Tiger thought to himself proudly that it was such a horse as he himself might have dreamed of as a lad and thought too good to be alive, and he looked eagerly at his son to catch the pleasure that must break into his eyes and smile.

But the boy did not come out of his gravity at all. He looked at the horse and said, composed as he always was,

"My thanks, my father."

And Wang the Tiger waited, but no light came into the boy's eyes, and he did not leap forward to seize the bridle nor to try the saddle, and he seemed waiting to be allowed to go away.

Then Wang the Tiger turned away in furious disappointment and he went into his room and shut the door and he sat down and held his head in his hands and yearned over his son with anger and with bitterness of unrewarded love. But when he had grieved awhile he hardened himself again in his old way and he said stubbornly,

"Yet what more can he want? He has all I dreamed of when I was his age and more than I dreamed. Yes, what would I not have given for a teacher so skilled as he has, and for a fine foreign gun such as he has, and now a little shining black horse and the saddle and bridle red, and a red whip set into a silver handle!"

Thus he comforted himself, and he commanded the lad's tutor to spare no teaching of this son of his, and not to heed the languors that the boy might have, for these are common to all lads who grow, and they cannot be heeded.

But at night when Wang the Tiger woke up and was restless he heard his son's quiet breathing in the room and a suffering tenderness filled his breast and he thought to himself over and over,

"I must do more for him—I must think of something more I can do for him!"

Thus did Wang the Tiger spend his years upon his son and he might have slipped all unknowing into age, so engrossed was he, had not a certain thing come about that shook him out of his too great fondness and stirred him up to war again, and to his destiny.

It was on a day in spring when his son was nearly ten years old, for so did Wang the Tiger measure the years now by his son, and he sat under a budding pomegranate tree with the boy. The lad had been rapt before the little flame-like new leaves of the tree and he had cried out suddenly,

"I do swear that to me these little fiery leaves are more beautiful than the whole flower, even!"

Wang the Tiger was looking at them, painstaking in his attention to see what his son saw if he could, when there came a great commotion at the gates and one came running to Wang the Tiger to announce someone coming. But before the serving man could get the words from his mouth Wang the Tiger saw his pocked nephew come staggering in, lame from his swift riding, and he was haggard and weary with his riding by night and day, and the dust had settled into his deep pocks so that he was very curious to see. Words came slowly to Wang the Tiger so long as he was not angry and he could but stare at the young man and the young man gasped forth,

"I came on a winged horse by day and by night to tell you that the Hawk is plotting to divide himself from you and he has set up your army for his own and he has taken for his base the very city you besieged, and he is in some league with the old robber chief who has been itching these years for his revenge. I have known he held back revenue these last

386

months and I feared some such outcome, but I have waited to make sure lest raising a false alarm the Hawk be offended and kill me secretly somehow!"

All this tumbled out of the young man's mouth and Wang the Tiger stared out of his deep eyes and his eyes seemed to recede beneath his forehead as his black brows drew down more heavily and he felt his good hot rage come up to help him and he roared out,

"That accursed dog and thief—and I raised him up from a common soldier! Everything he owes to me, and he turns on me like the wild cur he is!"

And feeling his good, war-like anger rise higher and higher in him Wang the Tiger forgot his son and he strode to the outer courts where his captains lived and his trusty men and some of his soldiers, and he roared that five thousand men were to prepare to follow him within the forenoon and he shouted for his horse and for his keen and narrow sword. Everywhere those courts, which had lain quiet and at peace with the spring, became now like a turmoiled pool, and out of the women's courts the children and the slaves peeped with frightened faces dismayed at so much shouting of weapons and war, and the very horses were excited and their hoofs clattered and pranced upon the tiles of the courts.

Then Wang the Tiger, when he saw all was astir as he had commanded, turned to the weary messenger and he said,

"Go and eat and drink and rest yourself. You have done very well and for this I shall raise you up. Well I know that many a youth would have joined the rebels, for it is always in the hearts of young men to rebel, but you have remembered our bond of blood to stay by me. Be sure I shall raise you up!"

Then the young man looked east and west and he whispered,

"Yes, but, my uncle, will you kill the Hawk? He will sus-

387

pect when he sees you come for I told him I was ill and must go back to my mother for a while."

Then Wang the Tiger promised in a great, furious voice, and he cried,

"You need not beg me, for I will burnish my sword upon his flesh!"

And the young man went away very content.

Then by forced marching Wang the Tiger led his men out the three days to the new territory and he led out his old and trusted men, and he kept at home those who had joined his ranks from the besieged city and the captain who had betrayed the robber chief lest they betray him also in his turn. He promised his good men that they should have their turn now to loot the city if they were brave for him, and he would give them besides a month's extra wage in silver, so they marched with good hearts and ready feet.

They did so well that before the Hawk had any idea of such a mishap he heard that Wang the Tiger was upon him. The truth was that the Hawk had no knowledge of how wily and full of clever guile was the young man who was Wang the Tiger's nephew, for the youth was so merry and his tongue so smooth and his pocked face so full of seeming ignorance except of a jest or of some bit of horseplay among the soldiers, that the Hawk thought all he did unseen. He was very glad when the youth said he was ill of some pain in his liver and that he must go home to his mother, and he planned that now he would put out his proclamations of rebellion and he would discover which men were loyal to him and the others he would put to death. To the men who would rebel with him he promised the freedom of the city for booty.

In these days, therefore, the Hawk fortified himself and he commanded food to be brought into the city, for well enough he knew Wang the Tiger's temper that he would not be still

and let things be, and in great terror the helpless people prepared themselves again for a siege. Even on that very day
when Wang the Tiger came into the city gate he saw farmers
coming by the score with their loads of fuel upon their poles
across their shoulders, and donkeys and mules came with
bags of grain crossed upon their backs, and men carrying
baskets of squawking fowls or driving herds of cattle and
carrying pigs trussed upon poles and squealing furiously as
they felt themselves borne along, their heads hanging and
feet up. And Wang the Tiger gnashed his teeth to see it all,
for he knew that if he had not been told in time of the plot,
he would have had a very difficult siege with all this food in
the city, and the Hawk was a far greater foe than the witless
old robber chief had been, for he was a clever man and very
fierce and he had besides the two foreign weapons of war and
he could set them on the city wall and turn them upon the
besiegers. When Wang the Tiger thought of all he had missed
so narrowly, his anger rose until his eyes were red and he
gnawed and chewed at his beard. He let his anger rise then
as deep and high as it would and he forced his horse on and
shouted to his men that they were to go straight to the courts
where the Hawk was encamped.

Now there were already those who had run to tell the
Hawk that he was undone, for Wang the Tiger was already
upon him, and the Hawk felt despair drop on him out of the
skies. He hesitated but a moment to think whether or no he
might brazen the hour out by guile, or whether he might
rather escape by a secret way, and he had no hope at all that
his men would dare to stand by him now, since Wang the
Tiger brought so vast an army in. He knew he stood alone.
But in that moment's hesitation he was lost, for Wang the
Tiger came galloping through the gates crying that the Hawk
was to be caught at any cost and held for him to kill, and he

turned himself off his saddle as he shouted and his men swarmed through the courts.

Then the Hawk, seeing his end was on him, ran and hid himself. Although he was a brave man, he ran and hid himself in the pile of grass in one of the kitchens. But what hope had he against the hordes that poured to find him who were fierce with their hopes of promised reward? Nor did the Hawk have any hope from his followers beyond that if one saw where he was hid, he would not tell it. He waited there in the grass, and if he hid, still did not tremble, for he was a brave man.

But he must be found, for they ran searching everywhere for him eager to find him and claim reward, and the gates front and back were guarded and the small gate of escape, and the walls to the courts were very high. So the Hawk was found by a handful of soldiers, and they saw an end of his blue coat in the grass and they ran out and clapped the door to, and yelled for others to come, and when some fifty men or so came running they went in cautiously, for they did not know what weapons the Hawk might have, although he was weaponless, except for a small, short dagger, useless against so many, for he had run out in distraction as he sat eating his morning meal. They fell upon him in a heap, then, and pinioned him and led him to their general, and the Hawk went sullenly, his eyes wild and the straw sticking in his hair and his clothes. Thus they led him to where Wang the Tiger sat in the great hall waiting, his sword drawn and shining like a narrow silver serpent stretched across his knees. He glowered at the Hawk from under his dark brows and he said harshly, "So you have turned traitor against me, who raised you up from a common soldier and made you all you are!"

The Hawk answered sullenly and without raising his eyes from the shining thing on Wang the Tiger's knees,

"You taught me how to rebel against a general, and what were you but a runaway son, and who raised you if not the old general?"

Now when Wang the Tiger heard so rude an answer he could not bear it, and he shouted to the crowded soldiers who stood to see all they could,

"I thought I would drive my sword through him, but it is too clean a death for him! Take him and slice his flesh into strips as they do to criminals and those too wicked to live, to unfilial sons and traitors to the state!"

But the Hawk, seeing his end was come, and before any could stop him, pulled his small short dagger out of his bosom, and he plunged it into his own belly and gave it a great twist and left it sticking there out of his belly, and he stood staggering a moment, and he looked at Wang the Tiger as he died, and he said in his hard and reckless way,

"I do not fear to die! Another twenty years and I shall be born again in some other body—again a hero!" And he fell with his dagger still twisted in his entrails.

And Wang the Tiger, staring at what had come about almost before he could draw a breath, felt his anger ebbing out of him as he stared. He had been cheated of his revenge and yet for all his anger he was remorseful, too, that he had lost so brave a man as this rebel. He was silent for a while and at last he said in a low voice,

"You to the right and left of me, take his dead body away and bury it somewhere, for he was a lone man. I do not know whether he had father or son or any home." And after a while he said again, "I knew he was brave but I did not know him so brave as this. Put him into a good coffin."

And Wang the Tiger sat on awhile and sorrowed, and the sorrow made his heart soft so that he held his men back for a time from the looting he had promised. While he sorrowed, the merchants of that city came and craved an audience of him, and when he let them in to see what they desired of him, they came and with courtesy and much silver they besought him not to allow his men to be free in the city, saying that the people were in great terror. And being soft for the time, Wang the Tiger took the silver and promised to give it to his men in lieu of booty, and the merchants were grateful and went away praising so merciful a lord of war as this.

But Wang the Tiger had an ado to comfort his soldiers, and he had to pay them each one a good sum and he ordered feasts and wines for them before they would leave off their sullen looks and Wang the Tiger had to call upon their loyalty to him and promise them some further chance some other time of war before they settled to themselves again, and ceased their curses of disappointment. And indeed Wang the Tiger had to send twice to the merchants for other sums of silver before the thing was settled and the men satisfied.

Then Wang the Tiger prepared to return to his home once more, for he longed exceedingly to see his son, for he had left in such haste he had scarcely thought to plan for him these days he was away. This time Wang the Tiger left his trusty harelipped man to hold the city with the soldiers until his nephew could return and the Hawk's men he led back with himself, leaving in their place certain tried and old men he had brought out when he came. And as precaution Wang the Tiger took the two great foreign guns with him, for he found the Hawk had had an ironsmith of the city make round balls for them and he had gunpowder to fire the guns, and Wang the Tiger took them so that he need never again fear them turned upon himself.

Now as Wang the Tiger marched back again through the streets of the city, the people looked as he passed and cast eyes of hatred upon him, for a tax had been levied upon every house to make up the vast sum that Wang the Tiger had needed to reward his soldiers and to pay his own cost of the expedition. But Wang the Tiger would not notice these looks, and he hardened himself and he reasoned in his own mind that these people ought to be willing to pay for peace, for if he had not come and delivered them they would have suffered greatly at the hands of the Hawk and of his men. For the Hawk was very cruel and men and women were nothing at all to him, and he had been used to wars from his childhood. The truth was Wang the Tiger felt that these people were very unjust to him, who had these days of hard marching, and they did not perceive they had been saved from anything and he thought to himself sullenly,

"They have no gratitude for anything, and I am too soft of heart."

He hardened his heart with such thoughts, therefore, and he was never quite so kind again to common people as he once had been. He narrowed his heart still more, and he took no trusty man in the Hawk's place for he said to himself drearily that not one could be trusted who was not of his blood, and in this narrowness he leaned yet more upon his beloved son and he comforted himself saying,

"There is my son, and he alone will never fail me."

He hastened his horse then, and hurried his march, yearning for the sight of his son.

As for the nephew of Wang the Tiger, he waited until he had heard the Hawk was killed and the news made him very blithe and merry and he went to his home for a few days and there he told everyone how brave and wily he had been, and how he had been too clever for the Hawk, although the Hawk was so clever and wise a warrior, and old enough to be another generation. So he boasted everywhere, and his

393

brothers and sisters stood about him in greatest delight to hear him, and his mother cried out,

"Even when this son suckled I knew he was no common child, for he did pull so hard and lustily at my breast!"

But Wang the Merchant sat and listened with his meager smile fastened upon his face, and if he was proud of his son he would not praise him and he said,

"It is a good thing to remember, nevertheless, that of the thirty-six ways out of difficulty the best way of all is to run away." And he said, "Good guile is better than good weapon."

And it was his son's guile that pleased him most of all.

But when the pocked youth went to his uncle's court to pay respect to Wang the Landlord and his lady, and he told his doughty tale there, Wang the Landlord was strangely jealous. He was jealous for his dead son, and he was jealous for these other two sons of his whom he admired for their lordly looks and ways and yet for whom he had vague fears, too, that there was something wrong in them. So although he seemed courteous when his brother's pocked son told his tale, yet he lent but one ear, and while the young man talked in his eager way, the old man kept calling out for tea and for his pipe, and that he was chill now that the sun was down and he would have his light spring fur robe. As for the lady, she inclined her head to her nephew the very least she could in decency of mannerliness, and she took up a bit of embroidery and feigned to be very busy with it, matching this silk to that in the pattern, and she yawned loudly and often, and asked her lord this and that of some matter in the house or about the tenants on the land they still had left. At last the young man saw she was weary of him and he stopped his tale and went away, somewhat dashed. And before he had gone far he heard the lady raise her voice and say,

"I am glad no son of ours is a soldier! It is such a low life and it makes a young man very coarse and common."

And Wang the Landlord answered listlessly, "Aye—I think I will go to the tea house for a while."

Now the young man could not know that these twain thought of their dead young son, and he felt his heart sore in him until he came to the gate. But there stood Wang the Landlord's second wife, her last babe in her arms. She had sat listening to the young man's tale, and had slipped out ahead of him and she said to him wistfully,

"But to me it was a very good, brave tale."

And the young man went back to his mother comforted.

Three times ten days did this pocked nephew of Wang the Tiger stay in his home, for his mother took this chance to wed him to his betrothed, the maid whom she had chosen for him a few years before. Now this maid was the daughter of a neighbor, who was a silk weaver, but not a poor and common weaver who hires himself to others. No, the maid's father had his own looms and he had twenty apprentices and made bolts of many-colored satin and flowered silks, and there were not many of his trade in the city, so that he did well at it. The maid, too, was clever at it, and she could, if the spring lingered on too chill, nurse the silkworm eggs against her own warm flesh until they hatched into worms, and she could feed the worms, as they should be fed to grow, upon the mulberry leaves the apprentices gathered, and she knew how to wind the silk from the cocoons. All such skill she had, a rare skill in that town, for the family had come the generation before from other parts. It was true that the young man she was to wed had no such use for her skill; still, Wang the Merchant's wife felt it was something for a maid to have such knowledge and it made her thrifty and busy.

As for the young man, it was little to him what the maid

could do, but he was glad to be wed, for he was now nearly twenty-four and troubled often with his desires, and he was pleased that the maid was neat and middling pretty and she seemed not to have any great temper of her own, and it was enough for him that she was so.

When the wedding was over, therefore, and it was good enough but without great display, he returned to the city to which Wang the Tiger had appointed him, taking his wife with him.

XXV

EACH spring that drew itself out of the long winter, Wang the Tiger felt in him the stirring of his ambition to greater wars and each spring he thought to look about him and see what he could do to enlarge himself. He sent out his spies to hear what the general wars of the year were likely to be and how he could fit some private war to the greater one, and he waited, he told himself, until the spies returned and until the year was warm enough and until the hour came when he could feel his destiny call him. But the truth was that Wang the Tiger was over his youth and now that he had his son he was held and content, and he had not that old restlessness in him to be out and at war. Each spring he told himself he must for his son's very sake go forth and achieve what he had set out to do in his lifetime and each spring there seemed to be some immediate good reason why he must put off his campaigns until another year. Nor were there any great and single wars in those years of his son's youth. There were but many small lords of war over that whole country, each holding his own small domain, and not any great man came out to be above them all. For this reason, also, Wang the Tiger felt it safe to wait another year and when the year came past its spring, yet another year, and he felt sure that some time or other when his destiny struck, he would still go forth to whatever victory he would choose.

There came on a certain spring, when his son was close upon thirteen years of age, a messenger from Wang the Tiger's two brothers, and he came upon a mission very grave, and it was no less than that Wang the Landlord's eldest son lay languishing in the city gaol of his town. The two brothers sent the messenger to beseech the aid at the provincial court of their brother, Wang the Tiger, so that the young man might be released. Wang the Tiger heard the tale, and it seemed to him a very good chance to test out his power at the provincial seat and his influence with the general of that province. He put off his war he had thought of, therefore, for yet another year, and he undertook to do what his brothers asked of him, and not without some pride, that they the elders had come to beg of him, the younger, and not without some scorn that a son of theirs could be cast into gaol, such a thing as never could befall his own good son.

Now the matter was thus and this was how Wang the Landlord's eldest son came to be put into a gaol.

This son of Wang the Landlord's was now in the twenty-and-eighth year of his age and he was not wed nor even betrothed. The reason for this very strange thing was that he had gone in his youth for a year or two to a new sort of a school in the town, and there he had learned many things, and one of the things he learned was that it was a vile slavery to an old custom for a young man to be wed by his parents to a maid they chose for him, and that all young men ought to choose their own maids to wife, maids whom they had seen and had talked with and could love. When, therefore, Wang the Landlord made a survey of all the marriageable maids to fix upon one for his eldest son, this son was very rebellious

397

in the matter and he flung himself about and pouted and said he would choose his own wife.

At first Wang the Landlord and his lady were outraged at this notion, and for once they were agreed upon a thing, and the lady cried out to her son with heat,

"And how can you see a decent maid so close as to talk with her and know if you like her or not? And who so able to choose as your parents who formed you and who know your every turn of mind and nature?"

But the young man was full of argument and temper and he pushed his long silken sleeves back from his white smooth hands, and he tossed the black hair back from his pale forehead and he cried out in his turn,

"Neither you nor my father know anything except old dead customs, and you do not know that in the south all the sons of wealthy and learned people let their sons choose for themselves!" And when he saw his father and mother look at each other, and when he saw his father wipe his brow with his sleeve and his mother purse up her lips, he cried again, "Well, and betroth me, then, and I will leave my home and never see you more!"

This frightened the parents beyond measure and Wang the Landlord said in haste,

"But tell us what maid it is you love and we will see if it can be arranged."

Now the truth was that the young man had seen no such maid as he could love for wife, for the women he had known were such as could be easily bought, but he would not tell that he had seen no maid he loved, and he only pouted out his red lips and stared sullenly down at his pretty finger nails. But he looked so violent and so wilful that this time and every time his parents spoke of the matter they pacified him in the end again and again by saying, "Well, well, let it be for now!" Twice, indeed, had Wang the Landlord need to cry off the bargain with some maid he had begun to negotiate for, because when the young man heard of this he swore he would hang himself on a beam as his brother had done, and this terrified his mother and father so that they gave in to him every time.

Yet as time went on both Wang the Landlord and his lady grew the more eager to see their son wed, for he was their eldest son and chief heir and his sons must be the chief among their grandsons. Well, too, did Wang the Landlord know that the young man went to this tea house and to that and spent his youth here and there, and while he knew that all young men are so who have no need to labor for what they eat and wear, still as Wang the Landlord passed out of his own lustiness into a quieter age, he grew very uneasy at this son of his and both Wang the Landlord and his lady feared that if their son did not wed soon he would come some day with an idle maid out of a tea house for wife, such an one as it is well enough to take for a concubine but is a shame for a wife. But the youth, if they spoke their fears to him, talked ruthlessly of how in these new days young men and women were freed from their parents' rule, and how men and women were free and equal, and he said many such foolish things, so that these two parents could do nothing but hold their peace, for the young man's tongue was so glib and swift there was no answering him and they early learned to be silent while he poured out his fiery discontents and flashed his eyes from one to the other of the old pair, and every second flung back his long cut hair and smoothed it back with his soft white hand. But after such speeches when he was gone again, for he was very restless and never there for long, the lady looked at her husband with reproach and she said,

"You have taught him these things with your own lewd

ways and he learned from his own father to satisfy himself with these flower girls instead of with an honest woman."

She drew her sleeve across her eyes as she spoke and wiped one eye and the other, and she felt herself very ill used. As for Wang the Landlord he was in great alarm for he knew that this mild beginning could lead up to a great storm, for the older the lady grew the more righteous and ill-tempered she grew also, and he rose hastily to go away and he said very meekly,

"You know that now as I pass into my age I do not go as once I did, and I try to hear your counsel, and if you have a way out of this turmoil, I promise I will follow what you say."

Now the truth was that this lady could not herself think of any way to manage this turbulent son, and she must ease herself somehow and Wang the Landlord saw that her temper was rising in her, so he made all haste to go away out of his house. And as he passed through his court he saw that other wife of his there in the sunshine nursing a child, and he said to her hastily,

"Go in and fetch something for your mistress, because she is waxing angry. Take her tea or one of her prayer books or something, and praise her and say some priest or other said this or that about her or some such thing!"

The woman rose obediently, holding her child in her arm as she went, and as he went out into the street and thought where he might turn, Wang the Landlord blessed the hour he saw this second woman of his, for if he had been alone with his lady it would have been ill for him. But this second woman grew with the years even milder and more placid than she had been, and in this Wang the Landlord was very fortunate, since two women with a common lord will often-times quarrel and lead a noisy life, especially if one of them or both of them love their lord.

But this second woman comforted Wang the Landlord in many small ways and she did things that the servants would not. For the servants knew who had the authority in this house of Wang the Landlord's, and when he roared for some servant, man or maid, the servant called out, "Oh, aye, aye!" but he lagged or did not come, and if Wang the Landlord grew peevish, the servant made excuse, "The mistress commanded me thus and thus," and so silenced his master.

But this second wife served him secretly, and she it was who comforted him. When he came back from his few lands out of humor and weary, she saw to it that he had hot tea in his pot or if it were summer that there was a melon cool in the well, and she sat by and fanned him while he ate, and she fetched water to bathe his feet and brought fresh hose and shoes. To her also he poured out all his grievances and his hatreds, and chief of these was the grievance he had against his tenants and he told her all his bitter tales and he would say,

"Yes, and today that old snag-toothed woman who is mother to the tenant on the west land poured water into the basket of grain the steward weighed—he is such a fool, or else knave, and they pay him not to see—but I saw how the scale leaped!"

To such she made answer, soothing him, "I do not believe they cheat you much, you are so clever and the cleverest wisest man I ever knew."

His bitterness against his rebellious son he poured out to her, too, and she soothed him there also, and now as he went along the street he planned how he would tell her his lady blamed him cruelly and he dwelled upon the sweetness of her answer, how she would say as she had many times,

"To me you are the best man, and I ask no better, and I swear my lady does not know what men all are and how you are better than them all!" Yes, out of the weariness of his son and his lady and all his troubles with the little land he had and dared not sell altogether, Wang the Landlord clung to this second woman of his and he thought in his heart, that of all the women he had followed only this one was comfortable to him and he said to himself, for reason, "She is the only one out of all I feed who knows me for what I am!"

And his heart swelled with especial bitterness against his son this day, because he had put fresh trouble upon his father.

Now as Wang the Landlord on this day walked along the streets so pondering, his son was on his own way to the house of a friend and it came about that in the strangest way he met the maid who could please him. This friend whom the young man sought was son of the chief of police of that town, and Wang the Landlord's son gamed with him continually in preference to all others, for since such gaming was against a new law that had been made, if there was trouble the son of the chief of police could escape and his friends could escape, since his father was so weighty a man in the town. On this day Wang the Landlord's son thought to game awhile and take the anger out of his heart and divert himself from the trouble his parents were to him, and therefore he went to his friend's house.

When the door was opened to him he gave his name to the serving man, and he sat and waited in the guest hall, brooding and impatient with all his troubles. Suddenly an inner door opened and a very pretty and young lady came in alone. Now if she had been a usual maid and had seen a young man sitting there alone, she must have covered her face with her sleeve and turned back with all speed. But she did not. She looked very calmly at Wang the Landlord's son, and she looked at him fully and slowly, but without coquetry, and she was not shy at all, and meeting this full calm look it was the young man's eyes which first fell. He saw, as anyone could see, that she was a proper maid enough for all her boldness, and she was such an one as belonged to the new times. Her black hair was cut short about her head and her feet were not bound, and she wore the long straight robe that new maidens wear, and since it was now late spring, the robe was made of a soft silk the color of a gosling's down.

Now for all his lordly talk, the truth was that this son of Wang the Landlord's had very little chance to meet with such maidens as he desired to wed. He spent his days when he was not gaming or feasting and playing somewhere in reading tales of love. Nor did he like the old tales, but he read most ardently the newly written tales of love that is free between man and maid, and he dreamed of well-born maidens who were not courtesans and yet were not shy and timid before men, but like men are with men except they be maids still, and such an one he sought. Yet he knew not one, for as yet such freedom was more in books than in truth. But now it seemed to him that here was truly the one he sought and his ready heart flamed to her cool, bold look, for that heart of his was like a fire laid and waiting for the torch to set it rushing into conflagration.

In that one moment he loved this maid so mightily that he was struck dazed, and although he said not one word and she passed on her way, he sat still dazed, and when his friend came in he gasped, his mouth dry, and his heart beating fit to burst against his breastbone,

"Who is the lady who passed?"

His friend said carelessly, "It is my sister who is in a foreign school in a coastal town, and she is home for the spring holiday."

Then Wang the Landlord's son could not but ask on, faltering,

"Is she not wed, then?"

The brother laughed and said, "No, she is the wilfullest maid, and she is forever quarreling with my parents on this, for she will not have any man they choose for her!"

Wang the Landlord's son heard this and it was like a cup of wine held to thirsty lips, he said no more and went on to his game. But as he played, he was distraught, for he felt the flames licking up about his heart and the fire burned in him. He excused himself soon and hastened to his home and to his own room and he shut the door and there alone he felt himself knit to this maid by every tie. And he murmured to himself that it was a shame she must suffer from her parents too, as he did, and he told himself he would not come to her except by such free means as men and women use in these free times. No, he would have no go-between, not parent nor even his friend her brother. Then in fever and haste he took out the books he had read and studied them to see what sort of a letter such heroes wrote to their free loves, and then he wrote her such a letter, too.

Yes, he wrote to that maid, and he put his name to what he wrote, and he began the letter with all the courteous proper words. But he said also that he was a free spirit and so he saw her, also, and she was therefore to him the very light of the sun, the very hue of a peony flower, the very music of the flute, and in an instant's time she had plucked his heart out of his bosom. Then when he had written this, he sent it by his own private servant, and having sent it he waited at home in such a fever that his parents did not know what was wrong with him. When the servant came back to say the answer would come later, the young man could but wait on, and yet he loathed his waiting and he hated all in the house and he slapped his younger brothers and sisters without mercy if they came near him and complained against the servants, and even the good-natured concubine his father had, cried out, "You behave as a dog that will go mad!" And she drew her own children out of his reach.

But after three days a messenger brought an answer, and the young man, who spent his days hanging about the gate, seized it and made off to his room and tore the letter in his haste to open it. He pieced the two torn parts together and made it out. She wielded her brush very boldly and prettily and when she had written words of courtesy and words to justify her boldness, she said, "I also am a free spirit, and I will not be forced by my parents in anything."

Thus delicately did she put her preference for him, and the young man was beside himself with pleasure.

In such a way, then, had the matter begun, and the two could not be content even with many letters, but they must meet somehow, and so they did meet a time or two at the side gate to the maid's house. They were both afraid, although they neither wished to show it, and in such hasty meetings and in many letters written back and forth and much bribing of servants and disguising of their names in their letters, this love burned hotter and hotter, and since neither man nor maid had ever done without anything they dearly wanted, so they could not now. At their third meeting the young man said very ardently,

"I cannot wait and I must wed you and so I will tell my father."

To this the maid answered very wilfully, "And I will tell my father I will poison myself if I am not to have you, too."

So they did tell their fathers, and while Wang the Landlord was glad enough to have his son's fancy fix itself on a maid of such a good house and set himself at once to arrange the match, the maid's father turned stubborn and he would not have the young man for his daughter. No, since he was chief of police it was his business to have his spies everywhere, and he knew things that others did not about this young man and he cried out at his daughter,

"What, that do-nothing of a dandy who spends his time in every idle house of pleasure?"

And he commanded his servants that his daughter was to be locked into her own courts until she went back to her school, and when she came flying in furiously to talk with him and implore him he would not pay any heed to her. No, he was a very calm man and while she argued he hummed a tune and read a book, and when she grew too angry and said things a maid should not, he turned on her and said,

"I always knew I should have held you in this house and not sent you to a school. It is this schooling that spoils maids now-a-days, and if I had it to do again, I would have kept you decent and ignorant as your mother is and so wed you early to a good man. Yes, and I will do it yet!" and he roared at her so suddenly that she faltered and was afraid.

Then these two young things wrote very pretty despairing letters to each other and the servants grew rich on bribes, and ran back and forth. But the young man pined in his home and did not go out to game or play, and his parents saw him pine and they did not know what to do. Wang the Landlord sent a secret bribe by devious ways to the chief of police, and though he was a man ready for a bribe, yet this time he was not ready, and so they all despaired. As for the young man, he would not eat and he talked of hanging himself and Wang the Landlord was distracted altogether.

Now one evening as the young man walked near the back of the house where his love lived, he saw the small gate of escape open, and the maid servant who carried her letters, squeezed through, and she beckoned to him to come. He came faltering and fearful, yet driven by his own heart, and when he was come, there inside the little court by the gate, stood his love, and she was very determined and wilful and full of plans. Yet now that they were face to face their words did not come easily either, and not nearly so easily as words upon paper, and the truth was the young man was much afraid lest he be discovered there where he ought not by any means to be. But the maid was wilful, and being learned, she would have her desire and she said,

"I will not heed these old ones. Let us flee together somewhere and when they see us gone, for very shame they will let us wed. I know my father loves me, for I am his only daughter and my mother dead, and you are your father's oldest son."

But before the young man could match his ardor to hers, the chief of police stood suddenly there at the door of the house that gave upon the court, for some servant that bore ill will to the young girl's maid had told for revenge, and the chief of police shouted to his attendants,

"Bind him and put him in gaol, for he has taken away my daughter's honor!"

Now it was a very unlucky thing for Wang the Landlord's eldest son that his love's father was chief of police and could throw whom he liked into gaol, for another man would not have had such power and must have paid money to have him imprisoned. But with the word the attendants haled the young man away, and the maid shrieked and hung herself upon the young man's arm, and cried she would not marry any other and that she would swallow her rings.

But that calm old man, her father, turned to the serving maids and said,

"See to her, and if she is left alone and by any chance does what she says, I will hold you for her death."

And he went away as though he did not hear her moans

and cries, and the serving maids did not dare to leave her, being afraid for themselves, and so the young girl had no choice but to live on.

As for the chief of police, he sent word to Wang the Landlord that his son was in the gaol because he had attempted the honor of his own daughter, and having sent this message he sat in his hall and waited. Then was the household of Wang the Landlord in the greatest confusion and Wang the Landlord was completely distracted and did not know what to do. He sent a good bribe immediately of all the silver he had about him, and he struggled into his finest robes and went to the chief of the police himself to apologize. But that man was in no mood to have the thing so easily settled, and he sent word out to the gate that he was ill from so much worry and could see no one, and when the bribe was brought in he sent it back again saying that Wang the Landlord had mistaken his character and he was not such an one as to be tempted thus.

Then Wang the Landlord went groaning back to his house, and he knew the bribe was too small, and since it was just before wheat harvest he was very short of silver, and he knew he must ask his brother's help. There was his son in gaol, too, and he suffered for that, and he must send food and bedding lest he suffer there. When this was done and Wang the Merchant called, Wang the Landlord sat in his own room and waited, and his lady forgot all usage and in her distress she came in where he sat leaning his head on his hands, and she called on this god and that to witness to all she had to bear in this house.

But for once Wang the Landlord sat not moved more than he was, for all her cries and reproaches, for he was frightened to his heart's bottom to have his son like this in the power of the chief of police. But Wang the Merchant came in very collected and he made his face smooth as though he did not know what was wrong, although the tale was flying everywhere, and being so good and nasty a tale, every servant knew it already and his wife knew it and had told him all and more than all, and she had said with greatest relish, over and over,

"Well I knew no good would come out of that woman's sons and their father so lustful as he is, too."

But now Wang the Merchant sat and listened to the tale as it came from the young man's father and mother, and they made his crime very light, and Wang the Merchant looked judicial and as though he took for granted the young man's innocence and thought only of some wily way to free him. Well he knew his elder brother wanted to borrow a vast sum, and he planned deeply as to how this could be avoided. When the tale was told and the lady was weeping freely at the end, he said,

"It is true that silver is very useful when dealing with officials anywhere, but there is one thing better still and it is power of arms. Before we spend all we have, let us beseech our brother, who is now a very high general, that he exert himself and use his influence in the provincial court and have a mandate sent down from above to our magistrate here who will command the chief of police to release your son. Then a little silver may be used here and there to help the cause."

Now this seemed a wonderful and good plan to them all and Wang the Landlord marvelled that it had not come to him, and on that very day and in that very hour he sent a messenger to Wang the Tiger and thus it was that Wang the Tiger heard of it.

Now Wang the Tiger besides the duty he had to help his brothers, saw it was a very good chance to test his power and influence. So he wrote a proper, humble letter to the

409

general of the province and he prepared gifts and he sent all by his trusty man and a guard to keep the gifts safe from robbers. Now that general when he received the gifts and read the letter, pondered awhile, and it seemed to him that here was a useful way to bind Wang the Tiger to him in case of a war and if he did this favor, Wang the Tiger would feel an obligation and it seemed a cheap way to secure this favor by letting a young man out of gaol and he cared nothing at all for so small a fellow as the chief of police in a single town. So he sent the word that Wang the Tiger asked, and then he told the ruler of that province, and the ruler sent a mandate down to the magistrate of the county, who sent his mandate down to the magistrate of the town where the House of Wang lived.

Now Wang the Merchant was more tricky than ever, and he was more clever, and he followed each step with enough silver so that every man who touched the affair felt himself rewarded but still not so much that a greedy spirit might be roused to look twice at the source of so much money. In his turn, the chief of police received the command also and Wang the Landlord and Wang the Second watched very carefully for this moment when it came, for they knew a man will not suffer being put to public shame, and so when they knew he had received the command, they went to him with goodly bribes and with many apologies and they begged the chief of police as though for their own sakes, feigning that they knew nothing of all that had passed from above. No, they made obeisances and they besought him as a man of mercy, and at last he accepted the money carelessly and largely as a man will who confers a favor. Then he ordered the young man released and he reproved him and sent him home.

As for the two brothers, they gave a mighty feast to the

chief of police and so the matter was ended, for the young man was free again, and his love somewhat the cooler for the gaol.

But that maid was more wilful than ever and she clamored anew to her father. This time he was somewhat more willing, now that he understood how powerful this family of Wang was, and how strong a lord of war one of the three brothers was, and how much money Wang the Merchant had, and he sent a go-between to Wang the Landlord and he said,

"Let us wed these two and seal our new friendship."

So the matter was carried through and the betrothal was made and the wedding on the first lucky day to be found thereafter and Wang the Landlord and his lady were filled with relief and happiness. As for the bridegroom, although he was somewhat dazed at this sudden turn, yet he felt some of his old ardor return and he was very well content and the maid was full of triumph.

But to Wang the Tiger the whole affair was of no great moment except for this; he knew himself now for a man of power in that province and he knew that the general held him to be one whose favor he wished to hold to himself, and his heart swelled with pride. When this whole matter was finished, the spring had turned well into summer and Wang the Tiger said to himself that since he had been so busy and the year was now so late, he would put off his planned war until yet another year. He did this the more easily, because he was now sure of his position, and yet more easily, because in the beginning of that summer his spies began to return to him and they said that some sort of war was rumored well to the south, but they did not yet know what war it was, nor who its head. When Wang the Tiger heard this he understood fully the value of his army to the provincial general and why he sought to hold his favor. And he waited then for another spring, to see what it would bring forth.

And as always he did, Wang the Tiger spent his life with his son. The lad came and went gravely about his duties and it was Wang the Tiger's pleasure to watch the lad in his silent way. Often he gazed at his son, and he loved to dwell upon his serious face, half child, half youth. Many a time when he thus studied his son's face as it bent over some book or task, Wang the Tiger was caught by a strange familiar look in the boy's high square cheek, or in the firmness of his mouth. It was not a beautiful mouth, but very firm and fixed for so young a lad.

And it came to Wang the Tiger one night that his son had his look from his grandmother, Wang the Tiger's own mother. Yes, Wang the Tiger knew it was his mother's look, although he could only remember her clearly when she lay dying, and the boy's ruddy face was very different, too, from her pale, dying face. But deeper in Wang the Tiger than any clear memory was some feeling that told him his son moved in his mother's slow and silent way, and that her gravity was upon his son's lips and in his eyes. And when Wang the Tiger felt this vague familiar thing in his son, it seemed to warm his heart the more, and he loved his son more deeply yet and for some reason he did not understand he was knit to him yet more closely.

XXVI

Now the son of Wang the Tiger was such a sort of lad as this; he was faithful in every duty and he did all that he was told to do. He studied to perform the feints of war and the postures that his teachers set before him, and he rode his horse well enough, if not easily as Wang the Tiger did. But the lad did all as though he had no pleasure in any of it and as though he forced himself to everything as a task. When Wang the Tiger asked the tutor how his son did, the tutor answered hesitating,

"I cannot say he does not do well, for he does all well to a point, and he does very exactly what he is told, but beyond that he never goes. It is as though he kept his heart back."

This answer troubled Wang the Tiger very much for it had seemed to him before this that his son had no good hearty anger in him, and he was never angry and he had neither hatred nor desire in him for anything, but only he went gravely and with patience to all he had to do. Now Wang the Tiger knew that a warrior cannot be so; no, a warrior must have spirit and anger and wilfulness in him and a ready passion and he grieved and wondered how to change his son in this.

One day he sat by and watched the lad in the court as he fired at a target under his tutor's direction, and although the lad stood quietly and lifted his arm quickly and did not hesitate to pull firmly upon the trigger when the call came, yet it seemed to Wang the Tiger that he saw his son brace himself and a look come over his smooth boy's face as though he hardened himself within, so that he might do what he must, because he hated it so much. Then Wang the Tiger called to his lad and he said,

"Son, put your heart into it, if you would please me!"

The lad looked quickly at his father then, the pistol still smoking in his hand, and a strange look stole into his eyes and he opened his lips as though to speak. But there sat Wang the Tiger, and he could not look gentle if he would, those brows of his heavy and black, and his mouth sullen in his stiff black beard even when he did not mean it so, and the lad looked away again and sighed a little and he said in his patient way,

"Yes, my father."

Then Wang the Tiger looked with vague pain at his son, and for all his stiff hard looks his heart was soft, but he did not know how to speak out of his heart. And after a while he sighed and he watched in silence until the lesson was over. Then the lad looked doubtfully at his father and he said,

"May I go now, my father?"

And it came to Wang the Tiger that this lad of his went often away somewhere alone and many times he slipped away and Wang the Tiger did not know where, except that he knew the guard he had appointed to follow his son wherever he went followed him doubtless. But Wang the Tiger on this day looked at his son with a question in his mind, whether the lad went where he should not, and he saw him that he was a child no longer, and smitten with a sudden jealousy, Wang the Tiger made his voice as gentle as he could and he asked,

"But where do you go, my son?"

The boy hesitated and hung his head and at last he said half afraid,

"To no one place, my father. But I like to go outside the walls of the city and walk about the fields awhile."

Now if the boy had said he went to some bawdy place Wang the Tiger could not have been so taken aback and he said astounded,

"Now what can be there for a soldier to see?"

And the boy kept his eyes down and he fingered his little leather belt and he said in a low voice, in his usual patient way,

"Nothing—but it is quiet and pleasant to see now when the fruit trees are abloom, and I like to talk with a farmer sometimes and hear how he plants his land."

Then Wang the Tiger was completely astonished and he did not know what to do with this son of his, and he muttered to himself, that here was a strange son for a lord of war to have, who had hated from his youth up the ways of farmers upon the land, and suddenly he shouted out more angrily than he meant to do, because he was somehow disappointed and yet he did not know why he was,

"Do what you will then, and what is it to me?" And he sat on awhile heavily, for his son had slipped, swift as a freed bird, away from his father.

Wang the Tiger sat on and he meditated painfully, and yet he did not know why his heart was so sore, either. At last he grew impatient and he hardened himself somewhat and he told himself that with such a son he ought to be content, since the lad was not profligate and he did what he was told, and so Wang the Tiger put the matter away from him once more.

Now during these several years there were rumors of some new great discontent shaping itself up into a war somewhere, and Wang the Tiger's spies brought back tales of young men and young women in the schools of the south shaping themselves in a war and they brought tales of common folk upon the land shaping themselves for war and such things had never been heard of before, because such things are the trade of lords of war and have nothing to do with common people. But when Wang the Tiger in astonishment asked why they did battle and in what cause his spies did not know, and Wang the Tiger told himself it must be some school or other where some teacher did a wrong, or if it were the common people it must be some magistrate too vile and the people could not endure him more and they rose to kill him and put an end to what they could not bear.

But at least until he could see how new war shaped and how he could fit himself to it Wang the Tiger waged no wars of his own. No, he conserved his revenues and he bought such tools of war as he wished. Nor did he need to ask his brother Wang the Merchant to help him for Wang the Tiger had now his own port at the river's mouth which he owned and he hired ships and smuggled his own weapons in from outer countries easily enough. If there were those above him who knew it they were silent for they knew he was a general on their own side and every gun he had was a gun for them in the struggle that must come one day, since peace cannot last forever anywhere.

In such ways did Wang the Tiger strengthen himself as he waited, and his son grew and came into his fourteenth year.

Now these fifteen years and more that Wang the Tiger had been a great lord of war he had been lucky in many ways and the chief way was that there had been no great whole famine in his regions. Small famines there had been in one place or another, for thus it must ever be under a cruel heaven, but there was no famine over all his regions together, so that if one part starved, he need not press hard upon it, but he could raise his taxes in some other part where the people did not starve, or at least not so bitterly. This he was pleased to do, because he was a just man and he did not willingly take from dying people the little they had as some lords of war will do. For this the people were thankful and they praised him, and many throughout his region said,

"Well, and we have seen worse lords of war than the Tiger, and since there must be such lords, it is lucky we have this one who only taxes us for his soldiers and he does not love feasting and women and the things that most such men love."

It was true that Wang the Tiger took care to be just to the common people as much as he could. To this day no new magistrate had come to take the old one's place in that court. There had been a certain one appointed, but hearing how fierce a man Wang the Tiger was he delayed his coming, saying that his father grew old and that he must wait until the old man died and was buried before he could come. So until he came Wang the Tiger very often dispensed his own justice in the court and he heard people who came before him and he defended many a poor man against a rich man or a usurer. The truth was that Wang the Tiger did not need to fear any rich man, and he would clap the rich man into gaol if he did not pay what Wang the Tiger would have of him, so that it came to be in that town that landlords and usurers and such people hated Wang the Tiger very heartily and they went to great lengths to avoid bringing a case before him. But Wang the Tiger cared nothing for their hatred, since he was powerful and did not need to be afraid. He paid his soldiers regularly and well and if he was harsh sometimes with a man who committed some liberty too great, still he paid them their monthly wage and this was more than many a lord of war did, who must depend upon a looting to keep his men about him. But Wang the Tiger was not driven to a war for the sake of his men, and he could delay if he pleased, and his position in that region among the people and among his own men was very good and secure by now.

But however well men do establish themselves, they have always a perverse heaven with which to reckon, and so also did Wang the Tiger. In the fourteenth year of his son's age, when he prepared the next year to send him to the school of war, there fell a very heavy famine upon every part of Wang the Tiger's regions, and it spread from one part to another like a dire disease.

It came about that the proper rains of spring fell in their season, but when the time came for their cessation, the skies rained on, and the rains held day after day and week after week, and even into the summer they held, so that the rising wheat mouldered in the fields and sank into the water, and all those fair fields were pools of muddied water. The small river, too, which was by nature but a placid stream, went roaring along swollen and furious, and it tore at its clay banks and overran them and rushed against inner dykes and burst them apart and then went sweeping down its course and poured all its mud into the sea, so that the clear green waters were sullied for many a mile out. As for the people, they lived in their homes at first, building up their tables and beds upon boards out of the water. But as the waters rose to the roofs of their houses and the earthen walls crumbled, they lived in boats and in tubs and they clung to such dykes and mounds as still stood above the water, or they climbed into trees and hung there. Nor did people so only, but wild beasts and the snakes of the fields also, and these snakes swarmed up the trees and hung festooned upon the branches and they lost their fear of men and came creeping and crawling to live among them, so that men did not know which was the greater terror, terror of water or terror of the crawling snakes. But as the days went on and the water did not fall, there was yet another terror and it was the terror of starvation.

Here was a very sore thing for Wang the Tiger to bear, and one that he had not known before. He was worse off than many another man, too, because where other men have but their own families to feed, here was he with a vast horde dependent on him and they all very ignorant men, ready to complain, and content only if they were well fed and well paid, and loyal only so long as they were given what they held to be their due. From one place and another in Wang the Tiger's territories the revenues ceased to come in fully and at last as the waters stayed through the summer and when autumn came and there was no harvest, then by the winter of that year there were no revenues except the one upon the opium which was smuggled into those parts, and even this was much shrunken, since people could not buy and so the smugglers took their goods to other places for the time. Even the salt revenues ceased, for the waters washed away the salt wells, and the potters made no more wine jars, since that year no new wine was brewed.

Now Wang the Tiger was in great distress and for the first time in all his years as a lord of war and ruler over territories, in the last month of that year he could not pay his men. When he saw what was come he knew he must save himself by harshness alone, nor dared he show pity lest they take it for weakness in him. He called his captains to him, therefore, and he shouted at them as though they had done some evil and as though he were angry at them,

"All these months you men of mine have been fed while others starved and you have had wage as well! Now your wage must be food only, for my silver is gone, and no revenues will come until these times are over. No, and in a month or so, I shall have no silver left even to feed you and I must borrow a vast sum from somewhere, if you are not to starve, and if I and my son are not to starve with you."

Now as he spoke thus Wang the Tiger made his face hard and he glared at his men from under his brows and he pulled at his beard angrily, but secretly he looked to see what his captains did. There were mutinous faces among them and when they had gone out in silence there were those whom he kept as spies about him always who came back to tell him,

"They say they will fight no war until their dues are given them."

When he had heard his spy whisper this Wang the Tiger sat gloomy for a while in his hall, and he thought on the hearts of men and how ungrateful they are, and he thought how he had fed his men well and as usual during all these hungry months when the people starved and died and they did not love him the better. Once or twice he had said to himself that he might even take some of that private store of silver that he kept for his own lest he be put to it hard in some retreat and vanquishment in some war, but now he swore his men might starve and he would not rob himself and his son for any of them.

Still the famine did not cease. Everywhere in that region the waters lay and men starved and since there was no dry land in which to bury them, their bodies were cast out upon the water and floated there. There were many bodies of children, because men grew desperate at the unceasing wail of hungry children who could not understand why they were not fed, and so in the darkness of night and despair some parents even laid their children into the water; some did it out of pity for their children, for it seemed a shorter, sweeter death, but some did it because of the little store of food they had left, and they would not divide it with any other, and when two were left in a family then sometimes those two schemed secretly as to which was the stronger.

By the New Year, and none remembered it was a festival, Wang the Tiger gave his men but half their usual food, and he himself ate no meat in his household, but only grain gruel and such poor stuffs. One day as he sat in his own room thinking on what a pass he had come to, and wondering that his good destiny was in such abeyance, there came a man out of his guard who stood day and night about his door, and the man said,

"There are six men to see you who come from your own army and to stand for all the others. They have something to say."

Then Wang the Tiger looked up sharply out of his gloom and he asked,

"Are they armed?"

To this the guard replied, "I do not see any arms on them, but who can know the heart of any man?"

Now Wang the Tiger's son sat in the room at a little desk of his own, and his head was bent over some book he studied diligently. Wang the Tiger looked at him, thinking to send him away. And the lad rose at that instant and made as though to go away. But when Wang the Tiger saw him so willing his heart hardened suddenly and he thought to himself that his son must learn how to deal with men who were rebellious or savage, and so he cried out,

"Stay!" And the lad sat down slowly, as though he did not know what to make of it.

But Wang the Tiger turned to the guardsman and he said,

"Call the whole guard to come in and stand about me, and let them bring their guns ready set as though to make attack, and call the six men in!"

Then Wang the Tiger sat himself in a great old armchair he had which had once been the magistrate's own chair, and there was a tiger skin thrown over the back of it for warmth. There Wang the Tiger sat, and his guards came in and stood to right and to left of him, and Wang the Tiger sat and stroked his beard.

The six men came in and they were young men, hardy and easily moved and daring as young men are. They came in courteously when they saw their general sitting there with his guards about him and the points of the guns glittering about his head, and the one who had been chosen to speak made his proper obeisance and he said,

"Most Merciful, we have been chosen by our comrades to come and ask for a little more food. Indeed, we are not fed.

We do not say anything of wage now, seeing the times are so hard, and we will not ask for arrears in our wage now. But we are not fed, and day by day we grow weaker, and we are soldiers and our whole trade stock is in these bodies of ours. We have but a poor loaf of bread a day. For this we come to you, to put the matter before your justice."

Now Wang the Tiger knew what ignorant men are and he knew that they must be kept frightened or they will not obey their leader. He stroked his beard furiously, therefore, and he coaxed his anger to rise in his breast. He thought of all his kindness to his men, how he had not used them hard in war and how he had gone against his will in letting them take their booty after siege, and how he had always paid them and seen them well clothed, and how he was himself a good man and not lustful and exorbitant in his desires as so many men are, and as he thought of all this he felt his good anger begin to rise in him that these men of his could not bear hardship with him when it was the will of heaven and no fault of his own, and the more he thought of this the more he fanned his anger and tried to increase it. When he felt some semblance of it rise in him he made haste to use its strength, for he knew what he must do, and he roared out,

"Do you come here to pull the tiger's whiskers? Shall I let you starve? Have I ever let you starve? I have my plans made ready and food is due at any hour from foreign lands. But no, you are rebels—you would not trust me!" And he gathered up all his anger and he gave a great shout to his guards, "Kill me these six rebels!"

Then those six young men fell on their faces to beg for their lives but Wang the Tiger did not dare to spare them. No, for the sake of his son and himself and his household and for the people of that whole countryside whom they might turn to maraud if he lost his command over his men, he dared not

422

spare them, and he would not let his mercy free now. He shouted,

"Shoot, you men, to right and left!"

Then those guards shot, and the whole great room was filled with roar and smoke, and when the smoke lifted, those six men lay dead.

And Wang the Tiger rose at once and he commanded, "Take them back now to those who sent them and tell them it is my answer!"

But before the guards could stoop to lift the bodies of the young men a strange thing happened. That son of Wang the Tiger's, he so grave a lad and seeming usually to see little of what went on around him, now he rushed forward in the wildest distraction such as his father had never seen upon him, and he bent over one of the young men and stared and he went from one to the other of the young men, touching them here and there swiftly, looking at them with great wild eyes, staring at their loose-flung limbs, and he cried out to his father, standing to face him, and not knowing what he did,

"You have killed them—they are every one dead! This one I knew—he was my friend!"

And he fixed such despairing eyes upon his father's eyes that Wang the Tiger was suddenly afraid in some strange way because of the look in his son's eyes and he looked down and he said to justify himself,

"I was compelled to it, or they might have led the others and risen against me and so killed us all."

But the boy choked and he muttered, "He did only ask for bread—" And suddenly his face broke into weeping and he rushed from that room, and his father stared after him stupefied.

As for the guards, they went to their business and when Wang the Tiger was alone again, he sent out of the room even the two men who were always with him day and night, and he sat alone and held his head in his hands for an hour or two and he sat and groaned and wished he had not had to kill the young men. When he could not bear it any longer he called out that his son was to come to him, and after a while the boy came in slowly, his face bent down and his eyes veiled from his father. Wang the Tiger called to him to come near, and when he was come he took the lad's strong slender hand and fondled it a little as he had never done before and he said in a low voice,

"I did it for you."

But the lad made no reply at all. He had hardened himself and bore his father's love silently and stiffly and Wang the Tiger sighed and let him go, for he did not know what to say to his son or how make his son understand his love. So Wang the Tiger's heart was very sore and it seemed to him that of all men he was the most alone in this whole world, and he suffered a day or two. Then he, too, hardened himself again and let this pass also, since he did not know what to do, and he planned that he would do something for his son to make him forget. Yes, he would buy him a foreign watch or a new gun or some such thing and so win the boy back to him. Thus Wang the Tiger hardened himself and thus he comforted himself, also.

Nevertheless, the coming of these six men out of the army did show Wang the Tiger in what dire straits the times had brought him, for he saw that he must find food if he was to hold his army true. He had said falsely that he had already found food for them from foreign parts, but now he knew he must go out somewhere and find such food. Then once more he thought of his brother, Wang the Merchant, and he told himself that in such an hour brothers must stand together and he would go and see how the times were in his father's house, and what help he could secure.

He sent out the word, therefore, among his men that he went to find food and silver for them and he promised them a plenty, and when they were all cheerful and expectant, and freshened somewhat in their hope and loyalty to him, he chose a good guard and put them over his house and he commanded his own guard to prepare for the journey, and on a day he had set he called for boats to be brought and with his son and his soldiers and their horses all in these boats, they prepared to ferry across the waters to those parts of the road where the dykes still held, and there they would mount their horses again and ride to the town where Wang the Tiger's brothers lived.

Upon those narrow dykes their horses took their pace slowly, for the water spread in a sea on either side, and the dykes were crowded with huddled people. And not people only, but rats and serpents and wild things struggled to share that space with the people, and these wild things forgot their fears and tried with all their feeble strength to contend for space. But the only life these people showed was in such brief angers as rose in them when the serpents and beasts grew too many and they struck at them spitefully. But sometimes for long spaces they did not even so contend and the serpents curled and crawled wherever they would, and the people sat in their stupor.

Through these Wang the Tiger marched, and he had need of his armed guard and of his guns, for these people would have fallen upon him otherwise. As it was, here and there and often a man rose, or a woman, and twined about his horse's legs in silence and despair, yet with a faint last hope. And Wang the Tiger was gentle enough in heart with them, and he drew his horse and would not trample them down. No, he waited until one of his guardsmen came and took the wretched creature away and threw him on the ground again, and Wang the Tiger passed on without looking back. Sometimes the man lay where he had been thrown, but sometimes he gave a wild howl and leaped into the water and so ended himself and his woe.

All the way the lad rode beside his father, and not one word did he say, nor did Wang the Tiger speak to him, since there was the coldness between them of the six dead men, and Wang the Tiger feared to ask his son anything. But the lad's face was bowed down except sometimes when he seemed to steal a look sidewise at the starving people, and such a look of horror came into his face that Wang the Tiger could not bear it and he said at last,

"These be but very common folk and they are used to this once in a few years or so, and there are tens of thousands of such as these and the ones that die are not missed in a handful of years. They spring up like new rice again."

Then the boy said suddenly, and his voice was changing now like a fledgling bird's, and it came out in a squeak because he was so charged with his feeling, and with his fear lest he weep before his father,

"Yet I suppose it is as hard for them to die as though they were governors and men like us." And as he spoke he tried to fix his mouth hard and firm, but indeed these were sorrowful sights and his lips quivered, do what he would.

Now Wang the Tiger would have liked to say some comforting word, but he was astonished at what his son had said, and it had not come to him that these common folk suffered as he might suffer, since men are born as they are born and one may not take the place of any other. And he did not wholly like what his son said, because it was too soft a thing for a lord of war who may not stop to put his own heart into

426

any man who happens to suffer hardship. So Wang the Tiger could not think of any comforting word, for it was true that nothing could be fed these days except the carrion crows that circled and whirled again slowly in great wheels above the waters, and he said no more than this,

"We are all alike under the cruel will of Heaven."

After this Wang the Tiger let his son be; seeing what thoughts the lad had, Wang the Tiger asked him no more of anything.

XXVII

Now Wang the Tiger wished very often upon that journey that he could have left his son behind. But the truth was he did not dare to do it, lest there be some among his men who were secretly sullen because of the six dead men. Yet almost as much as he feared death for his son he feared too to take him to his brothers' courts. He feared the softness of the young men there, and he feared the coarse love of money that tradesmen have. He commanded his son's tutor, therefore, whom he had brought also, and he commanded his trusty harelipped man, that they were not to leave their young master at all, and besides these he told off ten seasoned and old soldiers who were to stay beside his son day and night, and he told his son he must study his books as ever he did at home. But he did not dare to say to him, "My son, you are not to go where there are women," for he did not know whether or not the boy had thought of such things yet. All these years when Wang the Tiger had his son by him in his own courts, there had been no women there, neither servant nor slave nor courtesan, and the lad knew no women at all except his mother and his sisters, and of latter years Wang the Tiger had not let him go alone even on the rare visits of duty he made to his mother, but had told off a guard to go with him. In such ways had Wang the Tiger fortified his son, and he was more jealous for this son of his than other men are for the women they love.

Yet in spite of his secret fears, it was a sweet moment for Wang the Tiger when he came riding to his brother's gates with his son riding beside him. It had pleased some fancy of Wang the Tiger's to have his tailors and sewing men cut his son's garments exactly like his own, and the lad wore just such a coat of foreign cloth, and such gilt buttons and such shoulder pieces of gilt, and a cap like Wang the Tiger's with a sign upon it. Wang the Tiger had even, upon the lad's fourteenth birthday, sent a man into Mongolia and found two horses exactly alike, except one a little smaller than the other, and both of them strong and dark and reddish in color, and their eyes white and rolling, and so even their horses were alike. It was sweetest music to Wang the Tiger's ears to hear the people upon the street cry out, as they stopped to stare at the soldiers pass,

"See the old lord of war and the little lord of war, as like as the two front teeth in a man's mouth!"

So they came riding up to the gates of Wang the Landlord, and the lad swung himself down from his horse as his father did, and clapped his hand to his sword's hilt as his father did, and marched gravely beside his father, without ever knowing that he did all like his father. As for Wang the Tiger, when he had been received into his brothers' house, and when his two brothers and their sons came in to give greeting, one after the other as they heard he was come, Wang the Tiger looked about on them all, and he drank in the looks of admiration they gave to his son as a thirsty man drinks down his wine. In the days thereafter while Wang the Tiger was in that house, he watched his brothers' sons

428

eagerly and scarcely knowing he did, hungry to be sure his own son was far better, and hungry to be comforted for his only son.

And Wang the Tiger could find much wherewith to comfort himself. The eldest son of Wang the Landlord was now well wed, although he had no children yet, and he and his wife lived in the same house with Wang the Landlord and his lady. This eldest son grew already somewhat like his father, and he was already a little round in the belly and his pretty body was coating itself with a soft deep fat. But he had a weary look, too, and it was true he had something to weary him, for his wife would not live pleasantly with his mother, the lady, but she was pert in her new wisdom and she cried out to her husband when they were alone and he tried to exhort her,

"What—am I to be a servant to that old proud woman? Does she not know we young women are free now-a-days and we do not serve our mothers-in-law any more?"

Nor did this young woman fear the lady at all, and when the lady said with her old majesty, "When I was young I served my mother-in-law as it was my duty to do, and I took her tea in the morning and I bowed myself before her as I had been bred to do," the daughter-in-law shook back her short hair and tapped her pretty unbound foot upon the floor and she said very impudently,

"But we women today do not bow down before anyone!"

Because of such strife the young husband grew often weary, nor could he solace himself with his old diversions, for his young wife watched him and would know his every play place, and she was so bold she did not fear to follow him out into the street and cry out that she would go, too, and that now-a-days women did not stay locked in the house, and men and women were equal and with such talk she so diverted the

429

people upon the streets that for very shame's sake the young husband gave up his old diversions, for he did believe her bold enough to follow him anywhere. For this young wife was so jealous that she would break off every habit and natural desire her husband had, and he could not so much as glance at a pretty slave and she would not let him go near a brothel with his friends without finding such a shrieking and weeping stirred up ready for him when he came home again, that it was an outrage in the house. Once a friend to whom he complained advised him saying,

"Threaten her with a concubine—it is very humbling for any woman!"

But when the young man tried this, his wife was not humbled at all, but she cried out and her round eyes flashed at him,

"In times like this we women will not endure such things!"

And before he knew what she did, she sprang at him with her little hands outspread and she clawed him on either cheek like a small cat, and there were four deep scratches red and bright on his two cheeks, and it was plain to anyone how he came by them, and he could not stir out for five days and more for shame. Nor dared he put her to any open shame, for her brother was his friend and her father chief of police and a man with power in the town.

Yet in the night he loved her still, for she could curl against him sweetly enough and coax him and be so seeming penitent that he loved her heartily then, and he softened to listen to her talk.

At such hours the burden of all her talk was that he must ask his father for a certain sum of money and they two would go away out of this house and go to some port city on the coast and live there in the new fashion and live among those of their kind. And she would fling out her pretty arms and hold him and wheedle him, or she would grow angry and weep or she would lie in her bed and refuse to rise or to eat until he would promise, and so in a thousand ways she wearied her husband, until at last he gave his promise. But when he had promised and had gone to his father, and when Wang the Landlord heard it he looked up out of his heavy old eyes and he said,

"Where shall I find such a sum as you say? I cannot do it." And after a while when he seemed sunken in the sleepy indolence in which he passed much of his life now, he spoke again and he said, "A man must bear with women, for the best of them are full of strife and contention. Learned or unlearned, they are so, but the learned ones are the worst for they do not fear anything. Let the women rule the house, I have always said, and I will seek my peace elsewhere. So you must do, also."

But the young wife would not have it settled so easily, and she forced her husband to go again and again to his father, and for peace's sake Wang the Landlord grew weak at last and he promised he would plan some way, although well he knew the only way he had was to sell the most of what land he still owned. As for the young wife, when she had even the half promise, she prattled of her going and made her every plan and talked so constantly of what many ways there were to find pleasure in the coast city, and how fine the women dressed themselves and how she must buy a new gown and a coat of fur, and how all the clothes she had were less than rags and fit only for such a country place as this, that with all her talking she stirred her husband up to some eagerness to be gone, too, and to see all the wonders of which she spoke.

Now Wang the Landlord's younger son was a man, too, and he had followed in his brother's footsteps, and he was eager in only one thing and it was that he should be given no less in anything than his elder brother had. He had a secret and mighty admiration for his pretty sister-in-law, and in his heart he determined that when his elder brother left home, he would storm to follow after and see that city where there were many ladies pretty and new as his sister-in-law was. But he was wise enough to say nothing of his plan until his brother was gone, and he only idled about the house and the town, waiting, and despising all he had and saw, now that he knew how wonderful a place the coast city was and how filled with new things and fine new people, learned in every foreign thing. And he even looked at Wang the Tiger's son as though secretly belittling him, and Wang the Tiger caught the look and hated the young man for it.

But in the house of Wang the Merchant the young men were outwardly more humble and when they came home at night from their shops they sat edgewise on their seats and stared at this uncle and at this cousin of theirs, and Wang the Tiger took secret pleasure in the looks these young tradesmen cast at his son, and he marked how they stared at the lad and at the little gilded sword he wore that he took off sometimes and held across his knee for the younger children to look at and to touch with their fingers.

At such times Wang the Tiger rejoiced mightily in his son and he forgot the lad had been cold to him. He rejoiced to see his son rise sharply and neatly as his tutor had taught him to do and make his salute to his father or to his uncle as he came in, and then sit down again in a very mannerly way when his elders had taken their places. And Wang the Tiger smoothed his beard and loved his son exceedingly and he grew more merry than he had ever been in his life when he saw how much taller for his years his son was than these clerks his brother had for sons, and how much harder his son's flesh was and how straight and true his body and not languid and curved and pale as his cousins were.

During all these days that Wang the Tiger was in the houses of his brothers he guarded over his son carefully. When the lad sat beside him at feasts Wang the Tiger himself saw to his son's wine, and when the serving men had poured three times, he would not let them pour again for his son. And when the lads who were his cousins cried out to him to come and play here or there somewhere, Wang the Tiger sent his son's tutor and the harelipped trusty man and the ten old soldiers with him everywhere. Every night Wang the Tiger made some excuse and he would not be at rest until he had gone himself to his son's room and seen the lad in his own bed and alone except for the guard who watched at the door.

Now in this house of his father where his two brothers still lived so easily and well, it was as though no famine were in the land and as though no waters stood upon harvest fields, and as though none starved anywhere. Yet well enough did Wang the Landlord know and well enough did Wang the Merchant know what went on outside their peaceful home, and when Wang the Tiger had told them his straits and why he was come and when he ended saying, "It is to your interest to save me out of my danger, because my power keeps you safe, too," they knew very well he spoke the truth.

For there were starving people outside of this city also, and many of them hated the two brothers very bitterly. They hated Wang the Landlord because he still owned land and those who worked on it must share with him, who did not labor at all, the bitter fruit they wrung from the earth, and to them it seemed, when they had bent over their fields in cold and heat and in rain and sun, that the earth and its fruit belonged to them. It was a very sore thing that at harvest time they

433

must give a good half of it to one who had sat in a town house and waited for it, and that in famine time he must still have his share.

It was true that in these years when Wang the Eldest had been landlord and while he sold the land, too, he was still no easy landlord. No, for a man so weak and soft as he was, he could curse and quarrel, and his hatred of the land vented itself against these people who tilled it for him and he hated them not only for the land's sake, but because he was so hard pressed often for money enough for his house's needs and his own needs and he was doubly bitter because it seemed to him his tenants wilfully held back what was his due and given him from his father. It came to such a pass that when his tenants saw him coming they would turn their faces to the sky and mutter,

"It must be we will have rain since the devils are out!"

And often they reviled him and said,

"You are no good son of your father, for he was a merciful man even in his age when he was rich, and he remembered that once he had toiled as we do, and he never pressed us for our rent, nor demanded grain of us in famine years. But you have never suffered and mercy has never been born in your heart!"

Such hatred had there been, and it was manifest in this hard year because in the night when the great gates were locked there were those who came and beat upon that gate and they lay on the steps and moaned out,

"We are starving and you still have rice to eat and rice to make into wines!" And others cried out upon the streets as they passed the gates, and they cried even in daytime, "Oh, that we might kill these rich men and take what they have robbed from us!"

At first the two brothers paid no heed, but at last they had hired a few soldiers of the town to stand about the gate and keep all off who had no proper business there. And indeed there were many rich men in that town and countryside who were robbed and despoiled as the year grew old, for robbers began to spring up, numerous and desperate, as they do in any evil time. Yet the two sons of Wang Lung were safe enough, because the chief of police and head of the soldiers of the town had married his daughter into that house, and because Wang the Tiger was near there and the lord of war. And so before that House of Wang the people did not as yet dare to do more than moan and curse.

Nor had they come to rob the earthen house which belonged to this family they hated. No, it stood up on its hillock out of the slowly receding waters, and Pear Blossom lived there safely enough through the bitter winter with her two. This was because Pear Blossom was well known by now for her pity, and they knew that she begged for stores out of the House of Wang and many came to her doors in their little boats and tubs and she fed them. Once Wang the Merchant had gone to her and said,

"In such dangerous times as these you must come into the town and live in the great house."

But Pear Blossom had replied in her tranquil, usual way,

"No, I cannot, and I am not afraid, and there are those who depend on me."

But as the winter grew deep and cold she did grow afraid at times because there were men made desperate by hunger and the bitter wind upon the icy waters where they lived in boats still or clung to tree tops as they could, and they were angry because Pear Blossom still fed the fool and the hunchback and they muttered before her very face, with her gifts in their hands,

"Shall those two still be fed, when good strong men, who have a whole child or two left, must starve?"

Indeed, such mutterings grew very loud and often, and Pear Blossom had just begun to wonder if she should not take these two into the town lest they be killed some time because of what they ate, and she too weak to defend them, when the poor fool, now more than fifty and two years of age, but still the same child she ever was, died in the sudden swift way such have of dying. One day she ate and played as ever she did with her bit of cloth, and she wandered out of the gate and into the water without knowing it was water and not dry land now where she usually sat, and Pear Blossom ran after, but the fool was already drenched and shivering with the icy water. From this she took a chill, in spite of every tenderness that Pear Blossom gave her, and in a few hours she was dead, since she died as easily as she lived without a will in anything.

Then Pear Blossom sent word into the town to Wang the Landlord for the coffin, and since Wang the Tiger was there, the three brothers came together, and Wang the Tiger brought his son, also. They stayed to see this poor thing put into her coffin, and she lay there for the first time in her life wise and grave with a dignity that death alone had given to her. And Pear Blossom truly grieving, was somewhat comforted to see how her child looked and she said in the quiet, murmuring way she had,

"Death has healed her and made her wise at last. She is like any of us now."

But the brothers had no funeral for her, seeing what she had been, and Wang the Tiger left his son in the earthen house while he went in the boat with his brothers and with Pear Blossom and the tenant's wife and a laboring man to the other high land where the graves of the family were, and there in a lowly place but still inside the earthen enclosure, they buried the fool.

When all was finished and they had returned to the earthen house and made ready to go back to the town again, Wang the Tiger looked at Pear Blossom and he spoke to her for the first time and he said in his calm, cold way,

"What will you do, now, lady?"

Then Pear Blossom lifted her face to him, brave for the first time in her life, knowing as she did that her hair was growing white, and her face no longer young and smooth, and she said,

"I have long said that when this child of mine was gone I would go into the nunnery near here, and the nuns are ready for me. I have lived close to them these many years and I have already taken many vows and the nuns know me and I shall be happiest there." Then she turned to Wang the Landlord and said, "You and your lady have already made the plan about this son of yours, and his temple is very near to mine and I will still tend him, seeing how old I am now and old enough to be his mother, and if he is ill or fevered as he often is, I can go to him. Priests and nuns, they worship together at morning and evening, too, and I can see him twice a day, too, even if we may not speak."

Then the three brothers looked at the hunchbacked lad who hung about Pear Blossom, lost now that the fool was gone, for whom he often cared with Pear Blossom. He was a man now, and he smiled painfully under their looks. Wang the Tiger was somehow touched because his own son stood so tall and strong and astonished at all this he had not known about before, and Wang the Tiger said very kindly, when he saw the son smile on the hunchback's face,

"I wish you well, poor lad, and if you had been able, I would have taken you gladly as I took your cousin and I would have

437

done as well for you as I have done for him. But as it is, I will add something to your fee in the temple and to yours, too, lady, for money always buys a place, and I daresay it is the same in temples as elsewhere."

But Pear Blossom replied softly and surely,

"I will take nothing for myself and need nothing, for the nuns know me and I know them, and all I have is theirs too when I go to cast my lot with them. But for the lad I will take something, for it will help him."

This she said in mild reproach to Wang the Landlord, for his sum he gave when he and the lad's mother decided upon this life for their son was too meager, but if he knew it for a reproach he gave no sign, and he only sat down to wait for his brothers, being very heavy and finding it a grievance if he must stand up. But Wang the Tiger still gazed at the hunch-backed lad and said once more to him,

"And would you still rather go to the temple than to any other place?"

Then the youth took his eyes off from his tall cousin at whom he stared very avidly, and he hung his head and looked down the short length of his crooked body and he said slowly,

"Yes, seeing I am as I must be." And he said after a moment, very heavily, "A priest's robe will hide my hump, perhaps."

He turned his eyes once more to his cousin, then suddenly it seemed he could not bear to look at him any more, and not even at his gilded sword, for he dropped his eyes and turned and limped quickly out of the room.

On that night when Wang the Tiger was returned to the house of his brothers, and when he went in to see his son in his bed, he found the lad awake and eager and he asked his father,

"My father, was that house my grandfather's house too?"

438

And Wang the Tiger answered in surprise, "Yes, and I lived there as a lad and until he founded this house and brought us all here."

Then the boy looked up out of his bed, and his head lay pillowed on his hands crossed under his head and he looked eagerly at his father and he said with ardor,

"I like that house. I would like to live in a house set in fields like that earthen house, and very quiet and trees there and the oxen!"

But Wang the Tiger answered with an impatience he could not understand, seeing that, after all, his son had said no great harmful thing,

"You do not know what you say! I know, for I was there as a lad, it is a very hateful ignorant life, and I longed every hour to be away from it!"

But the lad said with some strange stubbornness,

"I would like it—I know I would like it!"

These few words his son said very ardently, and so ardently that Wang the Tiger felt some strange small anger in him and he rose and went away. But his son lay and dreamed that night that the earthen house was his home and that he lived there among the fields.

As for Pear Blossom, she went to that nunnery and the son of Wang the Landlord went to his temple, and the old earthen house stood empty of the three who had lived there these many years. Of the family of Wang Lung no one lived there on his land, and there were but the old tenant and his wife, and these two lived on alone. Sometimes the old woman took a withered cabbage she had hid in the earth or a handful of meal she had saved, and she tied it up in a kerchief and went to the nunnery to give it to Pear Blossom, because in her years of service she had learned to love the gentle, silent woman. Yes, even in these hard times the old woman took what little thing she had, and she would wait at the gate for Pear Blossom to come out, clothed as she was now in the grey nun's robe, and she would whisper to her,

"I have a new-laid egg from that one hen I still have and it is for you!"

Then she thrust her hand into her bosom and brought out a small egg and she covered it in her hand and she held it to Pear Blossom's hand and tried to slip it in and she coaxed her, whispering,

"Eat it, mistress! I swear there would be many nuns who would do it, for all their vows, and I have seen many priests eating meat and drinking wine. Stand here where none will see you and eat it fresh—you are so pale!"

But Pear Blossom would not. No, she had made her true vows, and she shook her shaven head in its grey cap and she pushed the old woman's hands gently away and she said,

"No, you must eat it, for you need it more than I, even if I could eat it, for I am well fed enough for my needs. But even if I were not fed, I could not eat it because I have taken my vows!"

Yet the old woman would not be satisfied and she forced it into Pear Blossom's bosom where her robes crossed at the throat, and then hastened into her tub and pushed it away from the door into the water so that Pear Blossom could not reach her, and she went away smiling and content. But Pear Blossom gave the egg away in the next half hour to a poor starving wretch who crawled out of the water at the temple gate. It was a mother, and she held a starveling to the shriveled bit of skin that had been once a full round breast, and pointing to it, she begged of Pear Blossom, who came at her feeble call,

"Look at these breasts of mine! Once they were round and

full and this child as fat as a god!" And she gazed down at the small dying creature whose lips were still pressed to the empty fountain. Then Pear Blossom took the egg out of her bosom and gave it to the woman and rejoiced she had so good a thing to give.

In such ways of peace did Pear Blossom live out her life from that time on, and Wang the Tiger never saw her more.

Now Wang the Merchant was very able to help Wang the Tiger in that year of straits if he would, for the truth was he had great stores of grain and if famine brought poverty to others to him and to others like him it brought yet greater riches. For, when he saw what the times were to be, he began to hoard vast bins of grains, and even though he sold some from time to time to the rich who were able to buy at the high prices he set upon it, yet he bought also of flour and of rice from other regions, and he sent his agents out even to the nearest foreign countries to buy such goods, and his granaries were heaped with food.

He had more silver now than ever he had, for as his grain flowed out to this rich house and to that market, the silver flowed back to him for it, and in this year Wang the Merchant was burdened with his silver and he was put to it to know what he could do with it and keep it safe. Being merchant, he wanted no more land, and yet there was no other security men could offer in such a time if they borrowed money of him except the land they had under the water. He took risks, therefore, at very high interest, and he put heavy mortgages upon the harvests of the future, and such mortgages that when the lands had drained themselves once more, it seemed that all the harvest of that whole region would pour into the granaries of Wang the Merchant. But not one knew fully how rich he was, for he kept even his own sons pressed

441

for the silver they wanted to spend, and he made poor face before every one of his sons, and held them to their clerkships in his shops and markets, so there was not one among his sons, except his eldest whom he had given to Wang the Tiger, who did not look for the day when his father was gone and he could leave the shop or the markets and spend something for the play and the good garments which Wang the Merchant would not let them have now.

Nor were his sons the only ones who hated their servitude, for there were certain of the farmers in that countryside, and one of them that shelf-toothed man who had bought largely of Wang Lung's land when he was dead, and now that the land was most of it under water, he pinched and starved and saw his children near to starvation before he would borrow from Wang the Merchant, and he waited for his land to come up out of the water and while he waited he took his brood and went south to some southern city, choosing such a life rather than to let Wang the Merchant get a hold upon his land.

But Wang the Merchant was righteous enough in his own eyes, for he told himself and all who came to borrow of him that men must not expect to borrow money or buy grain in times of scarcity at the prices not higher than usual, else what profit can there be to a man who is a merchant? He did no more, therefore, than what was just in his own eyes.

Yet he was wise man enough, and he knew that men do not think of justice in such times and he knew he was very heartily hated, and he knew that Wang the Tiger was of some service to him even in the very fact that he was lord of war. He exerted himself, therefore, and he promised certain very large stores of grain to Wang the Tiger and he lent him a great sum at not very great interest, and not above twenty per cent or so on a silver piece. When they sealed the bargain one day in the tea house, Wang the Landlord, who sat by, sighed heavily and he said,

"My little brother, I wish I were rich as this merchant brother of ours, but the truth is I grow poorer every year. I have no good business such as he has, and nothing but a little money loaned and a little land left out of all my father's fields. It is a good thing for us all that we have one rich man among us!"

At this Wang the Merchant could not forbear a very sour smile and he said plainly, for he had no grace of tongue nor any wit at courtesy,

"If I have a little it is because I have worked and I have held my sons to the shops and they do not wear silk, and I have only one woman."

But Wang the Landlord would not have any such plain talk as this, although his temper had dwindled very much too, in these later years, for he knew his brother reproached him because he had sold off a large portion of such land as he had left so that his two sons could go out to the coast as they wished, and he sat and swelled awhile in himself and at last he said loudly, rousing himself,

"Well, and a father must feed his sons, I believe, and I hold my sons a little too precious to make them spend their good young strength at a counter somewhere. If I honor my father's grandsons, shall I let them starve? It is my duty to feed my children, I believe, but perhaps I do not know my duty when I keep my sons as a lord's sons should be kept!" He could not say more, for a hoarse, constant cough troubled him these years and it came rumbling out of his bosom now, and racked him. Being speechless awhile, he could only sit swelling and angry, and his eyes were sunken in his fat cheeks, and the red mounted slowly up his thick neck. But Wang the Merchant let a little smile creep upon his own thin and

443

withered cheeks, for he saw his brother understood himself reproved, and no more need be said.

Now when the bargain was signed and sealed, then Wang the Merchant would have it written down, and at this Wang the Tiger shouted out,

"What—are we not brothers?"

And Wang the Merchant said, as though in apology, "It is for my own memory—I have such a feeble memory now-a-days!"

But he held the brush to Wang the Tiger so that he must perforce take it and put his name down. Then Wang the Second said, still smiling,

"Is your seal about you, too?"

Then Wang the Tiger must take out the seal he carried in his girdle that had his name carven on the stone, and he must stamp that too upon the paper before Wang the Merchant would take it and fold it and thrust it carefully into his own girdle bag. And watching him, Wang the Tiger grew angry, even while he had what he wanted, and he swore to himself that he must enlarge his territories somehow and he wished he had not let these years slip by as he had so that once again he was dependent upon this brother.

But for the time Wang the Tiger's men were saved, and he called for his son to be made ready and for his guardsmen to gather themselves and they would go home. It was now well upon spring and the lands were drying rapidly and everywhere men were eager for new seed to put into their lands, and everywhere men forgot the winter and all the dead and they looked forward hopeful again to the spring.

So also did Wang the Tiger feel himself eager for new things and he told his brothers farewell. Then the two brothers gave him a feast of departure, and after the feast Wang the Tiger went into that place where the tablets of his

444

ancestors were kept, and he lit incense there. He had his son by him as he lit it, and while the dense sweet smoke curled upwards, Wang the Tiger made his obeisances to his father and to his father's fathers, and he bade his son bow also. Watching the gallant figure of his son thus bowing, Wang the Tiger felt a strong sweet pride rise in him, and it seemed to him that the spirits of those dead gathered close to see so fine a one as this descended from their line, and he felt he had done what he should in his family.

When all was finished and the incense burned to the ashes in the urn, Wang the Tiger mounted his horse, and his son mounted his own horse, and with their guardsmen, they rode back by dry land to their own regions.

XXVIII

In the spring of the year when Wang the Tiger's son was fifteen full years of age the tutor whom Wang the Tiger had hired for his son came to him one day as he walked in his court alone, and he said,

"My general, I have taught the young general, your son, all that I can alone, and he needs to go into a school of war where he will have comrades with whom to march and to fight and to practice war."

It seemed to Wang the Tiger, although he knew this day must come, as though a dozen years had passed as the turn of a hand. He sent for his son to come to him there in the court and he felt suddenly weary and old and he sat down upon a stone seat that was under a juniper tree and waited for his son. When the lad came through the round gate between the courts, walking with his steady somewhat slow step, Wang the Tiger looked at him newly. It was true that the lad was tall and nearly as high as a man, and his face had already taken on rougher curves and he kept his lips folded firmly and well together. It was a man's face rather than a child's. And as Wang the Tiger looked at this only son, he remembered with a sort of wonder that once he had been impatient for his son to be grown and a man, and once his babyhood had seemed endless. Now it seemed rather that he had leaped straight out of his babyhood into this new manhood. Then Wang the Tiger sighed and he thought to himself,

"I wish that school were not in the south. I wish he had not to go among those little southerners to learn!" And aloud he said to the tutor who stood pulling at a few short hairs he grew on his upper lip, "And you are sure he had better go to that school?"

The tutor moved his head to signify assent, and Wang the Tiger stared on at his son painfully and at last he asked the lad, "And yourself, my son, you wish to go?"

Now it was very rarely that Wang the Tiger ever asked his son what he liked, because he knew so well what he wanted for his son, but he had a small weak hope that if the boy refused to go he could use it as an excuse. But the boy looked up quickly, for he had been looking at a patch of white lilies that grew there under a juniper tree, and he said,

"If it were so that I could go to another school, I would like that very well."

But this answer did not please Wang the Tiger at all and he drew down his brows and pulled at his beard and said pettishly,

"Now what school is there to which you could go except a school of war, and what use would stuff out of books be to you, who are to be a lord of war?"

The boy answered diffidently and in a low voice, "There

446

be schools I have heard in these days where they learn how to till land and such things as have to do with the land."

But Wang the Tiger was astounded at such foolishness, and he had never heard of such a school and he roared suddenly,

"Now here is foolishness, if it be true there are such schools! Well, and so every farmer must needs learn how to plow and sow and reap these days! Well, and I remember very well my father used to say a man needed not to learn to farm, for he had but to look at what his neighbor did!" Then he said very harshly and coldly, "But what has this to do with you or me? We are lords of war, and you shall go to a school of war or to no school at all, but stay here and take my army after me."

His son sighed then and shrank away a little as ever he did when Wang the Tiger roared, and he said quietly and with some strange patience,

"I will go then to the school of war."

Yet there was something in this patience which still made Wang the Tiger angry and he stared at his son and pulled at his own whiskers and he wished his son would speak out and yet he knew he would be angry if he heard what his son had in his heart, and he shouted,

"Prepare yourself, for tomorrow you shall go!"

The lad saluted him then as he had been taught to do and turned upon his heel and went away without a word more.

But in the night when he was alone in his room Wang the Tiger fell to thinking of his son going so far from him and a sort of terror came on him for what might befall his son in those parts where men were so tricky and deceitful, and he called out to his guard that his trusty harelipped man was to come in to him. When he was come Wang the Tiger turned to look at the hideous faithful face and he said, half pleading and not as master to man,

447

"That son of mine, my only son, is to go to a school of war tomorrow and even though his tutor goes, how do I know what that one's heart is who has spent so many years in foreign parts? His eyes are hid behind his spectacles and his lips behind his hairs, and he seems strange to me when I think my son must trust wholly to him. Now you shall go with my son, for I know you, and there is no one else whom I know as I do you, who have been with me when I was poor and alone and you were then what you are now that I am rich and strong. My son is my best possession and you are to watch over him for me."

Now here was a strange thing, for when Wang the Tiger said this the harelipped man spoke up stoutly and he was so earnest his words came whistling through his teeth,

"My general, in this one thing I will not obey you, for I will stay by you. If the young general must go, I will pick fifty good true men, not young, and I will teach them their duty to him, but I will stay where you are. You do not know how you need a true man near you, for in an army so great as yours there are always discontents and festerings and this man angry and that man talking of some better general, and there are very ugly rumors now of some new strange war gathering out of the south."

To this Wang the Tiger answered stubbornly,

"You hold yourself too dear. Have I not the Pig Butcher yet?"

Then the harelipped man grew very scornful and he twisted his face frightfully in his agitation and he said,

"That—that fool! Yes, he is well enough at picking flies out of the air, and if I tell him whom to strike and when to strike he can deal a blow with his great fist, but he has not wit enough to see anything until he is told where to look!"

He would not be moved at all, and Wang the Tiger commanded him and bore with his rebelliousness as he would never have borne with such refusal in any other, and at last the harelipped man said over and over,

"Well, and I can fall on my sword, then—well, I have my sword and my throat here together."

In the end there was nothing to do but to give in to this man and when he saw Wang the Tiger would do so, he grew very cheerful although a moment before he had been doleful and talking of dying. He ran out that very night and chose his fifty men and he rounded them out of their sleep and he cursed them soundly as they stood dazed and yawning and shivering in the chill spring air in the court and he shouted at them through his split lip,

"If so much as a tooth aches in the young general's mouth it will be your fault, O you who ought to die, and your whole business is to go with him wherever he goes and stand about and guard him! At night you are to lie about his bed, and in the day you are not to trust anyone or listen to anyone, no, not even to him. If he grows wilful and says he will not have you and that you encumber him you are to answer, 'We are under the old general, your father, and he pays us and we must hear him only.' Yes, you are to guard him against his own self." And he cursed the fifty men very richly and completely to frighten them well, and make them know how grave their duty was and at last he said, "But if you do well, you shall receive a good reward, for there is no more generous heart than our old general's heart, and I will speak for you myself."

Then they roared out their promise, for they knew this trusty man was nearer to their general than any except his own son, and the truth was they were pleased enough to go to foreign parts and see what they had not seen.

Then when the morning came Wang the Tiger rose from

his sleepless bed and he let his son go and he went with him a way because he could not bear to part with him. Yet it was but a small respite and a little putting off of what must come, and when he had ridden awhile beside his son, he drew rein and said abruptly,

"Son, it has been said from ancient times that though a man go with his friend three thousand miles, yet must the parting come, and so it must be with you and me. Farewell!"

He sat very stiffly upon his horse then, and he received the obeisances of his son, and he sat and watched the lad leap into the saddle again and ride away with his fifty men and his tutor. Then Wang the Tiger turned his horse about and he rode back to his empty house, and he looked no more after his son.

Three days did Wang the Tiger allow himself to grieve, and he could not set his hand to do anything nor his heart to any planning until the last of the men he had sent out with his son as messengers came back to make report. They came back every few hours from different places upon the road and each brought his own report. One said,

"He is very well and rather more gay than his wont is. Twice he dismounted from his horse and stepped into a field where a farmer was and talked with him."

"And what could he have to say to such an one?" asked Wang the Tiger, astonished.

And the man replied, remembering faithfully, "He asked him what seed he planted and he looked to see the seed, and he looked to see how the ox was tied to the plow, and his men laughed to see him, but he did not care and stared sturdily at the ox and how it was tied."

Then Wang the Tiger was puzzled and he said, "I do not see why a lord of war should care to see how an ox is tied or what seed it is," and he waited and then said impatiently, "Have you no more to say than this?"

The man thought awhile and answered, "At night he stopped at an inn and he ate heartily of bread and meat and some soft rice and fish and he drank but one small bowl of wine. There I left him and came back to bring the news."

Then another came and another with such news of how his son did and what he ate and drank and so they reported until the day when the lad reached the place where he was to go by boat upon the river to the sea. Then Wang the Tiger could but wait for some letter to come, for further than this men could not follow.

Now whether or not Wang the Tiger could have borne his restlessness without his son he did not know, but two matters came to divert and draw his heart out of himself. The first was that spies came back with strange news out of the south and they said,

"We hear a very curious war is coming up out of the south and it is a war of some sort of overturning and revolution and not a good and usual war between lords of war."

Then Wang the Tiger answered somewhat scornfully, for he was very surly these days,

"It is not new at all. When I was young I heard of such a war of revolution and I went to fight in it, thinking I did a noble deed. Yet it was but a war after all, and while the lords of war united for a time against the dynasty, when they were successful and overthrew the throne they fell apart and for themselves again."

Nevertheless, the spies returned all with the same tale, and they said,

"Nay, it is some sort of a new war and it is called a people's war and a war for the common people."

"And how can common people have a war?" answered Wang the Tiger loudly, raising his black brows at these silly spies of his. "Have they guns and will they wage war with sticks and staves and forks and scythes?" And he glared so at his spies that they were discomfited and coughed and looked at each other, and at last one said humbly,

"But we only tell what we hear."

Then Wang the Tiger forgave them with majesty and he said,

"It is true, that is your duty, but you have heard nonsense." And he dismissed them. Nevertheless, he did not wholly forget what they said, and he told himself he must watch the war and see what it truly was.

But before he could take much thought there arose another affair in his own regions which pressed upon him and drove out any other thought.

The summer drew near, and since nothing is so changeful as the heaven above men, it was a beauteous summer, with mingled rains and sun, and the waters receded and left the earth open and fertile, and wherever men could find a little seed they had but to thrust it into this warm, panting earth, steaming under the sunshine, and life leaped up out of that earth, and the harvest promised food and plenty for all.

But while they waited for harvest there were many men still hungry and that year robbers again grew rife in Wang the Tiger's regions and worse than he had ever known them to be. Yes, even in his regions where he maintained his great army fed and paid, there were men so desperate they dared to form into robber bands and to defy him, and when he sent his soldiers after them, they were not to be found. They were like a band of ghosts, for Wang the Tiger's spies would run back and tell him,

"Yesterday the robbers were to the north and they burnt

the village of the Ch'ing family." Or they would say, "Three days ago a band of robbers fell upon merchants and killed them all and took their goods of opium and silks."

Then Wang the Tiger grew exceedingly angry to hear of such lawlessness and he was angry most of all because he was defrauded thus of his own revenues from merchants, which he needed sorely to make him free from Wang the Merchant and he grew so angry that he longed to kill someone. Then he rose up in his courts and shouted that his captains were to partition out his soldiers over that whole region and for every robber's head they brought in he would give a reward of a piece of silver.

Yet when his soldiers rushed out, enticed by the reward, to seize the robbers they found none. The truth was many of these robbers were simple farming folk, and they only came out when they were not pursued. But if they saw the soldiers after them they dug and hoed in the fields and told sorry tales to the soldiers of how they had suffered at the hands of such and such a band and they told of any band except their own, and their own they never mentioned, or if they heard another mention it, they looked vacantly about and said they had never known such a band as that nor ever heard such a name. But because of the reward Wang the Tiger had promised and because many of his men were greedy, they killed any man they could and brought his head in and said it was a robber's head, and none could say it was not, and so they received the reward. There were thus many men killed who were innocent, but no one dared to complain, for they knew that Wang the Tiger sent his men out in a good and lawful cause, and if they complained it might anger some soldier and draw attention to him who complained and put it in the soldier's mind that this one who complained had a head also.

But one day in the midsummer when the sorghum cane

453

was very high and much higher than men standing, the robbers spread everywhere like a sudden blaze of fire, and Wang the Tiger was angry to such a pitch that he rose up one day himself against the robbers, although he had not gone out thus for many a day and year. But he heard of a certain small band in a village, and his spies had watched and they had seen that by day the villagers were farmers and by night they were robbers. It seemed the lands these villagers had were very low and the village lay in a great hollow and the farmers had not been able to plant even so soon as others and so they were still not fed, such as had not starved in the winter and spring.

Now when Wang the Tiger had this certain knowledge of how evil these men were and how they went by night to other villages and robbed them of their food and killed those who resisted, his anger swelled up in him and he went himself with his men to that village and he commanded them to surround the village and leave no way open for any to escape. Then with other men he went galloping in and they seized every man, a hundred and seventy-three men in all, young and old. When they were caught and held and tied together by ropes, Wang the Tiger commanded them to be brought to a certain large threshing floor before the head villager's house and there from his horse he glowered upon these wretched men. Some of them wept and trembled, and some were the color of clay, but some stood sullen and fearless having already known despair. Only the old men were tranquil and accepted whatever must come, since now they were so old, and every one of them expected death.

But Wang the Tiger when he saw he had them all, felt his killing anger cool in him. He could not kill as lustily as once he did; no, he had been secretly weaker since he killed the six men and saw his son's look. And to hide his weakness now he drew down his brows and pursed his lips and he roared at them,

"You deserve to die, every man of you! Have you not known me these many years that I will not have robbers in my lands? Yet I am a merciful man. I will remember your old parents and your little sons, and this time I will not kill you. No, I will save death for the next time you dare to disobey me and rob again." Then he called to his own men who surrounded the villagers and he said, "Draw out your sharp girdle knives and cut off their ears only, for a warning that they may remember what I have told them this day!"

Then the soldiers of Wang the Tiger stepped forward and they whetted their knives upon the soles of their shoes and they cut off the ears of the robbers and heaped the ears upon the ground before Wang the Tiger. And Wang the Tiger looked at the robbers, every man with two streams of his blood running down his cheeks, and he said,

"Let these ears of yours be sign of remembrance!"

Then he turned his horse and galloped away. And as he went his heart misgave him that perhaps he ought to have killed the robbers and finished them clean and so cleansed his regions, for such a death would have warned others, and his heart misgave him that perhaps he grew weak and too merciful, now as he grew old. But he comforted himself by saying to himself,

"It was for my son's sake I saved those lives, and some day I will tell him how for his sake I did not kill an hundred and seventy-three men, and it will please him."

XXIX

IN these ways did Wang the Tiger fill the months his son left him empty and alone in his house. When he had put down the robbers once more in his regions and when the harvests came on and helped him because the people were fed again, he took a small half of his army and in the autumn when it was neither cold with winds nor hot with sunshine, he went over all his lands once more, and he told himself he must see that all was ordered for his son when he returned. For now Wang the Tiger planned that when his son came back he would give over to him the generalship in these parts and he would give to him his vast army, keeping only a little guard for himself. He would be fifty and five years old and his son would be twenty years old, and a man. Dreaming such dreams Wang the Tiger rode over his lands and with his inward eye he saw here his son's son, and with his outward eye he marked the people and the land and what revenues there were and what promise of good harvest. Now that the famine had died away once more the lands did well, although land and people still showed the shadows of those two famine years, the land because it was not fully grown yet to crops, and the people because there were many still hollow cheeked and there were too few of old and young. But life had begun once more and it comforted Wang the Tiger to see many women great with child again and he said to himself, pondering,

"It may very well be that Heaven sent the famine to show me my destiny again, for I have rested too much in these last years and been too content with what I had. It may be the famine was sent to stir me up that I should be greater yet with such a son as I have to inherit all I do and gain."

For if Wang the Tiger was wiser than his old father had

been in his time and did not believe in a god of earth, yet he did believe in destiny and in heaven, and he would have said in all that befell him there was no chance at all, not in life nor in death, but that every life and every death was purposed and meet and came from heaven thus.

In this ninth month of the dying year he rode with his soldiers joyous behind him, and everywhere men greeted him somehow, because they knew him for a mighty man who had long ruled over them and justly, too, and they put smiles on their faces and if he stopped in a town, a feast was made for him by the elders of that town or village. Only the common farming folk were not courteous, and many a farmer when he saw the soldiers coming turned his back to the road and worked doggedly on in his field, and when they were passed he spat and spat again to free his heart of hatred. Yet if any soldier had asked him fiercely why he spat he would have covered his face with vacant innocence and answered,

"Because of so much dust that blew into my mouth from under the horses' feet that passed."

But Wang the Tiger did not need to care for any man, in town or countryside.

Now in his journeying he came to that city he had once besieged where his pocked nephew had lived these many years for him and Wang the Tiger sent messengers ahead to announce his coming, and he looked keenly to right and to left to see how this town had done under his nephew's rule.

This young man was no longer young; he was a man now, and with the silk weaver's daughter he had for wife he had begotten a son or two already, and when he heard his uncle came and was even at the city gates he was in greatest consternation. The truth was this fellow had lived many peaceful years here and he had lived very peacefully, and almost he had forgotten he was a soldier. He was always merry and easy in his ways, eager after pleasure and some new thing, and he liked his life here, for he had authority so that men were courteous to him, and he had no great work to do except to receive revenues and he grew fat. In these last years he had even taken off his soldier's garb and put on easier robes, and he looked like a prosperous merchant. Indeed, he was very good friends with merchants in the town, and when they paid their taxes into his hand for Wang the Tiger, he made his little profits too, as tradesmen do, and he used his uncle's name sometimes for a light tax on some new thing. But if the merchants knew it they did not blame him, seeing it is but what any man of them would do himself, and they liked the pocked fellow and they gave him gifts sometimes, knowing he might report what he pleased to his uncle and let evil descend upon them.

So Wang the Tiger's nephew lived this merry life, and his wife pleased him, for he was not over lusty, and not often tempted outside his own bed except on the few nights when some friend or other gave a feast more vast than usual and for a special treat had hired pretty maids for part of the night. To such feasts this man was always invited, both for his position in the town and for his own sake, because he was a witty clown and he had a tricky tongue that could make men roar with glee, especially if they were somewhat drunken.

Now when he heard his uncle came he hurried and bade his wife find his soldier's garb out of some box or other where she had thrust it, and he mustered out his soldiers who had lived too easily, too, and had been his servants more than soldiers, and as he pushed his fat legs into the garments he wondered how he ever had borne to wear such stiff hard garb. His belly had grown more full, too, than when he was a youth, and his clothing gaped there, so that he must needs tie a wide girdle about his middle to hide himself. But so garbed

458

somehow and his soldiers mustered somehow, too, they waited for Wang the Tiger to come in.

Now Wang the Tiger saw in a very few days all that had taken place and he saw the meaning of the vast feasts the merchants gave him and the magistrate also, and he saw very well that his nephew sweated in his soldier's garb, and he smiled coldly to himself one day when the winds died and the sun shone very hot and his nephew took off his coat he was so hot, and there his clothing gaped beneath his ill tied girdle. And Wang the Tiger thought to himself,

"I am glad I have a son who is a lordly man, and not like this one, my brother's son, who is but a tradesman after all!"

And he was negligent toward his nephew and did not praise him much and he said coldly,

"Your soldiers you control for me have forgot how to handle their guns. Doubtless they need a war again. Why do you not lead them out next spring and make them used to war?"

At this his nephew stammered and sweated, for the truth was that although he was no coward and he could have been a soldier if he had his life laid that way for him, he was not one to lead out men and make them fear him and he loved this life best now. When Wang the Tiger saw his uneasiness, he laughed his silent laugh and clapped his hand to his sword suddenly and he roared out,

"Well, Nephew, since you live so well and the town is so rich, doubtless we can raise our taxes! I am at mighty expense for my son in the south and I think to enlarge myself for him while he is away, and sacrifice yourself a little therefore and double my taxes for me!"

Now this nephew of his had made a secret bargain with the merchants that if his uncle sought to raise taxes he would cry poverty and hard times, and if he could persuade his uncle, he was to have a goodly sum for his reward. So he

459

began feebly to do now but Wang the Tiger was not moved at all by any such moan and he cried at last very roughly,

"I see what has come about here, and there are more ways of working against me than the way the Hawk had, but my remedy is the same!"

Then with a very rueful face for the good silver lost him, the nephew made report to the merchants and they sent in their own plaint and said,

"Yours is not the only tax. We have the city tax and the state tax, and yours is already higher than any, and it scarcely profits us to do any business."

But Wang the Tiger saw it was time to show his sword and he said bluntly, after courteous words had been spoken, "Yes, but power is with me, and I will take what is not given when I ask for it courteously."

In such ways did Wang the Tiger chasten his nephew and set him down in his place again, and in such ways did he make secure his hold over that city and over all his regions.

When all was sure and settled he went back to his house and he waited for the winter to end, and he busied himself sending out his spies and in making his plans and he dreamed of great conquests in the spring, and he dreamed that even now in his age, perhaps he could yet seize the whole province for his son.

Yes, all through that long winter Wang the Tiger held himself to that dream. It was the loneliest winter, so lonely that now and again almost he went into his women's courts he was so beside himself. But there was nothing for him there, for his ignorant wife lived alone with her daughters and Wang the Tiger had nothing to say to them, and so he only sat heavily on and alone and scarcely felt them his. Sometimes he wondered of his learned wife, but she had not come home these many years but she lived near her daughter who was

460

at some school. Once she sent a picture of herself and this young girl to Wang the Tiger, and Wang the Tiger had stared at it awhile. The girl was pretty. She had a small pert face and she looked boldly out of the picture, her eyes black and bold under her short hair, and he could not feel her his. Well he knew she would be one of those merry, talkative maids there were now-a-days, and he was speechless before them. Then he looked at that learned wife of his. He had never known her at all; no, not even in those days when he went to her in the night. He looked at her longer than at her daughter, and out of the picture she looked back at him and he felt again that unease he used to feel in her presence, as though she had something to say to him he would not hear, as though she made a demand on him for that he had not to give. And he muttered to himself, putting the picture out of his sight,

"A man has not time in his life for all these things—I have been very busy—I have had no time for women."

And he hardened himself a little and he thought it a virtue in him that not for many years had he gone even to his wives. He had never loved them.

But the loneliest hours were the hours when he sat alone in the night by his brazier. In the day he could busy himself somehow but here were the nights once more, and they hung on him dark and sad as once they had in the past. At such times he doubted himself and he felt himself old and he doubted whether even in the spring he could make any great new conquest. At such times he smiled painfully into the coals and gnawed his beard and he thought to himself sadly,

"It may be that no man ever does all he says he would," and after a while he thought again and said, "I suppose a man when his son is born, plans enough for three generations in his own lifetime."

But there was Wang the Tiger's old harelipped trusty man and he watched over his old master, and when he saw Wang the Tiger brooding over the coals in the night and without zest for his soldiers in the day so that he let them idle and do as they would, then the old trusty man came in without much speech and he brought with him a jug of hot good wine and a few salty meats to make thirst, and in many small ways he coaxed his master to ease. After a while Wang the Tiger did come out of himself and he drank a little and then more and he was cheered and could sleep. When he thus drank he thought before he slept,

"Well, and I have my son and what I cannot do in my one life, he will do."

In that winter without knowing it Wang the Tiger came to drink more wine than ever he had, and it was a great comfort to the old trusty man who loved him. If Wang the Tiger sometimes pushed the jug away the old man coaxed him earnestly,

"Drink, my general, for every man must have some little comfort when he grows old, and some little joy, and you are too hard with yourself."

To please him, then, and to show he valued him, Wang the Tiger would drink. Therefore he could sleep, even in this lonely winter, because he was eased like this, and when he had drunk he put his faith very ardently in his son and it slipped from his mind that there had been a difference between them. In these days it never came into Wang the Tiger's mind that his son's dreams might not be his own, and he lived for the spring.

But there came a night before the spring and Wang the Tiger sat in his room, warm and half sleeping, and his wine cooled on a little table at his hand, and he had unfastened his sword and laid it beside the jug of wine.

Suddenly out of the deep quiet of the winter's night he heard in the court a commotion of horses and soldiers' feet rushing in and stopping there. He rose up half standing, his hands upon the arms of his chair, not knowing whose soldiers these could be, and wondering if he dreamed. But before he could move further, one ran in and cried gladly,

"The little general, your son, is here!"

Now Wang the Tiger had drunk very deeply that night because of the cold and he could hardly come all at once to himself, and he drew his hand across his mouth and muttered,

"I thought in my dreams it was some enemy!"

He struggled out of his sleep, then, and stood up, and went out to the court by the great gate. It was light with the flaring of torches held by many hands, and in the midst of this brightness he saw his son. The young man had come down from his horse and he stood there waiting, and when he saw his father he bowed, but as he bowed he threw him a strange, half hostile look. Wang the Tiger shivered in the cold and he drew his coat closer and he faltered a little and asked his son, amazed,

"Where is your tutor—why are you here, my son?"

To this the young man replied, scarcely moving his lips,

"We are estranged. I have left him."

Then Wang the Tiger came out of his daze somewhat and he saw there was some trouble here not to be told before all these common soldiers who came pressing about and who were ever ready to hear a quarrel, and he turned and called his son to follow him. Then they went into Wang the Tiger's own room and Wang the Tiger commanded everyone to go out, and he was alone with his son. But he did not sit down.

463

No, he stood, and his son stood and Wang the Tiger looked at his son from head to foot, as though he had never seen this young man, who was his son. At last he said slowly,

"What strange garb is that you wear?"

To this the son lifted his head and he answered in his quiet, dogged way,

"It is the garb of the new army of the revolution." And he passed his tongue over his lips and stood waiting before his father.

In that instant Wang the Tiger understood what his son had done and who he now was, and he understood that this was the garb of the southern army in that new war he had heard rumored, and he shouted,

"It is the army of my enemy!"

He sat down suddenly then, for his breath caught in his throat and choked him. He sat there and felt his old murderous anger rise up in him as it had not since he killed the six men. He seized his narrow, keen sword from where it lay and he shouted in his old roaring way,

"You are my enemy—I ought to kill you, my son!"

He began to pant heavily, because this time his anger was strange and it came up in him so swiftly and strangely that it made him suddenly sick, and he swallowed again and again without knowing he did.

But the young man did not shrink now as he had been used to do when he was a child. No, he stood there quiet and dogged and he lifted his two hands and opened his coat and bared his smooth breast before his father. When he spoke it was with a deep bitterness, and he said,

"I knew you would want to kill me—it is your old and only remedy." He fixed his eyes on his father's face and he said without passion, "Kill me, then." And he stood ready and he waited, his face clear and hard in the candlelight.

464

But Wang the Tiger could not kill his son. No, even though he knew it was his right, and even though he knew any man may kill a son disloyal to him, and it will be counted to him for justice, yet he could not do it. He felt his anger checked at the flood, and then it began to stream out of him. He flung his sword upon the tiled floor, and he put his hand over his mouth to hide his lips, and he muttered,

"I am too weak—I am always too weak—after all, I am too weak for a lord of war—"

Then the young man, who saw his father sitting with his mouth thus covered under his hand and the sword flung down, covered his breast, and he spoke in a quiet and reasonable way, as though he reasoned with an old man.

"Father, I think you do not understand. None of you men who are old understand. You do not see our nation whole and how weak and despised—"

But Wang the Tiger laughed. He forced that silent laugh of his out and he made it loud and he said loudly, except he did not take his hand away,

"Do you think there never was such talk before? When I was young—you young men, you think you are the only ones—"

And Wang the Tiger forced out that strange, unused laugh of his that his son had never heard aloud in all his life. It goaded him as a strange weapon might, and it woke an anger in him his father had never seen and he shouted suddenly,

"We are not the same! Do you know what we call you? You are a rebel—a robber chief! If my comrades knew you they would call you traitor—but they do not even know your name—a petty lord of war in a little county town!"

So Wang the Tiger's son spoke, who had been patient all his life. Then he looked at his father, and in that same moment he was ashamed. He fell silent and the dark red came up his neck, and he looked down and began to unbuckle his leathern belt slowly and let it fall to the ground, and its bullets clattered there. And he said no more.

But Wang the Tiger answered nothing. He sat motionless in his chair, his mouth behind his hand. These words of his son's entered his understanding and some power began to ebb out of him and forever. He heard his son's words echo in his heart. Yes, he was only a petty lord of war—yes, a little lord of war in a small county town. Then he muttered behind his hand, feebly and as though from some old habit,

"But I have never been a robber chief."

His son was truly ashamed now, and he replied quickly, "No—no—no—" and then as though to cover his shame he said, "My father, I ought to tell you, I must hide away when my army comes north to victory. My tutor trained me well these many years and he counted on me. He was my captain— he will not easily forgive me that I chose you, my father—" The young man's voice dropped, and he glanced quickly at his father, and there was a secret tenderness in his look.

But Wang the Tiger made no answer. He sat as though he had not heard. The young man went on speaking, and he glanced every now and again at his father as though beseeching him for something.

"There is that old earthen house where I might hide. I could go there. If they went to seek me and found me they might look and see in a common farmer no son of a lord of war!" The young man made a little smile at this as though he hoped to coax his father to something through the feeble jest.

But Wang the Tiger made no answer. He did not understand the meaning of his son's words when he said, "I chose you, my father." No, Wang the Tiger sat still and over him rolled the bitterness of his whole life. He came out of his dreams in that moment as a man comes suddenly out of mists in which he has walked for a long time, and he looked at his son and saw there a man he did not know. Yes, Wang the Tiger had dreamed his son and shaped him faithfully to his dream, and here the son stood and Wang the Tiger did not know him. A common farmer! Wang the Tiger looked and saw his son, and as he looked he felt an old, known helplessness come creeping over him again. It was the same sick helplessness he had been used to feel in the days of his youth when the earthen house was his gaol. Once more his father, that old man in the land, reached out and laid his earthy hand upon his son. And Wang the Tiger looked sidewise at that own son of his and he muttered behind his hand, as to himself,

"—No son of a lord of war!"

Suddenly it seemed to Wang the Tiger that even his hand could no longer stay the trembling of his lips. He must weep. And so he must have done except at that instant the door opened and his trusty old harelipped man came in, bearing a jug of wine, and the wine was freshly heated, smoking and fragrant.

This old trusty man looked at his master as ever he did when he came into his room, and now he saw that which made him run forward as fast as he was able, and he poured the hot wine into the bowl that stood empty upon the table.

Then at last Wang the Tiger took his hand away from his lips and he reached eagerly for the wine and put it to his lips and he drank deeply. It was good—hot, and very good. He held the bowl out again and whispered,

"More."

—After all, he would not weep.

A HOUSE DIVIDED

I

IN this way Wang Yuan, son of Wang the Tiger, entered for the first time in his life the earthen house of his grandfather, Wang Lung.

Wang Yuan was nineteen years old when he came home from the south to quarrel with his father. On a winter's night when snow drifted now and again out of the north wind against the lattices the Tiger sat alone in his great hall, brooding over the burning coals in the brazier, as he loved to do, and always he dreamed that his son would come home one day, a man, grown and ready to lead out his father's armies into such victories as the Tiger had planned but had not seized because age caught him first. On that night Wang Yuan, the Tiger's son, came home when none expected him.

He stood before his father, and the Tiger saw his son clothed in a uniform new to him. It was the uniform of the revolutionists who were the enemies of all lords of war such as the Tiger was. When its full meaning came to the old man he struggled to his feet out of his dreaming, and he stared at his son and he fumbled for the narrow keen sword he kept always beside him and he was about to kill his son as he might kill any enemy. But for the first time in his life the Tiger's son showed the anger he had in him but which he had never dared to show before his father. He tore open his blue coat and he bared his smooth young breast, brown and smooth, and he cried out in a loud young voice, "I knew you would want to kill me—it is your old and only remedy! Kill me, then!"

But even as he cried the young man knew his father could not kill him. He saw his father's upraised arm drop slowly down and the sword fell mildly through the air, and staring at his father steadily, the son saw his father's lip tremble as though he would weep, and he saw the old man put his hand to his lips to fumble at his mouth to steady it.

At this moment when the father and son stood thus facing each other, the old trusty hare-lipped man, who had served the Tiger since both were young, came in with the usual hot wine to soothe his master before he slept. He did not see the young man at all. He saw only his old master, and when he saw that shaken face, and that feeble changing look of anger suddenly dying, he cried out and running forward, he poured wine quickly. Then Wang the Tiger forgot his son and he dropped his sword and with his two trembling hands he reached for the bowl and he lifted it to his lips and he drank again and again, while the trusty man poured out more and yet more from the pewter jug he held. And again and again the Tiger muttered, "More wine—more wine—" and he forgot to weep.

The young man stood and watched them. He watched the two old men, the one eager and childish in the comfort of the hot wine after his hurt and the other bending to pour the wine, his hideous split face puckered with his tenderness. They were only two old men, whose minds at even such a moment were filled with the thought of wine and its comfort.

The young man felt himself forgotten. His heart, which had been beating so hard and hot, turned cold in his bosom, and a tightness in his throat melted suddenly into tears. But he would not let the tears fall. No, some of the hardness he had learned in that school of war served him now. He stooped and picked up the belt he had thrown down, and without a word he went aside, holding his body very straight as he went, into a room where he had been wont to sit as a child to study with his young tutor, who later was his captain in the school of war. In the darkness of the room he felt to find the chair beside the desk, and he sat down, and he let his body be slack, since his heart was so dashed.

It came to him now that he need not have let himself be so passionate with fear for his father—no, nor so passionate with love for him, either, that for this old man's sake he had forsaken his comrades and his cause. Over and over again Wang Yuan thought of his father as he had just seen him, as he even now was in that hall where he sat drinking his wine. With new eyes he saw his father, and he could scarcely believe this was his father, the Tiger. For Yuan had always feared his father and yet loved him, though unwillingly and always with a secret inner rebellion. He feared the Tiger's sudden rages and his roarings and the swift way he thrust out the narrow bright sword he kept always near at hand. As a little lonely lad Yuan waked often in the night, sweating because he dreamed he had somehow made his father angry, although he need not have been so fearful, since the Tiger could not be truly angry with his son for long. But the lad saw him often angry or seeming angry with others, for the Tiger used his anger as a weapon with which to rule his men, and in the darkness of the night the lad shivered beneath his quilts when he remembered his father's rounded, glaring eyes and the way he jerked his coarse black whiskers when he raged. It had been a joke among the men, a half-fearful joke, to say, "It is better not to pull the Tiger's whiskers!"

Yet with all his angers the Tiger loved his son only, and Yuan knew it. He knew it and he feared it, for this love was like an anger, too, it was so hot and petulant and it lay so heavy on the child. For there were no women in the Tiger's courts to cool the ardor of his heart. Other lords of war when they rested from their battles and grew old took women to amuse them, but Wang the Tiger took not one. Even his own wives he did not visit, and one, the daughter of a physician who, being an only child, had inherited silver that her father gave her, was years gone to a great coastal city where she lived with her own daughter, the only child she ever bore the Tiger, to give her learning in a foreign

3

sort of school. Therefore to Yuan his father had been everything of love and fear, and this mingled love and fear were hidden hands upon him. He was held imprisoned and his mind and spirit were fettered often by this fear of his father and the knowledge of his father's only, centered love.

Thus had his father held him fast, although the Tiger did not know he did, in that hardest hour Yuan had ever known, when in the southern school of war his comrades stood before their captain and swore themselves for this new great cause, that they would seize the very seat of government of their country and put down the weak man who sat there, and wage a war for the good common people who now were at the cruel mercy of the lords of war and of the foreign enemies from abroad, and so build the nation great again. In that hour when youth after youth so swore his life away, Wang Yuan drew apart, held by fear and love of his father, who was such a lord of war as these cried against. His heart was with his comrades. A score of harsh memories were in his mind of the suffering common people. He could remember their looks when they saw their good grain trampled down by the horses of his father's men. He could remember the helpless hate and fear upon an elder's face in some village when the Tiger demanded, however courteously, a tax of food or silver for his men. He could remember dead bodies lying on the ground and meaningless to his father and his men. He could remember floods and famines, and once how he had ridden with his father on a dike, and water was everywhere about, and that dike was dark with lean hunger-ridden men and women, so that the soldiers must be ruthless lest they fall on the Tiger and his precious son. Yes, Yuan remembered these and many other things and he remembered how he had winced to see these things and hated himself that he was a war lord's son. Even as he stood among his comrades he had so hated himself, even when for his own father's sake he withdrew secretly from the cause he would have liked to serve.

4

Alone in the darkness of his old childish room, Yuan remembered this sacrifice for his father, and to him at this hour it was all a waste. He wished he had not made it, since his father could not understand it and did not value it. For this old man had Yuan left his own generation and their comradeship, and what did the Tiger care? Yuan felt himself misused and misunderstood his whole life long, and suddenly he remembered every little hurt his father ever gave him, how he had forced his son out to see his men do their feints of war when the lad was reading a book that he loved and was loath to leave it, and how his father had shot down the men who had come to beg for food. Remembering many such hateful things, Yuan muttered behind his closed teeth, "He has never loved me all his life long! He thinks he loves me and that he holds me the only dear thing he has, and yet never once has he asked me what I really want to do, or if he did, it was to refuse me if what I said was not his wish, so that I always must take thought to say what he wanted and I have had no freedom!"

Then Yuan thought of his comrades and how they must despise him, and how he now would never have a share with them in making his country great, and he muttered rebelliously, "I never did want to go to that school of war at all but he must force me to go there or nowhere!"

This soreness and loneliness grew in Yuan so that he swallowed hard and blinked his eyes quickly in the darkness and he muttered furiously as a hurt child mutters to himself, "For all my father knows or cares or understands, I might as well have turned a revolutionist! I might as well have followed after my captain, for now I have no one—no one at all—"

So Yuan sat on alone, feeling himself the loneliest soul and very dreary, and none came near him. Throughout the hours left of the night not even one serving man came near to see how he did. There was not one who did not know that Wang the Tiger, their master, was angry with his son, for while the two quarrelled

5

there were eyes and ears at the lattices, and now none dared to turn that anger on himself by comforting the son. It was the first time Yuan was paid no heed, and so he was the more lonely.

He sat on and would not search for any way to light a candle nor would he shout for any serving man. He folded his arms upon the desk and put down his head upon them and he let the waves of melancholy sweep over him as they would. But at last he slept because he was so weary and so young.

When he woke it was faint dawn. He lifted up his head quickly and looked about him; then he remembered he had quarrelled with his father, and he felt all the soreness of it in him still. He rose, and he went to the outer door upon the court and looked out. The court was still and empty and grey in the wan light. The wind was dead and the snow had melted as it fell in the night. By the gate a watchman slept, huddled in a corner of the wall for warmth, his hollow bamboo and his stick with which he beat upon it to frighten thieves away laid down upon the tiles. Looking at the man's sleeping face, Yuan thought with gloom how hideous was its slackness, the jaw loose and hanging and open to show the ragged teeth; although the man was at heart a very kindly fellow and one to whom in his childhood, and not many years ago, either, Yuan had often turned for sweets and toys at street fairs and such things. But to him now the man seemed only old and hideous and one who cared nothing for his young master's pain. Yes, Yuan now told himself, his whole life had been empty here and he was suddenly wild with rebellion against it. It was no new rebellion. It was the breaking of the secret war he now felt had always been between him and his father, a war grown he scarcely knew how.

In his childish early days Yuan's western tutor had taught him, trained him, plied him with the talk of revolution, of reshaping the nation, until his child's heart was all afire with the meaning of the great brave lovely words. Yet he always felt the fire dis

6

when his tutor dropped his voice low and said most earnestly, "And you must use the army that is one day to be yours; for country's sake you must use it, because we must have no more of these war lords."

So unknown to Wang the Tiger did this hireling subtly teach his son against him. And the child looked miserably into the shining eyes of his young tutor, and he listened to the ardent voice, moved to his core, yet checked by words he could not speak, although the words shaped too clearly in his heart, "Yet my father is a lord of war!" Thus was the child torn secretly throughout his childhood, and none knew it. It made him grave and silent and always heavy-hearted beyond his years, because though he loved his father, he could take no pride in him.

In this pale dawn, therefore, Yuan was wearied past his strength with all these years of war within himself. He was of a mind to run away from it, and from every war he knew, from cause of every kind. But where might he go? He had been so guarded, so kept within these walls by his father's love, that he had no friends and nowhere he could turn.

Then he remembered the most peaceful place he had ever seen in all the midst of war and talk of wars in which he had been from childhood. It was the small old earthen house in which his grandfather once lived, Wang Lung, called the Farmer until he grew rich and founded his house and moved it from the land so that he was called Wang the Rich Man. But the earthen house still stood on the edge of a hamlet and on three sides were quiet fields. Near it, Yuan remembered, were the graves of his ancestors set upon a rising bit of land, Wang Lung's grave, and other graves of his family. And Yuan knew, because once or twice or more, he had passed there as a child when his father visited his two elder brothers, Wang the Landlord and Wang the Merchant, who lived there in the nearest city to the earthen house.

Now, Yuan told himself, it would be peaceful in that small old house and he could be alone, for it was empty except for the

7

aged tenants his father let live there since a certain still and grave-faced woman Yuan remembered had gone to be a nun. He had seen her once with two strange children, one a grey-haired fool who died, and one a hunchback, his elder uncle's third son, who became a priest. He remembered he thought the grave woman almost a nun even when he saw her, for she turned her face away and would not look at any man, and she wore grey robes crossed upon her breast; only her head was not yet shaven. But her face was very like a nun's face, pale as a waning moon is pale, the skin delicate and tightly stretched across her small bones, and looking young until one came near and saw the fine and hair-like wrinkles on it.

But she was gone now. The house was empty except for the two old tenants and he might go there.

Then Yuan turned into his room again, eager to be off now he knew where to go, and he longed to be away. But first he must take off his soldier's uniform he hated, and opening a pigskin box, he searched for some robes he used to wear and he found a sheepskin robe and cloth shoes and white inner garments, and he put them on in haste and gladly. Then silently he went to fetch his horse, stealing through the brightening court, past a guardsman sleeping with his head pillowed on his gun, and Yuan went out, leaving the gates ajar, and he sprang upon his horse.

After Yuan had ridden awhile he came out from the streets and into lanes and alleys and out from those into the fields, and he saw the sun come slipping up beneath a blaze of light behind the distant hills, and suddenly it rose, nobly red and clear in the cold air of that late winter's morning. It was so beautiful that before he knew it some of his dolefulness was gone and in a moment he felt himself hungry. He stopped then at a wayside inn, from whose door, cut low in earthen walls, the smoke streamed out warmly and enticingly, and he bought hot gruel of rice, a salty fish and wheaten bread sprinkled thick with sesame, and a brown pot of tea. When he had eaten everything and had drunk the tea and rinsed his mouth, and paid the yawning keeper of the inn, who combed himself the while and washed his face cleaner than it had been, Yuan mounted on his horse again. By now the high clear sun was glittering on the small frosty wheat and on the frosty thatch of village houses.

Then being after all young, on such a morning Yuan felt suddenly that no life, even his, could be wholly evil. His heart lifted and he remembered, as he went on, looking over the land, that he always said he would like to live where trees and fields were, and with the sight and sound of water somewhere near, and he thought to himself, "Perhaps this is now what I may do. I may do what I like, seeing that no one cares." And while he had this small new hope rising in him before he knew it words were twisting in his mind and shaping into verse and he forgot his troubles.

For Yuan in these years of his youth found in himself a turn for shaping verses, little delicate verses which he brushed upon the backs of fans and upon the whitewashed walls of rooms he lived in anywhere. His tutor had laughed at these verses always, because Wang Yuan wrote of soft things such as leaves dropping down on autumn waters, or willows newly green above a pool or peach blossoms rosy through the white spring mists or the dark rich curls of land newly ploughed, and all like gentle things. He never wrote of war or glory, as the son of a war lord should, and when his comrades pressed him to a song of revolution until he wrote it, it was too mild for their desire, because it spoke of dying rather than of victory, and Yuan had been distressed at their displeasure. He murmured, "So the rhymes came," and he would not try again, for he had a store of stubbornness in him and much secret willfulness for all his outward quietude and seeming docility, and after this he kept his verses to himself.

Now for the first time in his life Yuan was alone and at the behest of no one, and this was wonderful to him, and the more because here he was, riding alone through such land as he loved to see. Before he knew it the edge of his melancholy was tempered. His youth came up in him and he felt his body fresh and strong and the air was good in his nostrils, very cold and clean, and soon he forgot everything except the wonder of a little verse rising shaped out of his mind. He did not hasten it. He gazed about him at the bare hills, now mounting sandy clear and sharp against the blue unspotted sky and he waited for his verse to come as clear as they, as perfect as a hill bare against an unclouded heaven.

So this sweet lonely day passed, soothing him in passing, so that he could forget love and fear and comrades and all wars. When night came he lay at a country inn, where the keeper was an old solitary man and his quiet second wife was not too young and so did not find her life dull with the old husband. Yuan was the only guest that night, and the pair served him well, and the woman gave him little loaves of bread stuffed with fragrant seasoned pork ground small. When Yuan had eaten and had supped his tea, he went to the bed spread out for him and he lay weary with good weariness, and though before he slept the memory of his father and the quarrel came stabbing once or twice, yet he could forget this, too. For before the sun had set that day his verse came clear as he had dreamed it, shaped to his wish, four perfect lines, each word a crystal, and he slept comforted.

After three such free days, each better than its yesterday, and all full of winter sunshine, dry as powdery glass upon the hills and valleys, Yuan came riding, healed and somehow hopeful, to the hamlet of his ancestors. At high morning he rode into the little street and saw its thatched earthen houses, a score or so in all, and he looked about him eagerly. About the street were the farmers and their wives and children, standing at their doorways, or squatting at their thresholds upon their heels, eating bread and gruel for their meal. To Yuan they seemed all good folk, and all his friends and he felt warmly to them. Over and over had he heard his captain cry the cause of the common people, and here they were.

But they looked back at Yuan most doubtfully and in great fearful wonder, for the truth was that although Yuan hated wars and ways of war, yet although he did not know it, still he looked a soldier. Whatever was his heart, Yuan's father had shaped his body tall and strong and he sat his horse uprightly as a general does, and not slack and anyhow as a farmer may.

So these people now looked at Yuan doubtfully, not knowing what he was and fearful always of a stranger and his ways. The many children of the hamlet, their bits of bread clutched in their hands, ran after him to see where he was bound, and when he came to the earthen house he knew, they stood there in a circle, staring at him steadily, and gnawing at their ends of bread, and pushing each other here and there, and snuffling at their noses while they stared. When they were wearied of such staring, they ran back one by one to tell their elders that the tall black young man had come down from his high red horse before the house of Wang, and that he tied his horse to a willow tree and that he went into the house, but when he went in he stooped because he was so tall the door of that house was too low for him. And Yuan heard their shrill voices shouting these things in the street, but he cared nothing for such children's talk. But the elders doubted him the more after they heard their children and none went near that earthen house of Wang, lest there be some evil about to come upon them from the tall black young man, who was a stranger to them.

So did Yuan enter as a stranger this house of his forefathers who lived upon the land. He went into the middle room and he stood there and he looked about him. The two old tenants heard the noise of his entering and they came in from the kitchen and when they saw him they did not know who he was and they too were afraid. Then seeing them afraid, Yuan smiled a little and he said, "You need not be afraid of me. I am son of Wang the General, called the Tiger, who is third son of my grandfather Wang Lung, who lived here once."

This he said to reassure the old pair to show them his right to be there, but they were not reassured. They looked at each other in greater consternation and the bread they held ready in their mouths to swallow went dry and stuck in their throats like stones. Then the old woman put down upon the table the stick of bread she held and she wiped her mouth with the back of her hand and the old man held his jaws still and he came forward and ducked his tousled head in a bow and he said, trembling and trying to swallow down his dry bread, "Sir and Honored, what can we do to serve you, and what would you have of us?"

Then Yuan sat down on a bench and smiled a little again and shook his head and answered freely, for he remembered how he had heard these people praised and so need not fear them, "I want nothing at all except to shelter myself here awhile in this house of my fathers—perhaps I may even live here—I do not know, except I have always had the strangest longing after fields and trees and water somewhere, although I know nothing, either, of such life on the land. But it happens just now I must hide myself awhile, and I will hide here."

This he said still to reassure them and again they were not reassured. They looked back and forth to each other and now the old man laid down his stick of bread, too, and he said earnestly, his wrinkled face anxious and his few white hairs trembling on his chin, "Sir, this is a very ill place to hide. Your house, your name, are so well known hereabouts—and, sir, forgive me that I am only a rude coarse man who does not know how even to speak before such as you—but your honored father is not loved well because he is a lord of war, and your uncles are not loved, either." The old man paused and looked about him and then he whispered into Yuan's very ear, "Sir, the people on the land here so hated your elder uncle that he and his lady grew afraid and with their sons they went to a coastal city to live where foreign soldiers keep the peace, and when your second uncle comes to collect the rents, he comes with a band of soldiers he has hired from the town! The times are ill, and men on the land have suffered so full their shares of wars and taxes that they are desperate. Sir, we have paid taxes ten years ahead. This is no good place for hiding for you, little general."

And the old woman wrapped her cracked, gnarled hands into her apron of patched blue cotton cloth, and she piped also, "Truly it is no good place to hide, sir!"

So the pair stood doubtful and eager and hoping he would not stay.

But Yuan would not believe them. He was so glad to be free, so pleased with all he saw, so cheered by the bright shining day, he would have stayed in spite of anything, and he smiled with his pleasure and he cried willfully, "Yet I will stay! Do not trouble yourselves. Only let me eat what you eat and I will live here awhile, at least."

And he sat in the simple room and looked about him at the plow and harrow set against the wall, at the strings of red peppers hanging there, and at the dried fowl or two and onions tied together, and he was pleased with everything, it was so new to him.

Suddenly he was hungry and the bread wrapped about garlic, which the old pair had been eating, seemed good to him, and he said, "I am hungry. Give me something to eat, good mother."

Then the old woman cried, "But, sir, what have I fit for a lord like you? I must first k ll a fowl out of our four—I have only this poor bread, not even made of wheaten flour!"

"I like it—I like it!" answered Yuan most heartily. "I like everything here."

So at last, although doubtful still, she brought him a fresh sheet of bread rolled into a stick about a stem of garlic, but she could not be content until she found a bit of fish she had salted in the autumn and saved, and this she brought him for a dainty. He ate it all, and it was good meat to him, good above any he had ever eaten, because he ate in freedom.

When he had eaten he was suddenly weary, although until then he had not known he was, and he rose and asked, "Where is a bed? I would like to sleep awhile."

The old man replied, "There is a room here we do not use commonly, a room where your grandfather lived once, and after that the lady who was his third, a lady we all loved, so holy good she turned a nun at last. There is a bed in that room where you may rest."

And he pushed a wooden door at the side and Yuan saw a little dark old room that had for window only a small square hole over which white paper was pasted, a quiet, empty room. He went into it and shut the door and for the first time in his guarded life he felt himself truly alone for sleep, and loneliness was good to him.

Yet as he stood in the midst of this dim, earth-walled room, for a moment he had the strangest sudden sense of some stout old life going on there still. He looked about, wondering. It was the simplest room he had seen in his life, a hemp-curtained bed, an unpainted table and a bench, the floor the worn and beaten earth where many feet had worn hollows by the bed and door. There was no one there except himself, and yet he felt a spirit near, an earthy lusty spirit he did not understand. . . . Then it was gone. Suddenly he ceased to feel the other life and he was alone again. He smiled and was so sweetly weary he must sleep, for his eyes were closing of their own will. He went to the great wide country bed, and he parted the curtains and he threw himself down, and he wrapped about him an old blue-flowered quilt he found rolled there against the inner wall. In the same moment he was asleep and so he rested in the deep quiet of the ancient house.

When at last Yuan awoke it was night. He sat up in the darkness and parted the curtains of the bed quickly and looked into the room. Even the square of pale light in the wall had faded, and there was only soft, silent darkness everywhere. He lay back again, resting as he had never rested in his life because he woke alone. It was good to him to see even no servant standing near to wait for his awakening. For this hour he would not think of anything, only of this good silence everywhere. There was no single noise, no grunting of some rough guardsman who turned himself in sleep, no clatter of a horse's hoofs upon a tiled courtyard, no shriek of a sword drawn suddenly from its scabbard. There was nothing but the sweetest silence.

Yet suddenly there came a sound. Out of the silence Yuan heard a sound, the sound of people moving in the middle room, of whispering. He turned himself upon the bed, and looked through the curtains to the ill-hung unpainted door. It opened slowly, a little, and then more. He saw a beam of candlelight, and in the beam a head. Then this head was pulled back again and another peered in, and beneath it more heads. Yuan moved then upon the bed so that it creaked and at once the door shut, softly and quickly, a hand pulling it closed, and then the room was dark again.

But now he could not sleep. He lay wondering and awake, and he wondered if already his father had guessed his refuge and sent someone to fetch him. When he thought of this, he swore to himself he would not rise. Yet he could not lie still either, being so full of his impatient wonder. Then suddenly he thought of his horse and how he had left it tied to a willow tree upon the threshing floor, and how he had not bade the old man feed or tend it, and it might still be waiting there, and he rose, for he was soft-hearted about such things more than most men are. The room was chill now and he wrapped his sheepskin coat closely around him, and he found his shoes and thrust his feet into

15

them, and he felt his way along the wall to the door and opened it and went in.

There in the lighted middle room he saw a score or so of farmers, both young and old, and when they saw him they rose, first this one and then that, all staring at him and when he looked at them astonished, he saw not one face he knew, except the old tenant's face. Then came forth a decent-looking, blue-clad farmer, the eldest of them all, his white hair still braided and hanging down his back in an old country fashion, and he bowed and said to Yuan, "We come to give you greeting, who are the elders of this hamlet."

Yuan bowed a little and he bade them all be seated, and he sat down, too, in the highest seat beside the bare table, which had been left empty for him. He waited, and at last the old man asked, "When does your honored father come?"

Yuan answered simply, "He is not coming. I am here for a while to live alone."

At this the men all looked at each other with pale looks, and the old man coughed again and said, and it could be seen he was spokesman for them all, "Sir, we are poor folk here in this hamlet, and we are much despoiled already. Sir, since your elder uncle lives in that far foreign city on the coast, he spends more money than he ever did, and rentals have been taken from us forcefully far more than we can pay. There is the tax we pay the lord of war, and the toll we pay the robber bands to keep them off us, and we have almost nothing left to live on. Yet tell us what your price is and we will pay you somehow so that you may go elsewhere and so spare us more sorrow here."

Then Yuan looked about him in amazement, and he said, with sharpness, too, "It is a strange thing I cannot come to my grandfather's house without such talk as this! I want no money from you." And after a moment, looking at their honest, doubtful faces, he said again, "It may be best to tell the truth and trust you. There is a revolution coming from the south, and it comes

16

against the lords of war in the north, and I, my father's son, could not take arms against him, no, not even with my comrades. So I escaped by night and day and with my guardsmen I came home, and my father was angry when he saw my garb, and so we quarrelled. And I thought I would take refuge here for a while, lest my captain be so angry with me that he search me out to kill me secretly, so I came here."

And Yuan stopped himself and looked about the grave faces, and again he said very earnestly, for now he was eager to persuade them, and a little angry at their doubtfulness, "Yet I did not come for refuge only. I came also because I have the greatest love for the quietness of land. My father shaped me for a lord of war, but I hate blood and killing and the stink of guns and all the noise of armies. Once when I was a child I came by this house with my father and I saw a lady and two strange children here, and even then I envied them, so that while I lived among my comrades at a school of war, I thought about this place, and how some day I might come here. And I envy you, too, who have your homes here in this hamlet."

At this the men looked at each other again, none understanding or believing that anyone could envy the life they had, because to them it was so bitter. They were only more filled with doubt of this young man who sat there speaking in his eager willful open way because he said he loved an earthen house. Well they knew how he had lived, and in what luxury, for they knew how his cousins lived, and how his uncles, the one like a prince in a far city, and Wang the Merchant, now their landlord, who grew rich so monstrously and secretly upon his usury. These two they all hated, while they envied them their riches, too, and they looked with coming hatred and with fear upon this young man, saying in their hearts they knew he lied, because they could not believe there was in the whole world a man who would choose an earthen nouse when he might have a great one.

They rose, then, and Yuan rose, too, scarcely knowing if he

need or not, since he was not used to rise except to his few superiors and he scarcely knew where to put these plain men, dressed in patched coats and in loose and faded cotton garments. But still he wished to please them somehow, so he rose, and they bowed to him and said a thing or two in courtesy, and they answered, their doubts clear enough upon their simple faces, and then they went away.

There were left only the old tenant and his wife, and they looked anxiously at Yuan and at last the old man began to plead, and he said, "Sir, tell us truly why you are here so that we may know ahead what evils are to come. Tell us what war your father plans, that he sends you out to spy. Help us poor folk, who are at the mercy of the gods and of the lords of war and of the rich men and governors and all such mighty evil ones!"

Then Yuan answered, understanding now their fearfulness, "I am no spy, I say! My father did not send me—I have told everything, and told it truly."

Still the old pair, too, could not believe him. The man sighed and turned away, and the woman stood in piteous silence and Yuan did not know what to do with them, and was about to be impatient with them, until remembering his horse he asked, "What of my horse?—I forgot—"

"I led him to the kitchen, sir," the old man answered. "I fed him with some straw and dried peas, and drew him water from the pond." And when Yuan thanked him, he said, "It is nothing —are you not my old master's grandson?" And at this suddenly he dropped to his knees before Yuan and groaned aloud, "Sir, once your grandfather was one of us upon the land—a common man like us. He lived here in this hamlet as we do. But his destiny was better than ours is, who have lived on poor and hardly always —yet for his sake who once was like us, tell us truly why you are come!"

Then Yuan lifted up the old man, and not too gently, either, because he began to be very weary of all this doubt, and he was used to being believed in what he said, being son of a great man, and he cried, "It is only as I say, and I will not say it over! Wait and see if any evil comes through me upon you!" And to the woman he said, "Bring me food, good wife, because I am hungry!"

They served him then in silence, and he ate the food. But it seemed not so good to him tonight as it had been earlier, and he soon had enough of it, and at last he rose with no more words and went again and lay down upon the bed for sleep. For a while he could not sleep, because he found an anger in him against these simple men. "Stupid fellows!" he cried to himself. "If they are honest, still they are stupid—knowing nothing in this little place —shut off—" And he doubted they were worth fighting for, after all, and he felt himself very wise beside them, and comforted by his greater wisdom he fell asleep again deeply in the darkness and the stillness.

Six days Yuan lived in the earthen house before his father found him, and they were the sweetest days of his whole life. No one came again to ask him of anything and the old pair served him silently and he forgot their doubts of him and he thought of neither past nor future, but only of each day. He did not enter any town nor go once to see his uncle in the great house, even. Each night at dark he lay down to sleep, and he rose early every morning in the sharp wintry sunlight, and even before he ate he looked out of the door across the fields now faintly green with winter wheat. The land stretched out before him, far and smooth and plain, and he could see, upon its smoothness, the flecks of blue which were men and women working to make the earth ready for the soon coming of spring, or some who came and went across the paths to town or village. And every morning he thought of verses, and he remembered every beauty of the distant hills, carved out of sandy stone and set against a blue cloudless sky, and for the first time he saw the beauty of his country.

All his childhood long Yuan had heard his captain use those two words "my country," or he said "our country," or sometimes to Yuan he said most earnestly "your country." But Yuan had felt no quickening when he heard them. The truth was Yuan had lived a very small, close life in those courts with his father. He had not often gone even into the camp where the soldiers brawled and ate and slept and even when the Tiger went abroad for war Wang Yuan lived on surrounded by his special guard of quiet men in middle years, who were bade to be silent near their young lord and tell no idle, lustful tales. So always there were soldiers standing near Yuan between him and what he might have seen.

Now every day he looked where he would, and there was nothing between him and all that he could see about him. He could see straight to where the sky met earth, and he could see the little wooded hamlets here and there upon the land, in the distance to the west the wall of the town, black and serrated against the porcelain sky. Thus looking every day as far and freely as he would, and walking on the earth or riding on his horse, it came into his mind that now he knew what "country" was. Those fields, this earth, this very sky, those pale, lovely, barren hills, these were his country.

And here came a strange thing, that Yuan ceased even to ride his horse because it seemed to lift him off the land. At first he rode because he had always ridden a horse, and to ride was to him the same as using his own feet. But now everywhere he went the farming people stared at him, and they always said to one another, if they did not know him, "Well, that is a soldier's horse, surely, and it never carried any honest load," and within two or three days' time he heard the gossip of him spread and people said, "There is that son of Wang the Tiger, riding his great high horse everywhere and lording it as all his family do. Why is he here? It must be he looks upon the land and tallies crops for his father and plans some new tax on us for war." It came to be that whenever Yuan rode by they looked sourly at him and then turned away and spat into the dust.

At first this scornful spitting made Yuan angry and aston-ished, for it was new to him to be so treated, who had never feared anyone except his father, and who had been used to ser-vants hurrying to his bidding. But after a time he fell to thinking why it was, and how these people had been so oppressed, for so he had learned in the school of war, and then he turned good-humored again and let them spit to ease themselves.

At last he even left his horse tied to the willow tree and walked and although it came a little hardly to him at first to use his own legs, yet in a day or two he was used to it. He put aside his usual leathern shoes and wore the straw sandals that the farmers wore, and he liked to feel beneath his feet the solid earth of path and roads, dry with the months of winter sunshine. He liked to pass a man and meet his stare as though he were any stranger and not a war lord's son to be cursed and feared.

In those few days Yuan learned to love his country as he never had. And being so free and lonely, his verses rose shaped and shining and ready to be written down. He had scarcely even to search out a word but only to write down what was in him. There was no book or paper in the earthen house, and only an old pen that once his grandfather had bought, perhaps, to set his mark on some purchase deed for land. Yet still the pen could be used, and with it and a broken bit of dried ink block he found Yuan brushed his verses on the whitewashed walls in the middle room, while the old tenant stared, admiring yet half fearful of the magic written unknown words. And now Yuan wrote new verses, not only of willows brushing silent pools, or of floating clouds and silver rains and falling flower petals. The new verses welled up from some deeper place within him, and they were not so smoothly written, for he told of his country and his new love of it. Where once his verses were pretty, empty shapes, like lovely bubbles on the surface of his mind, now they were not so pretty, but were filled more full of some meaning which he struggled with, not understanding wholly, coming with rougher rhythm and uneven music.

Thus the days passed, and Yuan lived alone with his great swelling thoughts. What his future might be he did not know. No clear form of anything came to his mind to make his future plain. He was content for this time to breathe in the hard bright beauty of this northern land, glittering in the cloudless sun, its very light seeming blue, it poured down from so blue a sky. He listened to the talk and laughter of the people in the little hamlet streets; he mingled with the men who sat at wayside inns, listening, seldom speaking, as one listens to a language scarcely understood, but very sweet-sounding to the ear and heart; he rested in the peace where there was no talk of war, but only of the village gossip, what son was born, what land was sold or bought and what its price, what man or maid was to be wed, what seed due to be sown, and such good common things.

His pleasure in all this grew greater every day, and when it grew too great, a verse came shaped into his mind, and he wrote it down also, and so was eased awhile, although here was a thing so strange it made him wonder at himself even, that while he found pleasure in these days, his verses came up out of him always not merry but tinged with deep melancholy, as though there were in him some hidden well of sadness, and he did not know why this was.

Yet how could he live on like this, the Tiger's only son? Everywhere the country folk were saying, "There is a strange tall black young man who wanders here and there like one witless. They say he is the son of Wang the Tiger, and nephew to Wang the Merchant. But how can son of men as great as these wander like this alone? He lives in that old earthen house of Wang Lung, and it must be he is out of his mind."

This rumor reached even to the ears of Wang the Merchant in

the town and he heard it from an old chief clerk in his counting house, and he said sharply, "Of course it is no brother's son of mine, for I have seen and heard nothing of him. And is it likely true that my brother would let free his precious only son in such a way? I will send out a serving man tomorrow and see who it is who lives in my father's tenant house. I gave no one such a leave to live there for my brother." And secretly he feared the sojourner might be some pretending, robber spy.

But the tomorrow never came, for those at the Tiger's camp had heard the rumor, too. That day Wang Yuan rose as his habit was now and even as he stood in the doorway eating bread and sipping tea, and looking out across the land and dreaming, he saw in the distance a chair borne upon men's shoulders and then another and about them walked a guard of soldiers, and he knew the soldiers for his father's by their garb. He went inside the door then, suddenly not able to eat or drink any more, and he put the food down on the table and stood waiting, and to himself he thought most bitterly, "It is my father, I suppose— and what shall we say to each other?" And he would have liked to run away across the fields like any child, except he knew this meeting must come upon some day or other, and he could not run away forever. So he waited very troubled, and forcing back his old childish fear, and he could eat no more while he waited.

But when the chairs drew near and were set down, there came out from them not his father nor any man at all, but two women; one was his mother, and the other was her serving woman.

Now could Yuan be astonished indeed, for he seldom saw his mother, and he never knew her to have left her house before, and so he went out slowly to make his greeting, wondering what this meant. She came towards him, leaning on her servant's arm, a white-haired woman in a decent garb of black, her teeth all gone so that her cheeks were sunken. But still there was good ruddiness upon her cheeks, and if the look upon her face was simple and a little silly, even, yet it was kind, too. When

23

she saw her son she cried out in a plain, country way, for she had been a village maiden in her youth, "Son, your father sent me to say that he is ill and near to death. He says you are to have what you will if only you will come at once before he dies. He says to say to you he is not angry, and therefore only come."

This she said loudly and for all to hear, and in truth even by now the villagers were clustering to see and hear a new thing. But Yuan saw none of them, he was so confused by what he heard. He had strengthened himself through all these days not to leave this house against his will, but how could he refuse his father if he were truly dying? Yet was it true? Then he remembered how his father's hands had shaken when he stretched them out in eagerness to take the comfort of the wine, and he feared it might be true, and a son ought not to refuse a father anything.

Now the serving woman, seeing his doubt, felt it her duty to aid her mistress, and she cried loudly, too, looking here and there upon the villagers to mark her own importance, "Ah, my little general, it is true! We are all half-crazed and all the doctors, too! The old general lies at the end of his life, and if you would see him living, you must go quickly to him. I swear he has not long to live—if he has, then may I die myself!" And all the villagers listened greedily to this and looked at each other meaningfully to hear the Tiger was so near his end.

But still Yuan doubted these two women, the more because he felt in them some hidden secret eagerness to force him home, and when the serving woman saw his continuing doubt, she threw herself upon the ground before him and cracked her head upon the hard-beaten threshing floor, and she bellowed in loud, feigned weeping, "See your mother, little general—see even me, a slave—how we beseech you—"

When she had done this a time or two, she rose and dusted off her grey cotton coat and cast a haughty stare about upon the crowded gaping villagers. Her duty now was done, and she stood

24

to one side, proud servant of a high proud family, and so above these common folk.

But Yuan paid no heed to her. He turned to his mother and he knew he must do his duty, however he might hate it, and he asked her to come in and seat herself and this she did, while the crowd followed after and edged into the door to see and hear. But she did not heed them, being used to common folk who always gape to see their betters.

She looked about the middle room, wondering, and said, "It is the first time I was ever in this house. I used in childhood to hear great stories of it and how Wang Lung grew rich and bought a tea house girl and how she ruled him for a while. Yes, the greatest tales of how she looked and what she ate and wore were told from mouth to mouth in this whole countryside, although it was a thing of the past, even then, for he was old when I was but a child. I mind now it was said Wang Lung even sold a piece of land to buy a ruby ring for her. But afterward he bought it back again. I saw her only once, upon my marriage day, and—my mother!—how fat and hideous she grew before she died at last! Eh—"

She laughed toothlessly and looked about her amiably, and Yuan, seeing how placidly and honestly she spoke, took heart to know the truth, and so he asked her plainly, "Mother, is my father really ill?"

This recalled her to her purpose and she answered, hissing through her toothless gums as she must do when she talked, "He is ill, my son. I do not know how ill, but he sits there, for he will not go to bed, and he drinks and drinks and will not eat until he is yellow as a melon. I swear I never saw such yellowness. And no one dares go near him to say a single word, for he roars and curses beyond even what he ever did. He cannot live if he will not eat, be sure."

"Aye, aye, it's true—he cannot live if he will not eat," the serving woman echoed. She stood beside her mistress's chair, and shook her head and took a melancholy pleasure in her words, and then the two women sighed together and looked grave and watched Yuan secretly.

Then when he had thought a little while in great impatience Yuan said, for he knew he must go if it were true his father was so ill, although he doubted still and thought to himself that what his father said was true and women all were fools, "I will go then. Rest here a day or two, my mother, before you come back, for you must be weary."

Then he made sure for her comfort, and saw her in the quiet room which seemed now his own so that he left it sadly, and when she had eaten, he put from him the memory of the pleasant, lovely days and mounting on his horse once more, he turned his face to the north and to his father and again he wondered at these two women, for they seemed too cheerful at his going, more cheerful than they should be if the lord of the house lay ill.

Behind him went a score or so of his father's soldiers. Once hearing them guffaw together at some coarseness he could not bear them any more, and he turned on them in anger, hating the familiar clatter of them at his horse's heels. But when he asked them fiercely why they followed him, they answered sturdily, "Sir, your father's trusty man bade us follow you lest some enemy take this chance and seize you for a ransom or even kill you. There are many robbers through the countryside, and you are an only, precious son."

And Yuan answered nothing. He groaned and turned his face northwards steadily. What foolishness had made him think of freedom? He was his father's only son, most hopelessly his father's only son.

And of the villagers and country folk who watched him passing there was not one who was not rejoiced to see him go away again, because they did not understand him or believe in him at all, and Yuan could see their great content that he must go, and this sight remained a darkness in the pleasure of those free days.

So Yuan rode against his will to his father's gates, the guard behind him. They did not leave him the whole way and he soon perceived they guarded him not so much from robbers as from himself, lest he escape them somewhere. It was on his lips a score of times to cry at them, "You need not fear me—I will not run from my own father—I come to him of my own will!"

But he said nothing. He looked at them in scorn and silence and would not speak to them, but rode on as fast as he could, taking a haughty pleasure in his quick horse that kept so easily before their common ones that they must press their poor beasts on and on. Yet he knew himself a prisoner, however he might go. No verse came to him now; he scarcely saw the lovely land.

At evening of the second day of this forced riding he reached his father's threshold. He leaped from his horse and suddenly weary to his very soul he went slowly towards the room in which his father commonly slept, not heeding all the secret stares of soldiers and of serving men, and answering no greeting.

But his father was not in his bed, although it was night by now, and a lounging guard said when Yuan asked him, "The general is in his hall."

Then Yuan felt some anger, and he thought to himself that after all his father was not very ill, and it was only a ruse to win him home. He nursed his anger at the ruse, so that he would not fear his father, and when he remembered the pleasant lonely days upon the land, he could keep his anger lively against his father. Yet when he entered the hall and saw the Tiger, Yuan forgot some of his anger, for eye could see here was no ruse. His father sat in his old chair, the tiger skin flung across the carved back of it, and before him was the glowing brazier full of coals. He was wrapped in his shaggy sheepskin robe, and on his head was set his high fur hat, but still he looked as cold as death. His

27

skin was yellow as old leather, and his eyes burned dry and black and sunken, and the unshaved hair upon his face was grey and harsh. He looked up when his son came in, and then down again into the coals and gave no greeting.

Then Yuan came forward and bowed before his father, saying, "They told me you were ill, my father, so I came."

But Wang the Tiger muttered, "I am not ill. It is woman's talk." And he would not look at his son.

Then Yuan asked, "Did you not send for me because you were ill?" And Wang the Tiger muttered again, "I did not send for you. They asked me where you were, and I said, 'Let him stay where he is.'" He looked down steadfastly into the coals and stretched his hands above their shimmering heat.

Now these words might have angered anyone and especially a young man in these days when parents are not honored, and Yuan might easily have hardened himself more and gone away again to do as he liked in his new willfulness, except he saw his father's two hands stretched out, pale and dry as old men's hands are, and trembling and seeking for some warmth somewhere, and he could not say a word of anger. It came to him now, as the moment must come to any gentle-hearted son, that his father in his loneliness was grown a little child again, and one to be dealt with as a child, with tenderness and no anger, in whatever petulance he spoke. This weakness in his father struck at the roots of Yuan's anger, so that he felt unusual tears come to his eyes, and if he had dared he would have put his hand out to touch his father except some strange natural shame restrained him. Therefore he only sat down sidewise on a chair nearby and gazing at his father, waited silently and even patiently for what he might say next.

But there was this freedom that the moment gave him. He knew his fear of his father was forever gone. Never more would he be afraid of this old man's roarings and his darkening looks and his black brows drawn down and all the tricks the Tiger

28

used to make himself fearful. For Yuan saw the truth, that these tricks were only weapons his father used; though he had not known it he had used them as a shield, or as men will take a sword and brandish it and never mean to bring it down on any flesh. So those tricks had covered the Tiger's heart, which never had been hard enough nor cruel enough nor merry enough to make of him a truly great lord of war. In this moment and its clearness Yuan looked upon his father and he began to love him fearlessly.

But Wang the Tiger, not knowing anything of this change in his son, sat brooding on, silent and seeming to forget his son was there. He sat long without moving and at last Yuan, seeing how ill his father's color was and how his flesh had dropped from him these last few days, so that the bones of his face stood out like rocks, said gently, "And would it not be better if you went to bed, my father?"

When he heard his son's voice again, Wang the Tiger looked up slowly as a sick man will, and he fixed his gaunt eyes upon his son and stared at him awhile and after another while he said hoarsely and very slowly, word for word, "For your sake once I did not kill an hundred and seventy-three men who deserved to die!" He lifted his right hand as though he would have held it over his mouth in a way he had, but the hand dropped of its own weight, and he let it hang and he said to his son again, still staring at him, "It is true. I did not kill them for your sake."

"I am glad, my father," said Yuan, moved not so much by the living men, although he was glad to know they lived, as by the childish longing he discerned in his father to please him. "I hate to see men killed, my father," he said.

"Aye, I know it; you were always squeamish," answered Wang the Tiger listlessly, and fell to silent staring at the coals again.

Once more Yuan thought how to urge his father to his bed, for he could not bear the look of illness on his face and in the dry and drooping mouth. He rose and went to where the old trusty

29

hare-lipped man sat on his haunches by the door, nodding as he sat, and whispered to him, "Cannot you persuade my father to his bed?"

The man started up and staggered to his feet, awake at this, and answered hoarsely, "And have I never tried, my little general? I cannot persuade him even to go to his bed at night. If he lies down he rises up again within an hour or so and comes back to this chair to sit and I can only sit here, too, and I am so filled with sleep now I am as good as dead. But there he sits, always awake!"

Then Yuan went to his father and coaxed him and he said, "Father, I am weary, too. Let us go and lie upon a bed and sleep, for I am so weary. I will lie near you, and you can call me and know that I am there."

At this the Tiger moved a little as though he would rise; then he sank back and shook his head and would not rise and he said, "No, I am not finished what I have to say. There is something else—I cannot think of it all at once—two things I counted on my right hand that I must say. Go sit somewhere and wait until my thought comes out."

The Tiger spoke with his old vehemence now, and Yuan felt the habit of his childhood on him to go and sit. And yet there was this new fearlessness in him too, so that now his heart cried out against its duty, "What is he but a very tiresome old willful man, and here must I sit and wait for his humors!" And his willfulness shone out of his eyes and almost he was about to speak when the trusty man saw him and hastened forward to coax him and said, "Let him have his way, little general, since he is so ill, and bear what he says as we all must do." So Yuan against his will, yet fearing it might indeed make his father worse if he were opposed at such an hour, who never had known opposition, went and sat down sidewise on a chair and sat now less patiently until the Tiger said suddenly, "It has come back to me. The first thing is that I must hide you somewhere, for I remember what you told me when you came home yesterday. I must hide you from my enemies."

At this Yuan could not forbear crying out, "But, father, it was not yesterday—"

Then the Tiger darted one of his old angry looks at his son and he clapped his dry palms once together and he cried, "I know what I say! How was it not yesterday when you came home? You did come home yesterday!"

And again the old trusty man stood between the Tiger and his son and called out pleadingly, "Let be—let be—it was a yesterday!" And Yuan turned sullen, and hung his head because he must be silent. For now it was a strange thing, but the first pity he had for his father was gone like a little quick mild wind passing over his heart, and these angry old looks his father gave him roused some deeper feeling in him than the pity. His resentments rose in him, he told himself he would not be afraid again, but he must be willful lest he be afraid.

And in his own old willfulness the father waited yet longer before he would speak on, he thought because he did not like his son to break into what he said, and so he waited longer than he would have otherwise. But the truth was the Tiger had something to say he did not like to say, and he waited. In that time of waiting Yuan's anger against his father leaped up more strongly than it ever had. He thought of all the times he had been cowed to silence by this man, and he thought of all the hours he had spent at weapons which he hated, and he thought of his days of freedom cut off once more, and suddenly he could not bear the Tiger. No, his very flesh shrank back from this old man and he loathed his father suddenly because he was not washed or shaven, and because he had let his wine and food dribble down upon his robe. There was not anything about his father that he loved, at least for this moment.

The Tiger not dreaming of all this hot loathing in his son's heart went on at last with what he had to say and it was this,

31

"But you are my only precious son. What hope have I except in your body? Your mother for once has said a wise thing. She came and said to me, 'And if he is not wed, from whence will come our grandsons?' I told her then, 'Go and search out a good hearty maid somewhere, and it does not matter what she is except she be lusty and quick to bear, for women are all alike and one is not better than another. And bring her back and wed him, and then he can go out to hide in some foreign country until this war is over. And we shall have his seed.'"

This the Tiger said very carefully, each word what he had thought before, and he gathered up his weary wits to do this duty for his son before he let him go. This was no more than any good father ought to do, and what every son must in reason expect, for any son should accept the wife so chosen for his parents' sake, and wed her and give her child, and then he is free to find his love elsewhere as he will. But Yuan was not a son like this. He was filled with the poison of new times and full of secret willful freedoms that he did not know himself, and full, too, of his father's hatred against women, and what with this hatred, and what with his willfulness he felt all his anger burst out of him now. Yes, his anger at this hour was like a checked flood in him, and all his life was gathered to its crisis now.

At first he could not believe his father truly said these words, for all his life he had been so used to hear the Tiger speak only of women as fools, or if not fools, then traitors and never to be trusted. But there the words were, spoken, and the Tiger sat and stared into the coals as before. Now Yuan knew suddenly why his mother and her serving woman had been so eager secretly to get him home, and pleased when he made ready to return, for such women think of nothing but of matches and of weddings.

Well, and he would not yield to them! He leaped up, forgetting that he ever had feared or loved his father, and he shouted, "I have waited for this—yes, when my comrades told me how they were forced to marriage—and many of them left their homes for this very cause—I used to doubt my own good fortune—but you are like all the others, all these old people who would keep us tied forever—tied through our bodies—forcing us to the women you choose—forcing us to children—well, I will not be tied—I will not have my body used like this to tie my life to yours—I hate you—I have always hated you—I know I hate you—"

Out of Yuan rushed such a stream of hatred now that he began to sob wildly, and the trusty man, in terror at such anger, ran and held him around the waist and would have spoken and could not, because his split lip was all awry. Yuan stared down and saw this man, and he was beside himself. He lifted up his hand and beat it down clenched upon that old hideous face, so that the man lay felled to the floor.

Now the Tiger rose tottering, not to his son—no, he had stared in a daze at Yuan, as though he could not comprehend what these words were, his eyes dazed and staring. When he saw his old servant fall, he went to lift him up.

But Yuan turned and fled. Not waiting once to see what was done, he ran through the courts and found his horse tied to a tree and ran through the great outer gate and past the staring soldiers there and leaped upon his horse and rode out of that place and to himself he cried it was forever.

Now Yuan had run out of his father's house in wildest anger, and this anger must cool from its very heat or he would die. And it did cool. He began to think what he could do, a lone young man, who had cut himself away from comrades and from father. The very day helped him to coolness, for the winter sunshine, which seemed so endless in the days Yuan spent in the earthen house, now was not endless. The day was turned to greyness, and the wind blew from the east, very chill and bitter, and the land through which Yuan's horse went slowly, for the beast was wearied with the days of travel, turned grey, too, and in its grey-ness Yuan felt himself swallowed up and cooled. The very people on the land took on this same greyness, for they were so like the earth upon which they lived and worked that their looks changed with it and their speech and all their movements quieted. Where in the sunshine their faces were live and often merry, now under the grey sky their eyes were dull and their lips unsmiling, and their garments dun-colored and their bodies slow. The little vivid colors of the land and hills, the blue of garments, the red of a child's coat, the crimson of a maiden's trousers, all these hues which commonly the sun would choose out and set alive, were now subdued. And Yuan, riding now through this dun country, wondered how he could have loved it so before. He might have turned back to his old captain and the cause, except he remembered the villagers and how they had not loved him, and these people whom he passed this day seemed so sullen that he cried to himself bitterly, "And shall I go and throw my life away for them?" Yes, on this day even the land seemed to him unsmiling. And as if that were not enough, his horse began to hobble and when he descended near a certain small city that he passed, he found the beast stone-bruised and lame and useless.

Now as Yuan had stopped and bent to look at the horse's hoof he heard a great roaring noise, and he looked up and there rushed past him a train, smoking mightily and full of haste. But still it did not pass too quickly for Yuan to see the many guests within, because he was so near and kneeling by his horse. There they sat so warm and so secure and thus went with such speed that Yuan envied them, and felt his own beast too slow and now useless and he cried to himself, and it seemed to him a quick clever thing to think, "I will sell this beast inside the city and take that train and go far away—as far as I can—"

On that night he lay at an inn, a very filthy inn it was, inside that little city, and Yuan could not sleep, the vermin crawled so on him, and he lay awake and while he lay he planned what he could do. He had some money on him, for his father always made him wear a belt of money next his body, lest he be too short sometime or other, and he had his horse to sell. But for a long time he could not think where he must go and what he must do.

Now Yuan was no common and untutored lad. He knew old books of his own people, and he knew the new books of the west, for so his tutor had taught him. From his tutor, too, he had learned to speak very well a foreign tongue, and he was not helpless and untaught as he might have been. So while he tossed his body on the hard boards of that inn bed, he asked himself what he should do with the silver that he had, and with his knowledge. To and fro in his own mind he asked himself if he had better go back to his captain. He could go and say, "I have repented. Take me back." And if he told that he had left his father and struck down the trusty man, it would be enough, since among this band of revolutionists it was a passport if a parent were defied and always proof of loyalty, so that some of these young, both men and women, even killed their parents to show their loyalty.

But Yuan, even though he knew he would be welcome, somehow did not want to go back to that cause.

The memory of the grey day was still melancholy in him, and he thought of the dusty common people and then he did not love them. He muttered to himself, "I have never in all my life long had any pleasure. All the little joys that other young men have I have not had. My life has been filled with my duty to my father and then this cause I could not follow." And suddenly he thought he would like some life he had not yet seen, a merrier life, a life with laughter in it. It seemed to Yuan suddenly that all his life he had been grave and without playmates, and yet there must be pleasure somewhere as well as work to do.

When he thought of play he remembered into his very early childhood, and he thought of that younger sister he once knew and how she used to laugh and patter here and there upon her little feet and how he used to laugh when he was with her. Well and why should he not seek her out again? She was his sister

35

they were one blood. He had been so knotted into his father's life all these long years that he had forgotten he had others too to whom he belonged.

Suddenly he saw them all in his mind—he had a score of kin folk. He might go to his uncle, Wang the Merchant. For a moment he thought it might be pleasant to be in that house again, and he saw in his memory a hearty merry face, which was his aunt's, and he thought of his aunt and of his cousins. But then he thought willfully, no, he would not go so near his father, for his uncle surely would tell his father, and it was too near. . . . He would take the train and go far away. His sister was far away, very far in the coastal city. He would like to live awhile in that city and see his sister and take pleasure in the merry sights, and see all the foreign things he had heard of and never seen.

His heart hurried him. Before dawn came he rose leaping up and shouted for the servant in the inn to fetch him hot water to wash himself and he took off his clothes and shook them well to rid them of the vermin, and when the man came he cursed him for such filth and was all eagerness to be gone.

When the serving man saw Yuan's impatience he knew him for a rich man's son, for the poor dare not curse so easily, and he grew obsequious and made haste, and so by dawn Yuan was fed and off, leading his red horse to sell. This poor beast he sold for very little at a butcher's shop. A moment's pang Yuan had, it is true, for he shrank a little to think his horse must be turned into food for men, but then he hardened himself against this softness. He had no need for horses now. He was no longer a general's son. He was himself, Wang Yuan, a young man free to go where he would and do what he liked. And that very day he mounted into the train that took him to the great coastal city.

It was a lucky thing for Yuan that he had sometimes read to his father the letters which the Tiger's learned wife sent him from that coastal city where she had gone to live. The Tiger as he was older grew more indolent about reading anything, so that, although as a youth he had read very well, in his age he had forgotten many letters and did not read with ease. Twice a year the letters came from this lady to her lord, and she wrote a very learned sort of writing which was not easy to read, and Yuan read the letters to his father and explained them. Now remembering, he could remember where she said she lived, in what street and in what part of that great city. So when at the end of a day and a night Yuan came down off that train, having crossed a river on the way and skirted by a lake or two and passed through many mountains and through much good planted land whereon the spring wheat was sprouting, he knew where he must go. It was not very near to where he was and so he hired a ricksha to pull him there, and thus he went through the lighted city streets alone and to his own adventure, and as he went he stared about him as freely as any farmer might, since no one knew him.

Never had he been in such a city as this was. For the houses rose so high on the sides of the streets that even with all the blazing lights he could not see their tops which ended somewhere in the darkness of the sky. But at the foot of the towering houses where Yuan was it was bright enough, and the people walked as though in the light of day. He saw the people of the world here, for they were of every race and kind and color; he saw black men from India and their women wrapped about with cloth of gold and with pure white muslin and with scarlet robes to set off their dark beauty. And he saw the swift-moving shapes of white women and their men with them all dressed the same always, and all their noses long, so that Yuan looking at the men wondered how these women told their husbands from other men, they looked so much the same except some were big-bellied or hairless on their scalps or had some other such lack in beauty.

Still most of the people were his own kind, and Yuan saw every sort of countryman of his upon these streets. There were the rich, who came riding in great machines to the door of some pleasure house, and they drove up with the great shrieking noise of horns, and Yuan's ricksha man must draw aside and wait until they passed, as in the old days kings might have passed. Where the rich were, there were the poor beside them, the beggars and the maimed and the diseased who made much of their woes to gain a little silver. But it was hardly gained, and the silver leaked from the purses of the rich in very small scanty pieces, for usually the rich passed on their way, their noses high and their eyes unseeing. In all his eagerness for pleasure, Yuan could feel a moment's hatred of these haughty rich, and he thought they ought to give a little to the beggars.

Through all this moving multitude Yuan went obscure enough in his humble vehicle until the man stopped panting before a certain gate set in a long wall, and like a score of other gates on either side. This was the place Yuan sought and so he came down and fetched out the coins he had promised to the man and gave them to him. Now Yuan had seen with indignation how little those rich men and ladies had heeded the cries of the beggars and how they had pushed past the scrawny hands thrust out before them. Yet when this working man cried humbly, trembling and sweating with his running, "Sir, add a little out of the kindness of your heart," for he had noted Yuan's robe of silk and his well-fed looks, it did not seem the same thing to Yuan at all. He did not feel himself rich and it is known that these men who pull at rickshas never are content. So he cried stoutly, "Is not the price agreed?" And the man answered, sighing, "Oh, aye, it is the price agreed—but I thought from your kind heart—"

But Yuan had forgotten the man. He turned to the gate and pressed a bell he saw there. Then the man seeing himself forgotten, sighed again and wiped his hot face with a filthy cloth he had about his neck and wandered down the street, shivering in the keen night wind which turned his sweat to ice upon his flesh.

When the manservant came to open the gate, he stared at Yuan as at a stranger and for a while would not let him in, because in that city there were many well-dressed strangers who rang at gates and said they were friends and relatives of those who lived there, and when they were bidden to come in they drew out foreign guns and robbed and killed and did what they would, and sometimes their fellows came and helped them and they seized a child or man and took him away to hold for ransom. So the servant quickly barred the gate again, and although Yuan cried out what his name was, there he must wait awhile. Then once more the gate opened, and this time he saw a lady there, a quiet grave-faced lady, large and white-haired, her robe of some dark plum-hued satin. Yuan looked at her as she looked at him, and he saw her face was kind, a full pale face, not wrinkled much, but never beautiful, since the mouth was too large and the nose large and flat between the eyes. Still the eyes were kind and comprehending and Yuan took courage, and he smiled a little in shyness and he said, "I need to ask your pardon that I come like this, lady, but I am Wang Yuan, the Tiger's son, and I have left my father. I ask nothing from you except, since I am alone, that I may come in and see you and my sister."

The lady had been looking at him very closely as he spoke, and she said mildly, "I could not believe the man when he said it was you. It has been so long since I saw you that I would not know you, except you are so like your father. Yes, none could fail to see you are the Tiger's son. Come in, then, and be at home."

And though the servant looked still doubtful the lady urged Yuan to come in and she was so mild and placid that she seemed not surprised at all, or in truth as though anything on this earth could surprise her now. No, she led him into a narrow hall, and then she bade the servant make a room ready with a bed in it, and asked Yuan if he had eaten and she opened a door into a guest hall, and asked him to be seated there and at his ease while she went to fetch certain things for his comfort in the room the servant made ready for him. All this she did so easily and with such ready welcome that Yuan was pleased and warmed and felt himself a welcome guest at last, and this was very sweet to him, wearied as he was with what had come about between his father and himself.

In this guest hall he sat himself down upon an easy chair and waited wondering, for it was not such a room as he had ever seen, but, as his way was, showing no wonder or excitement on his grave face. He sat quietly, wrapped in his long robe of dark silk, looking a little about the room, yet looking not so much that if one came in he would be surprised at such a thing, for he was of a nature which hated to seem strange or ill at ease in any new place. It was a small, square room and very clean, so clean that on the floor a flowered woolen cloth was spread, and even this had no soil upon it. In the center of this cloth a table stood, and on the table another cloth of red velvet, and in this center a pot of pink paper flowers, very real to see, except the leaves were silver and not green. There were six chairs such as the one he sat on, soft in the seat and covered with pink satin. At the windows were hung white strips of fine cloth, and on the wall was hung a picture of a foreign sort behind a pane of glass. This picture showed high mountains very blue, a lake as blue, and on the mountains foreign houses such as he had not seen. It was very bright and pretty to the eye.

Suddenly a bell rang somewhere, and Yuan turned his head to the door. He heard quick footsteps, and then a girl's voice high and full of laughter. He listened. It could be perceived she spoke to someone, although he heard no answering voice, and many words she used he scarcely understood, ripples interspersed of some foreign tongue.

"Ah, it is you?—No, I am not busy— Oh, I am tired today, I danced so late last night— You are teasing me— She is much prettier than I— You laugh at me— She dances much better than I do—even the white men want to dance with her— Yes, it is true I did dance with the young American— Ah, how he can dance— I will not tell you what he said!—No, no, no!—Then I will go with you tonight—ten o'clock! I will have dinner first—"

He heard a pretty rill of laughter and suddenly the door opened and he saw a girl there, and he rose to bow, his eyes dropped down in courtesy, avoiding a direct look at her. But she ran forward swiftly, graceful as a darting swallow and as quick, her hands outstretched. "You are my brother Yuan!" she cried gaily in her little soft voice, a voice high and floating seemingly upon the air. "My mother said you were here all of a sudden—" She seized his hands and laughed. "How old-fashioned you are in that long robe! Shake hands like this—everybody shakes hands now!"

He felt her small smooth hand seize his, and he pulled his own away, too shy to bear it—staring at her while he did it. She laughed again and sat down on the arm of a chair and turned her face up at him, the prettiest little face, three-cornered as a kitten's, the black hair smooth and curled upon her rounded cheeks. But it was her eyes that held him, the brightest, blackest eyes shot through with light and laughter, and beneath them was her red little mouth, the lips very full and red and yet small and delicate.

"Sit down," she cried, a little imperious queen.

He sat then, very carefully upon the edge of a chair, not near her, and she laughed again.

"I am Ai-lan," she went on in her light fluttering voice. "Do you remember me? I remember you so well. Only you have grown up better than you were—you used to be an ugly little boy—your face so long. But you must have some new clothes—all my cousins wear foreign clothes now—you would look nice in them—so tall! Can you dance? I love to dance. Do you know

41

our cousins? My eldest cousin's wife dances like a fairy! You should see my old uncle! He'd like to dance, but he is so old and hugely fat, and my aunt won't let him. You should see him when she scolds him for staring at pretty girls!" Again she laughed her restless, flying laughter.

Yuan stole a look at her. She was slighter than any creature he had ever seen, as small as any child about the body, and her green silk robe fitted as tightly to her as a calyx to a bud, the collar high and close about her slender neck, and in her ears were little rings of pearls and gold. He looked away and coughed a little behind his hand.

"I came to pay my respects to our mother and to you," he said.

She smiled at this, mocking his sedateness, a smile that set her face twinkling, and she rose and went to the door, her step so swift it seemed like a light running.

"I'll go and find her, brother," she said, making her voice solemn to mock his. Then she laughed again and flung a teasing look at him from out her black kitten's eyes.

The room was very quiet with her going, as though a little busy wind had suddenly ceased to blow in it. Yuan sat astonished, not able to comprehend this girl. She was not like anyone he had ever seen in all his soldier's life. He set his brain to remember how she was when they were small together before his father made him leave his mother's court. He remembered this same swiftness, this prattle, this darting of her great black eyes. He remembered, too, how dull his days had seemed at first without her, how lifeless were his father's courts. Remembering it, even now this room seemed too quiet and lonely and he wished she would come back to it, and he was eager to see her more, because he wanted more of laughter like hers. Suddenly he thought again how his whole life long had been without laughter, always filled with a duty of some kind or other, and how he had never play and merriment such as any poor child has upon the street and such as any crowd of laboring men has if they stop a moment to rest in the sunshine of noon and eat their food together. His heart beat a little quickly. What had this city for him, what laughter and what gaiety such as all young men must love, what new shining life?

When the door sounded again, therefore, he looked eagerly towards it but now it was not Ai-lan. It was the lady, and she came in quietly and as one who made her house ready and full of good ease and comfort for all. Behind her came the serving man bearing on a tray some bowls of hot food, and she said, "Set the food here. Now, Yuan, you must eat a little more if you would please me, for I know the food upon the trains is not like this. Eat, my son—for you are my son, Yuan, since I have had no other, and I am glad you have sought me out, and I want you to tell me everything and how you are come here."

When Yuan heard this good lady speak kindly and when he saw her face honest in its look and meaning and when he heard her comfortable voice and saw the inviting look her little mild eyes had when she put a chair for him beside a table, he felt foolish tears come to his eyes. Never, he thought passionately within himself, had such gentle welcome been made for him anywhere—no, no one was so kind to him as this. Suddenly the warmth of this house, the gayness of the colors of the room, the remembered laughter of Ai-lan, the comfort of this lady, rose up and wrapped him round. He ate eagerly, for he found himself very hungry and the food was seasoned carefully and not scant of fat or sauces as foods are when they are bought, and Yuan, forgetting how once he had eaten eagerly of country fare, thought now this was the best, most heartening food he ever ate, and he ate his fill. Yet he was quickly satisfied because the dishes were so fat and highly seasoned, and he could eat no more in spite of all the lady's urging.

When it was over and the lady waited while he ate, she bade him sit in the easy chair again, and then warmed and fed and comforted, Yuan told her everything and even things he scarcely knew himself. Now he met the lady's gaze, a full, waiting gaze, and suddenly his shyness dropped from him and he began to speak and tell her all he wanted—how he had hated war and how he wanted to live upon the land, not ignorantly, as the peasants did, but as a wise husbandman, one learned enough to teach the peasants better ways. And he told how for his father's sake he ran from his captain secretly and now in some new understanding of himself those wise eyes gave him while they rested on him, he said, troubled, "I thought I ran because I would not go against my father, but now as I tell it, lady, I see I went partly because I hate the killing my comrades must do some day even in their good cause. I cannot kill—I am not brave, I know. The truth is I cannot hate wholly enough to kill a man. I always know how he feels, too."

He looked at the lady humbly, ashamed to show his weakness. But she answered tranquilly, "Not everyone can kill, it's true else would we all be dead, my son." And after a while she said more kindly still, "I am glad you cannot kill, Yuan. It is better to save life than take it, and so I think, although I serve no Buddhist god."

But it was not until he told haltingly and half ashamed how the Tiger would have him wed anyhow to any maid that the lady was fully moved. Until now she had listened to him kindly and full of comprehension, murmuring small assents now and then when he waited for a moment. But when he hung his head and said, "I know he has the right to do it—I know the law and customs—but I could not bear it. I cannot—I cannot—I must have my body for my own and free—" And then troubled by his own memory of his hatred against his father and needing to confess it somehow he said further, for he wanted to tell everything, "Almost I understand how sons kill their fathers in these days—not that I could really do it, but I understand the feeling in those with a readier hand than mine."

He looked at the lady to see if this were too hard for her to bear, but it was not. She said with a new force and with more certainty than she had yet spoken, "You are right, Yuan. Yes, I always tell the parents of the youth nowadays, the fathers and the mothers of Ai-lan's friends, and even your uncle and his lady, who complain unceasingly against this generation, that in this at least the young are right. Oh, I know very well how right you are. I will never force Ai-lan to any marriage—and I will help you, if need be, against your father in this thing, for here I am sure you are truly right."

This she said sadly, but with some secret passion gathered from her own life, and Yuan wondered to see her small quiet eyes change and sparkle so, and her whole placid face grow moved. But he was too young to think long of any other than himself and the comfort of her words joined to the comfort of this quiet house, and he said longingly, "If I could stay here for a while until I can see what I must do—"

"And so you shall," she answered warmly. "You shall stay here as long as you have need. I have ever wanted a son of my own and here you are."

The truth was the lady suddenly loved this tall dark youth and she liked the big honest look upon his face and she liked the slow way he moved, and though he might not be pretty by the measure of the usual guess, being too high-cheeked and his mouth too big, still he was taller than most young men are, and she liked a certain shyness and a delicacy he had about him when he spoke, as though even if he were willful he was not too sure of his own abilities. Yet this delicacy was only in his speech, for his voice was deep and good and a man's voice.

And Yuan saw her liking and was yet more warmed by it and it made this house his home. When they had talked a little more, she led him to a small room which was to be his own. It was up a stair and then up another smaller winding stair, and under the roof it stood, clean and with all the things he needed. When she was gone and he was alone, he went and looked out of the

45

window and there was the light upon the many streets and all the city lay glittering and shining and in the high darkness he seemed looking into a new heaven of some sort.

Now began for Yuan a new life indeed, a full new life such as he had never dreamed for himself. In the morning when he rose and washed and clothed himself, he went down the stairs and there the lady waited for him, and she had her same beaming look this morning to set him at fresh ease. She led Yuan in to where the breakfast was upon the table, and at once she began to tell him what her plans were for him, but always very carefully too, so that she might not say a thing against his will. First, she said, she must buy him some garments, since he came forth in only what he had upon him, and then she must send him to a school for young men in that city. She said, "There is no great haste, my son, for you to work. It is better in these days to have your fill of this new learning, or else what you will earn will be very little. Let me treat you as my son. Let me give you what I had planned for Ai-lan if she would have had it. You shall go to this school here until it is clear what your place is in your books, and when you are finished here, then you may work, or you may even go to some foreign country for a while. Nowadays the young men and women are all zealous to go abroad, and I say it is a good thing for them to go. Yes, though your uncle cries out it is a waste and that they all come back too full of their own skill and abilities so that there is no living with them, I say still it is well for them to go and learn what they can and come back and give it to their own country. I only wish Ai-lan--" Here the lady stopped and looked sorrowful for a while and as though she had forgotten what she spoke of because of some inner trouble of her own. Then she made her face clear again and said resolutely, "Ai, I must not try to shape Ai-lan's life— If she will not, then she will not—and do not let me shape you, either, son! I

46

only say that if you would—if you will—why, then I can think of a way to do it."

Now Yuan was so dazed at all this newness that he could scarcely take it all into him, and he stammered forth joyfully, "Be sure I can only thank you, lady, and I do most gladly what you say—" And he sat down and in his young new hunger and in all the joyfulness of a heart at rest and a place to be his home he ate a mighty breakfast, and the lady laughed and was pleased and said, "I swear I am glad you are come, Yuan, if for nothing else than that I shall see you eat, for Ai-lan is so fearful lest she put a little flesh upon her bones she dares not eat at all, scarcely, and not more than a kitten does, and she will not rise from her bed in the morning lest seeing food she crave it. She cares for beauty more than for anything, that child of mine. But I like to see the young eat!"

So saying she took her own chopsticks and searched out the best bits of the fish and fowl and condiments for Yuan, and took far greater pleasure in his healthy hunger than in anything she ate herself.

So began Yuan's new life. First this lady went out to great shops of silks and woolen stuffs sent from the foreign countries, and she called tailors to the house and they cut and measured all the stuffs and made robes for Yuan according to the city fashions. And the lady hastened them, because Yuan still had his old robes on, and they were cut too wide and in a country style and she would not let him go to see his uncle and cousins while he wore them, and when they heard he was come, for be sure Ai-lan must tell them that he was there, they bid him come to a feast of welcome. But the lady held them off a day until his best robe was finished, a robe of satin peacock blue and flowered in the same color and a short jacket, sleeved, of black satin. And Yuan was glad she did, for when he clothed himself in the new garment and had called a city barber to come and cut his hair and shave the young soft hairs from off his face and when he had put on his feet the new leather shoes the lady bought for him, and had drawn on the black short silken jacket and put on his head a foreign hat of felt such as every young man wore, he could not but know, as he stared into the mirror on the wall in his own room, that he looked a very fine young man, and like all the young men in this city, and it was only nature to be glad of this.

Yet this very knowledge made him shamefaced, and he went down very shyly to the room where the lady waited for him, and Ai-lan was there, too, and she clapped her hands to see him and cried out, "Ah, you are a very beautiful young man now, Yuan!" And she laughed so teasingly that Yuan felt the blood rush up to make his face and neck red, so that she laughed again. But the lady rebuked her mildly and turned him about to see that all was right, and it was, and she was pleased again with him, because his body was so straight and strong it paid her to see how well her pains were rewarded in his better looks.

On the second day after this one the feast was set, and Yuan went with his sister and with the lady whom already he called mother—and the word came to his tongue more easily than it did for his own mother, somehow—to his uncle's house. They went in a vehicle not drawn by horses, but forced by an engine in its vitals and driven by a serving man, and Yuan had never sat in such a thing before, but he liked it very well because it ran as smoothly as though it went on ice.

While they went and before they ever reached his uncle's house Yuan knew much about his uncle and his aunts and cousins, for Ai-lan chattered of them, telling this thing and another, laughing as she told, and with such sly looks and twistings of her little round red mouth as added point to every word. And as she talked Wang Yuan could see the very pictures of their kin and in spite of his decorum he laughed, she was so witty and so mischievous. He saw his uncle as she told him off, "A very mountain of a man, Yuan, holding such a paunch before him I swear he needs to grow another leg to carry it on, and jowls down to his shoulders, and bald as any priest! But far from any priest, Yuan, and only sore against his fat, because he cannot dance as his sons do—though how he thinks to clasp a maid and have her near him—" At such a thought the maid burst into laughter and her mother cried out mildly, but her eyes twinkled, too, "Ai-lan, take care of your words, my child. He is your uncle."

"Yes, and so I say what I like," she answered pertly. "And my aunt, Yuan, his first lady, she hates it here and longs to go back to the country. And yet she fears to leave him lest some maid catch him for his money, and being modern will not be his concubine but his true wife, and so push her to one side. His two ladies join in this one thing at least, they will not let him take a third—a sort of women's league these days, Yuan— And my three cousins— Well, the eldest is wed as you know, and my cousin's wife is the man there and rules him furiously, so that my poor cousin must take his pleasure all secretly and then she is so clever that she smells a new perfume on him, or finds a dash of powder on his coat, or hunts his pockets for a letter, and he is his own father over again. And our second cousin Sheng—he is a poet, a pretty poet, and he writes verses for the magazines and stories about death for love, and he is a rebel of a sort, a gentle, pretty, smiling rebel, always newly in some love. But our third cousin is the real rebel, Yuan. He's a revolutionist—I know he is!"

At this her mother cried out in earnest, "Ai-lan, be careful what you say! Remember he is our kin, and that word is dangerous in this city in these days."

"He told me so himself," said Ai-lan, but she put her voice low, and glanced at the man's back who drove the vehicle.

So much she said and much more, and when Wang Yuan went in his uncle's house, he knew each one there because of what his sister said.

It was a different house indeed from the great house Wang Lung had bought and left his sons in that old northern country

49

town. That house was aged and great, and the rooms were vast and deep and dark, or small and dark and set about the courts, and there was no upper story to it, but room upon room sprawled out, and space was plenty and the roofs were high and beamed and old, and the windows latticed with a sort of shell sent from the south.

But this new house in this new foreign city stood in a street with others like it which pressed hard against it. They were foreign houses, tall, high, narrow, without a single court or garden, and the rooms were close together, small, and very bright with many glass windows without lattices. The sunlight poured into the rooms, hard and shining and lightening every hue and color on the walls or on the flowered satin-covered chairs and tables, and the bright silks of women's clothes and the vermilion of their painted lips, so that when Yuan entered the room where all his kin folk were, he felt a glitter there which was too much for beauty.

Now his uncle rose, his hands lifting his huge belly from his knees, and from it his brocaded robes hung down like curtains, and he gasped out to greet his guests, "Well, sister-in-law, and my brother's son, and Ai-lan! Well, eh, this Yuan is a great tall black lad, too, like his father—not like, no, I swear—gentler than a tiger somewhat, perhaps—"

He laughed his rolling gasping laugh and heaved himself into a seat again, and his lady rose and Yuan looking sidewise saw her a neat, grey-faced lady, very plain and proper in her black satin coat and skirt, her hands crossed into her sleeves, and her little bound feet holding her unsteadily. She gave greeting to them, and she said, "I hope I see you well, sister-in-law, and brother's son. Ai-lan, you are grown thin—too thin. These maids nowadays will starve themselves and wear their little straight-cut dresses that are bold as men's robes. Pray sit down, sister—"

Near her stood a woman Yuan did not know at all, a woman with a scrubbed rosy face, her skin shining with soapy washing and her hair drawn straight from her brow in a country fashion, and her eyes very bright but not too wise. No one thought to say this woman's name, and Yuan did not know if she were a servant or not, until his lady mother said a kind greeting to her and from it Yuan knew this was his uncle's concubine. He moved his head a little then and the woman blushed and bowed as country women will, her hands folded in her sleeves, but she said nothing.

Then when greetings were all given, the cousins called out to Yuan to come and drink his tea aside in another room with them, and he and Ai-lan did, glad to be free of their elders. And Yuan sat silently and heard the chatter of those who know each other well, to whom only he was stranger, though he was their cousin.

Very well he marked them one by one, his eldest cousin not young any more, not slender either, but his belly growing as his father's did. He was half foreign in his dark woolen foreign garb, and his pale face was handsome still, his soft hands smooth-fleshed, and his wandering restless glance lingered over-long even on his girl cousin, so that his pretty sharp-voiced wife recalled him with a little sneer she slipped sidewise into something else she said. And there was Sheng the poet, his second cousin, his hair straight and long about his face, his fingers long and pale and delicate, his face studied in its look of smiling meditation. Only the young third cousin was not smooth in his looks and ways. He was a lad of sixteen years or so, clad in a common school uniform of grey, buttoned to the neck, and his face was not beautiful at all, shaped anyhow and pimpled, and his hands were angular and loose and hung too long from out his sleeves. He only said nothing while the others chattered, but he sat eating peanuts from a dish nearby, eating hungrily and yet with such a look of young gloom upon his face that one would say he ate them against his will entirely.

About the room and among the feet of all of them ran younger children, a lad or two of ten and eight, two little girls, and there

51

was a screaming two-year-old looped in a band of cloth held by a serving woman, and a babe in arms suckling at the breast of a wet nurse. These were the children of Yuan's uncle's concubine, and of his elder cousins, but Yuan was shy of children and he let them be.

At first the talk was among them all, and Yuan sat silently, for while they bade him eat as he would from varied sweetmeats that stood near in dishes on small tables, and while his elder cousin's wife called to a serving maid to pour out tea, they forgot him seemingly, and paid no heed to courtesies in which he had been taught. So he cracked a few nuts noiselessly and sipped his tea and listened, and now and then he shyly gave a nut meat to a child who gobbled it gracelessly and with no word of thanks.

But soon the talk fell quiet among the cousins. The elder cousin, it is true, asked Yuan a thing or two, such as where he would go to school, and when he heard Yuan might go abroad he said enviously, "I wish I might have gone, but my father never would spend the money on me." Then he yawned and put his finger in his nose and fell to moody thinking, and at last he took his youngest lad upon his knee and fed him sweets and teased him for a while and laughed to hear him grow angry and laughed yet more when the child beat him with little furious fists. Ai-lan fell to talking in a low voice with her cousin's wife, and the cousin's wife spoke in an angry tone which she made low, but still Yuan could hear her and perceive the speech was of her mother-in-law and how she demanded things no woman nowadays would give another.

"With this house full of servants she will call to me to pour her bowl of tea, Ai-lan—and she blames me if a measure more of rice is used this month than last! I swear I cannot bear it. Not many women nowadays will live in the house with their husband's parents, and no more will I!" And much more of such women's talk.

Of all of them Yuan looked most curiously at his second cousin,

52

Sheng, whom Ai-lan called the poet, and this was partly because Yuan himself loved verses and partly because he liked the grace about the youth, a slender grace, made quicker and more marked because he wore the dark and simple foreign garb. He was beautiful, and Yuan loved beauty very well, and he could scarcely keep his eyes from Sheng's golden, oval face and from his eyes, as apricot in shape as any maid's, and soft and black and dreaming, for there was some feeling in this cousin, some look of inner understanding, which drew the heart of Yuan and made him long to speak with Sheng. But neither Sheng nor Meng said anything and soon Sheng read a book, and when the nuts were gone Meng went away.

But in this crowded room no speech was easy. The children wept at anything, and the doors squeaked with constant passing of the servants coming in with tea and titbits and there was the whispering of his elder cousin's wife, and Ai-lan's laughter and mocking interest in the tales she heard.

So did a long evening pass. There was a mighty dinner at which the uncle and the elder cousin ate beyond belief, complaining together if some dish fell below their hopes, and comparing the cooking of meats and sweets, and praising loudly if a dish were good, and calling for the cook to come and hear their judgments. The cook came, his apron very foul and black with all his labors, and he listened anxiously, his oily face all smiles if he were praised and he all promises and hanging of his head if he were blamed.

As for the lady, Yuan's uncle's wife, she was distraught on her own account to find out if any dish were meat or cooked with lard or had an egg in it, for now that she was old she took the Buddhist vow against all flesh, and she had her own cook, who served up vegetables in every sort of cunning shape of meats, so that a dish that one would swear was pigeons' eggs in soup, would have no pigeon egg at all, or a fish would come so like a fish with eyes and scales in such cunning imitation that one must believe

53

it was a fish until he cut and saw there were no flesh and bones The lady kept her husband's concubine busy to see to all this, and she did it ostentatiously, saying, "Lady, it ought to be a task my son's wife does for me, but in these new days the son's wives are not what they were. I have no daughter-in-law at all or good as none."

And her son's wife sat straight and stiff, very pretty but cold in looks, and pretended she heard nothing of all this talk. But the concubine, being easy in her temper and one to keep the peace always, answered amiably, "I do not mind, lady. I like to be busy."

So she did busy herself about a score of little things and kept the peace for all, a ruddy, plain woman, healthy and sound and always smiling, whose great happiness was to be left for a little while to do embroideries upon her shoes or upon the shoes of her children. She kept by her always her bits of satin, her fine-cut paper patterns for flowers and birds and leaves, and all her many colored silks she hung ready about her neck, and around her middle finger always was her brass ring thimble, so always there, that many times at night she forgot and slept with it, or she would search for it and wonder and then find it still on her finger and burst into loudest merry childlike laughter at herself until all must laugh who heard her.

In all this family talk and noise, the whines of children and the bustle of the food, the learned lady maintained her quiet dignity, answering if one spoke to her, eating delicately but without undue heed to what she ate, and courteous even to a child. Her mild grave eye could by its very meditative gravity check Ai-lan's too quick tongue and too shining eyes that must see any cause for laughter, and somehow in this whole company her presence sat, beneficent and kind, and made them all more kind and courteous. Yuan saw it and respected her the more and was proud to call her mother.

For a little time Yuan lived carefree as he never had dreamed a life could be. He trusted everything to the lady and obeyed her as though he were her little child, except he obeyed her joyfully and eagerly, because she never laid a command on him at all but always asked him if a certain plan she had was what he liked best to do, and she put it so kindly that to Yuan it seemed always what he would have chosen himself if he had thought of it first. She said to him one early day, when they sat alone at the morning meal to which Ai-lan never came, "My son, it is not kind to leave your father ignorant of where you are. If you like it, I will write a letter to him myself and tell him you are safely with me, and that you are safe from his enemies, since here in this coastal city we are under the government of foreigners, and they do not let wars come here. And I will beg him to let you free from this marriage and let you choose some day for yourself as the young do nowadays, and I will tell him that you are to go to school here and that you are well and that I will care for you, for you are my own son."

Yuan had not been all at ease about his father. In the daytime, when he went here and there upon the streets to see the sights, when he was swept among the strange city people or when he was in this clean and quiet house and busy with the books he had bought to go to the new school, he could remember to be willful and he could cry out it was his right to live this free life and his father could not force him to come back. But in the nights or when in the dark morning he awoke, not being used yet to the noise that came up early from the streets, then freedom seemed' a thing impossible, and some of the old childhood fear came back on him and he cried to himself, "I doubt I can stay on here. What if he comes and fetches me back again with his soldiers?"

At such times Yuan forgot all his father's many kindnesses and much love, and he forgot his father's age and illness, and he only remembered how his father often was angry and that he was always bent upon having his own will, and then Yuan felt the

55

old sad careworn fears of childhood come on him again. Many times already he had planned how to write his father, and how to make the letter pleading, or if his father came, how he could hide again.

So now when the lady said this, it seemed the easiest, surest way, and he cried gratefully, "It is the best thing, mother, to help me." And when he had thought a little while as he ate, his heart released itself, and he dared to be a little willful and he said, "Only when you write, write very plainly, because his eyes are not so good as they were, and be sure you make it plain I will not come back to be wed by him. I will never go back again, not even to see him, if I am to be in danger of such slavery."

The lady smiled peaceably at his passion, and she said mildly, "Aye, I will say it, but more courteously," and she seemed so calm and sure that Yuan let his last fears go and trusted her as he might have had he been born of her own flesh. He feared no more, but felt his life here safe and sure, and he turned ardently to all its many parts.

Hitherto Yuan's life had been most simple. In his father's courts there were but the few things he could do that he had always done, and in the school of war, the only other place he knew, there had been much the same simplicity of books and studied warfare, and the bickering and friendship of the lads he knew in the few short hours they had for play, for there they were not allowed to wander at their will among the people, but were schooled most sternly for their cause and the coming warfare for it.

But in this great noisy hurried city Yuan found his life like a book whose pages he must read all at once, so that he lived a score of different kinds of life, and he was so greedy and so kindled and so eager that he could not bear to let any of them pass him by.

Nearest to him in this house was the merry life he craved. Yuan, who had never laughed with other children or played or forgot his duty, now found a new late childhood with his sister Ai-lan. These two could bicker without anger and could play at some game or other of their own and set each other laughing until Yuan forgot everything except his laughter. At first he was shy with her, and only smiled instead of laughing, and his heart was hindered so it could not come out freely. He had been so long taught that he should be sober and should move with dignity and slowness and keep his face grave and straight and answer with full thought, that he did not know what to do with this teasing maid who mocked at him and copied his grave looks upon her little shining face, and made it look so like his own long one that the lady could not but smile, and even Yuan must laugh, although at first he did not quite know if he liked to be so mocked or not, since no one had ever done it before. But Ai-lan would not have him grave at all. No, she would not rest until she had him answering her wit, and she was just enough to cry applause when he said a good thing, too.

One day she cried, "Mother, this old sage of ours is growing young again, I do declare! We'll make a boy of him again. I know what we must do—we must buy him some foreign clothes, and I will teach him to dance and he shall go with me sometimes to dance!"

But this was too much for Yuan's new-found merriment. He knew that Ai-lan went out often for this foreign pleasure called dancing, and he had seen it sometimes at night in passing by some gay lighted house, but it always made him look away, it seemed so bold a thing to do that a man should clasp a woman to him closely, who was not his wife, and even though she were his wife it seemed a thing not to be done thus publicly. But when Ai-lan saw his sudden gravity, she grew very willful and persisted in her notion, and when he said shyly in excuse, "I could never do it. My legs are too long," she answered, "The legs of some foreign men are longer than yours are and yet they do it. The other night I danced with a white man at Louise Ling's house, and I swear my hair kept catching on his waistcoat button, and yet he danced like a tall tree in the wind. No, think of some other reason, Yuan!"

And when he was too shy to speak the real reason, she laughed and shook her little forefinger in his face and said, "I know why it is—you think all the maids will fall in love with you and you are afraid of love!"

Then the lady said gently, "Ai-lan—Ai-lan—not too bold, my child," and Yuan laughed in some discomfort and let the moment pass.

But Ai-lan would not so let it pass, and each day she cried at him, "You shall not escape me, Yuan—I'll teach you to dance yet!" Many of her days were so filled with hours for merry-making that when she ran in from school, she threw down books and changed her garments to some of gayer hue, and went out again to see a theatre or some picture made so like life that the people moved and spoke, and yet even in these days when she saw Yuan but a moment or two, she could tease him that she would begin tomorrow or tomorrow and he must harden himself to the thought of love.

What it might have come to between himself and Ai-lan, Yuan could not have said, because he was still afraid of the pretty chattering girls who came and went with Ai-lan and whom, though she told him their names and said to them, "This is my brother Yuan," he still did not know, they all looked so alike and all so pretty. And he was afraid too of something deeper in himself than even these pretty maids, some secret power in himself he feared their little careless hands might stir alive in him.

But one day there came a thing to help Ai-lan in her mischief. There was an evening when Yuan came out of his room to eat the evening meal and he found the lady whom he called his mother waiting for him alone at the table, and the room very quiet since Ai-lan was not there. This was no surprise to Yuan, for often these two ate alone while Ai-lan went to some merry-making with her friends. But this night the lady said in her quiet way, as soon as he had set himself at table, "Yuan, I have wanted for a long time to ask a thing of you, but knowing how busy you have been and eager to get on in all your books, rising early and needing all your sleep, I have not done it. But the truth is I am at the end of my own ability in a certain matter. I must have help, and since I have looked on you as son in truth, I can ask of you what I cannot ask of any other."

Then Yuan was in great surprise, for this lady was so sure and quiet always, very safe in her content and understanding, that one could not think she needed any sort of aid from anyone. He looked up at her from over the bowl he held and said wondering, "Be sure, mother, I am ready to do anything, because you have been more than own mother to me since I came here. There is not any kindness I have not had from you."

At the plain goodness in his voice and look, some gravity in the lady broke. Her firm lips trembled and she said, "It is your sister. I have given my life to this girl of mine. I suffered first because she was not a boy. Your own mother and I conceived near together, and then your father went away to a war, and when he came back, we both had given birth. I cannot tell you how much I wanted you, Yuan, to have been mine. Your father never —he never looked at me. I always felt a power for some feeling in him—a strange, deep heart he has, but none has ever had it that I know, except you. I do not know why he hates women so. But I used to know how he longed for a son, and all the months he was away I used to tell myself that if I bore his son—I am not foolish, Yuan, as most women are—my father taught me all his learning. I always thought that if your father would only look at what I really am, see what my heart is, he might have taken comfort in me for the little wisdom I have had. But no, to him I was ever no more than a woman who might bear a son for him—and I bore no son, only Ai-lan. When he came home from war and victory he looked at you, Yuan, in your country mother's arms. I had dressed Ai-lan as bravely as a boy in red and silver, and she was the prettiest babe. But he never saw her. Time and time again I sent her to him on some pretext or took her to him, for she was so clever and so forward for her age, I felt he must see what she was. But he has the strangest shyness toward all females. He only saw she was a girl. At last in my own loneliness, Yuan, I told myself I would leave his courts—not openly, but with the excuse of schooling for my daughter, and I was sure that I would let Ai-lan have everything a son would have, and do my best against this bondage of a woman's birth. And he was generous, Yuan—he has sent me money—there has been nothing lacking except he did not care if I were dead or living, or my daughter either. . . . I help you, not for his sake, but for your own, my son."

She cast a deep look at him when she said this, and Yuan caught the look, and was confused because he saw thus into this lady's life and thoughts, and he felt shy and speechless at such knowledge because she was his elder. Then she went on, "So have I spent myself for Ai-lan. And she has been a lovely, merry child. I used to think she must one day be great, perhaps, a great painter or poet, or best of all a doctor as my father was, for there are women doctors nowadays, or at least some leader in this new day for women in our land. It seemed to me this one child I have given birth to must be great and all that I would have been—learned and wise in everything. I never had the foreign learning as I craved to have it. I read her school books now that she has thrown by, and I grieve to see how much there is in them that I can never know. . . . But I have come to understand now that she will never be very great. Her only gift is in her laughter and in her mockery and in her pretty face and in all her winning ways of gaining hearts. She will not work much at anything. She loves nothing very well except her pleasure—kind she is, but without any depth to kindness. She is kind because life is more pleasant when she is kind than not. Oh, I know my child's measure, Yuan—I know the stuff I have had to shape. I am not deceived. My dreams are gone. Now all I ask is that she wed wisely somewhere. For she must be wed, Yuan. She is such a one as must be in a man's care. And she has been bred in such freedom that she will not wed where I might choose, and she is willful, and I live in misery lest she cast herself away on some lad or on some foolish man too old for her. There is even some perverseness in her that for a while made her even look twice at a white man and think it an honor to be seen with him. But I do not fear this now. She has taken another turn. I fear rather a man she is with continually. I cannot always follow her and I do not trust these cousins nor the cousin's wife. Yuan, to please me, go with her sometimes at night and see if she is safe."

At this instant while her mother talked so long, Ai-lan came into the room dressed for her merry-making. She wore a long straight robe of deep rose bound about with silver and on her feet were silver shoes, foreign and high at the back, and the collar was cut away from her gown in the newest fashion and her soft neck showed as slim and smooth and golden as a child's, and the sleeves were cut away, too, just below the shoulder and left bare her pretty arms and hands, slender, yet with no bones to be seen and covered with the softest and most delicate of flesh. Upon her wrists, slight as a child's yet round as any woman's, she wore carved silver bracelets, and on each middle finger of her hands were rings of silver and of jade, and her hair was curled about her lovely painted face, as smooth and black as jet. About her shoulders, but not fastened, was a cloak of softest whitest fur, and when she came in she threw this back, and looked smiling, first at Yuan and then at her mother, knowing very well how fair she was and innocently proud in all her beauty.

Both of them looked at her and could not move their eyes away and this Ai-lan saw too, and laughed a little cry of pure delighted triumph. This broke the mother's gaze and she said quietly, "Whom do you go with tonight, my child?"

"With a friend of Sheng's," she answered gaily. "A writer, mother—and famous for the tales he writes, too—Wu Li-yang!"

It was a name that Yuan had heard of sometimes—a man in truth famous for his tales written in the western manner, tales very bold and free and full of talk of love between man and maid, and ending very often in death somewhere, and Yuan was not a little curious to see him, although his tales were such that Yuan read them secretly and even so he was ashamed to read them.

"Some time you might indeed take Yuan," the mother said mildly. "He works too hard, I tell him. He ought to have a little pleasure sometimes with his sister and his cousins."

"So you should, Yuan, and I have been ready for a long time," cried Ai-lan, smiling lavishly and looking at him from her great black eyes. "But you must buy the clothes you need. Mother, make him buy foreign clothes and shoes—he will dance better with his legs free from those robes. Oh, I like to see a man in foreign clothes—let's go tomorrow and buy him everything! You're not ugly, you know, Yuan. You'd look as nice as any man in foreign clothes. And I'll teach you to dance, Yuan. I'll begin tomorrow!"

At this Yuan blushed and shook his head, but not with his first decision, for he felt what the lady had been telling him, and he could not but think how kind she had been to him, and this was a way to repay her. Then Ai-lan cried, "What will you do if you cannot dance? You can't sit keeping alone at a table— we all dance, we younger ones!"

"It is the fashion, true enough, Yuan," the mother said, half sighing, "a very strange and dubious fashion, I know, brought over from the West, and I hate it and I cannot think it wise or well, but so it is."

"Mother, you are the oddest, old-fashioned soul, and yet I love you," said Ai-lan, laughing.

But before Yuan could speak the door opened and Sheng came

in, dressed in the black and white of foreign clothing, and with him another man, whom Yuan knew was the story teller, and with them was a pretty girl, dressed exactly like Ai-lan except in green and gold. But to Yuan all girls looked the same these days, all pretty, all slight as children, all painted, and all with tinkling voices and little constant cries of joy or pain. He did not see the maid, therefore, but he looked at the famous young man, and he saw a tall smooth man, his face large and smooth and pale and very beautiful with narrow red lips and black and narrow eyes and straight narrow black brows. But the man was notable most for his hands which he moved incessantly even when he did not speak; large hands they were, but shaped like a woman's hands, the fingers pointed at the ends and thick and soft at the base, and the flesh smooth and olive and oiled and fragrant,—voluptuous hands, for when Yuan took one in his own for greeting, it seemed to melt and flow warmly about his fingers and Yuan hated suddenly the touch of it.

But Ai-lan and the man drew together intimately in their looks and his eyes told her boldly what he thought of her beauty and seeing it the mother's face was troubled.

Then they were suddenly gone, like a flower-laden wind, the four of them, and in the quiet room Yuan sat alone again with the mother, and she looked at him straightly.

"You see, Yuan, why I ask you?" she said quietly. "That man is already wed. I know. I asked Sheng to tell me, and at first he would not, but at last he made light of it and told me it was not thought now, if the man's wife were old-fashioned and chosen by his parents, a dishonor if he walked with other maids. But I wish it were not my maid, Yuan!"

"I will go," Yuan said, and now he could forget what had seemed wrong to him, because he did it for this lady's sake.

Thus it came about that Yuan was bought the foreign clothes and Ai-lan and her mother went with him to the foreign shop

63

and there a tailor measured him and stared at his shape, and fine black cloth was chosen for one suit and a dark brown rough stuff for a suit to wear by day. And leather shoes were bought and a hat and gloves and such small things as foreign men may wear, and all the time Ai-lan was chattering and laughing and putting out her pretty fluttering hands to pull at this or push that away, and she put her head on one side and looked at Yuan to see what would make him prettiest, until Yuan, half shy and shamed, was laughing too, and merrier than he had ever been his life long. Even the clerk laughed at Ai-lan's talk and glanced at her secretly, she was so very free and pretty. Only the mother sighed while she smiled, for this maid did not care what she said or did, and thought only to make people laugh at her and she searched, not knowing it, to see what was in anyone's eyes and if he found her pretty, and he always did, then she grew more merry still.

So Yuan was garbed at last, and the truth was that once he was used to a certain feeling of nakedness about his legs, where he had been accustomed to his swinging robes, he liked the foreign clothing very well. He could walk freely in it, and he liked the many pockets where he could store small things he needed every day. It was true, too, that it was pleasant to him the first day he put his new garb on himself to see Ai-lan clap her hands and hear her cry, "Yuan, you are handsome! Mother, look at him! Doesn't it become him? That red tie—I knew it would sit well beneath that dark skin of his and so it does— Yuan, I'll be proud of you!—Look, here we are— Miss Ching, this is my brother Yuan. I want you to be friends. Miss Li, my brother!"

And the maid pretended so to introduce him to a row of pretty girls and Yuan did not know how not to yield to his shyness and he stood smiling painfully, the dark blood in his cheeks as red as the new tie. But still it was somehow sweet, too, and when Ai-lan opened a music machine she had and set the music beating through the room, and when she seized him and laid his arm about her and took his hand and gently forced him to a

64

movement, he let her do it, half confused, and yet finding it very pleasant. He found a natural rhythm in himself, so that before very long his feet were moving of their own accord to the pace the music set, and Ai-lan was delighted at the ease with which he learned how to move himself to music.

Thus Yuan began this new pleasure. For he found it was a pleasure. Sometimes he was ashamed of a craving it aroused in his blood, and when this craving came, he must restrain himself because he longed to seize closer the maid he held, whatever maid it was, and give himself and her to the craving. Indeed it was not an easy thing for Yuan, who until this hour had never touched even a maid's hand, nor spoken to any maid who was not his sister or his cousin, to move to and fro in warm lighted rooms to the strange twisting foreign rhythms of music, and in his very arms a maid. At first, the first evening, he had been so torn with fear lest his feet betray him and go astray that he could not think of anything else except how to set them properly.

But soon his feet moved of their own accord and smoothly as any other pair of feet, and the music was their guide, so Yuan did not need to think of them again. Among the people of every race and nation who gathered in the pleasure houses of that city, Yuan was only one, and he was lost among their strangeness, who did not know him. He was alone, and he found himself alone and with a maid against his body and her hand in his. He saw no maid better than another, in these first days, and they all were pretty and they all were friends of Ai-lan's and willing, enough, and anyone did as well for him as any other, and all he wanted was a maid to hold and to set his heart burning with a slow sweet smothered fire to which he dared not yield.

If afterwards he was ashamed, when he was cooled by daylight and the soberness of school rooms, still he need not tell himself the thing was dangerous for him and he should avoid it, because there was his duty to the lady, and he could say he was helping her.

It was true he did most carefully watch his sister, and at the end of every evening's pleasure he waited until Ai-lan was ready to come home, and he never asked another maid to go with him, lest he must take her home and leave Ai-lan. Especially was he so careful because he must justify to himself these hours he spent thus, and he was very zealous and the more because it was true that the man Wu did meet Ai-lan very often. This one thing could make Yuan forget the sweet sickness that stole into him sometimes when the music swayed too much and the maid he held clung closely to him, and it was if he saw Ai-lan turn aside to any other room with that one named Wu, or if she sought a balcony for the coolness. Then he could not rest until the dance was ended and he could go and find her and stay near her.

But be sure Ai-lan did not always bear it. Often she pouted at him, and sometimes she cried in anger, "I wish you would not stick so close to me, Yuan! It is time you went alone now and sought out maids for yourself. You do not need me any longer. You dance as well as anyone. I wish you would let me be!"

To this Yuan answered nothing. He would not say out what the lady had told him and Ai-lan would not press the thing too plainly, either, not even in her anger. It was as though she feared to tell something she did not want told, but when she was not angry she could forget and be as merry a play-fellow as ever with him.

At last she grew cunning and even was not angry with him. Rather she laughed and let him follow her as he would, as though she wanted to keep him friendly to her. For everywhere Ai-lan went, the story teller was. He seemed to know the maid's mother did not like him, for now he never came to her house. But always at other houses, whether public or of friends, there he was near Ai-lan, as if he knew where Ai-lan was to be. And Yuan began to watch Ai-lan dancing with this man, and he saw at these times her little face was grave. This very gravity sat so strangely on her that Yuan was troubled by it often, and once or twice he was about to tell the lady of it. Yet there was nothing true to tell, for Ai-lan danced with many men, and one night when they came home together Yuan asked her why she was so grave with that one man, and she said lightly, laughing while she spoke, "Perhaps I do not like to dance with him!" And she drew down her mouth and thrust out her little red painted lips to Yuan to mock at him.

"Then why do it?" Yuan put to her bluntly, and she laughed and laughed at this, some hidden mischief in her eyes and at last she said, "I can't be rude, Yuan." So he let it pass from his mind, though doubtfully, and it remained a darkening on his pleasure.

There was another thing to mar his pleasure, too, a small thing and usual, and yet there it was. Each time Yuan came out of the heated brilliant midnight rooms where flowers were and food and wine spilled out and more than anyone had needed, he seemed to step out into that other world he wanted to forget. For in the darkness or in the grey dawn, the beggars and the desperate poor stood huddled by the doorways, some to try and sleep, but some to steal, like street dogs, into the pleasure houses after the guests were gone, and grovel under tables to snatch at the broken bits of food that were thrown there. It could be but a brief moment only, for the serving men roared and kicked at them and dragged them out by the legs and barred the gates against them. These piteous creatures Ai-lan and her playmates never saw, or if they saw they paid no heed to them and were as used to them as to stray beasts, and they went laughing and calling to each other from their vehicles, and so went gaily to their homes and beds.

But Yuan saw. Even against his will he saw them, and it came to be that even in the midst of the night's pleasure, in the midst of music and of dancing, he remembered with great dread the moment when he must go into the grey street and see the cringing figures and the wolfish faces of the poor. Sometimes one of these poor stretched out a hand in despair at such deafness as these merry rich people had, and the hand would lay hold upon a lady's satin robe and cling to it.

Then a man's lordly voice would shout out, "Your hand away there! How can you lay your filthy hand upon my lady's satin robe and soil it?" And a policeman of those who stood there would rush forth and beat the taloned filthy hand away.

But Yuan shrank and bent his head and hurried on, because he was so formed in spirit that he felt as upon his own flesh the beating of the wooden club, and it was his own starved hand that winced and fell down broken. At this time of his life Yuan loved pleasure, and he was unwilling to see the poor, and yet he was so shaped within that he saw them all even while he wished he did not.

But there were not only such nights in Yuan's life now. There were the sturdy days of work in school among his fellows, and here he came to know better his cousins Sheng and Meng, whom Ai-lan called the Poet and the Rebel. Here in the school these two were their true selves, and in the classrooms or in throwing a great ball about upon the playground, they all, these three young cousins, could forget themselves. They could sit in the decorous listening rows of desks, or leap and shout at their fellows and roar with laughter at some faulty play, and Yuan came to know his cousins as he never did at home.

For as young men at home among their elders are never their true selves, so were not these two, Sheng always being silent and too good for everybody, and secret as to his poems, and Meng always sulky and prone to knock against some small table or other too full of small toys and bowls of tea, so that his mother cried constantly against him, "I swear no son of mine has ever

68

been so like a young buffalo in my house. Why can you not walk smooth and silent as Sheng does?" And yet when Sheng came home so late from pleasure that he could not rise in time the next morning for his school she would cry at Sheng, "I ever say I am the most suffering mother in the world, and all my sons are worthless. Why can you not stay decently at home at night as Meng does? I do not see him slipping out at night dressed like a foreign devil and going I do not know to what evil place. It is your elder brother leads you wrong, as his own father did lead him. It is your father's fault at bottom and I always said it was."

Now the truth was that Sheng never went to the same pleasure houses as his elder brother did, for Sheng liked a daintier sort of pleasure, and Yuan saw him often in the pleasure houses where Ai-lan was. Sometimes he went with Yuan and Ai-lan, but often he went alone with some maid he loved for the time, and they two would dance together the whole evening through in silence and in perfect pleasure.

Thus the brothers went their own ways, each absorbed in some secret life of this great multitudinous city. But, although Sheng and Meng were two such diverse souls that they might easily have quarrelled, more easily than either with the elder brother, who was too far older than they were, since there were two between, one dead by hanging himself in his youth, and the other given to the Tiger, yet they did not quarrel, partly because Sheng was a truly gentle laughing youth who held nothing worth a quarrel, and he let Meng have his way, but also because each was in the other's secret. If Meng knew Sheng went to certain places, Sheng knew Meng was a secret revolutionist and had his own certain hidden meeting places, too, though in a different cause, yet in a more dangerous one. And so the two kept silence for each other and neither defended himself before the mother at the expense of the other. But each, as time went on, came to know Yuan and to like him the more, because he told to neither of them what one might tell to Yuan alone.

And now this school began to be the great pastime of Yuan's days, for he truly did love learning. He bought his great heap of new books and held them piled beneath his arms, and he bought pencils and at last he proudly bought a foreign pen such as all the other students had, and fastened it upon his coat's edge, and he laid aside forever his old brush, except when he wrote to his father once a month.

All the books were magic to Yuan. He turned their clean, unknown pages eagerly, and he longed to print each word upon his mind, and learn and learn for very love of learning. He rose at dawn if he could wake and read his books, and he memorized the things he did not understand; whole pages he put to his memory like this. And when he had eaten his early breakfast—solitary, because neither Ai-lan nor his mother rose as soon as he did on school days, he rushed off, walking through the still half-empty streets and was the first to reach his classrooms always. And if a teacher came a little early, too, then Yuan took it as a chance for learning and he overcame his shyness and put what questions that he could. If sometimes a teacher did not come at all, then Yuan did not, as the common students did, rejoice in an hour for holiday. No, rather he took it as a loss he could not happily bear, and spent the hour in studying what the teacher might have taught.

This learning was the sweetest pastime therefore to Yuan. He could not learn enough of history of all the countries of the world, of foreign stories and of verses, of studies of the flesh of beasts; most of all he loved to study the inner shapes of leaves and seeds and roots of plants, to know how the rain and sun can mould the soil, to learn when to plant a certain crop, and how select its seeds, and how increase its harvest. All this and much more did Yuan learn. He begrudged himself the time for food

70

and sleep except that his great lad's body was always hungry, too, and needing food and sleep. But this the lady mother watched, and while she said nothing, yet she watched him, although he scarcely knew it, and she saw to it that certain dishes which he loved were often set before him.

He saw his cousins often, too, and they were daily more a part of Yuan's life, for Sheng was in a classroom with him, and often had his verses or his writing read aloud and praised. At such times Yuan looked with humble envy at him, and wished his verses were as smoothly rhymed, although Sheng looked down most modestly and pretended it was nothing to him to be praised. And he might have been believed, except that on his pretty mouth a little smile of pride sat very often and betrayed him when he did not know it. As for Yuan, at this time he wrote very little verse, because he lived too occupied for any dreaming, and if he did write, the words came roughly and he could not make them grouped and as they used to be. It seemed to him that his thoughts were too big for him, unshaped, not easily to be grasped and caught into a form of words. Even when he smoothed and polished and wrote them over many times, his old scholar teacher often said, "It interests me, it is fair enough, but I do not catch just what you mean."

Thus he paused one day when Yuan had written a poem about a seed, and Yuan could not say what his meaning was exactly, either, and he stammered out, "I meant—I think I meant to say that in the seed, in that last atom of the seed, when it is cast into the ground, there is an instant, a place perhaps, when seed becomes no longer matter, but a sort of spirit, an energy, a kind of life, a moment between spirit and material, and if we could catch that transmuting instant, when the seed begins to grow, understand the change—"

"Ah, yes," the teacher said, doubtfully. A kindly, aged man he was who kept his spectacles low on his nose and stared across them now at Yuan. He had taught so many years he knew exactly what he wanted and so what was right, and now he laid Yuan's verses down and he pushed his spectacles and said half-thinkingly, and picking up the next paper, "Not very clear, I fear, in your mind. . . . Now, here's a better one, called 'A Walk on a Summer's Day'—very nice—I'll read it." It was Sheng's verse for that day.

Yuan fell to silence and kept his thoughts to himself, listening. He envied Sheng his pretty, swiftly running thoughts and pure rhymes; yet it was not bitter envy, either, but very humble and admiring envy, even as Yuan loved secretly his cousin's handsome looks, so much more clearly handsome than his own.

Yet Yuan never knew Sheng's self, for with all his smiling courteous seeming openness, none ever knew Sheng well. He could give anywhere the gentlest words of praise and kindness, but though he spoke often and easily, yet what he said never told his inner thought. Sometimes he came to Yuan and said, "Let us go and see a picture today after school—there is a very good foreign picture at the Great World Theatre," yet when they both had walked there together and sat three hours through and come away again, and though Yuan had liked being with his cousin, still when he thought of it he could not remember that Sheng had said anything. He only could remember in the dim theatre Sheng's smiling face and his shining, strangely oval eyes. Only once Sheng said of Meng and his cause, "I am not one of them—I never shall be a revolutionist. I love my life too well, and I love only beauty. I am moved only by beauty. I have no wish to die in any cause. Some day I shall sail across the sea, and if it is more beautiful there than here, it may be I shall never come back again—how do I know? I have no wish to suffer for the common people. They are filthy and they smell of garlic. Let them die. Who will miss them?"

This he said in the most tranquil pleasantness while they sat in the gilded theatre and looked about upon the well-dressed men and women there, all eating cakes and nuts and smoking foreign cigarettes, and he might have been the voice of all of them speaking. Yet though Yuan liked his cousin very well, he could not but feel a coldness in him at the calmness of these words, "Let them die." For Yuan still did hate death, and though at this time in his life the poor were not near him, he did not want them to die, nevertheless.

But these words of Sheng's that day prompted Yuan to ask another time more concerning Meng. Meng and Yuan had not talked very often together, but they played on one side of the game of ball, and Yuan liked the fierceness of Meng's thrust and leaping. Meng had the hardest tightest body of them all. Most of the young men were pale and slackly hung and they wore too many clothes they did not take off easily, so that they ran anyhow as children do, and fumbled at the ball, or threw it sidewise as a girl might, or kicked it mildly so that it rolled along the ground and stopped very soon. But Meng sprang at the ball as though it were his enemy and he kicked it with his hard leather-shod foot, and up it soared and came down with a great bound and flew up again, and all his body hardened at the play, and Yuan liked this as well as he liked Sheng's beauty.

So one day he asked of Sheng, "How do you know Meng is a revolutionist?" and Sheng answered, "Because he tells me so. He has always told me something of what he does, and I am the only one he tells, I think. I live in a little fear for him, too, sometimes. I dare not tell my father or my mother, nor my eldest brother even, what he does, for I know they would accuse him, and he is so fiery and so angry in his nature that he would run away forever. He trusts me now and tells me very much and so I know what he is doing, although I know there are secrets that he will not tell, for he has taken some wild oath of patriotism, and he has cut his arm and let his blood and written down his oath in blood, I know."

"And are there many of these revolutionists among our school-mates?" Yuan asked, somewhat troubled, for he had thought

73

that here he was safe enough, and now it seemed he was not safe, for this was the very thing his comrades in the school of war did, and still he did not want to join them.

"Many of them," answered Sheng. "And there are maids among them, too."

Now Yuan stared indeed. For there were maidens among the students in his school, this being the custom in this new and forward coastal city, that in many schools for men the law allowed young women to come also, and though there were not many maids yet who dared to be learned, or whose fathers let them be, yet there were a score or two in this one school, and Yuan had seen them here and there about the classrooms, but had paid no heed to them, nor counted them as any part of his life there, since they were not often beautiful and were always bent on books.

But after this day being troubled at what Sheng had said he looked at them more curiously, and now every time he passed a maid, her books beneath her arm and her eyes downcast, he wondered if so demure a creature could be part of all the secret plotting. One especially he noted, for she was the only one of her kind in the class which he and Sheng shared. She was a slender creature, bony as a little hungry bird, her face delicate and peaked, the cheek bones high, and the narrow lips pale and fine beneath the straight nose. She never spoke in class and what her thoughts were none knew, because she wrote neither good nor ill, and drew no comment from the teacher. But she was always there and sat listening to every word he said, and only in her narrow sombre eyes her interest seemed to shine sometimes.

Yuan looked at her curiously, until one day the maid felt his stare and looked back, and thereafter when Yuan looked at her he found her always watching him with her secret steady eyes, and so he looked no more. But he asked Sheng about her, since she moved withdrawn from anyone, and Sheng laughed and answered, "That one! She is one of them. She is a friend of

Meng's—she and Meng are always in some secret talk and planning—look at her cold face! The cold ones make the steadiest revolutionists. Meng is too hot. He is all hot today and in despair tomorrow. But this girl, she is always cold as ice and same as ice and hard as ice. I hate girls to be so same and cool. But she cools Meng when he is hot and makes some too early showing of the plans, and when he despairs, her sameness pulls him up again. She comes from an inland province where there is revolution already."

"What do they plan?" asked Yuan curiously, his voice made low.

"Oh, when the army comes they plan to meet it triumphantly," said Sheng and he shrugged himself and walked with seeming indolence away from any who might hear them. "Most of all they work among the mill folk here who get a few pence only for their daily wage, and they tell the pullers of the rickshas how downtrodden they are and how these foreign police oppress them cruelly and all such things, so that if this day of triumph comes these low people will be ready to rise and seize what they may wish. But wait, Yuan,—they'll come and see if they can win you. Meng will come and see you some day. He asked me only the other day what sort you were, and if you were a revolutionist at heart."

At last one day Yuan perceived that Meng did seek him out, and he laid his hand on Yuan and caught him by his clothes and said in his usual sulky way, "You and I are cousins, yet we seem strangers still, never meeting much alone. Come with me to the tea shop at the school gate, and let us eat together."

Now Yuan could not well refuse, for it was the last class hour of that day, and all were free now, and so he went with Meng. They sat awhile, speechlessly, but after all it seemed Meng had nothing he cared to say, for he only sat and stared out into the street and watched the passers-by, and if he spoke at all it was to make a bitter joke at something that they saw. He said,

75

"Look at that great fat lord in that motor car! See how he eats and how he lolls! He is an extortionist—a usurer or a banker or he has a factory. I know the very look! Well, he does not know he sits upon a hidden fire!"

And Yuan, knowing what his cousin meant, said nothing, though in honesty he thought to himself that Meng's own father was somewhat fatter still than this man was.

Or Meng said, "See that man toiling at his ricksha—he is half-starved—look, he has broken some little law. He's newly come from the country and he does not know he must not cross the street when that policeman holds his hand so. There, see what I said! Look at that policeman beat him—see him force the ricksha down and seize its cushions! Now that poor man has lost his vehicle and his day's earnings. And yet he must pay out just the same tonight at the place where he hires the ricksha!"

And when he saw this thing and watched the ricksha man turn away drooped in despair, Meng's voice grew shaking and Yuan looked and to his wonder he saw this strange lad was weeping angrily and struggling against his tears uncouthly. When Meng saw Yuan looking at him with such sympathy, he said, half choking, "Let's go where we can talk. I swear I cannot bear it if I do not talk. I swear I could kill these stupid folk for bearing their oppression so patiently."

And Yuan to soothe him took him to his own room and shut the door and let the lad talk.

This talk with Meng stirred deep in Yuan a sort of conscience that he wished not to remember. Yuan loved so well the ease of these days, the merriment and stir, the rest from duty, the doing only what he liked to do. These two women in the house, the lady and his sister, gave him lavishly their praise and tenderness, and he lived in warmth and friendliness. He would have forgotten that there were others who were not warmed or fed. He was so happy that he would not think of any sorrowful thing, and if sometimes in the dark dawns now he remembered that still his father might have power over him, he put the thought away, because he trusted to the lady's resourcefulness and care for him. Now these poor of whom Meng must talk brought an old shadow over him again, and he drew away from shadows.

. . . Yet through such talk Yuan learned to see his country as he had not. In those days in the earthen house he saw it as spreading, lovely lands. He saw the fair body of his country. Even then he had not deeply felt the people. But here in these city streets, Meng taught him how to see the country's soul. Through the younger lad's angry notice of every smallest slight put on any lowly man or laborer, Yuan learned to notice, too. Since always where the very rich are there are the very poor, too, Yuan as he came and went upon the streets saw many more of these, for most were poor—the poorest starving children, blind and foul with disease and never washed, and in the fairest brightest streets, faced on both sides with great shops of every sort of merchandise, and fluttering silken banners overhead and hired musicians to play in balconies and draw their crowds of purchasers, even on these streets the filthiest beggars whined and wailed, and most faces were too pale and thin, and there were scores of prostitutes who came out even ahead of night to ply their hungry trade.

He saw everything and in the end this notice went far deeper in him than it could in Meng, for Meng was one of those who must serve some cause, who bend everything to serve the cause. Whenever he saw a starved man, or if he saw the poor clustered at the gate where rotten eggs are thrown outside the gates of factories where eggs are sent in ships to foreign lands, and these poor buying bowlfuls for a penny and drinking down the stuff, or if he saw men straining at great loads too heavy even for beasts, or if he saw rich and idle men and silk-clad painted women, laughing and taking pleasure while the poor begged, then his anger burst from him, and for everything he felt, he had this cry for cure, "These things will never be better until our cause is gained. We must have revolution! We must have all the rich thrown down, and these foreigners who force us cast out again, and the poor shall be lifted up, and only revolution can do it. Yuan, when will you see this light and join our cause? We need you—our country needs us all!"

And Meng turned his burning, angry eyes on Yuan as though he would fasten them in him until he gave his promise.

But Yuan could not promise because he feared the cause. It was the same cause, after all, from which he had escaped.

And Yuan could not somehow trust to any cause to cure these ills, nor could he hate a rich man hot and properly as Meng could. The very plumpness of a rich man's body, the ring upon his finger, the fur lining of his coat, the jewels in his lady's ears, the paint and powder on her face, could send Meng wildly deeper in his cause. But even against his will Yuan must see a kindly look if it were on a rich man's face, or he could see a look of pity in a painted woman's eyes, who gave a bit of silver to a beggar, even though she wore a satin coat, and he liked laughter, whether it was from rich or poor; he liked the one who laughed even if he knew him evil. The truth was, Meng must love or hate men for being white or black, but Yuan could not for his life say, "This man is rich and evil, and this man is poor and good," and so he was spoiled for any cause-making, however great the cause.

He could not even hate as Meng hated them the foreigners who mingled with the city crowds. For the city, being very great in trade with all parts of the world, was filled with foreigners of every hue and tongue, and anywhere upon the streets Yuan saw them, some gentle, but some loud and evil and often drunken, and many poor and rich among them. If Meng hated any rich men worse than others it was rich foreigners; he could bear any cruelty better than this, if he saw a drunken foreign sailor kick a ricksha puller or a white woman buying something from a vendor and bent on paying less than she was asked, or any of those common sights that may be seen in any coastal city where men of many nations meet and mingle.

Meng grudged these foreigners the very air they lived upon. If he passed one, he would not give way a foot of path before him. His long sour lad's face grew darker still and he would thrust his shoulders out, and if he pushed the foreigner, even though a woman, from his way, then so much the better, and he muttered full of hate, "They have no business on our land. They come to rob and plunder us. With their religion they rob our souls and minds, and with their trade they rob us of our goods and money."

One day Yuan and Meng walking home from school together passed upon the street a slight slender man whose skin was white and his nose high as white men's are, but his eyes and hair were very black and not like white men's. Then Meng cast the man a furious look and he cried to Yuan, "If there is a thing I hate above another in this city, it is such men as these who are nothing wholly, but are mixed in blood and untrustworthy and divided in their hearts! I never can understand how any of our race can so forget himself, man or woman, as to mix his blood with blood of foreigners. I would kill them all for traitors and kill such fellows as the one we passed."

But Yuan must remember the man's gentle look and how his face was patient in spite of paleness and he said, "He looked kind enough. I cannot think he must be evil only because his skin is pale and his blood mixed. He cannot help what his parents did."

But Meng cried out, "You ought to hate him, Yuan! Have you not heard what white men have done to our country, and how they hold us hard as any prisoners with their cruel, unjust treaties? We cannot even have our laws—why, if a white man kills a countryman of ours, he is not punished scarcely—he will not go before our court—"

While Meng cried out thus, Yuan listened, smiling half in

79

apology, because he was so mild before the other's heat, and feeling perhaps it was true he ought to hate for country's sake, but he was not able.

Therefore Yuan could not yet join Meng's cause. He said nothing when Meng begged him, smiled in his shy way, and could not say he would not, but he put forth the reason that he was so busy—he had no time for even such a cause, and at last Meng let him be and even ceased to talk with him, and gave him but a surly nod or two in passing. On holidays and patriotic days when all must go forth with flags and singing, Yuan went too, as they all did, lest he be cried a traitor, but he joined no secret meetings and he made no plots. Sometimes he heard some news of those who plotted, how this one had been found with a bomb hidden in his room to throw at some great man, and once a band of plotters went and beat a certain teacher whom they hated for his friendship with the foreigners, but when he heard such things Yuan turned more steadfastly to his books and would not lend his interest elsewhere.

The truth was at this time Yuan's life was pressed too full for him to know what any one thing was at bottom. Before he could think clearly to the end of rich and poor, or before he could comprehend the meaning of Meng's cause, or even take his fill of gaiety, some other thing came to his mind. There was all he knew at school, the many things he learned and did, the strange lessons that he had, the magic of a science opening to him in a laboratory. Even in the chemistry he hated because its stinks offended the delicacy of his nose, he was charmed by the hues of potions that he made and wondered at the way two mild passive fluids cast together could suddenly foam up into a new life, new color and new odor, and so make a different third. Into his mind these days there poured every sort of thought and perception of this great city where the whole world met, and there was not time in day and night to see what each one meant.

He could not give himself to any single knowledge because there were so many, and in his heart sometimes he envied his cousins and his sister very much, for Sheng lived in his dreams and loves, and Meng lived in his cause, and Ai-lan in her prettiness and pleasure, and to Yuan this seemed easy living, since he lived in such diversity.

Even these city poor were so unlovely in their poverty that Yuan could not feel them wholly pitiful. He did pity them, and he did want them fed and clothed, and nearly always if he had a penny and a beggar laid his claws upon Yuan's arm, he gave the penny. But he feared he gave it not all in pity either, but partly to buy his freedom from that filthy clinging hand and from the whining voice beside his ear, "Have a kind heart, young sir—a kind heart, sir, lest I starve, I and my children!" There was only one more hideous sight than a beggar in this city, and it was their children. Yuan could not bear the puling children of the very poor, their little faces set already in the whining look of beggary, and worst of all were starveling babes half-naked and thrust into the naked skinny bosoms of the women. Yes, Yuan drew shudderingly from them all. He threw his pennies at them and averted his eyes and hastened on his way. And to himself he thought, "I might join Meng's cause if they were not so hideous, these poor!"

Yet there came something, too, to save him from complete estrangement from these of his own people, and it was his old love of lands and fields and trees. In the city during the winter that love receded and Yuan often forgot it. But now as spring drew on, he felt a restlessness come on him. The days grew warm, and in small city gardens the trees began to bud and leaf, and on the streets came vendors carrying on their poles' ends baskets of blossoming plum trees, twisted into dwarfish shapes, or great round bunches of violets and spring lilies. Yuan grew restless in the mild spring winds and these winds made him remember the little hamlet where the earthen house stood, and he had a craving in his feet to stand on earth somewhere instead of on these city pavements. So he entered his name in the new spring term into a certain class of that school where teachers taught of cultivation of the land and Yuan, among others, was apportioned a little piece of earth outside the city, for practice at the land to test what they had learned in books, and in this bit of land it was part of Yuan's task that he must plant seeds and keep the weeds out and do labor of this sort.

It so happened that the piece Yuan had was at the end of all the others, and next to a farmer's field, and the first time Yuan came out to see his plot of land he went alone, and the farmer stood there staring, his face alight with grinning, and he shouted, "What do you students here? I thought students only learned in books!"

Then Yuan answered, "In these days we learn in books of sowing and reaping too, and we learn how to make the land ready for the sowing, and that is what I do today."

At this the farmer laughed loudly and said with a mighty scorn, "I never did hear of such a learning! Why, farmer tells his son and his son tells his son—one looks only at his neighbor and does what his neighbor does!"

"And if the neighbor is wrong?" said Yuan, smiling.

"Then look at the next neighbor and a better one," said the farmer and then he laughed over again and fell to hoeing in his own field and he muttered to himself and stopped to scratch his head and shake himself and laugh again and cry out, "No, I never did hear such a thing in all my days! Well, I'm glad I sent no son of mine to any school, to waste my silver to have him learn of farming! I'll teach him more than he can learn, I'll swear!"

Now Yuan had never held a hoe in his two hands in all his life, and when he took up the long-handled clumsy thing it felt so heavy that he could not wield it. However high he lifted it he could not bring it down in such a way as to cut the packed

82

soil and it always came down sidewise, and he sweat most fearfully and still he could not do it, so that although the day was cold for spring and biting windy, his sweat was pouring down him as though it were summer.

At last in despair and secretly he glanced at the farmer to see how he did it, for the farmer's steady strokes went up and down and made a mark each time the hoe's point fell, although Yuan hoped the farmer would not see him glance, for indeed he was a little proud. But soon he saw that the farmer did see him, and had seen him all along and was laughing in himself to see the wild way Yuan flung his hoe about. Now catching Yuan's glance he roared with fresh laughter and striding over clods he came up to Yuan and cried, "Never tell me you are watching what a neighbor farmer does, when you have learned it all in books!" And he laughed and cried again, "Has not your book told you even how to hold the hoe?"

Then Yuan struggled a little over a petty anger, for to his own surprise he found it was not easy for him to hear the laughter of this common man, and he had his own rueful knowledge that indeed he could not even dig this bit of land, and how could he hope to plant the seed in it? But his reason overcame his shame at last and he let his hoe drop and he grinned, too, and bore the farmer's laughter and wiped his dripping face and said sheepishly, "You are right, neighbor. It is not in the book. I'll take you for my teacher if you'll let me learn of you."

At this simple speech the farmer was very pleased and he liked Yuan and he stopped his laughing. In truth he was secretly proud that he, a humble farmer, had something he could teach this young man, a youth from the schools, as anyone could see, and learned in his speech and looks. And so, importantly and with a sort of pompousness upon him, the farmer eyed the young man and said seriously, "First, look at me and at yourself, and ask which one is free to wield the hoe without such sweating."

And Yuan looked and saw the farmer, a man strong and

brown, stripped to the waist, his legs bare to his knees, his feet in sandals, his face brown and red with winds and weather, his whole look good and free. Then Yuan said nothing, but he smiled and without a single word he took off his outer heavy coat and then his inner coat, and rolled his sleeves up to his elbow and stood ready. This the farmer watched, and suddenly he cried again, "What woman's skin you have! Look at this arm of mine!" And he put his arm by Yuan's and outstretched his hand. "Put out your hand!—Look at your palm all blisters! But you hold your hoe so loosely it would have rubbed a blister even on my hand."

Then he picked up the hoe and showed Yuan how to hold it in his two hands, the one hand firm and close to keep the handle sure, and the other farther on, to guide the swing of it. And Yuan was not ashamed to learn, and he tried many times until at last the iron point fell true and hard and clipped away a piece of earth each time it fell, and then the farmer praised him and Yuan felt as glad as he did if he had a verse praised by his teacher, although he wondered that he did, seeing the farmer was but a common man.

Day after day Yuan came to work upon his plot of land, and he liked best to come when all his fellows were not there, for when they came the farmer would not draw near at all, but worked in some more distant field of his. But if Yuan were alone he came and talked and showed Yuan how to plant his seed and how to thin the seedlings when they sprang up, and how to watch for the worms and insects that were eager and ready always to devour each seedling as it came.

And Yuan had his turn in teaching, too, for when such pests came he read and learned of foreign poisons that would kill them and he used these poisons. The first time he did this the farmer laughed at him and cried out, "Remember how you watched me, after all, and how your books have not come true nor showed you how deep to lay your beans or when to hoe them free of weeds!"

But when he saw worms shrivel up and die upon the bean plants under the poison then he grew grave and wondering and said in a somewhat lower tone, "I swear I would not have believed it. So it is not a thing willed by gods, these pests. It is something man can do away with. Something there is in books, after all—yes, more than a little even, I can say, because planting and sowing are of no use if worms devour the plants."

Then he begged some poison for his own land, and Yuan gave it gladly, and in such giving these two became friends after a fashion, and Yuan's plot was best of all, and for this he thanked the farmer, and the farmer thanked Yuan that his beans throve and were not eaten as his neighbors' fields were.

It was well for Yuan to have this friend and to have this bit of land to work upon. For often in the springtime as he bent himself upon the earth, some content rose up in him which he had never known. He learned to change his clothes and wear a common garb such as the farmer wore, and even to change his shoes to sandals, and the farmer let him be free in his home, for he had no unwed daughter, and his wife by now was old and ugly, and Yuan kept his clothes for work there. So every day he came he changed himself into a farmer, and he loved the earth more even than he thought he would. It was good to watch for seeds to sprout, and there was a poetry in it too, a thing he scarcely could express, although he tried to do it and made a verse about it. He loved the very labor of the land, and when his own was done, he often went and labored on the farmer's land, and sometimes at the farmer's asking he would eat a meal on the threshing floor where as the days grew warmer the farmer's wife would spread the table. And he grew hard and brown until Ai-lan cried at him one day, "Yuan, how is it you grow blacker every day? You are black as any farmer!"

Then Yuan grinned and answered, "So I am a farmer, Ai-lan, but you never will believe me when I say so!"

For often at his books or even in the midst of an evening's pleasure, when he was far away from that bit of land, it came suddenly to his mind and while he read or while he played, he planned some new seed he could sow or he would wonder if perhaps a vegetable he had would be fit for gathering before the summer came, or he would be troubled because he remembered a yellow withering beginning upon a plant's tip.

To himself Yuan thought sometimes, "If all the poor were like this one man, then I might be willing to join Meng's cause and make it mine."

It was well that Yuan had this solid and secret content in this little plot of land lent him. It was secret, for not if he would could he have told anyone why he liked to work on land, and at this time of his youth he was even a little ashamed of this liking, because it was the fashion of these city youths to laugh at country men and call them louts and "big turnips" and many names like these. And Yuan cared what his fellows said. Not even to Sheng therefore could he speak of this, though with Sheng he could talk of many things, such as a beauty they both saw in a sudden color or shape somewhere; still less to Ai-lan could he have told what strange deep solid pleasure he had in this bit of land. He might have spoken if there had been need to tell, to this one whom he called his mother, for though they did not speak much of inward things, still at the mealtimes they had alone in the house, the lady did talk often, in her grave way, of things she liked to do.

For this lady was full of quiet good works, and did not give herself over completely to gaming or feasting or going to see running horses and dogs, as many ladies did in this city. These were not pleasures to her, although if Ai-lan wished it, she went with her and sat and watched it all, apart and elegant, and as though it were a duty and nothing to be done for its own sake. Her real pleasure was in a certain good work she did for children, those female children, newly born, who are cast away unwanted by the poor. These when she found them she gathered into a home she kept and she hired two women to be mothers to them, and she herself went there daily, too, and taught them and watched to see those who were ill or wasted, and she had nearly twenty of these little foundlings. Of this good work she talked to Yuan sometimes and how she planned to teach these girls some good honest livelihood and wed them to such honest men as might be found, farmers or tradesmen or weavers, or whatever man might want good, working maids.

Once Yuan went with her to the home, and he was amazed to see the change that came upon this grave staid lady. It was a poor plain place, for she had not much money to spend there, since even for these she would not rob Ai-lan of any pleasure, but once within the gate the children fell upon her, crying out she was their mother, and they pulled her dress and hands and loved her eagerly, until she laughed and looked shyly at Yuan, and he stood staring, for he had not seen her laugh before.

"Does Ai-lan know of them?" he asked.

At this the lady was suddenly grave again, and nodded, saying only, "She is busy with her own life now."

And then she led Yuan here and there about the plain home; from court to kitchen all was clean though poor, and she said, "I do not want much money for them, for they are to be the wives of working men." To this she added presently, "If I find one, even one, among them, who might be what I planned for Ai-lan . . . I will take her apart then to my own home and spend myself upon her. I think there is this one—I do not know yet—" She called and a child came out to her from another room, a child older than the rest, a child of a certain gravity of look, although not more than twelve or thirteen years of age. She came with confidence and put her hand into the lady's hand

and looked at her and said in a clear voice, "Here I am, my mother."

"This child," the lady said, most earnestly, looking down into the child's upturned face, "has some spirit in her but I do not yet know what it is. I found her my own self, laid at this door, when she was newborn, and I took her in. She is the eldest and the first I found. She is so quick at letters, so true to every teaching, so to be depended on, that if she continues thus, I shall take her to my own home within a year or two. . . . So, Mei-ling, you may go."

The child gave her a smile, a quick, lighting smile, and she threw Yuan a deep look, and though she was only yet a child Yuan did not forget the look, it was so clear and questioning, straightly put, not as though to him more than to another. Then she went away again.

To such a lady, then, Yuan might have spoken, but there was no need for speech after all. He only knew he liked the hours he put upon the land. They joined him to some root he had, so that he was not, as were many others, rootless and floating upon the surface of the life in this city.

Again and yet again Yuan, when he suffered unrest or questioning of some sort, went to this bit of land, and there sweating in the sun or wet with cool rain, he worked in silence or talked quietly of common things with his neighbor farmer. Although such work, such talk, seemed nothing or of no great import of any kind while it was being done, yet when night came Yuan could go home and he was cleansed and freed of all inward impatience. He could read in his books and meditate upon them happily, or he could go with Ai-lan and her friends and spend the hours in noise and light and dancing, and not be disturbed, having in himself some quietness he learned upon his land.

And he well needed this quietness the land gave him, the steadiness and root it gave him. For in this spring his life was given a twist he had not dreamed it could be given.

88

in one thing Yuan was very far behind Sheng and very far behind Ai-lan, and behind even Meng. These three lived in a warmer air than Yuan ever had. In this great city they had spent their youth, and all its heats poured into their blood. There were here a hundred hundred heats for youth; the pictures of love and beauty painted on the walls, the pleasure houses where the pictured loves of strange men and women in foreign lands were shown, the halls of dancing where for a little silver a woman may be bought for a night, these were the crudest heats.

Above these somewhat were the printed tales and stories and verses of love that could be found for sale in any little shop. In the old days these were counted all for evil, and understood for what they were, a torch to light the fires in man or maid, and none would read them openly. But now in this day, the subtlety of outer nations had crept in and under guise of art and genius and such fair names the young read these writings everywhere and studied them; yet for all the fairness of the names, the torch was there still and the old fires were lighted.

Young men grew daring and maids, too, and old modesties were gone. Hands touched, and it was not counted evil as it used to be, and a youth himself might ask a maid to be betrothed to him, and her father did not sue his father at a court of law as once he might and still would in an inland city where the evil ways of foreigners were unknown. And when the two were openly betrothed, they came and went as freely as though they were savages, and if sometimes, as it must happen, blood ran too hot and high and flesh met flesh too soon, then the two were not killed for honor's sake, as would have happened in their parents' youth. No, only the marriage day was hastened forward, and so the child was born in wedlock, and the young pair were as careless as though they both were honorable, and parents, if they were miserable, could but look at each other in sick privacy and bear it as they could, for this was the new day. But many a father cursed the new day for his son's sake and the mother for her daughter's sake. But still this was the new day and none could turn it back.

In this day Sheng had lived and Meng his brother, and Ai-lan, too, and they were part of it and did not know another. But Yuan was not so. Him the Tiger had reared in every old tradition and in his own added hatred of all women. And Yuan had never dreamed of women, even. Or if inadvertently he did dream in his sleep he woke in hottest shame at it, and sprang out of bed and fell to furious labor on his books or else he walked the streets awhile or did some such thing to clear his mind of evil. Some day, he knew, he must wed as all men did and have his sons in decency, but it was not a thing to think of when he had so much to learn. He craved learning only now. He had plainly told his father and he was not changed yet.

But in the spring of this year, he was harassed with nightly dreaming, plagued by dreams. It was the strangest thing, for by day he never let his thoughts go to love or women. Yet his thoughts asleep were filled with such lewdness that he awoke and sweat with shame, and he was cleansed only when he went striding to his bit of land and worked there desperately, and on the days when he could work there longest, in the nights of such days, he dreamed the least and slept the sweetest. So he turned yet more ardently to labor there.

Now although he did not know it Yuan was as hot as any youth within, and hotter far than Sheng, who diffused his heart into a hundred pretty languors, and hotter, too, than Meng, who had his cause to burn for. And Yuan had come out of the cold courts of his childhood into this heated city. He who had never even touched a maid's hand could not yet put his arm about a maid's slight body and hold her hand in his with no rebuke, and feel her breath upon his cheek, and move her as he would to sounds of music, without the sweet sickness in him which he loved and feared. And though he was decorous, until Ai-lan teased him without pity, and he scarcely touched the hand he

90

held, and never rested the maid's body against his own, as many men were eager to do, and did it unreproved, too, still Ai-lan's very teasing set his thoughts moving as they would not have dared to move and as he wished they would not.

She cried sometimes, pursing out her pretty lips, "Yuan, you are so old-fashioned! How can you dance well if you push the girl away from you like that? Look, this is the way to hold a maid!"

And there in the room where they all sat in the rare evenings when she was home with her mother, she set the music going in its box and she pressed herself into his arms and let her body follow all the lines of his, her feet weaving in and out with his. And she did not fail to tease him with the other maidens by, too, and she cried, laughing, if one were there, "If you would dance with my brother Yuan you must force him to hold you rightly. What he would like best would be to set you up against a wall somewhere and do his dancing all alone!" Or she would say, "Yuan, you are handsome, we all know, but not so fearfully handsome you need to fear every maid! Doubtless there are some of us who have our loves already set!"

And with such raillery before her friends she set them all to merriment so that bold maids grew bolder and pressed themselves against him shamelessly, and though he would have stopped their boldness he feared the sharp merriment of Ai-lan's further speech, and bore it as he could. And even timid maids grew smiling when they danced with him and bolder than they were with bolder men, and they, too, added upturned eyes and smiles and warmer handclasps and the touch of thigh to thigh and all those wiles which women know by nature.

At last he grew so troubled by his dreams and all the freedom of the maids he knew for Ai-lan's sake, that he would never have gone with her again except that the mother still said so often, "Yuan, it comforts me to know you are with Ai-lan; even though she has another man to take her where she goes, I feel the better if I know you are there, too."

And Ai-lan was willing enough for Yuan to go with her, for she was proud to show him off, for he was a tall youth, and not ill to look at, and there were maids she knew to whom it was a favor that she brought him with her. Thus were the fires ready in Yuan against his will but he laid no torch to them.

Yet was the torch laid and in no way he could foresee, nor, indeed, that any could foresee.

And thus it was. One day Yuan lingered in the classroom to write down a foreign poem which his teacher had set upon the wall for a task, and he lingered until every other one was gone, or so he thought. It so happened that this was the class that he and Sheng sat together in, and also that pale maid who was a revolutionist. Now as Yuan finished what he wrote and closed his book and put his pen into his pocket and stirred himself to rise, he heard his name called and one spoke thus, "Mr. Wang, since you are here, will you explain to me the meaning of those lines set there? You are more clever than I am. I thank you if you will."

This Yuan heard said in a very pleasing voice, a maid's voice, but not tinkling with affectation as even Ai-lan's voice was, or those of her friends. It was rather somewhat deep for any maid, very full and thrilling in its tone, so that any casual word it spoke seemed to take on more meaning than the mere word had. Yuan looked up in haste and great surprise, and there beside him stood that maid, the revolutionist, her pale face paler still than he remembered it, but now that she stood near him, he saw her dark narrow eyes were not cold at all but filled with inward warmth and feeling, and they belied the set coldness of her face, and burned there in its paleness. She looked at him steadfastly, and then with calmness set herself beside him and waited for him to answer, as cool as though she spoke on any day to any man.

He somehow answered, stammering while he did, "Ah, yes, of course—only I am not sure. 1 think it means—a foreign verse is always difficult—it is an ode—a sort of—" and so he stammered on, speaking something, somehow, and conscious always of her deep and steadfast look, now on his face, now on the words. And then she rose and thanked him, and again she spoke the simplest words and yet somehow her voice freighted them with a great load of gratitude, far more, Yuan thought, than any service could deserve. Then naturally they drew together as they left the room and walked together down the silent halls, for it was late afternoon and every student eager to be gone, and so they walked out to the gate and the maid seemed content to be silent until Yuan asked a thing or two for courtesy's sake.

He asked, "What is your honored name?" and he asked in the old-fashioned courteous way he had been taught. But she answered crisply, the words short and curt seemingly, and without the return courtesy, except that voice of hers gave meaning to everything she said.

At last they reached the gate, and Yuan bowed deeply. But the maid gave a quick nod and went her way, and Yuan looking after her, saw her a little taller than most women as she walked sure and swift among the crowds until he lost her. Then he leaped wondering into a ricksha and went home, and he wondered what she really was, and wondered at the way her eyes and voice said other things than did her face and words.

On this slight beginning a friendship grew. Now Yuan had never had a maid for friend, nor in truth had he many friends, for he had not, as some did, a little special group in which he took a natural place. His cousins had their friends, Sheng his friends among young men like himself, who fancied they were the poets and the writers and the young painters of a modern day, and they followed zealously after leaders such as the one surnamed Wu, at whom Yuan glanced sidewise while he danced with Ai-lan. And Meng had his secret group of revolutionists. But Yuan belonged to none, and though he spoke to a score or so of young men as he passed them, and though he knew this maid or that of Ai-lan's friends to talk lightly with a little while, he had no bosom friend. Before he knew it this maid came to be his friend.

And thus it came about. At first it was always she who pressed the friendship, coming as any wilier maid might do to ask his explanation or his advice on something or other, and he was deceived as all men easily are by even such simple wile as this, for after all he was a man and very young and it was pleasant to him to advise a maid, and he came to helping her to write her essays and at last it came about that with one excuse or another they met somehow every day, although not openly. For if any had asked Yuan what he felt for this maid he would have said he felt friendship only, nothing more. She was in truth a very different maid from any he thought fair—thought even a little fair, because there was no maid to whom he gave a real thought yet in his life, and to himself if he meditated on any maid at all it was to see some pretty flowery maid like Ai-lan, with little pretty hands and lovely looks and dainty ways, and all these qualities he saw in Ai-lan's friends. Yet he had not loved one of them— he had only said in his heart that did he ever love, the maid must be pretty as a rose is pretty, or a budded plum flower or some such delicate useless thing. So had he written secret verses sometimes to such maids, a line or two and always unfinished, because the feeling was so slight and vague and there was no one single maid who stood enough to him as the one to write to above all others. It was rather that his love was diffused like a dim coming light before the sunrise.

Certainly he never thought of one to love like this maid, severe and earnest and clothed always in her dark straight robes of blue or grey, and wearing leather shoes, and bent always on her books and cause. Nor did he love her now.

But she loved him. At which hour he found this out he scarcely knew. Yet he knew, too. One day they met at a distance to walk upon a quiet street along a canal's edge, and it was evening and the time of twilight, and they were about to turn homeward, when suddenly he felt her looking at him and he caught her look and it was changed, a deep clinging burning look it was, and then her voice, her lovely voice that never seemed a part of her, came forth and said, "Yuan, there is one thing I'd rather see than anything."

And when he faltered out to know what it was, his heart beating very thickly of a sudden, although he had not thought of loving her, she said on, "I want to see you in our cause. Yuan, you are my very brother—I want to call you comrade, too. We need you—we need your good mind, your strength. You are twice what Meng can ever be."

Suddenly Yuan thought he saw why she had come to friendship with him, and he thought angrily that she and Meng had planned it, and his rising feeling checked itself.

But then her voice said again, very soft and deep-sounding in the twilight, her voice said, "Yuan, there is another reason."

And now Yuan dared not ask her what it was. But a faintness in him rose and choked him nearly, and he felt his body tremble, and he turned and said, half whispering, "I must get home—I promised Ai-lan—"

And so with no other word they both turned and walked homeward. But when they parted they did that they never had done; scarcely meaning it, and certainly not planning so to do. They clasped their hands together, and with that touch some change came into Yuan, and he knew they were no more friends, not now friends any more, though still he did not know what they were.

But all that evening when he was with Ai-lan, when he spoke to this maid, danced with that one, he looked at them as he never had and puzzled over how maids in the world can be so differing, and that night when he went to bed he lay a long time pondering on this, the first time he had even thought of any maid. For now he thought long of this one maid and he thought about her eyes, how he had once thought them cold like dull onyx in the paleness of her face. But now he had seen them brighten into warm beauty of their own when he spoke to her. Then he remembered how her voice was always sweet, and how its richness seemed unsuited to her quietness and seeming coldness. And yet it was her own voice. So pondering he wished that he had had courage to ask her what that other reason was. He would have liked to hear her voice tell him such a reason as he guessed.

But still he did not love her. He knew he did not love her.

And last he came to the memory of that touch of her hand to his, the heart of her hand pressed against his hand's heart; so, palm to palm, they had stood an instant in the darkness of the unlit street, so fixed a ricksha swerved to pass them, and they did not see it until the man cursed them, and still they did not care. It had been too dark for him to see her eyes, and she had said nothing, nor had he. There was only that close touch to think on. And when he thought of it the torch was lit. Something flamed inside him, though what it was puzzled him no little, for still he knew he did not love her.

Now if it had been Sheng who touched this maid's hand he would have, if he liked, smiled and forgotten it, for he had touched many maids' hands warmly for a moment, or if he liked he would have touched it again and yet again, as often as he would if he found the maid loved him, or at least until he wearied of it and he would have written a tale or two or made a verse and then forgot her the more easily. And Meng would not have dreamed long of it either, for in this cause of his were maids enough, and they made it a purpose, youths and maids, to be bold and free together, and to call each other comrade, and Meng heard much talk and made some talk, too, about men and women being equal always and free to love each other as they would.

Still, with all this freedom, there was not overmuch true freedom, for these maids and youths, as Meng did, burned with another cause than lust, and the cause burned them clean. And Meng was cleanest of them all, for he had grown so filled with loathing of lust, having seen his own father's heats and his elder brother's wandering eyes, that he scorned all vain pastime spent with women, because to him it seemed they wasted mind and body that should be spent for cause. As yet Meng had never touched a maid. He could speak as well as any on free love and rights of love without a rule of marriage, but he did none of it.

But Yuan had no burning cleansing cause. He had not the safety of Sheng's idle, pleasant ways with maidens either, and so when this one maid touched Yuan's hand as none had ever touched it he could not forget it. Here was a thing to wonder at, too, that this hand of hers, when he remembered it, was hot and moist in the palm. He had not thought her hand could be hot. Thinking of her pale face, of her cool pale lips that moved so little when she spoke, he would have said, if he had thought of it before, that her hands would be dry and cool and the fingers loose to hold. But this was not true. Her hand had held to his hand, close and hot and clinging. Hand and voice and eyes—those spoke of her hot heart. And when Yuan began to think what her heart might be, the heart of this strange maid who was so bold and calm, yet shy as he could know her shy through his own shyness, then he tossed upon his bed and longed to touch her hand again and yet again.

Nevertheless, when at last he fell asleep and woke in the cool morning of the spring, he knew he did not love her. He could think in the cool morning and remember how hot her hand was, and say to himself that even so he did not love her. And on that day in the school in great shyness he avoided every glance at her, and he did not linger anywhere and at the earliest hour after noon he went out to his land and worked there feverishly, and to himself he thought, "This feel of earth upon my hands is better than the touch of any maid's hand." And he remembered how he had lain and thought in his bed the night before and he was ashamed and glad his father did not know.

Before long the farmer came by and he praised the clever way Yuan felled the weeds about his turnips and he laughed and said, "Do you remember that first day you hoed? If it had been today, you would have felled each turnip with the weeds!" And he laughed mightily, and then he said to comfort Yuan, "But you will make a farmer yet. It is told in the muscle of your arm and in the bigness of your back. Those other students—such a puny lot of pale weeds I never saw—their spectacles and dangling little arms and their gold teeth and their sticks of legs stuck into foreign trousers—if I had such bodies as they have I swear I'd wrap me in robes somehow and hide myself." And the farmer laughed again and shouted, "Come and smoke awhile and rest yourself before my door!"

And so Yuan did, and he listened, smiling, to the farmer's loud constant voice and to all the farmer's scorn of city men and especially did the farmer hate the young men and the revolutionists, and he cried down every mild good word Yuan said for them and he shouted, "And what good can they do me, then? I have my bit of land, my home, my cow. I want no more land than I have, and I have enough to eat. If the rulers would not tax me so hard, I would be glad, but men like me have always been so taxed. Why should they come and talk to me of doing good to me or mine? Whoever heard of good coming out of strangers? Who will do good for any man except those of his own blood? No, I know they have something they want for themselves—my cow, perhaps, or else my bit of land."

And then he cursed awhile, and cursed the mothers who could bear such sons and grew merry at the expense of all who were not like himself and praised Yuan for working on the land so well, and then he laughed and Yuan laughed and they were friends.

From this robustness and from the cleanness of the earth Yuan went home again and to his bed, and he would not go out that night for any pleasure even, because he wanted nothing of any maid, and he desired to touch no maid at all, but only to do his work and learn his books, and so this night he slept. In this way the land healed him for a time.

Yet in him were the flames already lit. Another day or two and his mood changed itself again, and he was restless and he turned his head secretly one day to see if that maid were in the schoolroom, and she was, and between the heads of others their eyes met, and her eyes clung to his although he turned back quickly. But he could not forget her. In a day or two again he said in passing through the door, although he had not planned it, "Shall we walk together again today?" And she nodded, her deep eyes looking down.

That day she did not touch his hand and it seemed to him she walked farther from him than she used to do, and was more silent, and talk came harder than it did. And here was something contrary in Yuan, which surprised himself. He would have sworn he would be glad not to be touched and that he did not want her very near. And yet when they had walked awhile he wished that she had touched him. He would not even at parting put out his hand, and yet he watched and longed to see her hand come forth, so he must meet it. But it did not, and he went home defrauded somehow, and yet angry that he felt so, and he was ashamed and swore he would not walk with any maid, and that he was a man with work to do. And he astonished a certain mild old teacher that day with his bitter writing of how men ought to live alone and strive after learning and keep away from women, and that night he told himself a hundred times that he was glad he did not love this maid. Each day thereafter for a while he went dogged to his land and would not let himself remember that he wanted any touch.

Then one day, some three days after that, he had a letter writ-

ten in a small square writing that he did not know. Now Yuan
had not many letters, and only one sometimes from a comrade he
had loved in the school of war who loved him still. And this letter
was not the hasty writing of his friend. He opened it, and there
within he found a page from the maid he did not love—a single
page, very short, and saying these words clearly, "Have I done
something to make you angry with me? I am a revolutionist, a
modern woman. I have no need to hide myself as other women
have. I love you. Can you then love me? I do not ask or care for
marriage. Marriage is an ancient bondage. But if so be you need
my love, you have it when you will." And then, very small and
cryptic, she twisted close together the shaping of her name.

So was love first offered to Yuan. Now must he think of love,
sitting in his room alone, this letter in his hand, and he must
wonder of all that love could mean. Here was a maid ready for
his taking if he would take her. And many times his blood cried
out that he might take her. He began to lose his childish youth
in those few hours, and manhood grew in him in rushing heart-
beats and in his ardent blood. His body was no more a lad's body
now. . . .

In a few days the heats within him ripened him and he was
full-grown and a man in his desires. But still he wrote no answer
to the maid, and at the school he avoided every sight of her.
Twice on different nights he sat down to write, and twice beneath his pen the words rose up, "I do not love you," but yet
those words he would not write because his curious body pressed
him to let it know what it desired. So in this dark confusion of
his blood and heart he wrote no answer and he waited for himself.

But he was sleepless and more nearly angry and full of impatience than he had ever been before, so that the lady, his
mother, looked at him most thoughtfully, and Yuan felt her
questioning. Yet he would say nothing, for how could he say
that he was angry because he could not take a maid he did not

love, and that he was angry because he could not love her since he wanted what she offered him? So he let the struggle wage itself in him and was as moody as his father ever was when any war was to be waged.

Now out of all this mingled life of Yuan's, wherein he was caught a little in everything and in nothing wholly, the old Tiger suddenly forced a clarity, and this without knowing at all what he did. These many months since the lady had written him first the Tiger had not answered anything. He sat there in his distant halls, silent and sulky against his son, and no word came out of him. Once again the lady wrote, and yet again, without telling Yuan she did, and if Yuan asked sometimes why she had no answer from his father, she answered soothingly, "Let be. As long as he says nothing, there can be no ill news." And indeed Yuan was very willing to let be, and every day his mind was more swallowed in his life, and at last he almost forgot that he had anything to fear at all from his father, or that he had run away from his father's power, it seemed so much his life here.

Then one day in the later passing spring the Tiger put forth his power again upon his son. He came out of his silence and he wrote a letter not to the lady, but to his own son. This letter he did not bid a letter writer write for him, either. No, with his own brush which he had not for long used the Tiger put down a few words to his son, and though the letters were sharply, rudely made, the meaning of them was very plain. They said, "I have not changed my will. Come home and be wed. The day is set for the thirtieth of this moon."

This letter Yuan found waiting for him in his room one night when he came in from an evening's pleasure. He came in all languorous and roused with pleasure, so that almost, while he swayed to this music and to that, he had made up his mind that night to take the love the maid had offered to him. He came in filled with this excitement, that the next day perhaps, or the next day but one, he would go with her where she would and do as she was willing—or at least he played with the thought that so perhaps he would. Then his eye fell on the table, and there the letter was, and very well he knew the superscription, and who had written it. He seized it and tore the tough old-fashioned paper of its envelope, and drew the inner paper forth, and there the words were, plain as though he heard the Tiger's shout. Yes, the words were like a shout to Yuan. When he had read them, the room seemed suddenly filled with silence as though after a great roar of noise. He folded the paper again and thrust it in the envelope again and sat down breathless in the silence.

What should he do? How answer this command his father laid upon him? The thirtieth? It was less than twenty days away. And then the old childhood fear fell on him. Despair crept up into his heart. After all, how could he withstand his father? When had he ever withstood his father? Always somehow in the end his father had his way, by fear or love, or some such equal force. The young never could escape the old. It came to Yuan weakly that perhaps it would be better if he did go back and yield to his father in this one thing. He could go back and wed the maid and stay a night or two and do his duty and come away and never go home again. Then might he by any law do as he pleased and it would not be counted to him for a sin. He could wed whom he pleased after he had obeyed his father. So thinking back and forth he lay down to sleep at last, and yet he could not sleep. All the warm flush of pleasure was gone clean out of him. When he thought of lending his body to his father, to the woman chosen now and waiting, he was as cold as though he lent a beast to breed.

In this mood of weakness he arose early, having not slept at all, and he went to find the lady and he roused her at her door and when she came to open it, he gave the letter to her mutely and waited while she read it. Her face changed at the words. She said quietly, "You are exhausted. Go and eat your breakfast. And force the food a little, son, for its heat will restore you, even though I know now you think you cannot swallow. But eat. I will come quickly."

Yuan did obediently what she said. He set himself before the table, and when the serving maid had brought the hot morning gruel of rice and the condiments and the foreign breads the lady liked to eat, he did force himself. Soon the hot food sent its heat into him, and he began to feel more cheered, and less hopeless than he had been in the night, so that when the lady came he looked at her and said, "Almost I am ready to say I will not go."

The lady sat down then, too, and took up a little loaf and ate it slowly, thinking while she ate, and then she said, "If so be you can say this, Yuan, I will stand by you. I will not put strength into you, to force your decision, for it is your own life and he is your father. If you feel your old duty to him stronger than the duty to yourself, then return to him. I will not blame you. But if you will not go back, then stay on, and I will help you somehow at every step. I am not afraid."

At these words Yuan felt courage coming into him again, a good rising courage, almost enough to make him dare against his father. But still it needed Ai-lan's recklessness to finish out his courage. When he came home that noon there Ai-lan was, playing in the parlor with a little dog she had had given her by the man Wu, a tiny furry black-nosed toy which she loved very well. When Yuan came in she looked up and cried out, "Yuan, my mother told me something today and bade me talk with you because I am young, too, and she thought it would be only just that you know what a maid would say these days. Why, Yuan, you would be a fool to listen to that old man! What if he is our father? How can we help that? Why, Yuan, not I nor any of my friends would think of such a folly as to go and wed a person we had never seen! Say you will not—what can he do? He cannot come and fetch you here with his armies. In this city you are safe—you are not a child—your life belongs to you—some day you will wed rightly as you like. You are too good for an ignorant wife who cannot write her name—and even she might have her feet bound! And do not forget these days that we new women will not be concubines. No, that we will not. If you marry such a woman as your father chooses, you are married to her. She is your wife. I would not bear to be a second wife. If I chose a man already married, then he must turn away his first wife and live with her no more, and I must be the only one. I have so sworn it. Yuan, we have a sisterhood, we new women, and we have so sworn that we will never marry rather than marry to be concubines. Better then if you do not obey your father now, for it will not be easier in the end."

These words of Ai-lan's did what Yuan could not do for himself. Listening to her voice, now made so earnest for all its soft willfulness, and thinking of the many like her in this city, he came to think under the magic of her brilliant, willful beauty, "It is true I do not belong to my father's time. It is true he has not this right nowadays over me. It is true—it is true—"

And under this new strength he went straight to his room and he wrote quickly while he felt courageous, "I will not come home for such a thing, my father. I have my right to live these days. These are the new times." And then Yuan sat and thought awhile, and doubted perhaps that the words were too bold, and he thought it might help them if he added a few milder ones and so he added, "Besides, it is the end of the term of school, and it is a very ill time for me to come, and if I come I miss the examinations, and my work of many moons is lost. Release me, therefore, my father, though the truth is I do not want to wed." So though he put at the first and last of the letter the proper courteous words, and he added these few mild words, still Yuan wrote his meaning plain. And he would not trust the letter to a serving man. He put the stamp on and himself went down the sunlit city street and thrust the letter in the box for it.

Once it was gone he felt stronger and at ease. He would not

recall what he had written, and going homeward again he was glad, and among all these modern men and women walking to and fro upon the streets he felt yet stronger and more sure. It was true that in these times what his father had required of him was an absurdity. These people on these streets, if he told them, would only laugh at such old dead ways, and cry him for a fool to feel any fear. Mingling thus among them Yuan felt suddenly very safe. This was his world—this new world—this world of men and women free and free to live in each his own way. He felt a darkness lifted from him, and suddenly he thought he would not go home yet to sit and study. He would be amused awhile at something. There beside him on the street was the great glitter of a pleasure house, and in letters of many languages a sign said, "Showing Today the Greatest Film of the Year, 'The Way of Love.'" And Yuan turned and joined the many who went into that wide-flung door.

But the Tiger was not so easily denied as this. In less than seven days he had written his answer back, and this time he wrote three letters, one to Yuan, one to the lady, and the third one to his elder brother. But they all said the same thing in different ways, although he had not written the letters himself, so the language was more smooth. Yet the very smoothness seemed to make the words more cold and angry. What they said was this, that his son Yuan would be wed on the thirtieth of that same moon, for the geomancer had said this was the lucky day to wed him. Because the young man his son could not return to his home on that day, since the examinations of the school were set for then, the parents had decided that he must be wed by proxy, and so a cousin would stand up for him who was Wang the Merchant's eldest son and who could answer in his place. But Yuan would be truly wed upon that day, as truly as though he came himself.

These words Yuan read in his letter. So did the Tiger have his will, and Yuan knew his father never could have been so cruel except that he was forced to it by anger, and Yuan felt that anger and was afraid of it again.

And now indeed the thing was too strong for Yuan. For by the old law the Tiger did no more than he had right to do, and no more than many fathers have done always. Yuan knew this very well, and that day when he had this letter, and the servant had given it to him as he came within the door, so that he stood there in the little hall alone and read it, he felt all his courage ebb away from him. What was he, one lone youth, to do against the gathered power of all these old centuries? He turned slowly and went into the parlor. Ai-lan's little dog was there and came and rubbed against him, snuffling, and when Yuan paid no heed to it, barked a short high bark or two. Still Yuan did not heed it, though commonly he could laugh at this little fierce lion of a dog. He sat down and leaned his head in his hands and let the dog bark on.

But the barking called the lady, and she came in to see what was wrong and if a stranger had come in, and when she saw Yuan, very well she knew what was wrong. She said soothingly, for she had her letter earlier, "You are not to give up, son. This is more than a matter for you now. I will ask your uncle here and your aunt and your elder cousin, and we will talk it over in a council to see what shall be done. Your father is not the only one in this family, nor even the eldest one. If your uncle will be strong, it may be we can divert your father's will by some persuasion."

But Yuan could only cry out when he thought of that old fat pleasure-loving lord who was his uncle, "And when was my uncle ever strong! No, the only strong men in this country, I swear, are those who have armies and guns—they force all the others to their will, and who knows it better than I? I have seen my father force his will by threat of death a hundred times—a hundred hundred times. Everybody fears him because he has swords and guns—and now I see he is right—it is such force as this which rules at last—"

106

And Yuan began to sob, because he felt so helpless. All his running away and all his willfulness were of no use now.

But after a while he yielded to the lady's urging and her comforting, and that very night she made a sort of feast and bid all the family there, and they all came, and when the feast was eaten, the lady told the matter forth, and they all waited to hear what was to be said.

Now Sheng and Meng and Ai-lan were there too, although they were given lower seats, since they were young, for at this time the lady had taken care to seat everyone as old custom taught, since this was a family gathering for counsel. But the young ones were silent and waited as they should. Even Ai-lan was silent, though her eyes sparkled to show she inwardly derided all this gravity, and would make a joke of it afterwards, and Sheng sat as though he thought inwardly of other pleasanter things. But Meng sat silentest of all and stillest. His face was fixed and very red and angry, and he thought of nothing but this thing and he suffered because he could not speak. . . .

It was Wang the Eldest's duty to speak first, but it could be seen he wished it were not, and Yuan, looking at him, gave up any little scanty hope he might have had that this man would say anything to help him. For Wang the Eldest was afraid of two. He was afraid of the Tiger, his younger brother. He remembered how he used to be a fierce young man, and he remembered that his own second son was in a very soft good life in a great inland city holding it almost as a governor in the Tiger's name, and this son was nearly always ready to send his father silver now and then when Wang the Eldest had such need, and when had he not this need in this foreign city where there was every sort of way to spend it? So Wang the Eldest had no desire to make the Tiger angry. Beyond this one he feared his own wife, the mother of his sons, and she had told him plainly what he must say. Before they left their home she called him to her room and said, "You shall not take sides with the son. In the first place we older ones must stand together, and in the second place it may be we shall need your brother's help some future time if this talk of more revolution comes to anything. We still have lands in the north to take thought of, and we cannot forget what we owe ourselves. Moreover the law is on the father's side, and the young man should obey."

These words she said so positively that now the old man sweat to meet her eyes she kept fixed on him, and he wiped his shaved head before he spoke, and drank a little tea, and coughed and spat once or twice and did all he could to put off what must come, but still they all waited, and so haltingly and gasping as he spoke, for he was always hoarse these days because his fat pressed inwards on him, he said, "My brother has sent me a letter and he says Yuan is to be wed. And I am told Yuan does not wish to wed. And I am told—I am told—"

Here he wandered off and met his lady's eye and looked away and sweat newly and wiped his head again, and Yuan at the moment hated him with all his heart. To such a one as this, he thought passionately, was his life committed! Then suddenly he felt his eye commanded and he looked and Meng's eyes were fastened upon him with great scornful question, and they said, "Have I not told you there is no hope for us in the old?"

But now the old man was forced on by his lady's fixed cold gaze and he said very fast, "But I think—I think—it is better for sons to obey—the Sacred Edicts say—and after all—" Here the old man smiled suddenly, as though here he did think of something of his own to say, "After all, Yuan, my son, one woman is truly much like another, and after it is over you will not mind much and it will only be a day or two and I will write a letter to the master of your school and beg him to excuse you from your examinations, and if you please your father it will be better, for he is such a fierce angry man, and after all, the time may come when we need—"

Here his eye wandered to his lady again, and she bade him in

108

such silent fierceness to be still that he ended suddenly and in great weakness, "It is what I think," and he turned to his eldest son and said in much relief, "Speak, son, for it is your turn."

Then the eldest son spoke, and he spoke with more reason, but on both sides, because he wished no offense to anyone. Yet he said kindly, "I understand Yuan's wish to be free. I was so in my youth, and I remember that in my time I made a great pother about my marriage and would have whom I would." He smiled a little coolly, and he spoke with more daring than he might have used if his sharp and pretty wife had been there, but she was not, for she was near the moment of a birth, and very angry these days that she must have another child after four already born, and she swore day and night that she would learn the foreign ways of not conceiving any more. So since she was not there he looked at his father and laughed a little and he said, "The truth is I often wonder why I made such a noise about it then, for in the end it is true what my father says, that women are the same, and marriage is the same, and the end is the same and sure to come. It is as well to marry cool at first, because it ends cold always, and love does not last so well as reason."

And this was all. None other spoke. The learned lady did not speak, for where was the use before these two men? She kept her words for Yuan alone. And none of the young spoke, for to them speech was useless, too. These young ones as soon as could be slipped out one by one into another room, and there they talked to Yuan, each in his own way. Sheng thought the whole thing to be laughed at, and so he told Yuan. He laughed and smoothed his hair down with his pretty pale hands and he said, laughing, "If it were I, I would not even answer that summons, Yuan. I do feel for you, and I am glad I know my parents would not treat me so, for however they may rail against the new ways, they are used now to living in this city, and they would not truly force us to anything, and all their power spends itself in talking. Pay no heed—live your own life. Say nothing angry, but do as you please. You need not go home again."

And Ai-lan had cried out vehemently, "Sheng is right, Yuan! You shall not think of it again. You will live here with us always, and we all belong to the new world and you can forget everything else. There is enough here to keep us all happy and amused our whole lives long. I swear I do not ever want to go anywhere else!"

But Meng kept silence until all the talk was over. Then he said with a slow dreadful gravity, "You all speak like children. By the law Yuan will be married on the day his father sets. By the law of this nation he will not be free again. *He is not free*—it does not matter what he says he is or thinks he is or how he amuses himself—he is not free. . . . Yuan, now will you join the revolution? Do you see now why we must fight?"

And Yuan looked at Meng and met his two burning savage eyes and caught the desperation of his soul. He waited for a moment and then from his own despair he answered quietly, "I will!"

So did the Tiger drive his son to be his enemy.

Now Yuan said to himself he could throw all his heart into this cause to save his country. Before this time, when it was cried to him, "We must save our country," though his heart was always stirred because it seemed something which ought to be done, yet he was checked because he never could wholly see how the country must be saved, or if saved, then from what, or even what this word country meant. Even in his early childhood days in his father's house when his tutor had so taught him he felt this impulse to save, and yet this bewilderment, so that while he would do something he did not know what to do. In the school of war he had heard of much evil done his country by foreign enemies, and yet his father was an enemy too and he could see nothing clearly still.

At this school it had been so also. He listened often to Meng's talk of the same thing, how the country must be saved, for Meng had no other thing to talk of, if he did not talk of his cause, and he scarcely heeded his books at all these last days he was so busy in his secret meetings, and he and his comrades were always shaping protests against some authority in school or city and they made parades and marched along the streets carrying banners to cry against their foreign enemies and against evil treaties and against the laws of the city and of the school and against anything which was not in accordance with their own wish. They forced many to parade with them, even though these went sometimes against their will, for Meng could force his fellows by looks as black as any war lord's, and he could roar and shout at a reluctant schoolmate, "You are no patriot! You are the running dog of foreigners—you dance and play while our country is destroyed by enemies!"

So Meng had even cried to Yuan one day when he pleaded he was busy and had no time for such parades. Sheng could laugh and jeer a little in his pleasant way if Meng came near him with his furious talk, for Meng was his younger brother first before he was the leader of young revolutionists, but Yuan was only cousin and he must evade the angry youth as best he could. And to this time the best hiding place had been his plot of land, for Meng and his comrades had no time for steady stupid plodding toil on land, and there Yuan was safe enough from them.

But now Yuan knew what it meant to save his country. Now he saw why the Tiger was an enemy. For, now, to save his country meant to save himself, and now he saw how his father was his enemy, and none could save him if he did not save himself.

Into the cause he threw himself. There was no need to prove his own sincerity since he was Meng's cousin and Meng swore for him. And Meng could swear him true, because he knew Yuan's reason for anger, and he knew the only surety of zeal for a cause is ever in such deep personal anger as Yuan now felt.

Yuan could hate the old because the old was now his particular enemy. He could fight to make his country free because only so could he be free. He went with Meng that same night, therefore, to a secret meeting held in a certain room in an old house at the end of a winding street.

This street was known as a street of prostitutes for poor men, and many men came and went there who were dressed anyhow and many young working men could come and go there and none remark them, because it was known what the place was. Down this street then Meng led Yuan. To the calls and noises of the place he paid no heed. He knew it well and did not even see the women who ran out from one door and another in search of trade. If one plucked at his sleeve too long he shook her hand away as though it were some senseless insect which annoyed him. Only when one laid too long a hold on Yuan did Meng shout out, "Let go of him! We have a certain place already—" He strode on, and Yuan beside him glad to be released, because the woman was so coarse and beastly in her looks and not young, so that she was very fearful in her leering fondness.

Then into a house they went where a woman let them in, and Meng turned up a stair and then into a room, and there were some fifty and more young men and women waiting. When they saw Yuan follow their leader in, the low talking ceased and there was an instant's doubting silence. But Meng said, "You need fear nothing. This is my cousin. I have told you how I hoped he would join our cause because he has much help to give us. His father has an army even that one day might be for our use. But he was never willing. He never felt the cause clearly until today he knows what I have told him is the truth, that his own father is his enemy—as all our fathers are our enemies. Now he is ready—he hates enough to be ready."

And Yuan, in silence listening to these words, looked round about on all those fiery faces. There was not one face there which was not somehow fiery, however pale it might be or however it was not beautiful, and the eyes of all looked the same. At these words Meng said, and at these eyes, his heart stopped a little. . . . Did he truly hate his father? Suddenly it was hard to hate his father. He wavered, stammering in his mind at that word hate—he hated what his father did—well enough he hated much his father did. At that very moment while he wavered someone rose out from a certain shadowed corner and came to him and put out a hand. He knew the hand and turning he looked into a face he knew. It was that maid, and she said in her strange lovely voice, "I knew some day you must join us. I knew there would be a thing to make you join us."

At this sight and this touch, at the hearing of her voice, Yuan was so warmed and welcomed that he remembered freshly what his father did. Yes, if his father could do such a hateful thing as make him wed a woman he had never seen, then he did hate his father, too. He grasped the maid's hand in his own. It was most wild and sweet to know she loved him. Because she was here and held his hand, he suddenly felt one of them. He looked quickly about the room. Why, they were all free here, free and young together! Meng was still talking. No one thought it strange that they two stood, a man and a maid, hand in hand, for here all were free. And Meng ended, saying, "I stand his guarantor. If he be traitor then I will die too. I swear for him."

And the maid, when he had finished speaking, led Yuan out a few steps still holding fast his hand, and she said, "I, too—I swear for him!"

So she bound him to her and to her fellows. Without a word against it then Yuan took his pledge. Before them all and in the silence of all, his own blood was let a little with a small knife Meng drew across Yuan's finger. Meng dipped a brush in the blood and Yuan took the brush and set his name in writing to the written pledge. Then they all rose together and received him and swore the pledge together, and gave a certain sign to Yuan to keep for proof of brotherhood and so was he at last their brother.

Now Yuan discovered many things he had not known. He found that this one brotherhood was netted to many scores of others everywhere and this net ran over very many provinces of that country and into many cities, and especially it ran southward, and the center of it all was in the great southern city where that school of war was. From that center there were given forth commands by secret messages. These messages Meng knew how to receive and read and he had his helpers who called together all the band, and then Meng told them what must be done, how a strike must be called or how a declaration must be written, and at the same time that he did this, in scores of cities was the same thing done, for thus were many young banded secretly in that whole country.

Every meeting of these brotherhoods was a step forward in the carrying out of a great plan of the future, and this plan was not so new to Yuan in truth, because he had heard of something much the same his whole life long. From his childhood his father had been used to say, "I will seize the seat of government and make a great nation. I will make a new dynasty," for the Tiger had these same dreams in his youth. Then Yuan's tutor had taught him secretly, "Some day we must seize the seat of government and make a new nation—" And in the school of war he heard it, and now he heard it still. Yet to many it was a new cry. To sons of merchants, sons of teachers, sons of quiet usual people, those sons who were beset with dull ordinary life, it was the mightiest cry that ever was. To speak of making a nation, of seeing the country rise to new greatness, of waging mighty wars against foreign peoples, made every common youth among them dream great dreams and see himself a ruler or a statesman or a general.

But Yuan was not so new to the cry, and often he could not shout so loudly as the others did, and sometimes he wearied them by asking overmuch, "How shall we do this thing?" Or he would say, "How can it save the country if we do not go to classes and spend our time only in parades?"

But he learned after a while to keep silence, for the others would not bear such talk, and it fell hard on Meng and on the maid if he did not do as the others did, and Meng told him privately, "It is not your right to question the orders that come through to us from above. We must obey, for only thus can all be ready for the great coming day. I cannot let you question thus, for the others may not, and they will say I favor my cousin."

So Yuan must push down the question rising in him even then, which was to ask where the freedom was if he must obey what he did not understand. He told himself doubtless they would have freedom later and he told himself that there was no other way to go, for it was sure he had no freedom with his father, and he had cast in his lot now with these others.

Therefore he did his duty as it was appointed to him these days. He made flags ready for the days of parade, and he wrote out the petitions to teachers for this thing or that, because his writing was clear and better than most, and he made himself stay out of class on days of strike when teachers would not grant what had been asked, although he studied secretly that he might not miss the learning, and he went to certain laborers' houses and gave them sheets of paper whereon were written for them sayings which told them how abused they were in their labor and how they were given too little wage and how their masters grew rich from them, and all such things they knew already. These men and women could not read, and Yuan read to them, but they heard him gladly and they looked at each other aghast to hear how they were oppressed even more than they had thought, and one and another would cry out, "Aye, it is true our bellies are never so full as they ought to be—" "Aye, we do work all the day and in the night and our children are not fed—" "There is no hope ahead for such as us. What is today is the same tomorrow and forever, for each day we eat all we make," and they looked at each other fiercely and in despair when they found how cruelly they were used.

And Yuan looking at them and hearing them could not but be sorrowful for them, for it was true they were used cruelly many times, and their children were not nourished but were starving pale and worked at looms and at foreign machinery for many hours every day and often died there and none cared. Not even their parents cared overmuch, since children are so easily made and born, and are always more than can be wanted in a poor man's house.

Yet with all his pity the truth was Yuan was glad when he could go away, because there was always such a stink about these poor and his nostrils were fastidious. Even after he went home and was cleaned and far away from them he seemed to have the smell about him. In his quiet room with his books alone, he lifted up his head and smelled that odor. Though he changed his coat he smelled it. Even if he went out to some house of pleasure he smelled it. Above the scent of the woman in his arms while he danced, above the fragrance of clean well-cooked foods he could discern the stink of the poor. It penetrated everywhere and he loathed it. There was in Yuan this old shrinking which still kept him from giving himself wholly anywhere, because in everything there was some small thing to strike too coldly on his senses, and although he was ashamed he was so small, he knew he was a little cold in the cause for the shrinking of his flesh from this stink.

There was another trouble, too, in this fellowship he now was in, and often this obscured the cause and made a cloud between him and the others. It was the maid. For since Yuan had joined the cause it seemed this maid felt it sure that he was hers, and she could not let him be. Now there were other pairs among these youths, who lived together boldly and it was taken as a thing which could be done, and no talk made of it among the others. They were called comrades, and the bond between any two held

116

only as long as the two wished it. And this maid so hoped that Yuan would live with her.

But here was a strange thing. If Yuan had not joined the cause, and had lived on his old pleasant dreaming life, not seeing the maid much, and only in the schoolroom, and only sometimes walking alone with her, then her boldness and her lovely voice and her frank eyes and hot-hearted hand might have in the end enticed him by strangeness and difference from the other usual maids he knew and saw more often who were friends of Ai-lan's. For Yuan was very shy with maids, and so shy that boldness could seem enticing to him.

But now he saw this maid every day and everywhere. She marked him for her own and waited for him after every class and walked away with him, so that others saw it and many of his fellows jeered at Yuan and cried out at him, "She waits—she waits —you cannot escape—" and such ribaldry was always in his ears.

At first Yuan feigned not to hear it, and then when he must hear it he smiled in a sickly fashion, and then he grew ashamed and tried to linger long or to go out by some other unexpected way. And yet he could not face her bravely and say to her, "I am weary of your always waiting." No, he could not but pretend to greet her, and when he went to the secret meetings, there she was, and always she had a place beside her saved for him, and all the others took it for a truth that they two were joined together in every fact.

And yet they were not, for Yuan could not love this maid. The more he saw her and the more she touched his hand, and now she took his hand often and held it long and made no secret at all of her longing, the less Yuan could love her. And yet he must value her because he knew her very faithful and truly loving to him, and though he was ashamed he did sometimes take advantage of this very faithfulness, for when he was commanded to do a thing he did not like to do, she was quick to see his reluctance and if it could be done, she cried out that it was what she wanted to do herself, and she managed it so that Yuan more often had what he liked best to do, some writing perhaps, or to go out to villages and talk to farmers there instead of to the city poor who did stink so vilely. So Yuan did not want to make her angry because he valued what she did for him, and yet he was man enough to be more than often ashamed because he took this service from her and still could not love her.

The more he denied her—though for long it did not come to words—the more passionate this maid's love grew, until one day it did come to words, as all such things must. It happened on that day Yuan had been sent to a certain village, and he had wanted to go alone and come back by his bit of land and see how it did, for he had been too busy with the added work of this cause to be there as often as he liked to be. It was a most beautiful day in the late spring of that year, and he had planned that he would walk to the village and sit and talk awhile with the farmer folk and give his little books out secretly, and then wind eastward by his own bit of land. He liked the talk with the farmers, and often he talked with them not to persuade them by force, but as he might talk to anyone and he listened to them when they said, "But whoever heard of such things as these, that the land is to be taken from the rich and given to us? We doubt it can be done, young sir, and we would rather it were not, lest afterwards we be punished somehow. We are better as we are. At least we know our troubles. They are old troubles and we know them." And among them often only those who had no land at all were those who thought the new times welcome.

But on this day when he had planned dreaming lonely pleasant hours, this maid found him and said in her sure way, "I will come with you and I will talk to the women."

Now there were many reasons why Yuan did not want her. He felt constrained before her to speak more violently for the cause, and he did not love such violence. And he feared her touch upon him if she were alone with him. And he could not go by his own bit of land, lest that good farmer be there, and he had never yet told that farmer he now was joined to the cause, and he did not want that man to guess it, and so he did not want to go there with this maid. Yes, and more, he did not want this maid to see he cared how the plants grew whose seed he had sown himself. He did not want her to see the strange old close love he felt for such things, lest she be amazed at him. He did not fear her laughter, for she was one who never saw a thing to laugh at, but he feared her surprise and lack of understanding and her swift contempt for all she did not understand.

Still he could not shake her off, for she had so contrived that Meng had given her the command, and she must go. Therefore they set off together, Yuan silent and keeping to his own side of the road, and if she came over to him, he in a little while found an excuse to seek a smoother walking on the other side, and he was glad when the city road changed to the smaller country one and then this changed to a little path where they two must walk one behind the other, and Yuan went first so that he could look about him and not see her before him.

But be sure this maid understood before long how he felt. She made her talk at first very quietly, and as though she would not heed his short replies, and then she fell into silence, and at last they walked only in silence. And all the time Yuan felt her feelings rising in her and he dreaded her, and yet must go doggedly on. Now they came to a certain turn of road where willow trees had been planted long ago, and they were very old and the branches had been often cut and so often that the new branches of each year grew thick and tufted as brushes and met above the path and made a deep green hiding shade. Then as they passed through this quiet lonely place Yuan felt his two shoulders laid hold on from behind, and this maid twisted him about and cast herself against him and she burst into dreadful weeping and she cried, "I know why it is you cannot love me—I know where you go of nights—I followed you the other night and saw you with your sister, and how you went into that great hotel and I saw the women there. You like them better than you do me— I saw the one you danced with—that one in the peach pink gown—I saw her shamelessness the way she hung herself upon you—"

It was true that Yuan still went sometimes with Ai-lan, for he had never told his sister or the lady that he joined this cause, and though he often made excuse that he was busy and so could not go for pleasure so much as she did, yet he must go sometimes or Ai-lan would wonder, and that lady still hoped to have him go and keep her eased. When this maid wept out these words he remembered that a night or two gone by he had gone with Ai-lan to a party given for her nearest friend's birthday at a great foreign hotel there in that city, and he had danced with this friend and there were vast glass windows in that hall which showed out upon the street, and doubtless it was true he could have been noted out from among the others by this maid's searching knowing eyes.

He stiffened his body now and was angry and he said resentfully, "I went with my sister, and I was a guest and—"

But the maid had felt him turn cold under her hot hands and she flung herself back and cried in anger greater than his, "Yes, I saw you—you held her and did not fear to touch her, but you **draw** from me as if I were a very snake! And what do you think would come to you if I should tell the others that you spend your time with the very people whom we hate and against whom we all work? Your life is in my hands!"

Now this was very true, and Yuan knew it. But he only answered quietly and with scorn, "Do you think it is a way to make me love you, to speak to me like that?"

Then she fell against him again, weakened, and she sobbed softly against him, and lifted up his two arms and by her own strength held them about her and so they stood, and Yuan after a moment could not but be moved by her sobbing, and be sorry for her, and when at last she said, "You have so won me, and if it is against your will it is against mine, too, for I did not want to be won by any man—yet I know I would leave the cause before I could leave you—I am so wicked and so weak—" he felt his pity rise very swiftly, and then, though unwillingly, he held his arms where she had put them.

After a while she quieted herself and moved away and wiped her eyes and they went on again and now she was very sad and quiet, and they did their work and she spoke no more on that day.

But Yuan knew and she knew how the matter was between them. And here was the perversity in Yuan, that until this time he never had looked twice at any friend of Ai-lan's, and they all looked alike to him, these pretty daughters of the rich, all with their high light merry voices and their tinkling laughter and their varied pretty clothes and jewels in their ears and smooth skin and painted fingernails and all such likenesses one to the other. He loved the rhythms of music and a maid added to the music and now he was not so disturbed as he had been at first by maids.

But this other maid's incessant jealousies drove him strangely to look at the very ones against whom she complained, and their merriment was sweet to him because she was never merry, and he found a sort of pleasure in their gaiety and lack of any cause except to find pleasure anyhow. He began to single out two or three maids he liked above others, one the daughter of an old prince who had lived for refuge in this city since the empire had fallen down, and she was the smallest pretty maid he had ever seen, so perfect in her little beauty that Yuan liked to see her now he had taken thought to do it, and another older maid, who liked his youth and looks and while she swore she would not wed and would do her business all her life, which was to own and manage a shop for women's garments in that city, still she liked to dally and Yuan pleased her, and he knew he did, and he found her sharp beauty, sword slender as she was, and her short black hair smooth as paint upon her head, a teasing prodding pleasure to him.

This little passing thought he took for these two maids and one or two more made him feel guilty when the other maid reproved him as she often did, and one day she was hot and pleading in her anger and another she was cold and hateful and Yuan was bound to her in strange comradeship, so that he felt tied, and yet he could not love her.

One day a few days before the day his father was to wed him in that far-off town he was thinking of it, and he stood melancholy and alone before the window in his room and looked down upon the city streets and thought distastefully that he must see that maid today, and then he thought, "I cry against my father, because he binds me, and yet what a fool am I that I have let her bind me, too!" And he was so struck that he had not thought of this before, how he had let his freedom go again, that he sat down and planned swiftly of what escape he now could have and how he might be free once more by some means from this new bondage, which in its way was as heavy as the other because it was so secret and so close.

Then suddenly he was freed. For all this time the cause had been strengthening itself in the south, and now the hour was struck, and out of the southern city the armies of the revolution marched swiftly through the very heart of that country. Suddenly as a great typhoon wind swings up the coast from the southern seas, those armies took on flesh and blood and truth, and they were filled with a power which made them more than human, almost, so that all about the country and into every city there ran ahead of them and behind them and on every side of them the tales of their strength and power and never-failing victories. For these armies were all young men, and among them were maids, too, all filled with secret power, so that they did not fight as soldiers do who only fight for pay. They fought for a cause which was their life, and so they were invincible, and the soldiers of the rulers, who were hirelings, ran before them like leaves before a bitter wind. Before them like a vanguard ran tidings of the terror of their strength and fearlessness and how death could not touch them, since they did not fear to die.

Then the rulers of the city were so much afraid they fell upon every revolutionist they knew within that city, lest these plot from within to join those who were to come, and there were many in other schools like Meng and Yuan and like that maid. This happened in three little days, that these rulers sent burly soldiers into every room where any student lived, and if anything were found, a book, a bit of paper, a flag or any symbol of the cause of revolution, then he was shot, and if it were a maid, then she was shot. In those three days there were so shot in that one city hundreds of such youths and maidens, and no one dared to say a word against it, lest he be held a friend of them and so lose his own life. And there were killed among the guilty many innocent, for there were evil men who had enemies who would not die, and these went and told secretly the names of those they hated and gave false witness of their being revolutionists, and on such bare word even were many killed, so great was the fear among the rulers that the revolutionists within the city would join the cause of those who came from outside to attack.

Then one day this thing took place without a warning. On a morning when Yuan sat in his class and at a very moment when he swore to himself he would not turn his head because he knew that maid was looking at him, and half he was about to turn because he felt somehow constrained to do it, suddenly there came into the room a band of soldiers and the captain of them shouted, "Stand and be searched!" Then every one of them stood dazed and wondering and frightened while soldiers passed their hands over their bodies and looked at their books, and one took down into a book the names of where they lived. In utter silence was this done, the teacher standing silent, too, and helpless. There was no sound except the clanking of the soldiers' swords against

123

their leather heels and the sound of their thick shoes upon the wooden floor.

Out of that silent, frightened roomful three were singled out because something was found upon their persons. Two were lads, but the third one was that maid, who had a guilty paper in her pocket. Those three the soldiers held before them, and when they turned to go, they prodded them with bayoneted guns to hasten them. This Yuan watched, staring dazed and helpless to see the maid go out like this. And at the door the maid turned back her head and gave him one look, one long, imploring, speechless look. And then a soldier touched her sharply with his pointed gun and pushed her on, and she was gone, and Yuan knew he would never see her any more.

His first thought was, "I am free!" and then he was half ashamed because he could not but be glad, and yet he could not but remember, too, that great tragic look the maid had given him as she went, and somehow he felt himself guilty for that look, because though with her whole heart she loved him, he had not loved her. Even while he justified himself and cried in his silent self, "I could not help it—could I help it if I did not want her?" there was another smaller weaker voice which said, "Yes, but if I had known she was to die so soon—could I have comforted her a little?"

But his questionings were soon stopped, for there could be no more work that day, and the teacher gave them dismissal and they all hastened away from that room. But in the hastening Yuan felt his arm taken and he looked and there was Sheng, and Sheng led him secretly aside where none could hear and he whispered, his smooth face for once all in a disarray of fright, "Where is Meng?—he does not know of this raid today and if he is searched—my father will die of it if Meng is killed."

"I do not know," said Yuan, staring back. "I have not seen him these two days—"

But Sheng was gone, his agile body slipping swiftly in and out among the throngs of silent, frightened students pouring now from every room.

Then Yuan went by small quiet streets to his own home and there he found the lady and he told her what had come about, and he said to ease her at the end, "Of course I have nothing I need fear."

But the lady's mind went more deeply than did Yuan's, and she said swiftly, "Think—you have been seen with Meng—you are his cousin—he has been here. Has he not left a book or paper or any least thing in your room? They will come here to search. Oh, Yuan, go you and look while I think what I am to do with you, for your father loves you, and if you should suffer anything it would be my fault because I did not send you home when he commanded it!" And she was in more fear than Yuan had ever seen upon her.

Then she went with him to his room to look at all he had. And while she looked at every book and in each drawer and on each shelf, Yuan bethought him of that old letter of love the maid had sent which he had never torn to pieces. He had kept it between the pages of a book of verse, not that he valued it but at first it was precious to him because after all it spoke of love—the first word of love in his whole life and so for a while magic for its own sake and then he had forgotten it. Now he took it out while the lady's back was turned, and he crushed it in his hand and made some excuse and left the room and slipped into another room and set a match to it. While it burned between his thumb and finger, he remembered that poor maid and how she had looked at him, the look a hare might give before the wild dogs fell upon it to devour it. And Yuan was filled with a great sadness when he thought of her, a sadness strangely deeper somehow, because even now, now more than ever, he knew he did not love her and that he never could have loved her, and he was not even sorry for her death, though he felt guilty that he was not. So the letter fell to ash between his fingers and then was dust

Yet even if Yuan had had a mind to grieve, he had not time for it, for scarcely was the letter burned before he heard the noise of voices in the hall, and the door opened and his uncle came in and his aunt and elder cousin and Sheng, and they all cried out to know if Meng had been seen. And the lady came in from Yuan's room, and they all put questions at each other and were frightened and the uncle said, his fat face trembling with fright and weeping, "I came here to be safe from those tenants on my land who are the cruelest wildest savages, and I thought here I would be safe with foreign soldiers to protect us, and I do not know what these foreigners are about that they allow such things to be, and now here is Meng gone, and Sheng says he was a revolutionist, although I swear I did not know it. Why was I not told of it? I would have seen to it long ago!"

"But, father," answered Sheng in a low, troubled voice, "what could you have done except to talk and noise it more about?"

"Aye, that he would have," said Sheng's mother sourly. "If anything is to be kept it is only I who keep it in our house. But I take it hard I was not told, either, and Meng my own favorite son!"

And the elder son, whose color was as pale as willow ashes, said anxiously, "For this one foolish boy's sake we are all in danger, for the soldiers will come and question us and suspect us."

Then the lady, Yuan's mother, said quietly, "Let us all think what we must do in such a danger. I must think of Yuan, since he is in my keeping. I have thought of this. He is to go abroad sometime anyway to foreign schools, and I will send him now. As quickly as it can be done and all the papers signed, I will send him, and in foreign parts he will be safe."

"Then we will all go," cried the uncle eagerly. "In foreign parts we will all be safe!"

"Father, you cannot," said Sheng patiently. "The foreigners will not let men of our race on their shores unless it be for study or some such special thing."

At this the old man swelled himself out and opened up his little eyes and said, "And are they not here upon our shores?"

But the lady said to soothe them all, "It is scarcely useful now to talk of ourselves. We old ones are safe enough. They will not kill such old staid folk as we are for revolutionists and scarcely you, eldest nephew, who have wife and children and are no longer young. But Meng is known and through him Sheng is in danger and so is Yuan, and we must somehow get them from the country to foreign parts."

So they planned how this could be done, and the lady bethought herself of a foreign friend whom Ai-lan knew, and how through him the many papers to be written and signed and hastened on could be written, and the lady rose and put her hand upon the door to call a servant to go fetch Ai-lan home from a friend's house where she had gone for a morning's gaming, for she was not willing to go to school these days of disturbance, because it made her sad, and she could not bear sadness.

Even as the lady put her hand upon the door a mighty noise rose up from the lower rooms, the noise of a bold rough voice shouting, "Is this where one Wang Yuan lives?"

Then they all looked at each other, and the old uncle turned as pale as the fat upon a butchered beef and looked about to hide himself. But the lady's quick thought was for Yuan first, and then for Sheng.

"You two," she gasped—"quick—into the little room beneath this roof—"

Now this room had no stairway to it, and its entrance was no more than a square hole let into the ceiling of this very room where they were gathered. But the lady even as she spoke had pulled a table beneath it and dragged at a chair, and Sheng sprang forward, being ever a little more quick than Yuan was, and then Yuan after him.

But none was quick enough. Even as they hastened, the door was flung open as by a gale of wind, and eight or ten soldiers stood there and the captain cried out, looking first at Sheng, "Are you Wang Yuan?"

Now Sheng was very pale, too. He waited for one instant before he answered, as though he took thought for what he should say, and then he answered very low, "No, I am not he."

Then the man roared out, "Then this other one is he— Aye, I remember now the maid said he was tall and very dark, and his brows were black above his eyes—but his mouth soft and red— it is this one—"

Without one word to deny himself, Yuan let himself be bound, his hands behind his back, and no one could stay the matter. No, although his old uncle wept and trembled and though the lady came up beseeching and said in her grave sure way, "You are mistaken—this lad is no revolutionist. I can swear for him—he is a studious, careful lad—my son—who has never taken any part in all this cause—"

But the men only laughed coarsely, and one great round-faced soldier cried out, "Ah, lady, mothers never know their sons! To know a man one must ask the maid—never his mother—and the maid gave his name and the number of this very house, and told his looks exactly—aye, she knew his looks very well, didn't she?— I swear she knows his every look!—and she said he was the greatest rebel of them all—yes, she was so bold and angry at first, and then she grew silent for a while, and then she gave his name of her own will, without a moment's torture for it!"

Then Yuan saw the lady look dazed at this, as at a thing she did not understand at all. He could say nothing. He kept silent but in his heart he thought dully to himself, "And so her love turned into hating! She could not bind me by her love—her hate binds me fast enough!" And thus must he let himself be led away.

Even at that moment Yuan feared with every certainty that he must die. These latter days, though it was never public, yet he knew the end of all such as were known to have been joined to the cause was death, and no proof could be surer than this of his guilt, that the maid herself had given his name. Yet though he told himself so, that word death could not seem real to him. Not even when he was thrust into a prison cell, full of other youths like himself, and not when the guard shouted at him when he stumbled on the threshold because it was so dark, "Aye, pick yourself up now, but tomorrow others must do it for you—" even then he could not understand the meaning of the word. The guard's words struck into his heart like the bullets waiting in the guns for tomorrow, and yet Yuan could take thought to look through the dimness of that crowded cell, and be eased because he saw none in it but men, and not one woman. He could think, "I can bear to die better than I could bear to see her here and have her know I am to die, and have her know she has me after all." This thing remained an ease to him.

All had come about so quickly Yuan could not but believe that somehow he would be saved from here. At first he thought that any moment he would be saved. He trusted very much the lady his mother, and the more he thought the more confident he was that she would think how to save him. The first hours he so believed, and the more because he felt, as he looked about upon his fellows, that he was much better than any of them, and they looked poor and less wise than he, and of families of less wealth and influence.

But after a while the darkness fell completely black, and in the black silence they all sat or lay upon the earthen floor. For none spoke, lest out of their own mouths they be committed by some word which might confirm their guilt, and each man feared the other and so long as face could see even the dim shape of face, there was no sound except the movement of a body changing its position, or some such voiceless sound.

Then night fell, when none could see another's face, and the darkness seemed to shut each into his own cell, and a first voice cried softly, "Oh, my mother—oh, my mother—" and broke into desperate weeping.

This weeping was very hard to bear, for each felt it might be his own self weeping, and a louder voice cried out, very loud and surly, "Be silent! What child is it who cries for its mother? I am a loyal member—I killed my own mother, and my brother killed our father, and we know no parents but the cause—eh, brother?"

And another voice out of the darkness answered, twin to that voice, "Yes, I did it!" And the first voice said, "Are we sorry?" And the second sneered and answered again, "Though I had a score of fathers I would gladly kill them all—" And another cried emboldened, "Aye, those old men and women, they only breed us to make sure they have servants for their old age to keep them warmed and fed—" But the first softest voice moaned on most steadily, "Oh, my mother—oh, my mother—" as though the one who cried these words heard nothing.

But at last as deep night wore on even such cries must be stilled. Yuan had not spoken once while others spoke, but after they were quiet the night stayed on and on forever with its deep exhausted stillness, and he could not bear it. All his hopefulness began to ebb away. He thought the door must open any moment and a voice shout forth, "Let Wang Yuan come—he is freed!"

But no voice called.

At last it seemed to Yuan some sound must be made because he could not bear the stillness. He spent himself in thought. Against his will he thought of all his life and how short it was and he thought, "If I had obeyed my father, I would not now be here—" and yet he could not say, "I wish I had obeyed him." No, when Yuan thought of it, some stubbornness he had made him say honestly, "Yet I do believe he asked a wrong thing of me—" And again he thought, "If I had forced myself a little and yielded to that maid—" And then again his gorge rose and he thought honestly, "Yet I did not like to do it—" And at last there was nothing else to do than to think ahead to what was to come, since the past was shaped and gone, and he must think of death.

Now did he long for any sound to come out of the darkness, and he longed even to hear that lad calling for his mother. But the cell was still as though it were empty, and yet the darkness was not sleeping. No, it was a living waiting wakeful darkness, full of terror and of silence. He had not been afraid at first. But in the deep night he grew afraid. Death, which had not been real until this hour, now grew real. He wondered, breathless suddenly, if he would be beheaded or if he would be shot. These days the gates of inland cities, he had read, were decorated with the heads of the dead young men and women who had joined the cause, for whom the armies of deliverance had not come swiftly enough, so that before the day of battle they were caught by the rulers. He seemed to see his own head—and then it came to him like comfort, "But here in this foreign sort of city they will doubtless shoot us," and then he wondered at himself with a bitter sort of mirth, even, that it could matter to him that he could keep his head on his shoulders when he was dead.

Now even as he sat crouched in this agony these hours through, his back thrust between two walls into a corner and his feet dragged close to him, so he sat huddled, the door opened suddenly and a grey beam of early light fell into the cell and showed the prisoners curled among each other like a heap of worms. The light stirred them into moving, but before any could move to rise, a voice roared forth, "Out with you all!"

And soldiers came into the cell, and pushing and prodding with their guns they roused them all, and now roused, that lad began his wailing, "Oh, my mother—oh, my mother—" and would not leave off even when a soldier smote him hard across the head with his gun's butt, for he moaned these words as though he breathed them and could not help it, and must draw his life in so.

Now as these staggered forth, in silence otherwise than for this one, each knowing what was coming and yet dazed, too, a certain soldier held up a lantern that he had and flashed its light across each face. Yuan was the last of all, and as he came the light flashed across his face. This brightness blinded him suddenly after the long darkness of the night, and in that moment's blindness he felt himself pushed back into the room, and pushed so hard he fell upon the beaten earth. Then instantly he heard the door lock, and there he was, alone and still alive.

Three times did this thing happen. For during that day the cell was filled again with new young men, and again through that night and two more nights Yuan must hear them, sometimes silent and sometimes cursing and sometimes whimpering and sometimes crying out in their madness. Three dawns came, and thrice he was thrust back into the cell alone and the door locked on him. He was given no food, nor was any moment given him for speech or question.

The first day he could not but have hope. And on the second day he had a lesser hope. But by the third day he was so faint and weak with no food and no water even to drink, that it seemed a little matter to him if he lived or died. That third dawn he could scarcely rise to his feet at all and his tongue was dry and swollen in his mouth. Yet the soldier shouted at him and prodded him and made him rise, and when Yuan clung to the door-frame with his two hands, again the light flashed across his face. But this time he was not thrust into the cell again. Instead, the soldier held him, and when the others were all gone their doomed and certain way, and when at last not even their footsteps could be heard echoing, the soldier led Yuan by another narrower passage to a place where a small barred door was set, and he drew back the bar and without a word thrust Yuan through that door.

Then Yuan found himself upon a small narrow street, such as wind through the inner, more secret parts of any city, and the street was still dim with early dawn and there was no one in sight, and out of his clouded mind Yuan could see this thing clearly, that he was free—somehow he had been freed.

Even as he turned his head this way and that to think how he could run, two came near out of the dusk, and Yuan shrank back against the door again. But one of the two was a child, a tall child, and she came running to him and came near and peered at him, and he saw her two eyes, very large and black and eager, and he heard this child call out in a low fervent voice, "It is he—here he is—here he is—"

Then the other came near, too, and Yuan saw her and knew it was his lady mother. But before he could speak, in spite of all his eagerness to speak and say it was he himself, he felt his body tremble on his feet and seem to melt away, and he suddenly could not see anything and the child's dark eyes grew larger and blacker and then faded. From some very far distant place he heard a voice whisper, "Oh, my poor son—" and then he fell and heard and saw no more.

When Yuan awoke again he felt himself upon some moving swaying thing. He lay in a bed, but this bed rose and fell beneath him, and opening his eyes he saw he was in a small strange room where he had never been. Someone sat there watching him beneath a light set in the wall, and when Yuan summoned all his strength to look he saw this was Sheng, his cousin. And Sheng was watching Yuan, too, and when he saw Yuan looking he rose and smiled his old smile, but now it seemed to Yuan truly the gentlest sweetest smile a face could have, and he reached to a little table and fetched some hot broth in a bowl there and he said, soothing Yuan, "Your mother said the moment you awoke I was to give you this, and I have been keeping it hot these two hours on a little lamp she gave me—"

He began to feed Yuan as he might feed a child, and like a child Yuan said not a word, he was so weary and so dazed. He drank the broth down, too weak to wonder how he came here and what this place was, and like a child accepting all that was come about. He only felt the warm liquid very succoring and pleasant to his dry and swollen tongue and he swallowed it as best he could. But Sheng talked quietly as he dipped the broth up with the spoon, and he said, "I know you wonder where we are and why we are here. We are on a small ship,—a ship our uncle merchant has used to carry his goods back and forth to the nearest islands, and by his influence we are on it. We are to go across the nearest seas, and stay in the closest port and there we are to wait for papers we must have to go on to foreign parts. You are free, Yuan, but at a mighty price. Your mother and my father and my brother have laid hold on every sum they could and they borrowed much money of our second uncle, and your father was beside himself, and they said he kept groaning how he had been betrayed by a woman, too, and he and his son were done with women this time and forever. And he has given up your marriage, and sent all the money for it and all he could get and all these moneys together bought your freedom and our escape on this ship. High and low money has been paid—"

When Sheng said these words, Yuan listened, and yet he was so weak he scarcely could perceive their meaning. He could only feel the ship rise and fall beneath him and feel the good heat of the food slip down into his starved body. Then Sheng said, suddenly smiling, "Yet I do not know if I could have left happily even in such a case if I had not known Meng was safe. Ah, he is a clever one, that lad! Look here! I went grieving for him and my parents were distracted between you and him, and not knowing whether it was worse to know where you were and that you were to be killed, or not know where Meng was and that he might be safe or killed already. Then yesterday when I was on the street between your home and mine, someone thrust this bit of paper in my hand, and on it is Meng's writing, saying, 'You are not to look for me or be anxious, and my parents need not think of me again. I am safe and where I want to be.' "

Sheng laughed and set down the empty bowl and struck a match to light a cigarette and he said gaily to Yuan, "I have not even relished smoking these three days! Well, that young rascal who is my brother is safe enough, and I have told my father, and though the old man is angry and swears he will not have Meng ever be as his son again, still I know by now he has let down his heart and gone to a feast tonight. And my elder brother will be at the theatre to see a new piece put on with a woman acting in her own right in this new fashion, and not a man dressed as a woman, for he is all agog to see the vileness in it. And my mother has been angry at my father for a while and so we are all ourselves again, now that Meng is safe and you and I are escaped." He smoked a little and then he said, more gravely than his wont was, "But, Yuan, I am glad that we are going to other parts even though we go like this. I say little of it, and I will not join in any cause and I take my pleasure where I can. But I am weary of my country and its wars and though you all think me a smiling laughing fellow only thinking of my verses, yet the truth is I am very often sad and hopeless. I am glad to go and see another country and know how its people live. I feel my heart lift just to be going away!"

But even as he talked Yuan could listen no more. The comfort of the food and the softness of this narrow swinging bed and the knowledge of his freedom covered him with comfort. He could only smile a little, and he felt his eyes begin to close. Sheng saw it too, and he said very kindly, "Sleep—your mother said I was to let you sleep and sleep—and you may sleep better than you ever have, now you are free."

Yuan opened his eyes once more at this word. Free? Yes, he was free of everything at last. . . . And then Sheng said once more, to finish out his thought, "And if you are like me, there is nothing much you do not want to leave."

No, Yuan thought, slipping into sleep—there was nothing he grieved to leave behind him. . . . At this instant of his sleep he

saw again that crowded cell, those writhing forms—those nights
—there was that maid turning to look at him before she went to
die. He dropped his mind away and fell into sleep. . . . And then
suddenly, in a great peace, he dreamed he was on his bit of land.
There was the little piece of land he had planted. He saw it suddenly as clear as any picture; the peas were forming in their pods,
and the green-bearded barley was coming to its height, and there
was that old laughing farmer, working next upon his own fields.
But here the maid was, too, and now her hand was very cold—
very cold. Her hand was so cold he woke again a little—and remembered he was free. What had Sheng said, that he was not
sorry. . . . No, the only thing he minded leaving was that little
piece of land.

And then before Yuan slept there came this comfort to him,
"But that land—it is one thing that will still be there when I come
back—land is always there—"

II

WANG YUAN was in the twentieth year of his age when he went away from his own country, but in many ways a boy still and full of dreams and confusions and plans half begun which he did not know how to finish, or even if he wanted to finish them. He had all his life long been guarded and watched over and cared for by someone, and he did not know any other thing than such care, and for all his three days in that cell, he did not know what sorrow truly was. He stayed six years away.

When he made ready to return again to his country in the summer of that year he was near to his twenty-sixth birthday and he was a man in many things, though no sorrow had yet come to put the final shape of manhood on him, but this he did not know he needed. If any had asked him, he would have said steadfastly, "I am a man. I know my own mind. I know what I want to do. My dreams are plans now. I have finished my years at school. I am ready for my life in my own country." And indeed to Yuan these six years in foreign parts were like another half of his life. The early nineteen years were the first lesser half, and the six were the greater, more valuable ones, for these years had taken him and set him fast in certain ways. But the truth was, although he did not know it, he was set in many ways of which he was not himself aware.

If any had asked him, "How are you ready now to live your life?" he would have answered honestly, "I have a degree of learning from a great foreign college, and I took that degree above many who were native to the land." This he would have said proudly, but he would not have told of a certain memory he had that there were those among his fellows in this foreign people who muttered against him saying, "Of course, if a man wants to be nothing but a grind he can carry off the honors in grades, but we owe more to the school than that. This fellow—he grinds at his books and that is all—he takes no part in the life—where would the school be in football and in the boat races if we all did it?"

Yes, Yuan knew these pushing, crowding, merry foreign youths who so spoke of him, and they took no great pains to hide the words, but said them in the halls. But Yuan held his head high. He was secure in the praise of his teachers and in the mention he received at times of prize-giving, when his name often came the first and always it was said by the one who gave the prize, "Although he works in a language foreign to him, he has surpassed the others." So, although Yuan knew he was not loved for this, he had gone proudly on, and he was glad to show what his race could do, and glad to show them that he did not value games so high as children did.

If again one had asked him, "How are you ready now to live your man's life?" he would have answered, "I have read many hundreds of books, and I have searched to find out all I could from this foreign nation."

And this was true, for in these six years Yuan lived as lone as a thrush in a cage. Every morning he rose early and read his books, and when a bell rang in the house where he lived he went downstairs and took his breakfast, eating usually in silence, for he did not trouble to talk much to any other in that house, nor to the woman whose it was. And why should he waste himself in speech with them?

At noon he took his meal among the many students in the vast hall there was for this purpose. And in the afternoons, if he had not work in the field or with his teachers, he did what he loved most to do. He went into the great hall of books and sat among the books and read and wrote down what he would keep and pondered on many things. In these hours he was forced to discover that these western peoples were not, as Meng had cried so bitterly, a savage race, in spite of the rudeness of the common people, and they were learned in sciences. Many times Yuan heard his own countrymen in this foreign country say that in the use and knowledge of materials these folk excelled, but in all the arts whereby men's spirits live, they lacked. Yet now, looking at the rooms of books which were all of philosophy, or all of poetry, or all of art, Yuan wondered if even his own people were greater, though he would have died before he spoke such a wonder aloud in this foreign land. He even found translated into western tongues the sayings of the earlier and later sages of his own people, and books which told of arts of the East, and he was aghast at all this learning, and half he was envious of these people who possessed it and half he hated them for it, and he did not like to remember that in his own country a common man often could not read a book, and less often could his wife.

Yuan had been of two different minds since he came to this foreign country. When he grew well upon the ship and felt his forces come back into him after those three days of death, he was glad to live again. Then as he grew glad to live he caught from Sheng his pleasure in the travel and in all the new sights they would see and in the greatness of the foreign lands. So Yuan had entered upon the new shores as eager as any child to see a show, and ready to be pleased by everything.

And he found everything to please. When first he entered into the great port city on this new country's western coast it seemed to him that all he ever heard was more than true. The houses were higher than he had heard and the streets were tiled and paved like floors of houses and clean enough to sit on or to sleep on and not be soiled. And all the people seemed most wonderfully clean. The whiteness of their skins and the cleanness of their garments were very pleasing to see, and they all seemed rich and

139

ted, and Yuan was glad because here at least the poor were not mingled among the rich. Here the rich came and went most freely on the streets and no beggars plucked at their sleeves and cried out for mercy and a little silver. It was such a country as could be enjoyed, for all had enough, and one could eat with joy because all so ate.

Thus Yuan and Sheng together in those first days could not but cry at much beauty to be seen. For these people lived in palaces, or so it seemed to these two young men who had not seen such homes. In this city away from the shops the streets stretched wide and shaded by great trees and families needed not to build high walls about them, but each grassy garden ran into the next man's, and this was a marvel to Yuan and Sheng, because it seemed every man so trusted his neighbor that he needed not to build against him or his thievery.

Thus at first all seemed perfect in that city. The great square high buildings were cut so clean against the blue metallic sky that they seemed mighty temples, only there were no gods inside. And between these ran at great speed the thousand thousand vehicles of that city all filled with rich men and their ladies, although even the people who went on foot seemed to do it out of joy and not because they must. At first Yuan had said to Sheng, "There must be something wrong here in this city, that so many people go at such speed somewhere." But when he and Sheng had looked awhile they perceived that these people looked very gay and often laughed, and their high clacking speech was more merry than it was mournful, and there was no trouble anywhere, and they went quickly because they loved swiftness. Such was their temper.

And indeed there was here a strange power in the very air and sunshine. Where in Yuan's mother country the air was often somnolent and soothing, so that in summer one must sleep long and in winter one wished only to curl into a close space for sleep and warmth, in this new country the winds and sunshine were filled with a wild driving energy, so that Yuan and Sheng walked more quickly than their wont was, and in the beaming light the people moved like shining mingling motes driven through the sunshine.

Yet already in those earliest two days when all was strange to them, and all to be enjoyed, Yuan found his pleasure checked by a certain moment. Even now after six years were gone Yuan could not say he had forgot that moment wholly, though it was a small thing, too. The second day upon the shore he and Sheng went into a certain common restaurant where many ate, and there were people not rich as some, perhaps, but still well enough to eat as they chose. When Yuan and Sheng passed through the doors from the street, Yuan felt, or thought he did, that these white men and women stared somewhat at him and at Sheng, and he thought they drew a little off from them, though the truth was Yuan was glad they did, because there was about them a strange alien odor, a little like a certain curd of milk they loved to eat, though not so foul, perhaps. When they went into that place to eat, a maid standing at a counter took their hats from them to hang among many others, for so the custom was, and when they came back to claim them this maid put many hats out at a time, and a certain man before Yuan could stay him, reached out his hand and seized on Yuan's hat, which was of a brown hue like his own, and he pressed it on his head and ran out of the door. At once Yuan saw what was the mistake, and hastening after he said with courtesy, "Sir, here is your hat. Mine, which is the inferior one, you have taken by mistake. It is my fault, I was so slow." And then Yuan bowed and held forth the other's hat.

But the man, who was no longer young, and who wore an anxious, sharp look upon his thin face, listened with impatience to Yuan's speech, and now he seized his own hat, and with great distaste removed from his bald head Yuan's hat. Nor did he stop except to say two words, and these he spat forth.

Thus Yuan was left standing holding his hat and wishing he

141

need not set it on his head again, for he had not liked the man's shining white pate—and most of all he did not like the hiss of the man's voice. When Sheng came up he asked Yuan, "Why do you stand as though you had been struck?"

"That man," said Yuan, "struck me with two words I did not understand, except I know they were evil."

At this Sheng laughed, but there was an edge of light bitterness in his laughter. "It may be he called you foreign devil," he said.

"Two evil words they were, I know," said Yuan, troubled, and beginning to be less joyful.

"We are now foreigners," said Sheng and after a while he shrugged himself and said again, "All countries are alike, my cousin."

Yuan said nothing. But he was not again so joyful and not so wholly pleased again with anything he saw. Inside he gathered steadfastly his own self, stubborn and resistant. He, Yuan, son of Wang the Tiger, grandson of Wang Lung, would remain himself forever, never lost in any millions of white alien men.

That day he could not forget his hurt until Sheng saw it again and laughed and said with a little smile of malice, "Do not forget that in our country Meng would have cried at that little man that he was a foreign devil, so the hurt might have been the other way." And after a while he told Yuan to look at this strange sight or that, until he had diverted Yuan at last.

In the next days and in all the years to come when there was so much to see and to make wonder over, he would have said he had forgotten that small one thing, except he had not. As clearly today, if he happened to take thought of it, as he had six years ago, he saw that man's angry look and he could still feel the wound, which seemed to him unjust.

But if he had not forgotten, yet the memory was often buried. For Yuan and Sheng together saw much beauty in those first days in the foreign country. They rode on a train which bore them through great mountains where, although spring was warm upon the foothills, yet snow was white and thick against the high blue skies, and between these mountains there were black gorges where deep waters foamed and frothed and Yuan staring down at all this mad beauty felt it almost too much and scarcely real, but like some wild painter's picture hung there beneath the train, foreign and strange and too sharply colored, and not made of earth and rocks and water of which his own country was compounded.

When the mountains were behind them, there were valleys as extravagant and fields big enough to be counties and machines struggling like huge beasts to make ready the fertile earth for gigantic harvests. Yuan saw it very clearly, and this was even more a marvel to him than the mountains. He stared at the great machines and he remembered how the old farmer had taught him to hold a hoe and fling it so it fell true to its set place. So did that farmer still till his land, and so did others like him. And Yuan remembered how the farmer's little fields were made, each neatly fitted to the other, and how his few vegetables grew green and heavy with the human wastes he saved and poured on them, so that every plant grew to its richest best, and every plant and every foot of land had its full value. But here none could take thought of single plants and any foot of land. Here fields were measured by the mile, and plants unnumbered, doubtless.

Thus in those first days everything except that one man's words seemed good to Yuan and better than anything in his own country could be. The villages were clean and very prosperous, and although he could recognize the different look of a man upon the land and a man who lived in any town, still the man upon the land did not go ragged in his coat, and the houses on this land were never made of earth and thatch, nor did the fowls and pigs stray as they would. These were all things to admire, or so Yuan thought.

Yet from those first days even Yuan felt the earth here strange and wild and not like his own earth. For as time passed and Yuan knew better what that earth was from walking often along country roads or tilling a piece for himself in the foreign school even as he had in his own country, he never could forget the difference. Though the earth which fed these white folk was the same earth which had fed Yuan's race, too, yet working on it, Yuan knew it was not the very earth in which his forefathers were buried. This earth was fresh and free of human bones, and so not tamed, since of this new race not yet enough were dead to saturate the soil with their essences as Yuan knew the soil of his own country was saturated with its own humanity. This earth was still stronger than the people who strove to possess it, and they were wild through its wildness and in spite of wealth and learning often savage in their spirits and their looks.

For the earth was uncaptured. The miles of wooded mountains; all the waste of fallen logs and rotting leaves beneath great trees ungarnered; the lands let free to grass and pasture for beasts; the carelessness of wide roads running everywhere; these showed forth the unconquered land. Men used what they wanted, they brought forth great groaning harvests, more than they could sell, they cut down trees and used only the fields that were best and left the others to waste, and still the land was more than they could use, and greater still than they.

In Yuan's own country the land was conquered and men were the masters. There the mountains were stripped of their forests in years long past, and in these present times were shaven even of the wild grasses to feed the fires of men. And men coaxed the fullest harvests from the tiny fields they had, and forced the land to labor for them for its fullest and into the land again they poured themselves, their sweat, their wastes, their dead bodies, until there was no more virginity left in it. Men made the soil out of themselves, and without them the earth would have been long since exhausted, and but an empty barren womb.

So Yuan felt when he mused over this new country and what

its secret was. On his own bit of land he thought first of what he had to put in before he could have hope of harvest. Here this foreign earth was enriched still by its own unused strength. For a little put in, it gave forth greatly, leaping into life too strong for men.

When did Yuan come to mingle hatred in this admiration? At the end of six years he could look back and see the second step he took in hatred.

Yuan and Sheng parted early and at the end of that first journey on the train, for Sheng fell into love of a great city where he found others of his own kind, and he said the schools there were better for such as he was who loved to learn of verse and music and of philosophies, and he cared nothing for the land as Yuan did. For Yuan set his heart to do in this foreign country what he had always hoped to do, to learn how to breed plants and how to till the soil and all such things, and the more steadfastly because he soon believed this people owed their power to their wealth of harvest from the land. So Yuan left Sheng behind in that city, and he went on into another town and to another school where he could have what he wanted.

First of all Yuan must find himself a place to eat and sleep and a room to call his home in this strange land. When he went to the school he was met courteously enough by a grey-haired white man who gave him lists of certain places where he might be housed and fed, and Yuan set forth to find the best one. The very first door at which he rang a bell was opened to him, and there stood a huge woman, one no longer young, and wiping her great bare red arms upon an apron that she wore about her vast middle.

Now Yuan had never seen a woman shaped like this one, and he could not bear her looks at this first instant, but he asked very courteously, "Is the master of this house at home?"

Then this female set her two hands on her thighs and she answered in a very loud-mouthed heavy way, "It's my house, and there is no man who owns it." At this Yuan turned to go away, for he thought he would rather try another place than this, thinking there must not be many even in this land so hideous as this woman, and he would rather live in a house where a man was. For this woman was truly more than could be believed; her girth and bosom were enormous, and on her head was short hair of a hue Yuan thought could not have grown from human skin except he saw it. It was a bright reddish-yellow color, dulled somewhat with kitchen grease and smoke. Beneath this strange hair her round fat face shone forth, a red again, but now of a different purplish red, and in this visage were set two small sharp eyes as blue and bright as new porcelain is sometimes. He could not bear to see her, and he let his eyes fall and then he saw her two spreading shapeless feet and those he could not bear either and he made haste away, and after courtesy turned to go elsewhere.

Nevertheless, when he had asked at another door or two where it was marked there were rooms for lodgers, he found himself refused. At first he did not know the reason why. One woman said, "My rooms are taken," although Yuan knew she lied, seeing that her sign of empty rooms was there. And so it was again and yet again. At last the truth was shown him. A man said bluntly, "We don't take any colored people here." At first Yuan did not know what was meant, not thinking of his pale yellow skin as being other than the usual hue of human flesh, nor his black eyes and hair what men's hair and eyes might always be. But in a moment he understood, for he had seen black men here and there about this country and marked how they were not held in high respect by white ones.

Up from his heart the blood rushed, and the man, seeing his face darken and glow, said half in apology, "My wife has to help me out in making our way in these hard times, and we have regular boarders, and they wouldn't stay if we was to bring in foreigners. There's places where they do take them, though," and the man named the number of the house and street where Yuan had seen the hideous female.

This was the second step in hatred.

He thanked the man therefore with deep proud courtesy and he went back again to that first house, and averting his eyes from her dreadful person, he told the woman he would see the room she had. The room he liked well enough, a small upper room against the roof, very clean, and cut off by a stairway. If he could forget the woman, this room seemed well enough. He could see himself there quietly at work, alone, and he liked the look of the roofs sloping down about the bed and table and the chair and chest it held. So he chose to stay in it, and this room was his home for the six years.

And the truth was the woman was not so ill as her looks and he lived in her house, year after year, while he went to that school, and the woman grew kind to him and he came to understand her kindness, covered as it was by her hideous looks and coarse ways. In his room he lived as sparsely and as neatly as a priest, his few possessions always placed exactly and this woman came to like him well and she sighed her gusty sigh and said, "If all my boys was like you, Wang, and as little trouble in their ways, I'd be a different woman now."

Then he found, as a few days went by, that this burly female creature was very kind in her loud way. Although Yuan cringed before the sound of her great voice, and shivered at the sight of her thick red arms bared to her shoulders, still he thanked her truly when he found some apples put in his room and he knew she meant kindness when she shouted at him across the table where they ate, "I cooked some rice for you, Mr. Wang! I reckon you find it hard eating without what you're used to—" And then she laughed freely and roared, "But rice is the best I can do—snails and rats and dogs and all them things you eat I can't supply!"

She did not seem to hear Yuan's protest that indeed he did not eat these things at home. And after a while he learned to smile in

147

silence when she made one of her jokes and he remembered at such times, he made himself remember, that she pressed food on him, more than he could eat, and kept his room warm and clean and when she knew he liked a certain dish she went to some pains to make it for him. At last he learned never to look into her face, which still he found hideous, and he learned to think only of her kindness, and this the more when he found as time passed by and he came to know a few others of his countrymen, in this town, circumstanced as he was, that there were many less good than she in lodging houses, women of acrid tongues and sparing of their food at table, and scornful of a race other than their own.

Yet when he thought of it here was the strangest thing of all to Yuan, that this gross loud-mouthed woman once had been wed. In his own land it might have been no wonder, for there youths and maidens wed whom they must before the new times came, and a man must take what was given him, even though it were an ugly wife. But in this foreign land for long there had been choosing of maid by the man himself. So once then was this woman chosen freely by a man! And by him, before he died, she had a child, a girl, now seventeen or so in age, who lived with her still.

And here was another strange thing,—the girl was beautiful. Yuan, who never thought a white woman could be truly beautiful, knew well enough this maid, in spite of all her fairness, must be called beautiful. For she had taken her mother's wiry flaming hair and changed it by some youthful magic in herself into the softest curling coppery stuff, cut short, but winding all about the shape of her pretty head and her white neck. And her mother's eyes she had, but softer, darker, and larger, and she used a little art to tinge her brows and lashes brown instead of pale as her mother's were. Her lips, too, were soft and full and very red, and her body slender as a young tree, and her hands were slender, not thick anywhere, and the nails long and painted red.

She wore, and Yuan saw it as all the young men saw it, garments of such frail stuff that her narrow hips and little breasts and all the moving lines of her body showed through, and well she knew the young men saw and that Yuan saw. And when Yuan knew she knew it, he felt a strange fear of her and even a dislike, so that he held himself aloof and would not do more than bow in answer to a greeting she might give.

He was glad her voice was not lovely. He liked a low sweet voice and hers was not low or sweet. Whatever she said was said too loudly and too sharply in her nose, and when he was afraid because he felt the softness of her look or if by chance when he took seat at table, where she sat beside him, his eyes fell on the whiteness of her neck, he was glad he did not like her voice. . . . And after a while he sought and found other things he did not like, too. She would not help her mother in the house, and when her mother asked her at mealtimes to fetch a thing forgotten from the table, she rose pouting and often saying, "You can never set the table, ma, and not forget something." Nor would she put her hands in water that was soiled with grease or dirt, because she valued her hands so much for beauty.

And all these six years Yuan was glad of her ways he did not like and kept them always clearly before him. He could look at her pretty restless hands beside him, and remember they were idle hands that did not serve another than herself, and so ought not maid's hands to be, and though he could not, roused as he once had been, avoid the knowledge sometimes of her nearness, yet he could remember the first two words he ever heard upon this foreign earth. He was foreign to this maid, too. Remembering, he could remember that their two kinds of flesh, his and this maid's, were alien to each other and he was set to be content to hold himself aloof and go his solitary way.

No, he told himself, he had had enough of maids, he who was betrayed, and if he were betrayed here in a foreign land, there would be none to help him. No, better that he stay away from maids. So he would not see the maid, and he learned never to look where her bosom was, and sedulously he refused to go with her if she begged it to some dancing place, for she was bold to invite him sometimes.

Yet there were nights when he could not sleep. He lay in his bed and remembered the dead maid, and he wondered sadly, yet with a thrilling wonder, too, what it was that burned so hot between a man and maid in any country. It was an idle wonder, since he never knew her, and she turned so wicked in the end. On moonlit nights especially he could not sleep. And when at last he did sleep he woke and then perhaps again, to lie and watch the silent, dancing shadows of a tree's branch against the white wall of his room, shining, for the moon was bright. He turned restlessly at last and hid his eyes and thought, "I wish the moon did not shine so clear—it makes me long for something—as though for some home I never had."

For these six years were years of great solitude for Yuan. Day by day he shut himself away into greater solitude. Outwardly he was courteous and spoke to all who spoke to him, but to none did he give greeting first. Day by day he shut himself away from what he did not want in this new country. His native pride, the silent pride of men old before the western world began, began to take its full shape in him. He learned to bear silently a foolish curious stare upon the street; he learned what shops he could enter in that small town to buy his necessities, or to have himself shaved or his hair cut. For there were keepers of shops who would not serve him, some refusing bluntly or some asking twice the value of goods, or some saying with a semblance of courtesy, "We have our living to make here and we do not encourage trade with foreigners." And Yuan learned to answer nothing, whether to coarseness or to courtesy.

He could live days without speech to anyone and it came to be that he might have been like a stranger lost in all this rushing foreign life. For not often did anyone even ask a question of him of his own country. These white men and women lived so enwrapped within themselves that they never cared to know what others did, or if they heard a difference they smiled tolerantly as one may at those who do not do so well from ignorance. A few set thoughts Yuan found his schoolfellows had, or the barber who cut his hair, or the woman in whose house he lodged, such as that Yuan and all his countrymen ate rats and snakes and smoked opium or that all his countrywomen bound their feet, or that all his countrymen wore hair braided into queues.

At first Yuan in great eagerness tried to set these ignorances right. He swore he had not tasted either rat or snake, and he told of Ai-lan and her friends who danced as lightly free as any maidens could. But it was no use, for what he said they soon forgot and remembered only the same things. Yet there was this result to Yuan, that so deep and often his anger rose against this ignorance that at last he began to forget there was any rightness or truth in anything they said, and he came to believe that all his country was like the coastal city, and that all maidens were like Ai-lan.

There was a certain schoolfellow he had in two of his classes where he learned of the soil, and this young man was a farmer's son, a lout of a very kind heart, and amiable to everyone. Yuan had not spoken to him when he dropped into the seat beside him at a class, but the youth spoke first and then he walked sometimes with Yuan away from the door, and then sometimes lingered in the sunshine and talked a little while with him, and then one day he asked Yuan to walk with him. Yuan had never met with such kindness yet, and he went and it was sweeter to him than he knew, because he lived so solitary.

Soon Yuan found himself telling his own story to this friend he had found. Together they sat down and rested under a tree bent over the roadside, and they talked on and very soon the lad cried out impetuously, "Say, call me Jim! What's your name? Wang. Yuan Wang. Mine's Barnes, Jim Barnes."

Then Yuan explained how in his country the family name came first, for it gave him the strangest reversed feeling to hear his own name called out first as this lad now did. And this amused the lad again, and he tried his own names backwards, and laughed aloud.

In such small talk and frequent laughter their friendship grew, and led to other talk, and Jim told Yuan how he had lived upon a farm his whole life, and when he said, "My father's farm has about two hundred acres," Yuan said, "He must be very rich." And then Jim looked at him surprised and said, "That's only ⊂ small farm here. Would it be big in your country?"

To this Yuan did not answer straightly. He suddenly could not bear to say how small a farm was in his country, dreading the other's scorn, and so he only said, "My grandfather had greater lands and he was called a rich man. But our fields are very fertile, and a man needs fewer of them to live upon."

And so through such talk he passed to telling of the great house in the town and of his father Wang the Tiger, whom he now called a general and not a lord of war, and he told of the coastal city and of the lady and Ai-lan his sister and of the modern pleasures Ai-lan had, and day after day Jim listened and pressed his questions and Yuan talked, scarcely knowing that he said so much.

But Yuan found it sweet to talk. He had been very lonely in this foreign country, more lonely than he knew, and the small slights put on him, which, if he had been asked, he would have said proudly were nothing to him, yet were something to him. Again and again his pride had been stabbed, and he was not used to it. Now it eased him to sit and tell this white lad all the glories of his race and of his family and his nation, and it was a balm to all his wounds to see Jim's eyes grow large and full of wonder and to hear him say most humbly, "We must look pretty

poor to you—a general's son and all—and all those servants and—
I'd like to ask you home with me this summer, but I don't know
as I dare, after all you've had!"

Then Yuan thanked him courteously, and with courtesy said,
"I am sure your father's house would be very large and pleasant
to me," and he drank in with pleasure the other's admiration.

But here was the secret fruit in Yuan of all this talk. He came
himself, without his knowing it, to see his country as he said it
was. He forgot that he had hated Wang the Tiger's wars and all
his lusty soldiery, and he came to think of the Tiger as a great
noble general, sitting in his halls. And he forgot the humble little
village where Wang Lung lived and starved and struggled up
by labor and by guile, and he only remembered from his childhood the many courts of that great house in the town, which
his grandfather had made. He forgot even the small old earthen
house and all the millions like it, shaped out of earth and
thatched with straw, and housing poor folk and sometimes even
beasts with them, and he remembered clearly only the coastal
town and all its riches and its pleasure houses. So when Jim
asked, "Have you automobiles like we have?" or if he asked,
"Do you have houses like ours?" Yuan answered simply, "Yes,
we have all these things."

Nor did he lie. In a measure he spoke the truth, and in a full
measure he believed he spoke the whole truth because as days
passed his own distant country grew more perfect in his eyes.
He forgot everything not beautiful, miseries such as are to be
found anywhere, and it seemed to him that only in his country
were the men upon the land all honest and content, and all the
serving men loyal and all masters kind and all children filial and
all maids virtuous and full of modesty.

So much did Yuan come to believe thus in his own distant
country that one day by force of his own belief he was driven to
say publicly a thing in her defense. It happened that to this town
and to a certain temple in it, which was called a church, there

came a white man who had lived in Yuan's country and announced he would show pictures of that far place and tell of its people and their habits. Now Yuan, since he believed in no religion, had never been to this foreign temple, but on this night he went, thinking to hear the man and see what he might show.

In the crowd then Yuan sat. From the first sight of the traveller Yuan did not like him, for he perceived him to be a priest of a sort of whom he had heard but had not seen, and one of those against whom he had been taught in his early school of war, who went abroad with religion as a trade, and enticed humble folk into his sect for some secret purpose, which many guessed at but none knew, except that all know a man does not leave his own land for nothing and with no hope of private gain. Now he stood very tall and grim about the mouth, his eyes sunken in his weathered face, and he began to speak. He told of the poor in Yuan's land and of the famines and of how in places girl babes were killed at birth, and how the people lived in hovels, and he told filthy, gruesome tales. And Yuan heard them all. Then the man began to show his pictures, pictures of the things he said he had seen himself. Now Yuan saw beggars whining at him from the screen, and lepers with their faces eaten off, and starving children, their bellies swollen though empty, and there were narrow crowded streets and men carrying loads too great for beasts. There were such evils shown as Yuan had not seen in all his sheltered life. At the end the man said solemnly, "You see how our gospel is needed in this sad land. We need your prayers; we need your gifts." Then he sat down.

But Yuan could not bear it. All through the hour his anger had been rising, mixed with shame and dismay, so to see revealed before this staring, ignorant foreign crowd his country's faults. And more than faults, for he had not himself seen the things this man had told of, and it seemed to him that this prying priest had searched out every ill that he could find and dragged it forth before the cold eyes of this western world. It was only greater shame to Yuan that at the end the man begged for money for these whom he disclosed thus cruelly.

Yuan's heart broke with anger. He leaped to his feet, he clenched his hands upon the seat in front· of him, and he cried loudly, his eyes burning black, his cheeks red, his body trembling, "These are lies this man has told and shown! There are not such things in my country! I myself have never seen these sights—I have not seen those lepers—I have not seen starved children like those—nor houses like those! In my home there are a score of rooms—and there are many houses like mine. This man has shaped lies to tease your money from you. I—I speak for my country! We do not want this man nor do we want your money! We need nothing from you!"

So Yuan shouted, and then he set his lips to keep from weeping and sat down again, and the people sat in great silence and astonishment at what had happened.

As for the man, he listened, smiling thinly, and then he rose and said, and mildly enough, "I see this young man is a modern student. Well, young man, all I can say is that I have lived among the poor, like these I have shown, for more than half my life. When you go back to your own country come into the little city in the inland where I live and I will show you all these things. . . . Shall we close with prayer?"

But Yuan could not stay for such mockery of praying. He rose and went out and stumbled through the streets to his own room. Soon behind him came the footsteps of others who went homeward too, and here was the final stab which Yuan had that night. Two men passed him, not knowing who he was, and he heard one say, "Queer thing, that Chinese fellow getting up like that, wasn't it?—Wonder which of 'em was right?"

And the other said, "Both of them, I reckon. It's safest not to believe all you hear from anybody. But what does it matter what those foreign folks are? It isn't anything to us!" And the man yawned and the other man said carelessly, "That's right—looks like rain tomorrow, doesn't it?" And so they went their way.

Then Yuan, hearing this, was somehow more wounded than if the men had cared. It seemed to him they should have cared, even if the priest had been right, but since he told lies they should have cared to know the truth. He went angry to his bed and lay and tossed and wept a little for very anger's sake, and vowed he would do something yet to make these people know his country great.

After such a thing as this Yuan's new friend assuaged him. He took sound comfort in this simple country youth and poured out his beliefs in his own people to him, and told him of the sages who had shaped the noble minds of his ancestors and framed the systems whereby men lived to this day, so that in that far lovely country there was not such wantonness and willfulness as was to be found here. There men and women walked in decency and ordered goodness, and beauty grew from out their goodness. They did not need laws such as were written in these foreign lands, where even children must be protected by a law and women sheltered under law. In his country, Yuan said earnestly, and he believed it, there needed not to be such laws for children were harmed by none, for none there would harm a child, he said, forgetting for the moment the foundlings even his lady mother had told him of, and he said women were always safe and honored in their homes. When the white lad asked, "So it is not true they bind women's feet?" Yuan replied proudly, "It was an old, old custom, like the one of yours when women bound their waists, and now it is long past and no more to be seen anywhere."

So Yuan stood in defense of his own land, and this was now his cause. It made him think of Meng sometimes, and now he could value Meng at his true worth and to himself he thought, "Meng was right. Our country has been defamed and brought so low we ought all to come to her support now. I shall tell Meng he saw more truly, after all, than I did." And he wished he knew where Meng was that he might write and tell him this.

He could write to his father, and so he did. And now Yuan found he could write more kindly and more fully than he ever had. This new love for his country made him love his family more, too, and he wrote saying, "I long often to come home, for no country seems as good to me as my own. Our ways are best, our food the best. As soon as I return I will come gladly home again. I stay here only that I may learn what is to be learned and use it for our country."

And when he had set after this the usual words of courtesy from son to father, he sealed and stamped the letter and went out upon the street to drop it in a box put there for such purpose. It was an evening of a weekly holiday and all the lights were lit in the shops and young men were rollicking and roaring out songs that they knew, and girls laughed and shouted with them. Yuan, seeing all this savage show, drew down his lips in a cold smile, and he let his thoughts follow after his letter into the dignity and stillness where his father lived alone in his own courts. At least his father was surrounded by hundreds of his own men, and at least he, a war lord, lived honorably according to his code. Yuan seemed to see the Tiger again as he had often seen him, sitting stately in his great carved chair, the tiger skin behind him, before him the copper brazier of burning coals, and all his guard about him, a very king. Then Yuan, in the midst of all the clattering ribaldry, the loud voices and the rude unmelodious music streaming out of dancing places, took greater pride in his own kind than he ever had before. He withdrew himself and went again alone into his room and fell upon his books most resolutely, feeling himself above all such men as were about him and that he came of old and kingly origin.

This was the third step he took in hatred.

The fourth step came soon, and from a different, nearer cause, and it was a thing Yuan's new friend did. The friendship between these two grew less warm than it was, and Yuan's talk grew cool and distant, always of work and of the things they heard their teachers say, and this was because Yuan knew now that often when Jim came to the house where he lived he came not to see Yuan but to see that daughter of his landlady.

The thing had begun easily enough. Yuan one evening had brought his new friend to his room, since the day was wet, and they could not go together to walk as their growing habit was. When they entered the house there was the sound of music from a front room and the door stood ajar. It was the landlady's daughter who made the music, and be sure she knew the door was open. But as he passed Jim looked in and saw the girl, and she saw him and cast him one of her looks and he caught it and whispered to Yuan, "Why didn't you tell me you had such a peach here?"

Yuan saw his leering look and could not bear it, and he answered gravely, "I do not understand you." But though he did not understand the word he understood all else and he felt a great discomfort in him. Afterwards he thought of it more gently and told himself he would not remember it, nor let so small a thing as that maid come to mar his friendship, since in this country such things were lightly considered.

But the second time this happened, or that he knew it happened, Yuan was so cut he could have wept. He came late one night, having eaten his night meal away, in order that his work might go on among the books, and when he came in he heard Jim's voice in a room used in common by them all. Now Yuan, being very weary and his very eyes aching with the long reading of the western books, whose lines run to and fro across the page and thus weary very much eyes used to lines from top to bottom, was glad to hear his friend's voice and he longed for an hour's companionship. He pushed open the door, therefore, which was ajar, and cried out gladly and with unwonted freedom in his manner, "I am back, Jim—shall we go upstairs?"

There in that room he saw only these two, Jim, in his hand a box of sweets at whose wrappings he was fumbling, a silly smile upon his face, and opposite him in a deep chair, lying in loose grace, the maid. When she saw Yuan come in, she looked up at him and tossed back her curly, coppery hair and said teasingly, "He came to see *me* this time, Mr. Wang . . ." And then seeing the look between the two young men, how the dark blood came slowly into Yuan's cheeks and how his face, which had been all open and eager, grew closed and smooth and silent, and how on the other's face a bright red shone out and how hostile that one looked as though he did a thing he could do if he liked, she cried petulantly, waving her pretty red-tipped hand, "Of course if he *wants* to go—"

A silence hung between the two men, and the girl laughed and then Yuan said gently and quietly, "Why should he not do what he likes?"

He would not look again at Jim, but he went upstairs and carefully closed his door and sat down for a while upon his bed and wondered at the jealous pain and anger in his heart—and most of all his heart was sick because he could not forget the silly look upon Jim's plain good face and Yuan was revolted at that look.

Thereafter he turned yet more proud. He told himself these white men and women were the loosest, lustiest race he ever heard of, and their whole inner thoughts were turned to each other wantonly. And when he thought this there rushed into his mind a hundred of the pictures in the theatres where they loved to go, the pictures blazoned on the highways of things to sell and always of some woman half unclothed. He could not, he thought bitterly, come back at night and not see an evil sight in any dark corner—some man who held a woman against him, their arms locked, hands touching in an evil way. Of such sights the town was full. And Yuan sickened at it all, and his very stomach turned proud within him at such coarseness everywhere.

Thereafter, he was never so near to Jim. When he heard Jim's

voice in the house somewhere he went silently alone up the stairs
to his own room, and fell to his books and he was formal in his
speech if Jim came in after a while, and very often he did so
because, in some strange way Yuan could not understand, his
feeling for the maid was no hindrance to his old friendship for
Yuan, so that he was as hearty in his way and seemed not to see
Yuan's silence and aloofness. Sometimes, it is true, Yuan forgot
the maid and let himself go free again in good talk and even
jesting gently. But at least now he waited first for Jim to come to
him. The old eager going out to meet him was no longer possible.
Yuan said quietly to himself, "I am here if he wants me. I am
not changed to him. Let him seek me if he wants me." But he
was changed, for all he said he was not. He was alone again.

To assuage himself Yuan began now to notice everything he
did not like about this town and school, and every small thing he
did not like came to fall like a sword-cut upon his raw heart.
He heard the clatter of the foreign tongue among the crowds
upon the street and he thought how harsh the voices were and
the syllables, and not smooth and like the running waters of his
own tongue. He marked the careless looks of students and their
stammering speech before their teachers oftentimes, and he grew
more jealous of himself and more careful even than he had been,
and planned his own speech more perfectly, even though it was
foreign to him, and he did his own work more perfectly than
they did, and for his country's sake.

Without knowing it he came to despise this race because he
wanted to despise them, and yet he could not but envy them their
ease and wealth and place and these great buildings and the many
inventions they had made and all they had learned of the magic
of air and wind and water and lightning. Yet their very wisdom and his very admiration made him like these people less.
How had they stolen to such a place of power as this, and how
could they be so confident of their own power and not know even
how he hated them? One day he sat in the library poring over

a certain very wonderful book, which marked out clearly for him how generations of plants could be foretold before even the seed was put into the ground, because the laws of their growth were known so clearly and this thing was so astonishing to Yuan, so far above men's usual knowledge, that he could not but cry out secret admiration in his heart, and yet he thought most bitterly, "We have in our country been sleeping in our beds, the curtains drawn, thinking it still night and all the world asleep with us. But it has long been day, and these foreigners have been awake and working. . . . Shall we ever find what we have lost in all these years?"

Thus Yuan fell into great secret despairs in those six years, and these despairs put into him what the Tiger had begun, and Yuan determined that he would throw himself into his country's cause as he never had, and he came to forget after a while that he was himself. He walked and talked among these foreigners and saw himself no longer as one Wang Yuan, but he saw himself as his people, and one who stood for his whole race in a foreign alien land.

There was only Sheng who could make Yuan feel young and not full of this mission. Sheng would not once in all the six years leave that great city he had chosen to live in. He said, "Why should I leave this place? There is more here than I can learn in a lifetime. I would rather know this place well than many places a little. If I know this city then I know this people, for this city is the mouthpiece of the whole race."

So because Sheng would not come to Yuan and yet he would see Yuan, Yuan could not withstand his letters full of graceful, playful pleading, and so it came about that these two spent their summers in the city together, and Yuan slept in Sheng's small sitting room, and sat and listened to the varied talk that was there often, and sometimes he added to it, but more often he kept silence, because Sheng soon saw how narrow Yuan's life was and that he lived too much alone, and he did not spare Yuan what he thought.

With a new sharpness that Yuan did not know was in him Sheng told Yuan all he ought to know and see, and he said, "We in our country have worshipped books. You see where we are. But these people care less for books than any race on earth does. They care for the goods of life. They do not worship scholars—they laugh at them. Half their jokes are told of their teachers, and they pay them less than their servants are paid. Shall you then think to learn the secrets of this people from these old men alone? And is it well enough to learn of only a farmer's son? You are too narrow-hearted, Yuan. You set yourself on one thing, one person, one place, and miss all else. Less than any people are these people to be found in their books. They gather books from all the world here in their libraries, and use them as they use stores of grain or gold—books are only materials for some plan they have. You may read a thousand books, Yuan, and learn nothing of the secret of their prosperity."

Such things he said over and over to Yuan, and Yuan was very humble before Sheng's ease and wisdom and he asked at last, "Then what ought I to do, Sheng, to learn more?" And Sheng said, "See everything—go everywhere, know all the kinds of people that you can. Let that small plot of land rest for a while and let books be. I have sat here listening to what you have learned. Now come and let me show you what I have learned."

And Sheng looked so worldly, so sure in the way he sat and spoke and waved the ashes from his cigarette and smoothed down his shining black hair with his graceful ivory-colored hand that Yuan was abashed before him, and felt himself as raw a bumpkin as a man could be. It seemed to him in truth that Sheng knew far more than he did in everything. How much Sheng had changed from the slender dreamy pretty youth he had been! In the few years he had grown quick and vivid; he had bloom d forth into sureness of his beauty and faith in himself.

Some heat had forced him. In the electric air of this new country, his indolence was gone. He moved, he spoke, he laughed as these others did, yet with this vividness were still left the grace and ease and inwardness of his own race and kind. And Yuan, seeing all that Sheng now was, thought surely there was never any man like him for beauty and for brilliance. He asked in great humility, "Do you still write the verses and the tales you did?"

And Sheng answered gaily, "I do, and more than I did. I have a group of poems now that I may make into a book. And I have hope of a prize or two for some tales I wrote." This Sheng said not too proudly, but with the confidence of one who knows himself well. Yuan was silent. It seemed to him indeed that he had done very little. He was as cloddish as he had been when he came; he had no friends; all that he could point to for his life these many months was a pile of notebooks, and some seedling plants upon a strip of earth.

Once he asked Sheng, "What will you do when we go home again? Shall you always live there in the city?"

This Yuan asked to feel and see if Sheng were troubled as he was by his own people's lack. But Sheng answered gaily and very surely, "Oh, always! I cannot live elsewhere. The truth is, Yuan, and we may say it here, what we cannot say before strangers, except in such cities there is no other fit place for men like us to live in our country. Where else can one find amusements fit for intelligence to enjoy, and where else cleanliness enough to live in? The little I remember of our village is enough to make me loathe it—the people filthy and the children naked in summer and the dogs savage and everything all black with flies—you know what it is—I cannot, will not, live elsewhere than in the city. After all, these western peoples have something to teach us in the way of comfort and of pleasure. Meng hates them, but I don't forget that left alone for centuries we didn't think of running clean water, or of electricity or motion pictures or any of these things. For me, I mean to have all good that I can and I shall live my life where it is best and easiest, and make my poems."

"That is, to live it selfishly," said Yuan bluntly.

"Have it so," Sheng answered coolly. "But who is not selfish? We are all selfish. Meng is selfish in his very cause. That cause! Look at its leaders, Yuan, and dare to say they are not selfish—one was a robber once—one has shifted back and forth to this winning side and that—how does the third one live except upon the very money he collects for his cause?—No, to me it is more honorable to say straightly, I am selfish. I take this for myself. I take my comfort. So be it that I am selfish. But also I am not greedy. I love beauty. I need a delicacy about me in my house and circumstances. I will not live poorly. I only ask enough to surround myself with peace and beauty and a little pleasure."

"And your countrymen who have no peace or pleasure?" Yuan asked, his heart seething in him.

"Can I help it?" Sheng replied. "Has it not been for centuries that the poor are born and famines come and wars break out, and shall I be so silly as to think that in my one life I can change it all? I would only lose myself in struggle, and in losing myself, my noblest self, this me—why should I struggle against a people's fate? I might as well leap in the sea to make it dry up into productive land—"

Yuan could not answer such smoothness. That night he could only lie awhile after Sheng had gone to sleep and listen to the thunder of that vast changing city beating against the very walls against which he lay.

Thus listening he grew afraid. His mind's eye, seeing through this little narrow wall of security between him and the strange dark roaring world beyond, saw too much and he could not bear his smallness and he clung to the good sense of Sheng's words and to the warmth of the room lighted by the street light, and to the table and the chairs and the common things of life. There was this little spot of safety in the thousand miles of change and death and unknown life. Strange how Sheng's sure choice of safety and of ease could make Yuan feel his dreams so great they were foolish to him! So long as he was near Sheng, Yuan was not himself somehow, not brave or full of hate even, but a child seeking certainty.

But Yuan could not always be thus closely and alone with Sheng. Sheng knew many in this city, and he went dancing many a night with any maid he could, and Yuan was alone even though he went with Sheng. At first he sat on the edge of all the merriment, wondering and half envious of Sheng's beauty and his friendly manner, and his boldness with a woman. Sometimes he wondered if he might follow and then after a while he saw something which made him walk away and swear he would not speak to any woman.

And here was the reason. The women Sheng made friends with in this fashion were women not often of his own race. They were white women or they were mixed in blood, and partly dark and partly white. Now Yuan had never touched one of these women. He could not for some strange reason of the flesh. He had seen them often in the evenings when he had gone with Ai-lan, for in the coastal city people of every hue and shade mingled freely. But he had never taken one to him to dance with her. For one thing, they dressed in such a way as to him seemed shameless, for their backs were bare, and so bare that a man in dancing must place his hand on bare white flesh and this he could not do, because it made a sickness rise in his blood.

Yet now there was another reason why he would not. For as he watched Sheng and all the women who smiled and nodded when he came near them, it seemed to Yuan that only certain women smiled, and that the best, less shameless ones looked sidewise or away from Sheng when he came near and gave themselves only to the men of their own kind. The more Yuan looked, the more true this seemed, and it even seemed to him that Sheng knew this, too, and that he only took the ones who smiles were sure and easy. And Yuan grew deeply angry for his cousin's sake, and somehow for his own sake and for his country's sake, although he did not understand fully why the women so behaved, and he was too shy and fearful of hurting Sheng to mention it, and he muttered in his own heart, "I wish Sheng were proud and would not dance with them at all. If he is not held good enough for the best of them, I wish he would scorn them all."

And then Yuan was in an agony of hurt because Sheng was not proud enough and took his pleasure anyhow. Here was a strange thing, that all Meng's angers against foreigners had not moved Yuan to hatred. But now seeing these proud women who looked sidewise when Sheng came near, Yuan felt that he could hate them and then that he did, and that because of these few he could hate all their kind. Then Yuan often went away and would not stay to see Sheng scorned and he spent his nights alone, at books, or staring into sky or into city streets and into the questions and confusions of his heart.

Patiently through these summers Yuan followed Sheng hither and thither in his life in that city. Sheng's friends were many. He could not go into the restaurant where commonly he bought his food without some man or maid calling out most heartily, "Hello, Johnnie!" For this was what they called him. The first time Yuan heard it he was shocked at such freedom. He murmured to Sheng, "How do you bear this common name?" But Sheng only laughed and answered, "You should hear what they call each other! I am only glad they call me by so mild a name as this. Besides, they do it in friendship, Yuan. The ones they like best they speak of with the greatest freedom."

And indeed it could be seen that Sheng had many friends. Into his room at night they came, twos and threes of friends, and sometimes twice as many. Piled together on Sheng's bed or on the floor, smoking and talking, these young men strove each with the other to see who could think the wildest quickest thoughts

166

and who could first confound what another had just said. Yuan
never had heard such motley talk. Sometimes he thought them
rebels against the government and feared for Sheng, until by
some new wind the whole several hours' talk might veer away
from this and end in the cheerfulest acceptance of what was
and in great scorn of any newness, and then these young men,
reeking of their smoke and of the stuff they brought to drink,
would shout their partings, grinning and content and with the
mightiest relish for themselves and all the world. Sometimes they
talked of women boldly, and Yuan, silent on a theme he knew so
little of,—for what did he know except the touch of one maid's
hand?—sat listening, sick at what he heard. When they were
gone he said to Sheng most gravely, "Can all we hear be true,
and are there such evil, forward women as they say? Are all the
women of this nation so—no chaste maids, no virtuous wives,
no woman unassailable?" Then Sheng laughed teasingly and
answered, "They are very young, these men—only students like
you and me. And what do you know of women, Yuan?"

And Yuan answered humbly, "It is true, I do know nothing
of them—"

Yet thereafter Yuan looked more often at these women whom
he saw so freely on the streets. They, too, were part of these people. But he could make nothing of them. They walked quickly,
were gay in garb and their faces were painted as gaily. Yet when
their sweet bold eyes fell on Yuan's face, the look was empty.
They stared at him a second and passed on. To them he was not
a man—only a stranger passing by, not worth the effort that a
man was worth, their eyes said. And Yuan, not understanding
this fully, yet felt the coldness and the emptiness and was shy to
his soul. They moved so arrogantly, he thought, so coldly sure
of their own worth, that he feared them greatly. Even in passing
he took care not to touch one of them heedlessly in any way, lest
anger come forth from the casual moment. For there was a shape
to their reddened lips, a boldness in the way they held their

shining heads, a swing their bodies had, which made him shrink away. He felt no lure of woman in them. Yet they did add their magic of living color to this city. For after days and nights Yuan could see why Sheng said these people were not in their books. One could not, Yuan perceived, his face upturned to the distant golden peak of one great building, put such a thing as that in books.

At first Yuan had seen no beauty in their buildings, his eye being trained to quiet latitudes of low tiled roofs and gentle slopes of houses. But now he saw beauty,—foreign beauty, it was true, yet beauty. And for the first time since he had come to this land, he felt a need to write a verse. One night in his bed, while Sheng slept, he struggled to shape his thought. Rhymes would not do, not usual, quiet rhymes, the rhymes he once had made of fields and clouds. He needed sharp words, rough-edged and cleanly pointed. The words of his own tongue he could not use, they were so round and smooth with long polished use. No, he must search out other words in this newer, foreign tongue. And yet they were like new tools to him, too heavy for his own wielding, and he was not accustomed to their form and sound. And so at last he gave it up. He could not shape the verse and there it lay unshaped in his mind to make him a little restless for a day or two, and longer, because at last he came to feel that if he could but shape it out of him, he could have caught between his hands the meaning of these people. But he could not. They kept their souls away from him and he moved only here and there among their swift bodies.

Now Sheng and Yuan were two very different souls. Sheng's soul was like the rhymes which flowed so easily out from it. He showed these rhymes to Yuan one day, beautifully written on thick paper edged with gold, and said with pretended careless-ness, "They are nothing, of course—not my best work. That I shall do some later day. These are only fragments of this country put down as they came to me. But my teachers give me praise for them."

Yuan read them carefully, one by one, in silence and reverence. To him they seemed beautiful, each word well chosen, fitted to its place as neatly as a stone set in a ring of gold embossed with gold. There were some of these verses, Sheng said lightly, which had even been set to music by a certain woman whom he knew. One day after he had spoken a time or two of this woman he took Yuan to her home to hear the music she had made of Sheng's verses, and here Yuan saw another sort of woman still, and still another life of Sheng's.

She was a singer in some hall, not quite a common singer, but still not so great by far as she conceived herself to be. She lived alone in a house where many others lived, each in his own little home in the great house. The room which she had made for herself to live in was dark and still. Although outside the sun shone brightly no sun came here. Candles burned in tall bronze stands. A scent of incense hung heavily upon the thick air. There was no seat hard or uncushioned, and at one end a great divan stretched. Here on this bed the woman lay, a long, fair woman, whose age was inscrutable to Yuan. She cried out when she saw Sheng, waving a holder that she held to smoke by, and she said, "Sheng, darling, I haven't seen you in ages!"

When Sheng sat easily beside her, as though he had sat there many times before, she cried again, and her voice was deep and strange and not like a woman's voice, "That lovely thing of yours—'Temple Bells'—I've finished it! I was just going to call you up—"

When Sheng said, "This is my cousin Yuan," she scarcely looked at Yuan. She was rising as Sheng spoke, her long legs careless as a child's, and with the holder in her mouth she flung a twisted word or two, "Oh, hello, Yuan!" and seeming not to see him, went to the instrument she had and laying down the thing from out her mouth, began to slide her fingers slowly from

169

one handful of notes to another—deep, slow notes such as Yuan did not know. Soon she began to sing, her voice deep as the music her hands made, shaking a little, very passionately.

The thing she sang was short, a little verse of Sheng's he had once written in his own country, but the music changed it, somehow. For Sheng had shaped the words wistfully and slightly, as slightly as bamboos shadowed in the moonlight on a temple wall. But this foreign woman singing these pretty little words made them passionate, the shadows black and hard, the moonlight hot. And Yuan was troubled, feeling the frame of music was too heavy for the picture the words made. But so the woman was. Every movement she made was full of troubled meaning—every word and every look not simple.

Suddenly Yuan did not like her. He did not like the room she lived in. He did not like her eyes too dark for the fairness of her hair. He did not like her looks at Sheng, nor how she called him by the name of "darling" many times, nor how when she had made the music she walked about and touched Sheng often as she passed him, nor how she brought the music to him written down and leaned over him and once even laid her cheek against his hair and murmured in her casual negligent fashion, "Your hair's not painted on, is it, darling? It shines so smoothly always—"

And Yuan sitting in completest silence felt some gorge in him rise against this woman, some healthy gorge his old grandfather had given him, and his father, too, a simple knowledge that what this woman did and said and how she looked were not seemly. He looked to Sheng to repulse her, even gently to repulse her. But Sheng did not. He did not touch her, it is true, or answer her words with like words, or in any way put out his hand to meet her hand. But he accepted what she did and said. When her hand lay upon his for an instant, he let it lie, and did not draw away from her as Yuan wished he would. When she sent her gaze into his eyes, he looked back, half laughing but accepting

170

all her boldness and her flattery until Yuan could scarcely stomach what he saw. He sat as large and stolid as an image, seeming to see nothing and hear nothing, until Sheng rose. Even then the woman clung to his arm with her two hands, coaxing Sheng to come to some dinner that she gave, saying, "Darling, I want to show you off, you know—your verses are something new—you're something new yourself—I *love* the Orient—the music's rather nice, too, isn't it? I want the crowd to hear it—not *too* many, you know—only a few poets and that Russian dancer—darling, here's an idea—she could do a dance to the music—a sort of Oriental thing—your verses would be divine to dance to—let's try it—" So she continued coaxing until Sheng took her two hands in his own and put them down and promised what she wished, seeming reluctant, yet as Yuan could see, only seeming.

When they were out away from her at last Yuan breathed in a time or two and out again and looked about him gladly at the honest sunshine. They two were silent for a while, Yuan fearing to speak lest he offend Sheng in what he thought, and Sheng absorbed in some thinking of his own, a little smile upon his face. At last Yuan said, half trying Sheng, "I never heard such words upon a woman's tongue before. I scarcely know such words. Does she then love you so well?"

But Sheng laughed at this and answered, "Those words mean nothing. She uses them to any man—it is a way such women have. The music is not bad, though. She gets my mood." And Yuan, looking now at Sheng, saw on his face a look Sheng did not know was there. It was a look which plainly said that Sheng somehow liked those sweet and idle words the woman had said, and he liked her praise of him and liked the flattery of his verses which her music made. Yuan said no more then. But to himself he said that Sheng's way was not his, nor Sheng's life his, and his own way for him was best, though what his way was, he scarcely knew, except it was not this way.

Therefore, though Yuan stayed on awhile in that city and

its sights to please his cousin, and saw its subterranean trains and all the streets of show, he knew that in spite of what Sheng said, not all of life was here. His own life was not here. He was lonely. There was nothing here that he knew or understood, or so he thought.

Then one day when it was very hot, and Sheng was indolent with heat and lay asleep, Yuan wandered forth alone, and riding on a public vehicle or two, he came into a region he had not dreamed was here in such a city. For he had been surfeited with its richness. To him the buildings were palaces, and every man took for matter of course that he had all he would of food and drink and garments and his needs were not for these things, for they were his due and only to be expected. Beyond these were the needs of pleasure and of better garments and food made not to live by but to take zest in. Thus were all the citizens of this city or so it seemed to Yuan.

But upon this day he found himself in another city, a city of the poor. He stumbled on it, unknowing, and suddenly it was everywhere about him. These were the poor. He knew them. Though their faces were pale and white, though some were black-skinned as the savages are, he knew them. By their eyes, by the filth upon their bodies, by their dirty scaly hands, by the loud screams of women and the cries of too many children, he knew them. There in his memory were the other poor he knew, very far away in another city, but how like these! He said to himself, recognizing them, "Then this great city, too, is built upon a city of the poor!" Ai-lan and her friends came out at midnight into such men and women as these were.

Yuan thought to himself, and with a sort of triumph, "These people, too, hide their poor! In this rich city, crowded secretly into these few streets, are these poor, as filthy as any to be seen in any country!"

Here then Yuan truly found something not in books. He walked among these people in a daze, staring into narrow shadowed rooms, choosing his footsteps among the garbage of the streets, where starved children ran half naked in the heat. Lifting up his head to look at misery on misery he thought, "It does not matter that they live in lofty houses—they live in hovels still —the same hovels—"

He went back at last, when darkness fell, and entered into the cool lit darkness of the other streets. When he came into Sheng's room, Sheng was gay again, awake, and ready with a friend or two to sally forth into the street of theatres to make merry there.

When he saw Yuan he cried out, "Where have you been, cousin? I nearly feared you lost."

And Yuan answered slowly, "I have seen some of the life you told me was not in the books. . . . Then all the wealth and strength of these people still cannot keep away the poor." And he told where he had been and a little of what he saw. And one of Sheng's friends said, careful as a judge, "Some day, of course, we will solve the problem of poverty." And the other said, "Of course if these people were capable of more they would have more. They are defective somehow. There is always room at the top."

Then Yuan spoke out quickly, "The truth is you hide your poor—you are ashamed of them as a man is ashamed of some secret vile disease—"

But Sheng said gaily, "We'll be late if we let this cousin start us on this talk! The play begins in half an hour!"

In those six years Yuan came near to three others who befriended him among all the strangers among whom he lived. There was a certain old teacher he had, a white-haired man, whose face Yuan early liked to see because it was very kindly marked by gentle thoughts and perfect ways of life. To Yuan this old man showed himself, when time went on, as more than a teacher only. He spent willingly much time in special talk with Yuan, and he read the notes Yuan wrote in planning for a book

173

he hoped to write, and with very mild correction he pointed out a place or two where Yuan was wrong. Whenever Yuan spoke he listened, his blue eyes so smiling and so filled with understanding that Yuan came at length to trust him greatly and at further length to tell him inward things.

He told him, among much else, how he had seen the poor in the city, and how he wondered that in the midst of such vast riches the poor could live so desperately. And this led him on to talk of the foreign priest and how he had besmirched Yuan's people by his vile pictures. The old man listened to it all in his mild silent way and then he said, "I think not everyone can see the whole picture. It has long been said we each see what we look for. You and I, we look at land and think of seed and harvests. A builder looks at the same land and thinks of houses, and a painter of its colors. The priest sees men only as those who need to be saved, and so naturally he sees most clearly those who need to be saved."

And after Yuan had thought of this awhile, unwillingly he knew it to be true, and in all fairness he could not quite hate the foreign priest as wholly as he did, or even as he wished he could, for still he thought him wrong, and still he said, "At least, he saw a very narrow part of my country." To which the old man answered always mildly, "That might be, and must be if he were a narrow man."

Through talk like this in field and schoolroom after others had gone home, Yuan learned to love this old white man. And he loved Yuan and looked on him with increasing tenderness.

One day he said to Yuan, half hesitating, "I wish you would come with me tonight, my son. We are very simple folk—only my wife and my daughter Mary and I—we three—but if you will come and take your supper with us, we'll be glad. I've told them so much about you, they want to know you, too."

This was the first time anyone had spoken thus to Yuan, in these years, and he was very moved by it. It seemed a warm and special thing to him that a teacher would take a pupil to his private home. He said shyly therefore in the courteous way of his own tongue, "I am not worthy."

To which the old man opened his eyes wide and smiled and said, "Wait until you see how plain we are! My wife said when I first told her it would be a pleasure to me if you came, 'I'm afraid he's used to much better than we have.'"

Then Yuan protested again in courtesy and yielded. Thus he found himself walking down the shaded street into a small square court-like yard, and thence to an ancient wooden house, standing back in trees, and set about with porches. There at the door a lady met him who made him think of the lady whom he called his mother. For in these two women, ten thousand miles apart, who spoke two different tongues, whose blood and bones and skin were not alike, there was yet a common look. The white smoothed hair, their full settled look of motherhood, their simple ways and honest eyes, their quiet voices, the wisdom and the patience graven on their lips and brows, these made them like. Yet it was true there was a difference in the two which Yuan could perceive after they were seated in the large main room, for about this lady there was an air of contentment and simple satisfaction of the soul which his lady mother had not. It was as if this one had her heart's desire in her lifetime, but the other had not. By two roads the two had come to a good tranquil age, but the one had come by a happy road and with companionship, while the other had come by a darker way and she walked alone.

But when this lady's daughter came in, she was not like Ai-lan. No, this Mary was a different sort of maid. She was, perhaps, a little more in years than Ai-lan was, much taller and not so pretty, very quiet, seemingly, and governed in her voice and look. Yet when one listened to the words she spoke, there was sense in all she said and her dark, grey-black eyes, somber in hue when she was grave, could flash out merrily to match a witty twist her words might take. She was demure before her parents, yet not afraid, and they deferred to her as to an equal, and Yuan perceived this.

Indeed Yuan saw very soon she was no common maid. For when the old man talked of what Yuan wrote, this Mary knew of it, too, and put a question so quickly and so aptly before Yuan that he was taken aback and asked her, wondering, "How is it that you know the history of my people so well that you can ask me of one so far away in history as Ch'ao Tso?"

To this the maid answered modestly but with a shine of smiling in her eyes. "Oh, I have always had a kinship with your land, I think. I have read books about it. Shall I tell you the very little I know about him? Then you will know I am a sham! I really know nothing. But he wrote about agriculture, didn't he?—in an essay. I remember I memorized a bit I read once in a translation. It was something like this, 'Crime begins in poverty; poverty in insufficiency of food; insufficiency in neglect of tilling of the soil. Without such tilling, man has no tie to bind him to the soil. Without such a tie he readily leaves his birthplace and his home. Then he is like the birds of the air or the beasts of the field. Neither battlemented cities nor deep moats, nor harsh laws, nor cruel punishments, can subdue this roving spirit that is strong within him.'"

These words, which Yuan knew very well, this maid now chanted in a round clear voice, for her voice was very full of meaning. It could be seen she loved the words, because a gravity came upon her face and into her eyes a mystery, as of one who again perceives beauty known before. Her parents listened reverently and in pride while she spoke and the old father turned to Yuan as one who cries out in his heart, only keeping back the words in decent courtesy, "Do you see what my child is for wisdom and intelligence, and have you seen one like her?"

Yuan could not but speak out his pleasure, and hereafter when she spoke he listened, too, and felt a kinship with her, because whatever she said, even if she said a small thing, was said fitly and well, and as he would have liked to have said it in her place.

Yet though he felt so used to this house he had entered for the first time this night, so used to these people that he forgot they were not of his kind, yet every now and again there came a strangeness of some sort, a foreign thing he did not understand. When they entered into a smaller room and sat about an oval table spread for the meal, Yuan took up his spoon to eat. But he saw the others hesitate, and then the old man bowed his head and so did the others except Yuan, who did not understand the thing, and while he looked from one to the other, to see what would happen, the old man spoke aloud as though to some god not to be seen, a few words only, but said with feeling, as though he thanked one for a gift received. After this, without further rite, they ate, and Yuan asked nothing at that time, but he gave and received in talk.

But afterwards, being very curious about this rite and never having seen it heretofore, he asked his teacher of it as they sat alone in the twilight on the wide veranda, and he asked so he might know what the courteous thing was he should do at such a time. Then the old man fell silent for a while, smoking his pipe and looking peacefully away into the shadowed street. At last he held his pipe in the cup of his hand and said, "Yuan, I have many times wondered how to speak to you of our religion. What you saw is a religious rite we have, a simple giving thanks to God for food daily set before us. In itself it is not important and yet it is a symbol of the greatest thing our lives hold—our belief in God. Do you remember you spoke of our prosperity and power? I believe it is the fruit of our religion. I do not know what your religion is, Yuan, but I know I should not be true to my own self or to you if I should let you live here and daily come and go in my classes and come often, I hope, to my home, and not tell you of my own faith."

While the old man spoke thus, the two women came out and

seated themselves there, the mother on a chair in which she rocked gently to and fro as though a wind were blowing it. There she sat listening to her husband, a mild agreeing smile upon her face, and when he paused a moment, for he went on to talk of gods and mysteries of gods made human flesh, she cried out with a sort of gentle passion, "Oh, Mr. Wang, ever since Dr. Wilson told me how brilliant you are in his classes, how able in all you write, I have counted you for Christ. What a great thing it would be for your country if you could be somehow won for Christ and go back to bear good witness!"

This gave Yuan great astonishment, for he did not know what all these words meant. But being courteous he smiled merely and bowed a little and was even about to speak when Mary's voice broke out sharp and clear as metal, and with a tone Yuan had not heard in it before. She had not sat herself in a chair but on the uppermost step and she had sat there silent while her father had talked, holding her chin in her two hands and listening seemingly. Now out of the dim light her voice came restless, strange, impatient, cutting like a knife across the talk, "Shall we go inside, father? The chairs will be more comfortable—and I like the light—"

To which the old man answered in a vague surprise, "Why yes, Mary, if you wish. But I thought you always liked to sit here of an evening. Every night we sit here awhile—"

But the young woman answered still more restlessly and with a sort of willfulness, "Tonight I want the light, father."

"Very well, my dear," the old man said, and rose slowly and so they went within.

There in the lighted room he spoke no more of mysteries. Instead his daughter led the talk, plying Yuan with a hundred questions of his own country, so quick and deep sometimes that he must in all honesty confess himself confounded by his own ignorance. And while she talked, he could not but feel a pleasure in her. For though he knew she was not beautiful, her face

178

was keen and quickened, and the skin was delicate and very white, her lips narrow and a little red, and her hair was smooth and very nearly like his own in blackness, but much finer than his was. Her eyes he saw were beautiful, now near black with earnestness, then changing to a lovely shining grey when she smiled, and she smiled often though she did not laugh aloud. Her hands spoke, too, being very restless, supple, slender hands, not small, and perhaps too thin and not smooth enough for beauty but nevertheless with a sort of power in their look and movement.

But Yuan took no pleasure in these things for themselves. For he saw she was one whose body seemed a thing not of itself but only a covering for her mind and soul. And this was new to Yuan, who had known no such woman. When he thought he saw a sudden beauty in her as suddenly it was gone and he forgot it in the flash of light her mind sent out or in a witty word her tongue spoke. The body was informed here by the mind, and the mind did not spend itself in thoughts upon the body. So Yuan saw her scarcely as a woman, but as a being, changeful, shining, eager, sometimes a little cold, even, and often suddenly silent. Yet not silent out of emptiness, only silent while her mind took hold of something that he said and pulled it delicately apart to question what it was. In such silence she often did forget herself and forgot that her eyes were still on Yuan's eyes, though he had finished speaking, so that in such silence more than once he found himself looking deep and deeper into the soft changing darkening blackness of her eyes.

Not once did she speak of mysteries nor did the elder two again either, until at last when Yuan rose to take his leave the old man clinging to his hand a little said, "If you wish, son, come to church with us next Sunday and see how you like it."

And Yuan, taking this as further kindness, said he would, and this he said more willingly because he felt it would be a very pleasant thing to see these three again, who made him like a son in the house, who was not even of their race or kind.

Now after Yuan had gone back to his room, when he lay in his bed waiting for sleep, he thought about these three and most of all he thought about the daughter of the old two. Here was a woman such as he had not seen. She was of a material different from any he had known, a stuff more shining than Ai-lan, and this in spite of all of Ai-lan's mirth and pretty kitten's eyes and little laughters. This white woman, though grave often, had some strong inner light, at times too hard, if one compared her to the vague soft kindness of her mother, but always clear. She made no misdirected movement, even, of her body. There were in her none of the constant useless movements of the body only, such as the landlady's daughter made continually to show her thigh or wrist or foot more clearly forth, blind movements of the flesh. Nor were her words, nor was her voice like that one's, who had set Sheng's pretty words to heavy, passionate music. For this Mary's words were not surcharged with oversubtle meaning. No, she spoke them out swiftly and with sharp clearness and each word had its own weight and meaning and no more, good tools of her mind, but not messengers of vague suggestion.

When Yuan thought of her he remembered most her spirit, clothed in color and in substance of her flesh, but not hidden by it. And he fell to thinking of what she said and how she said sometimes things he had not thought upon. Once she said, when they spoke of love of country, "Idealism and enthusiasm are not the same thing. Enthusiasm may be only physical—the youth and strength of body making the spirit gay. But idealism may live on, though the body be aged or broken, for it is the essential quality of the soul which has it." And then her face had changed in its quick, lighting way and looking at her father very tenderly, she said, "My father has real idealism, I think."

And the old man answered quietly, "I call it faith, my child."

To which Yuan now remembered she had answered nothing. And so thinking of these three he fell asleep in more content of soul than he had ever had in this foreign country, for to him they seemed actual and to be comprehended.

When the day came, therefore, for the religious rites of which the old teacher had spoken Yuan dressed himself with care in his better garments and again he went to the house. At first he felt some timidity, because the door opened and there Mary stood. It was plain she was surprised to see him, for her eyes darkened and she did not smile. She was moreover clothed in a long blue coat and a small hat of the same hue, and she seemed taller than Yuan remembered her and somehow touched with an austerity. Therefore he stammered forth, "Your father invited me to go with him to his religious place today."

She answered gravely, searching out his eyes with some troubled look within her own, "I know he did. Will you come in? We are almost ready."

So Yuan went in again to the room where he had remembered such good friendship. But this morning it did not seem so friendly to him. There was no fire burning on the hearth as there had been that night, and the hard cold sunshine of the autumn morning fell through the windows and showed the wornness of the rugs upon the floor and of the stuffs upon the chairs, so that whereas by night and firelight and lamplight what had looked dark and homely and used, by this stern sunshine seemed too worn and aged and needing newness.

Yet the old man and his lady were very kind when they came in, clothed decently for their devotions, as kind as they had been. The old man said, "I am so glad you came. I did not speak again, because I do not want to influence you unduly."

But the lady said in her soft, overflowing way, "But I have *prayed!* I prayed you would be led to come. I pray about you every night, Mr. Wang. If God will grant my prayer how proud it will make me, if through us—"

Then sharp as a ray of the piercing sunlight across the old room the daughter's voice fell, a pleasant voice, not unkind, but very clear and perfect in its tone, a little colder yet than Yuan had heard it, "Shall we go now? We have just time to get there."

She led them out and sat herself by the guiding wheel in the car which was to take them to the place they went. The old two sat behind, but Yuan she placed beside her. Yet she did not say any word while she turned the wheel this way and that. And Yuan, being courteous, did not speak, either, nor did he even look at her, except as he might turn his head to see a strange sight passed. Yet, without looking straightly at her, he saw her face sidewise against and in front of that which he looked. There was no smile or light in that face now. It was grave even to a sort of sadness, the straight nose not small, the sharply cut, delicately folded lips, the clearly rounded chin lifted out of a dark fur upon her collar, her grey eyes set direct and far upon the road ahead. As she was now, turning the wheel quickly and well, sitting there straight and silent, Yuan was even a little afraid of her. She seemed not that one with whom he had once spoken freely and easily.

Thus they came to a great house into which many men and women and even children were passing. With these they entered and seated themselves, Yuan between the old man and the young woman. Yuan could not but look about him curiously for this was only the second time he had been in such a temple. Temples in his own land he had seen often, but they were for the common and the unlearned, and for women, and he had never worshipped any god in his life. A few times he had entered for curiosity and stared at the vast images, and had listened to the deep warning solitary note the great bell gave forth when it was struck, and he had seen with contempt the grey-robed priests, for his tutor taught him early that such priests were evil and ignorant men who preyed upon the people. So Yuan had never worshipped any god.

Now in this foreign temple he sat and watched. It was a cheerful place, and through long narrow windows the early autumn sunshine streamed in great bars of light, falling upon flowers at an altar, upon the gay garments of women, upon many faces of varied meaning, although not of many young. Soon music flowed out into the air from some unknown source, at first very soft music, then gradually growing in sound and volume until all the air was throbbing with that music. Yuan, turning his head to see what its source was, saw beside him the figure of the old man, his head bowed before him, his eyes closed, upon his face a smile, sweet, ecstatic. And Yuan, looking about, observed others also in this bound speechless silence, and in courtesy he wondered what he should do. But when he looked at Mary, he saw her sitting as she had been at the wheel, straight and proud, her chin lifted, and her eyes opened and fixed in the distance. When he saw her sitting thus, Yuan also therefore did not bow his head in any unknown worship.

Now, remembering what the old man had said, that in the power of their religion these people had found their strength, Yuan watched to know what this power was. But he could not easily discover it. For when the grave music fell soft once more and at last withdrew itself into the place where it hid, a robed priest came out and read certain words to which all seemed to listen decorously, although Yuan, observing, could see that some paid heed to their garments or to others' faces or to some such thing. But the old man and his lady listened carefully, although Mary, her face still set as to a far distance, did not change her look with anything she heard so that Yuan could not know if indeed she listened. Again and again there was music, and there was chanting of words Yuan could not understand, and the robed priest exhorted those in the temple out of the great book from which he had read.

To this Yuan listened, and it seemed a good harmless exhortation by a pleasant, holy man who urged his countrymen to be more kindly to the poor and to deny themselves and to obey their god, and such talk he made as priests do anywhere.

When he had finished, he bade them bow while he cried out a prayer to this god. Again Yuan looked to see what he should do, and again he saw the old pair bow themselves in their devotion. And again the woman by him held her proud head high, and therefore he also did not bow. He held his eyes open and looked to see if any image would be brought forth by the priest, since the people were bowed ready to worship. But the priest brought forth no image and no god was seen anywhere, and after a time when he had finished his speaking, the people waited no more for the god to come, but stirred and rose and went to their homes, and Yuan went back also to his own place, not understanding anything of what he had seen or heard, and out of all of it remembering most the clear line of that proud woman's head, which had not bowed itself.

Yet out of this day grew the next new thing in Yuan's life. For one day when he returned to his room from the field where he was now planting seeds of winter wheat, to see which did best in various rows where he placed them, he found a letter upon his table. Letters were very rare in Yuan's solitary life in this foreign country. Once in three months he knew his father's letter would lie on that table, each time its letters brushed to say the same words nearly, that the Tiger did well, but rested until next spring when he would go out to war again, that Yuan must study hard at what he wished most to know, and that he must come home as soon as his years of study were complete, since he was only son. Or else a letter might lie there from the lady, Ai-lan's mother, a quiet good letter, telling small things that she did, how Ai-lan she thought was to be wed, now three times promised, by her own will, but each time willfully refusing to be wed to the one promised, so that Yuan smiled a little when he read of Ai-lan's willfulness, and when the mother had spoken of it, she often added as though for her own comfort, "But Mei-ling is my stay. I have taken her into the home with us, and she learns so

184

well and does everything so rightly, and is so filled with every proper sense of fitness, that almost she might be the child I should have had, and sometimes more my daughter than my Ai-lan is."

Such letters Yuan could look for, and once or twice Ai-lan had written, letters mixed in two languages and full of willfulness and teasing and pretty threats if Yuan did not bring her back some western baubles, and vows that she expected perhaps a western sister-in-law. Or Sheng might write, but very seldom and never surely, and Yuan knew, half sadly, that his life was filled with all the many things a young man has who is beautiful in body and skilled in pretty speech, whose foreignness added grace to him in the eyes of those city dwellers who sought restlessly and everywhere for every new thing they could find.

But this letter was none of these. It lay white and square upon the table and his name was there marked clearly in black ink. So Yuan opened it, and it was from Mary Wilson. There her name was, plain and large at the bottom, yet with an energy and keenness in its shape, and very far from the rude letters that he landlady shaped upon her monthly bills. The letter asked Yuan to come for a special purpose on any day he could, since she who wrote it had been troubled since the day they went to church together, and had something unsaid which she wanted said, so she could be free of it toward Yuan.

Then Yuan, wondering very much, dressed himself in his dark better clothes and washed himself free of the stain of earth and that night when he had eaten he went out. And as he went his landlady cried out after him that she had put a letter from a lady on his table that day, and now she reckoned that he went to see her. And all the company laughed aloud, and the young girl laughed loudest of them all. But Yuan said nothing. He was only angry that this rude laughter should come even as near as this to Mary Wilson, who was too high for such as these to touch her name. And Yuan felt his heart grow hot against them and he swore to himself that none should ever hear her name from him, and he wished he had not that laughter and these looks even in his mind when he went to her.

But there the memory was, and it put a constraint upon him when he stood again before that door, so that when the door opened and she stood there, he was cool and shy and did not touch her hand when she put it warmly forth, but feigned he did not see it, he was so fastidious against the coarseness of those others. And she felt his coolness. A light went from her face, and she put away the little smile she had to greet him, and asked him gravely to come in and her voice was quiet and cool.

But when he went in the room was as it had been that first evening, warm and intimate and lit with the flames that burned upon the hearth. The old deep chairs invited him and the very stillness and the emptiness received him.

Nevertheless Yuan waited to see where she would seat herself, so that he might not be more near her than he ought to be, and she, not looking at him, dropped with a careless grace upon a low stool before the fire, and motioned to a great chair near. But Yuan, as he sat in it, contrived to push it back somewhat, so that while he was near to her, near enough so that he could see her face clearly, yet, if he put forth a hand, or if she did, their hands could not touch each other. So he wished to have it, and know more surely that the laughter of those common folk was coarse laughter only.

Thus these two sat alone. Of the old pair there was nothing seen or heard. But without telling of them, the woman began to speak directly and with abruptness, as if what she said was hard to say, and yet necessary to be spoken. "Mr. Wang, you will think it strange of me that I asked you to come here tonight. We are really strangers, almost. And yet I have read so much about your country—you know I work in the library—and I know a little of your people and admire them a great deal. I asked you here, not only for your own sake, but for your sake

186

as a Chinese. And I speak to you as a modern American to a modern Chinese."

Here she paused, and gazed awhile into the fire, and at last took up a little twig caught among a heap of logs upon the hearth, and with this she stirred half idly the red coals which lay beneath the burning logs. And Yuan waited, wondering what was to be said, and not wholly easy with her, since he was not used to being alone with a woman, until she went on.

"The truth is I have been much embarrassed by my parents' efforts to interest you in their religion. Of them I say nothing, except they are the best people I have ever known. You know my father—you see—anyone can see—what he is. People talk of saints. He is one. I have never seen him angry or unkind in all my life. No girl, no woman, ever had better parents. The only trouble is that my father, if he did not give me his goodness, did give me his brain. In my time I have used that brain, and it has turned against the religion, the energy that feeds my father's life, really, so that I myself have no belief in it. I cannot understand how men like my father, with strong, keen intellect, do not use it upon their religion. His religion satisfies his emotional needs. His intellectual life is outside religion, and—there is no passage between the two. . . . My mother, of course, is not an intellectual. She is simpler—easier to understand. If father were like her, I should be merely amused when they try to make a Christian out of you—I should know they never could."

Now the woman turned her honest eyes straight upon Yuan, and let her hands grow still, the twig hanging in her fingers, and looking at him she grew still more earnest. "But—I am afraid —father may influence you. I know you admire him. You are his pupil. You study the books he has written, he has been attracted to you as he seldom has been to any pupil. I think he has a sort of vision of you going back to your country as a great Christian leader. Has he told you he once wanted to be a missionary? He belongs to the generation when every good earnest boy or girl was faced with the—the missionary call, as it was named. But he was engaged to my mother, and she wasn't strong enough to go. I think both of them have felt ever since a sense of—of some frustration. . . . Strange, how generations differ! We feel the same thing about you, they and I"—there were her deep lovely eyes, looking straight into his, unashamed, with no coquetry—"and yet how we differ! They feel because you are what you are, how glorious to win you to their cause! To me, how presumptuous to think you could be made more than you are—by a religion! You are of your own race and your own time. How can anyone dare to impose upon you what is foreign to you?"

These words she said with a sort of ardor streaming from her, and Yuan was stirred, but not grossly, towards her. For she seemed to see him not only as himself, one man, but as one of his whole race. It was as though through him she spoke to millions. Between them was a wall of delicacy, of mind, of a withdrawal native to them both. And he said gratefully, "I understand very well what you mean. It doesn't, I promise you, weaken any admiration I feel for your father to know he believes a thing my mind cannot accept."

Her eyes were turned upon the flames again. The fire had sunk into coals and ashes, and the glow was steadier now upon her face and hair, upon her hands, upon the dark red of her dress. She said thoughtfully, "Who could not admire him? It was a hard thing for me, I can tell you, to put aside my childish faith in what he had taught me. But I was honest with him—I could be—and we talked again and again. I couldn't talk to mother at all—she always began to weep, and that made me impatient. But father met me at every point—and we could talk—he always respected my disbelief, and I always respected—more and more—his faith. We would reason very much alike up to a certain point—when the intellect must stop and one must begin to believe without understanding. There we parted. He could take that at a leap—frankly believing, in faith and hope—I couldn't. My generation can't."

Suddenly and with energy she rose and taking a log flung it upon the bed of coals. A mass of sparks flew up the wide black chimney, and again a blaze burst forth, and again Yuan saw her shining in the fresh light. She turned to him, standing above him, leaning against the mantel, saying seriously, yet with a little half smile at the corners of her mouth, "I think that's what I wanted to say—that sums it up. Don't forget that I do not believe. When my parents try to influence you, remember their generation—it is not mine—not yours and mine."

Yuan rose, too, very grateful, and as he stood beside her, thinking what to say, words came up unexpectedly out of him, which were not what he would have planned to say.

"I wish," he said slowly, looking at her, "that I could speak to you in my own language. For I find your speech never wholly natural to me. You have made me forget we are not one race. Somehow, for the first time since I entered your country I have felt a mind speaking to my mind without a barrier."

This he said honestly and simply, and she looked back at him as straight as a child, their eyes level to each other's, and she answered quietly, but very warmly, "I believe we shall be friends— Yuan?"

And Yuan answered, half timidly and as though he put his foot out to step upon an unknown shore, not knowing where he stepped or what was there, but still he must step forth, "If this is your wish—" and then still looking at her he added, his voice very low with shyness—"Mary."

She smiled then, a quick, brilliant, playful smile, accepting what he said and then stopping him as clearly as though she spoke the words "We have said enough for this day." They spoke then for a while of small things in books or elsewhere until there were steps heard upon the porch and she said at once, "Here they come—my precious two. They went to prayer meeting—they go every Wednesday night."

And she walked swiftly to the door and opened it and welcomed the old two, who came in, their faces fresh and reddened by the chilly autumn air. Soon they were all before the fire, and more than ever they made Yuan one of them, and bade him sit down again, while Mary brought fruit and the hot milk they loved to drink before they slept. And Yuan, though his soul loathed the milk, yet took it and sipped a little of it to feel more one with them, until Mary perceived how it was and laughed and said, "Why didn't I remember?" And she brewed a pot of tea and gave it to him, and they made a little merriment about it.

But the moment which afterwards Yuan thought of most was this. In a pause of talk, the mother sighed and said, "Mary dear, I wish you had wanted to come tonight. It was a *good* meeting. I think Dr. Jones spoke so well—didn't you, Henry?—about having faith enough to carry us even through the greatest trials." And then she said kindly to Yuan, "You must feel very lonely often, Mr. Wang. I often think how hard it must be to be so far from your dear parents and they, too, how hard it is for them to let you be so far. If you feel you'd like it, we'd love to have you take supper with us Wednesdays and go to church with us."

Then Yuan, perceiving how kindly she was, said only "Thank you," and as he said it his eyes fell on Mary, who sat again upon the stool, so now her eyes were beneath the level of his own, and very near. And there in her eyes and upon her face he saw a lovely tender half-merry meaning, tender towards the mother, but very comprehending too toward Yuan, so that this look bound them together in a sort of mutual understanding, wherein they two were quite alone.

Thereafter Yuan lived with a sense of secret, hidden richness. No longer was this people alien to him wholly nor its ways altogether strange and often he forgot he hated them, and he thought he had not so many slights put on him as before, either. He had now two gateways whereby to enter. The one was the outer gateway, and it was this one house into which he could come and go always with freedom and welcome. The worn brown room became home to him in this foreign place. He had thought his loneliness very sweet and the thing he wanted most, yet now he came to this further knowledge, and it was that loneliness is only sweet to a man if it rids him of presences irksome and unwanted, and it is no longer sweet when the beloved presences are discovered. Here in this room did Yuan discover such beloved presences.

There were the little presences of used books, seeming so small and silent, and yet when sometimes he came alone into this room, and sat alone, the house being empty for the time, he took up a book and he found himself spoken to most mightily. For here books spoke more nearly to him than they did anywhere, because the room enfolded him in learned quiet and in friendliness.

And there was here often the beloved presence of his old teacher. Here more than in any classroom or even in the fields Yuan came to know the full beauty of this man. The old man had lived a very simple childlike life, a farmer's son, a student, then a teacher, many years, and he knew so little of the world that one would say he had not lived in it. Yet did he live in two worlds of mind and spirit, and Yuan, exploring into those two worlds with many questions and long listening silences when he sat and heard the old man speak out his knowledge and beliefs, felt no narrowness here, but the wide ranging simple vastness of a mind unlimited by time or space, to which all things were possible in man and god. It was the vastness of a wise child's mind, to which there are no boundaries between the true and magical. Yet this simplicity was so informed with wisdom that Yuan could not but love it, and ponder, troubled, on his own narrowness of understanding. One day, in such trouble, he said to Mary, when she came in and found him alone and troubled, "Almost your father persuades me to be a Christian!"

And she answered, "Does he not almost so persuade us all? But you will find, as I did, the barrier is the—almost. Our two minds are different, Yuan—less simple, less sure, more exploring."

So she spoke, definitely and calmly, and linked thus with her Yuan felt himself pulled back from some brink towards which he had been drawn against his will, and yet somehow with his will, too, because he loved the old man. But she drew him back each time.

If this house was the outer gateway, the woman was the gateway to its inner heart. For through her he learned of many things. For him she told the story of her people and how they came to the shores of the land upon which they lived, gathered out of every nation and tribe nearly upon the earth, and how by force and by guile and by every measure of war they wrested the land from those who possessed it and took it for themselves, and Yuan listened as he had been used to listen to tales of the Three Kingdoms in his childhood. Then she told how her forefathers forced their way always to the farthest coasts, boldly and desperately, and while she talked, sometimes in the room by the fire, sometimes walking in woods when the leaves fell now before winter, Yuan seemed to feel in this woman for all her outward gentleness the inner hardness which was in her blood. Her eyes could grow brilliant and daring and cold, and her chin set beneath her straight lips, and she would kindle as she talked, very proud of the past of her race, and Yuan was half afraid of her.

And here was the strangest thing, that at these times he felt in her a power that was man, almost, and in himself a lesser, leaning quality which was less than man, as though they two together might make man and woman, but interfused, and not clearly he the man and she the woman. And there was sometimes in her eyes a look so possessive towards him, as though she felt herself stronger than he, that his flesh drew back until she changed her look. So while he often saw her beautiful, her body arrowy and light with all her energy, and while he could not but be moved by her darting mind, yet he never could feel her quite flesh to his flesh, or as a woman to be touched or loved, for there was that in her which made him a little afraid of her, and so held back growing love.

He was glad of this, for he still did not wish to think of love or woman, and while he could not keep away from this woman, since there was much in her which drew him, yet he was glad he did not want to touch her. If any had asked him even now he would have said, "It is not wise nor well for two of different flesh to wed each other. There is the outer difficulty of the two races, neither of which likes such union. But there is also the inner struggle against each other, and this pull away from each other goes as deep as blood does—there is no end to that war between two different bloods."

Yet there were times, too, when he was shaken in his sureness that he was safe against her, for sometimes she seemed not wholly foreign to him even in blood, for she could not only show him her own people, but she showed him his people, too, in such a way as he had never seen them. There was much Yuan did not know of his own kind. He had lived among them in a way, a part of his father's life, a part of the school of war and of young men filled with ardor for a cause, a part of that earthen house, even, and a part too of the great new city, but between these parts there was no unity to make them into one world. When any asked him of his own country or his people, he spoke out of knowledge so separated and disjointed, that even while he spoke he remembered something against what he said, and at last it came about that he did not speak at all of it except to deny such things as the tall priest had shown, for pride's sake.

But through this western woman's eyes, who had never even

seen the earth upon which his people had their life, he saw his country as he wished to see it. Now, for his sake, he knew, she read everything she could about his people, all books and sayings of travellers, the stories and the tales which had been put into her language, and the poems, too, and she pored over pictures. From all this she formed within her mind a dream, an inner knowledge, of what Yuan's country was, and to her it seemed a place most perfectly beautiful, where men and women lived in justice and in peace, in a society framed soundly upon the wisdom of its sages.

And Yuan, listening to her, saw it so, too. When she said, "It seems to me, Yuan, that in your country you have solved all our human problems. The beautiful relationship of father to son, of friend to friend, of man to man—everything is thought of and expressed simply and well. And the hatred that your people have for violence and war, how I admire that!" And Yuan, listening, forgot his own childhood and remembered only that it was true he did hate violence and war, and since he did, he felt his people did, and he remembered the villagers, how they had besought him against any wars, and so her words seemed true to him and only true.

And sometimes when she gazed at a picture she had found and saved for him to look at with her, a picture perhaps of a slender tall pagoda, flung up against the sky from some craggy mountain top, or perhaps a country pool fringed about with drooping willows and white geese floating in the shadows, she caught her breath to cry softly, "O Yuan—beautiful—*beautiful!* Why is it when I look at these pictures I seem to feel they are of a place I have lived in and know very well? There is a strange longing in me for them. I think yours must be the most lovely country in the world."

Yuan, staring at the pictures, seeing them through her eyes, and himself remembering the beauty he had seen those few days upon the land, where he had seen such pools, accepted what she said most simply and he answered honestly enough, "It is true; it is a very fair land."

Then she, looking at him troubled, said on, "How crude we all must seem to you, and how crude our life—we are so new and crude!" And Yuan suddenly felt that this, too, was true. He remembered the house in which he lived, the brawling woman there, often angry at her daughter, so that in many bickering ways she filled the house with anger, and he remembered the poor in the city, but he said only very kindly, "In this house, at least, I find the peace and courtesy to which I am accustomed."

When she was in a mood like this, Yuan almost loved her. He thought proudly, "My country has this power over her, that when she thinks and dreams upon it, she grows soft and quiet, and her hardness goes away, and she is all a woman." And he wondered if it might be one day that he would love her in spite of his own wish. Sometimes he thought it so, and then he reasoned thus, "For if she lived in my country, which she has already so much made her own, she would always be like this, gentle and womanish and admiring, and leaning on me for what she needs."

And Yuan at such times thought it might be sweet to have it so, and it would be sweet to teach her how to speak his tongue; sweet, too, to live in the home that she could make, a home like this one he had learned to love very well, its comforts and its homeliness.

But as surely as he let himself be drawn thus, he would come one day to find this Mary changed again, her hardness flashing out, her dominating self the uppermost, so that she could argue and condemn and judge and drive a point home with a keen word or two, even to her father, for she was gentler with Yuan than with anyone, and then he was afraid of her again, and he felt a wildness in her that he could not subdue. So did she draw him to her and so thrust him from her many times.

Thus through the fifth year and the sixth did Yuan continue in this bondage to this woman, and always she was either more

195

than woman to him so that he was afraid of her, or less than woman so that he did not desire her, and yet he never could wholly forget she was a woman. Nevertheless, at last it came about, that with his deep, too narrow nature, she was his only friend.

Thus was it more sure that soon or late he must draw closer to her still, or else grow colder towards her, and he drew away and it came about over a thing not great in itself.

Now Yuan was one who never could take part in all the fooleries of his fellows. There came to the school that last year two brothers who were of his own race, but from the southern parts, where men are light in speech and heart, and variable in mind and laugh too easily. These were two youths so debonair, who so easily lent themselves to the lesser life about them that they were well beloved and often sought for such occasions as demanded what they could do, and they had learned to sing as well as any clown the roaring songs or tricky, halting rhythms which the students loved, so that when they came before a crowd they grinned and danced like clowns and loved the clapping hands of any crowd. Between them and Yuan there was a chasm deeper than between him and the white men, and not only was it that their native language was not his, since south and north have not the same tongue, but because Yuan was secretly ashamed of them. Let these white men, he thought, shake their bodies hither and thither in foolishness but not his countrymen before these foreigners. And when Yuan heard the loud laughter and the roars of praise his own face grew still and cold, because he discerned, or was sure he did, a mockery beneath the merriment.

One day especially he could not bear it. There had been an evening set for amusement in a certain hall and thither Yuan went, inviting with him Mary Wilson, for she now would often go with him to public places, and there they sat with all the others. These two Cantonese appeared in their turn that night, tricked out as an old farmer and his wife, the farmer with a long false queue hung down his back, and the wife coarse and loud as any bawdy woman. And Yuan must sit there and see those two play the fool, in pretense quarrelling and cursing over a fowl made of cloth and feathers which they held between them and divided bit by bit, and they spoke so all could understand and yet seemed somehow to be speaking in their own tongue, too. Indeed the sight was very funny, and the two so witty and so clever that none could keep from laughing, and even Yuan smiled a little sometimes, in spite of an uneasy heart, and Mary laughed often and when the two were gone she turned to Yuan, her face still bright with laughter, "It might have been a bit straight out of your country, Yuan! I am so glad to have seen it."

But these words drove the laughter from him. He said very stiffly, "It was not my country at all. No farmer there wears queues in these days. It was as much a farce as any comedian upon your own stage in New York."

Seeing he was somehow very hurt, she said quickly, "Oh, of course I see that. It was only nonsense, but there was a flavor to it, nevertheless, Yuan?"

But Yuan would not answer. He sat gravely through the evening until it was over, and at the door he bowed and when she asked him to come in he would not, although of late he had looked forward eagerly to coming in and staying awhile in the warm room with her. When now he refused, she looked at him questioningly, not knowing what was wrong, yet knowing something was; suddenly she was a little impatient with him, and felt him foreign and different and difficult, and she let him go, saying only, "Another time, perhaps." Then he went away more hurt because she had not urged him and he thought somberly, "That clownishness made her think less of me, because she saw my race so foolish."

He went home and he was so angry in himself, thinking of her coolness, too, that he went to the house where those two clowns slept and knocked and went into their room and surprised them as they stood half dressed, preparing for sleep. Upon the table were the false queue and the long false whiskers and all the things they used for disguise, and seeing these, Yuan could not but add earnestness to what he said. He said very coldly, "I come only to say I think it wrong that you did what you did tonight. It is not true love of country so to hold one's own up for cause of laughter to a people always too ready for such laughing at us."

At this the two brothers were wholly taken aback, and first they stared at each other and at Yuan, and then one burst into laughter and then the other, and the elder said in the foreign tongue, since they and Yuan spoke differently in any other tongue, "We let you hold up the honor of the country, elder brother! You have dignity enough for a million others!" At this they roared again and Yuan could not bear their wide lips and little merry eyes and their squat bodies. He looked at them while they laughed and then without a word went out and shut the door behind him.

"These men of the south," he muttered, "to us true Chinese they are no kin—petty tribes—"

Lying in his bed that night, the bare branches of the trees patterned in shadows upon the white moonlit wall, he was glad he had no dealings with them, glad he had not even in the old days stayed on in their school of war, and he felt in this foreign country very far away from these very ones whom others counted of his race and nation. He stood alone, he thought, proudly, himself the only one to show forth what his people really were.

Thus Yuan gathered all his pride to strengthen him, for he was delicate in feeling this night, because he could not bear, knowing he valued most Mary's praise of him, to have her see his kind in any foolish light. To him it was as though she saw himself thus, and this he could not endure. He lay, therefore, very proud and solitary, more solitary because from these two even of his countrymen he felt alien, and more solitary because she had not begged him to come into her house. He thought bitterly, "She looked at me differently. She looked at me almost as though I had been myself one of those two fools."

And then he resolved he would not care, and he fostered in himself every memory of her that was not dear, how she could be hard sometimes and her voice incisive as a blade of steel, and how sometimes she was positive as a woman should not be before men, and he remembered her at the wheel of her car, driving it as though it were a beast she owned and forced to great speed and greater, her face set as stone. All these memories he did not love, and at last he ended them by saying in his haughty heart, "I have my work to do, and I will do it well. On the day when I finish what I have to do, I swear there shall not be a name above my name in the lists. Thus is my people honored."

And so he slept at last.

But for all his loneliness, he could not draw again into his solitude, for this Mary would not let him. She wrote him after three days again, and he could not but know his heart stirred strongly in him when he saw the square letter on his table. He felt his loneliness more heavily than he had before, and so now he took up the letter quickly, eager to know what she would say. When he tore it open he was a little cooled, because the words inside were very usual, and not as though she had not seen a friend for three days, whom she had grown used to seeing every day. There were only four lines and they said only that her mother had a certain flower in early bloom which she wished Yuan to see, and would he come the next morning? It would by tomorrow be in full bloom. . . . That was all.

At that moment Yuan was nearer to love for this woman than he ever had been. But her coolness pricked him, too, and he said to himself with a touch of his old childish willfulness, "Well, if she says I am to see her mother, why, then I will see her mother!" and in his little pique he planned that the next day he would devote himself to the mother.

And so he did, and when, as he stood by the flower with the lady, and gazed into its clear whiteness, Mary came by, drawing on her gloves, he only bowed his head a little without speech. But she would not have his coolness. No, although she did not stop except to say some common household thing to her mother, she threw her full look on Yuan, a look so calm and free from any meaning other than her friendship that Yuan forgot his hurt and afterwards, though she was gone, he suddenly found the flower lovely, and he took a new interest in this old mother and in what she had to say, though until this time he thought her usually too full in her speech, too quick to words of praise and of affection which she poured out, or so it seemed to Yuan, too easily on everyone alike. But now he thought in the garden she was only herself, a simple woman, very kind, and always tender to a young thing, so that she could touch a seedling struggling through the soil as tenderly as though it were a little child, and she could almost weep if a young shoot were snapped inadvertently from a rose tree, or if one stepped by accident upon a plant. She loved to feel her two hands in the earth among roots and seeds.

Here today Yuan could share her feelings, and after a while in this dewy garden he helped her pull the weeds and showed her how to move a seedling so it need not wilt but spread its small roots confidently to the new soil. He even promised he would find some seeds from his country, and would see if he could find a sort of cabbage, very green and white and well-flavored, and he was sure she would like it very well. And this slight thing made him feel more again part of this house, and now he wondered how he ever had thought this lady was too free of speech or ever anything other than warm and motherly.

Yet even today he had not much to say to this lady except the little talk of flowers or vegetables she planted. For he soon knew her mind was as simple in its own way as his own country mother's mind, a kindly narrow mind which dwelt on a dish to be cooked or a friend's gossip or the garden and its welfare, or on a bowl of flowers upon the dining table. Her loves were love of God and of her own two, and in these loves she lived most faithfully and so simply that Yuan was confounded sometimes by this simplicity. For he found that this lady, who could read well enough to take up any book and comprehend it, was as filled with strange beliefs as any villager in his own land. By her own talk with him he knew it, for she spoke of a certain festival in spring and she said, "We call it Easter, Yuan, and on this day our dear Lord rose from the dead again and ascended into heaven."

But Yuan had not the heart to smile, for well he knew that there are many tales like this among folk of every nation, and he had read them in his childish days, although he could scarcely think this lady did believe them, except he heard the awe in her kind voice and saw the goodness in her truthful eyes, blue and placid as a child's eyes, under her white hair, and he knew she did believe.

These hours in the garden finished what the quiet full look from Mary's eyes had begun, and when she came back, Yuan had put by all his hurt, and he said nothing of it, but met her as though there had been no three days apart. She said, smiling, when they were alone, "Have you spent all these two hours with mother in her garden? She is merciless if once she gets you there!"

And Yuan felt her smile free him and he smiled back and said, "Does she believe the tales she tells of rising from the dead? We have these stories but they are not believed often, even by women if they are learned."

To this she answered, "She does believe it, Yuan. And will you understand me when I say I would fight to keep you free from such beliefs because for you they would be false, and at the

201

same time I would fight to keep my mother in those same beliefs because for her they are true and necessary? She would be lost without them, for by them she has lived and by them she must die. But you and I—we must have our own beliefs to live and die in!"

As for the lady, she grew that morning to like Yuan very well, so well indeed that often later she forgot his race and kind and would say in mild distress, if he spoke of his home, "Yuan, I declare I forget most of the time now that you are not an American boy. You fit in so well here."

But to this Mary answered quickly, "He will never be quite American, mother." And once she added in a lower voice, "And I am glad of it. I like him as he is."

This Yuan remembered, for when Mary spoke with some secret energy, the mother for once answered nothing, but she looked with trouble in her eyes upon her daughter, and Yuan fancied at that moment she was not quite so warm as she had been towards him. But this passed when he had been with her a time or two more in her garden, for in that early spring a sort of beetle fell upon the rose trees, and Yuan helped her zealously and forgot her little chill towards him. But even in so small a thing as killing beetles Yuan felt a confusion in himself; he furiously hated the cruel tiny things, destroying beauty of bud and leaf with every hour they lived, and he wanted to crush them every one. And yet his fingers loathed the task of plucking them from the trees and his flesh was squeamish afterwards, nor could he wash his hands enough. But the lady had no such feelings. She was only glad for every one she plucked away, and killed them gladly for the plague they were.

So did Yuan come to friendliness with the lady, and he drew near, too, to his old teacher, as near as he could. But the truth was that none drew very near to this old man, who was so strange a compound of depth and simplicity, of faith and intelligence. Yuan could and did talk often with him of his books and of the thoughts there, but often even in the midst of learned talk of some scientific law, the old man's thoughts would steal away into a farther nebulous world, where Yuan could not follow him and he would muse aloud, "Perhaps, Yuan, such laws as this are only keys to unlock a door to a closed garden, and we must throw the key recklessly away and go forth into that garden boldly by imagination—or call it faith, Yuan—and the garden is the garden of God—God infinite, unchangeable, in whose very being are wisdom, justice, goodness, and truth—all those ideals to which our poor human laws try to lead us."

So he mused, until Yuan, listening and comprehending nothing, one day said, "Sir, leave me at the gate. I cannot throw away the key."

To which the old man smiled a little sadly and answered, "You are just like Mary. You young people—you are like young birds—afraid to try your wings and fly out of the little world you know. Ah, until you cease to cling to reason only and begin to trust to dreams and imaginations there will come forth no great scientists from among you. No great poets—no great scientists— the same age produces both."

But Yuan out of all these words remembered most the one saying, "You are just like Mary."

It was true he was like Mary. Between these two, born ten thousand miles apart, and of two bloods never mingled, there was a likeness, and it was twofold, the likeness of youth to any youth in any age, alike in their rebellions, and the other likeness, which is that between a man and maid in spite of time or blood.

For now as the full spring drew near and the trees grew green again and in the woods near the house little flowers sprang out from under the dead winter leaves, Yuan felt in himself a new freedom of the blood. Here surely in this home there was nothing to make his flesh shrink back. Here he forgot he was an alien. He could look at these three and forget their difference, so that the blue eyes of the old pair were natural to him and Mary's eyes were lovely for their changefulness and no longer strange.

And she grew more lovely to him. Some mildness came upon her always now. She was never sharp, her voice even not incisive as it used to be. Her face grew a little fuller, her cheeks less pale, and her lips were softer and not so tightly pressed together and she moved more languidly and with some ease she had not before.

Sometimes on Yuan's coming she seemed very busy, and she came and went so that he seldom saw her. But as spring came full in this she changed, and, not knowing that they did it, each began to plan to meet every morning in the garden. There she came to him, fresh as the day was, her dark hair smooth about her ears. To Yuan she was most lovely when she was dressed in blue, so one day he said, smiling at her, "It is the blue the country people wear in my land. It suits you." And she smiled back and answered, "I am glad."

One day Yuan remembered, for he came early to take his morning meal with them, and while he waited in the garden for her he bent over a bed of small pansy seedlings to take the weeds carefully from their roots. Then she came and stood there watching him, her face strangely warm and lighted, and as he looked, she put forth her hand and took from his hair a leaf or bit of weed lodged there, and he felt her quick hand touch his cheek as it dropped. He knew she did not touch him purposely, for she was always careful against such touching, so that she seemed to draw away even from an aid given her at some roughness in the road. She did not, as many maids will do, put forth a hand to touch a man for any small cause. It was in truth the first time he had ever felt her hand, except in the cool casual touch of greeting.

But now she did not excuse herself. By her frank eyes and by the sudden faint red in her cheeks he knew she felt the touch and that she knew he did. They looked at each other quickly, and turned away again, and she said tranquilly, "Shall we go in for breakfast?"

And he answered as tranquilly, "I must just wash my hands."

So the moment passed.

Afterwards he thought a little of it and his mind flew to bring him the memory of that other touch so long ago, given by the maid now dead. Strangely, beside that ardent open touch, this new light touch seemed less than nothing and still the other burned more real. He muttered to himself, "Doubtless she did not know she did it. I am a fool." And he resolved to forget it all, and to control his mind more sternly against such thoughts, for he truly did not welcome them.

So through the months of that last spring Yuan lived in a strange double way. Within himself he held a certain place of his own, secure against this woman. The softness of the new season, the mildness of a moonlight night when he and she might walk together down the street under the budding new-leaved trees into lonely roads leading to the country, or the stillness of a room where sometimes they sat alone while the musical steady rains of spring beat upon the window panes, even such hours alone with her could not break through into that place. And Yuan wondered at himself, not knowing how he could be so stirred as he sometimes knew he was and yet not want to yield.

For in some ways this white woman could stir him and yet hold him off, and by the same things he loved and did not love. Because he loved beauty and never could escape it, he often saw her beautiful, her brow and neck so white against her dark hair. And yet he did not love such whiteness. He often saw her lighted eyes, clear and grey underneath her dark brows, and he could admire the mind which made them shine and flash, and yet he did not love grey eyes. So, too, with her hands, quick, vivid, speaking, moving hands, beautiful and angular in strength. But he did not love such hands somehow.

205

Yet was he drawn to her again and yet again by some power in her, so that over and over in that busy spring he would pause in the midst of his work in fields or in his room or in the hall of books, to find her suddenly in his mind. He came to ask himself at such times, "Shall I miss her when I go away? Am I bound somehow to this country through this woman?" He dallied with the thought that he might stay on and study more, and yet he could ask himself plainly, "Why do I really stay? If in truth for this woman, to what end, seeing I do not want to wed one of her race?" Yet he felt a pang when he thought further, "No, I will go home." Then he thought further that perhaps he would never see her again, once he was gone, for how could he return again? When he thought he might never see her again, then it seemed he must indeed put off his going.

So might the questioning have dragged itself into an answer and he stayed on, except there came across the sea news which was like his country's voice demanding him.

Now these years while Yuan had been away he had scarcely known how his country did. He knew that there were little wars, but to these he paid no heed, for there had been always little wars.

In these six years Wang the Tiger wrote him of one or two such petty wars he undertook; one against a little new bandit chieftain, and a second time against a lord of war who passed unbidden through his regions. But Yuan passed quickly over such news, partly because he never loved wars, and partly because such things seemed not real at all to him, living in this peaceful foreign country, so that when some fellow pupil called out blithely, "Say, Wang, what's this new war you're getting up in China? I see it in the papers. Some Chang or Tang or Wang—" And Yuan, ashamed, would answer quickly, "It is nothing—no more than any robbery anywhere."

Sometimes his lady mother, who wrote him faithfully once a season, said in her letters, "The revolution grows apace, but I do

not know how. Now that Meng is gone we have no revolutionists in our family. I only hear that at last from the south the new
revolution breaks. But Meng cannot yet come home. He is there
among them, for he has written so, but he dares not yet come
home, even if he would, for the rulers here are afraid and still
very bitter in their hunting of those like him."

But Yuan did not lay aside wholly the thought of his own
country and as he could he followed all the news he could find
of that revolution, and he seized eagerly on every little printed
line which told of some change, such as, "The old calendar of
the moon is changed to the new western calendar," or he read,
"It is forbidden any more to bind the feet of women," or he read,
"The new laws will not let a man have more wives than one,"
and many such things he read in those days. Every change Yuan
read with joy and believed, and through all he could see his
whole country changing, so that he thought to himself and wrote
to Sheng so also, "When we go back next summer we will not
know our land. It seems not possible that so soon, in six short
years, so great a change has been brought about."

To which Sheng wrote back after many days, "Do you go
home this summer? But I am not ready. I have a year or two
yet I want to live here, if my father will send the money for it."

At these words Yuan could not but remember with great discomfort that woman who put Sheng's little poems to such languid
heavy music, and then he would not think of her. But he wished
Sheng would hasten and go home. It was true he had not yet
won his degree, although he had spent more time at it than he
should, and then troubled, Yuan thought how Sheng never spoke
of the new things in their own country. But he excused Sheng
quickly, because indeed it was not easy in this rich peaceful land
to think of revolutions and of battles for a cause, and Yuan did
too forget these things often in his own days of peace.

And yet, as he knew afterwards, the revolution was even then
coming to its height. Surely in its old way, up from the south,

while Yuan spent his days upon his books, while he questioned himself what he felt for this white woman whom he loved and did not love, the grey army of the revolution, in which Meng was, crossed through the heart of his country to the great river. There it battled, but Yuan, ten thousand miles away, lived in peace.

In such great peace he might thus have lived forever. For suddenly one day the warmth between him and the woman deepened. So long they had stood where they were, a little more than friends, a little less than lovers, that Yuan had come to take it as a thing accepted that every evening for a while they walked and talked together after the old pair slept. Before these two they showed nothing. And Mary would have said very honestly to any question, "But there is nothing to tell. What is there between us except friendship?" And it was true there had never been a speech between them which others could not hear and wonder nothing at it.

Yet every night these two felt the day not ended unless they had been alone a little while together, even though each talked idly only of the day's happenings. But in this little hour they grew more to know each other's minds and hearts than by days of other hours.

One night in that spring, they walked thus together up and down between the rose trees planted by a certain winding path. At the end of this path there was a clump of trees, six elm trees once planted in a circle and now grown large and old and full of shadows. Within these shadows the old man had placed a wooden seat, because he loved to come and sit there for meditation. On this night the shadows were very black, because it was a night of clear moon and all the garden was full of light except where the six elms grew. Once did the two pause within the circle of shadow and the woman said half carelessly, "See how dark these shadows are—we seem lost once we step within them."

In silence they stood and Yuan saw with a strange, uneasy

pleasure how clear the moonlight was and he said, "The moonlight is so bright one can almost see the color of the new leaves."

"Or almost feel the shadow cold and the moonlight warm,"
said Mary, stepping out again into the light.

Yet again they paused when they had walked to and fro, and
this time Yuan paused first and he said, "Are you cold, Mary?"
For now he spoke her name easily.

She answered, "No—" half stammering, and then, without
knowing how it came about, they stood uncertain in the shadow
and then quickly she moved to him, touched his hands, and Yuan
felt this woman in his arms, and his arms about her, too, his
cheek against her hair. And he felt her trembling and knew he
was trembling and then as one they sank upon the bench, and
she lifted up her head and looked at him and put up her two
hands and held his head, her hands upon his cheeks, and she
whispered, "Kiss me!"

Then Yuan, who had seen such things pictured in amusement
houses but never had he done it, felt his head drawn down and
her lips hot against his lips, and she was pressed and centered on
his lips.

In that instant he drew back. Why he must draw back he
could not tell, for there was that in him, too, which wanted to
press on and on, deeper and long. But stronger than that desire
was a distaste he could not understand, except it was the distaste
of flesh for flesh that was not its own kind. He drew back, and
stood up quickly, hot and cold and shamed and confused together. But the woman sat on, amazed. Even in the shadow he
could see her white face upturned to him, amazed, questioning
him why he drew back. But for his very life he could say nothing, nothing! He only knew he must draw back. At last he said
half above his breath, and not in his usual voice, "It is cold—
you must go in to the house—I must go back."

Still she did not move, and then after a little time she said,
"You go if you must. I want to stay here awhile—"

And he, feeling himself somehow lacking in what he should have been, yet knowing he had done only what he must do, said in attempted courtesy, "You must come in. You will be chilled."

She answered deliberately without moving at all, "I am chilled already. What does it matter?"

And Yuan, hearing how cold and dead her voice, turned quickly and left her there and went away.

But hour after hour he could not sleep. He thought of her only, and wondered if she still sat there in those shadows alone and he was troubled for her and yet he knew he had done only what he must. Like any child he muttered to excuse himself, "I did not like it. I truly did not like it."

How it might have been between them after that Yuan did not know. For as though she knew his plight his country now called him home.

The next morning he awoke, knowing he must go to see Mary, and yet he delayed, half fearful, for now in the morning still there were these truths clear to him, that he had somehow failed her, though he knew he could have done no other thing than what he did.

But when at last he went to the house he found the three of them in great gravity and consternation over what they saw in a paper. The old man asked anxiously as Yuan came in with him, "Yuan, can this be true?"

Yuan looked with them at the paper and there in great letters were the words that the new revolutionists had fallen upon the white men and women in a certain city in his land and had driven them from their homes and even killed some among them, a priest or two, an old teacher and a physician, and some others. Yuan's heart stopped, and he cried out, "There is a mistake here—"

And the old lady murmured, for she had sat waiting for his word, "Oh, Yuan, I *knew* it must be wrong!"

But Mary said nothing. Though Yuan did not look at her when he came in, and not now, either, yet he saw her sitting there, silent, her chin resting on her crossed hands, looking at him. But he would not look at her fully. He read quickly down the page, crying over and over, "It is not true—it cannot be true—such a thing could never happen in my country! Or if it did there is some dreadful cause—"

His eye searched for that cause. Then Mary spoke. She said, and now he knew her well enough to perceive her heart from the very way she spoke, her words clipped and clear and seemingly careless, her voice a little hard and casual, "I looked for the cause, too, Yuan. But there is none—it seems they were all quite innocent and friendly people, surprised in their homes and with their children—"

At this Yuan looked at her, and she looked at him, her eyes as clear and grey and cold as ice. And they accused him and he cried out to her silently, "I only did what I could not help!" But they steadily accused him.

Then Yuan, trying to be his usual self, sat down and talking more than was his wont, said eagerly, "I shall call up my cousin Sheng—he will know, being in that large city, what the truth is. I know my people—they could not do a thing like this—we are a civilized race—not savage—we love peace—we hate bloodshed. There is a mistake here, I know."

And the old lady repeated fervently, "I know there is a mistake, Yuan. I know God could not let such a thing happen to our good missionaries."

But suddenly Yuan felt his breath stopped by this simple speech, and he was about to cry out, "If they were those priests—" and then his eyes fell on Mary again, and he was silent. For now she was looking at him still and it was with a great speechless sadness, and he could not say a word. His heart longed for forgiveness from her. Yet his very heart drew back, lest in seeking forgiveness it yield to that to which his flesh did not wish to yield.

He said no more, and none spoke except the old man, who, when he was finished, said to Yuan as he rose, "Will you tell me, Yuan, what news you learn?" Then Yuan rose, too, suddenly not wanting to be left alone with Mary, lest the lady leave them so, and he went away very heavy of heart, afraid because he did not want the news to be true. He could not bear to be put to such shame, and this the more because he felt the woman judged him secretly for his withdrawal and counted it for weakness in him. Therefore the more must he show his people blameless of this thing.

Never again were these two near to each other. For as day passed into day, Yuan was swept into this passion to show his country clear, and he came to feel that if he could do it, he would be justified himself. In all the busy ending weeks of that year of school he so busied himself. Step by step he must prove it not his country's fault. It was true, Sheng said, his voice coming calm and like itself across the wires that first day, it was true the thing was done. And Yuan cried back impatiently, "But why—but why?" And Sheng's voice came back so careless Yuan could almost see him shrug himself, "Who knows? A mob—communists—some fanatic cause—who can know the truth?"

But Yuan was in an agony. "I will not believe it—there was a cause—some aggression—*something!*"

And Sheng said quietly, "We can never know the truth—" and changing he asked, "When shall we meet again, Yuan? I have not seen you in too long—when do you go home?"

But Yuan was able only to say "Soon!" He knew that he must go home; if he could not clear his country, then he must go home as quickly as he could finish what remained to be done.

Thereafter he went no more into the garden, nor were there hours alone with Mary any more. They were friendly outwardly, but there was nothing to be said between them, and Yuan planned so he need not meet her. For more and more as he could not prove his country blameless, he turned somehow against these very friends of his.

The old pair perceived this and though they were still gentle with him always, yet they drew themselves a little apart, too, not blaming him at all, and sensitive to his distress, though not understanding it.

But Yuan felt they blamed him. Upon his shoulders he carried the weight of all his country did. Now as he daily read the papers and read of things that any army does in victory and marching through a vanquished country, he felt himself in agony. Sometimes he wondered about his father, for the army moved steadily towards the northern plains, everywhere victorious.

But his father seemed very far away. Near, too near, were these gentle silent aliens, to whose home he must sometimes still go, for they would have it so, who never spoke one word of what the papers said, sparing him all mention of what they knew must torture him with shame. And yet in spite of all their silence, they accused. Their very silence accused. The woman's gravity and coolness, the prayers of the old two, for sometimes before a meal to which they pressed him the old man would say low and troubled words and he would add to his thanks such words as these, "Save them, O God, who are Thy servants in a distant land, who live in such peril of their lives." And the lady would add to it most earnestly her soft "Amen."

Yuan could not bear this prayer, nor this amen, and he could bear it less because even Mary, who had warned him against the faith of the old pair, now bowed her head in new respect of them, not, he knew, that she believed more than she did, but only because she felt the dangers against which they prayed. So was she leagued with them against him, or so he thought.

Again Yuan was alone, and alone he worked to the year's finish and to the hour when with the others he stood for his degree. Alone among them all, the single one of his own people, he received the symbol of his scholarship. Alone he heard his name mentioned for high honors. There were a few who came to give him congratulations, but Yuan told himself he did not care if they came or not.

Alone he packed his books and clothes. At the last it came into his mind that the old pair were even glad to see him go, although their kindness did not change, and then Yuan in his pride thought to himself, "I wonder if they have been uneasy lest I wed their daughter, and so are glad to see me go!"

He smiled bitterly and believed this so. And then thinking of her he thought to himself again, "But I have this to thank her for—she saved me from turning a Christian. Yes, once she saved me—but once, too, I saved myself!"

III

EVEN as Yuan had loved and hated his father in his childhood, so now he left that foreign country loving and hating it. He could not but love it, however unwillingly, as anyone must love a thing beautiful and young and strong. He loved beauty and so he must love the beauty of trees upon mountains, and of meadows free from graves of the dead and beasts upon the land fed and healthy and content and cities clean of human refuse. Then he did not love these very things because if they were beautiful he was not sure if there could be beauty in the bare hills of his own country and he felt it wrong that the dead should lie in the good land of the living so that their graves were in the midst of fields, and he remembered such things there. When he looked upon the rich countryside passing him in the train, he thought, "If this were mine I would love it very well. But it is not mine." He could not, somehow, love wholly a beauty or a good that was not his. He could not like very greatly the people even who possessed this good which was not his.

When once more he went upon the ship and turned to his own country again, he spent much time in questioning himself what gain he had from these six years away. He had gained, doubtless, in learning. His brain was stuffed with useful learning, and he had a small trunk full of notebooks and books of other sorts, and there was a long dissertation he had made himself upon a theme of the inheritance of certain strains of wheat. He had, moreover, little bags of seed wheat, which he had chosen carefully from other seeds he had planted himself in experiment, and he planned to put this seed into his own ground, and raise more and then more until there was enough to give to others, and so might all harvests be improved. Such things he knew he had.

He had more than this. He had some certainties. He knew that when he wed, the woman must be of his own flesh and kind. He was not like Sheng. For him there was now no magic in white flesh and pale eyes and tangled hair. Wherever his mate was she was like him, her eyes black as his, her hair smooth and straight and black, her skin the hue of his. He must have his own.

For, ever after that night beneath the elms, the white woman whom in some ways he knew very well had become to him completely strange. She was not changed, she maintained herself day after day as she had always been, steady, courteous always, quick to understand what he said or felt, but a stranger. Their two minds might know each other, but their minds were housed in two different habitations. Only for one moment had she striven to draw near to him again. She went with him, and the old pair also, to see him at his train and when he put forth his hand to say farewell, she held it for an instant strongly, and her grey eyes warmed and darkened and she cried in a low voice, "Shall we not even write to each other?"

Then Yuan, never able to give pain for any cause, and confused by the pain in her darkening eyes, said, stammering, "Yes—of course—why should we not?"

But she, searching his face, dropped his hand and her look changed, and she said no more, not even when the old mother broke in quickly, "But of course Yuan will write to us."

Then again Yuan promised that he would write and tell them everything. But he knew, and as the train drew away and he must look at Mary's face, he saw that she knew also that he would never write and tell them anything. He was going home, and they were aliens, and he could tell them nothing. As though he cast aside a garment no longer to be used, he cast aside these whole six years of his life except the knowledge in his brain and his box of books. . . . Yet now upon the ship when he thought of the years, there was the unwilling love in his heart, because this foreign country had so much he would have, and because he could not hate these three, since they were truly good; but the love was unwilling because now he was turned homeward he began to remember certain things he had forgotten. He remembered his father, and he remembered small crowded streets, not clean or beautiful, and he remembered the three days he had spent once in prison.

But against these things he argued thus, that in these six years the revolution had come about and doubtless all was changed. Was not all changed? For when he left Meng had been a fugitive, and now Sheng told him Meng was a captain in the army of the revolution and free to go anywhere and everywhere. There was more changed, too, for on this ship Yuan was not the only one of his kind. There were a score or so of young men and women who returned to their own land as he did, and they all talked much together and ate together at the same tables, and they talked of all that was come about, and Yuan heard how old narrow streets were torn away and great streets, as wide as any in the world, were driven through the old cities, and how there were motor vehicles far in the country along country roads, and farmers rode in them who used always to plod afoot, or at best sit across an ass's back, and he heard how many cannon and how many bombing planes and how many weaponed soldiers the new revolution had, and they told how men and women were equal in these days, and how it was against the new law to sell or to smoke opium, and how all such old evils were now gone.

They told so many things Yuan had not heard that he began to wonder why he ever had those old memories, and he grew more than ever eager to be in his new country. He was glad of his youth, in these days, and among these of his own kind he said one day as they sat at a table together and his heart leaped within him when he spoke, "How great a thing it is that we are born now when we may be free and do as we will with our own lives!"

And they all looked at each other, these young eager men and women, and they smiled in exultation, and one girl thrust out her pretty foot and said, "Look at me! If I had been born in my mother's time, do you think I could have walked on two good sound feet like these?" and they all laughed as children do over some little joke of their own. But the girls' laughter had a deeper meaning in it than only merriment, and one said, "It is the first time in our people's history that we are all free—the first time since Confucius!"

And then a merry youth cried out, "Down with Confucius!" And they all cried, "Yes, down with Confucius!" and they said, "Let's put him down and keep him down with all those old things which we hate—him and his filial piety!"

Then at other times they talked more gravely and at these times they grew anxious to think and plan what they could do for country's sake, for there was not one of these companions of Yuan's who was not filled with yearning so to serve his country. In every sentence they made, the words "country" and "love of country" could be heard, and they seriously weighed their faults and their abilities and compared them to those of other men. They said, "Those men of the west excel us in inventiveness, and in the energy in their bodies, and in their dauntlessness to go ahead in what they do." And another said, "How do we excel?" and they looked at each other and took thought, and they said, "We excel in patience and in understanding and in long endurance."

At this the girl who had thrust out her pretty foot cried impatiently, "It is our weakness that we do endure so long! For myself, I am determined to endure nothing—nothing at all I do not like, and I shall try to teach all my countrywomen not to endure anything. I never saw any woman in the foreign country

218

endure anything she did not like and that is how they have come as far as they have!"

And one who was a wag cried out, "Yes, it is the men who endure there, and now it seems we must learn it, brothers!" and then they all laughed together, as the young will laugh easily, but the wag looked secretly with admiration at the bold pretty impatient girl, who must have her own way.

So did all these young men and women and Yuan among them pass the days upon the ship in the highest good humor and most eager expectation of their home-coming. They paid no heed to any except themselves, for they all were filled with the strength of their sureness of their own youth and sufficient to themselves in their knowledge and zest to be going home again, confident each one that he was significant and marked for some special value and service to his times. Yet for all their pleasure in themselves, Yuan could not but see how the very words they used were foreign words, and how even when they spoke their own tongues they must add words of a foreign sort to supply some idea they had for which there was no suited word in their own tongue, and the girls were half foreign in their dress, and the men all foreign, so that if one saw another in the back, it could not be said what his race was. And every night they danced, man and maid together, in the way foreigners did, and even sometimes as shamelessly, cheek pressed to cheek, and hand put into hand. Only Yuan did not dance. In such small ways he held himself apart even from these his own people when they did that which was foreign to him. He said to himself, forgetting he used to do it, "It is a foreign thing, this dancing." But partly he drew back because now he did not want to take one of these new women in his arms. He was afraid of them because they put out their hands so easily to touch a man, and Yuan was always one who feared a clinging touch.

So those days passed, and Yuan wondered more and more

what his country would seem to him after all these years. On the day when he was to reach it, he went alone to the front of the ship and there watched the coming of the land. The land put forth its shadow into the ocean long before it could be seen. Into the clear cold green of ocean water Yuan looked down and saw the yellow line of clay which was the earth the river tore away in its passing through thousands of miles of land, and carried turbulently down to throw into the sea. There the line was as clearly as though a hand had drawn it, so that every wave was pushed back and held away. Yuan one moment saw himself upon the ocean, and the next moment, as though the ship had leaped a barrier he looked down into swirling yellow waves and knew himself at home.

When later he went to bathe himself, for the day was in the midst of summer and of great heat, the water rushed out yellow, and Yuan thought first, "Shall I bathe myself in it?" For at first it seemed to him not clean. Then he said, "Why should I not bathe myself in it? It is dark with the good earth of my fathers," and he did bathe himself and felt himself cooled and cleansed.

Then the ship crept into the river's mouth, and there the land was on either side, stolid and yellow and low and not beautiful, and on it were the small low houses of the same color, and there was no making it beautiful, as though that land did not care if men found it beautiful or not. There it was as it always was, low yellow banks the rivers had laid to push the sea back and claim more for their own.

Even Yuan must see it was not beautiful. He stood upon the decks among the many others of every race and kind upon the ship, and they all stood staring at this new country, and Yuan heard some cry, "It's not beautiful, is it?" "It is not as pretty as the mountains of other countries." But he would not answer anything. He was proud and thought to himself, "My country hides her beauty. She is like a virtuous woman who puts on sober clothes before strangers at the gates, and only within the walls of her own home does she wear colors and put rings on her hands and jewels in her ears."

For the first time in many years this thought shaped itself into a small poem, and he felt the impulse to write four lines down, and he drew out a little book he kept in his pocket, and instantly the verse was there, and this flying moment added its point of brightness to the exultation of this day.

Then suddenly out of the flat grave country towers arose, and these towers Yuan had not seen when he went away, awaking as he had within a ship's cabin at night with Sheng. Now he gazed on them as strangely as all these other travellers did, and they rose glittering in the hot sunshine, tall out of the flatness, and Yuan heard a white man say, "I did not dream it was such a big modern city," and he marked with secret pride the respect in the man's voice, though he said nothing and he did not let his face move, but only leaned as he was upon the rail and looked steadfastly at his country.

But even as this pride rose in him, the ship was docked and instantly a horde of common men leaped on the ship, fellows from the wharf and docks who pressed about to find a little work to do, a bag or box to hoist upon their backs, or some such lowly task. And in the harbor small dingy boats crept out into the hot summer sunshine, and in these boats beggars whined and held up baskets on long poles, and of these beggars many were diseased. Among these common fellows, too, many were half naked for the heat, and in their eagerness for work they pressed rudely among the delicately gowned white women, their bodies grimed and sweating.

Then Yuan saw those white women draw back, some afraid of the men and all afraid of dirt and sweat and commonness, and Yuan felt a shame in his heart, for these beggars and these common fellows were his own people. And here was the strangest thing, that while he hated these white shrinking women very much, suddenly he hated the beggars and the naked common fellows, too, and he cried passionately within himself, "The rulers ought not to allow these people to come out and show themselves like this before everyone. It is not right that all the world should see them first, and some never see any but these—"

He resolved he must set himself to right this wrong somehow, for he could not bear it; small as it might seem to some, it was not small to him.

Then suddenly he was soothed. For now he stepped from the ship, and he saw his mother there to greet him, and with her Ai-lan. There among many they stood, but in one look of his eyes, Yuan saw with a great flush of pleasure that there was none among all the many who could compare to Ai-lan. Even as he gave greeting to his mother, and felt the joy of her steadfast hand against his, and the great welcome in her eyes and smile, he could not but see how the eyes of all from that ship turned to Ai-lan, and he was glad they had her to see, who was his own race and blood. She could wipe out the sight of all the poor and common men.

For Ai-lan was beautiful. When Yuan had seen her last he was still a boy and he had not valued all her prettiness. Now as they lingered on the docks he saw Ai-lan truly could have stood among the beauties of the world and lost nothing.

It suited her well that she had lost the kitten-like coquettishness of her young girlhood. Now, although her eyes were bright and quick, her voice as light and flexible as ever, she had learned somehow a softer, finished dignity, from out of which only sometimes her laughter sparkled forth. About her warm lovely face her short hair was black and smoothly shaped. She did not curl it as some do, but kept it straight and smooth as ebony and cut across her forehead. On this day she wore a long straight silver gown of newest fashion, high-collared, but the sleeves short to her pretty elbows, and it was shaped to her body, so that without a breaking line, there flowed the smooth perfection of shoulder, waist, thigh, ankle.

So Yuan saw her proudly, comforted for much by her perfection. There were such women as this in his own land!

A little behind his lady mother there stood a tall girl, no more a child, but still not wholly maiden. She was not beautiful as Ai-lan was but she had a clear and noble gaze, and if Ai-lan had not been by, she would have seemed fair enough, for though she was tall, she moved gracefully and well, and her face was pale and oval, and the black eyes wide and set truly beneath full straight brows. Now no one thought in all the talk and welcoming laughter to say anything to Yuan of who she was. But even as he was about to ask the question, it came to him that she was the child Mei-ling who had cried out at the prison gate that day because she had seen him first. He bowed to her in silence, and she to him in the same way, though Yuan took time to know her face was one not easily forgotten.

There was one other who was the story teller whom Yuan remembered even still, the one surnamed Wu, against whom the lady had asked Yuan to guard his sister. Now he stood confidently among these others, very debonair in western garb, a small moustache beneath his nostrils, his hair as waxed and black as though it had been polished so, and in his whole look a sort of sureness that he was where he had a right to be. This Yuan soon understood, for after the first cries of greeting and the bows were over, the lady took this young man's hand delicately and took Yuan's, and she said, "Yuan, here is the man who is to wed our Ai-lan. We have put off the wedding day until you came, for Ai-lan chose it so."

Now Yuan, remembering very well how the lady felt against this man, wondered that she never wrote of this, and yet now he could say nothing here except kind things, and so he took the other's smooth hand and shook it in the new fashion and he smiled and said, "I am glad I can be at my sister's wedding—I am very fortunate."

And the other laughed easily and a little indolently, and he let his eyelids droop in a way he had and he looked at Yuan and drawled out in English of a modish certain sort, "It is I who am fortunate, I am sure!", and across his hair he passed his other hand, whose strange loveliness Yuan remembered, now he saw it again.

Yuan, not used to this speech, dropped the hand he held, and turned away uncertainly, and then he remembered this man had been already wed to some other woman and he wondered yet more and resolved to ask his mother secretly how all this came about, since now nothing could be said. Yet when a few minutes later they all walked out to the street to where the cars awaited them, Yuan could not but see how very fairly mated these two were, and each like their race, and yet somehow they were not, too. It was almost as though some old sturdy rooted tree had put forth exquisite blossoms from its gnarled and knotted trunk.

Then the lady took Yuan's hand again and said, "We must go home because the sun is so hot here shining up from the water," and he let himself be led into the streets, and there were motors waiting for them. His lady mother had her own to which she led Yuan, still clinging to his hand, and Mei-ling walked on her other side.

But Ai-lan stepped into a small scarlet motor shaped for two, and with her was her lover. In that glowing vehicle these two might have been god and goddess for their beauty, for the top of it was thrown back, and the sun fell full upon their black and shining hair, upon the faultless smoothness of their golden skins, and the brightness of the scarlet did not daunt their beauty but only showed more clearly the flawless perfect shape and grace in which their bodies grew.

And Yuan could not but admire again such beauty and feel the pride of race rush to his heart. Why, never once in that foreign land had he seen clear beauty like to this! He needed not to be afraid to come home.

Then even as he gazed a beggar writhed himself out of the

gaping multitude who stood to see these rich folk pass, and he rushed to the lordly, scarlet car and laid his hands upon the edge of the door and clung there whining the old cry of his kind, "A little silver, sir, a little silver!"

At this the young lord within shouted very harshly, "Remove your filthy hands!" But the beggar continued to whine yet more earnestly and at last when he would cling so, the young man reached down and slipped from his foot his shoe, his western shoe, hard and leathern, and with its heel he struck down upon the beggar's clutching fingers and he struck with all his force so that the beggar murmured, "Oh, my mother!" and fell back into the crowd and put his wounded hands to his mouth.

Then waving his beautiful pale hand to Yuan the young man drove off his car in a roar of noise, and the scarlet thing leaped through the sunshine.

In the first days in his own country Yuan let his own heart stay in abeyance until he could see in proportion what was about him. At first he thought with a relief, "It is not so different here—after all, my country is like all other countries of this day, and why was I afraid?"

And indeed so it seemed to him, and Yuan, who had secretly feared to find that houses and streets and people might seem poor and mean to him, was pleased he did not find them so. This was the more true because in these years while he had been away the lady removed herself from the small house where she used to live into a good large house built in a foreign fashion. On the first day when Yuan came with her into it, she said, "I did it for Ai-lan. She felt the other house too small and poor to have her friends come to it. And I have done, moreover, what I said I would. I have taken Mei-ling to live with me. . . . Yuan, she might be my own child. Did I tell you she will be a physician as my father was? I have taught her all he taught me, and now she goes to a foreign school of medicine. She has two more years to learn, and then she must work in their hospital for more years. I say to her do not forget that for internal humors it is we who know best our own frames. Nevertheless, it cannot be denied that for cutting and sewing up again the foreign physicians are best. Mei-ling will know both. And she helps me besides with my girl babes whom I still find unwanted in the streets—and many of them these days, Yuan, after the revolution, when men and maids have learned to be so free!"

Yuan said, wondering, "But I thought Mei-ling only a child— I remember her only a child—"

"She is twenty years old," the lady answered quietly, "and very far past childhood. In mind she is much older than that, and older than Ai-lan, who is three years more than twenty—a very brave quiet maid Mei-ling is. I went one day and saw her help the doctor who cut a great thing from a woman's neck, and her hands were as steady as a man's to do it, and the doctor praised her because she did not tremble and was not frightened by the gush of blood. Nothing frightens her—a very brave quiet maid. Yet she and Ai-lan like each other, though she will not follow Ai-lan to her pleasures, and Ai-lan would not see the things that Mei-ling does."

By now they sat in the lady's sitting room alone, for Mei-ling had gone away at once, and no one was near except the servant who brought tea and comfits in and out, and Yuan asked curiously, "I thought this Wu was bound to another wife, my mother—"

At this the lady sighed and answered, "I knew you would wonder. I have been through such a trouble with Ai-lan! Yuan, she would have him and he would have her, and there was nothing to be said,—no way to persuade her to anything. That was the reason why I took this greater house, because I thought if they must meet it might be here—since meet they would, and all that I could do was to fend off more until he could divorce his old wife and be free. . . . And it was true she was an old-fashioned woman, Yuan, one his parents had chosen for him and wed to him when he was sixteen. Ai, I do not know whom to pity most, the man or that poor soul! I seem to feel in me the sorrows of them both. I was wed like that, too, and not loved, and so I felt myself her. And yet I promised myself I would let my daughter wed where she would because I know what it is to be not loved, and so it is that I feel the troubles of them both. But it is arranged now, Yuan, in the way such things are arranged—too easily, I fear, nowadays. He is free, and she, poor woman, returns to the inland city of her birth. I went to see her at the last, for she lived here with him—though not really, she said, with him. There she was with her two maids putting her garments in the red leathern boxes she had bought as part of her marriage portion. And all she said to me was, 'I knew this end must come—I knew this end must come,'—a woman not beautiful and older by five years than he, speaking no foreign tongue, as all must speak these days, and even with her feet once bound, though she strove to hide this in big foreign shoes. For her indeed it is the end—what is left to her now? I did not ask. I must think. most of Ai-lan now. We can do nothing in these days, we old ones, except let the new sweep us on as it will. . . . Who can do anything? The country is upset, and anyhow, and there is nothing left to guide us—no rule, no punishment."

Yuan only smiled a little when she ended thus. She sat, old and quiet and always a little sad, her hair white, and she said the things the old always say.

For in himself he felt only courage and hopefulness. In the day he had been back, in the few hours even, this city somehow gave him courage. It was so busy and so rich. Everywhere even in his quick passing he saw great new shops were raised up, shops to sell machines, and shops to sell goods of every kind from all parts of the world. No longer were there many humble streets lined with the low-roofed simple shops of homely merchandise. The city was a center of the world, and new buildings heaped on buildings, higher and higher. In the six years he had been gone a score of mighty buildings had flung themselves up against the sky.

That first night before he slept he stood at the window of his room and looked out across the city, and he thought, "It looks almost like the city where Sheng is abroad." There about him were blazing lights and noise of motors and the deep hum of a million humans and all the rush and throb of restless growing pushing life. This was his country. The letters hung in flame against the moonless clouds were letters of his own tongue, proclaiming goods his own countrymen were making. The city was his own, and great as any in the world. He thought for a moment of that woman pushed aside to make way for Ai-lan, but he hardened himself as he thought, and in his heart he said, "So must all be pushed aside who cannot stand in this new day. It is right. Ai-lan and the man are right. The new cannot be denied."

And in a sort of hard clear joy he laid himself to sleep.

Now Yuan went everywhere these few first days in this lift of joy through this great city. It seemed to him his fortune was good beyond his dreams, for he left this country from a prison, and now he was truly home again, and it seemed to him that all the prison gates were opened, not only his own prison, but all the bondages. It was an evil dream forgotten that his father had ever said he must wed against his will, and it was an evil dream that youths and maidens had once been seized and shot for seeking freedom. This freedom for which they died, why, now it was achieved for all! Upon the streets of the city he saw the young come and go, their looks free and bold and ready to do what they would, men and women, too, and there was no bondage anywhere. And in a day or two a letter came from Meng which said, "I would have come to meet you, but I am tied here at the new capital. We make the old city new, my cousin, and we tear down the old houses and we have put up a great new road which sweeps through the city like a cleansing wind, and we shall build more streets everywhere, and we have planned to tear down old unwanted temples and put schools in them, for the people have no need of temples any more in these new days. We teach them science instead. . . . As for me, I am a captain in the army, and near to my general, who knew you once, Yuan, in that school of war. He says, 'Tell Yuan there is a place here for him to do his work.' And so there is, my cousin, for he has spoken to a man above him very high, and that one has spoken in a place of influence, and in the college here there is a place where you may teach what you like, and you can live here and help us to build this city."

Then Yuan, reading these bold swelling words, thought to himself with exultation, "This is from Meng, who was in hiding —and see what he is come to!" It was a warmth in Yuan that already his country had a place for him. He turned it over in his mind a time or two. . . . Did he indeed wish to teach young men and women? It might be the quickest way to serve his people. He put the thought into his mind to wait a day or two or more, until his duty was fulfilled.

For first he must go and see his uncle and his household, and then there was Ai-lan's wedding three days off, and then he must go to see his father. Yuan found two letters from his father waiting at the coast for him, and when he saw the square trembling letters, scrawled upon a page or two, big and uncertain as old men write, he was touched with an old tenderness, and he forgot he had ever feared or hated his father, for now in this new day the Tiger seemed as futile as an old actor on a forgotten stage. Yes, he must go and see his father.

Now if the six years had made Ai-lan more beautiful and had led the child Mei-ling into womanhood, they had laid old age heavily upon Wang the Landlord and his lady. For where Yuan's lady mother seemed to hold herself at much the same place all these years, her hair only a little whiter, her wise face a little more wise and more patient and a little less round, these other two Yuan found were truly old. They lived now no more in their own house, but with their elder son, and thither Yuan went and found them, the house a western house the son had built and set into a pleasant garden.

In this garden the old man sat beneath a banana palm tree, and Yuan found him there as placid and as happy as any aged saint. For now he had given up all his seeking lustful ways, and the worst he did was to buy a picture now and then whereon was painted a pretty maid, so that he had some hundreds of these pictures, and when he felt inclined he called to a servant that they be brought to him, and he turned the pictures over one by one and gazed at them. So he sat when Yuan came, and the maidservant who stood beside him to fan off flies turned the pictures for him as she might have turned pages for a child to see.

Yuan scarcely knew him for his uncle. For this old man had by his very lustiness fended off his age until the last moment, so that whether it was because he now sometimes smoked a little opium as the old will often do, or what it was, when his age was come at last upon him it came as suddenly as a withering blast, shriveling him and driving off his fat, so that now he sat as loosely in his skin as though it were a garment cut too largely for him. Where his fat had stood out firm and full, folds of yellow skin hung down. His very robes he had not changed, and they also hung too loose upon him, very rich in textured satins, but still his old robes cut to suit his old fullness, and now gathered round his heels and the sleeves falling over his hands and the collar hanging to show his lean wrinkled throat.

When Yuan stood before him the old man gave him vague greeting and said, "I sit here alone to look at these pictures, because my lady will have it that they are evil." And he laughed a little in his old leering way, but it was ghastly laughter somehow on his ravaged face, and when he laughed he looked at the maidservant and she laughed with false heartiness to cheer him, while she stared at Yuan. But to Yuan the old man's very voice and laughter seemed thinner than they used to be.

And after a while the old man asked again, while he still looked at his pictures, "How long is it since you went away?" and when Yuan told him he asked, "And how does my second son?" and when Yuan told him, he muttered as though it were a thing he always thought when Sheng was in his mind, "He uses too much money in that foreign country—my eldest son says Sheng uses too much money—" And he fell into a gravity until Yuan said to cheer him, "He returns next summer, he tells me," and the old man murmured, staring at another picture of a maid beneath a young bamboo, "Oh, aye, he says he does." Then he bethought himself of something and he said suddenly with great pride, "You know my son Meng is a captain?" And when Yuan smiled and said he did the old man said proudly, "Yes, he is a very great captain now, and he has a fine large wage, and it is a good thing to have a warrior in the family somewhere in time of trouble—my son Meng, he is very high these days. He came to see me and he wore a soldier's garb such as they wear abroad, they tell me, and he had a pistol in his belt and spurs to his heels—I saw them."

Yuan held his peace, but he could not keep the smile from his face to think how in these few years Meng had turned from a fugitive against whom his father cried aloud into this captain of whom his father boasted.

All the time the two had talked the old man seemed not at ease with Yuan and he kept beginning little courtesies such as one does to a guest and not to a nephew, and he fumbled at his teapot on a little table there beside him, making as though to pour tea for Yuan until Yuan stopped him, and he fumbled in his bosom for his pipe for Yuan to smoke until at last Yuan perceived that indeed this uncle felt him like a guest, staring at him with troubled old eyes, and at last the old man said, "You look like a foreigner somehow—your clothes and how you walk and move make you look foreign to me."

Now though Yuan laughed he was not overpleased at this, and a constraint came on him since after all he could not answer it. And very soon, even though he had been six years away, he knew he had nothing to say to this old man, nor this old man to him, and so he took his leave. . . . Once he looked back, but his uncle had forgotten him. He had settled himself in sleep, his jaws moving a little and then dropping open and his eyes closing. Even as Yuan looked at him he was asleep, for a fly settled on his cheek bone while the maid stared at Yuan's foreignness and forgot to wave her fan, and it wandered down to his old hanging lips and the old man did not move.

When Yuan had left him thus he went in search of his aunt, to whom also he must pay his respects, and while he waited he sat in the guest hall and looked about him. Since he had returned he found himself measuring everything he saw in new ways, and always, although he did not know it, the standard by which he measured was what he had seen in the foreign country. He was very well content with this room, which it seemed to him was finer than anything he had seen anywhere. Upon the floor was a large carpet covered with beasts and flowers in a very rich confusion, red and yellow and blue together, and on the walls were foreign pictures of sunny mountains and blue waters, all set in bright gold frames, and at the windows were heavy curtains of red velvet, and the chairs were all alike, red, very deep and soft to sit upon, and there were little tables of fine black carven wood set about here and there, and the very spittoons were not a common sort, but were covered with bright blue painted birds and gold flowers. At the farther end of the room between the windows there were hung four scrolls painted for the four seasons, red plum blossoms for spring, white lilies for summer, golden chrysanthemums for autumn, and the scarlet berries of heavenly bamboo lying under snow for the winter.

To Yuan this seemed the gayest richest room he had ever seen, full enough of things to amuse a guest for hours, for on every table were set little carven images and toys of ivory and silver. It was far more to see than that distant worn brown room he had thought warm and friendly for a while. He walked about, waiting for the maidservant to return and tell him he might go in, and while he waited a roar of a vehicle stopped at the doors, and his cousin and his wife came.

Both these two looked prosperous beyond anything Yuan had remembered. The man was in his middle years, and gaining all his father's flesh, and he looked even fatter than he was, since he wore the foreign dress, which hid nothing of his shape, and above its severity, which shaped clear his large belly, his round smooth face was like a ripe yellow melon, for against the heat he had shaved away even his hair. Now he came in mopping the sweat from himself, and when he turned to give his straw hat to a servant, Yuan saw his neck in three great rolls of flesh beneath his shaven crown.

But his wife was exquisite. She was no longer young, and she had had five children, but none would know it, since after every childbirth, as the custom was with such ladies of fashion in the city, she gave her child to some poor woman to be nursed and she bound her breasts and body back again into slenderness. Now Yuan saw her slender as a virgin, and though she was forty years of age, her face was pink and ivory, her hair smooth and black, her whole look untouched by any care or age. Nor did the heat touch her. She came slowly forward, greeting Yuan prettily and gravely, and only in the quick look of distaste which she cast at her huge sweating husband could Yuan see the petulance she used to have. But she was courteous to Yuan for she looked on him no longer as a raw youth from the small old home city, and only a child in the family. He was a man now who had been abroad, and he had won a foreign degree and he saw it mattered to her what he thought of her.

233

Then to while the time away when they were seated after courtesies, and his cousin had shouted for tea to be brought, Yuan asked, "What do you now, elder cousin? For I see your fortunes have risen."

At this the man laughed and was well pleased and he fumbled at a thick gold chain hung across his great belly, and he answered, "I am a vice president of a newly opened bank now, Yuan. There is good business these days in banks in this foreign place where wars cannot touch us, and they have opened everywhere. People used to put their silver into land. I remember our old grandfather never rested until all he had was made over into land and yet more land. But land is not so sure as it once was. There are even places where the tenants have arisen and taken land from landlords."

"Are they not stopped?" asked Yuan, astonished.

And the lady thrust in sharply, "They ought to be killed!"

But the cousin shrugged himself a little in the tightness of his foreign coat and flung up his pudgy hands and he said, "Who shall stop them? Who knows how to stop anything these days?" And when Yuan murmured, "Government?" he repeated, "Government! This new confusion of warlord and student and that we call government! What can they stop? No, each man for himself these days, and so the money pours into our banks and we are safe enough guarded by foreign soldiery and under foreign law. . . . Yes, it is a good prosperous place I hold, and I have it through the grace of friends."

"*My* friends," his lady put in quickly. "If it had not been for me and that I grew friends with a great banker's wife and through her came to know her husband and begged for you—"

"Yes, yes," the man said hastily. "I know that—" and he fell into silence and discomfort of a sort, as though there were something there he would not discuss too clearly, and as though he had paid some secret price for what he had. Then the lady asked Yuan very prettily, for there was a sort of cool polished prettiness

234

in all she said and did now, as though she had said and done everything before a mirror first, "So, Yuan, you are home again and a man and you know everything!"

When Yuan smiled mutely to deny his knowledge, she laughed a little set laugh and put her silken kerchief to her lips and said again, "Oh, I am sure you know much you will not tell of, for you have not come out of such years knowing as little as you did when you began them!"

What Yuan would have said to this he did not know and he felt uneasy, as though his cousin's wife was false and strange, and as though she were encased about with falseness so he could not know how she really was, but at this moment a servant came in leading her old mistress, and Yuan rose to greet his aunt.

Into this rich foreign room the old lady came, leaning on her servant. She was a thin upright figure, her hair still black, but her face wrinkled into many crossing lines, though her eyes were as they were, very sharp and critical of all they saw. To her son and son's wife she paid no heed, but she let Yuan bow to her and took his greeting and sat down and called to the servant, saying, "Fetch me the spittoon!"

When the servant had so done, she coughed and spat very decently, and then she said to Yuan, "I am as sound as ever I was, thanks to the gods, except that I have this cough and the phlegm comes up in me especially in the mornings."

At this her daughter-in-law looked at her with great distaste, but her son said soothingly, "It is always so with the aged, my mother."

The lady paid no heed to him. She looked Yuan up and down and asked, "How does my second son in that outer country?" And when she heard Yuan say Sheng was well she said positively, "I shall wed him when he comes home."

Now her daughter-in-law laughed out and said uncautiously, "I do not see Sheng being wed against his will, my mother—not as the young are nowadays."

235

The old lady cast a look at her daughter-in-law, a look which showed she had spoken her feelings against her many times and now it was no use, so she said on to Yuan, "My third son is an official. Doubtless you have heard. Yes, Meng is now a captain over many men in the new army."

This Yuan heard again, and again he smiled secretly remembering how this lady had once cried against Meng. His cousin saw the smile and put down the bowl of tea he had been sipping loudly and he said, "It is so. My brother came in with the triumphant armies from the south, and now he holds a very good high place in the new capital and has his own soldiers under him, and we hear very brave and ruthless tales of him. He could come any day now to see us, for he is safe enough since the old rulers are swept so clean and flown to every foreign land for safety, only he is busy and cannot be spared."

But the old lady would not suffer any talk but her own. She coughed and spat again loudly and then she asked, "What position shall you take, Yuan, now that you have been abroad? You ought to win a very good high pay!"

To this Yuan answered mildly, "First, as you know, Ai-lan is to be wed three days hence and then I go to my father, and then I shall see how the way opens up before me."

"That Ai-lan!" said the old lady, suddenly, fastening on the name. "*I* would not let my daughter wed a man like that! I would put her in a nunnery first!"

"Ai-lan in a nunnery!" cried her son's wife, hearing this, and she laughed her little false and bitter laugh.

"If she were my daughter, so I would!" the old lady said firmly, staring at her daughter-in-law, and she would have said more except that she choked suddenly, and she coughed until the servant must rub her shoulders and strike her back to let her breathe again.

At last Yuan took his leave, and when he went homeward through the sunny streets, choosing to walk this fair day, he thought how good as dead this old pair were. Yes, all the old were good as dead, he thought joyously. But he was young and the times were young, and on this brilliant summer's morning it seemed to him he met none but young in this whole city—young laughing girls in light-colored robes, their pretty arms bare in the new foreign fashion, and young men with them free and laughing. In this city all today were rich and young, and Yuan felt himself one of these rich and young, and his life was good to him.

But soon none had time to think of anything these days except Ai-lan's wedding. For Ai-lan and the man were well known everywhere among the young rich of the city not only of their own race, but among those of other peoples too, and there were bidden to the marriage more than a thousand guests, and to the feast afterwards very nearly as many. Yuan had no time for any speech with Ai-lan alone, except for a little hour on the first day when he came back. Yet even then he felt he did not truly talk with her. For her old teasing laughing self was gone, and he could not penetrate into the lovely finish and assuredness that wrapped her about now. She asked him with what seemed her old frank look, "You are glad to be home, Yuan?" But when he answered he saw that her eyes, for all they looked at him, did not see him at all, but were turned inward in some thought of her own, and they were only lovely shapes of dark liquid light. So through all the hour, until Yuan was bewildered by the distance all about her and he asked uneasily, blurting out the words, "You are different—you do not seem happy—do you want to marry?"

But there the distance still was. She opened her pretty eyes very widely and made her voice very cool and silvery and laughed a small clear laugh and said, "Am I not so pretty, Yuan? I have grown old and pale and ugly!" And Yuan said hastily, "No—no—you are prettier, but—" and she said, mocking him a little as she used to do, "What—shall I be so bold as to say I want to be wed and must be wed to this man? Did I ever do anything I did not want to do, brother? Have I not always been naughty and willful? At least I hear my aunt say so, and mother is too good to say it, but I know she thinks it—"

But Yuan, although she made her eyes mischievous and arch in shape and twisted her pretty brows above them, still saw her eyes were empty and he said no more. Thereafter he spoke no more alone with her, for each night of those three days she went forth in a new dress and wrapped about with silks of every hue, and even if Yuan was bidden with her as a guest, he saw her only in the distance, a lovely, brilliant figure, strange to him these days, engrossed in her own self and seeing everyone as in a dream. She was silent as she had never been before—her laughter only smiles now, her eyes soft instead of bright, and all her body round and soft and gentle, moving slowly and with cool grace, instead of with her old light leaping merriment. She had cast aside the charm of her gay youth, and had learned this new charm of silence and of grace.

By day she slept exhausted. Yuan and the mother and Mei-ling met and ate alone, and moved gently about the house and all noise was shut out until nightfall when again Ai-lan came forth to meet her love and go forth with him to some house where they were bidden as guests. If she rose earlier it was only that she might have fitted to her form, by the many tailors who came for this, the gowns of silk and satin that she wanted, and among them was the pale peach-hued satin wedding gown with its trailing silvery foreign veil.

Now Yuan noted how silent and how grave the mother was through the few days before the marriage. She spoke very little to anyone except to Mei-ling, and on her she seemed to lean for many things. She said, "Did you take the broth in to Ai-lan?" Or she said, "Ai-lan must have soup to drink or that dried foreign milk she likes when she comes in tonight. I thought her pale."

Or she said, "Ai-lan wants two pearls to hold the veil, you know. Bid a jeweller send what he has for her to see."

Her mind was full of all these many small things for Ai-lan, and Yuan knew it natural for a mother to be so and he was glad she had this young girl to help her. Once when the mother was not there and they two happened to be alone in the room and waiting for the meal to come, Yuan said to Mei-ling, not knowing what to say and feeling something must be said, "You are very helpful to my mother."

The girl turned her honest look on him and said, "She saved me in my babyhood." Yuan answered, "Yes, I know," and he was surprised because there was no shame at all in the girl's eyes, such shame as she might have had to say she was a foundling, of what parents she did not know. And then Yuan, feeling her like one of his house, because of her feeling to his mother, said, "I wish she seemed happier to see my sister wed. Most mothers are glad, I thought, if their daughters wed."

But to this Mei-ling answered nothing. She turned her head away and at that moment the servant came in with bowls of meats, and she went forward herself to set them on the table. Yuan watched her do it, and she did it very simply and not at all as though she shared a servant's task. He watched her, forgetting that he did so, and he saw how slight yet strong her lithe body was, how firm and quick were her hands, not making one useless movement, and he remembered how not once when his mother asked if a thing were done or not, had it been undone.

Thus the days drew on quickly to Ai-lan's marriage day. It was to be a very great wedding, and to the largest and most fashionable hotel in the whole city the guests were bidden to come at an hour before noon. Since Ai-lan's father was not there, and since the old uncle could not stand so long, her elder cousin took his place, and beside her was her mother, who never left her at all.

This marriage was according to a new fashion, and very different from the simple way in which her grandfather Wang Lung had taken his wives, and very different too from the old formal weddings of his sons in ways set and appointed by the forefathers. In these days the city people wed their sons and daughters in many ways, in some more old and in some more new, but be sure Ai-lan and her lover must have the very newest. Therefore there was much music from foreign instruments hired for the day and there were flowers set everywhere, and these alone cost many hundreds of silver pieces. The guests came in all the various garb of their races, for Ai-lan and her lover counted such people among their friends. These all gathered in a vast hall of the hotel. Outside, the streets were choked with their vehicles and with the idle and the poor who pressed to see what they could, and to try what they could do to gain something from the day, to beg or to slip their hands unseen into pockets of the throng and take what they found there, although guards had been hired to hold them back.

Through this great throng Yuan and the mother and Ai-lan rode, the driver incessantly sounding his horn lest some be crushed, and when the guards saw their vehicle and the bride within, they darted forward shouting out, "Make way—make way!"

Through all this din Ai-lan rode proudly, silent now, her head bent a little beneath the long veil held to her head by the two pearls and by a circle of small fragrant orange flowers. She held between her hands a great cluster of white lilies and small white roses, very fragrant.

Never had there been so beautiful a creature. Even Yuan was awed by her beauty. A little cool set smile hung on her lips, though she would not let it out, and her eyes glittered black and white beneath her lowered lids, for well she knew her own beauty, and there was not one whit of it she did not know and had not fostered to its utmost height. The very crowd fell silent before her, and when she stepped out, its thousand eyes fastened on her hungrily and drank in all her beauty, at first silently and then with restless murmurings,—"Ah, see her!" "Ah, how fair, how fair!" "Ah, never such a bride was seen!" And be sure Ai-lan heard it all, but she made as if she did not.

So, too, when she came into the great hall, when the music set the moment, did all the crowded guests turn their heads and that same wondering silence came upon them. Yuan, who had gone first and stood with the man who was to wed her, saw her coming slowly between the guests, two little white clad children before her scattering roses for her to tread upon, and maidens with her, too, clad in silks of many hues, and he could not but share the wonder at her beauty. Yet, even so, even at that moment, although he did not know it until afterward, he saw Mei-ling very clearly, for she was with Ai-lan as attendant.

Yes, after all the wedding was over, and the contract read between the two, and when they had bowed to those who stood for the two families, and bowed to the guests and all to whom such courtesy was due, when all was over, the mighty feast and the merry-making and the wedded pair were gone to have a holiday together, then thinking of it all upon his return to his home, Yuan remembered, and he was surprised he did, the girl Mei-ling. She had walked alone before Ai-lan, and even Ai-lan's radiance had not made Mei-ling seem unnoticeable. Now Yuan remembered very well she wore a soft long robe of apple green, the sleeves cut very short, and the collar high, so that above the color her face looked clear and somewhat pale and resolute. The very difference to Ai-lan made her hold her own against such beauty. For Mei-ling's face owed nothing to its color or to its changefulness or sparkling eyes or smile, as Ai-lan's did. Its good high look was from the perfect line of bone beneath the firm clear flesh, a line which, Yuan thought, would keep its strength and nobleness long past its youth. She looked older now than her age was. But some day in her age her straight low nose, her clean oval cheeks and chin, her sharp-cut lips, the straightness of her short black hair shaped smoothly against her head, would give her youth again. Life could not greatly change her. Even as now a certain gravity was hers, so in her maturity she would still be young.

Yuan remembered this gravity. Of all that wedding party only two were grave, the mother and Mei-ling. Yes, even at the feast, when wines of every foreign sort were poured out, and all the tables full of guests were crying out such wit as they did not know they had before, when glass was lifted high to glass, and the bride and groom joined in the laughter as they made their way between the guests, even then Yuan saw at his table that the mother's face was grave, and so was Mei-ling's. These two talked together in low tones often and directed the servants here and there, and took counsel with the master of the hotel, and Yuan thought they were grave because of all these cares, and he let it pass and looked about the brilliant hall.

But that night when they were alone after all was over, and the house was silent save for servants passing here and there to set covers right again and bring order everywhere, the lady sat in her chair so silent and downcast that Yuan felt he must say something to make her lift her heart up somehow, and so he said kindly, "Ai-lan was beautiful—the loveliest I ever saw—the loveliest woman."

The lady answered listlessly, "Yes, she was beautiful. She has these three years been counted the most beautiful among the young rich ladies of this city—famous for her beauty." She sat awhile and then she said with strange bitterness, "Yes, and I wish it had not been so. It has been the curse of my own life and of my poor child's that she has been so beautiful. She has needed to do nothing. She has not needed to use her mind or hands or anything—only to let people look at her, and praise flowed in upon her and desire and all that others work to gain. Such beauty only a very great spirit can withstand, and Ai-lan is not great enough to bear it!"

At this Mei-ling looked up from a piece of sewing she had in her hands and cried softly and beseechingly, "Mother!"

But the lady would say on, as if for once her bitterness was more than she could bear, "I say only what is true, my child. Against this beauty have I fought my whole life, but I have lost. . . . Yuan, you are my son. I can tell you. You wonder that I let her wed this man. So may you wonder, for I do not like or trust him. But it had to be—Ai-lan is with child by him."

So simply did the lady say these dreadful words. Yuan, hearing them, felt the beating of his heart stop. He was yet young enough to feel the horror of this thing, that his own sister . . . He glanced in great shame at Mei-ling. Her head was bent over the bit of cloth she held, and she said nothing. Her face was not changed, only more grave and quiet.

But the lady caught Yuan's glance and understood it. She said, "You need not mind, for Mei-ling knows everything. I could not have borne my life if I had not had her. She it was who helped me to plan and know what I must do. I had no one, Yuan. And she stayed a sister to my poor pretty foolish child, and that one leaned upon her, too. She even would not let me send for you, Yuan. Once I thought I must have a son to help me, for I am not used in all these new ways of divorce, and I could not tell your eldest cousin even, not anything, for I was ashamed. But Mei-ling would not let me spoil your years abroad."

Still Yuan could not say a word. His blood flushed up to his cheeks and he sat confused and shamed, and angry too. And the lady, understanding very well this confusion, smiled sadly and said once more, "I dared not tell your father, Yuan, whose only simple remedy is killing. And even if he had not been so, I could not tell him. It is a sorry end to all my care for Ai-lan, to train and school my daughter in such freedom as this! Is this the new day, then? In the old days the two would have suffered death for such a sin! But now they will suffer nothing. They will come back and live merrily and Ai-lan's child will come too soon, but none will whisper more loudly than behind their hands, because today many children come too soon. It is the new day."

The lady smiled a mirthless smile but there were tears in her eyes. Then Mei-ling folded up the bit of silk she sewed and thrust her needle in it and came and said soothingly, "You are so tired you do not know what you say. You have done everything for Ai-lan and well she knows it and so do we all. Come and sleep and I will fetch a broth for you to drink."

Then the lady rose obedient to the young girl as though it were a thing she had often done, and went out leaning on her shoulder gratefully, and Yuan watched the two go, still having nothing he could say, so confounded was he by what he had heard.

So Ai-lan, his own sister, had done so wild a thing! Thus had she used her freedom. Into his own life through her had come again this hot wild thing which he had twice escaped. He went slowly to his own room, very troubled, and troubled in his old divided way, as though nothing could ever come clearly and simply to him, neither love nor pain. For now half he was ashamed of Ai-lan's recklessness, because such things ought not to happen to his own sister, in whom he wanted to have nothing but whole pride, and yet half he was troubled because there was a hidden sweetness in this wild thing and he wanted it for himself. It was the first doubtfulness to fall upon him in his own country.

When this marriage day was over Yuan knew he must not in decency delay his going to his father, and he was eager to be gone, and the more eager because he found it sad in this home now. The mother was more quiet even than she ever had been and Mei-ling devoted her time steadfastly to her school. In the two days while Yuan made ready to go away, he scarcely saw the girl. Once he thought she avoided him, and then he said to himself, "It is because of what my mother said of Ai-lan. It is natural for a maid so modest to remember that," and he liked this modesty. Yet when the time came when he must set forth and take the train north, he found he wanted to bid Mei-ling good-bye, and not leave to be away the month or two and not see her again. He even waited, therefore, and chose a later train by night, so that he could see her come home from her school, could dine alone with the lady and with her and talk a little quietly with them before he went.

And as they talked he found he listened for the girl's speech, very clear and soft and pleasant, always, and not shy and giggling as the laughter of maids is sometimes. She seemed always busy at some bit of sewing, and once or twice when a servant came in to ask a question of the next day's meats or some such thing, Yuan heard her ask Mei-ling instead of the lady, and Mei-ling gave directions as though she had done it many times. Nor was she shy in speech. This night, since the lady was more quiet than usual, and Yuan silent, too, Mei-ling talked on and told of what she did in school, and how she had long hoped to be a doctor.

"My foster mother made me think of it at first," she said and threw her quiet beaming look upon the lady. "And now I like it very well. Only it has meant a long time to study, and a great cost, and this my foster mother has done for me, and I shall always care for her in return; where I am she shall be, too. I want a hospital of my own one day in some city, a place for children and for women, and I want a garden in the center, and round it buildings full of beds and places for the sick,—not too large, not more than I could do, but all very clean and pretty."

So this young woman planned out her wish and in her earnestness she let her sewing lie, and her eyes began to beam and her lips to smile, and Yuan watching her, his cigarette between his fingers, thought in surprise, "Why, this maid is fair enough," and he forgot to listen to her while he looked at her. Suddenly he felt he was not pleased and when he looked into himself to see why it was, he found he did not like to hear this maid plan out a life alone for herself and so sufficient that she needed no

245

one else in it. It seemed then to him that women ought not to think it well to have no thought of marriage in their minds. But even as he was so thinking, he saw the lady's face. For the first time since the marriage day her eyes were lit with interest and she heard all the young girl said. And now she said warmly, "If I were not too old I would myself do something in that hospital. It is a better day than mine was. It is a very good day when women are not forced to wed!"

This Yuan heard her say, and while he believed it, or would have said he did, still it made him feel a little strangely, too. Somehow he took it as a thing not to be gainsaid or questioned that all women ought to wed, although it was not what a man could talk about with two women. Yet their eagerness for freedom left a little coolness in him, so that when he said farewell he felt less warmly than he thought he would and bewildered in himself because he was hurt somewhere within him, but he did not know just where or how the hurt was.

Long after he had lain himself down in the narrow berth of the train he thought of this, and of the new women of his country, and of how they were, Ai-lan so free she made her mother sad, and yet this same mother rejoiced in all Mei-ling's great free plans for her life. Then Yuan thought with a little bitterness, "I doubt she can be so very free. She will find it hard to do all she plans. And she will want a husband and children some day as all women do, doubtless."

And he remembered the women he had known, how in any land they turned at least secretly to a man. Yet, when his memory searched Mei-ling's face and speech, he could not truly say he had ever seen one sign of that searching in her look or voice. And he wondered if there were some youth she dreamed about, and he remembered that in the school she went to there were young men, too. Suddenly as a wind blows out of a still summer's night he was jealous of those youths he did not know, so jealous he could not even smile at himself or ask himself why he should care what Mei-ling dreamed. He planned soberly how he must hint to the lady that she ought to warn Mei-ling, and how she ought to guard the young woman better, and he took a heed for her he never had taken for any living soul, and never once did he think to ask why he did.

So planning, as the train swayed and creaked beneath him, he fell into a troubled sleep at last.

There came much now to drive all these thoughts from Yuan's mind for a while. Since his return from the foreign country he had lived only in the great coastal city. Not once had he seen any other thing than its wide streets, filled by day and night with vehicles of every sort, with motors and with public tramways and with people warm and brightly dressed and busy each in his own way. If there were poor ones, the sweating ricksha pullers, the lesser vendors, yet these in summer seemed not so piteous and there were not the winter beggars, who had fled from flood or famine to try a life in city streets. Rather the city seemed very gay to Yuan, a place measuring well beside any he had seen any-where, and in it there was the comfort and the wealth of his cousin's new house and the display of the marriage and all the shining wedding gifts. And as he left the lady had pressed into his hand a thick folded heap of paper which he knew was money, and he took it easily, thinking that his father sent it to her for him. He had almost forgotten now that there were poor even in the world, his own house seemed so rich and easily fed.

But when he woke in the train the next day and looked out of the window, it was not to see such a country as he thought was his. The train had stopped beside a certain mighty river, and there all must descend and cross in boats and take up their jour-ney again on the other side. So Yuan did also, crowding with the others on an open, wide-bottomed ferry boat, which still seemed not wide enough for all the people on it, so that Yuan, coming last, must stand upon the outside near the water.

He remembered very well that he had crossed this river when he went south before, but then he did not see what he now saw. For now his eyes, long shaped to other sights, saw these things newly. He saw upon the river a very city of small boats, tightly packed together, from whence a stench rose that sickened him. This was the eighth month of the year, and though it was scarcely more than dawn the day was thick with heat. There was no great light from the sun, the sky was dark and low with clouds, pressing down so that it seemed to cover the water and the land, and there was no least wind anywhere. In the dull sluggish light the people pushed their boats aside to make way for the ferry, and men scrambled out of little hatches, nearly naked, their faces sunk and sodden with the sleepless night of heat, and women screamed at crying children and scratched their tangled hair, and naked children wailed, hungry and unwashed. These crowded tiny boats held each its fill of men and women and many children, and from the very water where they lived and which they drank the stench arose of filth they had poured into it.

Upon this, then, Yuan suddenly opened his eyes that morning. The picture lasted scarcely a moment and was gone, for the ferry boat swung clear of the little boats against the shore, into the cleanness of the middle of the river, and as suddenly Yuan was looking no more into sodden faces but into the swift yellow water of the river. Then almost before he could grasp the change, the ferry half turned against the current, and crept past a vast white-painted ship, rising as clean as a snowy peak against the grey sky, and Yuan and all the crowd looked up to see above them the prow of a foreign ship, and the hanging blue and red of a foreign flag. But when the ferry had crept through to the other side, there were also the black points of cannon and these were foreign cannon.

Then Yuan forgot the stench of the poor and their little crowded boats. He looked up and down the river as he went on and upon its yellow breast he counted seven of these great foreign ships of war, here in the heart of his country. He forgot all else for this moment as he counted them. An anger rose in him against these ships. Even as he stepped on shore he could not but look back on them with hate and question why they were there. Yet they were there, white, immaculate, invincible. Out of those black cannon, aimed steadily at shore and shore, had more than once leaped fire and death upon the land. Yuan remembered very well that it was so. Staring at the ships, he forgot everything except that out of those cannon fire could come upon his people and he muttered bitterly, "They have no right to be here—we ought to drive them out of all our waters!", and remembering and in bitterness he mounted into another train and took up his way again to his father.

Now here was a strange thing that Yuan found in himself; so long as he could maintain his anger against these white ships and remember how they had fired on his people, and so long as he could remember every evil thing whereby his people had been oppressed by other outer peoples, and these were many, for he had learned in school of evil treaties forced upon the emperors of old by armies sent to ravage and to plunder, and even in his lifetime had there been such things, and even in the great city while he had been away young lads had been shot down by white guards for crying out their country's cause—so long as he could remember all these wrongs that day, he was happy enough and filled with a sort of fire, and he thought in all he did, while he ate, and while he sat and looked out over the passing fields and villages, "I must do something for my country. Meng is right and better than I am. He is more true than I am because he is so single. I am too weak. I think them all good because of one good old teacher or—or a woman clever with her tongue. I ought to be like Meng and hate them heartily, and so help my people by my strong hating. For only hate is strong enough to help us, now—" So he thought to himself, remembering the alien ships.

But even as Yuan would have clung to this wish of his, he

249

could not but feel himself grow cooler, and this coolness grew in little subtle ways. A great fat man sat in the seat across from him, so near that Yuan could not always keep his eyes away from his mighty bulk. As the day wore on to greater heat, the sun burning through the windless clouds upon the metal roof of the train, the air within grew burning, too, and this man took off all his garments, save his little inner trousers, and there he sat in all his naked flesh, his breasts, his belly rolls of thick yellow oily flesh, and his very jowls hanging to his shoulders. And as if this were not enough, he coughed, in spite of summer, and he made much of his cough and rumbled at it all he could and spat his phlegm out so often, that stay where he would Yuan could not avoid it always. So into his right anger for his country's sake crept his petulance against this man who was his countryman. At last a gloom came into Yuan. It was almost too hot for life in this shaking train, and he began to see what he did not want to see. For in the heat and weariness, the travellers were past caring for anything except how to live to the journey's end. Children wailed and dragged at their mothers' breasts and at every station flies flew into open windows and settled on the sweating flesh and on the spittle upon the floors and on the food and on the children's faces. And Yuan, who never noticed a fly in his youth because flies were everywhere and why should they matter, now that he had been elsewhere and learned the death they carried, was in an agony of daintiness against them, and he could not bear to have one settle on his glass of tea or on a bit of bread he bought from a vendor or on the dish of rice and eggs he bought at noon from the servant in the train. Yet he could not but ask himself what use was all this hatred against the flies when he saw the blackness of the servant's hands, and the sticky grime upon the cloth with which the man wiped the dish before he poured the rice in. Then in his bitterness Yuan shouted at him, "Leave the dish unwiped rather than touch it with such a rag as that!"

At this the man stared and grinned most amiably and then at

this moment feeling how very great the heat was, he took the cloth and wiped his sweating face and hung it on his neck again where he carried it. Now Yuan indeed could scarcely bear to touch his food. He put down his spoon and cried out against the man and he cried out against the flies and all the filth upon the floor. Then the man was outraged at such injustice and he cried out for heaven to witness and he said, "Here am I, one man, and I have only one man's work to do, and floors are not my work and flies are not my work! And who can spend his life in summer to kill flies? I swear if all the people in this nation spent all their lives to kill the flies they could not prevail against them, for flies are natural!" Then rid of his anger thus the man burst out laughing very heartily, for he was of a good temper even under anger, and he went his way laughing.

But all the travellers, being so weary and ready to look at anything or listen anywhere, had listened to everything said, and they all took part against Yuan and with the servant and some cried out, "It is true there is no end of flies. They come from none knows where but they have their life to live too, doubtless!" And one aged lady said, "Aye, and they have a right to it. As for me, I would not dare to take life even from a fly!" And another said scornfully, "He is one of those students come back from abroad to try his little foreign notions on us!"

At this the large fat man near Yuan, who had eaten mightily of rice and meats and was now drinking tea very gravely, belching loudly as he drank, said suddenly, "So that is what he is! Here I have sat my whole day through staring at him to see what he was and making nothing of him!" And he gazed on at Yuan in pleased wonder, now that he knew what he was, drinking as he stared and belching up his wind until Yuan could not bear to see him, and looked steadfastly away into the flat green country.

He was too proud to answer. Nor could he eat. He sat on looking out of the window hour after hour. Under the hot cloudy sky the country grew more poor, more flat, more flat with wastes

251

of water as the train sped north. At every station the people looked to Yuan more wretched, more plagued with boils and sore eyes and even though there was water everywhere they were not washed, and many of the women had their feet bound still in the old evil way he thought was gone. He looked at them and he could not bear them. "These are my people!" he said bitterly within himself at last, and he forgot the white foreign ships of war.

Yet there was one more bitterness that he must bear. At the far end of the car sat a white man whom Yuan had not seen. Now he came past to descend from the train, at a certain little mud-walled country town where he lived. And as he passed Yuan he noted him and his young sad face, and he remembered how Yuan had cried out against the flies, and he said in his own tongue, meaning to be kind and seeing what Yuan was, "Don't be discouraged, friend! I fight against the flies, too, and shall keep on fighting!"

Yuan looked up suddenly at the foreign voice and words. There he saw a small thin white man, a little common-looking fellow in a grey cotton suit of clothes and a white sun helmet, and with a common face, not newly shaven, though the pale blue eyes were kind enough, and Yuan saw he was a foreign priest. He could not answer. This was the bitterest thing to bear, that here was a white man to see what he had seen, and know what he had known this day. He turned away and would not answer. But from his seat he saw the man get off the train and trudge through the crowd and turn towards the mud-walled city. Then Yuan remembered that other white man who had said, "If you would live as I have lived—"

And Yuan asked himself accusingly, "Why did I never see all this before? I have seen nothing until now!"

Yet it was only the beginning of what Yuan must see. For when at last he stood before his father, Wang the Tiger, he saw him as he never knew he was. There the Tiger stood, clinging to the door post of his hall waiting for his son, and all his old strength was gone, even his old petulance, and there was only an old grey man, whose long white whiskers dropped down sparsely on his chin, and whose eyes were red and filmed with age and with too much wine-drinking, so that until Yuan came near he could not see him, but must listen for his voice.

Now Yuan had seen with wonder how weedy were the courts that he came through and how few the soldiers were who stood about, a few ragged idle fellows, and how the very guard at the gate had no gun and let him come in as he would and asked no questions and gave no courteous greeting as he should to his general's son. But Yuan was not ready to see his father look so gaunt and thin. The old Tiger stood there in an old robe of grey stuff, and it was even patched upon the elbows where his bones had worn through upon the arm of his chair, and on his feet were slippers of cloth and the heels turned under, and his sword was not in his hand now.

Then Yuan cried out, "My father!" and the old man answered trembling, "Is it really you, my son?" And they held each other's hands, and Yuan felt tears rush to his eyes to see his father's old face, the nose and mouth and dimmed eyes all somehow bigger than they used to be and too big in the shrunken face. It seemed to Yuan, staring at the face, that this could not be his father, not the Tiger whom he used to fear, whose frowns and black brows were once so terrible, whose sword was never far from his hand, even when he slept. Yet it was the Tiger, for when he knew it was Yuan he called out, "Bring the wine!"

There was a slow stirring and the hare-lipped trusty man, himself aged now, but still his general's man, came forward, and he gave his greeting to his general's son, his crooked face beaming, and he poured out wine, while the father took the son's hand and led him in.

Now did another show himself, and yet another whom Yuan

253

had not seen before, or thought he had not, two grave little prosperous men, one old, one young. The elder was a small, shriveled
man, dressed very neatly in an old fashion of long robe of dark
grey small-patterned silk, and on his upper body was a sleeved
jacket of dull black silk, and on his head a little round silk cap
and on it a white cord button denoting mourning for some near
relative. About his ankles, too, higher than the black velvet shoes
he wore, his trousers were tied with bands of white cotton cloth.
Above this sombre garb his small old face peered out, smooth as
though he still could not grow a beard, but very wrinkled, his
eyes as shining sharp as a weasel's eyes are.

The young man was like him except his robe was dull blue,
and he wore the mourning that a son wears for his dead mother,
and his eyes were not sharp, but wistful as an ape's little hollow
eyes are when it looks at human men to whom it is akin and
yet not near enough to understand them or be understood. This
was the other's son.

Now as Yuan looked at them uncertainly, the elder said in his
dried high voice, "I am your second uncle, nephew. I have not
seen you since you were a lad, I think. This is my eldest son, your
cousin."

At this Yuan gave surprised greeting to the two, not too gladly,
because they were very strange to him in their staid old-fashioned
looks and ways, but still he was courteous, and more courteous
than the Tiger, who paid no heed to them at all, but only sat now
and stared joyfully at Yuan.

And indeed Yuan was much moved by this childlike pleasure
his father had in his return. The old Tiger could not take his eyes
from Yuan, and when he had stared awhile he burst into silent
laughter, and rose from his seat and went to Yuan and felt his
arms and his strong shoulders and laughed again and muttered,
"Strong as I was at his age—aye, I remember I had such arms I
could throw an eight-foot spear of iron and wield a great stone
weight. In the south under that old general I used to do it of an

evening to amuse my fellows. Stand up and let me see your thighs!"

Yuan stood up obediently, amused and patient, and the Tiger turned to his brother and laughed aloud and cried in some of his old vigor, "You see this son of mine? I'll swear you have not one to match him out of all your four!"

Wang the Merchant answered nothing to this, except he smiled his little forbearing meager smile. But the younger man said patiently and carefully, "I think my two younger brothers are as large, and my next brother is larger than I, since I am smallest of them all, although the eldest." And he blinked his mournful eyes at them as he made his report.

Now Yuan, listening, asked curiously, "How are these other cousins of mine and what do they do?"

The son of Wang the Merchant here looked at his father, but since that elder sat silent, and wore the same small smile, he took courage and answered Yuan. "It is I who work to aid my father with his rents and grain shop. Once we all did it, but the times are very evil now in these parts. The tenants have grown so lordly that they will not pay the rents they should. And the grain, too, is harvested in lesser quantities. My elder brother is your father's, for my father gave him to my uncle. And my next brother, he would go out to see the world and he went and is in a shop in the south, an accountant, because he fingers the abacus very well, and he is prosperous, since much silver passes through his hands. My third brother is at home, and his family, and the youngest, he goes to school, for we have a school now in our town of a new sort, and we expect him to be wed as soon as it is decent, for my mother died a few months back."

Then Yuan remembering, remembered a great blowsy lively country woman he had seen in his uncle's house the once his father took him there, and how she made merry always, and he wondered to think she must lie still and dead while this little creeping man, his uncle, lived on and on so little changed. He asked, "How did it happen?"

Then the son looked at his father and they were both silent until the Tiger hearing what was asked answered, as if here were a thing which had to do with him, "How did it happen? Why, we have an enemy, our family has, and now he is a little wandering robber chieftain in the hills about our old village. Once I took a city from him in the fairest way, by open guile and siege, but he has not forgiven me for it. I swear he settled near our lands on purpose and he watched for my kin, I know. And this brother of mine is cautious and found out this robber hated us and he would not go himself to take his share of crops and taxes from the tenants, but he sent his wife, she being only a woman and the robbers caught her on her homeward way, and robbed her and cut her head off and rolled it down beside the road. I tell my brother, 'Wait a few months now until I gather up my men again. I swear I'll search that robber out—I swear I'll—I swear I'll . . .'" The Tiger's voice dragged in weakening wrath and he put out his hand blindly, searching, and the old trusty man standing near put a wine bowl in it and said drowsily, as if from long habit, "Quiet yourself, my general. Do not be angry, lest you grow ill." And he shifted on his tired old feet and yawned a little and stared happily at Yuan, admiring him.

Now though Wang the Merchant had said nothing during all this tale, when Yuan looked at him to speak some courteous comfort, he was surprised to see his uncle's little old shining eyes were wet with tears, and still silent, the old man took the edge of first one sleeve and then the other and carefully wiped each eye, and then in his spare stealthy fashion he drew his dry old hand across his nose and Yuan was so astonished he could not speak, to see this cold old man shed tears.

The son saw it, too, and with his small wistful eyes upon his father he said mournfully to Yuan, "The servant who was with her said if she had been silent and more obedient to them they

256

would not have been so quick to kill. But she had a very swift loud tongue and all her life long she had used it as she liked, and she had a temper always quick to boil, and she shouted at the very first, 'Shall I give you my good silver, you sons of cursed mothers?' Yes, the servant ran as fast as his feet could take him when she cried so loudly, but when he looked back her head was off already, and we lost the whole of those rents with her for they took everything."

Thus the son spoke in the evenest little garrulous voice, the words running out one like another in flatness, as though he had his mother's loose tongue inside his father's body. But he was a good son, too, who had loved his mother, and now his voice broke and he went out to the court and coughed to ease himself and wipe his eyes and mourn a little.

As for Yuan, not knowing what else to do, he rose and poured a bowl of tea for his uncle and felt himself in a dream here in this room, a stranger with these folk who were his own blood. Yes, he had a life to live they could not conceive, and their life was small as death to him. Suddenly, though why he did not know, he remembered Mary, of whom for a long time he had not thought. . . . Why now should she come to his mind as clearly as though a door were opened to show her there, as he had been used to see her on a windy day in spring across the sea, her fine dark hair blown about her face, her skin white and red, her eyes their steady grey? She had no place here. This place she could not know. The pictures of his country she had been used to speak of, the pictures she had made for her own mind, were only pictures. It was well, Yuan thought passionately, staring at his father and at these others, sunk back in themselves, now that the first keen edge of meeting was over,—oh, it was very well he had not loved her! He looked about the old hall. There was dust everywhere, the dust long left by a few old careless servants. Between the tiles upon the floor, the green mold grew, and there were stains upon the tiles of spilt wine and of old spittle and of ashes and of dripped greasy food. The broken lattices of shell had been mended with paper, hanging now in sheets, and even in this daylight rats ran to and fro upon the beams above. The old Tiger sat nodding, his warm wine drunk, and his jaw dropped and all his great old body slack and helpless. Above him on a nail his sword hung in its scabbard. Now for the first time Yuan saw it, although he had missed its shining nearness the first moment when he saw his father. It was still beautiful, though sheathed. The scabbard was beautiful in spite of dust in all the carven patterns on it and although the red silken tassels hung down faded and gnawed by rats.

. . . Ah, he was very glad he had not loved that foreign woman. Let her keep her dreams of what his country was! Let her never know the truth!

A great sob rose in Yuan's throat. . . . Had the old passed forever from him? He thought of the old Tiger, and of the little shriveled mean-faced man, his uncle, and his son. These, these were still his own and he was tied to them by the blood in his own veins, which he could not spill out if he would. However he might long to be free of all their kind, their blood must run in him so long as he lived.

It was very well that Yuan should know his youth was over and that he must be a man now, and look only to himself, for on that night while he lay alone in the old room where he had slept as a child and as a lad, his guards about him, and where he had sat alone and wept himself to sleep when he ran home from the school of war, the old trusty man came creeping in. Yuan had but just lain himself down to sleep, for his father had made a little feast for him that night and he had bidden his two captains in and they had eaten and drunk together for welcome to Yuan. Afterwards Yuan had let his father lean on him and taken him to his own door before he came to bed himself.

For a while, lying in his bed before he slept, he listened to what he never used to hear, the night sounds of the little town where his father had lived so long encamped. He thought to himself, "If I had been asked I would have said there were no sounds in this little town at night." And yet there were the barking of the dogs up the street, the crying of a child, a murmur of voices not yet stilled in sleep, a solitary tolling note now and again of some temple bell, and clear and wailing above it all, although not near, the crying agony of some woman's voice seeking for the wandering soul of her child now dying. No sound was loud, for there were silent courts between him and the gate, and yet Yuan, somehow newly keen to everything because he felt himself a stranger here where once he was not strange, heard each separate sound.

Then suddenly there was the squeak of his door upon its wooden hinges and the flare of a candle, and he saw the door open and there was the old trusty man, who bent and set his candle carefully on the floor, and panting a little because his back was stiff he stood again and closed the door and thrust the bar through. Yuan waited, wondering in surprise what he had to say.

He came on his slow old feet up to Yuan's bed, and seeing Yuan had not drawn the curtains he said, "You are not sleeping, young sir? I have something I must say."

Then Yuan, seeing how this man's old body bent at the knees, said kindly, "Sit, then, while you speak." But the man knew his place and was unwilling for a while, until at last he yielded to Yuan's kindness, and sat down on the footstool beside the bed and he began to hiss and whisper through his split lip and though his eyes were kind and honest, he was so hideous that Yuan could not bear to see him, however good he was.

Yet soon he forgot how the old man looked, in his dismay at what he heard. For out of a long, winding, broken story Yuan's mind began to discern something more and more clearly, and at last the old man put his two old hands upon his dried old knees and whispered loudly, "So every year, little general, your father has borrowed more heavily of your uncle. First he borrowed a great sum to set you free out of that prison, little general, and then every year to keep you safe abroad he borrowed more. Well, and he let his soldiers go and let them go until now I swear he has not a hundred left to fight with. He could not go to war; his men have left him for other lords of war. They were but hirelings and when the wage is stopped, shall hirelings stay? And the handful he has left are not soldiers. They are ragged thieves and wastrels of his army who live here because he gives them food, and the townspeople hate them because they go from door to door demanding money, and having guns they must be feared. Yet they are only armed beggars. Once I told the general what they did, because he has always been so honorable, he has never let his men take more than their due for booty, and never did he let them take from people in times of peace. Well, and then he went out and roared and drew his brows down and pulled his whiskers at them, but what of that, little sir? They saw him old and shaking even while he roared, and though they pretended to be afraid, when he was gone I saw them laugh and they went straight out again to their begging and still they do as they like. And what use to tell my general more? It is better for him to have peace. And so he borrows money every month, I know, because your uncle comes here often now, and he would not if it were not something for money. And your father gets money somehow, because he has it and I know people do not give him much tax these days, and his soldiers who force what is given keep most of it, and he could not have enough if your uncle did not give it."

But Yuan could not believe it all at once and he said in dismay, "Yet if my father has dispersed his army as much as you say he has, and he gives only food to his men now, he cannot need so much money as he did. And his father left him land, I think."

Then the old man bent close and he whispered piercingly,

"That land is all your uncle's now, I swear—or else as good as his, for how will your father pay him what is owed? And, little general, do you think it has cost nothing for you to go to foreign countries? Yes, he has let your own mother do with little enough, and your own two sisters have been wed to tradesmen in this little town, but every month your father has sent this money to that other lady for you."

In this moment Yuan perceived how childish he had been all these years. Year after year he had taken it as a thing not to be doubted that his father should pay for all he had wanted. He had not been wasteful and he had not gamed or wanted many fine garments or done those things that young men sometimes do to waste their parents' goods. But year after year his least needs had cost his father hundreds of pieces of silver. And now he thought of Ai-lan's silken gowns and of her wedding, yes, and of the lady's house and of her foundlings. And while Yuan knew the lady had some silver left her from her own father, whose only child she had been, so that he left her no mean sum of money, yet Yuan doubted if it could pay for all.

Then Yuan felt his heart rush out to his old father that all these years he had made no complaint, but by borrowing and contriving he had not let his son suffer for a want of silver. And Yuan said in the gravity of his new manhood, "I thank you that you have told me. Tomorrow I will see my uncle and my cousin and know what has taken place and what their hold is on my father—" and then as though this suddenly came to him as a new thought he added, "and on me!"

Through the night Yuan could not forget this thought. Again and again he woke and though he might comfort himself and remember that after all they were of one blood, and therefore debt is not really debt, yet Yuan felt a weight upon him when he thought of these two. Yes, they were his flesh and blood though he felt himself as alien from them as though his were another race. Once, pondering on this in the black loneliness of night, it came to him that here in his own childhood bed, within his father's house, he felt as foreign as he had across the sea. It struck with a sudden bleakness, "How is it I have no home anywhere?" And all the days upon the train and all he had seen rose up to sicken him again and make him shrink away and he said suddenly aloud in a low whispering cry, "I am homeless!"

Then he hastened his heart from that cry, for it was dreadful to him and he could not bear to understand it.

So on the next day he reminded himself many times that these were his own blood after all, and that he was no true stranger, and this his own blood could not harm him. Nor would he blame his old father. He told himself he knew easily how his father had been compelled by age and by his very love for his son to go into debt, and who better to borrow of than his own brother? So in the morning Yuan comforted himself. But he was glad it was a fair day, very fair and cool with little winds of coming autumn, for he felt it easier to find comfort when the sun shone into the courts, and the heat was blown out of the rooms by the stirring winds.

Now after they had eaten, on the next morning the Tiger went out to see his men, and this day he made a show before Yuan that he was very busy for his men, and he took down his sword and shouted to the trusty man to come and wipe it clean and he stood quarrelling because it was so dusty, so that Yuan could not but smile and comprehend a little sadly, too, what was the truth.

But when he saw his father gone it came to Yuan that here was a good time to talk privately with his uncle and his cousin and so he said frankly, after courtesies, "Uncle, I know my father owes you certain moneys. Since he is older than he was, I want to know what burdens are on him, and do my share."

Now Yuan was prepared for much, but he was not prepared for such obligations as he now found. For those two men of business looked at each other and the younger went and fetched an account book, such a book as is used to tally moneys in a shop, a large soft paper-covered book, and this he gave with both hands to his father, and his father took it and opened it and began to read forth in his dry voice the year, the month, the day, when the Tiger had begun to borrow sums from him. And Yuan listening, heard the years begin with that one when he had gone south to school, and it continued even until now, the sums mounting every time and with such interest that at the end Wang the Merchant read forth this sum, "Eleven thousand and five hundred and seventeen pieces of silver in all."

These words Yuan heard and he sat as though he had been struck down by a stone. The merchant closed up the book again and gave it to his son and his son placed it on the table and the two men waited. And Yuan said in a voice smaller than his was usually, though he tried to make it his own, "What security did my father give?"

Then Wang the Merchant answered carefully and drily, scarcely moving his lips at all, as his way was when he spoke, "I did naturally remember that he is my brother, and I required no such security as I might from a stranger. Moreover, for a while your father's rank and army were a safeguard for me, but now no longer. For since my son's mother died as she did, I feel my safety is all gone when I go out into the countryside. I feel no one fears me any more, and all know your father's power is not what it once was. But truly, no war lord's power is what it once was, with the new revolution in the south and threatening to press its way even here to the north. The times are very evil. There is rebellion everywhere and tenants are bold upon the land as they have never been. Yet I remember that your father is my brother, and I have not even taken his land for security, though indeed it is not enough for all the silver I have given your father for you."

At these last two words, "for you," Yuan looked at his uncle but he said nothing. He waited for the uncle to go on. And the old man said, "I have preferred to put my moneys out for you, and let you be security in what ways you could be. There are many things you can do for me, Yuan, and for my sons, who are your kin."

So this old man spoke, not unkindly, either, but very reasonably and as any elder in a great family may to his junior. But when Yuan heard these few words and heard the dry small voice and saw his uncle's little weazened face, he was dismayed, and he asked, "And what can I do, uncle, who have not even any work yet fixed for myself?"

"You must find that work," the uncle replied. "It is well known these days that any young man who has been to foreign countries can ask a very high wage, as much wage as in the old days a governor could hope for. I have taken pains, before I lent so much for you, to know this from my second son who is accountant in the south, and he tells me it is so, that this foreign learning is as good a business nowadays as can be found. And it is best of all if you can find a place where money passes by, because my son says there are higher taxes taken now for all the new things to be done than ever have been taken from the people, and the new rulers have the highest plans of great highways and mighty tombs for their heroes and foreign houses and every sort of thing. If you could find a good high place where silver must go in and out, it would be easy for you and a help to us all."

This the old man said, and Yuan could answer nothing. He saw before him in this clear instant the life his uncle planned for him. But he said nothing, only stared at his uncle, yet not seeing him, either, only seeing the narrow mean old mind shaping these plans. He knew that according to the old laws his uncle might so plan and might so claim his years, and when he remembered this, Yuan's heart rose as it never had against the miserable rights of those old times, which had been like logs chained to the feet of the young, so that they might never run swiftly. Yet he did not cry this forth. For when he thought of this, he thought of his old father, too, and how not in any willfulness the old Tiger had bound his son like this, but only because there was no other way whereby he could find money to give Yuan his desire. So in uncertainty Yuan could only sit and loathe his uncle secretly.

But the old man did not catch the young man's loathing. He went on again in the same flat little voice, "There are also other things that you may do. I have my two younger sons who have no livelihood. The times are so ill now that my business is not what it was, and ever since I heard how well my elder brother's son does in a bank, I have wondered why my sons should not, too. So when you have found a good place for yourself, if you will take my two younger sons with you and find places for them under you, it will be part payment of the debt, and so I shall consider it, depending on the size of the sum they have each month."

Now Yuan cried out bitterly, and he could no longer hold back his bitterness, "So I am sold as security—my years are yours!"

But the old man opened his eyes at this and answered very peaceably, "I do not know how you mean those words. Is it not a duty to help one's own family as one can? Surely I have spent myself for my two brothers, and one of them your father. I have been their agent on the land these many years, and I have kept the great house which our father left us, and paid all taxes, and done everything for the land which our father left to us. But it has been my duty and I have not refused to do it, and after me this eldest son must do it. Yet the land is not what it was. Our father left us enough in lands and rents so that we were accounted rich. But our children are not rich. The times are hard. Taxes are high and tenants pay little and they fear no one. Therefore my two younger sons must seek places for themselves even as my second son has, and this is your duty in your turn to help your brother-cousins. From ancient times the most able in a family has helped the others."

So was the old bondage laid upon Yuan. He could make no

answer. Well he knew that some young men in his place would have refused the bondage, and they would have run away and lived where they pleased and cast aside all thought of family, for these were the new times. And Yuan wished most passionately that he could be free like that; he longed, even as he sat there in that dark old dusty room, looking at these two who were his kin, to rise and shout out, "The debt is not mine! I owe no debt except to myself!"

But he knew he could not shout it. Meng could have said it for his cause's sake, and Sheng could have laughed and seemed to accept the bondage, and then he would forget it, and live as he liked in spite of it. But Yuan was differently shaped. He could not refuse this bondage which in ignorant love his father had set upon him. Nor could he blame his father still, nor when he pondered yet more upon it, think of any other way his father could have done.

He stared down on a square of sunlight falling through the open door, and in the silence he heard a twittering quarrel among the little wild birds in the bamboos in the court. At last he said somberly, "I am really your investment, then, my uncle. You have used me as a means to make your sons and your old age safe."

The old man heard this and considered it and poured out a little tea into a bowl and sipped it slowly and then he wiped his dried old hand about his mouth and said again, "It is what every generation does and must do. So will you when your own sons come."

"No, I will not," said Yuan quickly. Never had he seen in his mind a son of his until this moment. But now these words of the old man seemed to call the future into life. Yes, one day he would have sons. There would be a woman for him and they would have sons. But those sons—they should be free—free of any shaping from him who was their father! They should not be made for soldiers, nor shaped for any destiny, nor bound to any family cause.

And suddenly he hated all his kind, his uncles and his cousins, —yes, and even his own father, for at this moment the Tiger came in, weary from his rounds among his men and eager to sit down before his bowl and look at Yuan awhile and hear him talk of anything. But Yuan could not bear it. . . . He rose quickly and without a word he went away to be alone.

Now in his own old room upon his bed Yuan lay weeping and shivering and weeping as he used to do when he was a lad, but not long, because the old Tiger stayed behind him only long enough to discover from the other two what had gone amiss, and he came after Yuan and pushed the door open and came as fast as his two old feet would carry him to Yuan's bed. But Yuan would not turn to his father. He lay with his face buried in his arms and the old Tiger sat beside him and smoothed his shoulder with his hand and patted it and poured forth eager promises and broken pleadings, and he said, "See, my son, you are not to do anything but what you like. I am no old man yet. I have been too idle. I will gather up my men once more and sally forth again to a battle and make the region mine again and have the taxes that robber lord has taken from me. I downed him once and I can again, and you shall have everything. You shall stay here with me and have everything. Yes, and wed whom you like. I was wrong before. I am not so old-fashioned now, Yuan—I know how young men do now. . . ."

Now the old Tiger had truly said the thing most needed to strengthen Yuan out of his weeping and his pity for himself. He turned over and he cried violently, "I will not let you battle any more, father, and I—"

And Yuan was about to cry out, "I will not wed." He had so long said it to his father that the words ran off his tongue of their own accord. But in the midst of all his misery he stopped. A sudden question came to him. Did he indeed not wish to wed? But not an hour ago he had cried out that his sons should be free.

Of course one day he would wed. He delayed his words upon his tongue and then more slowly he told his father, "Yes, some day I will wed the one I want to wed."

But the old Tiger was so pleased to see Yuan turn his face about and cease his weeping that he answered merrily, "You shall—you shall—only tell me who she is, my son, and let me send the go-between and do it, and I will tell your mother—after all, what cursed country maid is worthy of my son?"

Then Yuan, staring at his father while he spoke, began to see a thing in his own mind he had not known was there. "I do not need a go-between," he said slowly, but his mind was not on these words. He began to see a face shape in his mind—a woman's young face. "I can speak for myself. We speak for ourselves, these days, we young men—"

Now it was the Tiger's turn to stare, and he said severely, "Son, what woman is there decent who can be so spoken to? You have not forgotten my old warnings against such women, son? Have you chosen a good woman, son?"

But Yuan smiled. He forgot debts and wars and all the troubles of these days. Suddenly his divided mind joined upon one clear way he had not seen at all. There was one to whom he could tell everything, and know what he must do! These old ones never could understand him nor his needs, they could not see that he belonged no more among them. No, they could not see any more than aliens could. But he knew a woman of his own times, not rooted in the old as he was and forever divided because he had no power to pull the roots up and plant them in the new and necessary times wherein his life must be—he saw her face clearer than any face in his whole life, its clearness making every face grow dim, dimming even his father's face that was before his very eyes. She only could set him free from himself—only Mei-ling could set him free and tell him what he ought to do. She, who ordered everything she touched, could tell him what to do! His heart began to lift within him out of its own lightness. He

268

must go back to her. He sat up quickly and put his feet to the floor. Then he remembered his father had put a question to him and he answered out of his dazing new joy, "A good woman? Yes, I have chosen a good woman, my father!"

And he felt such an impatience as he had not known before in all his life. Here were no doubts and no withdrawals. He would go at once to her.

And yet for all his sudden new impatience Yuan found he must stay his month out with his father. For when Yuan thought how he might find excuse to go away, the Tiger grew so hurt and downcast that Yuan could not but be moved and draw back the hints he had put forth of some business calling him to the coastal city. And he knew it was not fitting that he should not stay to see his mother, who during these days had been in the country where her old home once was. For this woman, ever since she had gone to the earthen house for Yuan, had returned to her childhood love of country life, and now that her two daughters were wed she went often to the village where once she had been a maid, and she found a home there with her eldest brother who suffered her willingly enough because she paid out silver and made a little lavish show as wife of a lord of war, and her brother's wife liked the show because it set her up above the other village women. Though the trusty man sent a messenger to tell the mother Yuan was come, yet she had delayed a day or two.

And Yuan was the more willing and even anxious to see his mother and make plain to her that he would choose his own wife, and that he had chosen her already, and it only remained that he tell her so. Therefore he could and did live on the month, and this more easily because his uncle and the son went back soon to the old great house and Yuan was alone with his father.

But this joyful knowledge of Mei-ling made it easier for Yuan

269

even to be courteous to his uncle, and he thought secretly with deep relief, "She will help me to find a way to settle off this debt. I will say nothing angry now—not until I have told her." And so thinking he could say to his uncle steadily at parting, "Be sure I shall not forget the debt. But lend us no more moneys, uncle, for now my first care when this month is past, will be to find a good place for myself. As for your sons, I will do what I can for them."

And the Tiger hearing it said stoutly, "Be sure, brother, that all will come back to you, for what I cannot do by war my son will do by government, for doubtless he will find a good official place, with all his knowledge."

"Yes, doubtless, if he tries," returned the merchant. But as he went he said to his son, "Put in Yuan's hand the paper you have written." And the son pulled a folded paper from his sleeve and handed it to Yuan and said in his little wordy way, "It is only the full counting out, my cousin, of those sums. We thought, my father and I, that you would want to know it all clearly."

Even then Yuan could not be angry with these two little men. He took the paper gravely, smiling inwardly, and with every outward courtesy he sent them on their way.

Yes, nothing was so confused now as it had been for Yuan. He could be courteous to these two, and when they were gone he could be very patient with his father in the evenings when the old man told long garrulous tales of his wars and victories. For his son the Tiger lived his life over, and made much of all his battles and while he talked he drew down his old brows and pulled at his ragged whiskers and his eyes grew bright, and after all to him it seemed as he talked to his son that he had lived a very glorious life. But Yuan, sitting in calmness, half smiling when he heard the old Tiger's shouts and saw his drawn brows and the thrust he made to show how he had stabbed the Leopard, only wondered how he ever could have feared his father.

Yet in the end the days passed not too slowly. For the thought of Mei-ling had come so suddenly to Yuan that he needed to live with only the thought for a while, and sometimes he was glad for the delay, even, and for the hours when he could sit and seem to listen to his father's talk. Secretly he wondered to himself that he had been so dull to his own heart that he had not known before, even on the day of Ai-lan's wedding, when, while he watched the marriage procession and had seen Ai-lan's beauty, he had seen Mei-ling and thought her still more beautiful. That moment he should have known. And he should have known a score of times thereafter, when he had seen her here and there about the house, her hands ordering all, her voice directing the helping servants. But he had not known, not until he lay weeping and in loneliness.

Across such dreaming broke again and again the Tiger's happy old voice, and Yuan could bear to sit and listen as he never could have done, had he not this new growing love inside himself. He listened in a dream to all his father said, not discerning at all between wars past or wars his father planned for the future, and his father prattled on, "I still do have a little revenue from that son my elder brother gave me. But he is no lord of war, no real lord. I dare not trust him much, he is so idle in his love of laughter—a born clown and he will die a clown, I swear. He says he is my lieutenant, but he sends me very little, and I have not been there now these six years. I must go in the spring—aye, I must make my rounds of battle in the spring. That nephew of mine, well I know he will turn straight over to any coming enemy, even against me he will turn—"

And Yuan, half listening, cared nothing for this cousin of his whom he scarcely could remember except his elder aunt liked to say, "My son who is a general in the north."

Yes, it was pleasant to sit and answer his father a little now and then, and think of the maid he knew he loved. And many comforts came to him in these thoughts. He told himself he would not be ashamed to have her see these courts, for she would understand his shames. They both were of a kind, this was their country, whatever its shames were. He could even say to her, "My father is an old foolish war lord, so full of tales he does not know which is false and which is true. He sees himself a mighty man he never was." Yes, he could say such things as those to her, and know she would comprehend. And when he thought of this simplicity she had he felt the false shames fall away from him. Oh, let him go to her, and be himself again, no more divided, but as he was those few days on the land, in that earthen home of his grandfather's, when he had been alone and free! With her he could be alone and free and once more simple.

At last he could think of nothing else than pouring out his need before her. So steadily did he know that she would help him, that when his mother came at last, he could greet her as he should and look upon her without suffering to think she was his mother and yet one to whom he had nothing to say. For she was now, for all her withered rosy healthy looks, a very plain old country woman. She looked up at him, leaning on a peeled staff she used these days to walk with, and her old eyes asked, wondering, "What is this I have for a son?"

And Yuan, tall and different in the foreign clothes he wore, looked down upon the woman in her old-fashioned coat and skirt of black cotton stuff and asked himself, "Was I indeed shaped in this old woman's body? I feel no kinship in our flesh."

But he did not suffer or now feel ashamed. To that white woman, had he loved her, he would have said with great shame, "This is my mother." But he could say to Mei-ling, "This is my mother," and she, knowing that a thousand men like him had sprung from such mothers, would not think it strange, for nothing was strange to her. To her it would be enough that it was so. . . . Even to Ai-lan he might feel shame, but not to Mei-ling. He could uncover all his heart to her and never be ashamed. This knowledge made him tranquil therefore, even in his impatience, and later on a certain day he told his mother plainly, "I am betrothed, or good as betrothed. I have chosen the maid."

And the old woman answered mildly, "Your father told me so. Well, I had talked of a maid or two I knew, but your father has always let you do what you wished. His son you have ever been, and scarcely mine, and he with the hottest temper ever was so I cannot go against him. Aye, that learned one, she could escape it and go out, but I have stayed and let him use me for his anger. But I hope she is a decent maid and can cut a coat and turn a fish as it should be turned, and I hope I may see her sometimes, though I know very well these new times are anyhow, and the young do what they will, and daughters-in-law do not even come to see their husband's mothers as they ought to do."

But Yuan thought she seemed glad she need not bestir herself beyond this and she sat and stared at nothing in a way she had and moved her eyes and jaws a little and forgot him, and slept gently, or seemed to do so. They were not of the same world, these two, and that he was her son was meaningless to him. In truth, everything was meaningless to him now, except that he come again into the presence of that one.

When his farewells had been said to his parents, and he forced himself to say them courteously and as though he grieved to leave them, he went again on the train south, and now it was strange how little he saw the travellers on that train. Whether they behaved fittingly or not was all one to him. For he could think of nothing but Mei-ling. He thought of all he knew of her. He remembered that she had a narrow hand, very strong, but narrow across the palm, the fingers very delicate, and then he wondered to think that hand could be swift and stern to cut away an evil growth in human flesh. Her whole body had this slender strength, the strength of good bones well knitted under the fine pale skin. He remembered again and again how able she was in everything and how the servants looked to her, and how Ai-lan had cried out that Mei-ling must say if a coat hung well about the edge, and only Mei-ling could do for the lady what she liked to have done. And Yuan said, comforting himself, "At twenty she is as able as many a woman ten years older."

For the maid had this double charm for Yuan when he remembered her. She had sedateness and gravity as the older women had, whom he looked to, his lady mother, his aunt, and all those reared in the old ways for rearing maids. And yet she had this new thing, too, that she was not shy and silent before men. She could speak openly and plainly anywhere, and be as easy, in her different way, as Ai-lan was. Thus in the turmoil of the train and while the fields and towns went past, Yuan saw nothing. He only sat and shaped his dreams of Mei-ling, and in his mind he gathered every least word and look of hers and made the precious picture whole. When he remembered all he could, he let his mind leap to the moment when he would see her and how he would speak and what he would tell her of his love. Perfectly as though the hour were there he could see her grave good look, watching him while he spoke. And afterwards—oh, he must remember still how young she was, and that she was no bold, ready maid, but gentle and very reticent. But still he might take that narrow hand of hers, that cool kind narrow hand. . . .

Yet who can shape an hour to his wish, or what lover knows how the hour will find even himself? For Yuan's tongue, which shaped the words so easily upon the train, could shape nothing when the hour was come. The house was quiet when he came into its hallway, and only a servant stood there. The stillness struck him like a chill.

"Where is she?" he cried to the servant, and then remembering, he said more quietly, "Where is the lady, my mother?"

The servant replied, "They are gone to the foundlings home to see to a babe newly left there who is ill. They may be late, they said."

So then Yuan could only cool his heart and wait. He waited and tried to turn his thoughts here or there, but his mind was not his own—it would turn back of its own will to the one great hope it had. Night came and still the two did not come, and when the servant called the evening meal, Yuan must go to the dining room and eat there alone, and the food was dry and tasteless on his tongue. Almost he hated the little child who so delayed the hour he had longed for all these weeks.

Then even as he was about to rise because he could not eat, the door opened and the lady came in, very weary and spent and downcast in her look, and Mei-ling with her, silent and sad as Yuan had never seen her. She looked at Yuan as though she did not see him and she cried out to him in a low voice, as though Yuan had not been away at all, "The little baby died. We did all we could, but she died!"

The lady sighed and sat down and said, grieving too, "You are back, my son? . . . I never saw a lovelier little newborn child, Yuan—left three days since on the threshold—not poor, either, for its little coat was silk. At first we thought it sound, but this morning there were convulsions, and it was that old ancient woe that curses newborn babes, and takes them before the tenth day is gone. I have seen the fairest, soundest children seized by it, as by an evil wind, and nothing can prevail against it."

To this the maid sat listening, and she could not eat. Her narrow hands were clenched upon the table and she cried angrily, "I know what it is. It need not be!"

But Yuan, looking at her angry face, more moved than he had ever seen it, perceived her eyes were full of tears. That anger and those tears were ice upon his hot heart. For he saw they closed the maid's mind against him. Yes, he thought of her and her only, but at this moment she did not dream of him; although he had been weeks away, she did not think of him. He sat and listened, therefore, and answered quietly questions that the lady mother put to him of his father's house. But he could not but see

275

that Mei-ling did not even hear the questions or how he answered them. She sat there strangely idle, her hands quiet in her lap, and though she looked from face to face, she said nothing at all. Only more than once her eyes were full of tears. And because he saw her mind was very far from him, on that night Yuan could not speak.

Yet how could he rest until he had spoken? All night he dreamed brokenly, strange dreams of love, but never love come clear.

In the morning he woke exhausted by his dreams. It was a grey day, too, a day when summer passes certainly into autumn. When Yuan rose and looked out of the window he saw nothing but greyness everywhere, a still smooth grey sky curved above the flat grey city and upon the grey streets the people moving sluggishly, small and grey upon the earth. His ardor seeped from him under this lifelessness, and Yuan wondered at himself that ever he could have dreamed of Mei-ling.

In such a mood he sat himself down to eat his breakfast, and while he ate listlessly, for the very food on this day seemed to him saltless and without flavor, the lady came in, too. She had not eaten or exchanged much more than morning greetings with Yuan before she saw something was wrong with him. So she began to press him gently with her questions. And he, feeling it not possible to speak of his new love, told her instead of how his father had borrowed so much silver of his uncle, and she was very taken back by this and cried out, "Why did he not tell me he was so hard pressed for money? I could have used less. I am glad I have used my own silver for Mei-ling. Yes, I had a sort of pride to do that, and my father left me enough, since he had no son, before he died, and he put his moneys in a good sound foreign bank where they have lain safely all these years. He loved me very well, and sold many of his inherited lands even, and turned them into silver for me. If I had known, I might have—"

But Yuan said dully, "And why should you have done it? No, I will seek out a place where what I have learned will serve me, and I will save my wage, as much as I can, and return it to my uncle."

Then it came to him that if he did this, how could he have enough to wed on and set up his house and do all those things for which a young man hopes? In the old days the sons lived with the father, and son's wife and son's children ate from the common pot. But Yuan in his day could not bear to do this. When he thought of the courts where the Tiger lived and of that old mother who must be Mei-ling's mother-in-law, he swore he would not live there with Mei-ling. They would have their own home somewhere, a home such as Yuan had learned to love, pictures on the walls and chairs easy to sit upon and cleanliness everywhere—and only they two in it to make it what they liked. And thinking of all this he fell into such longing before the lady's very eyes that she said very kindly, "You still have not told me everything."

Then suddenly Yuan's heart burst from him and he cried, his face all red and his eyes so hot he could feel them burning underneath their lids, "I have more to tell—I do have more to tell! I have somehow learned to love her and if I do not have her I shall die."

"Her?" asked the lady, wondering. "What her?" And she cast about in her mind. But Yuan cried, "And who but Mei-ling?"

Then the lady was full of astonishment, for she had not dreamed of such a thing, since Mei-ling was to her only a child yet, the child she had lifted up from the street one cold day and taken into her own home. Now she looked at Yuan and was silent for a while and she said thoughtfully, "She is yet young and full of her plans." And then she said again, "Her parents are unknown. I do not know how it will be with your father if he knows she was a foundling."

But Yuan cried in impatience now, "My father can say nothing on this thing. In this day I will not be bound by their old ways. I will choose for myself."

The lady bore this mildly, being by now very well used to all such talk, since Ai-lan had cried it often, and she knew from talk with other parents that all young men and women said the same thing and their elders must bear it as they could. So she only asked, "And have you spoken to her?"

Then Yuan forgot his boldness straightway and he said, shy as any old-fashioned lover, "No, and I do not know how to begin." And after a little thought he said, "It always seems as though her thoughts are set on some busy matter of her own. Other maids begin somehow with eyes or even touch of hands, or so I have heard, but she never does."

"No," the lady answered proudly, "Mei-ling never does."

Now even as Yuan sat in his dejection this came to him. He would ask the lady to speak for him. And after all, his mind said swiftly to itself, it was really better so. Mei-ling would listen to the lady whom she so loved and honored and it would be something for him.

So it seemed better to him suddenly not to say the words himself in spite of the new times. This would be a sort of new and yet an old way, and the maid, being so young yet, might like it more, too. All this Yuan thought, and he said to the lady very eagerly, "Will you speak for me, my mother? It is true she is very young. It may be if I speak it would frighten her—"

At this the lady smiled a little and she gazed with some tenderness at Yuan and answered, "If she wants to marry you, my son, let it be so, if your father will let it be. But I will not compel her. That one thing I will never do—compel a maid to any man. It is the only great new good these times have brought to women —that they need not be compelled to marriage."

"No, no—" cried Yuan.

But he did not dream the maid would need compelling, because it is natural for all maids to wed.

Now while they talked and finished the meal as they did, Mei-ling came in, very fresh and clean to see in her robe of a dark blue silk she wore to school, and her short straight black hair brushed behind her ears and no jewels in her ears or on her hands, such as Ai-lan must always wear or feel herself unclothed. Her look was quiet, the eyes cool and steady, and her mouth curved and not very red in hue, as Ai-lan's always was, and her cheeks pale and smooth. Yet though Mei-ling was never ruddy, she had always a clear gold skin which was full of health, it was so fine and smooth. Now she gave greeting courteously, and Yuan saw the night's sleep had taken the yesterday's distress away from her, so that she was tranquil again and ready for this day.

Even as he watched her seat herself and take up her bowl to eat, the lady began to speak out, a small half smile upon her lips and in her eyes. Suddenly if Yuan could have stopped her or chosen another hour, he would have done so. He wished any how to put the moment off, and a shyness rushed upon him and he dropped his eyes and sat all hot with misery. But the lady said, and the secret smile was shining in her eyes now for she saw how Yuan was, "Child, here is a question I have to put to you. This young man, this Yuan, for all he is a mighty modern and will choose his wife, turns weak at the last moment and goes back to old ways and asks a go-between after all. And I am the go-between, and you are the maid, and will you have him?"

As baldly as this the lady put it, in a very dry bald voice, and Yuan almost hated her because it seemed to him it could not have been worse done, and enough to frighten any maid.

And Mei-ling was frightened. She set her bowl down carefully and put her chopsticks down and stared at the lady in a panic. Then in a very small low voice she whispered, *"Must* I do it?"

279

"No, child," the lady answered and now she was grave. "You need not if you do not wish it."

"Then I will not," the maid answered joyfully, her face all lit with her relief. And then she said again, "There have been others of my schoolmates who have to wed, mother, and they weep and weep because they must leave school to wed. And so I was frightened. Ah, I thank you, mother," and this young woman Mei-ling, who was always so quiet and contained, rose quickly from her seat and went and fell before the lady in the old obeisance of gratitude and bowed herself down. But the lady lifted her up and held her by an arm about her.

Then the lady's eyes fell on Yuan, and there he sat, his hot blood all flying from his face and leaving him pale, his very lips pale that he bit between his teeth to hold them still, for he would not weep. And the lady pitied him, and she said kindly, looking at the girl, "Still, you like our Yuan, Mei-ling?"

And the girl answered quickly, "Oh, yes, he is my brother. I like him, but not to wed. I do not want to wed, mother. I want to finish school and be a doctor. I want to learn and learn. Every woman weds. I do not want only to wed and take care of a house and children. I have set my heart to be a doctor!"

Now when Mei-ling said these words, the lady looked at Yuan in a sort of triumph. And Yuan looking back at the two women, felt them leagued against him, women leagued against a man, and he could not bear it. There was something good about the old ways, after all, for it was the natural right thing that women should be wed and bear children and Mei-ling ought to want to marry, and there was some perversion in her that she would not. He thought to himself, angry in his manhood against these women, "It is a strange thing if women are like this nowadays! Whoever heard of a girl not marrying when the time comes? A very strange thing if young women are not to wed—a sorry thing for the nation and the next generation!" He thought, after all, how foolish even wisest women are, and he looked and met Meiiing's calm eyes and for once he thought them hard and cold to be so calm and sure, and he looked at her angrily. But the lady answered for her very certainly, "She shall not marry until she wishes. She shall use her own life as seems best to her, and you must bear it, Yuan."

And the two women looked at him, even hostile in their new freedom, the younger held within the circle of the elder's arm. . . . Yes, he must bear it!

Later in that gloomy day Yuan left his room where he had thrown himself upon the bed, and he went wandering through the streets, his mind all confusion once again. He had even wept and wept in his distress, and his heart sat in his side aching with an actual pain, as though it had been too hot and now was too cold and could not beat as it should.

What should he do now? Yuan asked himself in dreariness. Here and there about the streets he wandered, pushed and pushing, and seeing no one. . . . Well, and if joy was gone, his duty still remained. There was the debt he owed. At least alone he could fulfill his debt. He had his old father left to think of and he cast about to think what he could do, and where find a place to work and live, and save his wage to pay his debt. He would do his duty, he said to himself, and felt himself most hardly used.

So the day wore on and he wandered everywhere throughout that whole city, and it grew hateful to him. He hated all its foreignness, the foreign faces on the streets, the foreign garments even his own kind wore, the very garb upon his own body. It seemed to him at this one hour at least that old ways were better. He cried furiously to his cold, stopped heart, "It is these foreign ways that set our women to all this stubbornness and talk of freedom, so that they set nature aside and live like nuns or courtesans!" And he remembered with especial hatred that landlady's daughter and her lewdness and Mary, whose lips had been too ready, and he blamed even them. At last he looked at every foreign female that he passed with such hatred that he could not bear them and he muttered, "I will get out of this city somehow. I will go away where I shall see nothing foreign and nothing new and live and find my life there in my own country. I wish I had not gone abroad! I wish I had never left the earthen house!"

And suddenly he bethought himself of that old farmer whom he once knew, who had taught him how to wield a hoe. He would go there and see that man and feel his own kind again, not tainted with these foreigners and all their ways.

At once he struck aside and took a public vehicle to hasten on his way, and when the vehicle was gone as far as it would, he walked on. Very far he walked that day searching for the land he once had planted and for the farmer and his home. But he could not find it until nearly evening, for the streets were changed and built up and full of people. When he reached at last the place he knew and recognized, there was no land to plant. There on the earth which only a few years ago had borne so fertilely, where the farmer had been proud to say his family had lived for a hundred years, now stood a factory for weaving silk. It was a great new thing, large as a village used to be, and the bricks new and red and many windows shone upon its roofs, and from its chimneys the black smoke gushed. Even as Yuan stood and looked at it, a shrieking whistle blew, the iron gates sprang open, and out of their vastness came a slow thick stream of men and women and little children, spent with their day's labor and with the knowledge of tomorrow's day to come and many days and many days which they must live like this one. Their clothes were drenched with sweat, and about them hung the vile stench of the dead worms in the cocoons from which the silk was wound.

Yuan stood looking at these faces, thinking half fantastically that one of them must be the farmer's face, that he must be swallowed, even as his land had been, by this new monster. But no, he was not there. These were pale city folk, who crept out of their hovels in the morning and returned to them at night. The farmer had gone elsewhere. He and his old wife and their old buffalo had gone to other lands. Of course they had, Yuan told himself. Somewhere they lived their own life, stoutly as they ever had. And thinking of them he smiled a little, and for the moment forgetting his own pain, he went thoughtfully to his home. So would he also somehow find his own life.

IV

Two things came on the next day to shape Yuan's life. The lady said to him very early in the morning, "My son, it is not fitting somehow that you live in this house for the time. Think yourself how hard it is for Mei-ling now to see you day after day knowing what is in your heart towards her."

To this Yuan answered with anger left from his angers of the day before, "I do know very well, for so I feel also. I feel I want to be where I must not see her every day, too, and where I need not remember every time I see her or hear her voice that she will not have me."

These words Yuan started bravely enough and in anger, but before he came to the end his voice trembled and however he tried to hold his anger and say he wanted to be where he could not see Mei-ling, yet when he thought of it he knew miserably that the truth was he had rather be where he could see her and hear her voice and this in spite of anything. But this morning the lady was her old mild self and now that she needed not to defend Mei-ling or the cause of women against men she could be gentle and comprehending, and she heard very well the tremble in Yuan's voice and marked how he broke off speaking and fell very quickly to his bowl of food, for it was at table they met now, only Mei-ling did not come. So she said to comfort him, "This is your first love, son, and it comes hardly. I know what your nature is, and it is very much like your father's and they all tell me he was like his mother who was a grave quiet soul, always holding too hard to those she loved. Yes, and Ai-lan is like your grandfather, and your uncle tells me she has his merry eye. . . . Well, son, you are too young to hold so hard on anything. Go away and find a place you like and a work of some sort, and set yourself to your debt to your second uncle, and know young men and women and after a year or two—" She paused here and looked at Yuan, and Yuan waited, looking back. "After a year or two perhaps Mei-ling will be changed. Who can tell?"

But Yuan would not be hopeful. He said doggedly, "No, she is not a changing sort, mother, and I can see she cannot bear me. It came to me all in a moment that she was the one I wanted. I do not want the foreign sort of maid—I do not like them. But she is right for me. She is the kind I like— Somehow she is new and old, too—"

At this Yuan stopped again suddenly and filled his mouth with his food, and then could not swallow it because his throat was stiff with tears he was ashamed to shed, because it seemed a childish thing to weep for love, and he longed to think he did not care.

The lady knew this perfectly and she let him be awhile and at last she said peaceably, "Well, let it be now, and we will wait. You are young enough to wait, and it is true you have your debt. It is a necessity that you remember you have a son's duty to do, and duty is duty in spite of all."

The lady said this with a purpose to stir Yuan out of his dejection and it did, for he swallowed hard a time or two and burst out, although it was only what he had said yesterday himself, but today he could not bear it, "Yes, that is what they always say, but I swear I am tired of it. I did my duty always to my father and how did he reward me? He would have tied me to an unlettered country wife and let me be tied forever and never know what he did to me. Now he has tied me again to my uncle, and I'll do what I did before—I'll go and join Meng and throw my life in against what old people call duty—I'll do it again—it is

285

no excuse that he did it innocently. It is wicked to be so innocent and injure me as he has—"

Now Yuan knew he spoke unreasonably and that if the Tiger had tried to force him, still he had freed him from the prison with all the money he could find to do it. He kept his anger high therefore and ready to meet the lady's reminder of this. But instead of her expected words she said tranquilly, "It would be a very good thing, I think, for you to go and live with Meng in the new capital." And in his surprise at this lack of argument from her Yuan had no words and so the matter lay and they spoke no more.

On the same day by chance a letter came again from Meng to Yuan, and when Yuan opened it he found first a rebuke from his cousin that no answering word had come and Meng said impatiently, "With difficulty I have held this position waiting for you, for in these days to every such chance a hundred men are to be found. Come quickly and this very day, for on the third day from now the great school opens and there is no time for writing back and forth like this." And then Meng ended ardently, "It is not every man who has this opportunity to work in the new capital. There are thousands here waiting and hoping for work these days. The whole city is being made new—everything is being made which any great city has. The old winding streets are torn away and everything is to be made new. Come and do your share!"

Yuan, reading these bold words, felt his heart leap and he threw the letter down upon his table and cried aloud, "I will, then!" At that instant he began to put together his books and clothing and all his notes and writings and so he made ready for this next part of his life.

At noon he told the lady of Meng's letter and he said, "It is the best way for me to go, since all is as it must be." And the lady agreed mildly that it was so, and again they talked no more, only the lady was her usual self, kindly and a little remote from what was before her.

But that night when Yuan came to take his evening meal with her as usual she talked of many common things, of how Ai-lan would be home that day fortnight, for she was gone with her husband to play a month away in the old northern capital, and half the month was gone, and she told of a cough that had come into her foundling home and spread from child to child until today eight had it. Then she said calmly, "Mei-ling has been there all day, trying a sort of medicine the foreigners use against this cough by thrusting a liquid drug through a needle into the blood. But I told her you might go away very soon, and I told her to come home tonight that we might be all together this one more evening."

Now underneath all his other thoughts and plans through this whole day Yuan had wondered many times if he would see Mei-ling again, and sometimes he hoped he would not, and yet when he felt so he thought again with a great rush of longing that he would like once more to see her when she did not know it, perhaps, and let his eyes cling to how she looked and moved, even though he did not hear her voice. But he could not ask to see her. If it happened, let it be so, but if she stayed so it could not happen, he must bear it.

For his thwarted love worked a sort of ferment in him. In his room he halted a score of times during that day and he threw himself sometimes on his bed and fell to melancholy thinking of how Mei-ling would not have him and he even wept, since he was alone, or sometimes he wandered to the window and leaned against it, staring out across the city, as careless of him as a merry woman and glittering in a shimmer of hot sunshine, and then he was angry in his heart that he loved and was not loved. He felt himself most bitterly used, until at one such time there came to him a thing he had forgotten, which was that twice a woman had loved him and he had given no love in return. When he thought of this he had a great fear and he cried in his heart, "Is it that she can never love me as I never did love them? Does she hate my flesh as I hated theirs, so that she cannot help it?" But he found this fear too great to be borne and he bethought himself very quickly, "It is not the same—they never loved me truly—not as I love her. No one has ever loved as I do." And again he thought proudly, "I love her most purely and highly. I have not thought of touching even her hand—well, I have not thought of it but a very little, and then only if she should love me—" And it seemed to him as if she must—she must—comprehend how great and pure was the love he gave her and so he ought to see her once more and let her see how steadfast he was even though she would not have him.

Yet now when he heard the lady say these words he felt his blood fly to his face, and for an instant he hoped in a fever that she would not come and now he did not want to see her at all before he went away.

But before he could devise an escape, Mei-ling came in quietly and usually. He could not look at her fully at first. He rose until she sat down and he saw the dark green silk of her robe and then he saw her lovely narrow hands take up the ivory chopsticks, which were the same hue as her flesh. He could say nothing, and the lady saw it, and so she said very usually to Mei-ling, "Did you finish all the work?"

And Mei-ling answered in the same way, "Yes, the last child. But I think with some I am too late. They are already coughing, but at least it will help it." Then she laughed a little, very softly, and said, "You know the six-year-old they call Little Goose? She cried out when she saw me come with the needle and wept loudly and said, 'Oh, little mother, let me cough—I'd so much rather cough—hear me, I cough already!' And then she coughed a loud false cough."

They laughed then, and Yuan a little, too, at the child, and in the laughter he found himself looking at Mei-ling without knowing it. And to his shame he could not leave off looking at her once he saw her. No, his eyes clung to hers, though he was speechless, and he drew his breath in hard, imploring her with his eyes. Then though he saw her pale clear cheeks grow red, yet she met his gaze very fully and clearly and she said breathlessly and quickly and as he had never heard her speak before, and as though he had asked a question of her, though he did not know himself what question it was, "But at least I will write to you, Yuan, and you may write to me." And then as though not able to bear his look any more she turned very shy and looked at the lady, her face still burning, but her head held high and brave and she asked, "Are you willing, my mother?"

To which the lady answered, making her voice quiet and as though she spoke of any common thing, "And why not, child? It is only letters between brother and sister, and even if it were not, what of it in these days?"

"Yes," said the maid happily, and she turned a shining look on Yuan. And Yuan smiled at her look for look, and his heart, which had been so confined all day in sorrow, found a sudden door of escape thrown open to it. He thought, "I can tell her everything!" And it was ecstasy, since not in his whole life had there been one to whom he could tell everything, and he loved her still more than he had before.

That night on the train he thought to himself, "I can do without love all my life, I think, if I can have her for a friend to whom to tell everything." He lay in the narrow berth and felt himself full of high pure thoughts and shriven by his love and filled with stoutest courage, as swept aloft by these few words of hers as he had been cast down before.

In the early morning the train ran swiftly through a cluster of low hills green in the new sunlight and then pounded for a mile or two at the foot of a vast old echoing city wall, and stopped suddenly beside a great new building shaped of grey cement and made in a foreign fashion. Yuan at a window saw very clearly against this greyness a man whom he knew instantly to be Meng. There he stood, the sun shining full upon his sword, upon a pistol thrust in his belt, upon his brass buttons, upon his white gloves, upon his lean high-cheeked face. Behind was a guard of soldiers drawn up exactly, and each man's hand was on the holster of his pistol.

Now until this moment Yuan had been no more than a common passenger, but when he came down out of the train and when it was seen he was greeted by so bold an officer, at once the crowd gave way for him and common ragged fellows who had been begging other passengers to let them hoist their bags and baskets on their shoulders now forsook them and ran to Yuan and besought him instead. But Meng, seeing them clamoring, shouted out in a great voice, "Begone, you dogs!" and turning to his own men he commanded them as sharply, "See to my cousin's goods!" And then without a word more to them he took Yuan's hand and led him through the crowd saying in his old impatient way, "I thought you would never come. Why did you not answer my letter? Never mind, you are here! I have been very busy or I should have come to meet you at your ship— Yuan, you come back at a fortunate time, a time of great need of men like you. Everywhere the country is in need of us. The people are as ignorant as sheep—"

At this instant he paused before a petty official and cried out, "When my soldiers bring my cousin's bags, you are to let them pass!"

At this the official, who was a humble anxious man and new in his place, said, "Sir, we are commanded to open all bags for opium or for arms or for anti-revolutionary books."

Then Meng grew furious and he shouted very terribly and made his eyes wide and drew down his black brows, "Do you know who I am? My general is the highest in the party, and I am his first captain and this is my cousin! Am I to be insulted by these petty rules made for common passengers?" And as he spoke he laid his white gloved hand upon his pistol, so that the little official said quickly, "Sir, forgive me! I did not indeed perceive who you were," and at that moment when the soldiers came, he marked his mark upon Yuan's box and bag, and let them go free, and all the crowd parted patiently to let them pass, staring open-mouthed. The very beggars were silent and shrank away from Meng and waited to beg until he was passed.

Thus striding through the crowd Meng led Yuan to a motor car, and a soldier leaped to open it, and Meng bade Yuan mount and then he followed and instantly the door was shut and the soldiers leaped upon the sides and the car rushed at great speed away.

Now since it was early morning, there was a great crowd in the street. Many farmers had come in with their produce of vege-tables in baskets upon their poles slung across their shoulders, and there were caravans of asses carrying great bags of rice crossed upon their swaying backs, and there were wheelbarrows loaded full of water from the river near by to take into the city and sell to folk, and there were men and women going out to work, and men going to teahouses for their early meal and every sort of person on his business. But the soldier who drove the car was very able to do it, and fearless, and he sounded his horn unceas-ingly with a great noise, and blew his way by force among the crowd, so that people ran to either side of the street as though a mighty wind divided them, and they jerked their asses hither and thither that they might save the beasts, and women clutched their children aside, so that Yuan was afraid, and he looked at Meng to see if he would not speak to go more slowly among the frightened common people.

But Meng was used to this swiftness. He sat erect and stared ahead and pointed out to Yuan with a sort of fierce exultation all there was to see.

"You see this road, Yuan? A bare year ago it was scarcely four feet wide and a car could not pass through it. Rickshas, sedan chairs, and that was all! Even in the best wide streets the only other mode was a small carriage pulled by a single horse. Now see this road!"

Yuan answered, "I do see it," and he stared out between the soldiers' bodies and he saw the wide hard street, and on either side were ruins of the houses and the shops which were torn down to make way for it. Yet along the edge of these ruins were already being built new shops and new houses from the ruins, frail buildings raised too quickly, but brave in their foreign shapes, and in bright paint and big glass windows.

But across this wide new street there fell suddenly a shadow, and Yuan saw it was the high old city wall, and here was the gate, and looking he saw at the foot of the wall, and especially in a sheltered curve it made, a cluster of small huts made of mats. In them lived the very poor, and now in this morning they bestirred themselves, and the women lit small fires underneath cauldrons set on four bricks, and picked over bits of cabbage they had found on refuse heaps and made ready a meal. Children ran out naked and unwashed and men came forth, still weary, to pull at rickshas or to drag great loads.

When Meng saw where Yuan's eyes were he said with irritation, "Next year they are not to be allowed, these huts. It is a shame to us all to have folk like that about. It is necessary that the great of foreign parts should come to our new capital—even princes come here—and such sights are shameful."

Now Yuan very well saw this, and he felt with Meng that these huts ought not to be there, and it was true these men and women were very low to see, and something should be done to put them out of sight. He pondered on this for a while and at last he said, "I suppose they could be put to work," and Meng said gustily, "Of course they can be put to work, and sent home to their fields, and so they shall be—"

And then Meng's look changed as though at some old remembered grievance and he cried very passionately, "Oh, it is these people who hold back our country! I wish we could sweep the country clean and build it only of the young! I want to tear this whole city down—this old foolish wall which is no use now when we make war with cannon instead of arrows! What wall can guard against an airplane dropping bombs? Away with it, and let us use the bricks to make factories and schools and places for the young to work and learn! But these people, they understand nothing—they will not let the wall be torn away—they threaten—"

Now Yuan, hearing Meng so speak, asked, "But I thought you used to grieve for the poor, Meng? It seems to me I remember you used to be angry when the poor were oppressed and you were always angry when a man was struck by a foreigner or by an official of the police."

"So I am still," said Meng quickly, turning to look at Yuan, so that Yuan saw how black and burning was his gaze. "If I saw a foreigner lay his hand even on the poorest beggar here I would be as angry as I ever was and more, because I fear no foreigner and I would draw my weapon on him. But I know more than I used to know. I know that the chief hindrance against all we do is these very poor for whom we do it. There are too many— Who can teach them anything? There is no hope for them. So I say, let famine take them and flood and war. Let us keep only their children and shape them in the ways of revolution."

So Meng spoke in his loud, lordly way, and to Yuan, listening and considering in his slower fashion, there was truth in what he said. He remembered suddenly that foreign priest who stood before the curious crowd and showed them those vile sights. Yes, even here in this new great city, upon this wide street, among the brave new shops and houses, Yuan saw some of the things the priest showed—a beggar with his eyes sightless and eaten by disease, these hovels, running filthy cesspools at their doors so that there was a stench already upon the freshness of the morning air. Then his angry shame against that foreign priest rose up in Yuan again, an anger stabbed through with pain, too, and he cried in his heart passionately as Meng had cried aloud, "It is true we must somehow sweep all this filth away!" and Yuan thought to himself resolutely that Meng was right. In this new day what use were all these hopeless, ignorant poor? He had been too soft always. Let him learn now to be hard as Meng was hard, and not waste himself on feeling for the useless poor.

So they came at last to Meng's quarters. Yuan, not being of the soldiers' company, could not live there, but Meng had hired a room in an inn near by, and he made apology somewhat when Yuan seemed doubtful because it was small and dark and not clean, and he said, "The city is so crowded in these days I cannot find a room easily at any price. Houses are not built quickly enough—the city grows beyond all power of keeping up with it." This Meng said in pride, and then he said proudly, "It is for the good cause, cousin,—we can bear anything for this time of building the new capital!" And Yuan took heart and said he could willingly, and that the room did very well.

The same night alone he sat before the small writing table beneath the one window in the room where he was now to live, and there he began his first letter to Mei-ling. He pondered long what to say at the beginning, and wondered if he should begin with all the old courteous words of greeting. But there was something reckless in him at the end of this day. The old houses lying in ruins, the little bold new shops, the wide unfinished street tearing its ruthless way through the old city, and all Meng's ardent, fearless, angry talk made him reckless, too. He thought a moment more and then began in the sharp foreign fashion, "Dear Mei-ling—" And when the words were set down black and bold, he sat and pondered on them before he wrote more and stared at them and filled them full of tenderness. "Dear"—what was that but beloved?—and Mei-ling—that was herself—she was there. . . . Then he took up his pen again and in quick sentences he told of what he had seen that day—a new city rising out of ruins, the city of the young.

This new city now caught Yuan up into its life. He had never been so busy or so happy, or so he thought. There was everywhere work to be done, and here was the pleasure in the work, that every hour of it was full of meaning for the future of many people. Among all those to whom Meng led him, Yuan felt this great same urgency of work and life. Everywhere in this city, which was the newly beating heart of the country, there were men, none much older than Yuan himself, who were writing plans and shaping ways of life not for themselves but for the people. There were those who planned the city, and the chief of these was a small fiery southerner, impatient in speech and quick in every step he took and in the movement of his small, beautiful, childlike hands. He, too, was a friend of Meng's, and when Meng said to him of Yuan, "This is my cousin," it was enough and he poured out to Yuan his plans of the city, and how he would tear down the old foolish city wall and use the ancient bricks, which after hundreds of years were still beautiful and whole as blocks of stone, and better than those which could be made nowadays. These bricks, he said, his little eyes kindling to points of light, should be made into new great halls for the new seat of government, worthy halls built in a new fashion. And one day he took Yuan to his offices, which were in an old sagging house and full of dust and flying cobwebs. He said, "It is not worth while to do anything to these old rooms. We let them go until the new ones are ready, and then these will be torn down and the land used for other new houses."

The dusty rooms were full of tables and at these tables were many young men drawing plans and measuring lines upon paper and some were coloring very brightly the roofs and cornices they drew, and even though the rooms were so old and ruined, they were full of life from these young men and their plans.

Then their chief called aloud and one came running, and he said in a lordly way, "Bring the plans for the new seat of government!" When these were brought he unrolled them before Yuan, and there were pictured very high noble buildings indeed, built of the old bricks, and set in large new lines, and from every roof flew the new flag of the revolution. There were the streets pictured forth, too, the trees green on either side, the people, very richly dressed, men and women together, walking by the sides of the streets, and in the streets there were no caravans of asses or wheelbarrows or rickshas, or any such humble vehicles as were to be seen now, but only great motor cars colored brightly in red and blue and green and filled with rich folk. Nor was there any beggar pictured.

Yuan, looking at the plans, could not but find them very beautiful. He said, entranced, "When can it be finished?"

The young chief answered certainly, "Within five years! Everything is moving quickly now."

Five years! It was nothing. Yuan in his dingy room again, musing, looked about upon the streets where as yet there was no such building as he had seen planned. No, and there were no trees and no rich people, and the poor still were brawling and struggling. But he thought to himself that five years were nothing. It was as good as done. That night he wrote to Mei-ling what was planned, and when he set it down and told in all detail what the picture of the new city was to be, more than ever it seemed as good as done, since all the plans were clearly made, so that the very colors of the roofs were planned in tiles of bright blue, and the trees planned and painted full of leaf, and he remembered there was even a fountain running before a statue of a certain hero in the revolution. Without knowing it he wrote thus to Mei-ling, as if all were finished, "There is a noble hall—there is a great gate—there are trees beside a wide street—"

It was the same in many other things also. Young men who were physicians learned in the foreign ways of cutting diseases out of people's bodies and who scorned the old doctoring of their fathers, planned great hospitals, and others planned great schools where all the children of the country folk even might be taught, so that in the whole land there would be no one who could not read and write, and some sat and planned new laws to govern other people, and these laws were written down in every detail, and prisons were planned for those who disobeyed them. And there were yet others who planned new books to be written in a free new way of writing, and full of the new free sort of love between men and women everywhere.

Among all the planning there was a new sort of lord of war who planned new armies and new ships of war and new ways of warfare and some day he planned a great new war to show the world his nation was now mighty as any, and this one was Yuan's old tutor, who was afterward his captain, and now general over Meng, to whose army Meng had escaped secretly when Yuan was betrayed to prison.

Now Yuan was uneasy when he knew Meng's general was this man, and he wished it could have been another, for he did not know how much the general would remember against him. Yet he did not dare to refuse him either when he commanded Meng to bring his cousin to him.

So on a certain day Yuan went with Meng, and though he kept his face straight and calm, his heart was doubtful.

Yet when he had walked through a gate at which guards stood, very cleanly and bravely dressed, their guns shining and ready in their hands and through courts cleaned and ordered, and when he went into a room and saw the general there, sitting at a table, he need not have been afraid. In a moment Yuan saw this old tutor of his would not call to speech any old grievance against him. He was older than when Yuan saw him last, and now a known and famous leader of the armies, and although his face

297

was not smiling or easy or lenient, yet it was not an angry face. When Yuan came in he did not rise but nodded his head towards a seat, and when Yuan sat edgewise on it, for he had once been this man's pupil, he saw the two sharp eyes he remembered gazing from behind the foreign spectacles, and the harsh voice he remembered, which was not unkind nevertheless, asked him abruptly, "So now you have joined us, after all?"

Yuan nodded and as simply as he used to speak when he was a child he said, "My father pushed me to it," and he told his story.

Then the general asked again, looking at him very keenly, "But still you do not love the army? With all I taught you, you are not a soldier?"

Yuan in a little of his old confusion hesitated and then decided willfully he would be bold and not fear this man and he said, "I hate war still, but I can do my share in other ways."

"What?" the general asked, and Yuan replied, "I shall teach in the new great school here for the present, for I have need to earn, and then I shall see how the road opens."

But now the general grew restless, and he looked at a foreign clock that was on his desk, as though his interest was no more in Yuan if he were not a soldier, and so Yuan rose, and waited while the general said to Meng, "Have you the plans made for the new encampment? The new military law calls for an increase of men levied from each province, and the new contingents come in a month from today."

At this Meng struck his heels together, for he had not sat in his general's presence, and he saluted sharply and he said in a very clear proud voice, "The plans are made, my general, and await your seal, and then they will be carried out."

So was the brief meeting over and Yuan, for all his old distaste which rose up in him strongly as he passed between many soldiers who now filed in from grounds where they had been practicing their ways of war, yet could not but see these men were different from his father's lounging, laughing followers. These were all young, so young that half at least were less than twenty. And they did not laugh. The Tiger's men were always full of brawling and of laughter, and when they straggled home to rest after practice they pushed each other in rude trickery and shouted and made jokes, so that the courts were full of rough merriment. Daily in his youth Yuan knew the hours for meals because he heard guffaws and curses and loud laughter outside his inner court where he lived with his father. But these young men came back silently, and their footsteps were in such solemn unison the sound was like a great single footstep. There was no laughter. Yuan walked past them, soldier after soldier, and he saw their faces, all young, all simple and all grave. These were the new armies.

That night he wrote to Mei-ling, "They looked too young to be soldiers and their faces were the faces of country boys." Then he thought awhile, remembering their faces, and he wrote again, "Yet they had a certain soldier's look. You do not know it, for you have not lived as I have. I mean their faces were simple, so simple that I knew, looking at them, they can kill as simply as they eat their food,—a simplicity fearful as death."

In this new city Yuan now found his own life and share. He opened at last his box of books and placed them in some shelves he bought. There were also the foreign seeds he had grown to fruition in the foreign country. He looked at them doubtfully, each kind still sealed in its packet, questioning himself how they would grow if he planted them in this darker heavier earth. Then he tore one packet open and shook the seeds into his palm. They lay in his hand, large, golden, waiting grains of wheat. He must find a bit of land in which to try them.

Now he was caught in a wheel of days and weeks and months, each following swiftly after the last. His days were spent in the school. In the morning he went to the buildings, some new, some old. The new buildings were gaunt grey halls, foreign-shaped, built too quickly of cement and slender iron rods, and already flaking into pieces, but Yuan had his classrooms in an old building, and since the building was old the leaders of that school would not so much as mend a broken window. The autumn drew out long and warm and golden, and at first Yuan said nothing when a door hung cracked with age and would not close. But autumn became sharp with winter and the eleventh month howled in on the wings of a mighty wind from the northwest deserts, and fine yellow sands sifted through every break. Yuan, wrapped in his greatcoat, stood before his shivering pupils and corrected their ill-written essays and with the sandy wind blowing through his hair he set upon the blackboard rules for them on writing poetry. But it was nearly useless, for all their minds were bent on huddling in their clothes, which were for many too scanty in spite of their huddling.

First Yuan made report of it by letter to his head, an official who spent five weeks out of seven in the great coastal city, but to such letters the man paid no heed, for he had many offices and his chief work was to collect all his salaries. Then Yuan grew angry and he went himself to the high head of the school and he told the plight of his students, how the glass was broken in the windows, and how there were boards so cracked in the wooden floors the fierce wind came up between their feet, and how doors would not close.

But the high head, who had many duties, said impatiently, "Bear it awhile—bear it awhile! Such money as we have must go to making new—not patching up the useless old!" These were the same words to be heard everywhere in that city.

Now Yuan thought the words rightly enough said, and he could dream of a new hall and fine warm rooms sealed against the cold, yet here were these days, and every day colder than the last as the winter deepened. If Yuan could have done it he would have taken his own wage and hired a carpenter and made the one room closed against the winter. For after a while he came to like this work he did and he felt a sort of love for these young boys he taught. They were not often rich, for the rich sent their sons to private colleges where they had foreign teachers everywhere and fires in the school houses to keep them warm and good food every day. But to this school, which was public and opened by the new state, there were no fees, and here sons of little merchants came, and sons of ill-paid teachers of the old classics and a few bright village boys who hoped to be more than their fathers were upon the land. They were all young and poorly clad and not well fed, and Yuan loved them for they were eager and strained to understand what he taught them, though very often they did not, for although some knew more and some less, still all knew too little. Yes, looking at their pale faces and eager watching eyes, Yuan wished he had the money to mend their schoolroom.

But he had not. Even his wage was not paid to him regularly, for those above him were given their pay first, and if the moneys were not enough that month, or if some had been stopped for another cause, for army or for a new house for some official, or if some stuck in a private pocket, then Yuan and the newer teachers must wait in what patience they could. And Yuan was not patient, for he longed to be free of his debt to his uncle. At least he could be free of one debt. He wrote and told Wang the Merchant, "As for your sons, I can do nothing for them. I have no power here. It is all I can do to hold my own place. But I will send you half of what I earn until all is paid my father borrowed. Only I will not be responsible for your sons." So he cast off in these new times at least so much of the bondage of blood kin.

Therefore he dared not use his money for his pupils. To Mei ling he wrote of it, and how he wished he could mend the room, and how cold the winter drew down, but he did not know what to do. She answered quickly that one time, "Why do you not take them out of that old useless house into some warm court? If it does not rain or snow, take them out into the sun."

Yuan, holding her letter in his hand, wondered he had not thought of this, for the winters were dry and there were many sunny days, and after that for many days he taught his pupils in a sunny place he found, where two walls met into a corner between two buildings. If some laughed in passing he let them laugh, for the sun was warm. He could not but love Mei-ling the more because so swiftly she had thought of a small simple thing to do before the new building was made. Then this swiftness taught him something. She always answered him more quickly when he put a question to her of a thing he did not know what to do about, and he grew cunning and poured out all his perplexities. She would not answer if he spoke of love, but she answered eagerly if he spoke of trouble, and soon letters flew back and forth between these two as thick as leaves blown by the autumn winds.

There was another way Yuan found to make blood warm these cold days of coming winter, and it was by labor on the land and by planting the foreign seeds in the land. He must in this school teach many things, for the teachers were not enough for all those young who wanted to learn. Everywhere great new schools were opened to teach every new foreign thing which had not been taught before, and the young crowded into the schools to learn, and there were not to be found teachers enough to teach them all they craved to know in these new days. Since Yuan, therefore, had been to foreign parts, he was given some honor and urged to teach everything he knew, and among the things he taught was the new way of planting and tending of seeds. A piece of land was given him outside the city wall, and near a little hamlet, and thither he led his pupils, forming them like a small army into fours, and he marched through the city streets at their head, but instead of guns he bought hoes for them, and these they carried over their shoulders. The people who passed stared to see them, and many paused in their business to stare and call out in wonder, "What sort of a new thing is this?" And Yuan heard one man shout, a very honest dull fellow who pulled a ricksha, "Well, I see a new thing every day in this city now, but this is the newest thing I ever did see, to go to war with hoes!"

Then Yuan grinned to hear this and he answered, "It is the newest army of the revolution!"

The conceit pleased him, too, as he swung along in the winter sunshine. This was truly a sort of army, the only sort of army he would ever lead, an army of young men who went out to sow seed on the land. As he walked he set his feet down in the old rhythm he learned in his childhood from his father's armies, although he did not know he did it, and his footsteps rang so loudly and clearly that the ragged marching of his followers began to shape evenly and to his pace. Soon the rhythm of their marching set a rhythm moving in his blood, and when they had passed through the dark old city gate, where the mossy bricks gave echo to their steps, and were come into the country, this rhythm began in Yuan's mind to shape into short sharp words. For very long this had not happened to him. It was as though he had gone through a confusion and now work made him tranquil again and made his soul come clear and distil itself into a verse. Breathless he waited for the words and as they came he caught them in the old remembered delight of the few days in the earthen house. And they came clear, three living lines, but he lacked the fourth. In sudden uneasy haste, for the road was nearly ended and the land in sight, he tried to force it and then it would not come at all.

Then he had to let it all drop from his mind, for now murmurings and complainings began to break from his followers, and they caught their breath and cried out that he led them too quickly and they could not walk so fast and the hoes were heavy, and they were not used to such labor.

So Yuan must forget his verse and he called heartily to console them, "We are here; there is the land! Rest a little before we begin to hoe."

And the young men threw themselves down upon a bank by the edge of the field, and it was true the sweat poured down their pale faces and their bodies heaved with their panting. Only the two or three country lads among them were not in such a plight.

Then while they rested Yuan opened up his good foreign seed, and each youth held his two hands cupped and into their hands Yuan poured the full golden grains. This seed seemed very precious to him now. He remembered how he had grown it ten thousand miles away on foreign soil, and he remembered the old white-haired man. He could not but remember also the foreign woman who had put her lips to his. Pouring the grain out steadfastly, that moment came again into his mind. He wished she had not! Yet that moment after all had saved him and sent him on alone until he found Mei-ling. He took up his hoe swiftly and began to swing it up and down into the earth. "See," he cried to the watching pupils, "so the hoe must be swung! At first it is possible to waste much strength because one does not wield the hoe like this—"

Up and down his hoe swung in the way that old farmer had taught him, its point flashing in the sunlight. One by one the young men rose and tried to swing as he did. But the last and slowest to rise were the two country lads, and they, although they very well knew how to swing their hoes, moved slowly and reluctantly. Then Yuan saw it and he called out sharply, "How is it you will not work?"

At first the lads would not answer, but then one muttered sullenly, "I did not come to school to learn what I have done all my life at home. I came to learn a better way to earn my living."

Now Yuan grew angry when he heard this, and he answered swiftly, "Yes, and if you know how to do it better you would not need to leave home to find a way to earn more. Better seed and better ways to plant it and greater harvests would have made your life better, too."

Now there had gathered about Yuan and these pupils of his a handful of farmers from the village, and they stood staring in great wonder to see these young students come out with hoes and seed. At first they were afraid and silent, but soon they began to laugh to see how the young men could not strike their hoes into the soil. When Yuan said these words, they felt at ease and one shouted out, "You are wrong, teacher! However man works himself and whatever seed he sows, the harvests rest with heaven!"

But Yuan somehow could not bear to be contradicted so before his pupils, and so he would not answer this ignorant man. Without seeming to have heard the foolish speech, he showed his pupils how to scatter the seed into the rows, and then how deep to press the soil above the seed, and how to put a sign at the end of each row to show the name of the kind of seed, and when it was planted and by whom.

All these things the farmers watched agape, making merry over such great care, and they laughed freely and cried out, "Did you count each seed, brother?" And they cried, "Have you given each little seed its name, brother, and marked the color of its skin?" And another cried, "My mother! And if we took such care of every little seed, we would not have time to reap more than one harvest in ten years!"

But the young men who followed Yuan were disdainful of these coarse jests, and the two country lads were angriest of all and cried out, "These are foreign seeds and not such common stuff as you plant in your fields!" And the jokes of the farmers made them work with more zeal than their teacher could.

But after a while the merriment died out of the watching men, and their looks grew sullen and they fell silent. One by one they spat as if by chance, and turned and went back to their hamlet.

But Yuan was very happy. It was good to sow seed again and to feel the earth in his hands. It was thick and rich and fertile, black against the yellow foreign grain. . . . So the day's work was done. Yuan felt his body fresh with good weariness, and when he looked he saw the young men, even the palest one, had a new healthy look, and all were warmed, although a sharp wind blew against them from the west.

"It is a good way to be warmed," Yuan said, smiling at them. "Better than any other fire." The young men laughed to please Yuan, for they liked him. But the village lads stayed sullen in spite of their reddened cheeks.

That night in his room alone Yuan wrote it all down to Mei-ling, for it had come to be a thing as necessary as food and drink to him to end his day by telling her what it held. When he was finished he rose and went to the window and looked out over the city. The dark tiled roofs of the old houses huddled here and there, black in the moonlight. But thrusting up everywhere among them sharply were the tall new houses, red roofed—angular and foreign, their many windows shining with inner light. Across the city the few great new streets flung out wide pathways of light and glitter and dimmed the moon.

Looking at this changing city, seeing it and yet not seeing it much either, because he saw most clearly Mei-ling's face, very clear and young before his mind, the city only a background for her face, suddenly the fourth line of his verse came to his mind as finished as though he saw it printed down. He ran to the table and seized the letter he had just sealed, and tearing it open he added to it these words, "These four lines came to me today, the first three on the land, but I could not find the last perfecting line until I came back to the city and I thought of you. Then it came as simply as though you had spoken it to me."

306

So Yuan lived in this city, his days full of his work, and his nights full of his letters to Mei-ling. She did not write so often to him. Her letters were sedately put, the words few and exact. But they were not dull, because her words, since they were so few, were full of her meaning. She told him Ai-lan had come back after her months away, for those two had stayed their month of play over several times and were only now come home, and Mei-ling said, "Ai-lan is more beautiful than ever, but some warmth has gone out of her. Perhaps her child will bring this back. It will be born in less than a month. She comes home often because she says she sleeps better in her old bed." And she told him, "Today I did my first real operation. It was to cut off the foot of a woman which had been bound in childhood until it was gangrened. I was not frightened." And she said, "I ever love to go and play with the foundling babes, of whom I am one. They are my sisters." And she told often of some merry childish thing they said.

Once she wrote, "Your uncle and his eldest son have sent a command for Sheng to come home. He spends too much silver, they say, since they can collect no rents these days from the old lands, and the eldest son's wife is not willing for her husband's wage to be sent abroad and there is no great sum to be found otherwise. Therefore Sheng must come, because he is to have no more money."

This Yuan read thoughtfully, remembering Sheng as he had last seen him, excellently clothed in new garments, swinging a small shining cane as he walked along a sunny street in that great foreign city. It was true he spent much money since he was careful of his beauty. Doubtless he must come home—doubtless it was the only way to make him come home. Then Yuan thought, remembering the fawning woman, "It is better for him to come home. I am glad he must leave her at last."

Always Mei-ling answered very carefully every question Yuan wrote to her. As the winter deepened she cautioned him to wear a thicker coat and to eat well, and he must sleep long and not work too hard. Many times she bade him take care against the winds in the old schoolroom. But there was one thing she never answered in his letters. He said in every letter, "I am not changed. I love you—and I wait." This she did not answer.

Nevertheless Yuan thought her letters very perfect ones. Four times a month, as certain as the day came, he knew he could expect to find upon his table when he went to his room at night the long shape of her letter and her writing on it, clear and somewhat small in shape. These four days in each month came to be his feast days, and for sheer pleasure in his certainty he bought a little calendar and marked ahead the days he would have her letters. He marked them in red, and there were twelve in all until the New Year, when there was holiday and then he might go home to her and see her face. Beyond that he would not mark because he had his secret hope.

Thus Yuan lived from seventh day to seventh day, scarcely caring to go elsewhere than to his work, and needing no friends because his heart was fed.

Yet Meng would come sometimes and force him forth and then Yuan sat in a teahouse somewhere for an evening and listened to Meng and his friends cry out their impatience. For Meng was not so triumphant as he seemed at first. Yuan listened and he heard Meng angry still, and still he cried out against the times, even these new times. On one such night in a teahouse newly opened in the new street Yuan sat at dinner with him and four young fellow captains, and these were all dissatisfied with everything. The lights above the table were first too bright and then not bright enough, and the food was not brought fast enough to please them, and they wanted a certain white foreign wine that was not to be had. Between Meng and the other four the serving man was in a sweat, and he mopped his shaven head and panted and ran to and fro, afraid not to please these young captains who carried shining weapons at their belts. Even when the singing girls came in and after the new foreign fashion danced and threw their limbs about, the young men would not be satisfied, but spoke loudly of how this one's eyes were small as any pig's eyes, and that one had a nose like a leek, and one was too fat and one too old, until the girls' eyes were full of tears and anger. And Yuan, though he did not think them beautiful, could not but pity them and so he said at last, "Let be. They have their rice to earn somehow."

At this one young captain said loudly, "Better they starve, I say," and laughing their loud bitter young laughter they rose at last with a great clatter of their swords and parted.

But that night Meng went on foot with Yuan to his room and as they walked along the streets together, he spoke his discontent and he said, "The truth is we are all angry because our leaders are not just to us. In the revolution it is a principle that we shall all be equal and all have equal opportunity. Yet even now our leaders are oppressing us. That general of mine—you know him, Yuan! You saw him. Well, and there he sits like any old war lord, drawing a great pay each month as head of the armies of this region, and we younger ones are kept always in one place. I rose quickly to be a captain, and so quickly I was full of hope and ready to do anything in our good cause, expecting to rise yet higher. Yet though I work and spend myself I stick here, a captain. We all can rise no higher than being captains. Do you know why? It is because that general fears us. He is afraid we will be greater than he is some day. We are younger and more able, and so he keeps us down. Is this the spirit of the revolution?" And Meng stopped beneath a light and poured out his hot questions at Yuan, and Yuan saw Meng's face as angry as it used to be in his sullen boyhood. By now the few passers-by were staring sidewise curiously and Meng saw them and he dropped his voice and went on again and at last he said very sullenly, "Yuan, this is not the true revolution. There must be another. These are not our true leaders—they are as selfish as the old lords of war. Yuan, we young ones, we must start again—the common people are as oppressed as they ever were—we must strike again for their sakes —these leaders we have now have forgotten wholly that the common people—"

Now even as Meng said this he paused and stared, for just ahead at a certain gateway to a very famous pleasure house there was a brawl arising. The lights from that pleasure house shone down as red and bright as blood, and in the light they saw a very hateful sight. A foreign sailor from some foreign ship, such as Yuan had seen upon the great river which flowed past the city, in half drunkenness was beating with his coarse clenched fists the man who had pulled him to that pleasure house in his vehicle. He was shouting in his drunkenness and anger and staggering stupidly upon his clumsy feet. Now Meng when he saw how the white man struck the other, started forward and he began to run swiftly and Yuan ran after him. As they came near they heard the white man cursing foully the ricksha puller because he dared to ask for more coin than the white man wished to give and under his blows the man cowered, shielding himself with his upraised arms, for the white man was large and rude in body, and his drunken blows were cruel when they fell.

Now Meng had reached them and he shouted at the foreigner, "You dare—you dare—!" and he leaped at the man and caught his arms and pinioned them behind his back. But the sailor would not submit so easily, and he did not care that Meng was a captain or what he was. To him all men not of his kind were the same and all to be despised and he turned his curses on to Meng, and the two would have jumped upon each other then and there in mutual hatred, except that Yuan and the ricksha puller sprang between them and fended off the blows, and Yuan besought Meng, saying in an agony, "He is drunk—this fellow—a common fellow—you forget yourself," and while he cried he made haste to push the drunken sailor through the gate to the pleasure house, where he forgot the quarrel and went on his way.

Then Yuan put his hand to his pocket and brought forth some scattered copper coin and gave them to the ricksha man, and so settled the quarrel, and the man, who was a small old weazened fellow, never fed well enough in a day, was pleased to have the thing end thus, and in his gratitude he cackled out a little laughter, and he said, "You understand the doctrines, sir! It is true enough one ought not to blame a child, nor a woman, nor a man drunk!"

Now Meng had stood there panting and very hot with anger all this time, and since he had not freed his anger fully on the sailor it was more than half in him still, and he was beside himself. When he saw how easily the beaten man was assuaged with a few copper coins and when he heard the poor laughter and the old adage he put into words again, Meng could not bear it. No, in some strange way his clean right anger against the foreigner's insult to his own kind soured and without a word his eyes blazed out anew now upon the ricksha puller, and he leaned and gave the man's face a blow across the mouth. Yuan saw Meng do this thing, and he cried out, "Meng, what is it you do!" And he made haste to find a coin again to give the man for such a cruel blow.

But the man did not take the money. He stood in a daze. The blow came so swiftly and without any expectation, that he stood with his jaw hanging, and a little blood began to stream out from the corner of his mouth. Suddenly he bent and picked up the shafts of the ricksha, and he said to Yuan simply, "It was a harder blow than any the foreigner gave me." And so he went away.

But Meng had not stayed a moment after he gave the blow. He strode off and Yuan ran after him. When he came up to Meng he was about to ask him why he gave the blow, but first he looked at Meng's face, and then he kept silent for to his astonishment he saw in the bright light of the streets that tears were running down Meng's cheeks. Through these tears Meng stared ahead, until at last he muttered furiously, "What is the use of fighting in any cause for people like these, who will not even hate the ones who oppress them,—a little money sets everything right for such as these—" And he left Yuan at that instant and turned without another word into a dark side street.

Then Yuan stood irresolute a moment, questioning if perhaps he should not follow Meng to see he did not do some further angry deed. But he was eager to reach his room, for it was the night of a seventh day, and he could see before him the shape of the letter waiting for him, and so once more he let Meng go his angry way alone.

At last the days drew near to the end of the year, and it came within a handful of days to the holidays when Yuan could see Mei-ling again. In those days whatever he did seemed only a means of waiting until the one day when he would be freed. His work he did as well as he was able, but even his pupils ceased for him to have any life or meaning and he could not greatly care if they did well or ill, or what they did. He went to bed early to hasten the night, and he rose early to begin the day and pass it over, and yet in spite of all he did, the time went as slowly as though a clock were stopped.

Once he went to see Meng and made a plan to take the same train homewards, for this time Meng was free for holiday, too, and though he always said he was a revolutionist and he cared nothing if he never saw his home again, yet he was very restless in these days, and eager for some change or other he could not make, and he was willing to go home, having nothing better then to do. He never spoke to Yuan again of that night he had struck the common fellow. It seemed he had forgotten the thing, for now he was full of a new anger, and here it was, that the common people were so willful they would not make the great feast day for the New Year on the day the new government had said it must be. The truth was the people were used to a year timed by the moon, and now these new young men would have it timed by the sun as it was in foreign countries, and the people were doubtful, and on the streets where there were placards put commanding all to make merry at the foreign new year, the people gathered to look or to listen, if they could not read, to some scholar in their midst, who read out the commands. Thus the people muttered everywhere, "How can the year be put anyhow like this? If we send up the kitchen god a month too soon, what will heaven think? Heaven does not count by any foreign sun, we swear!" And so they stayed willful and women would not make their cakes and meats and men would not buy the mottoes of red paper to paste upon their doors for good fortune.

Then the new young rulers grew very angry at such willfulness, and they made mottoes of their own, not of old foolish sayings of the gods, but of the sayings of the revolution and they sent their own hirelings and pasted these mottoes on the doors by force.

Of this Meng was full on the day when Yuan went to see him, and he ended all the story triumphantly, "So whether they will or not the people must be taught and forced out of old superstitious ways!"

But Yuan answered nothing, not knowing indeed what to say, since he could see the two sides of the thing.

In those next two days left, Yuan looked and it was true he saw everywhere the new mottoes being pasted upon doors. There was no word said against it. Everywhere men and women watched the new red papers put upon their doors and they stayed silent. A man here and there might laugh a little, or he spat into the dust, and went his way as though he were full of something he would not tell, but men and women worked as usual everywhere and as though there was no feast day for them in that whole year anywhere. Though all the doors were gay and newly

313

red, the common people seemed not to see anything at all, but went with ostentatious usualness to their usual work. And Yuan could not but smile a little secretly, although he knew Meng's anger had a cause, and although if he had been asked he would have acknowledged the people ought to obey.

But then Yuan smiled more easily these days about any small thing because somehow he felt Mei-ling must be changed and warmer. Though she had not answered any word of love he wrote, at least she read the words and he could not believe she forgot them all. For him at least it was the happiest gayest year he ever had begun in his life, because he hoped much from it.

In such expectation Yuan began his holidays that Meng's angers even could not throw a cloud upon him, although Meng came as near to a quarrel with Yuan upon that day's journey as Yuan would let him. The truth was that Meng was in some such fierce secret inner discontent that nothing pleased him and in the train he was inflamed immediately against a rich man who spread his fur robes to take twice the space he should upon a seat, so that a lesser-seeming man must stand, and then he was inflamed as much against the lesser man because he bore it. At last Yuan could not forbear smiling and he made a little thrust at Meng half merrily and said, "Nothing will please you, Meng, not rich because they are rich, nor poor because they are poor!"

But Meng was too sore secretly to hear any merriment at all about himself. He turned furiously on Yuan then and said in a fierce low tone, "Yes, and you are the same—you bear anything—you are the lukewarmest soul I ever knew—never fit to be a true revolutionist!"

At Meng's fierceness Yuan could not but grow grave. He answered nothing, for all the people stared at Meng, and though he made his voice too low to let them hear what he said, still his face was so angry and his eyes so blazing under his black brows drawn down that they were afraid of such a one, who had a pistol thrust into his belt besides. . . . Therefore Yuan sat silent. But in his silence he could not but acknowledge Meng spoke the truth and he was wounded a little, although he knew Meng was angry at some hidden thing and not at him. So Yuan sat in soberness for a while as the train wound its way through the valleys, hills and fields, and he fell to thinking and to asking himself what he was and what he wanted most. It was true he was no great revolutionist, and never would be, because he could not hold his hates long, as Meng could. No, he could be angry for a while and hate for a moment, but not for long. The thing he truly wanted was a peace in which to do his work. And the work he loved best was what he did now. The best hours he had spent were those he used to teach his pupils—except his hours of writing to his love. . . .

Across his dreaming Meng's voice broke scornfully, saying, "What are you thinking of, Yuan? You sit there smiling as silly as a boy who has had barley sugar thrust unawares into his mouth!"

Then Yuan could not but laugh shamefacedly, and curse the heat he felt rush into his face, for Meng was not one to whom he could tell such thoughts as now were his.

Yet what meeting can ever be so sweet as it is dreamed? When Yuan reached his home on the evening of that day he leaped up the steps and into the house. But again there was only silence, and after a moment a serving woman came and gave him greeting and said, "My mistress says you are to go at once to your eldest cousin's house, where there is a family feast made for the homecoming of the young lord who has been in foreign countries. She awaits you there."

Now above his interest in this news of Sheng's coming home was Yuan's eagerness to know if Mei-ling was gone with the lady or not. Yet however he longed to know he would not ask a servant of her, for there is no mind so quick as a servant's mind to put a man and a maid together. Therefore he must make his heart wait until he could get to his uncle's house and see for himself if Mei-ling were there.

All during these many days Yuan had dreamed of how he would first see Mei-ling, and always he dreamed it that he saw her alone. They met, magically alone, inside the door as he stepped into the house. Somehow she would be there. But she was not there, and even if she were at his cousin's house, he could not hope to see her alone, and he dare not seem other to her than cool and courteous before the eyes of his family.

And so it was. He went to his cousin's house and into the large room which was full of rich foreign ornaments and chairs and there were they all gathered. Meng was before Yuan, and they had only finished making welcome for him when Yuan came in and fresh welcome must begin for him. He must go and bow before his old uncle, now wakeful and very merry with all his sons about him except the one he gave the Tiger and the one who was hunchback and a priest, but these neither he nor his lady counted any more as sons. There the old pair sat in their best holiday robes, and the lady was full of her place and dignity and she smoked very gravely a water pipe a maid stood and filled for her every puff or two, and in her hand she held a rosary, whose brown beads she passed constantly between her fingers, and still she took it on herself to say a balancing moral word to every jest the old man made. When he had given reply to Yuan he shouted, his old loose face in a thousand wrinkles, "Well, Yuan, here is this son of mine home again as pretty as a girl, and all our fears of a foreign wife were needless—he is still un-wed!"

At this the aged lady said very sedately, "My lord, Sheng was ever much too wise to think of such wickedness. I pray you do not speak foolishly in your age!"

But for once the old man would not be afraid of the lady's tongue. He felt himself the head of this house, and head of all these goodly young men and women in this rich house and he grew waggish and he was made bold by the presence of others and he cried, "It is nothing untoward to speak of marriage for a son, I suppose? I suppose Sheng will be wed?" To which the lady answered with majesty, "I know what is the proper way in these new days, and my son need not complain that his mother forced him against his will."

Then Yuan, who had listened half smiling to this bickering between the old pair, saw a strange thing. He saw Sheng smile a little cold sad smile and he said, "No, mother, I am not so new after all. Wed me as you like—I do not care—women are the same to me anywhere, I think."

At this Ai-lan laughed and said, "It is only because you are too young, Sheng—" And in her laughter the others joined and the moment passed, except Yuan did not forget Sheng's look, the look in his eyes while he steadily smiled and while the others laughed. It was the look of one who greatly cares for nothing, not even for what woman he is to wed.

Yet how could Yuan think deeply on this night of Sheng? Before even he had bowed to the old pair, his eyes sought and found Mei-ling. He saw her first of all, standing very still and quiet beside the lady, her foster mother, and for one flying second their eyes met, although they did not smile. But there she was, and Yuan could not be wholly disappointed even though it was not as he dreamed. It was now enough that she was here in this room, even though he did not say a word to her. Then he thought he would not say a word to her—not now, not in this crowded room. Let their true meeting be afterwards and in some other place. Yet though Yuan looked at her very often, he never caught her eyes after that one first time. But the lady his mother gave him very warm greeting, and when he went to her she caught his hand and patted it a little before she dropped it, and Yuan stayed by her a moment, although when he did Mei-ling made excuse to slip away to fetch some small thing she wanted.

Nevertheless, although he gave himself to all these others, there was the warmth of knowing her presence, and when he could do it he let his eyes find her again and again as she moved to pour tea into some bowl or to give a sweetmeat to a child.

All the talk and greetings were mostly for Sheng this night, and Meng and Yuan were soon only part of the others. Sheng was more beautiful than ever and so beautiful and seeming so to know everything and be at ease in all he said and did, that Yuan was shy before him as he always used to be and he felt himself a youth again before this finished man. But Sheng would not have it so. He took Yuan's hand in his old friendly way and held it, and Yuan felt the touch of Sheng's smooth graceful fingers, shaped so like a woman's hands, and the touch was pleasant and yet somehow distasteful, and so was the look Sheng had now in his eyes. For all its sweet seeming frankness there was in these days something near to evil in Sheng's face and way, as there is in a flower too fully blown and whose scent is heavy with something more than fragrance, but why this was Yuan did not know. Sometimes he felt he imagined it, and yet again he knew he did not. For Sheng, although he laughed and talked and his laughter was always nicely, rightly made, and his voice even as a bell, not high nor low, but very softly toned, and although he seemed to enter into all the family gossip with readiness and pleasure, yet Yuan felt Sheng himself was not there at all but somewhere very far away. He could not but wonder if Sheng were sorry to be home again, and once he seized a chance when he was near to ask him quietly, "Sheng, were you sorry to leave that foreign city?"

He watched Sheng's face for answer, but the face was smooth and golden and untroubled, and his eyes as smooth as dark jade, and telling nothing more, and Sheng smiled his lovely ready smile and answered, "Oh, no, I was ready to come home. It makes no difference to me where I am."

Again Yuan asked, "Have you written more verse?" And

318

Sheng answered carelessly, "Yes, I have a little book printed now of my verses, a few of them you saw, but nearly all new since you left— If you like, I will give you a copy before you go tonight." And he only smiled when Yuan said simply he would like to have them. . . . Once more Yuan asked a question and he asked, "Shall you stay here to live or come to the new capital?"

Then only did Sheng answer quickly and as though here were one thing which mattered to him, and he said, "Oh, I stay here, of course. I have been so long away I am used to modern life. I could not, of course, live in so raw a city as that is. Meng has told me something, and though he is so proud of the new streets and houses, still he had to tell me when I asked him, that there is no modern way to bathe one's self, no amusement houses worth the name, no good theatres—nothing in fact for a cultivated man to enjoy. I said, 'My dear Meng, what *is* there, pray, in this city of which you are so proud?' And then he went into one of his glowering silences! How little Meng has changed!" And all this Sheng said in the foreign tongue he now spoke so easily and well that it came more quickly to his tongue than his own native one.

But his elder brother's wife found Sheng very perfect, and so did Ai-lan and her husband. These three could not look at him enough, and Ai-lan, though she was then big with child, laughed more in her old merry way than she did usually, nowadays, and made free with Sheng and took great delight in him. And Sheng answered all her wit and paid her praise, and Ai-lan took it willingly, and it was true she was still as pretty as she ever was in spite of her burden. Yes, when other women grow thick and dark in the face and sluggish in their blood, Ai-lan was only like a lovely flower at its height, a rose wide in the sun. To Yuan she cried a lively greeting as her brother, but to Sheng she gave her smiles and wit, and her handsome husband watched her carelessly and lazily and without jealousy, for however beautiful Sheng might be, he still thought himself more beautiful and more to be preferred by any woman and most of all by the one whom he had chosen. He loved himself too well for jealousy.

So in the talk and laughter the feast began and they all sat together, not as in ancient times divided into old and young. No, in these days there was not such division. It is true the old lord and his lady sat in the highest seats, but their voices were not heard in the laughing back and forth of Ai-lan and Sheng and of the others who took part sometimes. It was a very merry hour, and Yuan could not but be proud of all these his blood kin, these rich well-clad folk, every woman in the finest gayest hue of satin robe cut to the hour's fashion, and the men, except the old uncle, in their foreign garb, and Meng haughty in his captain's uniform, and even the children gay in silks and foreign ribbons, and the table covered with dishes of every foreign sort and foreign sweets and foreign wines.

Then Yuan thought of something and here it was. These were not all his family. No, many miles in from the sea the Tiger, his own father, lived as he ever did, and so did Wang the Merchant and all his sons and daughters. They spoke no foreign tongue. They ate no foreign thing, and they lived as their own forefathers did. If they were brought into this room, Yuan thought, half troubled, they would be very ill at ease. The old Tiger would soon be pettish because he could not spit as freely as he was used, for on this floor was spread a flowered silken carpet, and though he was not a poor man, he was used at best to brick or tile. And the merchant would be in a misery at all this money spent on pictures and on satin-covered seats and little foreign toys, and all those foreign rings and trinkets which the women wore. Nor could this half of Wang Lung's house have borne the life the Tiger lived, nor even the life in the home where Wang the Merchant lived, which Wang Lung had left for his sons in that old town. These grandchildren and great-grandchildren would hold it too mean to live in, cold in winter except where the southern sun struck in, and unceiled and not modern anywhere, and not a fit house for them. As for the earthen house, it was no more than a hovel, and they had forgot it was, even.

But Yuan did not forget. In the strangest flash of memory, sitting at this feast and looking all about the table, white-clothed in the new foreign fashion, he suddenly remembered that earthen house and when he remembered it, he liked it, somehow, still. . . . He was not wholly one of them, he thought slowly— not with Ai-lan, not with Sheng. . . . Their foreign looks and ways made him wish to be less foreign even than he was. Yet he could not live in that earthen house, either,—no, though he liked something about it very deeply, he knew now he could not live there as his grandfather once had lived in content, and feel it home. He was between, somehow, and it was a lonely place—between, as he was, this foreign house and the house of earth. He had no real home, and his was a very lonely heart which could not be wholly here nor there.

His eyes rested on Sheng a moment. Except for his gold skin, and for his dark, pointed eyes, Sheng might be completely foreign. The very movements of his body now were foreign, and he spoke as a man from the west does. Yes, and Ai-lan liked it, and so did the cousin's wife, and even the eldest cousin felt Sheng very new and full of something modish, and he was silent and abashed and somewhat envious and for solace he ate heavily in silence.

Then quickly and secretly Yuan looked at Mei-ling, jealous because he had thought of a thing when he saw the praise of Sheng in Ai-lan's eyes. Did Mei-ling also watch Sheng as the other younger women did and laugh at all he said to make them laugh, and admire him with her eyes, too? He saw her look at Sheng calmly, and turn her gaze away again tranquilly. His heart eased itself. Why, she was like himself! She was between, too, not wholly new, and yet different from the old. He looked at her once more, hot and longing, and he let the waves of talk and laughter break over him and for a moment took his fill of her through his eyes. There she sat beside the lady, and now she leaned and with her chopsticks picked a bit of white meat daintily from a central dish and put it on the lady's dish, and smiled at her. She was, Yuan said most passionately within himself, as far from Ai-lan and her kind as a lily growing wild beneath bamboos is different from a forced camellia. Yes, she was between, too,—well, then he was not lonely!

Suddenly, Yuan's heart was so warm and ready that he could not believe Mei-ling would not be ready, too. In this one love of his his heart flowed out and all his many feelings fused most ardently into this one swift course.

That night he went to bed and lay sleepless, planning how he would talk with Mei-ling alone the next day and feel how her heart was to him now, for surely, or so he thought, the many letters he had written must mean some change in her to warmth. He planned how they would sit and talk, or perhaps he might persuade her to a walk with him, even, since many maids walked alone these days with young men whom they knew and trusted. And he bethought himself how he might say he was a sort of brother to her if she hesitated, and then quickly he rejected this excuse and he said stoutly in himself, "No, I am not her brother, whatever else I may not be." Only at last could he fall asleep and then to dream awry and without completion of any dream.

But who could foretell that this was the night when Ai-lan would give birth to her child? Yet so it was. When Yuan woke in the morning it was to hear confusion through all the house, and the noise of servants running here and there, and when he rose and washed and clothed himself and went to the dining room, there was the table only half set for the meal, and a sleepy maidservant moved to and fro languidly, and the only other in the room was Ai-lan's husband, who sat there dressed as he had been the night before. When Yuan came in he said gaily, "Never be a father, Yuan, if one's wife is the new sort of woman! I have had as hard a time as though I bore the child—sleepless, and Ai-lan crying out and making such a wailing I thought her near her end, except the doctor and Mei-ling promised me she did very well. These women nowadays bear their children very hardly. Lucky it is a boy, I say, because Ai-lan has already called me to her bed this morning to swear me there will never be another child from her!" He laughed again, and passed his beautiful smooth hand across his laughing, half-rueful face, and then he sat down to eat with great appetite the food the serving maid set there for he had been father several times before this, and so it was no great thing to him now.

Thus was Ai-lan's child born in this house, and all the household was absorbed and busied in it, and Yuan caught no glance at Mei-ling scarcely beyond a passing moment here and there. Three times a day the physician came, and nothing would please Ai-lan except a foreign one, and so he came, a tall red-haired Englishman, and he saw her and talked with Mei-ling and the lady and told them what Ai-lan must eat and how many days she must rest. There was the child, too, to be cared for, and Ai-lan would have it that Mei-ling must do this herself, and so Mei-ling did, and the child wept much, because the milk of the nurse they hired at first was not suited to its needs, and so this one and that must be found and tried.

For Ai-lan, like many of her kind these days, would not feed her son from her own breasts, lest they grow too large and full and spoil her slender looks. This was the only great quarrel Mei-ling ever made with her. She cried accusingly to Ai-lan, "You are not fit to have this good sweet son! Here he is born strong and lusty and starving, and your two breasts running full, and you will not feed him! Shame, shame, Ai-lan!"

Then Ai-lan wept with anger, and she pitied herself, too, and she cried back at Mei-ling, "You know nothing of it—how can you know who are a virgin? You don't know how hard it has been to have a child in me for months and months and my clothes hideous on me, and now after all my pain am I to go hideous another year or two? No, let such coarse work be done by serving women! I will not—I will not!"

Yet though Ai-lan wept, her pretty face all flushed and distraught, Mei-ling would not give in so lightly, and this was how Yuan heard of the quarrel, for Mei-ling carried it to Ai-lan's husband and Yuan was in the room. While she besought the father Yuan listened in enchantment, for it seemed to him he never had seen how true and lovely Mei-ling was. She came in swiftly, full of her anger and without seeing Yuan she began to speak earnestly to the father, "Will you let this be? Will you let Ai-lan hold back her own milk from the child? The child is hungry, and she will not feed it!"

But the man only laughed and shrugged himself and said, "Has anyone ever made Ai-lan do what she would not? At least I have never tried, and could not dare it, now, most certainly. Ai-lan is a modern woman, you know!"

He laughed and glanced at Yuan. But Yuan was watching Mei-ling. Her grave eyes grew large as she held them to the man's smiling face, and her clear pale face went paler and she said quickly beneath her breath, "Oh, wicked—wicked—wicked!" and turned and went away again.

When she was gone the husband said affably to Yuan, as men may speak when no women are by, "After all, I cannot blame Ai-lan,—it is a very binding thing to nurse a brat, and force one's self to be home every hour or two, and I could not ask her to give up her pleasure, and the truth is, I like to have her keep her beauty, too. Besides, the child will do as well on some servant's milk as hers."

But when he heard this, Yuan felt a passionate defense of Mei-ling. She was right in all she said and did! He rose abruptly to leave this man whom somehow now he did not like. "As for me," he said coldly, "I think a woman may be too modern, some-

324

times. I think Ai-lan is wrong here." And he went slowly to his room, hoping on the way to meet Mei-ling, but he did not.

Thus one by one the few days of his holidays crept past, and not on any one day did he see Mei-ling above ten minutes or so, and never then alone, for she and the lady were always bent together over the newborn babe, the lady in a sort of ecstasy, because here was the son at last she had so longed for once. Though she was so used to new ways, yet now she took a sweet half-shamed pleasure in a few old ways, too, and she dyed some eggs red and bought some silver trinkets and made ready for his month-old birthday feast although the time was still far off. And in every plan she made she must talk with Mei-ling, and almost she seemed to forget Ai-lan was the child's mother, she depended so on the foster daughter.

But long before this birthday was come Yuan must go back to the new city to do his work. Now as the days passed, they passed very empty for him, and after a while he grew sullen and then he told himself that Mei-ling need not be so busy and that she could make time for him if she would, and when he had so thought for a day or two, while the last day drew very near, he grew sure he felt rightly and that Mei-ling did what she did on purpose not to see him any time alone. And in her new pleasure in the child even the lady seemed to forget him and that he loved Mei-ling.

So it was even until the day he must go back. On that day Sheng came in very gaily and he said to Yuan and to Ai-lan's husband, "I am bid to a great merry-making tonight at a certain house, and they lack a youth or two in number, and will you two forget your age for once and pretend you are young again and be partners to some pretty ladies?"

Ai-lan's husband answered with ready laughter that he would very willingly, and that he had been so tied to Ai-lan these fourteen days he had forgot what pleasure was. But Yuan drew back somewhat, for he had gone to no such merry-making for years now, and not since he used to go with Ai-lan, and he felt the old shyness on him when he thought of strange women. But Sheng would have him and the two pressed him, and though at first Yuan would not go, then he thought recklessly, "Why should I not? It is a stupid thing to sit in this house and wait for the hour that never comes. What does Mei-ling care how I make merry?" So forced by this thought he said aloud, "Well, then, I will go."

Now all these days Mei-ling had not seemed to see Yuan, so busy had she been, but that one night when he came out of his room dressed in his black foreign clothes which he had been used to wear at evening, she happened to pass him, holding in her arms the little new boy who was asleep. She asked wonderingly, "Where are you going, Yuan?" He answered, "To an evening's merry-making with Sheng and Ai-lan's husband."

He fancied at that moment he saw a look change in Mei-ling's face. But he was not sure, and then he thought he must be wrong, for she only held the sleeping child more closely to her and said quietly, "I hope you have a merry time, then," and so she went on.

As for Yuan, he went his way hardened against her, and to himself he thought, "Well, then, I *will* be merry. This is my last evening and I will see how to make it very merry."

And so he did. That night Yuan did what he had never done before. He drank wine freely and whenever anyone called out to him to drink, and he drank until he did not see clearly the face of any maid he danced with, but he only knew he had some maid or other in his arms. He drank so much of foreign wines to which he was not used, that all the great flower-decked pleasure hall grew before his eyes into a sort of swimming glittering moving maze of brightness. Yet for all this he held his drunkenness inside him very well, so that none knew except himself how drunken he truly was. Even Sheng cried out in praise of him, and said, "Yuan, you are a lucky fellow! You are one of those who grow

326

paler as he drinks instead of red as we lesser fellows do! I swear it is only your eyes that betray you, but they burn as hot as coals!"

Now in this night's drinking he met one whom he had seen somewhere before. She was a woman whom Sheng brought to him, saying, "Here is a new friend of mine, Yuan! I'll lend her to you for a dance, and then you must tell me if you have found one who does so well!" So Yuan found himself with her in his arms, a strange little slender creature in a long foreign dress of white glittering stuff, and when he looked down at her face he thought he knew it, for it was not a face easily forgotten, very round and dark, and the lips thick and passionate, a face not beautiful, but strange and to be looked at more than once. Then she said herself, half wondering, "Why, I know you—we were on the same boat, do you remember?" Then Yuan forced his hot brain and he did remember and he said, smiling, "You are the girl who cried you would be free always."

At this her great black eyes grew grave and her full lips, which were painted thick and very red, pouted and she answered, "It is not easy being free here. Oh, I suppose I am free enough—but horribly lonely—" And suddenly she stopped dancing and pulled Yuan's sleeve and cried, "Come and sit down somewhere and talk with me. Have you been as miserable as I? . . . Look, I am the youngest child of my mother who is dead, and my father is next to the chief governor of the city. . . . He has four concubines—all nothing but singsong girls—you can imagine the life I lead! I know your sister. She is pretty, but she is like all the others. Do you know what their life is? It is gamble all day, gossip, dance all night! I *can't* live it—I want to *do* something— What are *you* doing?"

These earnest words came so strangely from her painted lips that Yuan could not but heed them. She listened restlessly after a while when Yuan told her of the new city and his work there, and how he had found a little place of his own and, he thought, a small work to do. When Sheng came and took her hand to bring her back into the dance, she thrust him pettishly away, and pouted her too full lips at him, and she cried earnestly, "Leave me alone! I want to talk seriously with him—"

At this Sheng laughed, and said teasingly, "Yuan, you would make me jealous if I thought she could be serious about anything!"

But the girl had turned already again to Yuan and she began to pour out her passionate heart to him, and all her body spoke, too, the little round bare shoulders shrugging, and her pretty plump hands moving in her earnestness, "Oh, I hate it all so— don't you? I can't go abroad again—my father won't give me the money—he says he can't waste any more on me—and all those wives gambling from morning to night! I hate it here! The concubines all say nasty things about me because I go places with men!"

Now Yuan did not like this girl at all, for he was repelled by her naked bosom and by her foreign garb and by her too red lips, but still he could feel her earnestness and be sorry for her plight and so he said, "Why do you not find something to do?"

"What can I do?" she asked. "Do you know what I specialized in in college? Interior decoration for western homes! I've done my own room over. I've done a little in a friend's house, but not for pay. Who here wants what I have? I want to belong here, it's my country, but I've been away too long. I have no place anywhere—no country—"

By now Yuan had forgotten this was an evening meant for pleasure, he was so moved by the poor creature's plight. There she sat before his pitying gaze, gay in her silly shining clothes, and her painted eyes full of tears.

But before he could think of a thing to say for her comfort Sheng was back again. And now he would not have refusal. He did not see her tears. He put his arm about her waist and laugh-

328

ing at her he swept her off with him into the whirling music, and Yuan was left alone.

Somehow he had no heart to dance more, and all the gaiety was gone from the noisy hall. Once the girl came by in Sheng's arms, and now her face was turned up to his, and it was bright and empty again and as though she had never spoken the words she had to Yuan. . . . He sat thoughtfully awhile, and let a servant fill his glass again and again, while he sat on alone.

At the end of that night of pleasure, when they went home again, Yuan was steady still, though it was true the wine burned inside him like a fever. Yet he could be strong enough to let Ai-lan's husband lean on him, for that one could not walk alone any more, he was so drunken, and his whole face was crimson and he babbled like a foolish child.

Now when Yuan struck at the door to be let in that night it opened suddenly and there by the manservant who had opened it was Mei-ling herself, and when the drunken man saw her he seemed to think of something he remembered between Yuan and Mei-ling, and he cried, "You—you—should have gone— there was a—a pretty rival—she wouldn't—leave Yuan—danger-ous, eh?" And he fell to laughing foolishly.

Mei-ling answered nothing. When she saw the two she said to the servant coldly, "Take my sister's lord to his bed, since he is so drunken!"

But when he was gone she held Yuan there with a sudden blaz-ing gaze. Thus were these two alone at last, and when Yuan felt Mei-ling's great angry eyes on him, it was like a sobering blast of cold north wind upon him. He felt the heat within him die down quickly, and for an instant he almost feared her, she was so tall and straight and angry, and he was speechless.

But she was not. No, all these days she had scarcely spoken to him, but now she did, and her words leaped from her, and she said, "You are like all the others, Yuan,—like all the other foolish idle Wangs! I have made myself a fool. I thought, 'Yuan is different—he is not a half-foreign fop, drinking and dancing all his good years away!' But you are—you are! Look at you! Look at your silly foreign clothes—you reek of wine—you are drunk, too!"

But Yuan grew angry at this and sulky as a boy and he muttered, "You would not give me anything—you know how I have waited for you—and you have made excuses and excuses—"

"I did not!" she cried, and then beside herself this maid stamped her foot and she leaned forward and gave Yuan's face a swift sharp slap, as though he were indeed a naughty child. "You know how busy I have been—who was that woman he told of?—and this was your last evening—and I had planned— Oh, I hate you!"

And she burst into weeping and ran quickly away, and Yuan stood in an agony, not comprehending anything except she said she hated him. So ended his poor holiday.

The next day Yuan returned to his work, and alone, for Meng had shorter holiday and was already gone. The rains of late winter were begun, and the train drove through the dark day, and the water dripped down the window pane, so that he could scarcely see the sodden fields. At every town the streets ran with liquid filth and the stations were empty except for the shivering few men who must be there for some duty, and Yuan, remembering how he had not seen Mei-ling again, for he left in the early morning and she was not there to bid him good-bye, said to himself this was the dreariest hour of his life. . . .

At last weary of watching the rain and in restless dreariness he took from his bag the book of verses Sheng had given him the first night, and which he had not read yet, and he began to turn the thick ivory paper, not caring much if he read or not. On each page were printed clear and black a few lines or words, a little group of strung phrases, seeming exquisite, Yuan thought, until he grew curious and half forgot his trouble, and read the

330

book again more carefully, and then he saw these little poems Sheng had made were only empty shapes. They were only small lovely empty shapes, all exquisite and empty although they were so fluent in their line and sound that almost Yuan forgot their emptiness until, the shape seized, he found there was nothing there within them.

He closed the pretty silver-bound book, and put it in its cover again and laid it down. . . . Outside the villages slipped past, dark and huddled in the rain. At doorways men looked sullenly into the rains that beat through the thatched roofs above their heads. In sunshine these folk could live outdoors as beasts do, and thrive merrily somehow, but days of rains drove them into their hovels and too many days of rain drove them half-mad with quarrelling and cold misery, and now they looked out with hate against heaven who sent such long rains down.

. . . The verses were of lovely delicacies, the light of the moon upon a dead woman's golden hair, an ice-bound fountain in a park, a faëry island in a smooth green sea, narrow between pale sands. . . .

Yuan saw the sullen beast-like faces, and he thought, very troubled, "As for me, I can write nothing. If I wrote these things Sheng does, which I can see well enough are exquisite, why, then I remember these dark faces and these hovels and all this deep under-life of which he knows nothing and will not know. And yet I cannot write of such life either. I wonder why I am so speechless and troubled?"

And so he fell to brooding and to thinking perhaps that no man can create anything who lives not wholly anywhere. He remembered how on that feast day he had thought himself between the old and the new. And then he smiled sadly, thinking how foolish he had been to think himself not alone. He was alone.

. . . So it rained on to his journey's end, and he came down from the train in rain and dusk, and in the rain the old city wall stood grim and black and high. He called a ricksha and climbed in, and sat chill and lonely while the man dragged the vehicle along the slippery running streets. Once the man stumbled and fell, and while he righted himself and waited for a moment to pant and wipe the rain from his dripping face, Yuan looked out and saw the hovels still clinging against the wall. The rains had flooded them and the wretched helpless folk within sat in the flood and waited silently for heaven to change.

Thus began for Yuan the new year, which he had thought would be his best and happiest year. Instead it began in every sort of evil. For the rains held that spring beyond all bearing, and though priests in temples made many prayers, nothing came of all their prayers and sacrifices except new evil, for such superstitions stirred up ardent angers in the young rulers who believed in no gods at all except their own heroes, and they commanded the temples in those parts to be closed, and ruthlessly they sent soldiers to live in those temples and drive the priests into the smallest worst rooms. Then this in turn made angry the farmer folk, who could be wroth enough against those selfsame priests for one cause or another when they came begging, but who feared now that the gods might be angry anew, and they cried that doubtless all these evil rains were because of these new rulers, and so for once they joined the priests against the young rulers.

For a month the rains held, and still they held, and the great river began to swell and rise and flow into the lesser rivers and canals and everywhere men began to see the coming of the same ancient floods, and if flood, then famine. Now the people had believed that the new times would bring them somehow a new heaven and a new earth, and when they found this was not true, and heaven behaved as carelessly as ever it did, and the earth gave forth no more for harvest in flood or drought than ever it did, they cried out the new rulers were false and no better than the old ones, and old discontents, stilled for a while by new promises of new times, began to rise again.

And Yuan found himself divided again, too, for Meng was pent in his narrow quarters all these many days and not able to spend the vigor of his young body in his usual training of his men, and he came often to Yuan's room and quarrelled with everything Yuan said and he cursed the rains and he cursed his general and he cursed the new leaders whom every day he said grew more selfish and careless of the people's good. He was so unjust sometimes that Yuan could not forbear saying one day, very mildly, "Yet we can hardly blame them that it rains so much, and even if there is a flood, we cannot blame them for that."

But Meng shouted savagely, "I will blame them, nevertheless, for they are no true revolutionists!" And then he let his voice drop and he said restlessly, "Yuan, I'll tell you something no one else knows. But I tell you because though you are so spineless and join in no cause clearly, still you are good enough in your way and faithful and always the same. Hear me—when one day I am gone, you are not to be surprised! Tell my parents not to be afraid. The truth is within this revolution there grows now another-a better, truer one, Yuan—a new revolution! And I and four of my fellows are determined to go and join it—we shall take our loyal men, and go into the west where the thing is shaping. Already thousands of young good eager men have joined secretly. I'll have my chance yet to fight against this old general who keeps me down so low!" And Meng stood glowering for a moment until suddenly his dark face grew bright, or bright as it ever did, for it was a sullen face at best, and then he said thoughtfully and more quietly, "That true revolution, Yuan, is for the people's good. We shall seize the country and hold it for the common people's good, and there shall be no more rich and no more poor—"

And so Meng talked on and Yuan let him talk in half-sad

silence. He had, he thought heavily, heard these words all his life somewhere, and still there were these poor, and still there were these words. He remembered how he had seen the poor even in that rich foreign country. Yes, there were always the poor. He let Meng talk, and when at last he was gone, Yuan went and stood by the window for a while and watched the few people trudging through the rain. He saw Meng come out and stride along the street, his head high even in the rain. But he was the only proud one. For the most part the only figures were the rain-soaked ricksha pullers, struggling over the slippery stones. . . . He remembered again what he never could wholly forget, that Mei-ling had not written to him once. Nor had he written to her, for, or so he said simply to himself, "There is no use in writing if she hates me so." And this set the seal of sadness to the day.

There remained therefore only his work, and into this he would have poured his strength, but even here the year did him evil. For the discontent of the times spread among the schools, and the students quarrelled with the laws laid down for them, and they felt too much the rights their youth gave them, and they quarrelled with their rulers and their teachers and refused to work and stayed out of school, so that often when Yuan went to his windy classroom, it was empty and there was no one for him to teach and he must go home again and sit and read his old books he knew before, for he dared not spend money for new ones, since steadfastly he sent half of all he earned to his uncle for his debt. In these long dark nights the end of that debt seemed as hopeless to him as the dream he once had had of Mei-ling.

One day in despair at his own idleness, for seven days on end he had gone only to find his schoolroom empty, he walked through mud and drifting rain out to the land where he had planted the foreign wheat that day. But even here there was to be no harvest, for whether the foreign wheat was not used to such long rains, or whether the black and heavy clay held the water beyond what the roots could bear, or what the wrong was, the foreign wheat lay rotting on the mucky earth. It had sprung up quick and tall and every seed had been alive and swift and eager to put forth. But the earth and skies were not native to it, and it took no deep natural root, and so it lay spoiled and rotted.

Even while Yuan stood and looked sorrowfully at this hope gone, too, a farmer saw him, and ran out in all the rain to cry out with malice and pleasure, "You see the foreign wheat is not good, after all! It sprang up very tall and fair, but it has no staying strength! I said at the time, it is not in nature to have such large pale seeds—look at my wheat—too wet, to be sure, but it will not die!"

In silence Yuan looked. It was true enough; in the next field the small strong wheat stood sturdily even in all the mud, scanty and short, but not dead. . . . He could not answer. He could not bear the man's common face and pleased stupid laughter. For one swift moment he saw why Meng struck the ricksha puller. But Yuan could never strike. He only turned in silence and went his own way again.

Now what would have been the end of Yuan's despair in this dull spring he did not know. That night he lay and sobbed on his bed he was so melancholy, although he wept for no one single cause. It seemed to him as he sobbed that he grieved because the times were so hopeless, the poor still poor, the new city unfinished and drab and dreary in the rains, the wheat rotted, the revolution weakened and new wars threatening, his work delayed by the strife of the students. There was nothing not awry to Yuan that night, but deepest awry of all was this, that for forty days there was no letter from Mei-ling and her last words still were as clear in his mind as the moment she spoke them, and he had not seen her again after she had cried, "Oh, I hate you!"

Once the lady wrote him, it is true, and Yuan seized the letter eagerly to see if perhaps Mei-ling's name was there, but it was not. The lady spoke only now of Ai-lan's little son, and how rejoiced she was because though Ai-lan was gone home again to her husband, she left the child with her mother to be cared for, since she felt the child too much trouble for her, and the lady said gratefully, "I am weak enough almost to be glad Ai-lan so loves her freedom and her pleasures, for it leaves this child to me. I know it is wrong in her. . . . But I sit and hold him all day long."

Now thinking of this letter as he lay in his dark and lonely room it added one more small sadness to him. The new little son seemed to have taken all the lady's heart so even she needed Yuan no more. In a great rush of pity for himself he thought, "I am not needed anywhere, it seems!" And so he wept himself at last to sleep.

Soon the discontents of these times were everywhere very widespread, and much more widely spread than Yuan could know, bound as he was by his solitary life in the new city. It was true he wrote dutifully once in every month to his father, and every other month the Tiger answered his son's letter. But Yuan had not been home again to visit him, partly because he wished to be steadfast to his work, the more because there were not many steadfast in these changing times, and partly because in the little holiday he had he longed most to see Mei-ling.

Nor could he have perceived clearly how the times were from the Tiger's letters, for the old man wrote only the same thing again and again without knowing he did, and always he wrote bravely of how in the spring he planned a great attack against the robber chieftain in those parts, for that robber was growing too bold by half, but he, the Tiger, vowed he would put him down yet with his loyal men, and for the sake of all good people.

Such words Yuan read scarcely heeding them any more. It did not make him angry now to hear his old father boast, and if he answered anything it was only to smile somewhat sadly because such boasting had once a power to frighten him, and now he knew it was only poor empty words. Sometimes he thought to himself, "My father grows old indeed. I must go to him in the summer and see how he does." And once he thought moodily, "I might as well have gone this holiday for all the good it did me." And he sighed and fell to reckoning how much of his debt could be paid by the summer, at the rate he could pay it, and hoping his wage would not be delayed or held back as it now was often in these troubled times which were not wholly old or wholly new and full of many uncertainties.

So there was nothing in the Tiger's letters to prepare his son for what befell him.

One day when Yuan had only just risen from his bed and stood half washed beside his little stove, where every morning he laid his own fire and lighted it for warmth against the cold wet air, there was at his door a knock, timorous and yet persistent. He cried out, "Enter!" and there entered the last man he would have said could stand there, and it was his country cousin, the eldest son of his uncle, Wang the Merchant.

Yuan could see at once that some evil had befallen this little reworn man, for there were black bruises on his skinny yellow throat, and deep bloody scratches on his small withered face, and he had a finger gone from his right hand, and a foul rag dark with blood was tied about the stub.

All these violent marks Yuan saw, and he stood speechless, not knowing what to say or think, he was so surprised. This little man, when he saw Yuan, began to sob but he held his sobs noiseless under his breath and Yuan saw he had some terrible tale to tell. He drew his garments quickly about him, therefore, and he made his cousin sit down, and he fetched some tea leaves in a pot, and poured water from the boiling kettle in the little stove and then he said, "Speak when you can and tell me what has appened. I can see it is some very fearful thing." And he waited.

Then the man caught his breath and he began, but in a lo

337

small voice, looking often at the closed door to see it did not move, and he said, "Nine days ago and one night the robber bands came against our town. It was your father's fault. He came to spend a while at my father's house and wait for the old moon year to pass and he would not be still as an old man ought to be. Time and again we besought him to be silent, but he would boast everywhere how he planned to go out to war against this robber chieftain as soon as spring was come and how he would down him as he had before. And we have enemies enough upon the land, for tenants hate their landlords always, and be sure those somehow told the robbers to incite them. At last the chieftain grew angry and he sent men out to cry everywhere in scorn that he feared no old toothless Tiger, and he would not wait for spring, but he would begin war now against the Tiger and all his house. . . . Even so, my cousin, we might have stayed him, for hearing this, my father and I, we made haste to send him a great sum of money and twenty head of oxen and fifty head of sheep for his men to kill and eat, and we made amends for your father's insult, and besought the chieftain not to heed an old man's talk. So I say it might have passed except for a trouble in our own town."

Here the man paused and fell into a fit of trembling and Yuan steadied him and said, "Do not hurry yourself. Drink the hot tea. You need not be afraid. I will do all I can. Tell on when you are able."

So at last the man could go on, subduing his shivering somewhat, and he said, his voice still strained low and half whispering, "Well, and the troubles in these new times I do not understand. But there is a new revolutionary school in our town nowadays, and all the young men go there and they sing songs and bow their heads before some new god whose picture they have hanging on the wall and they hate the old gods. Well, and even that would not matter much, except they enticed one who was once our cousin before he took vows—a hunchback—you never saw him, doubtless." Here the man paused to make his question, and Yuan answered gravely, "I have seen him once, long ago," and he remembered now that hunchbacked lad, and he remembered his father had told him he believed the boy had a soldier's heart in him because once when the Tiger passed by the earthen house the hunchback would have his foreign gun and he took the weapon and looked at its every part as fondly as though it were his own, and the Tiger always said, musing, "If it were not for that hump of his, I would ask my brother for him."—Yes, Yuan remembered him, and he nodded and said, "Go on—go on!"

The little man went on then, and he cried, "This priest cousin of ours was seized by this madness, too, and we heard it said he was restless and not like himself for these last two years, ever since his foster mother, who was a nun nearby, died of a cough she had for long. When she lived she used to sew his robes and bring him some sweetmeats sometimes she made which had no beast's fat in them, and then he lived quiet. But once she died he grew rebellious in the temple and at last he ran away one day and joined a band of a new sort I do not understand, except they entice the farming folk to seize the land for their own. Well, and this band joined with the old robbers and filled our whole town and countryside with confusion beyond any we have ever had, and their talk is so vile I cannot tell you what they say except they hate their parents and their brothers, and when they kill they kill first their own households. And then such rains as never were have fallen on the lands this year, and the people knowing flood sure and famine after, and made more fearless by the weak new times, have thrown aside their decency—"

Now the man grew so long at his tale and began trembling so again that Yuan could not bear it and he grew impatient and forced him on, saying, "Yes, yes, I know—we have had the same rains—but what has happened?"

At this the little man said solemnly, "This—they all joined together, robbers old and new and farming folk, and they fell on our town and sacked it clean, and my father and my brothers and our wives and children escaped with nothing but the little we could hide about us—and we fled to my eldest brother's house, who is a sort of governor in a city for your father—but your father would not flee—no, he still boasted like an old fool, and the most he would do was to go to the earthen house on the land which was our grandfather's—"

Here the man paused and then shivering more violently he said breathlessly, "But they were soon there—the chieftain and his men—and they seized your father and tied him by his thumbs to a beam in the middle room where he sat, and they robbed him clean and they took especially his sword which he loved, and left not one of his soldiers except his old hare-lipped servant who saved himself by hiding in a well—and when I heard and went secretly to his aid, they came back before I knew it and they caught me, and cut my finger off, and I did not tell them who I was or they would have killed me, and they thought me a serving man and they said, 'Go and tell his son he hangs here!' So I am come."

And the man began to sob very bitterly and he made haste and unwrapped from his finger the bloody rag, and showed Yuan the splintered bone and ragged flesh, and the stump began to bleed again before his eyes.

Now Yuan was beside himself indeed and he sat down and held his head, trying to think most swiftly what he must do. First he must go to his father. But if his father were already dead—well, he must have hope somehow since the trusty man was there. "Are the robbers gone?" he asked, lifting up his head suddenly.

"Yes, they went away when they had everything," the man replied, and then he wept again and said, "But the great house— the great house—it is burned and empty! The tenants did it— they helped the robbers, the tenants, who ought to have joined to save us—they have taken it all from us—the good house our grandfather—they say they will take back the land, too, and divide it—I heard it said—but who dares go to see what the truth is?"

When Yuan heard this it smote him almost more than what his father suffered. Now would they be robbed indeed, he and his house, if they had no land left. He rose heavily, dazed by what was come about.

"I will go at once to my father," he said—and then after further thought he said, "As for you, you are to go to the coastal city and to this house whose directions I will write for you, and there find my father's lady and tell her I am gone ahead, and let her come if she will to her lord."

So Yuan decided and when the man had eaten and was on his way Yuan started the same day for his father.

All the two days and nights upon the train it seemed this must be only an evil story out of some old ancient book. It was not possible, Yuan told himself, in these new times, that such an ancient evil thing had happened. He thought of the great ordered peaceful coastal city where Sheng lived out his idle pleasant days, where Ai-lan lived secure and careless and full of her pretty laughter and ignorant—yes, as ignorant of such tales as these as that white woman was who lived ten thousand miles away. . . . He sighed heavily and stared out of the window.

Before he left the new city he had gone and found Meng and took him aside into a teahouse corner, and told him what had happened, and this he did in some faint hope that Meng would be angry for his family's sake and cry he would come too, and help his cousin.

But Meng did not. He listened and he lifted his black brows and he argued thus, "I suppose the truth is my uncles have oppressed the people. Well, let them suffer, then. I will not share their suffering who have not shared their sin." And he said further, "You are foolish, to my thought. Why should you go and

341

risk your life for an old man who may be dead already? What has your father ever done for you? I care nothing for any of them." Then he looked at Yuan awhile, who sat silent and wistful and helpless in this new trouble, and Meng, who was not wholly hard in heart, leaned and put his hand on Yuan's as it lay on the table and he made his voice low and said, "Come with me, Yuan! Once before you came, but not with your heart—join now and truly in our new good cause— This time it is the real revolution!"

But Yuan, though he let his hand lie, shook his head. And at this Meng took his hand off abruptly and he rose and said, "Then this is farewell. When you come back, I shall be gone. It may be we meet no more. . . ." Sitting in the train, Yuan remembered how Meng looked, how tall and brave and impetuous he looked in his soldier's uniform, and how quickly when he said these words, he was gone.

The train swayed on its way through the afternoon. Yuan sighed and looked about him. There were the travellers who seem always the same on any train, fat merchants wrapped in silk and fur, the soldiers, the students, mothers with their crying children. But across the aisle from his seat were two young men, brothers, who were, it could be seen, newly come home from foreign parts. Their clothes were new and cut in the newest foreign way, loose short trousers and long bright-colored stockings and leather shoes of a yellow color, and on their upper bodies they wore thick garments of knitted yarn, and on their breasts were sewed foreign letters, and their leather bags were shining and new. They laughed easily and spoke freely in the foreign tongue and one had a foreign lute he strummed, and sometimes they sang a foreign song together and all the people listened astonished at the noise. What they said Yuan understood very well, but he made no sign of understanding for he was too weary and downhearted for any talk. Once when the train stopped he heard one say to the other, "The sooner we get the factories started the better it will be, for then we can get these wretched creatures at work." And once he heard the other rail against the serving man for the blackness of the rag he hung across his shoulder with which he wiped the tea bowls, and they both threw fiery looks at the merchant who sat next to Yuan when he coughed and spat upon the floor.

These things Yuan saw and understood, for so had he spoken and felt once, too. But now he watched the fat man cough and cough and spit at last upon the floor and he let it be. Now he could see it and feel no shame nor outrage, but only let it be. Yes, though he could not so do himself, he could let others do as they would these days. He could see the serving man's black rag and not cry out against it, and he could bear at least in silence the filth of vendors at the stations. He was numbed and yet he did not know why he was, except it seemed without hope to change so many people. Yet he knew he could not be like Sheng and live for his pleasures only, nor like Meng and forget his old duty to his father. Better for him, if he could, doubtless, be wholly new and careless as they were each in his own way and see nothing they did not like to see, and feel no tie which was irksome. But he was as he was, and his father was his father still. He could not so lay aside his duty to that old which was his own past, too, and still somehow part of him. And so he went patiently to the long journey's end.

The train stopped at last at the town near the earthen house, and Yuan descended and he walked through the town quickly, and though he stayed to see nothing, he could not fail to see it was a town which robbers had possessed not long since. The people were silent and frightened, and here and there were burned houses, and only now did the owners who were left dare to come and survey ruefully the ruins. But Yuan went straight through the chief street, not stopping at all to see the great house, and he passed out of the other gate and turned across the fields

343

towards the hamlet he remembered and so he came again to the earthen house.

Once again he stooped to enter the middle room upon whose walls he saw his young verses still as he brushed them. But he could not stay to see how they seemed to him now; he called, and two came to his call, and one was the old tenant, now withered and toothless and very near his end and alone, for his old wife was dead already, and the other was the aged trusty man. These two cried out to see Yuan, and the old trusty man seized Yuan's hand without a word, not even bowing to him as to his young lord, he was in such haste, and he led him into the inner room where Yuan had slept before, and there on the bed the Tiger lay.

He lay long and stiff and still, but not dead, for his eyes were fixed, and he kept muttering something to himself continually. When he saw Yuan he showed no surprise at all. Instead, like a piteous child, he held up his two old hands and said simply, "See my two hands!" And Yuan looked at the two old mangled hands and cried out, agonized, "Oh, my poor father!" Then the old man seemed for the first time to feel the pain and the cloudy tears gathered in his eyes and he whimpered a little and said, "They hurt me—" And Yuan soothed him and touched the old man's swollen thumbs delicately and said over and over, "I know they do—I am sure they do—"

And he began to weep silently, and so did the old man, and so the two wept together, father and son.

Yet what could Yuan do beyond weeping? He saw the Tiger was very near his death. A dreadful yellow pallor was on his flesh, and even while he wept his breath came so short that Yuan was frightened and besought him to be tranquil, and forced himself not to weep. But the Tiger had another trouble to tell and he cried again to Yuan, "They took my good sword—" Then his lips trembled afresh, and he would have put his hand to them in the

344

old habit he had, but the hand pained him if he moved it, and so he let it lie, and looked up at Yuan as he was.

Never in all his life had Yuan felt so tender as he now did to his father. He forgot all the years passed and he seemed to see his father always as he was now with this simple childish heart, and he soothed him over and over, saying, "I will fetch it back somehow, my father—I will send a sum of silver and buy it back."

This Yuan knew he could not do, but he doubted if tomorrow the old man could live to think of his sword and so he promised anything to soothe him.

Yet what could be done after soothing? The old man slept at last, comforted a little, and Yuan sat beside him and the trusty man brought him a little food, stealing quietly in and out, and speechless lest he wake his master's light sick sleeping. Silently Yuan sat there, and so he sat while his old father slept, and at last he laid his head down upon the table by him and slept a little too.

But as night drew near, Yuan awoke and he ached in every bone so that he must rise, and he did, and he went noiselessly away into the other room and there the old trusty man was, who, weeping, told him again the tale he already knew. Then the old man added this, "We must somehow leave this earthen house, because the farmers hereabouts are full of hatred, and they know how helpless my old master is and they would have fallen on us, I am sure, little general, if you had not come. Seeing you come, young and strong, they will hold off awhile perhaps—"

Then the old tenant put in his word, and he said doubtfully, looking at Yuan, "But I wish you had a garment not foreign, young lord, for the country folk hate these young new men so much these days because in spite of all their promises of better times rains are come and there will be certain floods, and if they see your foreign clothes such as the others wear—" He paused and went away and came back with his own best robe of blue cotton cloth, not patched more than once or twice, and he said coaxingly, "Wear this to save us, sir, and I have some shoes, too, and then if you are seen—"

So Yuan put on the robe, willing if it made more safety, for he knew the wounded Tiger could not be taken anywhere now, but must die where he had fallen, though he did not say so, knowing the old trusty man could never bear to hear the word death.

Two days Yuan stayed beside his father waiting, and still the old Tiger did not die, and while he waited Yuan wondered if the lady would come or not. Perhaps she would not, since she had the child to care for whom she loved so well.

But she did come. At the end of the afternoon of the second day Yuan sat beside his father, who lay now as though he slept continually unless he were forced to eat or move. The pallor had grown darker, and from his poisoned dying flesh a faint stench passed off into the air of the room. Outside, the early spring drew on, but Yuan had not once gone out to see sky or earth. He was mindful of what the old men said, that he was hated, and he would not stir that hatred now, for the Tiger's sake, that at least he might die in peace in this old house.

So he sat beside the bed and thought of many things, and most of all how strange his life was and how confused and how there was not one known hope to which to hold. These elders, in their times, they were clear and simple—money, war, pleasure—these were good and worth giving all one's life for. And some few gave all for gods, as his old aunt did, or as that old foreign pair across the sea did. Everywhere the old were the same, simple as children, understanding nothing. But the young, his own kind, how confused they were—how little satisfied by the old gods and gains! For a moment he remembered the woman Mary and wondered what her life was,—perhaps like his; perhaps marked for no clear great goal. . . . Out of all he knew there was only Mei-

346

ling who put her hand surely to a certain thing she knew she wanted to do. If he could have married Mei-ling. . . .

Then across this useless thinking he heard a voice and it was the lady's. She was come! He rose quickly and went out, greatly cheered to hear her. More than he knew he had hoped for her coming. And there she was—and by her, with her, there was Mei-ling!

Now Yuan had never once thought or hoped for this and he was so astonished, he could only look at Mei-ling and stammer forth, "I thought— Who is with the child?"

And Mei-ling answered in her tranquil, sure way, "I told Ai-lan for once she must come and see to him, and the fates helped, because she has had a great quarrel with her husband over some woman she says he looked at too often, and so it suited her to come home for a few days. Where is your father?"

"Let us go to him at once," said the lady. "Yuan, I brought Mei-ling, thinking she would know by her skill how he did." Then Yuan made no delay, but he took them in and there they three stood beside the Tiger's bedside.

Now whether it was the noise of talking or whether it was the sound of women's voices to which he was not used, or what it was, the old Tiger came for a passing moment out of his stupor, and seeing his heavy eyes open on her the lady said gently, "My lord, do you remember me?" And the old Tiger answered, "Aye, I do—" and drowsed again, so they could not be sure whether he spoke the truth or not. But soon he opened his eyes once more and now he stared at Mei-ling, and he said, dreamily, "My daughter—"

At this Yuan would have spoken who she was, but Mei-ling stopped him, saying pityingly, "Let him call me daughter. He is very near the last breath now. Do not disturb him—"

So Yuan stayed silent after his father's glance wavered again to him because even though he knew the Tiger did not know clearly what he said, it was sweet to hear him call Mei-ling by that name.

347

There they three stood, united somehow, waiting, but the old Tiger sank deeper into his sleep.

That night Yuan took counsel with the lady and with Mei-ling and together they planned what must be done. Mei-ling said gravely, "He will not live through this night, if I see rightly. It is a wonder he has lived these three days—he has a stout old heart, but it is not stout enough for all he has had to bear, to know himself defeated. Besides, the poison from his wounded hands has gone into his blood and made it fevered. I marked it when I washed and dressed his hands."

For while the Tiger slept his half-dead sleep Mei-ling in the skilfulest fashion had cleansed and eased the old man's torn flesh, and Yuan stood by humbly watching her, and all the while he watched he could not but ask himself if this gentle tender creature was that same angry woman who had cried she hated him. About the rude old house she moved as naturally as though she lived always in it, and from its poverty she found somehow the things she needed for her ministration, such things as Yuan would not have dreamed could be so used,—straw she tied into a mat and slipped under the dying man so he could lie more easily upon the boards, and a brick she took up from the edge of the small dried pool and heated in the hot ashes of the earthen oven and put to his chilling feet, and she made a millet gruel delicately and fed it to him and though he never spoke he did not moan so much as he had. Then Yuan, while he blamed himself because he had not done these things himself, knew humbly that he could not do them. Her strong narrow hands could stir about so gently that they seemed not to move the great old fleshless frame, and yet they eased it.

Now when she spoke he listened, trusting all she said, and they planned, and the lady listened when the old trusty man said they must go away as soon as the death was over, because ill-will gathered blacker every day about them. And the old tenant put his voice to a whisper and he said, "It is true, for today I went about and heard and everywhere there was muttering because they said the young lord was come back to claim the land. It is better for you to go away again, and wait until these evil times are over. I and this old harelip will stay here and we will pretend we are with them, and secretly we will be for you, young lord. For it is evil to break the law of the land. The gods will not forgive us if we use such lawless means—the gods in the earth, they know the rightful owners—"

So all was planned, and the old tenant went into the town and found a plain coffin and had it carried back by night while folk slept. When the old trusty man saw this coffin, which was such as any common man had at his death, he wept a little because his master must lie there and he laid hold of Yuan and begged him, saying, "Promise me you will come back one day and dig up his bones and bury him as he should be buried in a great double coffin—the bravest man I ever knew and always kind!"

And Yuan promised, doubting, too, it ever could be done. For who could say what days lay ahead? There was no more surety in these days—not even surety of the earth in which the Tiger must soon lie beside his father.

At this moment they heard a voice cry out, and it was the Tiger's voice, and Yuan ran in and Mei-ling after him, and the old Tiger looked at them wildly and awake, and he said clearly, "Where is my sword?"

But he did not wait for answer. Before Yuan could say his promise over, the Tiger dropped his two eyes shut and slept again and spoke no more.

In the night Yuan rose from his chair where he watched and he felt very restless. He went first and laid his hand upon his father's throat as he did every little while. Still the faint breath came and went weakly. It was a stout old heart, indeed. The souls were

349

gone, but still the heart beat on, and it might beat so for hours more.

And then Yuan felt so restless he must go out for a little while, shut as he had been these three days within the earthen house. He would, he thought, steal out upon the threshing floor and breathe in the good cool air for a few minutes.

So he did, and in spite of every trouble pressing on him the air was good. He looked about upon the fields. These nearest fields were his by law, this house his when his father died, for so it had been apportioned in the old times after his grandfather died. Then he thought of what the old tenant had told him, how fierce the men upon the land were grown, and he remembered how even in those earlier days they had been hostile to him and held him foreign though he did not feel it then so sharp. There was nothing sure these days. He was afraid. In these new times who could say what was his own? He had nothing surely of his own except his own two hands, his brain, his heart to love—and that one whom he loved he could not call his own.

Even while he so thought, he heard his name called softly and he looked and there stood Mei-ling in the doorway. He went near her quickly and she said, "I thought he might be worse?"

"The pulse in his throat is weaker every time I feel it. I dread the dawn," Yuan answered.

"I will not sleep now," she said. "We will wait together."

When she said this Yuan's heart beat very hard once or twice, for it seemed to him he had never heard that word "together" so sweetly used. But he found nothing he could say. Instead he leaned against the earthen wall, while Mei-ling stood in the door, and they looked gravely across the moonlit fields. It was near the middle of the month, and the moon was very clear and round. Between them while they watched the silence gathered and grew too full to bear. At last Yuan felt his heart so hot and thick and drawn to this woman that he must say something usual and hear his voice speak and hers answer, lest he be foolish and put forth

350

his hand to touch her who hated him. So he said, half stammering, "I am glad you came—you have so eased my old father." To which she answered calmly, "I am glad to help. I wanted to come," and she was as quiet as before. Then Yuan must speak again and now he said, keeping his voice low to suit the night, "Do you—would you be afraid to live in a lonely place like this? I used to think I would like it—when I was a boy, I mean— Now I don't know—"

She looked about upon the shining fields and on the silvery thatch of the little hamlet and she said, thoughtfully, "I can live anywhere, I think, but it is better for such people as we are to live in the new city. I keep thinking about that new city. I want to see it. I want to work there—perhaps I'll make a hospital there one day—add my life to its new life. We belong there—we new ones—we—"

She stopped, tangled in her speech, and then suddenly she laughed a little and Yuan heard the laughter and looked at her. In that one look they two forgot where they were and they forgot the old dying man and that the land was no more sure and they forgot everything except the look they shared. Then Yuan whispered, his eyes still caught to hers, "You said you hated me!"

And she said breathlessly, "I did hate you, Yuan—only for that moment—"

Her lips parted while she looked at him and still their eyes sank deeper into each other's. Indeed, Yuan could not move his eyes until he saw her little tongue slip out delicately and touch her parted lips, and then his eyes did move to those lips. Suddenly he felt his own lips burn. Once a woman's lips had touched his and made his heart sick. . . . But he wanted to touch this woman's lips! Suddenly and clearly as he had never wanted anything, he wanted this one thing. He could think of nothing else except he must do this one thing. He bent forward quickly and put his lips on hers.

She stood straight and still and let him try her lips. This flesh was his—his own kind. . . . He drew away at last and looked at her. She looked back at him, smiling, but even in the moonlight he could see her cheeks flushed and her eyes shining.

Then she said, striving to be usual, "You are different in that long cotton robe. I am not used to see you so."

For a moment he could not answer. He wondered that she could speak so like herself after the touch upon her, could stand so composed, her hands still clasped behind her as she stood. He said unsteadily, "You do not like it? I look a farmer—"

"I like it," she said simply, and then considering him thoughtfully she said, "It becomes you—it looks more natural on you than the foreign clothes."

"If you like," he said fervently, "I will wear robes always."

She shook her head, smiling again, and answered, "Not always—sometimes one, sometimes the other, as the occasion is— one cannot always be the same—"

Again somehow they fell to looking at each other, speechless. They had forgotten death wholly; for them there was no more death. But now he must speak, else how could he longer bear this full united look?

"That—that which I just did—it is a foreign custom—if you disliked—" he said, still looking at her, and he would have gone on to beg her forgiveness if she disliked it, and then he wondered if she knew he meant the kiss. But he could not say the word, and there he stopped, still looking at her.

Then quietly she said, "Not all foreign things are bad!" and suddenly she would not look at him. She hung her head down and looked at the ground, and now she was as shy as any old-fashioned maid could ever be. He saw her eyelids flutter once or twice upon her cheeks and for a moment she seemed wavering and about to turn away and leave him alone again.

Then she would not. She held herself bravely and she straightened her shoulders square and sure, and she lifted up her head and looked back to him steadfastly, smiling, waiting, and Yuan saw her so.

His heart began to mount and mount until his body was full of all his beating heart. He laughed into the night. What was it he had feared a little while ago?

"We two," he said—"we two—we need not be afraid of any·thing."